# THE FROZEN HEART

## Almudena Grandes

## Also by Almudena Grandes

The Ages of Lulu
The Wind from the East

# THE FROZEN HEART

## Almudena Grandes

*Translated from the Spanish by Frank Wynne*

Weidenfeld & Nicolson
London

First published in Great Britain in 2010 by Weidenfeld & Nicolson
An imprint of the Orion Publishing Group Ltd
Orion House, 5 Upper St Martin's Lane
London WC2H 9EA

An Hachette UK Company

First published in Spain in 2007 by Tusquets Editores

 This work has been published with a
subsidy from the Directorate General of
Books, Archives and Libraries of the
Spanish Ministry of Culture.

978 0 297 84488 4 (cased)
978 0 297 84489 1 (trade paperback)

This book proof printed and bound in
Great Britain by CPI Antony Rowe

The Orion Publishing Group's policy is to use papers that are
natural, renewable and recyclable products and made from wood
grown in sustainable forests. The logging and manufacturing
processes are expected to conform to the environmental
regulations of the country of origin.

www.orionbooks.co.uk

*To Luis.*
*To Mauro, to Irene and to Elisa*
*I watch over you.*

*One of the two Spains*
*will freeze your heart*

Antonio Machado

# I

# HEART

I am tired of not knowing where to die. This is the greatest sadness of the emigrant. What is there to connect us to the cemeteries in the countries in which we live? […]

Don't you understand? We are the ones who have observed each and every thought for thirty years. For thirty years we have longed for a lost paradise, a paradise that is unique, special, that is ours. A paradise of crumbling houses and collapsing roofs. A paradise of deserted streets, of unburied dead. A paradise of razed walls, fallen towers and devastated fields […] We are the exiles of Spain […] Leave us our ruins. We must begin again from the ruins. We will get there.

María Teresa León, *Memoria de la Melancolía*
(Buenos Aires, 1970)

What distinguishes man from the animals is that man is an heir, not simply a descendent.

José Ortega y Gasset

The women weren't wearing tights. Their fat, fleshy knees bulged over the elastic of their socks, peeking out from under the hem of their dresses, which were not really dresses but shapeless, collarless smocks made of some lightweight fabric I could not name. I looked at them, planted like squat trees in the unkempt cemetery, wearing no stockings, no boots, and with no other coat than the coarse woollen jackets they kept closed by folding their arms across their chests.

The men weren't wearing overcoats either, but their jackets - made of a darker shade of the same coarse wool – were buttoned up to hide the fact that they had their hands in their pockets. Like the women, they all looked identical – shirts buttoned to the throat, heavy stubble, hair close-cropped. Some wore caps, others were bare-headed, but, like the women, they adopted the same stance: legs apart, heads held high, feet planted firmly in the ground like stout trees, ancient and strong, impervious to cold or catastrophe.

My father, like them, had had no time for people who were sensitive to the cold. I remembered that as I stood with the icy wind from the sierras slashing at my face – "a bit of a breeze", he would have called it. In early March the sun can be deceitful, pretending to be riper, warmer, on one of those late winter mornings when the sky seems like a photograph of itself, the blue so intense it looks as though a child had coloured it in with a crayon - a perfect sky, clear, deep, translucent; in the distance, the mountains peaks still capped with snow, a few pale clouds ravelling slowly, their unhurried progress completing this perfection illusion of spring. "A glorious day", my father would have said, but I was cold as the icy wind whipped at my face and the damp seeped through the soles of my boots, my woollen socks, through the delicate barrier of skin. "You should have been in Russia, or Poland, now that was cold", my father would say when as kids we grumbled about the cold on mornings like this. "You should have been in Russia, or Poland, now that was cold". I remembered his words as I stared at these men, these hardy men who did not feel the cold, men he had once resembled. "You should have been in Russia, or Poland," and the voice of my mother saying "Julio, don't say things like that to the children…"

"Are you all right, Álvaro?"

I heard my wife's voice, felt the pressure of her fingers, her hand searching for mine in my coat pocket. Mai turned to me, her eyes wide, her smile uncertain; the expression of someone intelligent enough to

10

know that, in the face of death, there is no possible consolation. The tip of her nose glowed pink and the dark hair that usually tumbled over her shoulders lashed at her face.

"Yes," I said after a moment, "Yes, I'm fine."

I squeezed her fingers and then she left me to my thoughts.

There may be no consolation in the face of death, but it would have pleased my father to be buried on a morning like this, so similar to the mornings when he would bundle us all into the car and drive to Torrelodones for lunch. "A glorious day, just look at that sky, and the Sierra! You can see all the way to Navacerrada. The air is so fresh it'd bring a dead man back to life…" Mamá never enjoyed these trips, though she had spent her summers in Torrelodones as a child and it was where she had met her future husband. I didn't enjoy them either, but we all loved him - his strength, his enthusiasm, his joy - and so we smiled and sang *'ahora que vamos despacio vamos a contar mentiras, ¡tra-la-rá!, vamos a contar mentiras'*, all the way to Torrelodones. It's a curious town: from a distance, it looks like a housing estate but as you draw nearer it seems to be nothing more than a train station and a scatter of buildings. "You know why it's called Torrelodones?" Of course we knew, it was named after the little fortress that perched like a toy castle on top of the hill, the Torre de los Lodones, yet every time we came he would explain it to us again. "The fortress is an ancient tower built by the Lodones, they were a tribe, a bit like the Visigoths…" My father always claimed he didn't like the town, but he loved taking us there, to show us the hills and the mountains and the meadows where as a boy he had tended sheep with his father, he loved to wander the streets, stopping to chat with everyone, and afterwards telling us the same stories: "That's Anselmo - his grandfather was my grandfather's cousin. That woman over there is Amada and the woman with her is Encarnita, they've been friends since they were little girls. That man over there, his name's Paco, he had a vicious temper, but my friends and I used to steal apples from his orchard…

At the slightest sound Paco would rush out of his house waving his rifle though he never actually shot at the boys who were stealing his cherries, his figs. Anselmo was much older than my father; by rights he should have been long dead, yet here he was at my father's funeral, and beside him Encarnita. Beneath the wizened mask of old age, I could still see the plump, friendly faces that had smiled into my childish eyes. It had been years - more than twenty years - since that last "glorious Sunday morning" when my father had taken us to Torrelodones for lunch. I hadn't been back since and the sight of all these people moved me. Time

11

had been cruel to some of them, gentler to others, but they had all washed up on the shore of an old age that was very different to my father's. At some other time, some other place, some other funeral I probably wouldn't have recognised them in the dark mass of huddled bodies, but that morning I stared at each of them in turn, at their powerful bodies, their solid legs, their natural, almost haughty, formality, their shoulders aged but not bowed, their dark, tawny skin, weathered by the mountain sun which burns but does not tan. Their cheeks were etched with long wrinkles, deep as scars. No delicate web of crow's feet round their eyes, but deep, hard lines as though time had carved their faces with a chisel thicker than the fine blade it had used on my father.

Julio Carrión González might have been born in a little house in Torrelodones, but he died in a hospital in Madrid, his skin ashen, his eldest daughter - an intensive care doctor - in attendance, and with every tube and monitor and machine available. Long ago, before I was conceived, his life had taken a different path from the lives of the men and women he had known as a boy, the people who had outlived him, who had come to his funeral as if from another time, another world, from a country that no longer existed. Life had changed in Torrelodones too. I knew that if they had time, if they knew someone with a phone, a car, these people would also die surrounded by tubes and monitors and machines. I knew that the fact that they still left the house without an overcoat, a purse, or tights said little about their bank balance, which had been steadily growing over the years thanks to the influx of people from Madrid prepared to pay any price for a plot of land barely big enough to graze a dozen sheep on. I knew all this, yet looking across the grave at their weather-beaten faces, the stocky frames, the threadbare corduroy trousers, the cigarette-butts clenched defiantly between the lips of some, what I saw was the abject poverty of the past. In the fat, bare knees of these women with nothing to keep out the cold but a coarse woollen jacket, I saw a harsher, crueller Spain.

We stood on the opposite side of the grave. His family, the well-dressed product of his prosperity, his widow, his children, his grandchildren, some of his colleagues, the widows of former colleagues, a few friends from the city I lived in, from the world I knew and understood. There weren't many of us. *Mamá* had asked us not to tell people. "I mean, Torrelodones, it's hardly Madrid", she said, "people might not want to come all that way…" We realised that she wanted only those closest to her at the funeral, and we had respected her wishes. I hadn't told my sisters-in-law, nor my mother's brothers, I hadn't even told Fernando Cisneros, my best friend since university. There weren't many of us, but we weren't expecting anyone else.

I hate funerals, everyone in the family knows that. I hate the gravediggers, their offhand manner, the predictable, hypocritical expression of condolence they put on when their eyes accidentally meet those of the bereaved. I hate the sound of the shovels, the grating of the coffin against the sides of the grave, the quiet whisper of the ropes; I hate the ritual of throwing handfuls of earth and single roses onto the coffin and the insincere, portentous homily. I hate the whole macabre ceremony which inevitably turns out to be so brief, so banal, so unimaginably *bearable*. That's why I was standing with Mai off to one side, almost out of earshot of the droning voice of Father Aizpuru, the priest *Mamá* had invited from Madrid. The man who, she claimed, had kept her children on the straight and narrow, the priest my older brothers still treated with the same infantile reverence he had cultivated when he refereed football matches in the schoolyard. I'd never liked him. In my last year in primary school, he was my tutor and he used to make us exercise in the playground stripped with the waist on the coldest days of winter.

"Are you men or are you girls?" Another image of Spain. He would stand there, his cassock buttoned up while I shivered like a freshly sheared lamb in the fine cold drizzle of sleet. "What are you - men or girls?" I never joined in the enthusiastic chorus shouting "Men!" because there was only one thought running through my head, "you bastard, Aizpuru, you fucking bastard". Naïve as I was, I tried to get my own my own back at the age of sixteen, as I sat stonefaced through Friday mass, refusing to pray, to sing, to kneel, "fuck you, Aizpuru, it's your fault that I lost my faith". Until finally he phoned my mother, called her into school after class and had a long chat with her. He told her to keep an eye on me. "Álvarito isn't like his brothers," he said, "he's sensitive, headstrong, he's weaker. Oh, he's a good lad, a first-rate student, responsible and clever too - maybe too clever for a boy his age. That's what worries me. Boys like that develop unhealthy friendships, that's why I think it might be best for you to keep an eye on him, keep him busy." That night my mother sat on the edge of my bed, ran her fingers through my hair, and without looking at me, said: "Álvaro, *hijo*, you do like girls, don't you?" "Of course, *mámá*, I like girls a lot". She heaved a sigh, kissed me and left the room. She never asked me about my sexual orientation again and never said a word to my father. I graduated top of my class, with the same refrain still ringing in my head, "you fucking bastard, Aizpuru, you fucking bastard", never suspecting that years later I would realise that he was right, not me.

"Álvaro, *hijo*, I know you didn't want to wear a suit and tie today, but

13

please, I'm begging you, at least be pleasant to father Aizpuru..." This was the one thing my mother had asked of me that morning, so I'd made sure I was the first to shake his hand so that my somewhat frosty greeting would be forgotten in the exaggerated fuss my brothers Rafa and Julio would make of him, hugging the fat old man who ruffled their hair, kissed them on both cheeks, all of them blubbering and crying. The Marist brotherhood of brotherly love, "I have two mothers, one here on earth, the other in heaven." A clever piece of bullshit. I said as much to Mai and received a swift kick for my pains. Clearly, my mother here on earth had had a word with my wife.

Farther Aizpuru was right, I wasn't like my brothers, but I was a good lad, always. I'd never been a problem child, never caused trouble the way they had. In the innumerate, unscientific world I'd grown up in, my better than average flair for mental arithmetic had bestowed on me a mythical intelligence that even I did not believe I possessed. Yes, I'm a theoretical physicist, and that's a job title that causes a few raised eyebrows when people first hear it. Until they discover what it means in reality – a professor's salary and no prospect of becoming what they would consider to be rich and important. That's when they realise the truth - that I'm just a normal guy. At least I was until that morning when my one phobia - my morbid aversion to funerals – propelled my mind from the profound, universal grief of the survivor into a curious state of heightened awareness. It probably had something to do with the pill Angélica had given me at breakfast. "You haven't cried," Álvaro, she said, "Here, take this, it'll help." She was right, I hadn't cried - I rarely cry, almost never. I didn't ask my sister what the pill was - and maybe my detachment was simply down to me refusing to deal with my grief - but as I stood there feeling strangely alert I turned my gaze from the fat, fleshy knees of the women from Torrelodones to the faces of my own family.

There they stood, and suddenly it was as though I didn't know them. Father Aizpuru was still blethering on, my mother was staring out towards the horizon, the sea-blue eyes of a young woman set in an old woman's face, her skin so translucent, so fine it seemed as though it might split from all the wrinkling, folding and fanning out. My mother's character was not in her wrinkles, however, but in her eyes, which seemed so gentle yet could be so harsh, their shrewdness masked by the innocence of their colour; when she laughed they were beautiful but when she was angry, they flared with a purer, bluer light. My mother was still a handsome woman, but when she was young Angélica Otero Fernández had been a beauty, a fantasy - blonde, pale, exotic. "Your

14

family must be from somewhere in Soria," my father used to say to her, "You have Iberian blood in you, they have blonde hair and pale eyes..." "Julio," my mother would say, "You know perfectly well that my father is from Lugo in Galicia, and my mother is from Madrid." "That may be, but somewhere in the distant past. Either that or your father had Celtic blood," he insisted, unable to think of any other reason for the superiority of my mother's genes which had produced a string of pale, blonde blue-eyed children; a string broken only once, when I was born.

"Gypsy", my brothers used to call me, and my father would hug me and tell them to shut up. "Don't pay them any attention, Álvaro, you take after me, see?" In time, that fact became increasingly obvious. Father Aizpuru had been right, I wasn't like my brothers, I didn't even look like them. I glanced over at Rafa, the eldest, forty-seven - six years older than me - still blonde, although he was now almost bald. He stood next to my mother, stiff and serious, conscious of the solemnity of the occasion. Rafa was a tall man, with broad shoulders in proportion to his height and a pot belly that stuck out from his skinny frame. Julio was three years younger but looked almost like his twin, though age had been kinder to him. Between them, came Angélica - now Doctor Carríon- who had extraordinary green eyes and who envied me my dark complexion, since she had pale, delicate skin that burned easily. The mysteries of the Otero/Fernández bloodlines had produced better results in the female of the species than the male. My brothers were not particularly handsome, but both my sisters were beautiful and Clara, the youngest, was stunning. She too was blonde, but her eyes were the colour of honey. Then there was me. In the street, at school, in the park, I looked completely unremarkable, but at home I was completely out of place, as though I were from another planet. Four years after Julio was born and five years before Clara, along I came, with my black hair, dark eyes and dark skin, narrow shoulders, hairy legs, big hands, and a flat stomach - the lost Carríon, shorter than my brothers, barely as tall as my sisters, different.

On the day of my father's funeral, I hadn't yet realised how painful that difference would turn out to be. Father Aizpuru went on murmuring and the wind went on blowing, "You should have been in Russia, or Poland...", my father would have said, because it was cold, I felt cold, in spite of my scarf, my gloves, my boots, I felt cold even though I had my hands in my pockets and my coat buttoned up, even though I wasn't blonde and fair-skinned, even though I wasn't like my brothers. They felt the cold too, but they hid it well, they stood to attention, hands clasped over their coats, exactly as my father must have stood at the last funeral he attended. He would have worn that same expression - so different from the patient resignation I saw in the eyes of Anselmo and Encarnita, who were in no hurry, who no longer expected to be surprised, bowed only by time, drawing strength from their terrible weariness so that they could look reluctantly on the lives of others. This, I thought was what my father had lost when his life diverged from theirs. He had been luckier than they had because although money does not make for a happy life, curiosity does; because although city life is dangerous, it is never boring; because if power can corrupt, it can also be wielded with restraint. My father had had a great deal of power and a great deal of money in his life and had died without ever being reduced to the vegetable, the mineral state of these men, these women he had known as a child and who, at the moment of his final farewell, had come to claim him as one of them.

He was not one of them. He had not been one of them for a long time. That was why I was so moved to see them, huddled together on the far side of the grave, not daring to mingle with us, Julito Carríon's widow and his children. If I had not stared at them, had not accepted the quiet challenge of their bare knees, the coarse woollen jackets, perhaps I might not have noticed what happened next. But I was still staring at them, wondering whether they had noticed that I didn't look like my brothers, when Father Aizpuru stopped talking, and turning to look at me, spoke the terrible words: "if the family would like to come forward."

Until that moment, I had not been aware of the silence; then I heard the sound of a car in the distance and was relieved as its dull roar masked the dirty clang of the shovels digging into the earth, the harsh grating that seemed to rebuke me, the cowardly son, Father Aizpuru's unruly pupil. "If the family would like to come forward", he had said, but I didn't move. Mai glanced at me, squeezed my hand. I shook my head and she went over to join the others. Next come the ropes, I thought, the wheezing and panting of the gravediggers, the brutal indignity of the coffin banging against the walls of the grave, but I heard none of this as the profane, reassuring sound of the engine drew closer, then suddenly stopped just as the shovels finished their work.

There were not many of us, but we weren't expecting anyone else. And yet someone had turned up now, at precisely the wrong moment.

"What will you have, *Mamá?*"
"Nothing, *hijo.*"
"*Mamá*, you have to eat something…"
"Not now, Julio."
"Well, I'll have the *fabada*, and then after that…"
"Clara!"

16

"What? I'm pregnant. I'm eating for two."

"Let her have whatever she wants. Everyone has to grieve in their own way."

"Really? In that case I'll have the eel."

"Don't even think about it!"

"But Papá, aunt Angélica said…"

"I don't care what aunt Angélica said, you're not having eel and that's final."

"Has everyone decided what they're having?"

"Yes. The boys will have lamb chops" - my nephews snorted but didn't dare to argue – "I'll take care of the main courses. *Mamá*, at least have some soup."

"I don't want soup, Rafa."

"Have a starter, then."

"No, Rafa."

"Tell her, Angélica…"

"Can I say something?"

"What is it Julia?"

"Well you said the boys had to have lamb chops, but I'm a girl and I want garlic chicken."

"OK, all those who want chicken put up their hands…"

My sister-in-law, Isabel, assuming her husband's rights as the first-born, took over and, ignoring the waiter, started to count hands; everyone fell silent as if someone had pressed 'PAUSE' on a film we had seen a thousand times: the Carríon Otero Family Meal, twelve adults - only eleven now - and eleven children, soon to be twelve.

"Mamá, who was that girl who showed up at the end?"

There was a long silence.

"What girl?" my mother threw the question back at me.

"What are you having, Álvaro? I haven't got you down here."

"Be quiet a minute, Isabel," Mamá's blue eyes sparkled with curiosity, "What girl, Álvaro?"

"There was a girl, about Clara's age, tall, dark with long straight hair… She turned up right at the end in a car, but she stayed by the cemetery gate. She was wearing trousers, huge sunglasses and a raincoat. You didn't see her?"

No one else had seen her. She had crept slowly into the cemetery, stepping carefully so that her high-heeled boots wouldn't sink into the mud, yet she wasn't looking at the ground or the sky, she was looking straight ahead, or rather, she was allowing herself to be looked at. She walked across the recently-mown grass as though walking down a red carpet; there was something in her bearing, in the way she moved, shoulders relaxed, arms gently swinging as she walked, utterly different from the involuntary, inevitable, almost theatrical stiffness common to mourners at a funeral, even if they did not really know the deceased. I couldn't see her eyes, but I could see her mouth, her lips were slightly parted, serene, almost smiling, though she did not actually smile. She drew level with me and stopped, far from the fur coats and the coarse wool jackets. Perhaps she knew I was her only witness, the only one who had noticed her, the only one who would later remember having seen her, perhaps not.

"I thought maybe she worked with you?" I turned to my brother Rafa, my brother Julio. "Maybe she was once Papá's secretary or - I don't know - maybe she worked for the estate agents."

"If she had, she would have come over and said something," Rafa looked from me to Julio, who nodded. "I certainly didn't mention the funeral to anyone at the office."

"Neither did I."

"Well… I don't know. But I did see her. Maybe she knew dad better than she knew us, perhaps she was a nurse at the hospital, someone who looked after him? Or she didn't feel comfortable coming over to talk to us…"

But these were things I had thought of afterwards to try to justify her departure, which had been as sudden and inexplicable as her arrival. At first, I stupidly thought that she had made a mistake, she hadn't know there was a funeral and had some other reason for being in that small, remote cemetery on that cold, Thursday morning in March. It wasn't just her attitude, the studied casualness of a woman with no particular place to go, a woman who simply wants to be seen. There was something worryingly incongruous about her presence at my father's funeral. Those present fell into two diametrically opposed groups: the people my father had known as a child, and those he had known as an adult. This woman was young, well dressed, wrapped up warmly, yet in spite of her expensive boots, her hair was loose and she was wearing no make-up. If she had been related to Anselmo or Encarnita - or to any of the people of Torrelodones - she would have gone over and said something to them. But she didn't. Instead, she had opened her handbag, taken out a packet of cigarettes and a lighter, lit one, taken off her sunglasses and stared at me.

"I don't know what to say…" My sister Angélica was slower to react. "I work at UCI, I know all the nurses there and she doesn't sound like anyone I know… Besides, even if she was too embarrassed to talk to

Mamá, she would have said hello to me."

"Well, all I know is that I saw her," I said again, looking around the table. "Maybe she's somebody's neighbour, or she went to school with one of us, she could have been at school with Clara…"

"Maybe she's a local," said Rafa as Clara shook her head.

"I thought that too, but she didn't look like she was from Torrelodones."

"That doesn't mean a thing, Álvaro," my mother said. "Maybe if she were my age, but nowadays young people all look the same whether they're from small towns or the city. It's impossible to tell them apart."

The woman had looked at me as though she knew me, or was trying to work out who I was, and it occurred to me then that this was why she had come - not to be seen, but to see us. I had looked into her large dark eyes, and she had held my gaze, patiently, resolutely as though she had been waiting a long time to see us again or simply to acknowledge us, to acknowledge me. I had smoked so much over the past two days that I had woken up that morning determined never to smoke again, but there was still a packet in my coat pocket, and watching her slowly smoke her cigarette, I was forced to break my resolution. By the time I had lit my cigarette, she had finished hers, and when I looked back, she was no longer looking at me, but staring straight ahead, at my mother who was sobbing gently as Rafa took a handful of earth and threw it onto the coffin, at Clara, who, in one last, heartbreaking gesture, threw flowers into the grave, at my little nephews in their suits and ties, awkward in these roles, these clothes, knowing that grown ups were watching. At that moment I realised that this woman knew exactly where she was and I felt a shudder of anxiety, of fear – not of danger but of the unknown. Then my mother collapsed. My brother Julio caught her and everyone clustered round, and I realised that it was over: the shovels, the prayers, the ropes. By the time I, too, finally stepped forward and took my place next to my family, my father had begun his journey towards oblivion.

"I saw her." My nephew Guille, Rafa's youngest son, stopped playing with his mobile phone and looked up at me. "She was wearing a checked jacket and those trousers people wear for horse riding. They were tucked into boots that came up to her knees?"

"Yes, that's her. I'm glad you saw her too…" I smiled at him and he smiled back, a fourteen-year-old pleased to be the centre of attention. "Did you see her leave?"

"No. She was right at the back. I thought she'd come up to us afterwards, but I didn't see her again. I only noticed her because… well, she was pretty, wasn't she?"

"It's strange..." my brother Rafa looked from his son to my mother and then to me.

"Could she be related to us, Mamá?" I persisted, "A distant cousin or something..."

"No," my mother snapped, then paused for a moment before saying, "Please, *hijo*, I think I'd recognise my own relatives. I may be old, but I'm not completely gaga."

"Yes, but..." I didn't dare continue, because I saw something in those eyes I did not expect. "It doesn't matter..."

"Álvaro, are you on something?" my sister Angélica interrupted in that slyly solicitous tone everyone in the family recognised from births, hospital visits and convalescences. "The pill I gave you this morning wouldn't make you act like this..."

I had been waiting to see the woman up close, to look into her eyes and see their colour, find out who she was, why she was there, why she studied us so closely - but all the fur coats and woollen jackets had converged, hugging friends and strangers, kissing smooth cheeks and cheeks, and the woman did not appear. Then my mother, looking more shattered than she had even in her husband's final hours, asked if one of us would help her back to the car. Julio and I had each slipped an arm around her, felt the astonishing weightlessness of her body, and manoeuvred her out of the cemetery. "Forty-nine years," she murmured, "forty-nine years we lived together, forty-nine years we slept in the same bed, and now..." "Now you have Clara's baby on the way, Mamá, you get to watch your grandchildren grow up," Julio babbled, "you have five children and twelve grandchildren, and we all love you and need you. We need you so we can go on loving Papá, so that Papá carries on living, you know that..." My mother walked slowly, Julio trying to console her with sweet, slow words. From time to time I kissed her, pressing my lips to her face as I glanced around to find the mysterious woman, although I suspected she was already gone. I was certain that this woman had known exactly what she was doing, turning up at the last minute when the mourners had their backs to the cemetery gates, when the family was gathered around the priest, leaving her free to watch the funeral from a distance, shielded by the last paroxysm of grief, only to disappear as those unaffected by the death came forward to offer their condolences. She had anticipated all this, but she could not have reckoned on me, my one phobia, the morbid aversion to funerals that had frustrated her clever plan. I had seen her - just me, and a fourteen year-old boy - and I might have forgotten all about her were it not for the fact that, as I left the cemetery, I became convinced that her appearance at the funeral had not

20

been an mistake, an accident, or any of the names we give to such chance events. She had come, and she had looked at us as though she knew us, and when I had looked at her, I had seen something familiar in her profile, a vague, fleeting impression I could not put my finger on, in the same way that I could not say what it was that had made my mother's eyes flare a deeper, purer blue when I had asked my innocent question.

"Why didn't you say something at the time, Álvaro?"

"Say something about what?" Miguelito was struggling in my arms like an animal as I tried to strap him into the child seat in the car. By the time I had managed to buckle him in, he was fast asleep.

"About the girl..." Mai started the car.

I slipped into the passenger seat. My sister Angélica, in her usual hysterical way, had insisted that I wasn't fit to drive. Besides, I didn't feel like it.

"You could have told me at the time, or when we went to pick up Miguelito, or on the way to the restaurant."

"I suppose so..." I couldn't think of anything else to say. "It just didn't occur to me."

We stopped at a traffic light and Mai smiled and stroked my hair. Then she leaned over and kissed me, and this warm, calm, and affectionate gesture rescued me from the cold and the worry of the morning, bringing me back to somewhere familiar, to the little patch of garden that was my life.

"It was strange, though..." she said after a moment, as we turned onto the motorway.

"Yes. I mean no," Death is strange, I thought. "I don't know."

Grandma Anita's balconies teemed with geraniums, hydrangeas and begonias, blooms of white and yellow, pink and red, violet and orange spilling out of the clay flowerpots, climbing the walls or tumbling over the railings. "In Paris, the frost used to get them every year", she said to her granddaughter as she stepped outside to water them. It was a difficult task, because the plants were constantly searching for space that did not exist, climbing over one another as they grew towards the light and only grandmother knew exactly when and where, how and how much to water each pot.

"Come over here into the sun with me, I'll comb your hair."

For Raquel, this was the prelude to the most glorious part of her Saturdays. She would rush over and sit very still, staring out at the balconies that looked like posters advertising happiness as her grandmother brushed her hair.

"Why do people call you Anita, grandma?"

Absorbed, as she watched as her nimble fingers divide and subdivide the tresses with almost mechanical precision, Grandma Anita hesitated a moment before answering.

"Because that was the name I was given."

"But you were named Ana, weren't you?"

"Of course. My father wanted to call me Placer, pleasure, but my mother didn't like it. She said Placer was no name for a decent, hard-working woman…"

Although Raquel could not see her face, she knew her grandmother was smiling although she had never understood why it was funny. "And as I was the youngest in the family, and I was never very tall, and I was only fifteen when we left… Well, everyone always called me Anita."

She finished braiding one side and began on the other: the plaits were perfect, the same length, the same thickness, not a single stray hair, and as symmetrical as ears of corn.

"What about you?" she asked after a moment, "Do you know why you're called Raquel?"

"Of course I know," Raquel took a deep breath and rattled off the answer. "Grandma Rafaela didn't like her own name, but she wanted Mamá to be able roll her Rs properly, so she wanted to find a different name beginning with R, and Raquel was the one she liked best, so she was called Raquel and Mamá and Papá liked it best too, and that's why they called me Raquel too, even though people say the thing about

22

rolling her Rs is just silly."

"Well, they're wrong," Grandma Anita took the girl by the shoulders, turned her round and studied her carefully, looking for some fault she never found, then kissed her cheeks, her forehead and the tip of her nose. "Now you look beautiful. Do you want to wake your granddad?"

"Yes!"

And Raquel dashed off into the darkness of the long hallway with its high ceiling and parquet floor, so different from her own apartment, until she came to the last door, the door to her grandparents' room, where light reigned once more. She had always loved this apartment from the first time she saw it, unfurnished and freshly painted with a blue and white 'For Sale' sign hanging from a forlorn balcony that could not possibly imagine its future splendour. "Look, Mamá," she said struggling to read the words, partly because, although she had learned to speak in Spanish, she had learned to read in French, and partly because she had something with a strange name that her father and some of her uncles, and cousins, also had, which made it hard for them to read or write in either language. "*Se Ven-de*, Mamá, look," but her mother was already making a note of the phone number. "Come on," her mother said, "maybe there's a caretaker." There was, and he had the key, "This way," he said, "We've just had a lift installed, see, they brought it all the way from Germany and, of course, these old houses, well, they're not geared up for all these new-fangled gadgets…"

They went up to the apartment in the strangest lift Raquel had ever seen in her seven short years. The lift was so small it looked like a toy, and they had to go in Indian file – first the caretaker, then Raquel, with her mother bringing up the rear. "You'll see," the man said, "It's a beautiful flat, it's just been done up. They took out the partition walls to make the rooms bigger, and put an extension on at the side – there used to be a little terrace there, and they put in a kitchen and a second bathroom…" In the month and a half they had been scouring Madrid for an apartment for her grandparents, they had heard this all before but this time, it turned out to be true. They stepped into a large rectangular living room with two large balconies and a round, wrought iron pillar in the centre. "It might get in the way a bit when they try to arrange the furniture," said her mother, "but it's nice." When she had first seen the apartment on that October afternoon in 1976, with the light of the weary sun thrown like a translucent gauze over the dying leaves of the trees, the room that Raquel had liked best was this room at the end of the corridor. It too had an iron pillar, with the same capital of leaves and tendrils, but here the pillar was not in the centre of the room, but slightly to one side.

23

Facing the wall where the bed would be, a row of windows opened onto a sea of rooftops and terraces, waves of red, ochre and yellow surging towards the distant horizon above what seemed to be an empty space, but was actually a large terrace, almost a garden, since the tops of the acacias reached the third floor.

From here, Raquel could look out over Madrid, the red roof tiles dancing between light and shadow, all alike and yet different, like scales or petals, cunning mirrors that absorbed the sunlight to reflect it on a whim. The slender, jagged spires of churches rose humbly over undulating cityscape which danced around them like a boat, like a dragon, like the ancient, throbbing heart of a sky more beautiful than any Raquel had ever seen. How big the sky is here, she thought, as she looked out at an infinite expanse of blue so intense, so pure, that it didn't seem to be a colour but a thing, the true image of every sky. A few high clouds formed a wispy veil so delicate that the light passed through unaffected, the clouds looked hand-picked, placed in the sky deliberately to accentuate the blue. This sky which had greeted her towards the end of the day was the same sky which, years ago, her grandfather Ignacio had bid farewell to at dawn, not knowing that he would carry it in his heart wherever he went for such a long time to come.

Raquel already knew that sun and light and blue were important to Spanish people. "I'm dying, Rafaela", her grandfather Aurelio, her mother's father, had said to his wife, stepping out of the surgery where the doctor had just diagnosed him with a serious, inoperable heart condition. "You heard me. I'm dying, and I want to die in the sun." Rafaela had not wanted to tell her only daughter the truth. Her daughter who had married here in France, before her brothers, and who had just fallen pregnant. "We're going back," she had said simply, "We're going to sell our house and buy a house by the sea, in Malaga maybe, or Torre del Mar, wherever your father wants…" We're going back, we're not going back, I think they're going back, I'd like to go back but my father doesn't want to, I think my family will go back sooner or later. Nobody ever said where they were going back to – they did not need to. Raquel, who was born in 1969 and grew up hearing sentences composed of every tense, mood and interpretation of the verb 'to go back', never asked why. That was simply how things were. The French moved, or went away, or stayed. Not the Spanish. The Spanish either went back or did not go back in the same way that they spoke a different language, sang different songs, celebrated different holidays and ate grapes on New Year's Eve.

Her maternal grandparents had gone back, and so, after her third birthday, Raquel was sent every summer to stay with them in the bright, cool house, which had a large terrace with a vine, where her grandfather would sit and stare out at the sea. She would climb on to his knees and sit there quietly, kissing her grandfather, who was very ill, though he did not seem ill, and every time he would say the same thing; it's nice here, isn't it, it's nice here. Later, in August, her parents would arrive and they would drive to Fuengirola for a picnic on the beach or to Mijas for a donkey ride, or to Ronda to see the bulls. On the last day of summer everyone would be sad, so much so that Raquel felt they were not 'going back', but they were leaving – leaving behind the scent of the bougainvilleas and the rosebays, the orange trees and the olive groves, the smell of the sea and the boats in the harbour, the whitewashed walls, the flowering window-boxes and shade of the vines, leaving behind the golden oil, the silver sheen of sardines, the subtle mysteries of saffron and cinnamon, leaving behind her own language, because to them, to go back did not mean to go home, one could only 'go back' to Spain.

And so, when Raquel's family arrived in Paris, Papá's parents – the ones who had not gone back – would invite them to dinner, and grandmother Anita would ask them lots of questions, tell me everything, where did you go, what did you have to eat, what did people say, what music did you listen to, was it very hot, were there many tourists, did you bring me the things I asked for? They had brought them – a huge box of sweet pepper and another of spicy, cans of tuna, anchovies, purple garlic, manchego cheese, a whole ham, chorizo from Salamanca, *morcilla* from Burgos, haricot beans, chickpeas, salt pork, and two huge bottles of olive oil they always bought in the village of Jaén on the way back. That's good, Anita would say then, that's good, and her eyes would fill with tears, and you remembered the aubergines, I'm glad, you can't get them here, they don't know how to cook them... Of course they know, Anita, grandfather Ignacio would interrupt her, they just don't make them the way you like them. I suppose you're right, she would say, and then, a little fearfully because they both loved him, they would look at Mamá and say, "And your father, how is your father?" Oh he's fine, she would answer, it's incredible but going back has done him a world of good, maybe it's the weather or... well, you know. Grandmother Anita would quickly nod and say, that must be it, because her husband was looking at her again as though he had been pricked with a long, sharp needle. It's just foolishness, Anita, and don't say it again, because I don't want to hear it.

Afterwards, grandmother would shut herself up in the kitchen and spend three days cooking, preparing a feast for the second weekend in September. Every year she and her husband held a dinner for their

Spanish friends and a few French friends who loved Spanish food – apart from her son-in-law, Hervé, aunt Olga's husband, who was charming, a kind man, very forward-thinking, but he was from Normandy and claimed that olive oil didn't agree with him. Grandmother was terribly offended, though she always prepared something special for him, an endive and walnut salad, or meat cooked in butter, an alternative menu that grew with each passing year because every year there were more French people and fewer Spaniards. The tenses of the verb 'to go back' accelerated, quickly moving from the future to the present. After years of inactivity, of the permanent listlessness of sleeping in another man's bed, everything suddenly began to change for the Spanish. Raquel was very young, but she understood.

We're going back, even her father used the verb, though he had been born in Toulouse and his wife had been born in Nîmes. We're going back too. It was September 1975, they had spent August in Torre del Mar and her father had found a job in Spain, not in Malaga where grandfather Aurelio lived, but in Madrid, grandfather Ignacio's city. I'm going to go out there next week, *Papá*, just me. Everyone else will stay until Christmas while I look for an apartment, a school and so forth. Since it's just Raquel and the boys, and since Mamá goes to work in Aubervilliers every day, I was thinking that, if you don't mind, they could stay with you for a few months, that way we wouldn't have to wait until the last minute to move our things. You wouldn't mind dropping the kids off at school and picking them up again would you Mamá?

Her brother Mateo was so young he wouldn't remember Paris, but Raquel was six years old and although they had not even left, she was already beginning to miss the place.

"What is it, niña, don't you want to go?" Grandma Anita, chopping nuts of uncle Hervé's salad, looked worriedly at her granddaughter who was quiet and withdrawn. "You'll be happy in Spain, you'll see, and don't worry about school. Do you remember how you cried when I told you you wouldn't be going back to kindergarten? And what happened? Nothing. You met lovely Mademoiselle Françoise and you made lots of friends. Well, it'll be the same in Spain, it'll be better, because it's your own country, our country. We're Spanish, you know that."

I'm not, she was about so say, you all might be, but I'm Parisian, I was born here and I don't want to go back, I'm scared of leaving my friends, my school, my home, the streets and the TV programmes. This is what she thought, and if in the end she resigned herself to voicing a more restrained objection, it was not because at six years old she could not clearly formulate her thoughts, but because she knew that in this house

26

such things simply were not said.

"I wish we were at least going to Malaga. My grandparents are there."

"So what? Your grandpa Ignacio comes from Madrid. Ask him, he'll tell you all about it."

"Why don't you come with us grandma?"

"Because... because some must work and some must play, that's why." She finished chopping the walnuts, tossed them into a bowl and put her hands on her hips. "Because your grandfather doesn't want to go, he's the most stubborn man in the whole world, and I should know I'm from Aragon, and they say we're stubborn as mules. When they wanted to make him a French citizen, he didn't want it, when we were able to save a bit of money, he refused to buy an apartment, and look at your grandpa Aurelio, with the little he made on the house in Villenueve, and even with everything he had to pay off, he still had more than enough to buy the place in Torre del Mar. But not your grandpa Ignacio, oh no. I've always had to lead him round by the nose. And for what? I ask myself. For nothing. Where's you grandpa Aurelio, the one who was stupid enough to put down roots in France? Back in Spain. And where's your grandpa Ignacio, the one who always refused to invest a centime here? In France. So here we are and here we'll stay."

"But you want to go back..."

"Of course..." her grandmother sat down and took the girl in her arms. "If I'd married a Frenchman like Olga, maybe not, but... I married your grandfather, I was lucky enough to marry your grandfather, because we've been very happy together, but always in Spanish, speaking Spanish, singing in Spanish, bringing up Spanish children, with Spanish friends, Spanish food, Spanish habits... I learned to cook just like my mother-in-law – *cocido* on Saturdays, paella on Sundays – I've gone on doing it all these years, and I loved her as if she were my own mother, because she was there for me when your father was born and we didn't know where Ignacio was, didn't know if he was alive or dead, and I wasn't even married. We had a hard time, back then, but everything was logical, it made sense, and now... Now I don't know what we're doing here, especially when you're going back. If it was up to me, we'd be in Madrid already."

"What about the town you grew up in?"

"Where I grew up? I don't ever want to set foot in that place..."

That was how strange, how absurd, how incomprehensible things were. Because they were Spanish. Raquel's father had been born in Toulouse, her mother had been born in Nîmes, at the age of fifteen, her grandmother Anita had left a village somewhere in Teruel, but her granddaughter never knew its name and never wanted to know, because Anita could not bring herself to say it. Near the Sierra de Albarracín, was all she would say, and that it was a miracle she was alive at all, because they had killed everyone, her father, her brothers, her brothers-in-law, everyone except her, on that one terrible day, when, barely fifteen years old but with the courage of a woman of thirty, she had set off down the road with a tubercular sister and a mother who, at fifty, was like an old woman, until eventually she reached Toulouse.

There, alone, she had been taken in by a married couple from Madrid, Mateo Fernández and his wife Maria, who had two sons, one had been executed by firing squad in Spain, the other was a prisoner somewhere in France, forcibly conscripted into a military work detail simply because he was Spanish. They also had two daughters, the elder girl, barely twenty years old, was widowed, her husband executed before the same adobe wall where his brother-in-law had been gunned down. Anita married the only boy in the Fernández family to survive the two wars, "our war and the other one", she would say, as though Spanish wars were better, different, more important, and it had made her very happy to see her eldest son paired off with Raquel Perea, daughter of a man from Malaga named Aurelio who was scared of nothing except thunderstorms. Aurelio had been about to cross the border into Spain, having escaped from the internment camp where he had met Ignacio Fernández alias 'the Lawyer', but at the last moment, when he was close enough to see uniforms of the *guardía civil,* he turned back, because we come from a country of bastards, that's the truth, what more can you say.

This was the same Aurelio who had now gone back because he wanted to die in the sun, and every year he seemed further from death, living in the shade of his vine; these thoughts brought tears to the eyes of the woman who now cradled his granddaughter in the kitchen of her house in Paris, grandma Anita, who in her whole life had never seen an Andalusian vine, had never been to Malaga, had never seen the Mediterranean except from the Côte d'Azur, who had lived in France for more than twice as many years as she had lived in the village in Aragón whose name she could not bring herself to utter, who was alive thanks to a miracle and who had probably saved her husband's life when, in 1945, he told her he was thinking of crossing the border because they needed men there, experienced men capable of fighting for the cause. "Please, I'm begging you, Ignacio," she had said to him, "whatever you do, don't go back, you've already given enough, and I have only you, I have no family now, no home, no village, no country, nothing, all I have is you and a son you did not meet until he was two years old, and another on the way, you've done enough already, leave it to others now." "Others have done as much as I have," he said. "But they can do nothing for us, and you can. You're needed here, Ignacio..."

This last argument, shot through with such love, such desperation, had kept the most stubborn man in the world in France, the man who had wanted to go back to Spain when his wife did not want him to go and who did not want to go back now when she wept, homesick for the shade of a vine she had never seen. This was how things were; little Raquel could not make sense of them, yet this emotional maze where dead end streets all led to a chalk-white house by the sea was the backdrop to her life, the life she had been given.

"I'm sick to death of the civil war," her father would sing when they went for a drive. Her mother would burst out laughing and add another verse, "and sick of the brave Spanish Reds, tralala" "I'm sick to death of Madrid," her father went on, "and sick of the battle of Guadalajara, tralala" her mother replied. "I'm sick to death of the Fifth Regiment, and sick of that photo of dad in the tank, tralala, tralala, tralala..." It was the same every Sunday, driving home after grandma Anita's paella, her parents falling about laughing, and yet her father was in Spain now, and her mother was packing their things and to every question she asked Raquel received the same answer, "because I say so, because we're Spanish." Until finally her grandpa Ignacio gave her a different answer.

"I could have died many times, you know. I could have died during our war, the civil war, or when I was locked up in Madrid, or when I escaped from prison. I could have died when they put me in Albatera, or when I was thrown off a train in Cuenca in the middle of nowhere, or when I took a van from Barcelona to Gerona. I could have been killed crossing the border, or I could have died in the camp in Barcarès - a lot of people died there - or when I deserted, or when Madame Larronde told my mother that my brother-in-law was about to turn me in, or afterwards when I went back to my battalion, when I escaped again, when I fought against the Germans, let's see..." he counted them off on his fingers. "Thirteen times I could have died, and I'm still here. What do you think?"

"What about when you wanted to go back to Spain and grandma wouldn't let you?"

"That doesn't count."

"And why were you escaping all the time."

"Because they were trying to kill me."

"Who was?"

"Everyone."

But that was after the sad, tropical November morning, cold outside and too warm inside, when she heard her mother screaming into the phone, Mamá, we already know, and heard it on the radio and I phoned my husband a while ago. Really? Good, but don't cry, Mamá, put Papá on the phone, Papá, don't shout, calm down or you're going to make yourself ill…"

Raquel could not tell the time, but she knew it wasn't early because the light was blazing through the blinds, and it was Thursday, she was sure of that, she had been counting off the days until aunt Olga would take her to the cinema with her cousins, and now there was only one day and one night until Friday. Then the doorbell rang and it was aunt Olga, and she was shouting too. Raquel was scared. She sat quietly in her bed trying to work out what had happened until she heard her brother Mateo crying and she got up. They were all in the kitchen, looking sad and solemn. Aunt Olga was blowing her nose and putting coffee on the stove, Mamá's eyes were puffy, and her grandmother was shaking her head, giving deep sighs as though she was finding it difficult to breathe. Her husband, sitting in front of the empty table, arms hanging limply at his sides, was the only one who saw Raquel come in.

"What's going on?" Raquel climbed onto his lap without asking permission.

"Franco is dead," he said and hugged her.

"Is there no school today?"

"Not for you. Today is a holiday."

"Why does no one look happy then?"

He seemed more upset that the others, but when he heard her say this, her grandfather burst out laughing and his wife, his daughter and his daughter-in-law joined in. It was then that the holiday started, a long, strange day – perhaps not the strangest day Raquel would experience between then and that May afternoon in 1977 – but the only one on which she could do whatever she liked from morning to night.

At lunch time, she was still wearing her nightdress, she hadn't had her glass of milk but had stuffed herself with a packet of chocolate biscuits, she had drunk two coca-colas, and had used her mother's make up, but nobody seemed to notice, they didn't seem to notice anything, yet they never stopped coming and going, and the phone and the doorbell rang and rang and people they knew and people she didn't know came in and kissed her and some of them stayed and some of them went away and some of them ate of someone of them didn't. Grandma Anita shut herself up in the kitchen as she always did when she was nervous, and kept popping into the living room with a tray, and later uncle Hervé showed up with her cousins, Annette, who was called Anne after her grandmother and Jacques who was called Jacques just because, and Raquel played, she put make-up on her cousin Annette, until they heard two loud claps and then her grandfather's voice shouting, "Come on, we're all going out."

It was half past four in the afternoon and nobody was crying now. Mamá had cleaned her face, smiling from ear to ear, even though Raquel was covered in smudges of every possible colour, then she dressed her up in a new outfit, and her outdoors coat and a silly hat that was really only a toy called a bonnet and was really horrible. Raquel was about to take it off and leave it on the hall table but she was distracted by Uncle Hervé offering to take her over to his house with his children, he was taking Mateo, and even more by her grandmother's reply, "No, let her come with us. She's old enough and this way she'll always remember today."

Raquel would always remember that day, but not because of the kisses and the hugs, the joy and the tears, the celebrations and corks popping from champagne bottles. Spanish *fiesta* flared behind a few select doors of Paris, singular places, strange and yet familiar, where her grandparents were welcomed, people calling out their names, suggesting they try a *tortilla de patatas,* and another, each one the last, for this was a night long filled with bottles of champagne and *tortillas de patatas,* of kisses and fierce embraces, of curses and nicknames, of public vengeance and private grudges, of toasts to absent friends and questions to no one in particular. Because we are Spanish, and the Spanish can never be completely happy, a disciplined, drunken variant of despair began to show in the moist eyes, at the edges of the faces of hard, unemotional men, exhausted by the constant exercise of their stubbornness, as one by one they raised their glasses and repeated, 'the dog is dead', and forced themselves to look happy, although they already knew that they would be dead long before their anger died.

Raquel would always remember that day, but not because of the miraculous transformation of her grandmother, who suddenly looked like a young woman, walking as though she were floating on air, as though she were dancing, nor because of the way her grandfather looked at his wife, his eyes wild, as if he were falling in love, thirty-three years after he had fallen in love with her the first time. They kissed each other long and hard as the dancing came to an end in a square where younger and very different Spaniards, the bitter fruit of Franco's Spain, students and self-imposed exiles, pseudo left-wing adventurers from respectable families and brusque labourers, had organised an impromptu *fiesta* with an Argentinean *bandoneon* player who knew how to play *pasodobles.*

"Spanish?" a young man staring at them asked aunt Olga. She took a long drink from the bottle before replying.

"Yes."

"Emigrants?" he asked. Olga took another drink and shook her head; she paused for breath and pointed to grandfather.

"This is my father," she said, "Ignacio Fernández Muñoz, alias The Lawyer, a public defender in Madrid, captain of the Republican Popular Army, he fought against the fascists during the Second World War, twice decorated for helping to liberate France, a Red and a Spaniard," her voice quivered with a pride which Raquel did not understand.

She had heard these things many times, this was her grandfather, the father of her own father, who sang 'I'm sick to death of the civil war' and fell about laughing, and his sister, who joined in the songs and laughed along with him, but that did not surprise Raquel as much as the reaction of this stranger, little more than a boy, who walked over to her grandfather, shook his hand and spoke to him, his voice thick with emotion, his body stiff, head held high.

"*Señor*, it is an honour to shake your hand."

Raquel, who would remember this day her whole life, watched the scene as though she were watching a movie. The accordion stopped playing, the dancers stood motionless, the singing quickly trailed off as a murmur moved through the crowd, fragmentary, reverential, almost liturgical whispers, *captain, republican, exile, red*, the noble words spoken in low voices.

Captain, republican, exile, red, words like precious jewels, like a spring of fresh water bursting forth in the middle of the desert. All eyes turned towards this tall, well dressed man, who looked no different than a Frenchman, since he was blonde and fair-skinned, and his wife, the short dark-skinned woman pressed against him, looked too sophisticated to be Spanish, with her hair cut short and dyed a deep red, and a modern coat that came down to her ankles. These boys, with their long hair, their round, wire-rim glasses, their shirttails hanging out and their duffle-coats unbuttoned and these girls who wore their hair loose but otherwise went around dressed like grandma Rafaela, their faces solemn, yearning, respectful as though they had been waiting for this moment their whole lives.

At first, her grandparents were so stunned that her grandfather did not manage to say anything as he clasped the first boy's hand. "I'd like to shake your hand too," said a second boy, the third called him comrade, and the fourth, a girl, thanked him, "We owe so much to people like you." At that point, grandmother, who had managed not to cry all day,

32

broke down and began to sob, the tears falling from her eyes with a gentle reserve, "I'm very proud to meet you, *señor*, it is a pleasure, an honour," until the last of them, a short lad with black curly hair who stood to attention in front of him like a soldier, at your service, captain, and grandfather closed his eyes, opened them again, and at last he smiled.

Is it possible, he murmured, shaking his head and repeating this phrase so typical of him, is it possible, he said it whenever something good or bad seemed impossible, the inevitable prologue to shocks and surprises, unexpected sorrows and joys, is it possible, he said, and rather than take the boy's hand, he hugged him.

At that moment, the whole square seemed to take a breath, inhaling and exhaling as one, the buildings and the people coming alive again. The accordion started up, grandma took her husband by the arm, "Dance with me, Ignacio," and they danced together, alone in the centre of the plaza, and when they finished, they kissed each other for a long time, as though they were finally, truly happy.

When they finished dancing, everyone clapped and clustered round them. Corks popped again, and everyone toasted the day and the night, and now they felt able to speak, to ask questions and answer the questions the grandparents asked. They came from all over: Catalonia, Galicia, there were half a dozen from Andalucía, someone from Murcia, a couple from Ciudad Real, a girl from the Canary Islands, a few Basques, two people from Asturias, an Aragonese man from Zaragoza and four or five people from Madrid, two of them, even claimed to be from Vallecas. They seemed a tight-knit group, although most of them had not met until that morning when they had wandered out into the streets where they gathered in twos and threes and went to find the bars where Spanish expatriates congregated. They had spent the whole day drinking and singing, dancing, rounding up a number of French people along the way, girls mostly, a couple of Chileans and the Argentinean who was playing the bandoneon, but Raquel did not know this because she had fallen asleep on a bench and had to be woken up for the photos.

She fell asleep again in the car and did not wake again until her mother tried to get her undressed and put on her nightie. After that, she could not get to sleep again. She could hear doors opening and closing, whispered goodbyes, a half-silence broken by the furtive sounds of someone else who was awake but attempting to be quiet. Raquel was alone in her bedroom that night as Mateo was sleeping at aunt Olga's. She got up, went out into the corridor and found the light was on in the living room. Her grandfather did not tell her off. Instead, he smiled, took her in his arms and told her how he might have died many times.

"And why did everyone want to kill you?"

"For being a republican, being a communist, being a Red, for being Spanish."

"And were you all those things?"

"Yes, and I still am. That's how I might have died many times, but I survived, and do you know why?" Raquel shook her head, her grandfather smiled again. "For nothing," he paused for a moment and then said it again. "For nothing. So I could dance the *pasodoble* with your grandmother in a freezing square in the Latin Quarter in front of a bunch of kids. Oh, they were good kids, generous, funny, great kids, but they don't know what they're talking about, they have no idea what they're saying."

"But that's not nothing."

"No, you're right. But it's not much. Not much at all." Her grandfather kissed her and looked down at her. He was still smiling, but Raquel had never seen a sadder smile than this. Her grandfather's sadness was the reason she would always remember this day, the night of 20 November 1975 – a deep, dark, smiling sadness, the remains of a day of laughter and shouting, of champagne and *tortillas de patatas*, a Spanish fiesta, wild and dark and joyous, and this tired old man smiling at this final defeat, a trivial defeat, definitive, cruel and ambiguous, the work of time and of chance, the victory of death and not of the man who had eluded it so many times.

Ignacio Fernández had not shed a single tear that day. He had watched his wife cry, his daughter and his daughter-in-law, had watched many of his friends and his comrades weep, men who like him might have died but had lived to see their enemy's corpse pass by. A toast, they said, because we come from a country of *hijos de puta*, a country of cowards, cads, of grateful stomachs, a shitty country, he had heard all these things and had not shed a single tear. Since we have not been able to kill him these past forty years, let's drink a toast, and he had said nothing, done nothing, but silently raised his glass over and over again. I want to die, Ignacio, said an old man who had hugged him in one of the many places he had been tonight. Don't fuck around with me, Amadeo, he had said, today is not a day to die, and now he was smiling, but his granddaughter did not understand.

"Don't talk like that, granddad," Raquel tried to say, as choking tears rose in her throat.

"Hey," Her grandfather held her at arm's length, frowning, then took her in his arms again, "What's the matter?"

"I don't know." And she didn't know. "It just makes me said when you talk like that."

"Don't worry. I'm happy, even if I don't seem like it. Now I can go back too."

The following morning, Raquel could not remember going back to bed, but she would never forget that conversation. She remembered her grandfather hugging her, lying down next to her, and the next thing it was morning, and Mamá was in her room, "Get up, Raquel, *mi hija.* Come on, breakfast." Later, her grandmother had taken her to school as if it was an ordinary day, and it was an ordinary day except for the fact that she was exhausted and fell asleep at break time, and later, when aunt Olga picked her up and took her and her cousins to the cinema, she fell asleep again and didn't see the film. As it turned out, this was lucky, because when she got back to her grandparents house she was wide awake and she immediately realised that the young man getting out of the taxi outside the door was her father, and this sparked off another *fiesta*, one that was private, and familial, sour, sweet, bitter, salty, one that was perfect.

"I wanted to be with you, Papá, with you and Mamá." Her father said simply. He handed out presents, a huge box for Raquel, a smaller one for Mateo, a bottle of perfume for his wife and one of olive oil for his mother, and a patient, detailed account of the events of the previous day as they had been witnessed at first hand. His father listened attentively, his expression solemn; he did not even smile when his eldest son admitted that he was still hung over after the epic drinking binge. He had had a few glasses of champagne at the office in the morning, and had continued the celebration with cider, white wine, rum and whisky. "It wasn't my fault," he said, "we had to mix our drinks, because by lunchtime, there wasn't a glass of champagne to be had in Madrid." Grandmother was already making plans, juggling dates, calculating how many bedrooms they would need, "we could live somewhere near you, what do you think Ignacio?"

Her husband did not reply at once. He drained the glass of brandy in front of him, got up from his chair and put his fists on the table; only then did he explode.

"What are you talking about Anita? Would you mind telling me what the hell you're talking about?" Grandmother lowered her eyes and said nothing, no one dared to speak although uncle Hervé, who was French and who had had his fill of these outbursts of Spanish passion, gave a weary shrug which his father-in-law did not notice. "You know who's giving the orders in Spain? Haven't you seen the *hijo de puta* crying?

35

Don't you know who he is? Phone Aurelio, go on, let him tell you, or call Rafaela, they know all about him in Malaga."

"But the other day, when you saw Ramón, you told me…"

"I know what I told you! I told you that Ramón told me that X said that Y had heard that Z had been informed at some secret meeting – though nobody knows when or where this meeting took place – that somebody, and we don't know who that somebody is, said they weren't going to do anything without us. And do you know what that means? It doesn't mean shit, what's what it means. It's possible, Anita, that right now, at this very moment, I'm not fucking Spanish any more. I don't have a Spanish passport, or a French passport or any other kind of passport. All I have are papers stating that I'm a political refugee and my membership card for the Spanish Communist Party, something that's even banned in France. Where do you want me to go with that?"

"But Aurelio…"

"Aurelio was ill, I'm not ill…"

"That has nothing to do with it."

"It has everything to do with it! Aurelio is retired, I'm not, I'm fifty-seven and I can't live on fresh air, Anita, I can't suddenly decide to get up and leave, and neither can you. You'll have to talk to the woman who runs the nursery school with you, decide what you're going to do, whether you're going to sell up or close the place, I have to find a job, I can't …"

"But you've already talked to Marcel and he…"

"He nothing! Marcel will do what he can, when he can, and right now he can't, right now we have to wait, to see how it goes, how things develop. At least that's what I'm going to do. If you want to go back before then, talk to your son, I'm sure he'd be delighted.

"Why are you so stubborn Ignacio?" Grandma Anita shook her head from side to side, having travelled this road so often before.

"I'm not stubborn," he replied, almost gently, "I'm realistic."

"Realistic my foot! You're stubborn, that's what you are, stubborn as a mule."

Her husband made no further attempt to defend himself. He simply went back to his seat, poured himself another brandy, and toyed with it for a moment.

"Anyway…" At the sound of her husband's voice, grandmother stiffened, but he was not talking to her now, but his son. "Where did you say you were living?"

"It's a small development, four apartment blocks with communal gardens near Arturo Soria."

"And where's that?"

"Well, I'm not sure how to explain… At the end of the Calle Alcalá, right at the end, past the bullring."

"In Ciudad Lineal?"

"No, further out, heading towards Canillejas."

"Canillejas?" Ignacio Fernández looked at his son, eyebrows raised, his face like that of a frightened child. "But that's miles outside Madrid."

"It used to be Papá. Nowadays it's part of Madrid. The city has grown a lot since you were there."

"But I never even thought I'd be living in Canillejas," he said and glanced at his wife, who gave him a curious smile, shaking her head as if to say she had been right all along.

"So what do you want?" his son was smiling too, "I don't think you're going to find a place back on the Glorieta de Bilbao."

"Well, if not there, at least somewhere nearby."

"What's the name of that square?" One year later, this was the first question Raquel asked the caretaker as he helped her take down the blue and yellow sign from the balcony which was clearly no longer for sale. "That's the Plaza de los Guardias de Corps," he told her. "That's difficult," she said as the man who had told Mamá that he realised the apartment was a little expensive, but in this neighbourhood, they wouldn't find anything better signed a piece of paper. "And how far is it to the Glorieta de Bilbao?" she asked him. "On foot?" She nodded. "About ten minutes if you're a slow walker… That's not far, now, is it? No. I'd say it was very close."

"You're going to love it, grandpa, you're going to love it", she had rushed to the phone as soon as they got home, eager to be the first to tell him the news, "You can't imagine how big the sky is from there."

In the hour and a half of my second class that morning, my mother managed to crash the voicemail system of my mobile. Álvaro, *hijo*, it's Mamá, don't forget to give Lisette the money for the gardener; Álvaro, *hijo*, remember to pick up the post, I know you'll probably forget; Álvaro, *hijo*, when you pick up the post, could you go through it and throw out the junk mail, because I don't have time for all that rubbish right now; Álvaro, *hijo*, instead of gorging on junk food... like you always do, why don't you ask Lisette to make something for you back at the house, you know what a good cook she is; Álvaro, *hijo*, call me when you're leaving La Moraleja, I might take your sister out shopping... I deleted the messages before leaving the campus, standing at the bar with a glass of beer and two *montaditos de lomo*, the house speciality, famous all over the Madrid's Universidad Autónoma, although some people said the secret ingredient was simply that the chef never cleaned the grill, then I left a message on Mai's voicemail – she was the scatty one – to remind her that I couldn't pick our son up from school that afternoon, since it was my turn to, 'keep an eye on things', as my mother put it, at her house.

It had been a little less than a month since my father's death, and I quickly worked out that she had previously delegated the task to my two brothers, working down the list by age and leaving out the women, as she always did. I did not know how my brothers had felt going back to a house that inevitably still bore traces of Papá, his things still strewn over his desk, his favourite chair still turned to face the television because we were all at that autistic, considerate stage of mourning, when everyone tries to avoid burdening others with his own grief and hopes they will do the same. Almost every afternoon, we spent some time with my mother, so we saw a lot more of each other than usual, but by virtue of the strict but tacit agreement between us, we avoided discussing the recent memories of our adult lives, settling instead for the shared memories of childhood, which were sweet and easier to digest.

In peacetime, I got along well with my brothers, when there were no external conflicts to trouble the comfortable, routine topics of conversation - the weather, the football, the kids. But lately, things had been anything but peaceful and a number of family meals, children's birthday parties, even Christmas 2003, had degenerated into blazing rows. Whereas previously, Papá's distaste for talking politics had put a brake on such things, now we found ourselves re-enacting on a smaller scale the tensions that divided the whole country. Divisions in the dining room echoed the balance of power in government, with the right-wing holding an overall majority, while the opposition – my mother, my brother-in-law Adolfo and me, with the passive support of my sister Angélica – was zealous and argumentative. The radicalism of one side fuelled radicalism on the other, to the point where I found myself haranguing my pupils about the evils of the government before the 2002 general strike, even though I had joined a union only to support my friend Fernando, and until then had adopted political views more out of instinct than necessity. My family had been at daggers drawn until that first day in March 2005, when collective grief at our father's death had brought us together. Now, however, the fault-lines had once more begun to show.

As happens in almost all large families, ours had been divided into two groups, the elders – Rafa, Angélica, Julio, and the 'little ones', my sister Clara and me. The fact that I was only four years younger than Julio but five years older than Clara had never seemed to matter, but over time, other factors had complicated this web of rifts and alliances for everyone but me.

Rafa and Julio worked together. Both had bowed to my father's wishes. He had wanted his first-born to study Business, his second to study Law and would have liked me to become an architect so that he could parcel out his various companies between his three sons. When I told him Architecture didn't appeal to me, and that I was thinking of doing Physics, he gave me a long and detailed lecture outlining the advantages of his strategy. Though he never reproached me for my decision, I still felt as though I had disappointed him. Angélica's vocation as a doctor, in a family with no paramedical precedents, appealed to him and Clara's unpredictability in embarking on two careers and finishing neither frustrated rather than upset him.

Faced with the professional common ground my brothers had shared almost since university, my sisters slowly began to forge an alliance based entirely on gender. For their part, Angélica and Julio shared the fact that both had divorced and remarried, and had had children by both partners. Although they had each married only once, Rafa and Clara shared the fact that both had married partners of a high social standing that our own, though in the case of my sister-in-law Isabel, who had blue blood on both her mother's and her father's side, the size of our family fortune somewhat took the shine off aristocratic names.

In each case, I had remained on the sidelines. I did not work for the family business, I had been the last to marry, my only wedding had taken place in a registry office, my wife worked as a civil servant, her family were practically paupers and my son was the only one of my parent's grandchildren to go to a state school. To top it all, I was the only member of the Carríon family to vote for the left until my sister Angélica, the perfect wife, capable of winding herself around the man by her side with the sinuous intimacy of an orchid to a tree, kicked off the twenty-first century by unexpectedly leaving her first husband – a rather dumb urologist who had already walked out on her a couple of times – for an oncologist who was more intelligent than she was, handsome, charming, a militant atheist and even more left-wing than me.

Since then, my brother-in-law Adolfo had sided with me in these arguments and my sister followed our lead, albeit with some difficulty, since she had previously had no interest in politics beyond an instinctive, I would almost say pathological, approach to law and order which consisted of blaming everything on the victims. Five years into her second marriage, she could just about keep this trait in check and I was grateful to her for having brought someone interesting into our family discussions.

My isolated position, meant that I could maintain a similar, equidistant relationship with all my siblings, including those like Rafa and Angélica whom I loved but did not get along with. Julio, who as a little boy had seemed destined to idolise and emulate the first-born, had adroitly managed to shed this role to become a very different man, someone whose moods veered from light to shade with equal intensity. He was very likeable, funny, he adored his children, and he knew how to get the most out of those pleasures in life that cost nothing. In addition, he was much weaker than Rafa, which to me seemed a virtue, and although we didn't have much in common, he was the closest thing to a friend I had among my brothers and sisters.

Clara and I still shared a special closeness, though I knew that there were times when she looked at me as though I were from another planet, wondering what I had done with her brother Álvaro. None of this bothered me much, until the day my father had another heart attack and the gravity of the prognosis meant we kept vigil into the long dark hours, the brothers- and sisters-in-law all vanishing, leaving me alone with Clara and Mamá in the waiting room of UCI. Then, perhaps because I had nothing else to do, I thought about my family, what we were, what we had been, about the things that brought us together and those that kept us apart, about the things that had endured and those which time had obliterated.

My father made it through the night; in fact he would live for almost a fortnight. From that moment, my sister and my mother became inexplicably important, almost indispensable to me, not simply for what they represented, but for that part of me contained in each of them. And I knew that this was simply a side effect of grief, a trap set by my tired brain, which was frantically, attempting to commit to memory every date, every place, every image of this man whom we could now do nothing to save. To remember my father was to remember us all, freshly washed and combed and dressed, posing for the camera in every family snapshot in the photo album which Mamá kept in the attic, along with the folders in which she kept our school reports. And I was thinking about this as I unwillingly, almost fearfully, prepared myself for my father's absence, his desk still littered with papers, his chair in front of the television, maybe even his toothbrush, or worse still the empty space where his toothbrush had once been. But I had not reckoned on Lisette.

"Álvaro!" I opened the gate with the remote control, but she was already standing outside the front door waiting for me, as though she had heard the car, "It's so lovely to see you!"

I gazed up at her for a moment for the simple pleasure of looking at her. Then, as I bounded up the half-dozen steps to the front porch, I wondered how she would greet me. In front of my mother, Lisette always addressed me formally and referred to me as 'señorito Álvaro'; in front of my wife, Lisette talked to me as a friend but did not kiss me when we met. That afternoon she kissed me on both cheeks, as she always did when it was just the two of us, and then hugged me, rocking me like a mother comforting her child.

"How are you, *niño*?"

"Fine," I said, but my smile faded as I realised what she meant, "Well…"

"I know…" Slowly she let the palms of her hands slide down the back of my neck before stepping away, "I know…"

"Your mother called to say you would be coming," she said as she walked into the house and headed towards the living room, "I've made you some sandwiches and a little salad…"

"Thanks Lisette, but I ate something at the university before I came."

"Oh," she seemed disappointed, "So I suppose you won't want some *crème caramel* after all the trouble I went to learning how to make it?"

"OK then," I smiled finally, "I'll have some of that."

Lisette herself was as rich and intense, as syrupy and golden as the crème caramel she now offered me. She had the face of an exotic doll, almond-shaped eyes with just a touch of make-up, full crimson lips, her body small and slender yet curvaceous with soft, velvety skin the colour of milky coffee. "Have you seen Mamá's new maid, the one from Santo Domingo?" my brother Julio had asked me at one of his kids' birthdays and when I told him I hadn't, he put his face in his hands "Jesus, she's sex on legs."

At that point I burst out laughing, although I didn't particularly pay him any attention since my brother was the kind of player who tripped over gorgeous women at least twice a day, even if he only went out to walk the dog. But when I saw Lisette I had to admit that, despite his somewhat shallow and indiscriminate taste, this time my bother had not been exaggerating. "Hey," I said when I next saw him, back when my father still wanted us all to go to a restaurant for Sunday lunch, "you were right!" "Right about what?" Julio asked, "That thing you said about the Caribbean," I replied, even though it was just us and Rafa at the bar and none of the women could overhear, "I was right?" I nodded "Boy were you right!" "Well, I did warn you," he shot back. "Incredible," I said, "Fucking incredible," he stressed, "Could you two just stop all that bullshit?" interrupted Rafa, who, according to Julio, had always been appropriately interested in women, that is to say, not very interested, "you sound like a couple of horny schoolboys." "Not schoolboys", Julio burst out laughing, "but definitely horny" and I laughed with him.

I liked women a lot more than Rafa did, but I was less obsessive than Julio. I didn't go looking for them, I didn't run around after them, I didn't chat them up in bars or chase after them at traffic lights. To me, women had always seemed to be a sort of gift, an extraordinary goodness that floated far above my head and rained down on me from time to time. I never felt that I had done anything to deserve the attention that some of them lavished on me, perhaps because, although I found them beautiful, funny, gentle, and infinitely arousing, I also found women strange. I never bothered to try to fathom the mysterious working of their minds, never doubted for a moment that they were the ones who did the choosing; I was content to watch them come and go, neither regretting those who were beyond my reach, nor believing that their preference was in itself valuable, but accepting their existence gratefully. In any case, I loved my wife.

Mai and I had been together for nine years and neither of us had yet shown any sign of growing tired of each other. She was still cheerful, tranquil and patient, did not meddle too much in those parts of my life that did not concern her, and valued her own independence. I was grateful that she was easygoing and was pleased that she did not seem to miss the intense, emotional ups and downs of the kind of love that catapulted many of her friends from abject depression to the dizzy heights, only to spiral inevitably back down into depression, their lives like a squall constantly about to break.

"She's a complete idiot, you'll never believe what she's done this time," Mai would say before she'd even hung up the phone, annoyed by histrionics I simply found amusing.

Then, she would lie next to me on the sofa and I would stroke her hair while she brought me up to date on the endless passions, the jealousies, the break-ups, the doubts, the reconciliations, the wild make-up sex, the business trips, more jealousy, more doubts, more break ups and I wondered if sometimes she too was prey to these strange, intense, feelings, beyond reason, something capable of dismissing common sense in favour of some mythic happiness as insubstantial as smoke. Or not.

I didn't know, because I was not the kind of person who felt this kind of suffering, that kind of happiness and so, sometimes as I sat there listening to Mai I wondered if she had the same doubts that I did, if she had ever wondered about the stability of our life together, what we were losing in return for this image of the perfect couple. I never saw the least indication that my wife was unhappy, not even the hypothetical plane in which I played out these timid conjectures. It only took a moment for me to remember how much I loved Mai, that I liked her, that we were happy together. This had always been enough in dangerous situations and although there were a number of isolated instances when I had succumbed to temptation, I had only ever cheated on her when I was away from home, and only with women I met by chance and did not find too attractive, at least not attractive enough to think of these nights as anything more than a moment of madness. Whenever I met a woman I thought I might grow attached to, I put up barriers.

Consequently, I did not suffer from any pangs that first summer Lisette spent at my parents' house, and since that time we had had a curious relationship, a sort of innocent flirtation that did not worry me in the slightest. This was a game that I knew how to play, something that the women I genuinely found attractive – Lisette, the secretary at the museum, one of my colleagues – realised immediately. Some of them, especially the younger women, were hurt by my lack of ambition, but for the most part we had fun.

"Delicious," I said as I finished the dessert, "You get better every day."

"Thanks," she smiled, "How is your mother?"

"Not great. She says she's fine, but... Staying with Clara has done her a world of good. She spends her whole time tidying: the kitchen cupboards, the wardrobes, the box room. My sister must be going up the walls, but it keeps Mamá busy."

"She will come back, won't she?"

"Of course she'll come back!" I said with exaggerated emphasis because I could hear a waver of anxiety in her voice and realised she was worried about her job. "She still doesn't really get on with Curro and sooner or later she's bound to get bored of reorganising things. Clara is due next month, so Mamá will probably hang around until the baby is born, but she'll be back here by the middle of June, when it starts to get hot. You know how much she likes to have her grandchildren over in the summer."

"I could go and stay with her there, help her with things," she pursed her lips, her face both puzzled and hurt, "but she doesn't want me to."

"Of course she doesn't, because she'll be coming back here, and she needs you to look after the place in the meantime, to pay the gardener and so on... That reminds me, I brought some money for you," From my wallet, I took out half a dozen sealed envelopes held together with an elastic band, each one carefully marked with my mother's elegant, old-fashioned, handwriting. "Has there been any post?"

"It's in your father's study," Lisette gave a shrug, "I always used to leave it there. I'll go and get it if you like..."

"No, I'll come with you..."

I did not know how my brothers had felt, I knew that I was going to find this very difficult, and yet I had not anticipated the aching sadness that breathed through every object, permeating the whole house with an invisible patina at once ancient and impossibly new. Heading towards his study, something I could have done blindfold, every step I took, every door I opened, every thing I touched jolted me with the realisation that this was a step, a door, a thing that still existed in a world where my father did not.

Matter has no spirit and yet, my soulless body ached at the implacable memory of this room, the antique wooden desk, the wine-coloured leather wing chair, the fading Persian rug and, at the far end of the room, the low table, pair of armchairs and sofa, its back to the huge glass-fronted bookcase. The study smelled of my father, it held the touch of his fingers, the sound of his voice, the gaze of those eyes that had looked around this room day after day, year after year. Some of the most important events in my life had taken place in this room. It was here that as a teenager I had phoned my girlfriends in secret and read illicit books, here that I had confessed that I did not intend to study architecture, here that I announced that I had received a scholarship to study for a doctorate at a university in America, here that I told my father I was going to marry

Mai and that I was going to have a child. Yet none of these things seemed important now, while the harsh glare of the furniture, the mathematical precision of the angles between desk and chair, stapler and letter-opener, appointment book and pencil holder all proclaimed the passing of this man who would never use them again. Standing in this impossibly lifeless, the certainty of the loss hit me again. I wondered how many more times it would happen, how long it would be before I would simply remember my father as I wanted, rather than feeling obliged to do so by rituals, by well-meaning words and ceremonies.

I love my father. I admire him, I need him, I miss him, but I had not yet learned to conjugate those verbs in the past tense. It wasn't easy. In death, we say, all men are equal, but it's not true, they are not equal in our memories. My father was more extraordinary than we, his children, would ever be and his strength, energy and integrity was reflected in us, doing more to keep us whole and united than all my mother's affectionate scheming. I knew this better than anyone, because I was the one who had drifted away the most, the only one who had not attempted to be like him. I regretted that now, in spite of the yawning gulf between my beliefs and his. He always knew that I loved him, that I admired him, that I needed him, but that was not enough to relieve the nagging feeling that I had ended up being the son he would never have wanted to have.

It was not easy being the son of a man like my father, a natural charmer, a born winner, a magician, the genie of his own magic lamp. I never met anybody who did not like him, did not submit eagerly and seek out his company. Nobody, that is, except me, when I saw myself reflected in him and felt overwhelmed by the difference, crushed by his superiority. I did not even manage to be taller than him, and the inch I never grew, the inch that would have made me as tall as him, expanded in my adolescent mind to become a symbol of my failure to live up to him.

Sometimes, I felt proud of myself, but I never felt that my father would be proud of me. And yet, despite the fact that I was the only one of his children to question him, the values that he stood for, he had always been more magnanimous to me than I had been to him, as though he could tell that my defiance was not a whim, but a need that grew out of my own sense of inferiority. It was not easy to be the son of a man like that, at least it had not been easy for me, and all that forgotten pain, long buried in the sands of all the days that had passed, since the time when he had been the most important person in my life, now spouted again with every memory of him. Death is terrible; it is savage and impious, insensitive and cynical but most of all it is dishonest.

45

"If that all there is?" Lisette nodded as I picked up the pile of letters which lay on the desk. "I'll take them into the living room."

I didn't want to sit in his chair, didn't want to lean over his desk and touch his things, but as I was leaving, I could not help but notice the empty spaces on the wall.

"Where are the photos?" I asked, referring to three framed portraits, one of my father in a German army uniform posing beside a plane, one in which he and my mother stood facing each other, smiling, she almost a girl, he already a man, the name and address of a photographer on the Gran Vía in the bottom right-hand corner, and a snapshot, yellowing at the edges, of my father standing between my two older brothers in their school football kit.

"Rafa took them," Lisette said, her voice hesitant until she saw my smile. "Julio took the photo of your mother on the desk, the one in the silver frame, you remember... The girls haven't been yet. Aren't you going to take anything?"

I took a moment to digest what she had said. Death, I realised, had magnified my brother Rafa's unconditional, extreme worship of my father's personality. I shook my head.

"Not now," I said at last, "I'll have to think about it."

It didn't take long to sort through the post, about thirty letters, the junk mail outnumbered by the smart white hand-addressed envelopes bearing yet more belated condolences. There were a few invoices, which I gave to Lisette to file with the others, and five letters from five different banks, four of them in ordinary window envelopes and the other in a sealed envelope which I opened in case it was just a leaflet offering a loan. When I realised it was a personal letter from a financial advisor, I put it with the others. I said goodbye to Lisette, kissing her absent-mindedly, and headed back to Madrid

The traffic was so heavy on the motorway to Burgos that as I passed Alcobendas, I was able to see that the interactive museum I had been working with for a few years had now taken down the banners that had advertised the exhibition on Mars on loan from a German museum. The next exhibition, on black holes, was one I had curated myself. I was happy with the way it had turned out, yet, long before I reached Madrid, I found myself thinking about the woman at the cemetery again, as I had done at some point every day for almost a month.

I thought about her and I thought about me, and when I did, I remembered the strange state I had been in when I saw her, that sudden heightened awareness which had fixed her in my memory like some posthumous facet, dark and secret, of my own father.

I didn't dare to talk to anyone about this, because I realised that there was something unhealthy about my curiosity, something I did not quite understand myself, but something that had led me to the town hall in Torrelodones to check that there had been no other funerals that day or the previous day. Two people had, however, been buried the following day – a nineteen-year-old motorcyclist killed in a traffic accident and an elderly woman who had been born in the village. The official who dealt with me, and who unquestioningly accepted my garbled excuses about some mix-up over the invoice for the hearse, told me that the population of Torrelodones had grown considerably, but that most of the newcomers were from Madrid, with families who tended to bring them back when they died. "Your father was different, of course, but then he was born here," he said.

I knew that there was something unhealthy about my fixation, but my visit to the town hall completely did away with the reassuring possibility that what had happened was down to chance, since a road accident was news and the relatives of someone who had died of old age would know each other in a village like that. The presence of a strange woman at my father's funeral was not a mistake, a slip-up, or a mix up of any kind. I should have been troubled, but I felt oddly reassured, almost happy at the thought. I didn't say anything to anyone, not even to Mai, and yet she was the one who unwittingly steered me in an unexpected direction.

"Álvaro," she said that night, when Miguelito was in bed and the two of us were eating together in the kitchen, "I've been thinking... How old was your father when he married your mother?"

"I don't know... Let me think... he was born in '22, and they were married in '56... Thirty four.

"Thirty four," she nodded slowly as though chewing over the number along with her salad, "That's what I thought."

"Why?"

"I don't know. It's just extraordinary, isn't it? A man who lived to be eighty-three, who didn't marry until he was thirty-four, who lived through so much, the civil war, the second world war... And it seems normal to us, obviously, because that is who he was, and we knew him. But there are lots of things we don't know about his life, or at least things I don't know. I mean, he must have had a lot of girlfriends before your mother, mustn't he, when he was in Russia and so on? Think about it... I wish we'd talked to him more about his life, I feel we've missed an opportunity to get to know him... Maybe it's just that I miss him," she reached across the table, took my hand and squeezed it, "I loved him very much, Álvaro, you know that..."

"And he loved you…" I said, squeezing her hand.

Mai had been one of my father's greatest conquests. When I met her, a few months after I came back from Boston, I was still getting over a complicated relationship with an Asian-American girl called Lorna, who could go from charming to insufferable, often in the same day, occasionally in the same hour and sometimes from one minute to the next. At first, I thought that this was what people meant when they talked about passion, but after a while I became convinced that it was more likely a nervous disorder of some sort, so I dumped her, and she set about trying to ruin my life. I had never really thought about spending the rest of my life in the United States, but Lorna was the deciding factor in my return to Spain. When I got back to Madrid, the last thing I wanted was another relationship, but I was thirty, I was single, and I was employed so the whole world was secretly plotting to pair me off. Mai had no part in this scheming, but she did sleep with me the first night I met her.

"What a shame!" she said the next morning, "but that's life I suppose. I've been waiting for years for an interesting man to appear and now that I'm almost engaged to someone else, you show up…" We kissed goodbye, a long, languid kiss filled with the melancholy of those destined never to meet again, but less than eight months later my friend Fernando, who was married to one of her cousins, invited me to another party.

"I've got a bad feeling," he said to me as I arrived, "But careful, this whole thing smells like a hunt to me, and I think they've got you down as the fox…"

I burst out laughing.

"What is it? Are you OK with this?" he said.

"I don't know," I answered, "You tell me, you're the expert on this family."

"Well," he said, "I've seen worse," and he raised his right hand, making the sign of the cross, giving me his blessing, "But don't say I didn't warn you."

"What happened to your fiancé?" I asked Mai when I saw her, though I had already worked it out from her appearance, she looked more sophisticated, more stylish than the last time. "Nothing," she said, "That's just the problem, nothing happened." She was stunning, wearing a short, brown low-cut dress, with bronze highlights in her hair and the wild brilliance that blazes in a woman's eyes when she is on the hunt. "I'm glad," I told her, "I've been thinking about you a lot." This would not have been totally true ten minutes earlier before professor Cisneros had taken me into his office to offer me the benefit of his wisdom, but it had been true ever since, as she tilted her head slightly to give me a sidelong smile, brazen, alluring, perfect. And I had no doubts. Not that night, nor the next morning, nor in the months that followed, when she let slip that she was thinking of moving in with me because she never slept at her place any more.

The one moment of hesitation occurred some time later, when I had finally used up every excuse imaginable for not taking her to meet my curious family. It was July and sweltering hot. As we drove through the gates, somewhat imposing in themselves, of my father's property in one of the most expensive parts of La Moraleja, she seemed so overwhelmed that, for a moment, I thought our relationship might not make it through the paella. "Jesus Christ," she said as I parked in the one space left by my brothers. Everyone was sitting on the porch, gathered around my father like magistrates at a tribunal. As we started up the steps, my father got to his feet, and bestowed on us a particularly captivating version of his famous radiant smile. At that moment, I thought my girlfriend, who was highly intelligent, might find this impeccable display of affection suspicious. But I was wrong.

In time, Mai became my father's favourite daughter-in-law, the only one worthy of receiving his constant, ambiguous attention to the end, an utterly paternal affection mingled with a sort of wistful flirtatiousness, the easy charm Julio Carrión always used to win over his sons' wives, so different from the manly complicity, the unspoken macho bond, he used with his sons-in-law. I was amused by the banter between my father and my wife, and even more amused to see that my mother was jealous, even my brothers were jealous, furious at the unexpected advantage this common girl – whom they had never thought of as a good match – gave me over them. In my family, we all competed for my father's attention, it had always been this way, and Mai had no problem with that. Rafa's wife was slightly ugly, fairly spiteful, and very very slow – too slow to keep up with her father-in-law's constant punning and word play. Papá would sometimes lose his patience and in a jokey tone which did nothing to mask his irritation, say, "Come on, Isabel, you're not stupid." He preferred Julio's first wife, Ann, who was cute, clever and gentle, but she was gone. In 1999, a few weeks before their tenth wedding anniversary, my brother dumped her for another woman, who, as far as my father was concerned, would always be the other woman.

"What? Have you actually met her?" he said to me once, when I dared to defend her as we watched Julio's car move down the driveway.

"Yes, Papá," I said and started to giggle, which did nothing to help my good intentions, "I was the first to meet her."

49

"I want to ask you a favour, Álvaro..." That morning I had noticed a nervousness in my brother's voice when he phoned, "you can't say no, this is really important to me." This preamble, somewhat more serious that his usual 'Listen, Álvaro, it's Julio, and since we're having dinner together, I need to talk to you about the business", alerted me to the exceptional nature of the situation, but it did not prepare from what came next. "You and Mai have to come round to dinner one of these days, I need to introduce you to my girlfriend." "Girlfriend?" I said, "Well, it's just that... I'm divorced." "Not yet, you're not," I objected, it was barely two weeks since we had heard about his separation, "Well, I'm getting divorced, it's the same thing, isn't it?" and he rattled off parrot fashion, "She's a wonderful girl, really, she's great, I really love her, I don't think I've ever been in love before, and you two are the trendy liberals in the family, Álvaro, I thought you'd be on my side..." he took a deep breath and then picked up again, "It's just that Veronica – her name his Veronica – she doesn't trust me", I'm not surprised, I thought, but I didn't say anything, "I'm serious about her, I swear, but she doesn't trust me because I told her that I was already divorced... so she's suspicious, you know, and I need to introduce her to someone in the family, and you're the only one I can ask, I thought you two wouldn't mind – I mean you didn't even have a church wedding. For Christ's sake Álvaro, don't fuck around, you're hardly going to tell me now that you think marriage is for life..." Mai didn't much like the urgency in my brother's request, but she agreed that we couldn't refuse, and in the end, despite her principals, she enjoyed the evening as much as I did.

Julio had invited us to dinner at the most expensive and exclusive restaurant he knew, an extravagance that did nothing to favour his twenty-six year old girl-friend, who was undeniably pretty, though Mai didn't think so. Verónica was passably educated, though you would not have thought it to look at her. She was wearing makeup that made her look ten years younger, her hair was carefully coiffed, her nails were painted with little purple moons, and she had squeezed herself into a miniskirt and jacket that were two sizes too small for her. From the denim embroidered with sequins, mirrors and coloured thread, Mai immediately recognised that the outfit was the work of a chic Italian designer, and more importantly, she told me, obscenely expensive.

But at that moment, she just looked like every other twentysomething and countless thirtysomething girls having dinner with rich men old enough to be their father. In an ordinary restaurant, despite the twelve-year age gap between them, Verónica would have attracted attention only because of her magnificent cleavage – "It's a push-up bra," Mai

50

whispered to me – but this black basque and its effects were hardly sufficient to justify the ruin of the family, although they were disturbing. I didn't say this to my wife, obviously. And if I sided with my brother, it was not because of his girlfriend's breasts, but because of her intelligence, though she hid it well. She looked at Julio as though he were a God and, for his part, he looked at her like a benevolent, all-powerful deity in thrall to her formidable gravity-defying breasts. Six weeks later, in spite of my shrewd advice that he should take things slowly, Julio showed up with her unannounced at father's birthday dinner. Papá was not taken in by her demure t-shirt.

"She's a cheap whore, Álvaro, Jesus Christ, you only have to look at her!" "It doesn't surprise me coming from your brother, Julio has always done his thinking with his dick, but come on! You're more intelligent than that. I think…"

"No Papá," I interrupted him gently, "OK, she does look like a tart, but I don't think she *is* one. She's a nice girl, seriously…"

"Well, I'm not saying she isn't… But she'll cheat on your brother, that's for sure. I give it a month."

"It's not like that, Papá," I insisted, "It's the other way round."

I was right, something I also found out before anyone else. "Álvarito, listen you need to come over, we need to talk about the business," It hadn't been a year since the wedding but Julio and Verónica were still together, still happy in their elemental, lopsided, effective way. Although she had had two children one after the other, both of whom were so young that she had to take them everywhere with her, she would occasionally dress the way she used to, and Julio would look at her like a Greek god in all his helpless omnipotence. Until one day my father had a heart attack and had to be hospitalised for the first time, six months before he would go in for the last time, and Julio showed up at the hospital crying like a baby because Verónica had twice caught him cheating on her, and now had packed her bags.

Between sobs, my brother told me what had happened, "Now you've got the house to yourself," she'd told him at the door, "You won't have to ask anyone for favours, you don't have to remember to erase the message on your mobile before you come home or hide the credit card statements. I'm leaving, so you can fuck whoever you like." I realised this was the first time I had seen Julio cry since we were young, and I asked him why he didn't cry a little less and try a bit harder to stop sleeping around. He shrugged his shoulders and went on crying. Verónica took the kids and left, she didn't complain, she didn't phone people to badmouth her husband, she didn't talk to a lawyer, she didn't

51

ask for money and she didn't plot her revenge. All she would say was: "I still love him, but I can't take it any more." The way she behaved - dignified, sober, firm – finally won over my mother and my brother Rafa, but it did not convince my father.

"I told you she was a cheap tart," he said offhandedly, when, after two months, Julio finally managed to convince her to come back, "Didn't I tell you?" I was so dumbfounded I couldn't think of anything to say.

His words pierced me like a hard, brittle splinter, fossilising inside me, in that perfect place we think of as the heart, and I have never been able to recall them without a shiver running through me. Maybe I should have asked him why he said it, by what criteria he had made a judgement which to me seemed inconceivable. But I did not dare to question him, maybe because I was afraid of what he might say.

"You're making a big deal out of nothing, Álvaro" Mai took my father's side, as always, "What do you expect? Your father is an old man… he probably can't accept that a woman would leave her husband, particularly when that husband is his son…" Alright, Julio had it rough for a while – in fact I thought there was a certain dignity in the way he humiliated himself, a sort of tragic nobility I never thought him capable of, just as I had never realised how much he loved Verónica even though he cheated on her again and again. And I knew that I had never experienced anything like this, but I felt close to my brother, his red eyes, his trembling hands, his forlorn face, his ashen skin, and sunken cheeks. And at that moment, I understood Verónica too, I could imagine how she had left a home that she would one day return to, could imagine her opening the front door of her rented flat to take the children to nursery only to find her husband sleeping there fully clothed. After this, my father did not leave hospital. He was too weak now. He had only four months to live and yet in spite of everything, in spite of the fact that his voice was a faint echo of my father's voice, he had still found the strength to say: "I told you she was a cheap tart."

I heard those words again when my wife said that there were things my father could have told us that we did not want to know, they came to me unexpectedly as I sat in the traffic jam on the Burgos motorway, because Mai's strange remark had merged with the image of the woman in the graveyard.

There was something unhealthy about my curiosity, I realised that, but my father's venom towards my sister-in-law seemed somehow to be tinged with guilt, when connected to the fleeting apparition in the cemetery, and the fact that no one else seemed to care did nothing to allay my fear. It had never occurred to me to wonder what kind of man my father might have been before he became the man I knew. Maybe he had a girlfriend when he was in Russia, Mai said, and my mind had lingered on the thought, teasing out this possibility and other, much stranger possibilities, yet none of them could wipe away the icy chill of his words, nor help me to understand the look on the face of a young woman who had looked at me unhurriedly, like someone with a mission to accomplish.

I parked the car in the garage and walked down to Calle Argensola where my sister Clara lived in the beautiful, spacious old apartment we had lived in as children. I loved that house, had thought of it fondly ever since my father had killed two birds with one stone by building on one of the plots he owned in La Moraleja, so that he would have a house befitting his position and be able to escape the upheavals that now plagued what until then had been one of the quietest areas in central Madrid. I was fifteen years old when we moved to the suburbs and I spent the next ten years commuting between the old house, which my father had not sold since my brothers argued that they could sleep in the Argensola flat on Friday and Saturday nights to avoid driving home drunk, and the new house, which I stopped going home to on weekends when I came of age and got my own key to the Argensola place. For the next five years, during which I spent most of my free time wondering how to find space for all the books in my tiny, cramped, disproportionately expensive flat in Boston, I felt even more homesick for the Argensola flat with its spacious rooms and high ceilings. By the time I came back, it was too late. Clara, the most precocious member of the family, had already booked a date for her wedding and was having the flat renovated. I had to make do with the nearest thing I could find to it in the area, a big, slightly dilapidated flat on the Calle Hortaleza, which was fine once it had been done up, but which did not stop me feeling a wave of sadness every time I stepped through the door of my sister's place.

"Look who it is! Álvaro," my mother opened the door and gave me a shy smile before kissing me hard on both cheeks, "I knew you wouldn't call me before you left."

"But, Mamá, you *knew* he was coming," Clara, her lips puffy, her ankles puffier still, came to meet me, greeting me with the joy of a besieged soldier watching the cavalry arrive. "And, anyway, Álvaro knew you'd phone Lisette to ask her what time he'd left."

"And how could he know that?"

"Because he knows you, Mamá," she said kissing me again, "Because he knows you."

"In any case, I don't know what was so important you couldn't call your mother."

Clara suggested that maybe we could all have coffee, so we went into the living room. I sat on the sofa beside my mother while she went through the post, slicing through the envelopes with a letter-opener that cut as cleanly as a scalpel. She seemed to be in much better health, physically, than she claimed. In spite of her delicate appearance, she was a strong woman who had never suffered a serious illness, and had always recovered quickly from minor ailments. We all believed she would eventually get over the shock, but by the time she read the second letter of sympathy her eyes were filled with tears, and when she finished reading the last of them, she fell back against the sofa, burying her head in the cushions and stayed there, absent, for a time. Clara arrived with the coffee and gave her a glance somewhere between worry and pity.

"You don't understand how much I want this all to be over."

"Of course we understand, Mamá," I said seeing in her the weariness I myself had felt a little earlier, the desperate need to simply remember my father as I wanted to, rather than feeling obliged to do so by rituals, by things, by well-meaning words and ceremonies.

My mother took my hand, nodded, heaved a sigh and sat up again, then, ignoring the cup that Clara had put in front of her, she began to look at the other letters in the pile.

"What's this?" she asked, holding up the letter with the Caja Madrid letterhead I had opened earlier.

"It's from someone in some bank or other, they want to talk to you about money, some investment fund Papá had with them. Give it here, let me have a look..." I read the letter again and paraphrased it for her, "That's what it is, Papá had invested money – it doesn't say how much here – in tax-deductible bonds. Anyway, this man wants to know whether you want to redeem the capital or reinvest it in bonds, which – not surprisingly – he thinks would be a much better option..."

"What's his name?"

"The guy who wrote the letter?" My mother nodded. "It says R Fernández Perea, I'm not sure, Ramón, Ricardo, Rafael..."

"I don't know him."

"Maybe Roberto," Clara chipped in.

"Or Remigio," I said. My sister started to laugh but she stopped our little game when she saw the look of impatience on my mother's face.

"No, I don't know anyone by any of those names. And what does this person expect me to do? Does he want me to call?"

"Let's see," I glanced back at the letter, "He says he is at your

54

disposal should you wish to meet with him personally, but you could just call him. The phone number is here."

"Go and see him, Mamá," Clara looked at her and then at me, "Since it's about money, I think that's better, don't you?"

"Of course," I agreed though I had no opinion.

My mother sipped her coffee slowly.

"One thing, Álvaro… These accounts or whatever they are, were they in your father's name or in the company's?"

"Looks like they were in Papá's, he's the only one mentioned."

"Well then, you go. Call him, meet with him and he'll explain everything."

"Me?" I tried to defend myself, "Why me? I don't know anything about that kind of thing. Let Rafa go, he knows about money."

"Rafa knows about company finance, not personal banking, and your father always kept those accounts separate. It's better that you go. Anyway, your brothers are always busy. It'll be easier for you to pop into the bank some morning, and …

"Mamá, I have a job too, you know."

"Yes, I know, but… It's not the same. It's not as if you teach every day, *hijo*."

"But…" I've got an exhibition about black holes in two weeks, so I'll have to be at the museum every day, I was about to say, "Alright…"

I gave up. It was a battle I could never win, just like the battle to convince my mother and my brothers that the State didn't pay me a monthly salary to sit around – an argument that wasn't helped when I started working as a consultant for the new Interactive Science Museum, so that I now earned more than my sister Angélica, the only other Carrión who worked in the public sector. Far from enhancing my prestige, this merely confirmed my family's opinion that my job was nonsensical. "And you're telling me some bank gave you money to set up this place?" my mother asked me the day I took her to the museum with my nephew Guille - whose opinion I was far more interested in, given that he was the brightest ten-year-old I knew. "Millions, Mamá, millions" I said. She raised her eyebrows. "But it looks like an amusement park," she said finally. "What did you expect? Tracts about Newton on the walls and cabinets full of medieval slingshots?" I asked. "Well at least then it might *look* like a museum," she replied. We didn't say another word to each other until Guille returned to us. "It's incredible, Álvaro," he said, "no, seriously, I love it, it's frigging fantastic!" My mother told off her grandson for talking like that and on the way home scolded me for wasting my talent on such rubbish.

55

"So you'll go and see the man at the bank?" she said at the door when I was hoping to get away with just a goodbye kiss.

"Yes, Mamá, I'll go…"

And that was it. My mother sent the wrong son to the meeting, and nothing would ever be the same again.

That afternoon, when she went to wake him, Raquel Fernández Perea found her grandfather Ignacio sitting up in bed with his glasses on, staring into the distance at some point suspended above the blue spring sky which hung like a tender promise over the city.

"It's five o'clock grandpa," the little girl announced, then, interpreting his smile as permission, she ran to the bed and lay down next to him. "Did you not get any sleep?"

"No," he said, only to correct himself immediately as though eager not to arouse suspicions. "Well, a little…"

"Where are we going today?"

Grandpa Ignacio treated his midday *siesta* as if night had come in the middle of the day: he undressed, put on his pyjamas, pulled down the blinds and closed all the doors before getting into bed. Grandma Anita preferred to doze in her rocking chair, with the television on, a cushion at her back, another behind her head and something to read – a book or a magazine – that would slowly slip from her fingers. "Ouf, I think I just nodded off!" she would say when she woke, refusing to believe her granddaughter when she said she had been sound asleep and snoring long before the farmer's wife – or was it the governor's daughter – was kidnapped in whatever movie was on Channel One. "Snoring?" she would say, "Snoring? You grandfather is the only one round here who snores…" This was true. Raquel could hear him halfway down the corridor, it sounded as if her grandparent's room was a den full of ferocious monsters that always vanished the moment she opened the door, pulled up the blinds and said, "It's five o'clock, Grandpa, where are we going today?"

So began the best part of every Saturday, which had been the best days in Raquel's life since her grandparents went back to Spain. It had not been easy, but it had been worth it. It had not been easy because they had been waiting for them for a long time, much longer than anyone expected. Ignacio Fernández Muñoz refused to set foot in Barajas airport until September 1976, and even then he made it clear it was only for a holiday.

"I'm just here on holiday," he said as he kissed his grandchildren. His voice betrayed no trace of emotion or uncertainty, as though he truly believed what he was saying, or as though he felt protected by the neutral territory of the airport. His every gesture, his every movement, from the elegant detachment of his gait to the polite curiosity with which he stared

57

at the tourists, at the suitcases, at the little plastic flamenco dancers staring back at him from every shop window, was so precise, so polite, so languid that it looked as though he had spent years practising in front of a mirror. Raquel was disappointed by the grace with which he pretended he had just landed in Switzerland, a distant, disinterested manner that would have led anyone watching to assume he had simply come along to keep his wife company. Because grandma on the other hand – grandma kissed the frame of the door leading into the arrivals hall. "Anita, please," he whispered as she did the same thing to the door at the main exit, "Anita, stop this foolishness, please, for pity's sake," and she cried and she laughed and she clapped her hands to her face and said strange things, stock phrases, clichés, non-sequiturs, talking about her mother without realising it, and hugging each of them in turn. But once they had reached the car, packed the suitcases into the boot and got inside, grandpa offered his greetings, still without losing his composure. The driver turned the key in the ignition and pressed the accelerator. As he was putting the car in reverse, his father stopped him:

"Where are we going?"

His son turned towards the man in the back seat and stared at him. It was half past twelve, the day was bright and sunny, with a gentle warmth that heralded the coming autumn.

"Well... home, to drop off your stuff."

"Absolutely not!" the passenger's voice was firm. "I'm telling you, I haven't waited thirty years to come back to Madrid in order to go straight to Canillejas..."

"Where do you want to go then?"

"Vistillas."

His son, smiling at his father's cavalier impulsiveness turned to look at him, suspecting he was about to make a fool of himself.

"And where is that - apart for somewhere in the lyrics of *Su majestad el chotis?*"

"What do you mean where is that! Where it's always been, at the far end of Calle Bailén, let's go..."

"OK..." but neither the car nor the driver's head moved, "And how do I get there?"

"Is it possible?" his father shook his head happily, as though in his son's ignorance he had discovered something he had lost long ago. "Let's see... You know La Puerta del Sol,"

"Of course, Papá,"

"OK, well when you get there, take Calle Arenal, turn off at Ópera, drive round the theatre, turn on to the Plaza de Oriente and then take a left…"

"Which Arenal - there are two of them, aren't there?"

"I'll let you know, *hijo*, I'll let you know."

Raquel, sitting next to her grandfather, heard him murmur, "It's all changed so much, I'd hardly recognise the place that… that can't be right, can it? I don't know, I'm completely lost, Anita…" until they came to a broad avenue with trees and fountains and cars speeding in all directions, and his voice grew louder, solemn and serious, almost angry.

"La Castellana," he said to grandma Anita, who was sitting by the other window with Mateo in her arms, and he took her hand and kissed it over and over.

"Do I turn here or not?"

"Of course you turn here!" His son's indecision rescued him from his emotions. "Head down to Cibeles and turn up onto Alcalá… God, look at it, they've ruined it… Look Raquel, when I lived here, there were mansions like that one – see? – all along the street. Some of them were bombed, because there were bombings every day… And you see that big building on the left? That's the Biblioteca Nacional, that hasn't changed. That street there is Calle Génova, I used to live down there, and there's Recoletas and the Café Gijón – and just look at that monstrosity!"

"I know." Raquel, who could not understand that her grandfather was using her to shield himself from his emotions, interrupted him, "I've seen the Cibeles fountain lots of times. We live here now grandpa."

"Of course…" he nodded, "of course."

And yet he took her to a place where she had never been, and taught her that a city could be more than a collection of streets and houses.

"Why did you want to come here, grandpa?" she asked, when she was tired of standing beside him while he gazed at everything in silence, as though trying to recognise every building, every rooftop, every bridge, every hill, tree, and knoll and every peak of the mountains rising in the distance.

"I don't know… the view is nice, isn't it?"

"Yes, but…" Raquel didn't want to contradict him, "There are prettier places, like El Retiro, or the Plaza Mayor."

"Yes," her grandfather looked at her, smiling, "But this was my last view of Madrid before I left, and I wanted to come back here." Then he turned to his wife, brought his face close to hers and whispered, "It was here that…"

"I know." Anita pressed her face to his and kissed him, "Don't think about that. Come on, let's have a drink."

Raquel did not know what their words meant, but she guessed that her grandmother's sudden desire to visit this café terrace was her way of changing her husband's ellipsis into a full stop. Yet this did not surprise her as much as the sudden tremor in her grandfather's voice, which seemed to fade like a poorly tuned radio as the waiter leaned closer and closer to him, unable to make out what he was asking for. "A glass of beer?" he suggested and grandpa shook his head, cleared his throat, swallowed and repeated his request. The waiter nodded and gave a smile of relief, "Ah, *vermú de grifo*, I'm sorry, I didn't quite hear you the first time, of course we have vermouth on tap…" Raquel did not know what this was, but if they served it here and it came out of a tap, it couldn't be anything unusual or expensive.

There were thousands of bars in Madrid, it was something she had noticed when they first arrived, and in every bar there were lots of bottles, hundreds of bottles, whole walls filled with bottles, and in the middle of every bar was a sort of metal contraption with wheels and levers operated by a waiter who never said a word and had a serious expression as though working the contraption was so difficult or important that no one dared to talk to him as he tilted a glass with one hand and pulled the lever with the other. At that moment, anyone would think that something great was about to happen, but all that happened was beer came out of the tap along with a lot of white foam. The man would scoop out half of the foam with a spatula, fill up the glass and bang it down on the bar. "There you go!" he'd say with a smile. Then the customer would smile back and say 'thank you' as if the barman had done something important.

That was how it always was. Raquel had witnessed this ceremony many times, she had watched as her parents learned to say "Thank you, Andrés", that was the name of the barman from the bar on the corner of their street. She had even looked with pity at the espresso machine, which stood at the far end of the bar wondering why no one treated it with the same reverence. She didn't know that you could get things out of bar taps other than beer, but that morning the waiter put an ordinary glass in front of her grandfather filled with a dark, brownish liquid with an ice cube and half a slice of orange in it, and her grandfather picked it up, sniffed it, looked at it, turning the glass between his fingers. He closed his eyes before he took a sip and when he opened them again they seemed bigger, brighter, clearer and so strange that Raquel was shocked.

She had never seen her grandfather cry, nor would she see him cry that morning, but from the emotion that shimmered in his eyes she could tell that what had happened here was important, although she did not understand why. There were so many bars in Madrid, so many levers and taps, so many barmen versed in the sacred ceremony of pouring beer, that this could not be anything special. It seemed just like all the others yet when her grandfather picked up one of the fried potatoes topped with an anchovy and ate it, he smiled. This was the first time that Raquel Fernández Perea had seen her grandfather smile, *really* smile, his lips curved in sheer happiness, with no pretence, no reticence, no fear and no pain. Her grandfather was smiling like a small child, an avid student, a brave soldier, a lucky fugitive, a quiet lawyer, a resigned wrestler, a *madrileño* far from Madrid, like every man who had ever felt, that for one fleeting instant, perhaps the time had come to make peace with himself. Raquel understood none of this, but she knew that something important was happening, she was certain of it when her grandfather took his wife's hand and squeezed it and her grandmother laughed.

"And what if they hadn't had vermouth on tap, eh?" Her grandmother was as happy as he was. "Really, Ignacio, you're so stubborn..."

That morning, Raquel did not yet know that, as a young man studying Law in the magnificent old building that housed the Universidad Central on Calle de San Bernardo, Ignacio Fernández Muñoz would head home after class, stopping at every bar along the way, and in every bar he would ask for a vermouth on tap, and with every glass he got a complimentary *tapa* or snack. His granddaughter had never heard him tell this story. For years, what her grandfather Aurelio had missed about Spain was the sea, not the huge waves, the vast expanses of sandy beach, the subtle evanescence of the horizon, but a tangible piece of sea, a small strip of water in Andalucía he could call his own, where he could sit in the shade of a vine on the patio of his shimmering whitewashed house surrounded by orchards, far from the town and the beach. Raquel knew this, and she knew that her grandma Rafaela had missed two things, grilled sardines and music. "I've always loved to sing," she would say, "I can't tell you how much I loved it, but you can't do it here, it's stupid but when I first started working as a cleaner for a doctor – he was a comrade, a good person – in Nîmes after our war I used to sing to myself while I was working and he'd always say, don't sing like that Rafaela, it sounds like you're in pain. Obviously, they never sing, they don't even sing at parties..."

Raquel had heard this story many times, and she had seen her grandmother in the kitchen of her house in Torre del Mar, dancing by herself to the radio. Her smile was like the smile of grandma Anita when she opened the parcel they brought back from Spain every September when half a dozen tins of anchovies and a string of dried peppers seemed to be transformed into something else, as if Spain itself, the air, the soil, the mountains, the trees, the language and the people could be glimpsed through the cracks in this cardboard box, as if its best, its purest essence were distilled in the purple of the aubergines whose skin her grandmother stroked with a tremor of longing. "Beautiful, *hijo*, beautiful, just look how beautiful they are…" Raquel knew that, as she looked at those aubergines, her grandmother Anita was happier that her little brother Mateo when he saw his Christmas presents. But not until that morning in September had it ever occurred to Raquel that her grandfather Ignacio, who was always so quick to tell his wife that of course they had aubergines in France, also missed something.

"The sky, I missed the sky," he told her that same afternoon when it finally occurred to her to ask him, and she listened as he rattled off a whole string of other things, as though he had spent the past thirty-six years secretly preparing for this conversation. "The light of morning especially in winter, the pure, dry air that slashes at your face and wakes you up inside. Tap water, the water here tastes better than any mineral water in the world. The first signs of spring in February, though they are also so fleeting, so illusory, and do not last long, but the joy of stepping out into the street to take the sun, with no umbrella, no coat, and the pavement cafés suddenly full of people…" He looked at her and shook his head. "I've often thought back to February in Madrid, you know. I thought about it every day of every February of every year I lived in France. And the bars, the streets, going out early in the morning when everyone is still asleep, buying the paper and having breakfast in a café at a table by the window, reading the paper while the regulars make comments on the news…"

"You like that?" his granddaughter interrupted him, surprised.

"Of course I do," he gazed at her thoughtfully for a moment and then laughed, "What is it? You think that's strange?"

"Very strange. It's much nicer to have breakfast at home in your pyjamas all toasty and warm…"

"That's exactly what your grandmother used to say, but I always hated having breakfast at home. Of course, there's something I hate more – bars that try to rush you, where they're eager to be rid of you, but that's why I missed the bars here in Spain where a long leisurely breakfast can run straight into the aperitif…" He paused for a moment. "It's not easy living without the aperitif… It's a ridiculous habit – a pointless little snack, my mother always said it was bad for you, because it doesn't whet your appetite, it fills you up, a couple of glasses of vermouth, a few anchovies, a few crisps, and so on until by the time you get home, you're full up, but you're so tipsy, so happy and relaxed, you go straight to bed, have a little nap and by nine o'clock you feel ready to start again. Spending your life in bars, that's what it means to be rich, what it means to really live. It's not like I got to enjoy much of life - three paltry years - because after that war broke out, the fascists moved quickly, they took Toledo and they kept advancing, then one night while we were having dinner we heard that the government was planning to leave Madrid, heading for Valencia, leaving us behind, because in their minds the city was as good as lost..."

By this point, Raquel had realised that her grandfather was no longer talking to her, to a seven-year-old girl who was only dimly aware that once upon a time in Spain there had been a war and that her family had lost the war and that's why they went to live in France which was just as well because the ones who stayed behind were all killed. She also knew that it had something to do with her grandmother Anita's two fixations – she wouldn't eat apricots and she refused to speak the name of the village where she was born – but Raquel went on listening to her grandfather with rapt attention, as though she understood what he was saying, because his eyes were shining like the eyes of a much younger man, and when he looked at her she felt warm inside.

"I'll never forget that night as long as I live. The news wasn't official, and a lot of people didn't think it was important, but we were politically aware, so for us the government leaving was really them running away, more than that, it was a betrayal, the first of many... My father, who was a staunch republican, had been in a foul temper for the past two weeks, he was livid that Azaña had fled to France - never forget, the President of the Republic was the first to run away. My brother Mateo, the one who found out the government had met with all the political parties to tell them that it was impossible to defend Madrid, was so furious he didn't even try to defend the war minister Largo who was a socialist just as he was... But the one who took it worst was my brother-in-law Carlos, who was married to my sister Paloma, *la bella Paloma* we called her, you remember her, don't you?"

"Yes," Raquel remembered her, an old woman with white hair who looked like she could be her grandparents' mother. She used to live with her sister María on the outskirts of Paris, but she seemed mad and never went out. "But I didn't think she was pretty."

"She was... She was very pretty, the prettiest woman I've ever known."

"Prettier than grandma?" his granddaughter asked, puzzled, because until that day Anita Salgado Pérez had held the title of the most beautiful woman in the family.

"Well… she was different. I love you grandmother, she is short, but she is a pretty little thing, like a perfect miniature. My sister was more of a woman, taller, more…" He paused for a moment, trying to find the words to explain himself. "Maybe it's just that the rest of the family were nothing much to look at, that's why Paloma stood out. My brother Mateo… well, his ears didn't stick out and he had extraordinary blue eyes, but the poor man had a face that would stop a clock. I suppose he looked alright, but María and I were quite ugly."

"You're not ugly, grandpa."

"Really?" He looked at his granddaughter in mock amazement making her giggle. "With my big jug ears and my stubby little nose and my neck like a stork's?"

"You're not that bad…" Raquel protested. "You're tall and you have a good body… I wouldn't mind being your girlfriend."

"Thank you," he kissed her on the forehead, "I'll bear that in mind."

"What about Paloma's husband?"

"He wasn't what you would call handsome either, but he was attractive, dark-skinned, very intelligent… He had character. He was madly in love with his wife and it showed. My mother used to say they looked like a couple of film stars."

"No, I meant what happened to him."

"He was executed by firing squad after the war. Paloma was a widow at the age of twenty-four."

"No, I didn't mean that either," Raquel grew impatient, "I know they shot him – they shot your brother Mateo too, didn't they? You've told me that before. I want to know what happened that night, the night you were talking about…"

"Oh!" he paused and looked at her. "You really want me to tell you?" She nodded so vehemently that her grandfather suddenly remembered he was talking to a seven-year-old girl. "You wouldn't understand…"

"It doesn't matter."

He smiled. "Well, it's up to you… That night, we were all at home, and even that was quite rare because Carlos and Mateo had already been fighting for three months. My brother-in-law had a two-day furlough – you can think of it like a holiday. My brother had been fighting in the mountains all summer, but his regiment had had orders to come back and fight for Madrid right here *in* Madrid, because the fascists were already at the gates – just at the other end of Calle Princesa… He'd been given permission to see his family, but he had to go back to the barracks at night. So, what happened was that Carlos, who was a socialist too…" He stopped, cupped his chin and stared into space as though seeking inspiration. "How can I explain it? Carlos was one of my best friends, he was more than that, he was my hero. He was also my Civil Law professor during my first year at university. It wasn't really his subject, but he'd just started teaching so he was prepared to take anything, because he was very young – I mean he was seven years older than I was, but for a professor he was very young, very clever and a bit of a drinker. I started to hang around with him, and we would go out drinking together, then I introduced him to my sister and they started courting, they got married almost immediately and we had been friends ever since. That night... I was moved when I saw him, when I heard him speak, because he was normally a quiet man. He had a great sense of humour, and was writing a book that he would never publish, but that night he flew into a temper – I've fought in two wars since then and I've never seen anyone as enraged as Carlos was that night, not even your grandpa Aurelio, who was famous for his rages all over the south of France – especially the night we captured the German tank..."

Raquel burst out laughing. This was something she could easily imagine, she had often heard the story of how her grandpa Aurelio had furiously grabbed the French soldier who tried to destroy the tank, how he had thrown the man clean across the room and screamed at the soldier in a language the man had never learned but which that night he understood. "I'm crossing the border in this tank, got that, you imbecile? I'm driving this tank back to my village."

"What about Carlos? Who did he fight?"

"Carlos? He didn't fight anybody, or rather he fought everybody, he fought the whole world. He was shouting 'Franco will never set foot in Madrid. The fascists won't set foot here, not even over my dead body, because even if they kill me, I'll come back from the grave and put a bullet between the eyes of every last one of them and when I'm finished I'll start on our heroes in Valencia and show them whether or not Madrid can be defended.' I was so moved by what he said, by the way he said it, that the next day I enlisted."

"To go to war?" and although this was something she had always known, although she had seen lots of photos of her grandfathers in uniform carrying guns, Raquel seemed so shocked by his words that he burst out laughing.

"Of course, where else would I be going? I was eighteen years old, and when I showed up at home with a rifle, my father gave me a piece of his mind... 'That's all we need,' he said, 'first your brother-in-law, then your brother, and now you, Ignacio, now you. You won't last two days. You're nothing more than a lad, you're irresponsible, a spoiled baby...'

That's what my father said to me. But by the time the government ran off and abandoned the people of Madrid, I was a rifleman with the Fifth Regiment. They gave me two days training and then they sent me off to the front, but I carried on, and Madrid carried on and Mateo carried on and even Carlos carried on, though barely, because a shell put him in hospital for months, but he'd said he was going to survive and he did. He was a cripple, and his right arm was almost useless so he had to learn to do everything again with his left hand. 'I don't care,' he'd say, 'it's better than my right hand ever was...' After that there was no more vermouth. Not until today..."

"Really?" Raquel was surprised. "Don't they have it in Paris?"

"Of course they do, but it's not the same... When I left, I didn't realise I was leaving for a world with no *tapas*, no vermouth on tap, no drinking binges where you're tipsy for three days on end and all you do is laugh. I've missed that, missed it terribly, missed the good things and the bad, the noise and the shouting and the dirt, it might sound strange but I even missed the badly dressed women and waiters who wipe down every table with the same filthy rag. I could never stand flamenco, because when I was a boy you heard it in every restaurant, on every street corner at every hour of day or night, but there I even missed flamenco. But mostly I've missed the sky. When you're born here and you leave, other skies seem so bleak, so fake, like a painted backcloth in a theatre."

Raquel was astonished that her grandfather had missed so many things for so long and had never wanted to speak of them, but she did not dare to ask him why. He was afraid. Afraid that he no longer belonged in this city, in this country, afraid he might not recognise himself in the mirrors of his childhood, afraid that he had stumbled too deep into the unending labyrinth of transitory people who do not have anywhere to belong. "I've lost so many things in my life that I was afraid that I had lost everything," he said finally, after he had asked his son to look for a house so he could move back permanently at Christmas. From time to time, his wife would timorously outline the advantages of living on the Canillejas road. "You should see how nice their place is, there's no noise, no traffic, they've got a parking space and a garden." But she never dared say more. Her husband loved the city so much that it would have been worse than cruel to tear him away from it now, and Canillejas would never be Madrid to Ignacio. Nor to his granddaughter.

In those September days, Raquel learned to see the city through her grandfather's eyes. Every afternoon, Ignacio Fernández borrowed his son's car and drove his granddaughter to one of the five or six areas which to him had always been, and would always be, Madrid.

Sometimes, if they were not going far, grandma Anita would go with them but grandfather almost always planned long trips. "Because if I don't," he said to Raquel, "Your grandma will have us stopping in front of every shop window." And the little girl, who would sigh and groan with every step whenever her parents tried to take her somewhere, would nod and smile, slipping her hand into her grandfather's.

Their weekends were ruined. The two of them would sit side by side on the sofa in the living room, sulking, because they had planned to go to the Rastro or the Plaza Mayor or back to Vistillas to have a glass of vermouth, and everyone else was determined to take them on a trip to El Escorial, Toledo, Segovia, Ávila, Aranjuez, Chinchón, "No way!" grandpa would say, "Not Chinchón, why would we want to go there?" But they went and they admired the streets and the mansions and ate suckling pig or roast lamb because grandma Anita had never been to the centre of Spain and wanted to see everything as quickly as possible.

"You still have one weekend left," her father drove during these excursions, calmly accepting the late Sunday afternoon traffic jams, "If you like we could go to your *pueblo*, mama, the place where you were born. I looked on the map and it's not..."

"Absolutely not," She cut her son off with the same skill with which she wielded a kitchen knife. "I'm not going back to my *pueblo*, I have no intention of ever setting foot in it again, I swore I would never go back, and when I make a promise, I keep it –not like your father."

"Because you're stubborn as a mule, Anita."

"You can talk!"

"What about me?"

"You're worse." She turned her head and looked out at the scenery, changing her tone of voice so that it was, coaxing, almost childish. "Now Teruel, I'd love to go to Teruel, and Zaragoza, especially Zaragoza. My grandparents lived there and mother always took me with her when she went to visit them. They always made a fuss of me because I was the youngest,. My poor mother..."

"OK..." her son hurriedly agreed before grandma burst into tears, which she inevitably did whenever she thought of her mother. "Next weekend I'll take you to Zaragoza."

"We didn't get to go to the flea market, grandpa," Raquel said when he came to kiss her goodnight.

"Don't worry," he said, "We'll get there... When I come back we'll have every weekend to enjoy ourselves."

And so it was. To the old customs Ignacio Fernández picked up once more in January 1977, he added a new one– every Saturday between nine o'clock and ten, he would collect Raquel from her house on the Carretera de Canillejas and take her to his house on the Plaza de los Guardias de Corps, opposite the place where the Conde-Duque de Olivares barracks had once stood. The mornings were always the same. He would leave the car in the garage and they would stop at the first newspaper stand, then buy some *churros* and chat for a while with the doorman before going up to the apartment where grandma Anita, who refused to have breakfast in a bar, would be waiting with freshly made coffee and a bowl of chocolate milk, eager to see her granddaughter. After breakfast she and Raquel would go shopping. Raquel loved pushing the shopping trolley around and talking to her grandmother, who would ask her advice about the fruit and the fish as if she were a grown up, and then explain how they would cook this or that. From time to time, a shopkeeper would make a mistake and say "You see how lucky your mother is to have you with her?" and they would both laugh. They were happy times, because her grandmother had set aside the time just for her.

With the money her partner had paid to buy out Anita's share in the nursery school in France, she had set up another business. She had two minor partners, both with lesser shares, but she kept it in the family – one of the partners was Raquel's mother and the other, one of the child's aunts, the wife of her mother's older brother whose name was Aurelio like his father. Both of them had worked in the same business, and together they convinced Anita to set up a small shop making custom frames for pictures. Aside from these commissions, they sold lithographs, posters and ready-made picture frames along with a few trinkets. Grandma had no experience of framing, but she had excellent taste and she enjoyed talking to the customers, advising them on the size of the mount and the moulding of the frame. She had nothing to do with the actual framing process because she said that she was now too old to learn a trade, but she loved the work. On Saturdays, however, Anita would not open the shop until half past five, leaving her husband with their granddaughter for three hours, which were the best hours of the best days in Raquel's life until that May afternoon when she found her grandfather sitting up in bed with his glasses on, staring into space.

"Where are we going today, grandpa?"

"Today we're going visiting," he said and gave her his old smile, the smile he had worn in Paris which looked like a mask.

"But where?"

"To visit a friend of mine."

"Really?" Raquel frowned, because Saturday afternoons were supposed to be just for the two of them. "Will it be fun?"

68

"Absolutely. They have lots of children, some of them are your age."

But she knew that it would not be fun, and it wasn't. It was strange and mysterious, but it was not fun. Raquel guessed this even before her grandmother opened the door, kissed them both quickly and said she had to hurry because she was running late. Her husband reminded her that they would pass by the shop to pick her up at about half-past eight and then the three of them would go out for dinner. This, too, had become part of their Saturday routine. On Sundays, when her parents came to her grandparents to have lunch and take her back home afterwards, Raquel, proud to have eaten out in a restaurant, would painstakingly relate every detail. And yet she did not tell her father, or her mother, or her grandmother Anita what happened that Saturday, which had seemed like every other Saturday but which had felt different from the moment her grandfather decided to wear a grey suit and a tie rather than the shirt and jumper he usually wore. Then, from a drawer in his desk, he took out a brown leather folder, the corners faded by time.

"What's that, grandpa?"

"It's a folder," He showed it to her, careful not to bring it too close, "See?"

"I can see that, but what's inside it?"

"Papers."

"What papers?"

Not only did her grandfather not answer her question, he behaved as though he hadn't heard it, and this too was new, because ordinarily he never asked her to be quiet, never asked her to leave him in peace, never once muttered under his breath "sometimes, you try my patience *hija*," the way her parents did. Grandpa Ignacio had always answered any question she asked and, unlike her mother, had never worried about his granddaughter's appearance. And yet, that afternoon, before they went out, he had looked her up and down, from her shoes to the satin ribbons on the perfect braids plaited by her grandmother, which of course, matched her dress, which matched her jacket.

"What are you looking at?"

"Nothing," He kissed her forehead. "Just admiring how pretty you look."

Then, as if to gloss over his strange attitude, he did his best to behave normally, explaining the names of the streets to her, or telling her stories about his childhood, stories about curious characters he had known or had heard about when he was a boy.

"Today we're going to a different district – or to be more precise, we're going all the way to the other end of this district. My friend lives on the Calle Argensola which is at the far end of the Calle de Fernando VI. You'll see, we've been there before on our way to the Paseo de Recoletos.

Her grandfather still had an astonishingly accurate memory of the city where he was born, of the location of streets, buildings, fountains and statues, of shops and cinemas, a memory so rich and detailed that his wife was convinced that he had spent years practising in secret. At first, he denied it, but later, having made fun of his wife for spending more than an hour trying to get her bearings in Zaragoza, he admitted that every night after he turned out the light, he would lie thinking about Madrid. He would choose a point of departure: a square, a church, a street corner and then, from memory, he would mentally reconstruct the Calle Viriato, the Plaza de Santa Ana or the Carrera de San Jerónimo until he fell asleep. If on his first attempt he did not succeed, the next day he would glance at a map and try again. Raquel had been the privileged, often the only witness to Ignacio Fernández's joy when the city accorded with his memory.

That afternoon, however, her grandfather was talking for the sake of talking. He would stop in mid-sentence and suddenly change the subject without finishing the story he had begun. He held her hand too tightly as he walked, straight and stiff, his head held high, his feet moving forward at a constant speed, each pace precisely the same length as the one before. Raquel struggled to keep up with her grandfather, as though chained to this automaton that had usurped her grandfather's body as they headed towards their destination. On that last, silent stretch, his granddaughter began to feel sorry for him, certain that this was not going to be fun and just as certain that the man her grandfather was visiting could not possibly be a friend.

"Here we are."

Ignacio Fernández stopped outside a great, dark doorway and turned to look at his granddaughter – not as he had looked at her in the apartment, but gazing into the depths of her eyes, into the soul of this intelligent eight-year-old girl, staring so hard that she sensed things she knew to be true although she could not understand them: that her grandfather was nervous, that he was wondering whether it might not be better to turn back, that at that moment her presence there was important to him. And since she did not know what to do, she did what she had seen grandma Anita do whenever her husband was angry or sad or upset: she took his right hand in both of hers and kissed it over and over. Her grandfather smiled at her, a sad smile Raquel knew all too well, he took her in his arms and hugged her hard. Then he smoothed down his suit, slipped the brown leather folder under his left arm, gave her his hand and together the two of them stepped into the house.

On the third floor there were two doors, large and tall, their dark wood gleaming. Only one of them had a brass plaque in the centre, and Raquel noticed that her grandfather had chosen this door although there was no name on the plaque. As he let go of her hand in order to ring the doorbell, she also noticed that his hand was trembling like a scrap of paper in a gale.

"Good afternoon. Can I help you?"

Grandfather did not have time to answer the maid because a lady, who looked to Raquel like a movie star, appeared beside her. She very supremely elegant, incredibly blonde, with deep blue eyes and pale white skin and she was dressed in a black sleeveless dress, high heels and lots of jewellery: there were rings on every finger, bracelets on her wrists, and half a dozen strings of pearls twined round her throat. She gave them a polite, superficial smile, which was the only relaxed expression that Raquel would see on her beautiful face that afternoon.

"It's all right, María," she said to the maid, "I'll take care of it."

"You must be Angélica," Ignacio mused aloud in greeting. His voice was his own again: clear, steady and calm, the voice of a man entirely in control of his own body.

"Yes…" the woman faltered, studying the visitor intently. "I'm sorry, I don't believe we've met."

"Of course we've met," Ignacio paused and gave a smile, "But you wouldn't remember me because the last time I saw you, you were three years old, but I'm sure you know who I am." He paused again, the pause longer and more dramatic, as though he were playing a part. "Your mother and I were cousins. My name is Ignacio Fernández."

Let's go grandpa, let's go, thought Raquel seeing the movie star grow pale, much paler than she had been, let's get out of here grandpa, please… the woman took two steps back, suddenly weak and powerless, as though every bone in her body had melted away, leaving her dangling like a puppet. Don't smile like that grandpa, don't smile… Raquel tried to speak but her lips refused to move. And the woman, struck dumb at the mention of the name – a name that had exploded inside her like a bomb, a patiently constructed time-bomb – no longer sparkled. Let's get out of here grandpa, please, but he smiled, his lips curved in a perfect expression of sorrow, and he seemed calm, as though a great weight had been lifted from his shoulders…

"Let's go…" Raquel finally managed to say, her voice almost a whisper.

"I've come to see Julio," her grandfather's voice countermanded hers. "Is he home?"

"No… No, he… He's gone out." The woman looked at him, looked at the little girl, playing for time. "He'll be back later."

"All right," Ignacio Fernández took a step forward, though no one had invited him in. "I'll wait for him, if you don't mind. It's been a long time…"

"Of course, of course." The lady of the house took a moment to react, "Do come in… and the little girl?"

"This is my granddaughter, Raquel."

"Isn't she sweet!" the movie star struggled to regain her composure, but her eyes had a glassy sheen which filled the girl with a pity far worse than fear.

"Would you like to come and play with my children for a while? They were just about to have their afternoon snack…"

Raquel squeezed her grandfather's hand in desperation, because she did not want to be parted from him for an instant, but looking up she knew she had no choice.

"What a good idea…" her grandfather kissed her on the head, "You go with them."

"María…" The maid had not gone far. "Could you show this gentleman into the study? I'll be there in a moment."

The blonde woman took Raquel's hand and led her down a long hallway lined with dark wooden furniture. There were paintings on the walls, some very old and very big, others small and clustered in groups. The carpets muffled their footsteps so completely that it took Raquel a moment to realise that the strange muffled, insistent noise she could hear was simply the sound of the woman breathing. She was panting as though someone were following her, as though she were running rather than walking, or was trapped somewhere unfamiliar, somewhere dark and dangerous instead of simply walking down the corridor in her own home. As they turned the corner, the corridor changed, there was no furniture now, no paintings or carpet, but light flooded in from two windows that opened onto an internal courtyard. At the end of the corridor was a double door. The woman pushed it open and led Raquel into a big kitchen containing white furniture and with a table in the middle set for afternoon tea.

"OK" The blonde woman finally let go of her hand, gave her a smile so tense it looked like a grimace, and nodded towards the two children sitting at the table. "These are my two youngest, Álvaro and Clara. Children, we have a guest, her name is Raquel, and she's your cousin, a distant cousin but still... No, actually... I think she's your niece, twice removed, I don't know, I always get mixed up with family. Anyway... You sit here. Would you like a hot chocolate? Fuensanta makes wonderful hot chocolate..."

She was so nervous that when she pulled out the chair she knocked a napkin on the floor. A fat, smiling woman of about fifty in a blue uniform with an immaculate white apron offered Raquel a spoon and said she would take care of everything.

"Thank you, Fuensanta... I'm just going to the bathroom for a minute... I have to... Jesus, where did I leave my cigarettes?"

Raquel looked at the children. They didn't look like brother and sister. He had short, thick black hair and dark eyes like bottomless pools, the girl was blonde with pink skin and golden eyes that shone like beads of honey. She seemed very pretty, more than that. She had the sort of beauty you see in television advertisements for shampoo or biscuits, the gentle charm of those who always play the lead role in the school play, that innate, magnetic beauty that determines the pecking order in the classroom and the playground. Even Raquel would not have been indifferent to her beauty, would have wanted to be her friend, would have invited her to her birthday party before anyone else had she met her on some other day when she did not need to watch her words, to fear for her grandfather, to protect him from a kind blonde women who invited you to have hot chocolate with her children. The boy fascinated her much less than the girl, but he seemed to be fascinated by her.

"You're my niece?" This was the first in a long series of questions.

"I don't know." This was the truth, because no one had ever mentioned this family to her.

"How old are you?"

"Eight."

"I'm seven," his sister chimed in.

"And I'm twelve," he thought for a moment then shook his head. "You can't be our niece, we're too little. You must be our cousin."

"I don't know," repeated Raquel, "But my grandpa told your mother that he was her cousin or something..."

"It would be good if you were our cousin, because we don't have any cousins," the little girl said.

"Really?"

"No," her brother confirmed, "Papá and Mamá were only children. Have you got cousins?"

"Yes, lots... Miguel and Luis who live in Málaga, Aurelio, Santi and Mabel who live near my other grandparents in Torre del Mar, Pablo and

Cristina who live here in Madrid, and then I have cousins in Paris, Annette and Jacques."

You've got cousins in Paris?"

"Yes. We used to live there. I was born in Paris."

"That means you're French."

"No, I'm Spanish. My parents are Spanish and my grandparents."

"That's weird." The boy stared at her as though he didn't believe a word she had said. "People who are born in France are French."

"Have you got any brothers or sisters?" asked the little girl.

"I have a brother, his name is Mateo, he's four. But I'm going to have another one in November."

"There are five of us," the boy said, "Clara is the youngest."

"And you're the second youngest, Álvaro, so there…"

Fuensanta served the hot chocolate, it was delicious, and she put two plates in the middle of the table, one with buns, and the other one with freshly made toast. "Don't eat them all," she warned, "Your brothers will be home soon and they'll be starving after the match…" When she couldn't eat any more, Raquel tilted her chair back and to her surprise, almost against her will, she experienced a moment of genuine contentment, as though the taste of the chocolate and the sweet buns had banished the feeling of being trapped in enemy territory.

"I have a train set," the boy told her, "I'll show you if you like."

They trooped out into the corridor, the boy leading the way, Raquel in the middle and the little girl behind, and headed to a bright, spacious room with two balconies that overlooked the street. There was a pile of toys in the middle of the floor and a door on either side.

"Is this your room?"

"No, this is the playroom. I sleep in there," He pointed to the door on the left, "with my brothers, and the girls sleep in the room opposite."

"Do you want me to show you my dolls?" said Clara, "I have lots of dolls."

"No, she doesn't want to see your dolls," Álvaro spoke to her with the contempt of an older brother, "She wants to see my train set. Look…"

The train set was laid out on a board between the two balconies, and it was beautiful, because it had a bridge and a tunnel and a train station with tiny little people standing on the platform and others sitting on benches, there were even little mountains and a town in the background. The set had two engines, an old, black train that pulled three wagons full of coal, and a newer one painted in bright colours, hitched to a long line of passenger carriages.

"It's not your train set, Álvaro, it belongs to the three of you," the little girl came over to Raquel carrying two almost identical dolls wearing identical clothes in different colours. She held them out as though she wanted Raquel to pick one. "Look, they're twins. Aren't they pretty? Here, you take one…"

The trains had started up and were chugging along in opposite directions, accelerating as they went, when a chorus of male voices erupted in the hall singing a victory song. *"Hemos Ganao! Hemos Ganao! el equipo colorao!"*

"Papá!" The two children cried out as a tall, plump, dark-skinned man – not young, but with the athletic build of a much younger man – came into the room preceded by a lanky blonde boy and another boy who looked a lot like the first but was older.

"Three-Nil!"

The father shouted the result, holding up three fingers of his left hand and making a zero with the thumb and index finger of his right to illustrate the score, then he scooped his two younger children into his arms and tickled them and they tickled him until all three of them collapsed onto the floor in a ball of arms and legs, barely stopping to catch their breath.

"And I haven't even told you the best bit. Julio scored two goals, he was great, wasn't he Rafa?" And then, with Álvaro still hanging onto his neck and Clara still clinging to his feet, he turned and stared at Raquel. "And who might you be?"

"She's our cousin," the little girl said, "Her name is Raquel."

He burst out laughing, kissed his daughter, and smiled at his pretend niece, and it was then that she realised that, aside from her blonde hair and her caramel coloured eyes, the reason Clara was so pretty was that she had her father's smile.

"We'll see, we'll see…"

As she watched him crawl towards her on all fours, with his dark eyes, his brilliant white teeth and an expression on his face like a overexcited child, Raquel instinctively felt that she liked this man and did not wonder why he radiated warmth and confidence, and something more, a feeling of closeness, of intimacy, as though she had always known him and could trust him.

"Tell me something…" he knelt beside her and talked to her gently, his voice seductive and soothing, as though no one else could hear them, "Do you like lollipops?"

"Yes." Raquel smiled without knowing why.

"Are you sure?" `He held out his empty hand, closed it and brought it up close to her face. Suddenly he looked amazed. "You must really like them, because you've got one in your ear…"

Raquel stared at him, open-mouthed, as though hypnotized. She heard a burst of nervous applause and laughing from the audience before she felt his fingers stroke her jaw.

"Look," he held up a lollipop wrapped in orange paper. "Take it, it's yours. I found it in your ear."

"Thank you," she said, grinning.

"But maybe you prefer strawberry lollipops. Let me have a look in your other ear…" He performed the same operation with his other hand and found another lollipop, this one wrapped in bright pink paper. "Wow, you're lucky! You've got lollipops growing out of your ears!"

Without thinking about what she was doing, Raquel threw her arms around his neck and kissed him on the cheek, and he hugged her back, and for a moment it was as though they had always lived together, as though she were another daughter for this father who went to cheer on his children at football games, who let his children tickle him and rolled on the floor with them, and pulled sweets out of their ears.

"Julio…" the voice of the blonde lady came from the doorway, breaking the spell. "Julio, we have a visitor."

"I can see that," he said, laughing, "I've just been introduced to my niece."

"Well yes, it's just… this is the granddaughter of Ignacio Fernández, you know, my mother's cousin. He's waiting for you in the study."

The man closed his eyes for a second and then opened them again, studying Raquel's face, he smiled at her, but it was not a smile of pleasure or affection. He slowly got to his feet, patted down his clothes and left the room without looking back.

"Papá! Papá! Don't go!" Álvaro called to him. "I've got both of the trains working at the same time, you have to see…"

"In a minute, *hijo*. I'll be right back."

But Raquel did not see him again. It was the blonde lady who came to fetch her. Raquel was bored of looking at the trains and was now playing with Clara and her twins. "I'll be their mummy and you can be their auntie, OK?" the girl said as she showed Raquel her impressive collection of accessories, the twin-size cot and the pram and the highchair and the wardrobe, and a bathtub big enough to fit both dolls. By now they had bathed them, put them to bed, woken them up, and fed them.

"It's time to go, Raquel, you grandfather is waiting," the blonde lady said, as pale and nervous as before.

"Oh, no Mamá! Please!" Clara protested, "We're having a great time!"

And this strange woman hugged her daughter, held her close and kissed her once or twice, but she didn't say anything. Then, she took Raquel's hand and they went back the way they had come earlier, through the bare, bright corridor and into the corridor full of paintings to the entrance hall where Ignacio Fernández, very tall and very stiff, very alone, stood waiting by the door for his granddaughter. Clara followed them all the way, whimpering and begging to be allowed to play a little longer, something Raquel knew would not happen, because the highly strung movie star was walking faster and faster, and because she turned around twice and told her daughter to shut up, screaming the second time, before they entered the hall.

"Raquel..."

Her grandfather called out her name, and at that moment she realised she was still clutching one of the dolls, the red-headed one in the green dress, and she froze, not knowing what to do, her right hand stretched towards her grandfather, her other stretched back towards Clara who was already running to get her doll when her mother stopped her with a gesture that was intended to look like a hug.

"You can keep it if you like."

"No!" her daughter tried to wriggle from her grasp but the woman held her tighter.

"Of course she can," the woman said and forced herself to smile. "It's a present."

"But Mamá, they're twins!" the little girl looked up into her mother's eyes and started to cry, genuine tears his time. "You don't understand..."

"It's true." Raquel thought that Clara was right, and held the door out towards the girl. "Anyway, I've got lots of dolls already."

"It doesn't matter," the blonde lady persisted in this arbitrary display of generosity, "Take it. I'll buy her another one."

"Mamá!"

Suddenly, Raquel found herself outside on the landing. Her grandfather had removed her from that house and closed the door without saying goodbye. This was strange, but she didn't' dwell on it because the scene in the hall had brought back the lump in her throat she had felt when they first arrived, when she was scared, when she had struggled for breath as though the air inside the apartment was thinner than the air outside. Then she remembered that this was not going to be fun, she had known that from the beginning. She wondered how she could have enjoyed the hot chocolate and the train set and the dolls and yet now, as her grandfather led her down the stairs rather than taking the lift, she felt relieved because with every step her breath seemed to come more easily, until, still hand in hand, the two of them reached the cold, high-ceilinged foyer and beyond the door the reward of a bright, clear, May afternoon, with a light breeze rustling the leaves on the trees and the sun warm on their faces.

"They have a very big house, haven't they?" She did not dare to speak until they were on the pavement walking at the same slow, relaxed pace they did every Saturday, "And it's pretty, too. They must be very rich."

Her grandfather did not answer straight away, he just kept walking, head high, eyes fixed on the horizon, his face seemed pale in the sunlight and there was a slight but steady quiver on his closed lips.

"They're sons of bitches, that's what they are."

He said this but did not look at her. They had come to an unfamiliar square with a large building at the far end. There were trees and a newspaper stand and a number of benches. Her grandfather chose an empty bench and sat down, as though he had forgotten about his eight-year-old granddaughter. He set down the battered brown leather folder, its edges faded by time, and took his face in his hands. For a moment, nothing happened. Then his head began to shake, slowly at first then more quickly, more vigorously so that his shoulders, his arms, the hands that were still pressed against his face, all began to shake too. The girl stood facing him, unable to believe what she was seeing – not him, not her grandfather Ignacio – as the hoarse, guttural sounds that trickled through his fingers grew louder, clearer, became irrefutably the sound of sobs, until she could no longer ignore the evidence of her eyes and ears.

This was the first time that Raquel Fernández Perea had seen her grandfather cry, the first and only time, though she did not feel privileged to be a witness to his grief, because her grandfather wept like a child, uncontrollably, forgetting his granddaughter, forgetting himself, forgetting the man he had once been, the man he still was, the man who might have died many times but who had survived to celebrate the death of his enemy by dancing a *pasodoble* with his wife in a square in the Latin Quarter in Paris, forgetting Ignacio Fernández, aka 'the Lawyer', defender of Madrid, Captain in the *Ejército Popular de la República*, combatant against the fascists during the Second Word War, twice decorated for his role in the liberation of France; just as his granddaughter would never forget this afternoon when she saw him cry, heart-broken and desolate, unable to hold back the tears he had not had time to shed while he was dodging death, while he was escaping from prisons, camps and trains, while he was fleeing the men hell-bent on killing him simply for being who he was, while he was reconciling himself to the perpetual disappointment of a prosperous life in an alien country and to the impossible dream that died a little every day of the city where he was born.

"Don't cry, grandpa... Please don't cry."

"What's the matter?" she wanted to ask, "What have they done to you, grandpa?" But she could not say a word, could not even tell him that she loved him, that sunny May afternoon that had taught her how much she loved him, that there was no one in the world she loved more than him. What hurts you, hurts me, this was what she thought, what she would have liked to say, but she couldn't because now she was crying too, inconsolably, the words she wanted to say dying in her throat, drowned by her sobs, though she did not know the reason for these tears that splintered every word she tried to say, although she sensed that these tears were bitter because they were his tears, because she had chosen to share the grief of a lifetime.

"Don't cry," she finally managed to say again, hugging his arms and burying her face in his neck. This time he responded. He squeezed her tightly and kissed her on the head, pressing his lips into her hair until they were both calm again. His eyes were red and swollen and the skin on his cheekbones suddenly seemed so fine, it looked like paper.

"This is the Plaza de las Salesas," he said, his voice still cloudy with tears, "The name comes from the fact that there used to be a convent here, and the church over there is called the church of Santa Barbara, because it was founded by Barbara of Braganza, who was Queen of Spain and daughter of the King of Portugal," he paused, wiped his eyes and smiled, "The street takes its name from her. Over there is where the tribunal took place that sentenced my brother-in-law Carlos, you remember? And the grey building behind the church – see it? – that's the Supreme Court. The entrance is on the Plaza de la Villa de París."

Raquel was quiet for a moment, she did not know what to say, how to take these words that seemed so warm and yet so cold, so she dried her eyes, blew her nose and said exactly what she would have said if nothing had happened that afternoon.

"And both of the plazas are square, because if they were round, they'd be called *glorietas.*"

"Exactly," for an instant, tears welled again in Ignacio Fernández Muñoz's eyes, but this time he held them back. "Promise me you won't say anything to your grandma, OK?"

"Promise."

He smiled at his granddaughter's seriousness as she raised her raised her right hand to reinforce her vow.

"Pick up your doll," he said, looking down, "You've dropped it."

"I don't want it." Raquel laid it on the bench, then fumbled in her pockets until she found the lollipops and laid them beside the doll, the orange on the left, the strawberry on the right. The doll looked so pretty, she thought as she said goodbye to it, with its red hair and green dress fringed with ruffles and lace. "I never wanted it."

"It looks like an offering," her grandfather commented.

"What's an offering?"

"Nothing. It was a silly thing to say... But some little girl will be very happy when she finds it. Let's go."

And then, as though nothing had happened that afternoon, he got to his feet, slipped the battered leather folder under his left arm, held out his right hand to his granddaughter and, calmly they strolled towards the Paseo de Recoletos, just as they did every Saturday.

"Do you want an ice cream?" he suggested when they arrived at Recoletos.

"Please. Strawberry, but just a little one, because I've just had a..." she was about to say "snack", but she held her tongue, she did not want to remember anything good about that afternoon.

Grandfather asked for a large vanilla ice cream and ate it slowly, savouring the taste and the view of the Paseo full of children on roller skates, mothers with babies, couples kissing on the benches and groups of friends gathered on the café terraces with tall glasses of beer. They could hear conversation and laughter, hear the children playing pat-a-cake and singing rhymes.

"What happened, grandpa?" she finally plucked up the courage to ask him as she finished the last crumbs of her ice cream cone.

"Oh, it's a long story. A very long, very old story. You wouldn't understand, and anyway... I think it's best if you don't know."

"Why?"

He slowly turned to look at her, look deep into her eyes, into the heart of this eight-year-old girl and Raquel sensed that he would not answer her question, but she was wrong.

"OK..." He hesitated at first, "We've come back to live here, haven't we? If things were different, if things had been normal, you would have lived here all your life. But to live here, there are some things it's better not to know. Things it's better not to understand," he paused and smiled at the look of concentration on his granddaughter's face as she tried to work out what he meant. "Tomorrow morning, we'll go to the flea market if you like. The weather's nice, and I'm sure your grandma will want to come with us. You know how much she loves to buy things..."

Ignacio Fernández might have died many times, but he had survived so that he could decide what was best for his granddaughter Raquel, what she should and should not know. Many years would pass and much would happen before she understood what he had meant by these mysterious words, before she saw them as luminous, honourable, the necessary truths we give up over time for love.

By that point, she had ceased to think of herself, of her parents, her family, as Spanish. Many years had passed, many things had happened and her brother Ignacio, the third Ignacio Fernández in the family, had been born in Madrid, just as the first had been. When it seemed as if life was settled, on a June afternoon like any other, while her grandfather Aurelio was sleeping, his face turned towards the little strip of the blue Mediterranean where he had come to die, Raquel headed towards the radiant white house where she had spent her childhood summers, not realising how much she had forgotten of those strange years, of her life before Spain. A life that seemed all the more strange every time she visited Paris – where Mateo, where she had been born, yet where it seemed impossible that they could ever have lived. She did not realise that waiting on grandma Anita's table, on that ordinary Sunday afternoon in the 1980s, would be a salad of endives and chopped walnuts with blue cheese dressing that she could not remember ever having seen before, a salad that, although it looked wilted and slightly revolting, tasted rather pleasant.

Many years had passed and much had changed in Spain, rapidly at first, more slowly later, as dreams and reality slotted into their new, if narrow, moulds, just as she learned to fit into an ordinary life, to modify her dreams to fit reality, she had wanted to become an actress, but had wound up studying Economics, she would have preferred a more interesting job now but worked in a bank, she had married, but was divorced, she longed for a child but had never found the right time or the right man, she was unhappy sometimes, but sometimes she was happy.

Many years had passed and much had changed, but Raquel Fernández Perea never stopped looking at the sky. And she never forgot the name of the man who had made her grandfather cry.

The day dawned cloudy and damp, but by nine o'clock sharp, when I dropped my son off at school, the sky had cleared and the sun was beginning to warm the air. Tomorrow was the last day of March, and the last chance to meet my deadline if I was to avoid a long series of pained reproaches "Álvaro, *hijo,* what is it, is it so difficult for you to go and talk to the man at that office, I don't know, I ask one little favour…"

My mother would never understand how much even the name of the office left me feeling tired and depressed, and vaguely indignant as I invariably felt when dealing with languages designed only to be understood by initiates, the sort of deliberately incomprehensible jargon that obscures the very idea it is supposed to explain. It could have been called the Department of Financial Consultants, or even just the Financial Consultancy, but no, of course not, that would be too easy, people might understand that. Instead, the consultant who was disinclined to part with the money which death had snatched from my father worked for the 'Department of Asset Management at the Administrative Society of Cooperative Investment Institutions' and that was no place to be on a beautiful spring morning.

Indeed the weather was so beautiful that, on a whim, I drove home, parked my car in the garage and, leaving my coat behind, I set off on foot for the Plaza de las Descalzas Reales. I was sure that the meeting would be a short one, given my complete ignorance of financial matters and my determination that I would not be the one to make any important decisions, and if it did drag on, I could always get a taxi to Recoletos and then a train from there to the University. Though I had sworn to myself that my mother would never find out, I had no classes that morning, but did have a meeting at noon with my research group.

I arrived at the bank in good humour though somewhat later than I had expected. I had no trouble finding the Department of Gobbledegook and walked straight up to the receptionist.

"Hello. I'm here to see Mr Fernández Perea."

The receptionist, a plump woman of about fifty who was wearing too much make-up, stubbed out her cigarette – although it was early and there was a 'No Smoking' sign posted above her head – and glared at me.

"Mrs," she said.

"Sorry?"

"Mrs Fernández Perea," she explained, "she's not married, but she doesn't like to be called Miss. I'm single and I don't like it either."

"Oh, I'm sorry," I replied as though I had done something to be sorry for. I felt so uncomfortable about having apologised that I took the letter out of my pocket and showed it to her, "The letter doesn't give her full name, so there was no way I could have known she was a woman from the letter."

"OK," she nodded, agreeing to a ceasefire. "Have you an appointment?"

"No. The letter didn't say I needed one."

"You don't say. And I don't suppose it said that it's a good idea to put on your clothes in the morning?"

I was about to turn on my heel and leave, but she pressed the button on the entry phone.

"Raquel... You have a visitor. I don't know his name. No, he doesn't have an appointment. Yes, wait a minute, reference number JCG 32... Right, straight away, I'll tell him." She released the button, handed me the letter and glared at me, "Go on in, she's expecting you. Third door on the left. There's a plate on the door," she attempted something approaching a smile, "with her *full* name on it."

Later, when I knew that her name was Mariví, that she had a stomach ulcer, that she hated men in general because one in particular had dumped her for another guy when she was a 22-year-old non-smoker who weighed seven and a half stone, I often thought of her as a frontier, a border, the last witness to what I had been like before Raquel. Mariví was a complete bitch, but not enough of a bitch for me to walk out, and she cut off my retreat before I realised the consequences. If she had been a little more stupid, a little more rude, I would have left, I would have gone home and picked up my car, driven to the university and then phoned my mother to tell her about the abortive meeting, "I'm no good at this kind of thing, Mamá, I've told you that before, now I've wasted a whole morning and I'm not about to waste another." She, of course, would have persisted for a while and then given up and phoned my brother Rafa, thinking that was probably what she should have done in the first place. After that, something would undoubtedly have happened, but I wouldn't even have heard about it because Rafa would have dealt with it on his own, with the legendary dignity and determination he had inherited from Papá. He had been waiting for an opportunity to play the martyred soldier, the one who solves everyone's problems and heaps all the responsibility, all the blame upon himself. I would have gone on living my life, this carefully tended patch of earth which required little effort and little thought. And so I often thought about Mariví later, when all around me seemed like an infinite expanse of scorched earth.

And yet, that morning, I stood wondering whether or not I should knock and thinking that I'd go in, listen to whatever tedious claptrap she had to say, nod politely, take down a few figures and then be out of there by ten. In the end, I knocked gently and got no answer, I knocked again, harder this time and a bright, confident voice said "come in". I stepped inside. It was a big office, bright and spacious with two distinct sections. In the background, was a large, simply designed, but clearly designer desk next to the floor to ceiling windows that looked out onto the street; in the foreground two sofas flanked a low table. Years working at the university meant I could immediately spot where my consultant fitted into the hierarchy. She was not a big fish – hardwood furniture, expensive carpets and a distance of at least three metres between desk and reception area – nor was she a minor functionary – tiny office with small table, a work station for the computer and a couple of chairs for visitors. It was a pleasant space with large plants and tastefully framed prints, glancing around gave me a moment to think before I looked up and found myself face to face with her: Raquel Fernández Perea, the woman who had turned up unexpectedly at my father's funeral, the strange woman who had suddenly ceased to be a stranger.

My body recognised her before I did, an involuntarily spasm I could do nothing to stop. But she didn't notice my sudden weakness, so overcome was she by her own astonishment, staring at me, mouth open, hands clenched into fists against the desk. We stared at each other, silent, bewildered, each trapped in mute immobility for what seemed to me to be a long time. Then she closed her eyes, forced herself to smile and apologised.

"I'm sorry, it's just... I was expecting your mother."

"Yes, I..." Who are you? Why did you get in touch with us? Why did you come to my father's funeral? To look at us? What are you doing here? What am I doing here? But I said none of these things. What I said, though I barely recognised my own voice, was "I came instead. And since your charming receptionist didn't even both to ask my name..."

"Yes," she smiled again, more convincingly this time, "Mariví is a real character. Please, take a seat."

Who are you? Why did you get in touch with us? Why did you come to my father's funeral to look at? Over and over the same questions kept running through my head as I moved to a sofa and sat down. I noticed that her hands were shaking, I saw her grip a green cardboard folder in a vain attempt to still them as she came over to me with her scary, businesslike smile. She leafed through the documents in the folder, until finally she looked up at me and I realised that whatever the situation we found ourselves, she was in control, not I.

"I'm sorry, I should have offered you a drink. Would you like a coffee?"

I nodded. She picked up the phone and asked for two coffees.

"You do take sugar? - Yes, thank you and some mineral water."

Then she began. "I know it can be difficult to focus on practical matters after the death of a loved one, but your father was one of our clients and our duty – our obligation – is to continue to look after his interests now just as we did before."

She was pretty, much prettier than she had seemed when I saw her at the cemetery. Guille, my nephew, had noticed it but I hadn't. "This is why we contacted you. First, we need to give you an account of all the investments entrusted to us by your father, which at the present time show considerable appreciation, a fact which may be relevant to his heirs." She was much more beautiful than she appeared at first, you had to look twice, it was a hidden beauty, mysterious, because there was nothing particularly beautiful about her face except her face itself, the surprising symmetry of her gentle but very ordinary eyes, her small but ordinary nose, a well defined but ordinary mouth, a finely chiselled but ordinary chin.

"I assume that you, by which I mean your mother, your brothers and sisters, and yourself, are your father's sole heirs, in which case you will have to decide what happens to these investments. But I feel I should point out that the investments I'm referring to benefit from a privileged fiscal status the advantages of which terminate should you choose to withdraw the capital."

She was in control of the situation, I was not, and her advantage grew with every second as she delivered the speech she had carefully honed in front of many other heirs who, to judge from the rising confidence of her voice, had surrendered long before I did. She didn't realise that I was the wrong son, that I was the brother who would never make an irrevocable decision, she also didn't acknowledge the fact that I was her only witness, the only person who had seen her and would remember her afterwards. At that moment there was a knock at the door and an assistant came in with the coffees and the mineral water. She set the tray on the table and left, and I found myself making a joke.

"Just as well Mariví didn't bring it."

She smiled. She had a gap between her front teeth, just like my mother.

"I'm scared to death of her." I added and she laughed, and when she laughed she was even more beautiful, and I felt almost proud to have

85

made her laugh. Then I wondered what I was playing at, what was happening to me. *Who are you?* I remembered. *Why did you get in touch with us? Why did you come to my father's funeral?* After a moment, she went on in the same soft, clear voice of a woman accustomed to getting her clients to agree with her. "That's why I got in touch with you. Of course I understand that this is a delicate matter, and you may not be in the right frame of mind to make a decision, but there's no hurry, I'd just like you, for your own interest, to bear it in mind…"

At this point, she floored the accelerator and began skipping whole sections of her carefully prepared speech. I've never believed I'm as clever as other people say, but I'm not stupid, and I know all about timing. It's very important in my job - and clearly in hers, too, because you didn't need to know much about Investments to work out that she was desperate for us not to move the funds. This was why she had come out from behind her desk to sit with me in a more intimate, neutral area, this was why she had offered me coffee, why she was trying to butter me up, why until now she had been trying to reassure me with her warm intelligent words. And yet now she put her foot on the accelerator, and I let her. I had expected her to give me figures, percentages, in depth analyses – *this is how much you would lose if you decide to withdraw the capital now, this is how much you could earn if you leave it in for a year, two years, ten years* – but she skipped over it, and I let her. I didn't ask any questions, request any figures, demand any explanation. I had never been in control of the situation, but now she no longer seemed to be in control either. And I didn't understand why, when, or how she had lost the self-assurance that had been supporting us both, that had given a sense of reality to this meeting which now seemed dreamlike, impossible.

"I've drawn up an outline," she said to me, "These things are easier to understand when they're written down in black and white."

She got up and walked over to her desk, she was wearing black jeans and a black t-shirt with white scribbles on it. She had a good body in spite of the fact that her hips seemed disproportionately wide compared to her waist, or maybe because of that, I didn't know. "Here it is," she said holding out an open folder so that I could see that it contained all the necessary information, the evaluations, all the figures regarding tax and interest that she had not explained to me.

"Take it home so you can study it in peace. It's been a pleasure." I took her outstretched hand and shook it, and in her eyes I could see a look of boundless relief.

"Goodbye," she said.

"'Bye," I said, and I left.

I don't know how I made it outside. That's something I also thought about afterwards. I must have gone back down the corridor, past the receptionist, walked to the lift, pushed one button, then another, and walked out through the ground floor, but all I remember is the light, the surreal brightness of neon lights reflected in the marble floor of the vast entrance hall, as though I had stepped out of the lift into another world. I remember standing, unable to make sense of that cold glare until I felt my feet begin to slip out from under me and almost fell. I watched people coming in to the bank, their hair wet, their clothes sodden, there was something unexpectedly sad in the jumpers soggy from the rain, a bitter tribute to the treacherous spring that had tricked me too.

It was pouring outside, the rain dashing against the cobblestones as if announcing some ancient Godlike wrath. The spectacle was so magnificent and so terrifying that no one dared to break the dense, damp silence that bound us together, a small multitude of strangers. When the rain finally slowed, a few brave souls ran outside and made a dash for the nearest shopping centre where a couple of hawkers were selling umbrellas for three euros. I didn't buy one. I put the folder in my briefcase, crossed the square and went into the nearest bar I could find.

By the time I got inside, I was soaking, but I didn't care. I ordered a coffee with a dash of brandy and took it over to a table by the window. The bar was fairly empty, but the coffee machine hissed and a jukebox kept playing *El Golpe* : *Quiéreme, cuídame, trátame muy bien*. The coffee was good, but I knocked it back quickly and was still shivering inside. It had been years since I'd had a drink in the morning, I didn't even drink beer until after work, but then I'd never been in a situation like this before. That's why I revived a ritual from my old student days and ordered a *Sol y Sombra*, brandy and anisette – the worst it could do was get me drunk and that would be a lot better than the uncertainty I was feeling at that moment.

I knocked back the drink, but it didn't get me drunk. The rain stopped at a quarter to eleven and ten minutes later the sun was glinting off the puddles as though it had all been a joke. Fifteen minutes later, my mobile phone rang. It was one of my scholarship students so I didn't answer. It rang again a minute later and I turned it off.

Then it occurred to me that I could just do nothing, I could hang on to the folder, whose innocuous contents I had read through carefully to make sure it contained nothing strange or suspicious, then catch my train, get to the university in time to attend the meeting, go home and in the afternoon, I could go round to Clara's flat and give the paperwork to my mother: "It wasn't a man, Mamá, it was a girl, she explained the whole thing to me but I've got it written down here, you'll have to decide what you want to do, I don't have an opinion but I'm sure whatever you decide will be fine."

It occurred to me that I could choose to do nothing, I could just file away the memory of that morning as one more inexplicable episode in life, along with the paranoid fantasies and the imaginary memories of things never experienced, with astounding coincidences, with the fears and the nightmares and the mysterious lights that turn themselves on and off until we realise that our little boy is playing with the light switch.

"You didn't see anything the day of the funeral, Álvaro," this was something else I thought, "You were out of it on painkillers, you were exhausted, in shock. You don't even know if it's the same woman, perhaps she just looks like the woman." But at half past eleven I got up, went to the bar and paid. I crossed the square and went back into the bank, took the lift to the third floor, walked straight past the receptionist.

"Don't worry, I know my way."

"Hey!" she called after me, "You can't just... You can't do that... Hey!"

I didn't knock, I simply opened the door. Raquel Fernández Perea was sitting at her desk, talking on the telephone and jotting something down on a piece of paper. She looked up, saw me, and as she had done that first time, she closed her eyes. She kept them closed for a long while, a conscious, deliberate gesture. When she opened them again I was still standing there. She said goodbye to the woman on the phone, telling her she had an unexpected visitor, then folded her arms across her chest.

"Sorry," I said, though I showed no sign of actually being sorry for bursting into her office like that, "But I needed to ask you some questions. There are things I don't understand."

"Take a seat, please." She waved towards the chair beside the desk. I thought I could sense a helplessness in her gesture, but her voice was consummately professional and polite. "So how can I help you?"

"Well, what I don't understand is... This place isn't like a bank, is it? I mean, the department you work in, someone can't just show up here and set up an investment fund the way you open a bank account, right?'

"Right."

She smiled at me, reassured, she didn't suspect where this was leading and her naïve smile stirred feelings in me I didn't know I was capable of, I felt the sudden thrill a hunter feels when he creeps up on his prey, savouring the shot he is about to fire.

"So," I went on, "my father wasn't directly a client of yours, was he?"

"No, we don't work that way," she relaxed a little more, leaning back in her chair and her voice took on the scholarly tone she had used earlier. "This is the central investment management office. Here we manage the investments of the customers from all the various branches. Now, obviously, we have an investment advisor in every branch who deals directly with the client. In this case, I assume your father dealt with his local bank manager when he set up the investment, and the local manager sent the details to us. We process the transaction, manage the funds and provide the branch managers with an account of how investments are performing. The customers generally get their information from the person who handles their account."

"So customers don't come here," I ventured.

"That depends. On the type of investment, the size of the capital. But in general, as you say, we never meet our clients face to face."

"Have you been managing my father's investments for long?" I smiled, allowing myself the luxury of politeness, "You look so young."

She acknowledged the compliment with a little laugh, as professional as everything else about her. "No, no I haven't. My supervisor used to handle your father but when he was promoted, his portfolios were shared out between a lucky few, and so I inherited your father, along with a number of other clients."

"And he never had the pleasure of coming to see you at your office."

"No. Well, I think I did meet him once, in my supervisor's office."

At that moment, she began to worry and her smile faded. Clever girl, I thought, the penny has dropped, too many questions for a curious relative. She was looking at me differently now and sat bolt upright in the chair, her legs crossed but her right foot tapping hard enough for me to follow the rhythm from the other side of the desk. It's over, I thought, and for a moment the hunter in me was disappointed.

"But you must have known my father somehow, because you were at his funeral," I paused and she looked at me pokerfaced, but she could not control her breathing. "I saw you there."

She held my gaze for a long moment, then looked down at the papers on her desk.

"Unless of course your bank customarily sends someone to attend its clients' funerals," I added, relishing the slow, exasperated tone of every word. "But it doesn't does it?"

"No," she said finally, the word almost a whisper.

"That's why, when I showed up, you said you'd been expecting my mother. Because you know us, you saw us all together at the cemetery. Otherwise your assumption would make no sense. I look a lot like my

89

father as I'm sure you know, but almost anyone looks more like my mother than I do. You for example. I don't know if you know this but she has a gap between her front teeth just like yours."

"No," she said again.

"No what?"

She lifted her head and looked at me almost defiantly and spun round in her chair angrily, like a little girl who feels that she has been unfairly punished but can do nothing about it. When she spoke, her voice was different, it was hard, harsh, callous.

"No, I didn't realise that your mother had a gap between her front teeth," the telephone rang, "And, yes, I was at your father's funeral."

"Why?"

"Just a minute," she picked up the phone, "Yes, yes, of course… No, no I hadn't forgotten. I'm really sorry, I'm just running a little late… If you could just hang on for one second…" she put her hand over the mouthpiece and looked at me. "I'm sorry, I can't talk to you right now. Tomorrow I'll be in a meeting all day, but if you want, we can meet on Monday. I finish at three."

She took her hand from the mouthpiece, swung her chair round and went back to her conversation, jotting down figures on a piece of paper as though I didn't exist. She didn't even look at me when I told her I would be back on Monday at three without fail.

My heart was in my mouth that Monday as I watched her step through the glass doors, in fact, it had been there for so long it didn't know how to find its way back to my chest, to the gentle, regular rhythm it had known until only three days before.

"You're exaggerating, Álvaro." That's what Mai would have said, which was why I said nothing to her, nor to anyone else. My unhealthy obsession, far from dissipating now that I knew the identity of the strange woman, seemed to grew with every passing second. I knew now that this woman had known my father, knew that whatever had passed between them was complicated, a connection that could not be explained in a few words something that would justify Raquel Fernández Perea showing up at a ceremony as personal, emotional and dreary as a funeral. The prospect that I was finally going to hear the answers to my questions did nothing to calm me, on the contrary. By Friday evening, when I took Mai and Miguelito with me to visit my mother, my head was exploding, although nobody else seemed to notice. "Actually, it wasn't a man, Mamá," I said as I gave her the green folder, "it was a girl, she was pleasant, quite pretty, she explained the whole thing to me but I've got it all written down here." You should meet her, I was tempted to add, I'm sure that her name would mean something to you.

That night I couldn't sleep. Tossing and turning, I tried to come up with some reasonable hypothesis to connect the two – Raquel Fernández Perea, about thirty-five years old, beautiful, clever, with a gap between her front teeth, employee of Caja Madrid, and Julio Carrión Gonzalez, RIP, 83, a successful businessman with impeccable credentials, CEO of a Real Estate company, customer of Caja Madrid – fitting the pieces of the puzzle together to form endless solutions, first daring, then anodyne then daring, until finally, at 6am I fell asleep.

Mai woke me four hours later. "Are you alright, Álvaro, you look terrible." "I just slept badly," I said, "I'm fine, don't worry." And she didn't worry, but that evening at my house while his wife, my wife and couple of friends were having a few drinks and watching the football on television, Fernando Cisneros grabbed my arm, dragged me into the hallway and asked me what was wrong.

"Nothing," I said, "Don't worry, everything's sorted. José Ignacio is going to sign and María…"

"I'm not talking about that, Álvaro, you've been acting strangely…" he shot me a cautious smile and I remembered that he knew me better than anyone, better even than Mai.

At university, we were known as "the odd couple" because we had nothing in common, but we agreed on everything, which was why I became his right hand man, his permanent campaign manager. Fernando had already been head of department, vice dean, then dean and was about to be appointed vice president of the university – with a bit of luck, in ten years he would be president. He was much more interested in politics than he was in physics – "That's why I need you," he'd say – but even the stress of the forthcoming election hadn't thrown him off the scent.

"There's something going on," he insisted, "What is it, some girl?"

I was about to tell him the truth. I would have done, but given we only had a moment, the story was too long, too complicated, so I told him I didn't know.

"You don't know?" he laughed.

"Some other time. I promise. There is a girl involved but not in the way you think. Really. It's to do with my father… Look, I'll tell you another time."

"Have it your own way," he said.

We went into the kitchen to get some ice and then returned to the living room. Javier was rolling a spliff. I told him I'd been having a hard time sleeping so he rolled another one just for me and I smoked it after everyone had left. Sunday didn't dawn until half one in the afternoon. "I'm sure you're coming down with something," Mai said. "You're probably right," I replied to avoid lying, "I don't feel great."

"I told you," she said, "Didn't I tell you yesterday?" She took Miguelito and they headed off to her parents place for lunch. I stayed in bed working on my two main hypotheses – one of them cheap and unpleasant, the other one genetic and devastating on so many levels

On Monday morning, I pretended to feel better, a recovery as phoney as my illness, and told Mai that I had lunch with the dean and that afterwards I'd be going to the museum. It was eight o'clock in the morning but my heart was already thumping.

"Hi," I realised that she had noticed me when she was halfway across the foyer. It was already ten past three. "Sorry I'm late."

"It doesn't matter."

But it did matter. She had put on lipstick and some foundation so close to her own skin tone it was almost invisible, together with subtle eyeshadow. I had not been standing close to her at my father's funeral, but at our previous meeting I had noticed that she was not wearing any make up. She could get away with it, she could get away with anything she wanted, and yet today she had decided to put on lipstick before meeting me. She was a clever girl, I remembered, and her make-up was a serious, a worrying, sign.

"I booked a table in a restaurant people from the bank often go to," she set off in the direction of Arenal, "It's small and old-fashioned, up here on the Calle Escalinata. Actually, I would have preferred Japanese, but I wasn't sure if you liked sushi…"

I couldn't think of anything to say and I stopped dead in the middle of the pavement. She turned and looked at me, putting her own interpretation on my awkwardness.

"What is it? You haven't eaten, have you?"

I was so dumbstruck I couldn't even answer this simple question. I felt as though everything was getting out of hand before it had even started.

"I should have checked with you, Álvaro" she said, "but I didn't have a phone number."

"No, it's not that…" I finally managed to say, "It's just I didn't realise we'd be having lunch."

"I know," she said and walked on. I followed her like a well-trained puppy. "That what I mean when I said I should have called you. But you needn't be so shocked," she smiled "People do eat at three o'clock in Spain, you know, or at least I do. I'm always starving by the time I leave

92

work. If you haven't had lunch, so much the better."

"It's just…"

"Don't worry," she laughed, "I'm not expecting you to pay, Álvaro. We'll go Dutch. After all, it is a business lunch of sorts."

"By the way, I do like sushi," I said after a moment.

"Glad to hear it. I'll bear that in mind the next time," she looked at me as though she already knew there would be other occasions. "I hope you didn't mind me using your Christian name?"

"It doesn't bother me."

We had almost arrived at Ópera, and were standing waiting for the traffic lights to change. She gave me an enigmatic smile and we didn't speak again until we got to the restaurant.

It wasn't a long walk – only three or four minutes – but it was enough for me to realise a few things. The first being that the woman I was walking alongside was not the same woman I had met the previous Thursday. She had the same face, the same hair, the same body, this time clothed in a cotton print dress which suited her better than the jeans. There seemed to be nothing left of her earlier vulnerability or her fake smile, and yet I was not entirely convinced by her sudden artlessness, the spontaneous faintly ironic candour which was clearly designed to be charming. And it was charming, but there was something too polished, too eloquent about it, something that reminded me of someone playing a well rehearsed role.

The second thing I realised was about myself, the memory of the thrill of the chase she had awakened in me, a feeling I had never had before and which had since faded, though not completely. I could still remember the sensation, could still feel the tingling of the hunter's excitement and the furious energy with which he tried to hide it. No one who saw us as we went down the short flight of steps that gave the Calle Escalinata its name would have believed that only four days earlier I – the tense man shuffling gingerly along the street – had had this tank of a woman, who now steamrollered all before her, cornered behind her desk. And yet I could still feel the thrill of being that man, a thrill that only she could awaken.

The third and most important thing I realised on that short walk to the restaurant derived from numbers one and two. But it was not a fact, merely an intuition – that neither of us was really the person the other thought we were.

"Here we are."

She pushed open the wooden door. I waved for her to go in first, she nodded gracefully and smiled before stepping inside. The restaurant was not full, but all the empty tables were reserved. Raquel didn't like the table that had been reserved for us and asked the maitre d' for a table in the corner by the window.

"Do you mind if we order first?" she went on talking without waiting to see whether or not I minded, "The place is half empty now, but at three-thirty when the people from Alcalá get here it's always jammed and it takes ages to be served." She looked up from the menu. "Do you fancy sharing something?"

Everything was so absurd, the conversation, the place, the food, the two of us sitting at the same table as if we knew each other, as if we had lunch together all the time, as if there was something more between us than a single question and a single answer, that this last question which sounded both terribly innocent and terribly intimate took on a grotesque meaning and I burst out laughing. I was nervous. She wasn't.

"I meant share something to eat," she smiled, "Come on."

"OK, I know what you meant," I opened the menu and scanned through the starters.

"The anchovies are extraordinary, I'm serious... What about deep-fried courgette flowers – have you ever tasted them?" I shook my head. "Oh, you've got to try them."

In the end, she chose what she wanted, she picked the wine, tasted it and held her glass out for me to take a sip.

"I think it's fine," she said, "but maybe it's a little too cold for you?"

"No, no, it's very nice," I said, because it was, although I had no intention of letting this new display of warlike intimacy pass unnoticed, ""But I'll stick to my own glass, if that's alright with you."

"Of course," she said, taking back her glass and filling mine. She put her elbows on the table and stared at me, "Do you want to know why I decided to call you by your Christian name?"

"Please."

"Well, first off, on account of your father," she paused to see what effect these words might have, but I didn't blink, "Your father and I were on first name terms, and you're his son. But, apart from that... When I realised the only thing to do was have lunch with you, because when I get off work I can't do anything without eating first, it seemed... I don't know. I've always thought that eating is something that should really be done in private, because eating with someone, no matter how discreet or polite you are, means showing them the insides of your body – your tongue, your teeth, your palate..." By now, I knew we were playing out a scene, and I felt vaguely flattered by the passion she brought to her role. "Have you ever thought that? When you eat with someone, they see you

94

chewing, swallowing, maybe even choking on your food if you're unlucky. I've always found eating with someone who's not a friend strange, doing something as intimate as eating when I don't even know their Christian name. Of course, I have to do it all the time for work, but I don't like it," she paused again, more briefly this time, fuck, you're in trouble now, I thought and she smiled as though she knew what I was thinking. "What I mean is, I don't eat with just anyone."

"Me neither. But I'm not used to being here, eating with you."

After this mutual confession, there was a silence I found uncomfortable but she found easier to deal with since there were lots of things she could do to fill the void: she picked up her bag, took out a pouch of tobacco, a lighter, her mobile phone, a PDA, "Excuse me a minute," she said tapping on the screen of her PDA with the plastic pen.

"What? I look like Bank-Manager Barbie with all the accessories, don't I?" she said and laughed but I didn't laugh with her. Too right, I thought.

"Why did you come to my father's funeral, Raquel?"

"Oh, for God's sake, Álvaro, don't be so impatient," she looked at me as though I'd said something startling, when all I had done was repeat a question I had asked her before. "I know you're probably expecting some terrible revelation, but, I'm afraid I'm going to have to disappoint you. It's a boring story. At the end of the day human beings are boring and predictable, our lives are pretty much the same, we all have about half a dozen things in common."

"Like what?"

She clicked her tongue and shot me a weary look. "Look, we've ordered now. This is a really good restaurant, but it's not cheap, so it would be a pity to waste our money. We've got an hour, maybe an hour and a half together, and what I have to tell you will only take about two minutes. I don't want you to be angry with me ahead of time. We've only just met, and you seem like a decent guy. Why don't we talk about you instead. You know lots about me, but I don't know anything about you. It doesn't seem fair."

At that moment, I stopped feeling nervous and I stopped feeling scared, because I was starting to feel like the most stupid, incompetent, needy, arrogant, fuckwit in the whole world. "Just walk away, Álvaro", I thought, furious with myself. "Fuck her!" But I didn't move. I looked at her, and I didn't move. She'd tricked me, she'd won me over to her side, by making me a promise that she might never keep, she was toying with me, playing me for a fool to make herself feel like she was in control, the same way she had decided where I was eating, what I was eating and with whom. "Just walk away, Álvaro," I thought, "Let her pay for everything – she ordered it!" But I stayed, because she had put on lipstick before leaving the office, because she held the answers to all my questions, and because I couldn't stop looking at her.

"What do you want to know?"

She answered with a radiant smile, as though she had been listening to my inner conflict and was celebrating her victory.

"I don't know... Tell me about the family business. What do you do?"

"Nothing," I said, and I felt much better.

"Nothing? But I thought..."

"I don't do anything," and for the first time I was the one to smile. "I'm the only one of us – well, of the brothers, I mean – who doesn't work for my father's business. My elder sister is a doctor, she works in intensive care. My little sister doesn't work – well, I suppose she'd say she was a homemaker."

"Oh!" She quickly tried to hide her disappointment, "And... and what do you do?"

"I teach," In spite of her efforts to hide it, I had to laugh at her reaction. "It's not that bad, you know, lots of people do it."

"I know, it's just that... I don't know... Of course, that's why you've always got that briefcase with you... What do you teach, secondary school?"

"No, I'm a professor," She seemed happier to hear this, "I teach at U.A.M., in the Physics department."

"Physics... And you enjoy it?"

"More than anything."

"I nearly always failed it at school... For someone who always got top marks in maths..."

"You had a bad teacher."

At that moment, the waiter arrived with the starters and she busied herself serving them out. She was rethinking her strategy, I realised, looking for another way to get the information she was interested in. But just as I was about to take pity on her, she came up with a question.

"And what *exactly* do you teach?" Anyone listening would have thought she really wanted to know.

"Well, this year, I'm teaching an introductory course called Principles of Physics, two one-term advanced courses and a doctoral course."

"Did you have a lecture today?"

I nodded.

"So, what did you talk about?"

"About the whole. And its complex relationship to its parts," I took one of the pieces of toast she had put on my plate and bit into it, "You were right, the anchovies are good…"

"I don't understand," she said, "How can the relationship between the whole and its parts be complicated? I mean, the whole is equal to the sum of its parts, isn't it? Even a child in primary school knows that. And it has nothing to do with Physics."

"Really?" I was enjoying this. I didn't yet realise how far I was about to fall, "Are you sure?"

It was obvious she'd just been playing for time, and whatever her plan had been, it had failed. But what she had said was also true. We'd already ordered, the waiter would bring the food and we'd eat, we had a whole hour ahead of us and we had to fill it with words, and I was the only one who could do it. So I decided to have some fun.

"From what you've said, I think I can work out that you studied that debased, theoretically redundant pseudoscience known as Economics, am I right?" She laughed and nodded. "OK. The problem with economists is that they are extraordinarily arrogant, utterly lacking in the intellectual humility you learn when you work on a broader scale. I'm not going to question the fact that Marx was a genius, or that money makes the world go round, but you have to remember that the world is only one thing in a vast universe, a simple pinprick in something whose totality we cannot begin to understand. Beyond the limited scope of Economics, which is confined to this world, the whole is not necessarily the sum of its parts. In fact, one might say that the whole is only the sum of its parts when those parts do not interact."

"Do you speak Sanskrit too?" She was enjoying this as much as I was.

"It's not that difficult. I'll explain it to you. I'll give you a classic example directly related to everyday life, the same example I gave my students this morning. They were only first years, so even though you're only an Economist, you should be able to follow it."

"I'll do my best."

"Let's assume we have two rooms with a connecting door. In the first room, there is a little boy crying. We'll call him A. In the other room is another little boy who is also crying, we'll call him B. The door is closed, and the sum of A plus B we will call X, this being the crying that we can hear," I paused while the waiter brought our main course, pan-fried Dorado for her, grilled veal sirloin for me. "Now, let's see what happens if we open the door, that is to say, if we allow the parts to interact with one another. Now things become more complicated, because A and B could decide to ignore each other and carry on crying. But it's also possible that when he hears B crying, A will be curious and stop crying

97

to go and see what's happening, or maybe B will stop crying when he hears A crying. Best case scenario, A or B will wander into the other room hoping to play with the other boy and if he manages to convince the other boy, there will be no more crying. Worst case scenario: A or B, angry at hearing the tantrum will attack the other boy, a fight will break out, they'll thump each other, and the crying will go on, louder and more desperate than before. Get it?"

"Yes. You're a good teacher."

"Of course I'm a good teacher," I smiled, "Consequently, I assume you've learned that X can be equal to, greater than or less than the sum of A plus B. It depends on the interrelation of the parts. This is why we can only ever state that the whole is equal to the sum of its parts when those parts do not interact."

"Fine. But what use is it?"

"I don't know how anyone puts up with you…" She laughed, she was much more beautiful when she laughed "What use is it? It's useful for knowing how things happen. It's useful for trying to formulate rules that alleviate the existential angst of our existence on this insignificant speck of dust lost in the infinite universe. But, to bring it down to basics that even an Economist can understand, it's useful for determining natural disasters, for example. A disaster is what happens when the whole is greater than the sum of its parts."

"Wonderful," she applauded, clapping politely.

"It is…" I said, "Much more wonderful that what my brothers do for a living. Though a lot less useful to you, I'm afraid."

At that moment, a symbolic bell announced the third and final round. She had won the first, I had won the second. The third was to be much longer than either of us could have known, there would be no winner, and it would change our lives forever.

"You think I've brought you here to get information from you about your father's business," she ventured cautiously after a moment, "Things you don't know, but your brothers could have told me."

"I don't think that," I answered, grateful for the fact that for once she had decided to meet me head on, "I know it. You told me so earlier."

"Not exactly." She seemed calm.

"But you knew my father through your work."

"Is that what you think?" she smiled.

"It's one of the theories I've considered," her smile had unsettled me, but I couldn't back out now, "…that my father was mixed up in some shady deal you were involved with. As his broker or his accessory or maybe just as a witness."

She weighed my words for a moment.

"Do you fancy dessert?" I shook my head. "Coffee, then?" She signalled to a waiter and ordered two coffees. "Your father was mixed up in some shady deals – every successful businessman is. But my relationship with your father had nothing to do with his business – shady or otherwise."

"Or..." I couldn't bring myself to finish the sentence.

"Or?" she asked.

"Or..."

I tried a second time, and for a second time I couldn't bring myself to say it. I had another theory, but I had been so sure that my first theory was right that the second had been no more than an act of masochism, a wild guess with nothing to back it up except that it was consistent with the evidence. The consequences, while not disastrous, nor beyond the bounds of possibility – in fact it was all too possible, especially in Spain, back then - would be difficult for my family to accept. I had had a nagging suspicion that had stayed with me since that moment when I first saw her in the cemetery at Torrelodones, before I even saw her up close, before I had had time to study her and notice a faint family resemblance in her profile, something vague and fleeting. Now that she was sitting opposite me, the feeling vanished like a bubble, and yet that first day something had prompted me to ask my mother whether she might be some distant relation, and that question had made her uncomfortable. Since then, I had become obsessed with the gap between her front teeth – something that linked her not to my father but to my mother, yet I could not get the idea out of my mind.

"Or..." I said eventually, "we could be related."

"Really?" she smiled at first, and then looked serious, "How?"

"No offence but... it occurred to me..." I took a deep breath and said, "You might be my father's daughter."

She was drinking water and her immediate reaction, halfway between a gasp and a giggle, sent a spray of water over the table, and me.

"Sorry," she laughed, wiping her face with her napkin. "You see? This is what happens when you have lunch with someone who doesn't trust you."

"So you're not my sister?" I said, relieved, as she reached over and, with a dry corner of her napkin, wiped my chin. At that moment, in spite of the tension that hung over the apparently light-hearted scene, I realised that – leaving aside Thursday's polite handshake – this was the first time Raquel Fernández Perea had touched me.

"No, of course not," she laughed again, "It's just that I thought about my father, poor man, and… My father's name is Ignacio, he's a telecommunications engineer and he's twenty years younger than your father. They have nothing in common, really, I mean it would be hard to imagine two more different men. My mother's name is also Raquel, she studied History of Art, she runs a picture framing shop and as far as I know she's always been a model wife."

I kept my mouth shut. She went on laughing and shaking her head. I thought she was protesting too much, but nothing could have prepared me for what came next.

"I have to say, Álvaro, that for a physicist, you have a vivid imagination…"

"Physics requires a great deal of imagination," I said solemnly, though I realised I had already lost any last shred of authority, "Without it, there would be no progress."

"In any case… I don't suppose I should have been too surprised. I was afraid you'd come out with something like that from the start," she looked at the waiter, scribbling in the air to indicate she wanted the bill, "I told you the story was trite and you'd be disappointed. At the end of the day human beings are boring and predictable… Besides, you explained it better than I ever could. The whole is only equal to the sum of its parts when the parts do not interact," she paused and looked at me, "Until now, you and I have been two parts of a whole, though we knew nothing about each other."

The waiter brought the bill, she glanced at it, dropped two notes onto the tray, put her belongings back into her bag and took out a large, flashy, state-of-the-art key with a blue plastic tag.

"Your father and I were lovers, Álvaro. So this…" she pushed the key across the table, "…this is yours. The address is on the keyring.

She looked at me one last time, then got up and walked out.

# II

# ICE

The Popular Front manifesto began with these words: "The Republic as conceived by the parties which make up the Popular Front is not a republic governed by motives of social or economic class, but a regime of democratic freedom motivated by the interests of the people and social progress."

Constancia de la Mora, In Place of Splendor<br>(New York, 1939 – Mexico, 1944 – Madrid 2004)

One night, in the café Gayango, we were drinking coffee Juan Tomás, then leader of the "*flechas*", airmen Terviño and Bergali and capitán Martínez from the Division. Díaz Criado arrived [...] Some moments later, a policeman arrived in a car - a man I had often seen at the Comisaría - with a folder. He sat beside him, took out some papers and started to read out a list of names. Díaz Criado nodded: "Him, him, OK. No, not him. That one, maybe, tomorrow." I remember perfectly that the policeman, so he would remember, made him clarify: "This one has a brother in custody too." "Yes, that one, yes." "He's the one you saw the other day, the fat, bald one." "No, not him. Hang on... That one too." [...]

He said that, once he got going, it was all the same whether he signed a hundred death warrants or three hundred, what was important was to "rid Spain of the Marxists". I heard him say: "Here, no one's moved in thirty years."

Antonio Bahamonde, A Year with Queipo de Llano<br>(Memories of a Nationalist)<br>(Barcelona – Buenos Aires, 1938 – Sevilla, 2005)

She has great legs. That was my first thought as I watched her walk away, say goodbye to the manager, and disappear through the door.

She fucked my father. That was my second thought, a split-second before a wave of words, ideas, images, memories, suspicions and feelings broke over me. I called the waiter over and ordered a whiskey, a double.

By the time I had downed half of it, I had remembered that I was not my brother Julio, nor was I my brother Rafa. So there would be no scandal, I said to myself, poor Papá, it was his life, who was I to judge him, but what a bastard – eighty three years old, fucking hell... Then I started to laugh, in a sort of euphoria mingled with astonishment, it was the only possible way I could react to news that shocking, so unexpected, so utterly irreconcilable with everything I knew, with the fragile, grief-stricken face of my mother as she told us over and over that she and my father had slept together for forty-nine years, forty-nine years in the same bed, and now what?

But, after all, what did I know? I thought about my own son Miguel, who wasn't even four years old when I had gone, in mid-November 2004, to La Coruña for a three day conference. I'd had no more desire to go than I had to throw myself out a window, because my father had just come out of hospital and I was worried and, more than anything, exhausted. But still, I went to La Coruña, because the guy organising it was a friend of mine and I didn't want to leave him in the lurch.

I'll try to wangle it so I'm only there for one day, I'd told Mai before I left, I'll see if they can bring the round table discussion forward, and I did, I talked to the secretary as soon as I got there but afterwards, over dinner, I ran into a delegate from Valencia I'd never met before but had heard a lot about from my colleagues – mostly bad things from the women, good things from most of the men, better than good in some cases. Naturally, I sided with the men on this one, not only was she attractive, she was intelligent, she was funny, she was married and she knew exactly what she wanted.

"I'm a completely different person at conferences, you know," she said to me over a drink in the bar later, "It's a strange phenomenon, I leave my house feeling good, feeling calm, but as soon as I arrive, I can't help it... I look around thinking, let's see... who am I going to fuck tonight? I'm mean, Physics conferences are full of men, and there are so few women. I've no idea how Art Historians survive these things," she added, "I suppose they end up slashing their wrists..."

She was so straight with me that I wondered if she had already slept with every other delegate at the conference, but I didn't care, because in situations like this it didn't matter to me if I was just another notch on someone's gun. The next morning, over breakfast, I realised that I'd been wrong, it became obvious that although many were called few were actually chosen. Though this did not change the way I saw things, it put me in a good mood, made all the better when the conference secretary told me that they could change the time of the round table but not the day, because one of the guests was not arriving until Friday morning. "Oh, never mind then!" I said, "I'll hang on, let's keep to the original schedule. "Don't worry about it," Mai said to me. "It's OK, Álvaro, it'll take your mind off things, try to have fun."

And I did have fun, so much fun that I didn't have time to look for a toy shop to buy a present for my son. I ended up buying him a truck at the airport just before my flight left. Next to it in the shop window I saw a velvet-lined shawl in tones of red with long silk fringes that looked perfect for my wife. I was so sure she would like it I bought it in spite of the price – more than half of what I'd earned from the conference and the round table put together. As I paid, I felt calm, sure of what I was doing and my reasons for doing it, and guilt was not one of them. I'd often brought Mai gifts from trips when it had never even occurred to me to hook up with someone; just as often I'd not brought her anything, including after a trip to the Universidad de la Laguna when I didn't even make back to my hotel room the whole weekend. Although it wasn't as much fun as La Coruña. Mai didn't care if I didn't bring her a present, but she always thanked me when I did. Although this shawl was something else.

This was why, when Raquel walked out that afternoon, leaving me alone with a double whiskey, I thought about Miguelito who wasn't even four years old when he'd watched his mother take off the shiny red wrapping paper, shriek, take the shawl delicately between her fingers, then throw her arms around my neck and cover me in kisses. My son didn't remember it, he would have been too young, but perhaps the image of that shawl was engraved on his memory, because Mai cared for it more than she cared for herself, and always put it on when got she dressed up to go out. If he did remember it, I thought, then he would realise that it had been a present from me, something beautiful, rare and expensive and it would never cross his mind that his father, who loved his mother so much he couldn't even walk past a shop window if he saw something she might like, had spent the previous three days fucking like an animal with some professor from Valencia.

Miguel will never know, I thought, he will never have to listen to his mother say in that calm, neutral tone as she had once told me "It's a big world out there, and life is very short, and very long". The first time I heard them, the words were like a healing balm after the Chinese water torture of Lorna's jealousy.

"There's no point in me hoping you'll never come across another woman you find attractive, Álvaro," and she seemed calm, sure of what she was saying, "There are so many women in the world, so many men, so many people... But what we have together is important. It's important to me, too important to throw it away over some stupid little thing, don't you think?"

"Um, I don't know. Yes..." I said, unsure of where this conversation was heading.

"Well then..." she smiled, "I've always thought it's better to do stupid little things and get them over with, otherwise if you bottle them up they grow into something much bigger. That's why all I ask is that you be loyal, that you love me, and do not humiliate me or degrade me, and whatever stupid little things you do with other people are not important to me."

The first time I heard them, these words were like a healing balm, the second time I liked them less, and the third time I asked why she always talked as if it was just me, why she never mentioned herself.

"Don't tell me you're jealous!" she said brightly, though I could not tell whether she liked the idea or found it inadmissible.

"No... I don't think so," I said, "I don't think I'm jealous, but I'd prefer not to find out."

Mai laughed and she never brought up the subject again. And when he grew up, her son, my son, Miguel, would have no memory of the hazy conditions of the pact that his mother had offered his father, the pact I had agreed to with a casual confidence that grew over time, and not only did I become sure that my wife's speech referred only to me, I also ceased to worry about whether or not she was really having dinner with friends each time she went out.

When I could no longer detect the distinctive taste of ice made with tap water in my glass, I looked up and realised that very soon only the waiters and I would remain, since the only other diners were already getting to their feet. I paid the bill and left quickly, but when I reached the street I had to stop and think what I was going to do next. I turned on my mobile and registered that I had eight missed calls and eight voicemails, two from Mai, three from my mother, one from Clara and two from Rafa. They were all about the same thing.

"I've just left the restaurant," I said to Mai, who was the first person I managed to get hold of. "I turned on my phone and found out I'm the most wanted man in Madrid."

"Yep," she laughed, "It's your mother, she wants to know if you can go to the solicitors office at six on Thursday afternoon for the reading of your father's will."

"Fuck!" I said. "What for? She must have a copy so presumably she already knows what's in it…"

"I don't know. That's your mother's business."

"And can you come on Thursday?"

"I'm not invited, Álvaro, it's only the children. There would be no bequests to sons- and daughters-in-law, we know that."

"She said that?"

"Her very words."

"That's nice," we both burst out laughing. "Well, I suppose I'll have to find a way to be there, though I don't know how…"

I realised that I wasn't ready to talk to my mother just yet, to hear her delicate but firm voice, that heartbreaking note of constant reproach, "Oh, Álvaro, where have you been, I seem to spend my whole life running round after you." My mother was a tough woman, but I didn't quite know how tough – I remembered the hard-headed discipline she had meted out to us as children, a discipline that alternated with intense surges of affection, which was a very different combination to that of my father, who seemed much more indulgent, except when he was angry, when he would explode into a furious rage that terrified everyone, even my mother. While Mai filled the silence, telling me about her day, how Miguelito's teacher was very happy with his work, though not so happy that he was constantly picking fights in the playground, I wondered how much my mother knew, whether Raquel was just the last in a long line of lovers whose existence she was aware of; I wondered whether my father's infidelity had hurt her, or hurt her only at first, or never hurt her, perhaps she had accepted it as an inevitable part of their marriage, or perhaps she had been suffering in silence for years.

"… and I told him no," my wife went on talking, "of course we don't encourage our son's violent behaviour, although I know what you're thinking, Álvaro, you're thinking that it's your fault, because you're always happy when he's rowdy and all you ever buy him is dinosaurs and robots covered in missiles…"

"Maybe…" I admitted, not prepared to enter into a discussion of the educational criteria of the most idiotic teacher I had ever come across. "Mai, can you do me a favour?"

"You want me to call your mother?" I could hear her smile. "That's it, isn't it?"

"Would you? Please? It's just that I'm really tied up right now. I still have to stop by the museum and I've no idea what time I'll get home… Call her and tell her I'll be there, then maybe she'll give me a bit of peace for a change."

It was true, I did have to stop by the museum, I thought as I hailed a taxi. I told the driver to take me to the Calle Jorge Juan, checking the street number on the keyring I'd been carrying in my left hand ever since I'd left the restaurant. "Is that between Velázquez and Núñez de Balboa?" the driver asked. I told him I had no idea, that I'd never been there before. But I was wrong.

I recognised the doorway even before I stepped inside, and suddenly I felt an icy chill running down my spine.

So it's true, I thought, though I hadn't even imagined for a moment that it might be a lie. But everything had been so weird, my meeting with Raquel, the lunch we had, what she'd told me, the way she'd told me that I hadn't really thought of it as anything other than one more theory, one more version of my father, that seemed surprising, comical at first, then bitter and hurtful, but certainly more moving than any of the theories I had come up with. The image of this old man, powerful to the last, determined to, cling to life with a strength all but spent, his hands flayed, his teeth gritted with the effort, banished all other thoughts, not simply his wife's face, but the possibility that he might fail, the inevitable humiliations his eighty-three-year-old body visited on his unbroken spirit. As I stepped through the door, walked across the foyer and waited for the lift, I could think of nothing else. I could think only of my father, how he had been a more extraordinary man than we, his children, would ever be. And it moved me to realise quite how much.

The key Raquel had given me easily opened the armour-plated door of Loft E, which together with Loft F covered the right-hand wing of the building, while on the other side, the same floor space had been carved into twice as many apartments. His heart was hammering as I stepped into the spacious hallway and saw, at the far end, an enormous living room and farther still, a terrace that seemed to rush headlong into space. I suddenly felt something almost like euphoria, but more tangible.

"God, you are such a bastard, Papá!" I said aloud, using the present tense, talking as if he was still alive, "What a complete prick…"

Because although this loft apartment was no more luxurious, it was twice the size of the one my brother Rafa had tried to palm off on me a couple of years earlier.

"We've just finished restoring a magnificent historic building, it's in the best part of Salamanca," he told me over the phone, "It's really special, I'd love to show it to you…"

"Why?" I asked, "I'm not in the market for an apartment."

"That's what you say now, but just wait until you see it…"

His persistence was suspicious. I didn't trust his far-fetched business ventures, but there was nothing I could do when, one afternoon, Mai answered the phone.

"I'd like to go and see it, Álvaro," she told me later, "If only out of curiosity. I mean, it's not as if we have to do anything, just meet up with Rafa some Saturday morning, see the apartment and that's that."

What we saw was more like the kind of luxury suite you see in films than an apartment someone might actually live in. It had a huge living room, an enormous bedroom that looked like an apse, a bathroom with more marble than a Persian mausoleum, a jacuzzi and a ridiculous 'American-style' galley kitchen tucked away in a cupboard.

"Well, it's certainly impressive," said Mai nodding her head.

"Impressive?" I said incredulously, but my brother ignored my scepticism.

"It could be yours," he said.

"Ours?" I asked.

"Of course," Rafa addressed me, "You can afford it…" He put his arm round my shoulder – uh-oh, I thought – then started trying to reel me in. "I mean, you've been saving, Álvaro, haven't you?"

He was right. When I had returned from the States, I'd found out that my father had begun to share out some of his profits with us, quite a large share in fact, amounting to between two and three million pesetas each. He had set my share aside, he was always scrupulous and would never have favoured one of his children over another, and I had invested it all in the house. Later, until Mai got pregnant, I squandered the money I got each year on long, impressive trip. When impending fatherhood put that to an end, I thought it would make more sense to buy somewhere at the beach, an apartment or a little house that might become a childhood paradise for my unborn son, so I asked my father to hang onto my share until I told him otherwise.

We were taking things slowly. Mai liked the idea of somewhere up north, but I wasn't keen. Miguelito was still very young and my parents' house at La Moraleja, with its servants, its vast garden and swimming pool, was too big and much too comfortable to give up just yet. So I had been saving for three years, that much was true. That year, my father had given us the same share as usual, but he told us there was more to come.

He had just sold his stake in a company he'd never liked at such a profit that he had decided to share that equally with us as well. We all knew this, but Rafa was probably the only one who knew exactly how much we were going to get.

"You see," he said to me as we were leaving, "Between the money you've saved and what Papá is going to give you any day now, you have more than enough for a deposit. You can buy it, put it on the market and then you'll make twice what you paid for it, because I'll sell it to you at cost. And with whatever you make you can pay off the balance and then buy a place at any beach you like."

"Yes, but the thing is, I don't…"

"I know, you don't know anything about business," he got in before me. "But this is the sweetest, easiest deal you'll ever be offered. Clara's going to take one of the others, and Julio would have too, but Verónica won't let him…"

"Look, Rafa, count me out."

"OK," he said with a pained look, "Whatever you say…"

He didn't say anything more about it, but when I got home, I began to think I might have made a mistake.

"Listen, I've had it up to here with your brother Rafa," My father roared down the phone. "I've told him a thousand times, not to get you involved, not to rip you off, but he won't listen. He needs money, of course he does, he always needs money, because he's got his fingers in too many pies, he doesn't even tell me the half of it… I've never met anyone as fanatical about money as your brother, not that you ever see him spending it."

"So you mean…" I was a little surprised by my father's vehemence, "you mean the apartments aren't worth…"

"The apartments are worth a fortune," he interrupted me, "Of course they are, that's why he's hanging onto them. He's sold three, two little ones to an American film distributor who'll rent them out to film stars when they have to stay in Madrid, and one of the large apartments to one of the directors of the Banco de Santander, who wants somewhere to screw his mistress, because if you've seen the apartments you'll know that's exactly what they're designed for."

"That hadn't occurred to me, but now you mention it…"

"The thing is, he's made his money, but he still has three apartments on his hands and he won't find it easy to get a buyer quickly. If he took his time he could make a fortune on them, but he seems to need the money fast – God knows why – and obviously millionaires don't grow on trees… That's why he thought about your idiot brother-in-law Curro, who said yes to him until I had a word with your sister. He wouldn't dare try it on with Julio, and Angélica still has to pay off half her mortgage, so that leaves you and Clara…" He sighed as if he were tired of constantly repeating himself, "Listen, you call him and tell him I said you're having nothing to do with the Calle Jorge Juan, let him sell you one of those new houses in Arroyomolinos at cost, a house for a normal family with two kids and a dog… You'll see, I'm the one who will end up having to buy one of those bloody apartments…"

I never did call my brother about buying a house in Arroyomolinos, but my father must have said something to Rafa, he didn't mention his bargain when I next saw him.

"So this is why you didn't want us buying here, isn't it Papá?

I crossed the vast expanse of the half-empty living room. I recognised the furniture: the three white leather sofas, the glass-topped coffee table, the dining table flanked by eight chairs, the teak deckchairs on the terrace, were the same ones I had seen in the apartment Rafa had shown me. "You even managed to get the furniture from the show flat", I thought, "Nice work…" But there were other details I recognised too, the big, healthy plants, the tastefully framed abstracts on the walls. It was obvious that nobody had actually lived here – that wasn't what these apartments were for, I remembered, but there were some well-thumbed books on a shelf above the television and a crystal ashtray on the coffee table, clean but clearly used.

The bathroom was much more instructive. On two chrome hooks beside the door were a pair of bathrobes, a large one in white and a smaller one in salmon pink. On the stand next to the washbasin were two toothbrushes, a tube of toothpaste, some jars of cream, a can of shaving foam and a tissue holder. In the drawers, I found a box of tampons, some aspirin, a make-up bag, some cotton face wipes and two different types of disposable razor in blue and pink. Through the shower screen, I could see gels, shampoos and a well worn washcloth. So far, nothing out of the ordinary, but when I came to the jacuzzi, which was even bigger than the one Rafa had showed me, and was almost entirely surrounded by a large picture window with a spectacular view of the city, I noticed dozens of half-burned candles sitting round the edge. Fucking hell, I thought, how tasteless, how tacky, and before I'd even finished the thought I realised my face was burning.

But the burning on my face was as nothing compared to the sudden, savage blaze raging inside me, the flames of innocent guilt, an infinite shame that did nothing to appease the heat. "Please, take a seat. I'm sorry, I should have offered you a drink. Would you like a coffee?" And

Raquel Fernández Perea, who was more beautiful than she seemed, lighting the last candle before slipping naked into the jacuzzi. Easing her thirty-five-year-old body, her skin, velvety as a rare peach, her gorgeous legs, those hips slightly too wide for her narrow waist, into the water so that my father could take her in his arms as he thought to himself that his son Álvaro was a bloody fool who didn't have the first idea about what was horrible or tasteless or tacky in this world. This new feeling, of being a naïve idiot, an inadvertent witness to a complexity I could not begin to understand simply added to the excitement and shame I had felt a moment before. And this is nothing, I thought, This is nothing.

At first glance, the bedroom shed no further light. The domed room was like an apse, making the king-size bed seem like some pagan altar, an effect reinforced by the two alcoves above the bedside tables. The tables themselves were beautiful, simple lines, slightly curving, like the matching chest of drawers against one of the side walls. There was an enormous, flat-screen television on the far wall and underneath, on a metal TV stand, was a DVD player and a neatly arranged pile of films.

"You'll see, Álvaro, I said as I looked through them, "you'll see."

I sat down on the bed and felt an absurd wave of delight when I noticed that it wasn't a water bed, but a common sprung mattress. Rich people have no taste, I thought to myself, though it seemed unnecessary given that the room screamed the fact aloud. I wondered which side my father would have slept on and thought that logically he would sleep on the same side as he did in his conjugal bed. I checked, and there were two remote controls on the table on the right hand side. I looked through the drawers of the other nightstand but found nothing but an instruction manual for the digital clock radio that sat next to the bedside lamp.

The clock was accurate. Out of curiosity, I pressed the button and discovered that the alarm was set for 7am. So she must have slept here sometimes, afterwards, I thought, and this simple image, the image of a young woman waking up to go to work in a bed she used to share with a man old enough to be her father – to be her grandfather – seemed monstrous, until I quickly remembered that Raquel Fernández Perea was not some poor defenceless orphan, she was a smart girl earning a fat salary. Whatever reason she might have had for getting involved with one of her clients, it didn't include penury.

In the top drawer of the right hand nightstand there were three things. The smallest was a rectangular silver pillbox, the lid badly scratched, which was similar, if not identical, to the one that my father took with him everywhere. The same was true of the simple, elegant stainless steel propelling pencil which could be seen in his pocket in every photograph of him I could remember. The third thing was a purple rubber dildo which looked as if it was filled with some kind of gel and smelled of soap and plastic.

"Fucking hell, Papá…"

Raquel Fernández Perea, who is much more beautiful than she seems, lying naked on a pile of pillows, her stunning legs spread wide, offering a strange, pornographic view of her slightly disproportioned body. Her perfect skin "Please, take a seat. I'm sorry, I should have offered you a drink." Her belly trembles slightly, though less than the hands of the old man holding the purple cylinder that slowly disappears inside her, as she smiles gratefully, showing the gap between her front teeth.

Blood was pounding in my temples as though the veins were about to burst. "I'm afraid I'm going to have to disappoint you. It's a boring story. At the end of the day people are boring and predictable." And she was right, we are, because I turned on the television, then the DVD player and saw exactly what I had expected to see. The woman was dark-skinned, she was wearing a red and black basque that left her breasts exposed, the men – because there were two of them – were wearing dark suits and ties, but both of them had their flies open and their cocks out. I didn't see any more. I turned off the TV and the DVD to spare myself the harsh, clinical sordidness of what was to come. I couldn't help making a joke. "The executive model, Papá," I thought, remembering his displeasure at my unwillingness to wear a tie. It was a joke, but I didn't find it funny.

I didn't want to be there any longer, prying into the private world of this old man who now seemed as weak, fragile, and scrawny as a stray dog, a poor man who was dead, who was alone, who was nowhere. For the first time in my life I felt responsible for my father, more grown up than he was, able to make decisions, shelter and protect him as he had protected me when I was a child. You had to die Papá, I thought, before you needed me. And this stark realisation shocked me.

In the pillbox there was one small white tablet, some larger round pills, and two blue ones I had never seen before. I put one of them in my pocket, then returned the pillbox to the drawer of the nightstand. I realised that I would have to come back soon, because this was not a secret I could tell my brothers, much less my mother. At the end of the day, it was lucky Mamá had sent me, the wrong son, to a meeting with her husband's last lover. It was then that I remembered the meeting that was to take place the following Thursday, the reading of the will, and I realised that I would have to sort the flat out sooner rather than later, get rid of the DVDs, the dildo, the candles, the make-up in the bathroom. It seemed like an ugly job, and as I crossed the threshold I felt a wrenching sadness. I wondered when he had last crossed this threshold and how he had felt, how much time he had left before he died.

Jesus, Papá, why did you have to go and die like that when you had a thirty-five year old lover and still so much life in you. Outside, the air was balmy but it could not warm the frozen layer of grief.

"Miguelito!"

My son scampered along the corridor, hurtling towards me with the astonished delight of a bull noticing an open gate. It was true, he was a little rowdy, and it was also true that I liked him that way.

"Were you a good boy today?" I asked, sweeping him up in my arms and covering him with kisses. "Were you?" He nodded solemnly. "Mamá said your teacher told her that you work hard in class but you're always hitting people."

"No I don't..." he shook his head, even more solemn now. "Adrian does, and so does Tito, pow, pow..."

"They hit you and you hit them back, is that it?" I asked. He smiled at me. "In that case, I think maybe you deserve a reward for working so hard in class... What do you think?"

Mai was in the kitchen, stirring the contents of a saucepan with a wooden spoon.

"Álvaro, you're home early!"

"Yes," I closed the door behind me.

"Miguel is..."

"Miguel is watching *Peter Pan*," I interrupted her, pressing myself against her back. "I just put it on. You know it's his favourite, and I don't think there's any harm in it, they're *friendly* pirates."

"But I thought you'd hidden the DVD? Álvaro..." She gave a nervous little laugh. "Álvaro, what are you doing?"

"Nothing," I slipped my right hand under her bra and my left hand under her skirt and kissed her neck slowly. "Well, maybe this..." I moved my fingers. "I decided to give the poor child a suspended sentence."

"Why?"

"What do you mean why?" I mimicked her, pressing against her. "What do you think?"

"Álvaro, I'm making *croquetas* for dinner... The bechamel is going to go all lumpy..."

We had a family-size pizza for dinner, with free garlic bread and I realised that my son thought that this was part of the reward that, in an inexplicable burst of generosity, I had bestowed on him. He ate

113

everything on his plate and went to bed without complaining about his capricious father.

When I came back into the living room, Mai was watching a film. I poured two glasses of wine and sat next to her, she snuggled up to me as she always did and I managed to retain my composure for ten minutes."

"Álvaro!" Her T-shirt was up around her armpits, her bra was unhooked and her skirt rucked up to the waist. From her voice – pitched somewhere between pleasure and shock – I could tell that she was happy but a little frightened. "What's with you today? You're impossible, really…"

"I don't know…" I said as I pulled her onto my lap. "It must be the spring."

But it wasn't the spring. And when I was finished, I was no calmer than I had been when I arrived home.


The whole can be greater or less than the sum of its parts, depending on the relationship established between the parts. Think carefully about that statement, because it's important, both in itself and because it leads to a second statement: we can only say with certainty that the whole is equal to the sum of its parts when the parts do not interact.

This is what I used to tell my students and they would eagerly write it down, smiling somewhat sceptically, wondering what I was getting at with all these boring lectures, fuck, it's not like they'd signed up for philosophy… But by mid-way through the course, the more intelligent ones had realised that physics too is also a system of thought with its own rules, rules that cannot be immediately deduced from arithmetic principles. Because 2 + 2 does not necessarily make 4, not always, not in all circumstances. When you understand that, I told them, you're ready to understand a whole lot more. Yet I also understood that with a lifetime of finding that two plus two does equal four, the notion became so ingrained it was difficult to dismiss, so I tried not to be too hard on them. Just as I tried not to be to hard on myself when I went back to my father's love nest and felt that it was all a sham, a set up.

I had spent two and a half days working myself into a state of near collapse, deliberately, because it felt good, not just because since the day I'd met Raquel I had done nothing but invent inaccurate theories, and because, after spending the afternoon at the museum talking with the workers and supervising the installation of the exhibition I would get home late and so tired that Mai would have nothing to worry about. My own sense of calm was nothing more than physical exhaustion and, perhaps, the relief of knowing a little more.

"I've been thinking of asking your wife for some advice," I took advantage of the break between my first and second lectures to call my brother-in-law Adolfo, "but I think maybe it's better if I talk to you."

"Man to man?"

"Um... yes, I suppose so."

"I'll do my best..." his sarcastic tone made me smile, "But nothing too difficult. Or too manly, if possible."

"Well, I'm afraid it's very manly... Look, last week, when it was raining, I went over to pick up the post for my mother at La Moraleja. I was only wearing a jumper and got soaked so Lisette lent me Papá's raincoat. There was a silver pillbox in the pocket, with a small white pill in it..."

"Cafinitrina, a sublingual nitroglycerin tablet, your father always had to have one with him because he'd had one serious heart attack and a couple of minor ones," he interrupted, not realising he wasn't telling me anything I didn't already know.

"OK. There were a couple of other white pills I didn't recognise, they were bigger and oval."

"I've no idea," Adolfo laughed, "Could be anything. If they're oval, then they're probably some kind of statin for his cholesterol. Your father suffered from high cholesterol – nothing too serious, but he had to be careful."

"And... and there were a couple of other tablets. They're sky blue," I looked at the tablet I was holding between my fingers and tried to be specific, "Well, not sky blue exactly..."

"And they're sort of diamond-shaped?"

"Yes."

"Viagra."

"Are you sure?"

"I'm not a chemist, but if that's what they look like, I'm pretty sure..."

"But wouldn't that be dangerous?"

"Look..." he hesitated for a minute, considering the question. "It's like anything, it depends. Obviously, a man in his condition wouldn't exactly be the ideal target market for Viagra... But your father was a strong man, Álvaro, and though it might sound strange, given he died of a heart attack, he was in better shape than most people with heart conditions – he didn't have high blood pressure, he wasn't diabetic... Clinics are up to their ears in men your fathers age with heart conditions *and* high blood pressure *and* diabetes who take Viagra all the time, although their doctors would never prescribe it for them. If they didn't take Viagra is it possible that they would live a little longer? Yes, of course. Would they feel less tired, have less risk of cardiac arrhythmia? Sure. Would they have a better quality of life. Not necessarily. It depends on what you mean by quality of life. If you're asking me, I'd have to side with the old guys, and when I'm their age, I'm sure I'll take it too. You live as long as you live."

"Wow... I've never even thought about it," I admitted when I finally stopped laughing.

"That's because you're ten years younger than me. But seriously, Álvaro. The first – let's say private – conversation I ever had with your father was about this. I'd just started going out with your sister, and he brought it up. It was two years before he turned eighty, he was in good health, and he was curious, so it made sense. Well I thought it did anyway. He didn't ask me if it would be OK for him to take it, but I thought that was what he might be getting at so I pre-empted him. If you want to try it Julio, go ahead, I told him, just let me know beforehand. It's not going to do you any harm, but you have to get the dose right, and at your age, it's best to be careful. Of course, he said. He never got in touch with me about it, but that's understandable. I was his daughter's boyfriend, then her husband, and if he didn't want people knowing, he must have had his reasons."

"Yes," I admitted, "I understand all that, but... can't Viagra cause a heart attack?"

"Viagra doesn't cause heart attacks, Álvaro. It's true that strenuous physical effort can put too much strain on the heart, but honestly I don't think that's what happened in your father's case..." But he paused nonetheless as though he wanted to weigh his words carefully. "He had the heart attack on the Friday afternoon, but he'd been fine that morning, and had gone to work. He was sitting quietly in his office when he started feeling pain, but nothing had happened in the meantime... anyway, had time to get home, put himself to bed, then your mother arrived... I don't know Álvaro, but don't beat yourself up over this. Any strenuous physical effort, something completely innocent, could have caused his heart to give out – mowing the lawn, playing with his grandchildren, getting angry suddenly, being worried. And even if he'd decided not to take it, his death wouldn't have been any easier, any purer, or better. Death is shit, Álvaro, your father's death and everyone else's. If he was taking Viagra at the time, it's no one's business, it was his life, his risk."

"I know, I know... Thanks, Adolfo. Seriously."

"Don't mention it. But I'm glad you talked to me about it. I think it's better if you don't say anything to Angélica. I don't think she'd find this

116

funny."

"Don't worry," I said and hung up without even stopping to think how such a charming guy could have fallen in love with for such an insufferable woman.

Two plus two equals four, that's the tradition, the illusion, the famous absolute truth and you can't shift an idea like that without encountering some resistance. Two plus two equals four and your books balance, you have natural, whole numbers and don't have to worry those niggling little decimal places. Two plus two equals four and suddenly my father wasn't a prick, a bastard, a hero, a champion, just a sad bastard addicted to benign but possibly lethal pharmaceuticals. Poor man, I thought, and was surprised to realise that until now I would never have dared to think of him in those terms; that this magician, this wizard, this snake-charmer I had been so in awe of was now reduced to a shrunken, anxious, little man sitting in the waiting room of an expensive private clinic where no amount of money could buy what he had come looking for.

Even in this he'd been exceptional, but the confidence of his ambition could not erase my last memory of his body, the withered knees, the ashen, flaking skin, the sagging flesh, the sparse hair on his chest, his calves. This body was my father's, but my memory would never have accepted it if Raquel Fernández Perea had not wandered into my life. And yet I felt moved his arrogant determination to haggle, to negotiate his own terms with what little scrap of life fate had dealt him. It had been difficult for me, being the son of a man like that and it was no easier, now that he died and finally needed me. Adolfo was right, I knew that, I had nothing to reproach him for. And I knew I had no right to judge him, but it was sad to think that to my father, the most important thing was not getting laid but knowing that the next time would not be the last – a battle so unequal, so one-sided, that it was lost before it even began.

The whole is equal to the sum of its parts only when the parts do not interact, and Raquel Fernández Perea and Álvaro Carrión Otero were now interacting. This - and the fact that I convinced myself that two plus two necessarily equal four - was why when I came back to the apartment, I had the sensation that the whole thing was a set up.

It was just that – a sensation. It wasn't an idea or a deduction, not even an intuition, just one of those simple, dangerous, deceptive sensations as brittle as dry straw

It was 3.30pm, I hadn't eaten and I was standing in that vast, empty living room where there was enough room between the furniture to dance a waltz. I was carrying a roll of large black bin bags and had stopped, dead, mid-way between the dining area, and the living area, for no better

117

reason than that I needed to know what was coming next, like a dog that refuses to move forward when it picks up the weak scent of something unusual. There was something here that I hadn't sensed three days earlier, something that wasn't exactly wrong, I concluded having studied everything carefully, something I hadn't been able to do on my first visit. This time I had opened the wardrobes, emptied the drawers, looked in the freezer and found more obvious, ordinary, predictable things: dressing gowns, slippers, pyjamas, nightgowns, blankets, sheets, towels, women's underwear – decent and indecent – tonic water, instant coffee, condensed milk, an electric juicer, a coffee machine, a rubbish bin, six water tumblers, four whiskey glasses, plates, cups, knives and forks, back issues of magazines, a half-empty box of chocolates, the March edition of a TV guide, a small lump of hash, a packet of cigarette papers and a pad of filters.

These last three items, which I'd found in the bottom drawer of the dresser in the bedroom, I'd stuffed into my pocket, then taken them out again because they were probably hers and I thought I should give them back. At that point I'd realised that what I ought to do was give her everything without even bothering to go through it because logically, with my father dead, Raquel probably owned everything in the apartment. As I thought about this, I brought my hand up to my face, an unconscious gesture. I don't know if I rubbed my eyes or stroked my chin or my forehead, but I noticed the smell of hash remained on my fingers which was when I realised what it was that didn't fit.

The place didn't smell of anything. The books were well thumbed, the ashtray had been used, the toothbrushes were worn, the candles half-burned, but the apartment didn't smell of anything, it had the nondescript smell of places that have never been lived in. And it was true, no one had lived here, but then Raquel didn't live in her office and yet when I went there I hadn't had this strange sensation. I couldn't remember what Raquel Fernández Perea's office had smelled of – probably coffee, printer toner and her perfume – but I was sure her office had had a smell. This realisation so amazed me that I sat on the bed for the longest time, trying to think of something that might refute it.

I looked at my watch, which now read 4.25pm. I didn't have much more time. As I dashed about, filling three large bags with the surprising number of things this seemingly empty apartment contained, I could still feel the same sensation of impropriety, of a carefully concealed pretence, but I also felt that I didn't care anymore, that the frantic series of secrets and coincidences that had had me reeling for the past week would all soon be over, everything would be in its place and once I was back in the little patch of garden I called my life, these details would gradually fade away, until they became just one of the routine little mysteries of an ordinary life. My father had had a lover. OK. At eighty-three. OK. I had met her. Fine. I liked her, actually I liked her a lot, but my father liked my wife, so that just meant we had similar tastes. So what? I had been to the apartment where they had met, had got rid of all trace of him, given her back her belongings, end of story. When I finally left at a quarter to six, I felt as if all I'd done was return the apartment to its rightful state.

I really believed that it was over, but the apartment was not on the inventory of my father's assets I found on the vast boardroom table as I sat in the chair Julio and Clara had saved for me. On the opposite side sat Rafa, Angélica and my mother.

"Sorry I'm late, Mamá," I said as I came in, "I couldn't get away."

"It doesn't matter, Álvaro," she said, "We haven't started yet. But you could at least have worn a suit and a tie, *hijo*…"

"It's just…" I smiled, "I'm sorry."

I was only ten minutes late – I'd quickly dumped one bag in the bin, stuffed the other two in the boot of the car and set off to walk to the address on Príncipe de Vergara, which I could have sworn was much closer. I'd stopped at a bakery and bought a couple of croissants which I ate as I walked and with every bite I savoured the relief of knowing that the key I had in my pocket was about to disappear, only to reappear in the real world, spotless and innocent, as just another key that opened the door to another apartment, one of the many my father had owned. I'd slip it into a drawer the next time my mother sent me to pick up the post at La Moraleja and eventually someone would find it – hey, here's another one we hadn't noticed. I smiled at the thought, but I didn't know then that to everyone in my family, except me, this apartment would never exist.

"This can't be happening…" I murmured when I first read through the inventory.

I read it again, more slowly this time, ticking off everything with a pencil, but still it wasn't there. This can't be happening. Fuck. It was supposed to be over, it should all have been over by now… And yet, there I sat, growing increasingly irritated, increasingly agitated. Don't fuck me around, Papá, I swore silently, I've got problems of my own, my son's getting into fights at school, the workmen are setting the exhibition panels upside down, this can't be happening… I was so angry, so nervous and tired, that without realising, I said this last phrase aloud.

"What can't be happening, Álvaro?" Not only was my sister Angélica suspicious, nit-picking and bossy, she could also hear a pin drop when it suited her.

"Nothing," I said, ignoring her frown. I turned to my brother, "Hey, Rafa, didn't Papá own one of those apartments you showed me? You know the ones..."

"On Calle Jorge Juan," he finished the sentence, "Yes. He bought one of the bigger ones, but he sold it."

"When?"

"Really, Álvaro!" my sister butted in. "This is the limit. What's the matter with you...?"

"Listen, Angélica!" I shouted, a surge of hot rage erupting from me. "There's nothing wrong with me. I'm not running a temperature, I don't have so much as a toothache, so just shut up and stop breaking my balls!"

"Álvaro!" My mother seemed more surprised than angry. "Don't talk to your sister like that!"

In the silence that followed, Julio put his hand on my shoulder, Rafa stared at me as though he couldn't believe his eyes, only Clara dared to defend me.

"It's no big deal, Mamá, come on..."

"It *is* a big deal, Clara," my mother cut her off and turned back to me. "I will not have you making a scene, Álvaro. I don't know what's got into you, *hijo*, but I don't like it. You're a different person."

"Maybe I am," I was fed up, tired of carrying my father around. "Maybe I am a different person, Mamá, and I'm sorry, but for God's sake can't I even ask Rafa a simple question without Angélica sticking her nose in?"

She took her time before answering, but then she nodded.

"In that – and only in that, mind – you're right. You did the right thing," she looked at each of us in turn. "This is the moment to ask about anything you want to know."

"Good. I'm sorry, Angélica, really I am. I've been on edge recently, stressed, even I have trouble putting up with me. Forgive me?" Only when she nodded did I go on. "So when did Papá sell the apartment Rafa?"

"I don't remember exactly, but not long ago, I don't know, maybe two or three months? He wouldn't tell me how much he got for it, but I'm sure he made a packet." He thought for a moment, remembering something that clearly upset him. "I still own one of them, so if..."

His words gave me back my true father, as he had always been, a wily old man, hard-headed, authoritative, and more extraordinary than we, his children, would ever be. You were right, Papá, I thought, you were always right, and this thought not only calmed me, it immediately led me to a more agreeable and less thorny conclusion. If the apartment didn't

120

belong to us, it must belong to Raquel, he must have given it to her, bequeathed it to her, after a fashion. There was no other explanation, and this knowledge stirred two conflicting feelings in me – relief that my father's secret would remain hidden, and annoyance that I could have spared myself the visits to the apartment and the ugly, dirty work I had spent that afternoon doing. My mother took a small notebook from her purse, flicked through it, and called us to order, seeming more alive than she had done since my father's death.

"Right, you've all had time to read through the inventory. If there are no more questions, I'll tell you what I was thinking of doing. As you've seen, I inherit two-thirds, but I'm going to share out more than half of that between you. I'm going to sell off all of Papá's investments – the bonds, the shares, though obviously I'm not going to touch the businesses – and I'm going to divide the money equally between you. I'm going to keep the properties for the moment because it's much more difficult to divide them up and I don't want you falling out. If you're going to fight among yourselves, I'd rather you did it after I'm dead. Álvaro, I'll give you the money Papá was setting aside for you now, along with the rest of it. I really don't think you need to be saving any more," I nodded and smiled at her. "One more thing, the money you owe, Rafa... If your brothers and sisters don't object, I've decided to split it in half. I'll take half from your share now and then you can owe me the other half, and you'll pay me back the same way you would have paid your father, agreed?"

"Thanks, Mamá," my older brother leaned over and kissed her on the cheek.

"Don't mention it, *hijo*," she kissed him and smiled. "Well, if that all seems fair, we can explain everything to the solicitor..."

I'd never imagined that my father had so much money. Clearly, I was the only one of his children who hadn't, since no one else so much as batted an eyelid as the solicitor gave the official reading of the will, tossing out random numbers that were so large I couldn't even remember them. It was all happening too fast for my well-ordered brain and when the meeting was over, I still had no real idea of how much I stood to inherit. I knew it was more than I had been expecting, but wasn't the most pressing thing on my mind.

When we left the building, I said goodbye to my mother, kissed her on both cheeks and hugged her hard. I was surprised to find that everything I'd discovered in the past week had not changed my relationship with her, as though the worry, the pity and the vague guilt I felt at having become her husband's posthumous co-conspirator, albeit reluctantly, was not strong enough to come between us, or change the mother/son relationship we had spent forty years perfecting. Since I knew she was hoping we might celebrate her generosity, I apologised again, and whispered a thank you in her ear. As I watched her walk away between Rafa and Clara, suddenly so small, so delicate, it seemed impossible that she could have had anything to do with the apartment on Jorge Juan, the blue tablets, the candles by the jacuzzi and the deep-rooted fear of the man who had slept in the same bed with her for forty-nine years.

"You in a hurry?" I asked my brother Julio, after we had said goodbye to Angélica.

"No," he said, "Why?"

"I don't know, I just don't fancy going home..." This was true. "Do you want to go for a drink?"

"Good idea. Maybe two." He put his arm round my shoulder as if he were trying to calm me, or at least to let me know he was on my side. Some part of the secret was clearly showing. "If you like, afterwards we can go and visit some whores and burn Madrid to the ground. We're rich."

"No," I smiled, "I think it's better if we leave Madrid as it is."

"OK," he smiled too, "But never let it be said that I'm chicken."

In the end, we didn't just have two drinks, we had quite a few.

"Hey, Julio..." I said as soon as the waiter had taken our order, skipping over the introduction I couldn't think of, "do you think Papá had mistresses?"

"What is this?" And although it was obvious what I was about to say, he looked at me a little suspiciously. "Am I supposed to be the expert in the family?"

"No, but you're the only one I can talk to, it's not the same thing."

I hadn't intended to say anything to anyone in the family, but as we had all sat with my mother in the solicitor's office, I had realised that every one of them would have a different take on my father and might be able to shed some light on different aspects, things I would never have noticed.

"I don't know..." he was silent for a moment, then continued, "I've often thought about it, believe me. I mean, on the one hand... well, it would be like him. What I mean is rich men - men of his generation, especially – used to keep mistresses, lovers in the old sense, they bought apartments for them, that kind of thing. It was traditional, and anyway, it would fit with his personality, the way he behaved... He liked to flaunt his power, you know that, and he wasn't religious, he wasn't much bothered by scruples, but still... I don't know. On the other hand, he was such a stickler…"

"Yes, but he was a ladies' man," I said. My brother nodded slowly as though it wasn't easy for him to admit that I was right. "And he was happy to admit it whenever the subject came up. Remember on Saturday nights he'd joke around with us, giving the dancers on TV marks out of ten."

"Yeah, yeah that's true. I'm not saying he didn't like women, it's just… on the other hand it wasn't like him at all, he didn't like to complicate his life. Though I suppose we knew him when he was older, by the time Clara was born he was nearly fifty. I suppose he must have done something at some stage? I mean everyone has an affair at some point. In any case, we'll never know now. Papá could always run rings around us. He was smarter than the whole lot of us put together. If he had mistresses, I'm sure he'd never have let himself be caught."

"Not alive, maybe…"

"What are you talking about?"

"Papá was taking Viagra, Julio."

His mouth dropped open, as though he couldn't process what he had just heard. Then he leaned forward and looked me straight in the eye."

"Papá?" he said "Viagra?"

"Papá," I confirmed.

"Fuck!" he was staring at some fixed point behind me. "Stop, I don't want to know. How did you find out?"

I told him the same story I'd told Adolfo, told him what Adolfo had said about the risks of taking the stuff, and that Papá had had a conversation with him about it over six years ago.

"He didn't think there was anything strange about it," I said.

"Well I do."

"Me too," I admitted, "but maybe Adolfo sees things more clearly than we do, because he's not as close."

"Right…" Julio looked at me and nodded slowly, "so that's why you went off on one, because you thought…"

"Exactly," I confirmed his suspicions, because neither of us wanted to go there.

"You know what it's like, Álvaro? It's like Papá was a lot of different men, not just one man, because… I don't know, every time I talk to Rafa about him – and obviously we've been talking a lot recently – we remember different things, sometimes contradictory things… Verónica says it's normal, she says it always happens when someone dies, but I don't agree with her. I'm sure that if Mamá died, for example, our memories of her wouldn't be so different…"

"But Rafa's view of Papá was always distorted, wasn't it?" I ventured, "To Rafa, Papá was like Superman, his idol…"

"That's true. But it's not just that…" he stopped for a minute and thought, "Well, maybe it does have something to do with that. Rafa couldn't stand the fact that after a lifetime of doing his best, you were still Papá's favourite, not him."

"Me? What are you talking about? I didn't study what he wanted me to study, I left when he wanted me to stay, I got married in a registry office…"

"So what?" Julio interrupted, "I've spent my whole life listening to him talking about you, Álvaro is like me, Álvaro is the brightest, Álvaro is the only one I don't have to worry about… You were his favourite… You and the girls, especially Angélica, though it seems strange given what a cold fish she is, but he liked her more than Clara, don't ask me why… He couldn't stand me because we were too much alike, we were always fighting, but it was mutual, believe me, and anyway, I was always Mamá's little boy so I didn't care, I don't think Clara did either, at the end of the day. But Rafa didn't take it well, seriously."

"I don't understand," I protested as much to myself as to him, "Really, I don't, and if you want to know the truth, it never even crossed my mind…"

"You see? That's what I mean when I say this whole thing with Papá is weird?"

"But… Rafa was his right hand man, wasn't he? The one who knew everything, the one who was closest to him?"

Just then, my uncertainty began to crumble, to give way under the pressure of something which a moment ago had seemed incredible and now seemed within the realms of possibility.

My father liked to dance with my sister Angélica. They danced so well together that they looked like a couple of professional dancers, but I had only ever seen him dance with Clara once, at her wedding reception. "You brother Julio thinks with his prick, I'm sick to death of your brother Rafa…" He'd never said anything like this to me. "You're the brightest of the lot, Álvaro." But he'd never given me any sign that he had favourites, he'd never taken me aside to talk to me. We didn't argue, we didn't fight, and of course, we loved each other. I loved him, he was my father; he loved me, I was his son. We got that far and not one step further, but I never thought that it was different for the others, or for his eldest son at least.

"Anyway…" I started again, "Rafa did business with Papá, didn't he? You heard what Mamá said earlier."

124

"Business?" Julio raised his eyebrows and laughed. "The only business Rafa had with Papá was debts. Debts, Álvaro, he was always asking Papá for money. Papá didn't given him a quarter of what he asked for, which is just as well, because Rafa was always going too far, but in the end... well, you know what happened, the straw that broke the camel's back," Earlier when Mamá said 'if the others have no objection', I wanted to say something. Because he'll go on doing it, you know that. He'll do it all the more, because Mamá is easier to convince, she's much more indulgent than Papá ever was, and no matter how much Rafa has inherited, he'll try to get his hands on more, I was about to say it... But then I thought, what good will it do me, fucking things up for Rafa, I'm not going to be any happier just because I have more in the bank... Did you ever ask Papá for money, Álvaro?"

"No. I thought about it when we were buying the house, but the mortgage was tax deductible, and I didn't have much in the way of outgoings, so in the end I didn't need to."

He looked at me, finished his drink, and signalled to the waiter for another. He seemed to be meditating on something, as if he was about to make a decision.

"What about you?"

"I asked him for money once," he held up his right index finger so there could be no doubt, "Just once. And he wouldn't give it to me."

"Why not?" I asked.

"I still don't know. Or, to be more precise, I'd prefer not to know." The waiter set down another glass in front of him, and he knocked back half of it in a single swig before continuing. "But I'll tell you something. Papá was a great man, a self-made man who started out with nothing and got to be where he was without any help, OK I'll give you that. And he was charming and likeable and interesting and intelligent, I'll give you that too. But Papá could be a hard-faced bastard too. Listen to what I'm saying, because I'm not like you, Álvaro, I don't think like you. I'm not just saying Papá was conservative or old-fashioned, I'm saying he was a bastard, an out-and-out bastard."

"Verónica," I said aloud, because it was something I had never forgotten either.

"No," my brother shook his head, "Or not just that. That was the first time, and anyway, he could be forgiven for that, he was an old man and the world he grew up in was very different... When I told him I was leaving Asun, he was really angry. 'Don't you get on?' he asked me, and I said yes, because it was true, it's still true, I've always got on well with Asun, but it's nothing like what I had with Verónica, what can I say?" He smiled and looked at me with a candour I envied then said something astonishing. "But then Vero is the love of my life and Asun isn't, and that's nobody's fault. 'It's not that, Papá,' I told him, 'I've fallen in love with someone else…' 'What?' he said and gave me a little smile that felt like a kick in the balls. 'I'm in love with someone else,' I said again, and then he laughed. 'In love, in love,' he said mimicking me, 'and what has that to do with anything?'"

"But…" I interrupted, not really knowing what I was going to say next.

"No buts, Álvaro. Make no mistake, Papá had no problem with me having an affair with Verónica. What he found stupid was that I would leave Asun for her. But, well, that seemed normal to me, that's why I forgave him… The other time came later, and it's something I've never forgiven him for.

There was a long pause, and I realised he felt awkward.

"I may be a bad husband, Álvaro, but I'm a good father. I'm a fucking good father. And I'm not saying that because I think I deserve a medal, because it's easy, that's the truth… I love my kids. I love being with them, I have fun when I'm with them, and if I don't spend more time with them it's because their mother doesn't want me to… That's why I never go anywhere on Saturdays, I never go away for the weekend unless its with them. Vero knew that from the start, before we even got together, back when our relationship was just three-star adultery in five-star hotels. Me and the kids, we come as a package, and if we're going to live together, then I can only take you for dinner in Paris on Tuesdays.

"And she agreed," I said, smiling.

"Yes, she agreed," he nodded, "But she also accepted everything that went with it, and she really loves the twins, that was what worried me most. I couldn't have lived with her if she didn't love my kids. Anyway on Saturdays… especially now that Asun has a boyfriend and she lets me have them for the whole weekend – on Saturdays, at nine o'clock, after they've had their bath and they're in their pyjamas, the five of us sit on the sofa, me in the middle, the boys on my left, the girls on my right, with a couple of pizzas and we watch a movie on the Disney Channel – you can't imagine the garbage I've sat through…"

"Of course I can…"

"Well, anyway… Lucía always falls asleep in my arms when she's having her bottle and then Julia who's the oldest twin by a couple of minutes likes to pretend she's in love with me and leans her head on my shoulder and puts her hand in mine. The next one to nod off is Pablo, who falls asleep on top of Enrique, his older brother who then slowly

126

edges over to me and I put my arm around him. By the time the movie is over, I have one twin's head on each shoulder, Lucía asleep across my left leg, Enrique sprawled almost upside-down across the other, and Verónica on the armchair. She always says the same thing, 'It sounds strange, Julio, but if anyone else saw you like this, they wouldn't believe it.' And she's right, but at that moment, I'm the happiest man alive, I swear..."

"I believe it, Julio."

I believed him. Because I had often seen him with his children. I'd seen my brother – the most feckless, sex-obsessed man I'd ever met and a hard-nosed businessman almost as ruthless and unscrupulous as Rafa – feeding his kids, helping them with their homework, playing with them patiently, never losing his nerve, his energy, his willingness to take another penalty. 'Just one more, Papá.' It was amazing to watch, but it was real and it was moving.

"Well then, you'll understand the rest... When Asun and I separated, I made it clear that I wanted us still to get on. She was devastated of course, and it was my fault, but there was nothing I could do about that, so when the lawyer said we had to take her pain and suffering into account I said fine, whatever she wants, anything except the kids. I'd fucked her over and now she wanted to fuck me over, that seemed fair, but I said let's keep the children out of this... I didn't want to go to court, I wanted us to sort things out amicably, go before the judge with a settlement he couldn't find fault with, and I managed it. It was hard work, believe me, I spent more than a month negotiating because I wanted us to agree on joint custody and split the weekends in half, rather than having Julia and Enrique every other weekend. 'That won't be possible', the lawyer told me, 'Oh. Really?' I said, 'How much?' I gave her my best grin. 'How much what?' she said. "How much will it cost me to make it possible?'... She stared at me as if she was offended. 'I'm afraid I don't understand what you're saying,' she said. I said, 'I'm a lawyer too, so let's cut the bullshit...'"

"I didn't know any of this, Julio," I interrupted him, "You never said."

"No," he smiled, "I didn't tell anyone. Why? Because in the end I got what I wanted, even if it bankrupted me... Asun, who conducted herself brilliantly at the time, much better than her lawyer ever did, told me that she didn't want monthly alimony payments, just a reasonable settlement upfront. I was thinking of selling a business at the time and this struck me as a great idea, completely sensible. I ended up giving her half of what she had asked for, but that was double what I had originally offered, and even that was generous. She knew I couldn't give her any more, she

127

knew how much money we had, but I didn't care. After all, what is money?"

He was staring at me, as though waiting for an answer.

"What do I know…" I ventured after a moment, "Power?"

"No, it's nothing. When you haven't got it, money is everything, but when you've got it, it's nothing, you understand? It doesn't create anything, doesn't do anything, it's just frittered away buying nice things and having fun, but it was going to do a lot more for me. After all, I was lucky enough to have a rich father," I realised then what he was trying to say, and realised that he was right, "a father who gave me a couple of million pesetas every year for no reason at all, a father who'd spent his life lending my older brother money to invest in whatever moronic idea he came up with – Portuguese hydroelectrics, petrol stations in Toledo, shares in cement works – so when Arun and I had agreed, I signed the papers. I signed first, then I went to see Papá."

"You should at least have done it the other way round," I laughed, because I still didn't realise what we were talking about, "If you were going to ask him for money…"

"I know that. I'm too impulsive, I don't think things through, you're right. But everything seemed so obvious, so clear to me that I signed the papers and then went to see him. And I told him the whole story. He didn't open a drawer, he didn't take out his chequebook, he didn't look at me and say 'How much do you need, *hijo*?' No, when I had finished, he just sat there with his arms folded. 'I don't understand, Julio,' he said, 'Honestly, I don't understand how you could do something so stupid – ruining your life for the sake of the twins… You love children? Fine, have more kids! You're with a younger woman now.'"

Julio had said all this very quickly, barely pausing for breath. When he finally looked at me, looked up from the glass he had been staring into as he told me about his conversation with Papá, he smiled, and I realised that he had already left all this behind. He could not know how I felt when these last words ripped a hole through my body.

"You're joking," I said, and I could feel the hollowness in my voice.

"I swear to you, Álvaro." His voice was firm. "I couldn't believe it either. I swear, I didn't believe it. I'd never felt so bad, so humiliated, I just sat there, nailed to the chair, waiting for something to happen, for the roof to fall in, for him to tell me it was a joke."

"And what happened?" I said, because it couldn't end like this, my father had to make things right, had to do something…

"Nothing," my brother quickly dashed my hopes, "He didn't say another word. 'Okay,' I said to him, I didn't say the rest, that he was happy to give Rafa money for his businesses but when it came to my kids, nothing. 'OK, Papá,' I said again and I got up and left. Fuck him, I thought, fuck him forever. My wife got everything I had, except for a Jeep we'd just had delivered to a garage because we were getting some extras fitted, and a little apartment in Miraflores de la Sierra we'd bought to rent out during the summer. I'll just sell it, I thought, and I'll sell the Jeep and in the meantime, I'll get an overdraft, and while I'm waiting to get the overdraft approved, I'll asked Rafa to lend me twenty thousand to keep me going... And that's what I did... That, and I talked to Mamá, who phoned me at all hours of the day and night to tell me that I was wrong, that I must have misheard, that Papá was exhausted, that he loved my kids, and he would never have said what I thought he'd said..."

"It's probably true, Julio," I reluctantly pleaded my father's case one last time, "You must have caught him at a bad moment, maybe he was worried or depressed about something, maybe something had gone wrong with the business, or he thought that it wasn't fair to do something for you he wouldn't do for the rest of us..." I realised I was talking shit, but I went on, in spite of my brother's patient expression, "He was an old man, he didn't like Verónica, maybe that's why... What do I know? I just find it hard to believe that..."

"I know," Julio's smile had not faded, nor his conviction, "I know what he said, and the way he said it, Álvaro. I was sitting as close to him as I am to you now. And I didn't give in. I didn't go to La Moraleja that Saturday. It was tough on the twins, especially after the separation, but I didn't go. And the following week I called Mamá 'I'm taking the kids to the circus,' I said to her, 'Do you want me to get you a ticket?' You get the idea... It was coming up to Christmas, and she started crying down the phone. The next Saturday she was still crying and she pleaded with me, she begged me... But I couldn't give in, Álvaro. I'm too proud, and he'd gone too far."

"But..." I thought about my father, about my brother, about my family gathered round him when he was ill, when he was dying, at his funeral, "But you made up in the end, didn't you?"

"Yes, but only because he finally came to see me. The Monday after I took the kids to the circus he came to see me at the office and slapped a fat wad of cash on my desk, twice what I'd asked him for. And then he did something that moved me even more, he said 'Forgive me, *hijo*, don't humiliate me,' that's what he said, 'don't humiliate me any more.' He was clever. He'd chosen his words carefully, because if he'd said it any other way, I might not have forgiven him, but he picked that word, and I knew him, he was as proud as I was, maybe more so, and when I looked at him he seemed so old, so broken... I loved him, Álvaro, how could I not love him? He was my father. So I got up and hugged him and it was as if it had never happened. I sold the apartment, I sold the jeep, I moved into a rented flat and within a couple of years I'd paid him back every penny. We never talked about it again, but I haven't forgotten. That's why I think all this stuff about Papá is weird. And if you want the truth, I don't really know what kind of man he was..."

He finished his drink and asked for the bill.

"I don't know," my brother added, "And I don't care."

June 24, 1941 was hot, an arid, ungodly heat which set a haze shimmering over the pavements. It was noon but already it seemed as though the long sweltering torment of the day would never end, the stifling heat turning the night into an endless tossing and turning. It was noon, Madrid felt like a foretaste of hell, but Julio Carrión González changed his clothes anyway.

"You're a fool, lad…"

His boss, the proprietor, was sick and tired of earning money, and shook his head with paternal irony when he saw the boy reappear, freshly washed, his hair combed, wearing the same shirt and trousers he had shown up in the garage that morning. Señor Turégano was wearing what he called his 'summer overalls', which were a couple of sizes bigger than those he wore in winter –to leave enough room for the air to circulate, he said – with the name of his garage emblazoned on the pocket and the zip open to his navel. He didn't care who saw him dressed like this. No one fucks with you because you're the boss, thought Julio listening to him, but he said nothing. He did not want to get on the wrong side of this man, and not simply because he was drawing a weekly salary, but because the man's warped concept of work and idleness suited him, the boss's obsession with supervising every last detail, never leaving the garage even for a moment, which made it possible for his favourite employee to escape from the filthy pit where he did oil changes and go for a walk around town every now and then. And Julio did care whether people saw him in his oil-stained overalls which were more black than blue and shiny with grease, even though he did not know anybody in the area, any of these well-dressed men walking arm in arm with elegant ladies who strutted along, stamping their high heels as if trying to crack the pavements of the Calle Alcalá or La Gran Vía. Sometimes, it felt as though the women really did break them, he had felt the ground tremble under their feet, had stood aside to let them pass, and had stood there watching them, placing little bets with himself that this one or that would turn and look back at him. No one ever had, but some day, he thought, one of them would turn and she would not see him standing there in a mechanic's overalls. This was why - because he trusted to his determination rather than his luck – whenever the boss sent him on an errand, he always changed his clothes before he left.

"The sun's splitting the stones out there, Julio, you must really like to sweat…"

It was true that the garage, in the basement of one of the old buildings that had survived the bombing, was as cool and dark as a cave, but it stank, it was filthy and it was far removed from the real world, the world of elegant streets and opulent shop windows, of beautiful women and money, as though the ramp that separated them from the Calle de la Montera was a symbolic barrier between what Julio Carrión possessed and what he desired. Nor was he alone in feeling this sordid, illusory exile. While his boss was explaining to him what he had to do that morning, Julio could feel the envious stares of his co-workers burning into the back of his neck, the three who were older that he was, the three who had been working here longer, though not one of them competed for his position as Señor Turégano's favourite, Señor Turégano who had hired him a year earlier, when no one in Madrid trusted anyone, though he did not know the boy from Adam.

"I'm looking for work, señor," he had said, or something like that... "How old are you, son?" the older man had asked. Señor Turégano was fat and bald and over fifty, he had three daughters and was secretly annoyed that he did not have a son. "I'm eighteen, sir," he said and smiled the way only he knew how to smile, with his eyes and lips, showing his perfect white teeth. "Truth is, I'm not really looking for anyone right now..." but then the boss wavered, "Where are you from?" Julio took a deep breath and told some lies and some truths, "Torrelodones, but I came to Madrid with my father before the war, it was just one of those things, you know, my mother was ill, tuberculosis, she was admitted to hospital here on July 18 and after that, what with one thing and another... Anyway, they went back to Torrelodones last year and they got back everything, the house, the land, my father is a very religious man, he's good friends with the parish priest and everyone knows him, but me... now I've had a taste of life here, sir, I stuck it out through the war and the food shortages and everything, and I've got a taste for it. And to be honest, I've always hated sheep." The man burst out laughing, "I'm from Segovia," he said, "and I don't much care for sheep either."

At that moment, Julio Carrión González knew he was in luck – other people are born rich or handsome or intelligent, he had been born likeable and he knew it and had learned how to make the most of his gift. "What I really want is to be a magician," he said, "I know loads of tricks." "Show me something," Señor Turégano said, and Julio did, he showed him the coin trick and the card trick and the one with the handkerchiefs. "You're pretty good," Señor Turégano said finally. "I am good," Julio replied without a trace of arrogance, "But I can't make a living doing magic, at least not yet, I need a job, any job, to start me off..." "I can't offer you much," Señor Turégano capitulated. "I don't mind," said Julio "anything will do me," but before the garage owner could firm up the deal, Julio told him the joke about the Mexicans and the dog, doing all the voices brilliantly and he watched as the man laugh until he cried. Since that day Julio Carrión had not only worked in the garage, he had become Señor Turégano's right-hand man, and the boss gave him all sorts of jobs aside from his real work, some of which were quite enjoyable, including collecting and returning the cars for customers who did not have time to do to themselves, or taking one of his daughters to the cinema.

"Listen," he said that morning, "go to the bank, have a word with Gutiérrez and deposit these two cheques for me, don't forget to bring back the receipt for the deposit, and get me change of two hundred..."

"OK," Julio said, "Do you want me to bring back a couple of beers?"

"If you can find some that are cold, and I mean ice cold. Get six of them and mind you stay in the shade on your way back, I don't want them getting warm. Go on, and don't get into trouble."

Before he set off, Julio looked over and winked at his co-worker, Paquito, who shot him a conciliatory smile in return. Both of them knew that out of the six beers, they would each get at least one, and Julio deserved the credit for suggesting it. In doing so, his co-workers forgave him for the fact that he would be gone for at least an hour, what with getting there and back, the queue at the bank and the slowness of Gutiérrez, as he'd say to Señor Turégano when he got back, 'It's incredible, he must be the stupidest man in the world', imitating the way the bank teller rubbed his hands together, the way his nose twitched like a rabbit, the tic he had of pushing his glasses up his nose with his index finger, and Señor Turégano would erupt with peals of laughter rather than checking his watch.

It was hot. The sun beat down fiercely, burning his face, but Julio smiled and looked around him as though only here, out in the street, was he truly alive. When he came to the Red de San Luis, he stopped in front of a shop window. He pulled down the lock of hair he liked to wear in a spit-curl over his forehead, opened the top two buttons of his shirt, rolled up the sleeves, turned up his collar and added a cigarette dangling from his bottom lip until he'd achieved the cocky, slightly roguish look he felt comfortable with. He had thought of heading down the Gran Via, to make eyes at the waitresses on the terraces, but before he got to the corner, he heard shouts and then saw a sea of blue shirts.

"Fuck. Just my luck," he muttered under his breath as he turned

133

slowly in case the change of pace made it look as though he were running away.

He hesitated for a moment before deciding against taking Caballero de Gracia and instead walked a little further towards Jardines, a dark, deserted street, a haven of calm – or desolation – in the bustling throng. "Just my luck," he said again as he strode along the empty pavement, rejecting with a shake of his head the offers of a couple of clever prostitutes who skulked in doorways waiting for clients. Once, in time-honoured fashion they would have accosted potential clients in the street, but this was a custom that no longer fitted in with the new regime. In times like this, everyone in Spain knew what was meant by 'fit in'. The whores knew it and had learned to flaunt their bodies without showing their faces in case they needed to make a quick escape across the terraced roofs, and Julio Carrión knew it, who that very morning had once more seen Mari Carmen, Peluca's daughter, when he left the boarding house at twenty to eight.

There she is, he thought when he saw her, fucking hell, and he'd hidden in a doorway like a street whore so she would walk by without seeing him, her face still half asleep, her long, glorious legs magnificently awake. Mari Carmen Ortega's legs had been the first monument Julio Carrión González had admired on arriving in Madrid one June afternoon in 1937 when his father had coaxed him through the labyrinthine streets of this vast, unfamiliar city as if he were a sheepdog on the farm.

"Julio, come on, not that way, are you stupid? over there, hurry up, follow me…"

The truck that had brought them from Torrelodones had dropped them on the Calle Mayor, but he had travelled in the back, surrounded by sacks and crates of ammunition and had seen almost nothing, only fleeting glimpses of buildings, some in ruins others intact, wooden beams propping up facades, holes in the ground and people, lots of people, rushing around as though they were late for something, the women with baskets, the men in half a dozen different styles of military uniform, children shooting at each other with bits of wood, as though they knew nothing about the real war.

"Thank you, lieutenant," when he got out of the truck, his father was saying goodbye to the man who was still sitting next to the driver.

"Don't mention it, Benigno," he gave Julio a sad look, the same look he had given him the previous day before he had tousled his hair and said, 'see you tomorrow, lad.'

"Have you got somewhere to go?"

"Yes, I'm going to try to stay at a boarding house on the Calle de la Sal run by a woman from the village. Her sister tells me she's still there, and it's still open, so we'll see..."

The lieutenant, a young man, said goodbye to them both. Julio stood there, a suitcase in each hand, a bundle of clothes wrapped in a quilt slung over his shoulder and the bird cage containing his father's bloody parakeet hooked over his little finger. His father was just as loaded down, but he knew his way around and set off with an energy his son had never witnessed before, an energy that was nothing more than useless fury.

"Here we are," he said finally, stopping in front of a door, glancing in every direction except ahead of him as though with a single glance he might recognise the face of every man and woman in the city. You're mad, father, thought his son, but he kept the thought to himself.

"Now we've got to get to the third floor."

The proprietor of the boarding house greeted them as though she had been expecting them. Julio remembered her as soon as he saw her, but this memory of a more pleasant trip was quickly subsumed by the look of pity the old woman gave him, the same look he had seen on the face of the lieutenant ten minutes earlier. At fifteen, Julio Carrión González did not tolerate pity from anyone.

"My sister told me everything, Benigno... but what are you planning to do?"

"I'll do whatever I have to," Julio's father replied as his former neighbour busied herself helping the boy with the bundle of clothes and the birdcage.

"This is madness," she said, "Madrid has gone completely mad, we don't have anything, no food, no peace, we don't even know if we'll be alive tomorrow morning. Look, there..." she waved towards her living room, "...opposite. They've all gone away. And now you show up. What for? Hunger, ruins and bombs, that's all you'll find here. Go back to the village, Benigno, listen to me. Do it for the lad."

"Look, Pilar, do you have a room for us or not?" She nodded intimidated by the tone of his voice. "Well then, shut up, give me the key and leave me in peace."

She knows, thought Julio as he listened to her, she said her sister told her, she found out the same day I did...

The boarding house was a large, ramshackle apartment. It was clean but there was little furniture, though dark outlines on the walls indicated the place where the furniture they had had to burn the previous winter to keep warm had once stood. Doña Pilar was telling the truth. In Madrid, there was no coal, no wood, although this was something Julio did not discover until winter returned, by which time he and his father were the only guests in the boarding house and Doña Pilar was so consumed with grief for her son, who had been shot in the head, and her other son who was imprisoned in Huelva, that she had not a shred of pity left for them. But on that warm June afternoon in 1937, Madrid's citizens were still ready to brave hunger, ruins and bombings and whatever else might come, still prepared to take pity on a poor villager who had chosen precisely the worst moment to go mad. And they all knew it, thought Julio as he followed his father down the corridor, watched him open the door, put down the suitcases and sit on the bed, watched him take off his cap and rub his trembling fingers over his forehead, then glare at him in furious despair, this was all Julio could think of, they knew it, everyone knew it, the lieutenant, Doña Pilar, the people they had left behind in the village, everyone knew that his mother had run away, that she'd left them, that she had abandoned them to go off to Madrid with the teacher from Las Rozas.

"What will we do now, father?"

"Just unpack the suitcases," he answered, "After that... I'll have to think."

Julio had never really loved his father. He feared rather than respected him, and his father seemed to revel in the distance created by that fear. When his son was born, Benigno Carrión was already an old man, more than old enough to have been the father of Teresa, his second wife, whom he had met shortly after his first wife died. It worried Julio to know that his father had had a wife before marrying his mother. He would secretly pore over pictures of her, particularly the photograph of her on their wedding day, a lady with black hair, black eyes, dressed in black lace, a black mantilla, she looked like a raven about to gobble up the young man Julio had difficulty recognising as his own father. Benigno never knew about the strange attraction these photos held for his son, but his mother had once caught the boy looking at them.

"Julio! Leave those alone!" she snatched the photographs from him and gently put them back into the manila envelope that usually lay hidden in the drawer under some clothes. "Your father will be furious..."

But nothing happened. With his mother, it was always the same. It was not that she did not scold him or punish him, because she did. Sometimes she would send him to bed without dinner, or not talk to him for a whole day, but she never shouted at him, never humiliated him and never hit him. And yet she always depended on him to do his homework, not play truant, learn his lessons, teach her French. Teresa González's parents had been teachers, and she had studied to be a teacher herself.

She would have become one, if her mother had not died suddenly and her father had not fallen ill shortly afterwards – with grief, she said – before moving to Torrelodones to take up what would be his last position. She was the youngest daughter, and the only one still unmarried, so she went with him to take care of him and help him with his students, and that was how she had met Benigno Carrión, who stood at the school gates every afternoon, though he had no children of his own, not even a nephew. He simply went there to see her, something her father realised before she did.

"Don't say that, Papá! Please!" she had said when he told her, waving her hands in front of her face, "He's an old man, a prude. He spends his whole day playing dominos with the priest and the sacristan…"

"But he's a good man," her father Don Julio objected, who took for granted his republican leanings, considering himself to be a modest freethinker. "Oh. really? And how do you know?" asked his daughter, surprised. "Because whenever I go into the café, he leaves his dominos, comes over and sits with me, and sooner or later we get round to talking about you, how pretty you are, how good, and all the things that might make a man love you." "Well," said Teresa, "I had no idea…"

The following day, when she left the school and found him standing there, cap in hand, she looked at him more attentively that she had ever done before. The first thing she noticed was that he seemed much older, but was strong for his age. He was a large, stout man, quite unlike the graceful leading men she fell for at the cinema, the kind that would keep a person warm on frosty nights. No more than that, thought Teresa. He was not ugly, nor was he handsome, though as a young man, before he went grey, he must have been attractive, with his rugged face and glittering black eyes, his slender nose and his surprisingly full, fleshy lips. She did not find him attractive, but she began to look at him differently.

One afternoon, he dared to speak to her and walked with her back to her house. This act of daring became a custom, and customarily he was invited in. As he sat drinking hot chocolate with her and her father, Teresa could feel the love emanating from this silent, almost awkward man, who found in himself a vein of unexpected eloquence, and spoke to her gently, affectionately, whenever Don Julio left them alone together, which he did more and more often. "I adore you, Teresa, I love you more than anything on earth, more than God, more than myself." And Teresa, an avid reader of poetry and novels who wept every time she read of beautiful, doomed Anna hurling herself beneath the train, of Heathcliff's agony as he listens to the ghost of Cathy at his window, who sang sad

137

songs about unequal loves, who played Schubert and Chopin badly on a cheap out-of-tune piano until some men came to take it away because her father could not afford the rental and did not dare tell her, trembled as she heard the words she longed to hear from lips that were younger, freer, more like her own. And yet she married him, not wanting to think that she would never have done so if her father had not died suddenly, leaving her with nothing but two dozen books, his fountain pen and two silver brushes that had belonged to her mother.

The everlasting adoration barely outlasted the wedding, but the bride's disappointment did not extend into being unhappy. For many years —she was not yet twenty-one when she became Benigno Carrión's wife – Teresa was resigned to her life. Her husband was a good man, hard-working, strict, but respectful in his way, and he loved and trusted her. They lived well, not luxuriously, but in greater comfort than the schoolmaster's daughter had ever known, and after the birth of their son, whom they named Julio in memory of his grandfather, they even employed a maid to deal with the heavy chores. Teresa felt a little guilty about this, because although she also worked hard, tending the vegetable garden and the chickens, her husband had no one to help him with the sheep. He would get up before dawn and come home after dark and that, she thought, explained why he was tired, and in part compensated for his lack of affection, his indifference to his children and the silent undemonstrative routine of their tame, conventional lovemaking on occasional Saturday nights when it did not even occur to them to undress before they began.

For many years, Teresa was resigned to her life, but she had been born with the century, was not yet twenty-one when she had married Benigno and no one, not even he, was to blame for what she felt was her true awakening. No one could stop the passing of the years, nor the fact that these were heroic, passionate, decisive years in which a few scant days might be worth a whole life. It was no one's fault that in November 1933, having laid the table for the family's breakfast, Teresa González had gone up to her bedroom and reappeared a little later dressed in the Sunday best she had always worn when she used to go to mass to please her husband, before the election campaign.

"Where are you off to so early, Teresa," asked Benigno, although he already knew.

"To vote," she replied, and kissed her son, then her daughter before walking past her husband.

"To vote?" he clenched his fists, but could not contain his indignation, "You'll go if I say you can go."

"I don't need your permission," Teresa adjusted her hat, put her hand on the door handle, then turned back towards them. "I have the right to vote and I intend to exercise that right."

"And who are you going to vote for, might I ask?"

"Whoever I like. I don't have to tell you, as you very well know."

The sound of the door slamming coincided with the shattering of crockery as Benigno dashed the cups and plates to the floor, oblivious to his daughter's sobs and the silence of his son's, who was holding his breath as he had learned to do in the two months since that October afternoon when things had begun to fall apart.

"Don't be so proud, Julio," his mother was sitting beside him at the kitchen table, helping him with his maths homework, "There's nothing worse than a proud ignoramus. You're a clever boy, but you're only eleven and that means you don't know everything, so let me show you..."

"But I *do* know..." the boy protested, more out of pride than conviction.

"No, you don't, because you're not getting the right answers, or hadn't you noticed? And if you don't learn now, you'll never know how to do it."

Just then, his father popped his head round the kitchen door as he did every afternoon, but instead of closing it again, as he usually did, he came and sat with them.

"Listen, Teresa," his father said, "I've just been talking to Don Pedro, and it occurred to him... You know that the elections next month are very important..."

"Very important," but somehow his mother's agreement sounded more like defiance.

"Good, well, we thought... since women will get to vote this time... It occurred to him, the priest, I mean, I didn't make any promises, but I would like it if..." Julio thought he had never seen his father look so nervous, so small, faced with his mother's aloofness, sitting majestically serene in her chair. "It's not that we want you to campaign, but you get on with everyone, Teresa, the women in the village all look up to you, they like you, and you know how pious they are, and that's not the priest's fault... Well, anyway, if you would talk to them, tell them who has their best interests at heart... I know you're not religious, but you're in favour of women's rights, aren't you? And I..."

"I can't believe what I'm hearing, Benigno," Teresa González slipped her right arm around her son's shoulders.

"I'd be very grateful to you, Teresa."

"I honestly can't believe what you're saying. You're asking me to campaign for CEDA...[i]"

"I'm not asking you to do that..."

"Of course that's what you're asking!" she stood up suddenly, making the chair behind her topple but she did not pick it up. "Do you think I'm a fool? Well I'm not a fool, Benigno, I'm more intelligent than you and your priest put together. You should know, you know me better that anyone, you know who I am and who my father was and I have no intention of doing anything that would make him curse me from his grave."

"You'll do whatever I tell you to do!" her husband raised his voice, making his son shrink back in his chair.

"No!" this time she shouted louder that he had. "No! Do you hear me? That voice might work when the dinner's cold or when I've forgotten to feed the chickens, but not for this, Benigno, no. I'll walk out of this house before I do such a thing, believe me."

Julio Carrión had never loved his father that much, but from that day on he loved him a little more and a little less than he had done, having discovered his weakness, his inability to impose his will on his own family, and the roots of his powerlessness which were nothing more than fear, fear that his wife would talk, would tell people in the market, in the shops, in the Casa del Pueblo that she went to every week, what went on in their home, now that divorce was legal and women had the right to vote, now that the world had been turned upside down.

You're a coward, father, thought Julio feeling a contempt tinged with a vague solidarity as he watched his father close his mouth, choke back his desire to scream, to beat his head against the wall every time his wife walked out of the house and slammed the door. And all this just so nobody would know, so that no one in the association would gossip, so that his wife would not leave him, and people would continue to greet him in the street with a respect he was not prepared to give up for anything. Honour, he called it, my honour, during the screaming matches with Teresa. "You honour?" she laughed, "I wouldn't worry about that, Benigno, I'm not sleeping with *anybody* you should know that better than anyone," this mockery wounded her son, the brazen sarcasm of a woman who has no need of anyone by her side. You're nothing but a coward, father, thought Julio, realising that he loved his mother a little more and a little less than he had before, more because it was impossible not to love her, less because she was the one he was now afraid of.

Julio did not know how to explain what was happening to Teresa, he did not have the words to describe the difference in her, the incredible, impossible way her face, her body, her mind seemed to be growing younger as though time were running backwards. The woman who had seemed too old to have a child as young as he, the well-dressed lady, her hair always perfect, who moved slowly, her body heavy, who was constantly tired and wore a hat whenever she came to collect him from school, then collapsed into a chair as soon as they got home, who waited for her husband to come home so she could serve dinner. That woman had vanished, had been shed like a useless skin to reveal the lithe, tireless body of a young woman with the face of a girl, her dark hair now worn loose and tousled.

This woman was not the same woman, though she was still his mother, and every night she slept a little less, and every day she worked a little more, and after her husband went to bed, she would sit in the rocking chair and read, or sit at the kitchen table with Don Julio's fountain pen and some paper working for hours, writing things down, scoring them out and rewriting them always beginning with the same word: Comrades. It was as though Teresa González had been reborn not only on the inside, but on the outside. She had no time now to get dressed up before going out and would leave the house in whatever she happened to be wearing, never had she cared less about how she looked and yet every day she seemed to grow younger, stronger and more beautiful. She was his mother, and every day she was more courageous, speaking in public, organising collections, appearing at demonstrations, eliciting the murmurs of affection and admiration from the men and women of the village as she passed by, murmurs of contempt and scandal from other men, other women who no longer greeted her. "Oh well, what a shame," she murmured as she passed them, head held high, though they still treated her husband with respect.

"Now listen to me, Teresa! This nonsense is over!" The first time he saw his wife's name in small but unmistakable letters among the list of those who were to speak at a meeting of the Popular Front – all the more humiliating for being the only woman – Benigno Carrión stood by the door with his rifle in his hand. "You are not setting foot outside this house today."

"Do you want a divorce, Benigno," she said in a mocking tone as she stood before the mirror in the hall for once doing her makeup. "I'll give you one, with pleasure."

"That's not what I meant!" he shouted, then he calmed down. "I don't want a divorce, I won't *let* you divorce me."

"In that case, stop talking such nonsense… And move away from the door, please, I don't want to be late."

141

Teresa González, utterly calm, stood in front of her husband, who raised his hand as if to slap her until she forced him to put it down.

"Don't you ever raise your hand to me, Benigno," she said looking straight into his eyes, her every syllable filled with a menacing, controlled rage, "Don't even think of laying a hand on me, or I swear you'll regret it."

"What could you do?" Her husband's voice quavered, "Tell your gangster friends and have them kill me?"

"Ha!" his wife smiled. "So I have gangster friends, do I? Well, well… You really have no shame, Benigno! Now move!"

She gave her husband a shove, opened the door, and left. Julio, who had seen everything, heard the clatter of her heels on the cobblestones and then nothing, nothing except his father's sobs, which he did not want to see or hear, did not want to have to remember this snivelling old man, struggling with his rifle every day, cleaning it, loading it, aiming it, now slumped on the floor, so beaten, so broken, that his fourteen-year-old son could not bear to look at him. A son who did, and did not, want everything to go back to the way it was.

"Father!" he shouted, so that his father would at least get up off the floor, but he received nothing in return but the bewildered look of an old man, with no future, he thought, no dignity. "Why don't you do something, father?"

His father looked at him as though he did not understand and his face crumpled.

"Shoot myself," he said finally, his voice thin, weak and foolish. "That's what I'm going to do."

"You're not even capable of that," muttered Julio, and for a moment he didn't know where to go.

But it was only a moment. Because then Julio Carrión González realised that there was only one place he could go. He ran to the Casa del Pueblo and got there five minutes before the time announced on the posters. There were so many people pushing and shoving that he did not think he would get in, but one of the men on the door recognised him.

"Hold up, lad," he shouted, "You're Teresa's son aren't you?"

"Yes, sir."

"Nobody calls me sir," the man laughed, "Have you come to listen to your mother?" Julio nodded. "Good lad, there aren't many like your mother. In you go, there are seats reserved in the front row, they're probably all taken now, but it doesn't matter. Just tell the comrades you're your mother's son and they'll let you through…"

Julio Carrión González had never felt so important. And his mother had never looked at him the way she did that afternoon as she saw him make his way through the people crowding the aisles until he reached the foot of the stage where she seemed to be enthroned, two men on her left, two others on her right, the order in which they were to speak. She had never tried to inveigle her son with bribes and punishments, as did her husband who would only give the boy his pocket money on Sunday after mass. She had never even talked to him about politics, unless Julio asked her something. She justified this minor weakness by reminding herself that the children already had enough on their plate, given who she was, and married as she was to Benigno Carrión, but that was not the whole truth. In her heart, Teresa González felt guilty, and though she knew inside out the lecture about the harmful vestiges of reactionary Catholic orthodoxy, how they infiltrated a woman's subconscious and had to be rooted out at all costs, she felt much more comfortable when she was not at home, indeed when she was as far from her family as possible. This was why she was so moved when she saw Julio sitting on the floor waiting to hear her speak. So certain was she of her cause that she did not even consider that there might be other reasons why her son had come, because he wanted to be by her side – not holding her hand, not following in her footsteps, not tied to her apron strings, but standing by her side, which was something much more precious. I just hope I don't put my foot in it, she thought, the one time they let me take the stand, and with two candidates from Madrid...

"You were great, Mamá!" said Julio when the meeting was over, as she hugged him to her.

"Really?" she asked, although she knew she had spoken well, everyone had applauded, "Did you like the speech?"

"I liked it a lot, everyone did. Some of them even came up and congratulated me!"

"They didn't really let me talk at all. Ten minutes, they told me when I got here. Ten minutes!" You're so beautiful, thought Julio, and you scare me so much. "But I'm under no illusions, I know they only asked me to speak because I'm a woman, they like to have a woman speak at every meeting to get the female vote and they were hoping to get someone important, but of course those women are all busy, and that's why they selected me... And they only wanted me to talk about women's issues, it's always the same, as if we don't have opinions about other issues... That's why I went on for twice as long as I should have, I talked about what I wanted to talk about. If I can stand up to your father at home, I have to stand up to them here, that's what I thought... But, you know, they didn't mind. I was a success."

143

And it was true. As they walked towards the door, people applauded, patted them on the back, offered congratulations and words of encouragement, to her, for being who she was, and to Julio for being her son. Julio had never felt so important, so proud of his mother. Nor had he ever felt so close to the abyss, when he realised that things were coming to their inevitable conclusion, because his home, his family, his life could not go on like this. He was no longer a child, but he was not yet a man and although he understood things he could not bring himself to take his mother's side, he could not do it because all he wanted was for things to go back to how they used to be.

"Anyway," she was still talking as they turned into their street, "that's not what's important right now, all that's important now is to win the elections..." And suddenly she stopped and looked at him. "What about your father?"

"He stayed at home."

"It's not that I'm not sorry, *hijo*, honestly, but there was nothing else I could do. Not now..." and she hugged him again, held him close for a long time until he thought she had nothing left to say. "I have no choice, I have to keep going or die."

Julio, too, was sorry the next day when he saw his father, silent, mortified, broken, unable to look his son in the eye. Why do you have to be such a weakling, father? was what he thought, and then he thought that it was humiliating to have a mother like his. From that day, his father confirmed his worst fears, slowly erasing himself, shutting himself away, a silent, impassive witness to his own ignominy. Now, it was his mother who shouted. She shouted when the leftwing Popular Front won the elections, when the treacherous conservative generals rebelled against the Republic, when the people begged for arms to defend themselves, when the first slogans blasted out - Every man at the front, Every women in the factory, Every effort to win the war, They shall not pass!

"I'm starting work tomorrow," Teresa informed her family over breakfast on the last day of September 1936, "I've been asked to be a teacher - teaching infants. I hope I can handle them. Their usual teacher has enlisted and is setting off for Madrid this afternoon."

Benigno Carrión said nothing, not then, nor some weeks later when the war finally arrived in Torrelodones in an unexpected form, not simply the uniforms of soldiers on leave, the military convoys driving through, the Command Post where farmers went to sell their vegetables and lambs, and the German planes that had begun to streak the sky twice a day - on their way to bomb Madrid, and on their way back. These had been the only signs of war in Torrelodones, but now there were people, hordes of people, whole fatherless families, women and children loaded down with furniture, mattresses, clothes, saucepans, a cow led by a rope, and old men who brought the contents of their offices in case they found work. The government had evacuated the towns nearest the capital: Pozuelo, Aravaca, Húmera, Las Rozas. Even Las Rozas.

"I have something to tell you," Teresa chose to be blunt, showing up one day at dinner time with a thin, dark-skinned man of about forty who carried a suitcase in each hand. "From today, we'll have a guest staying with us. His name is Manuel Castro, he was a teacher in Las Rozas. He came with the rest of the people from the village and he'll be teaching the children who've been evacuated. They asked if anyone could put him up and I said of course, because there's nothing in the attic room... Are you listening to me, Benigno?"

"Yes, of course. Welcome." Julio watched as his father stood up, shook hands with the stranger and gave a feeble smile, before adding, in a whisper his wife did not hear, "For as long as it lasts..."

It was the evening of 13th November and the revolutionaries of the Nationalist army were about to enter Madrid at any moment. There had already been too many delays. In fact two weeks earlier, Don Pedro, the priest, had laughingly told his friend Benigno that a Seville newspaper had announced that Franco was 'a four-and-a-half peseta taxi ride from the Puerta del Sol.' Julio knew this because his father had told him 'everything will be all right, you'll see, after we win the war, I'll sort your mother out...'

Julio had not liked his father's words, or his tone of voice, there was something sinister about his father's sudden resurrection, something cruel in the way he bared his teeth as he smiled. You needed Franco to show up to save your bacon, father, he thought and despised him all the more, but he also believed him, and he feared for his mother, not for her cause, nor for her friends, her comrades, the people who had filled her head with rubbish and had ripped him from his life. But it would not be long before he discovered his fears were unfounded, because his father was a weakling to the last.

"It's only a matter of hours, days, weeks," his father said, and the hours and the days and the weeks passed and nothing happened. "Whenever they like," he said, "they can march into Madrid whenever they like." Bullshit, thought Julio. "They're purifying the city, they have to raze it to the ground, bring it to its knees, so that it can rise again, pure and clean," Bullshit, thought Julio. "They haven't given up on Madrid, oh no! But first they want to take El Escorial, it makes sense, El Escorial is the spiritual heart of the empire." Bullshit, bullshit, bullshit.

145

"Whenever they like," said Benigno, "I don't know what they're waiting for, but they know, that's for sure, and there's more to Spain than Madrid."

"Look, father," Julio finally interrupted him when he could stand it no longer, "Have they taken El Escorial?"

"No, but..."

"Well then shut up! They haven't taken it because they can't. End of story.

"You're wrong, *hijo*, you don't know how wrong you are."

In January 1937, Julio's life began to change once more, not in the way he had hoped, but branching off in a direction he could not possibly have foreseen. As the days, the hours, the weeks pushed back his retribution to distant horizons his faith could not curtail, Benigno Carrión disappeared from the day to day existence of his wife and his children, becoming a sort of ghost, a flesh and blood apparition that vanished in the early morning and did not return until they were asleep, drunk on anisette and slogans heard on Radio Castilla de Burgos which he listened to secretly in the rectory. And so he did not realise that at home no one missed him. Not even Julio.

"Watch carefully... the hand is quicker than the eye."

Manuel carefully tore a sheet of newspaper in half and then tore each half into little pieces, his fingers tracing arabesques in the air, he stuffed the pieces into his fist and blew on it, then with slow, mysterious gestures he unfolded the paper crumpled in his fist to reveal whole, untouched, magical, the very page he had started with. Teresa and her children, his only audience, clapped until their hands hurt.

"How did you do it?" asked Julio.

"I can't tell you that," he smiled, "A magician never reveals his secrets. Here, pick a card, but don't show it to me – show it to your mother and your sister. OK? Good, now put it back into the pack, anywhere you like."

The two Teresas, mother and daughter, saw the Jack of Pentacles before Julio hid it carefully in the pack. Manuel's face was turned away although even if he had been facing them he could not have seen the card because his victim held it carefully in the palm of one hand, covering it with the other, as he slipped it back into the deck.

"Let's see..." said Manuel, studying the cards and frowning as he deliberately misled them, "This is difficult, very tricky, I'm not sure... Could it be the ace of spades, no, no it's not that. The seven of clubs maybe, but no, it's not that either... And it's not the three of diamonds... So it has to be the jack of diamonds, doesn't it?"

Manuel Castro was Leonese, from La Bañeza, but he had left his village at the age of six when his father, who worked on the railways, was posted as station master to Las Matas. When he arrived in Torrelodones, he had just turned thirty-nine and had been a socialist for almost twenty years. When he was being serious, he looked older, because he had a long, grave, angular face, but when he smiled his face lit up like a greedy child watching someone unwrap a toffee. Being scrawny rather than thin, though not remotely frail, he was convalescing from a bout of osseous tuberculosis that had all but killed him – "That's why I'm here," he would explain, "they wouldn't let me enlist." He had many reasons to worry, but Julio saw him smile every day. His wife and daughters had gone to Valencia and wrote long detailed letters to him, but each of his replies was shorter than the last. So as not to be too sad, thought Julio, so that he could preserve his energy, not lose the smile that had made their home liveable again. Julio liked Manuel, admired his strength because it was an inner strength, with none of the bragging or the pathetic theatrics his father used, and he also liked his serenity, his slow way of thinking that managed to calm, and even prevail over, his mother's vehemence. Above all, he liked the man's composure, his ability to control his own reactions without having to raise his voice or resort to any tricks other than those in which the hand was quicker than the eye.

"Where did you learn to do magic?"

"My father-in-law taught me. He is a real magician, you know. He used to work for one of the finest Italian circuses and he travelled half the world, even went to America. But then he came home and he met my mother-in-law, they got married and went to live in Madrid. I met him before I met his daughter. I saw him perform one night, in a theatre and was really impressed, so afterwards I waited around outside to say hello to him. I never thought about giving up my job and taking up magic, but it was something I'd always loved ever since I was a boy. I started learning tricks myself, but I wouldn't have got far without him."

"So why don't you teach me?"

"Do you really want to learn?" Julio looked into his eyes and nodded solemnly. "OK then, I'll tell you what we'll do. This is what my father-in-law did to me. I'll let you come up close, right in front of me and I'll do some tricks a little more slowly, but only a little. We'll do that for... let's say a week. If you can see what's happening, if you can guess the trick, I'll teach you. If you can't – no deal. OK?"

"You're on!"

That night, Julio concentrated until his eyes hurt, but he didn't see anything. But the next day, he concentrated on the position of one of Manuel's thumbs which was not always visible although he was waving his fingers about so you thought you could see ten when actually there were only nine. It took a couple more sessions before Julio understood what he was seeing, and he did not quite guess everything, but it was enough.

"That's exactly what I noticed," said Manuel, smiling broadly.

The hand is quicker than the eye, especially when it deceives the eye, makes it focus on some irrelevant detail. A perfect illusion is nothing more than skill, cunning and misdirection, Julio discovered that afternoon, in fact, the eye is always quicker than the hands. Never forget that, and take your time. "You're better that I am," Manuel began to say, "and you'll learn to be even better still." He suggested Julio might perform with him, assisting him at the events held in the Casa del Pueblo every Saturday night, at schools when they held parties to take the children's minds off the horrors they saw every day, and in the barracks when he performed for the soldiers of the Popular Front.

Julio accepted eagerly, making sure he knew exactly what to do and for a few months he was happy, happier and less happy that he had been before. Happier, because he liked Manuel and it was fun travelling with him, along with his mother and sister, to the outlying villages where the girls did nothing to hide the fact that they fancied him, and would come up after the show and ask him his name, how he did the tricks and when he was coming back. Less happy because he discovered the truth, the shallow foundations on which his happiness was built.

Teresa gazed at her houseguest with an utterly covetous devotion, a look Julio had never seen before in his mother's eyes. Manuel was always attentive to her, eager to have her around, to protect her, not to lose sight of her as they moved through the crowded streets, and every morning, at breakfast, he would make a little paper bird and give it to her and she would smile gratefully, too gratefully, as though she had much more to be grateful for. Julio could see them, hear them, comrade this, comrade that, innocent almost insignificant words but which, on their lips, seemed loaded with a meaning he could understand. And he could have given in, could have believed the simple version, the polite, version in keeping with the war, with the terrible, raging atmosphere of the world around them, but he did not want to; he was too proud to give up on what was his, to play a minor role in a dream that was not his. Several times Manuel gave him the opportunity, but he did not want to take it.

"What's the matter with you," he asked, and Julio was aware that Manuel was treating him as an adult, a man, but he could not bring himself to feel grateful.

"Nothing."

"Do you want to talk?"

"No."

If he had talked to him, everything would have been different. If he had talked to him, they would not have left him behind. But in the lawless country where Julio Carrión lived the hand was still quicker than the eye, quicker than war, quicker than fear, uncertainty, shame, and all the rest was skill, cunning and misdirection, in reality the eye is much quicker than the hand, Julio, never forget that, and he would never forget it after that May afternoon when he came face to face with the truth he had been attempting to ignore.

He was on the main square, flirting with some girls, when he realised he had lost the green handkerchief. He looked for it everywhere, asked his sister Teresa who was playing with her friends nearby to help him look, but they didn't find it. In fact, he didn't need it, he could do the trick with four handkerchiefs, but there had been five and he had lost the green one. I'll go and borrow Manuel's, he thought. The house was close by and he ran all the way. As he went in he called out, "Hi, it's me! Anyone home?" but he was not expecting an answer. At that time of day, his mother was usually busy with one of the innumerable committees that included Manuel and almost everyone in the street, and his father would be out, as usual. Afraid of getting back and finding his audience gone, he dashed up the stairs to the attic, so excited that at first he thought that the noise he could hear was his own breathing. But it was not him. For a moment, he thought about turning around and leaving, he had four handkerchiefs, one red, one white, one blue, one yellow, the trick would be just as good with four, but he did not turn back. There was a small window between the stairwell and the attic, it was very high, but sunlight streamed through it as there was no curtain. The hand is quicker than the eye and Julio found a stool he could stand on. The eye is quicker than the hand, and so it proved for him in the end as he watched his mother, naked, smiling, at the height of a beauty that constantly seemed to be gainsaying time itself, sitting astride Manuel, naked too, the fingers of his hands – ten this time, no tricks, no misdirection – caressing her waist, her hips, before seizing her and pulling her down on top of him. The hand is not quicker than the eye, it is nothing but illusion, cunning, misdirection. Nothing but shit, though Julio Carrión González, nothing but shit.

"Julio, *hijo*, are you still here?" His mother, having looked all over the house for him, finally found him stretched out on his bed; they had a function to go to that night. "Hurry up, we're going to be late."

"Leave me alone, mother."

"Mother?" Teresa sat on the edge of the bed and attempted to stroke his hair, but gave up when her son pushed her hand away.

"You are my mother, aren't you?" he said with a harshness he had never felt before, "Among other things. So I'll address any way I like."

He cut them off. Later, when he began to miss them, when he gave in to temptation, he tried to find some other explanation for things, felt that it was they who had abandoned him, but he knew that was not the truth. They hurt him. They hurt him so much that he preferred to lose them rather than face the misery of his own life which had been trampled on, torn and ruined. He was the one they had betrayed, thought Julio, he had loved them, admired them, had been happy with them even if he did not side with them. It did not even occur to him to see things the other way round. He was too arrogant, too proud, too selfish and he did not know everything.

There's a man in this house, and I don't mean my father, he thought. There's a man in this house, and that man is me. Afterwards, when it was too late, he realised it had been a mistake, but only afterwards, when there was no way back, when his schemes, his tactics, his furious tyrannical plan were shattered by a cardboard suitcase and an envelope containing his mother's letter "For Julio" at the foot of his bed. It was 2nd June and the house was deathly silent. There was no one left to make a sound.

"This soup is cold, mother," he had said to her a few nights earlier, tasting it and dropping his spoon into the bowl.

"It's not true, Mamá," said his sister Teresita, "Tell him. It's not cold, Julio why are being horrible to Mamá?"

"Shut up, you little brat." As Julio said this, Manuel sat back in his chair and glared at his disciple in warning; Julio, with all the pride he could muster, held his gaze. "If I say it's cold, it's cold. Heat it up for me, mother."

"Heat it yourself," said Teresa the firmness in her voice belied by the tears in her eyes.

"No!" Julio stood up. Manuel stood up too, but Julio was not afraid, not yet. "You heat it up for me, that's your responsibility, you're the lady of the house, aren't you? The least you can do is keep up appearances even if everyone knows you're nothing but a tart."

"Don't speak to your mother like that!"

By the time he heard the words, Julio was already sprawled on the floor, Manuel towering over him. His face stung with rage and pain as he got to his feet ready to rush Manuel who, though he was no stronger than

150

the boy, was quicker and had been in many fights, so he managed to send the boy sprawling again before Julio had a chance to land a blow. He had not intention of giving the boy another chance. He threw himself on top of Julio, held him down with his left hand and slapped him with his right, a humiliating slap full of contempt.

"Who do you think you are, you little fool?" he said, "You're nothing but a coward, Julio, a little shit, nothing more, nothing less... Your father's son."

"Leave him alone," Teresa separated them, "He's only fifteen, Manuel, please let him go."

It was the last time he ever spoke to them. As soon as he could, he got to his feet and rushed out, running around the back of the house until he came to a narrow, filthy alleyway nobody ever used, and there he slumped to the ground and started to cry. You'll see, he muttered, surprised to hear his own voice ragged with sobs, filled with the same bewildered, desperate helplessness he heard when his father cleaned his rifle. You'll see who I am you fucker, I'll show you, take my word for it, I'll kill you... He stayed there for a long time, calming himself, and only then did he go back to the house. He sat on the bench beside the front door, intending to wait up for his father, but he fell asleep and was wakened by the cold before Benigno came home. Nor did he see his father the next day, because he stayed in bed until he was sure everyone had gone. He spent the whole day out and when he came back after dark, he found a hunk of bread and some cheese and took it to his room. He did not speak to them, but they were not speaking to him either: this he realised the following day when he woke up to find an empty house, a cardboard suitcase filled with handkerchiefs, , decks of marked cards, and boxes with secret compartments, and the last words his mother would ever address to him. 'My darling Julio, please forgive me for all the pain I have caused you, I never meant to hurt you, because I have always loved you and I will go on loving you until the day I die. And maybe someday, when you grow up and you fall in love with a woman and you know what heartbreak is, you'll understand...'

"Mamá!" Julio could not bear to read on. "Mamá!"

Without knowing what he was doing, he jumped out of bed, threw on some clothes and searched for them all over the house, opened every door, every wardrobe, every drawer and found nothing but bare wood, some crumpled, dusty tissue paper and some old shoes thrown in a corner. Then he went out and looked for them at the school, on the square, in the Casa del Pueblo, asking people if they had seen them, but no one seemed to know anything. "They'll be back this afternoon, or your mother will, at least," one of the teachers told him, "The Evacuee Support Committee is meeting at seven o'clock and she's the president..." At a quarter to eight, the committee was called to order without Teresa González, but her son Julio went on waiting until the last woman left, the teacher who had told him she would be there. "Go home," she said, "Maybe she wasn't feeling well, or something happened, and she had to go straight home." He already knew he would not find her there, but he took the woman's advice, and went back and stared at the bare wood, the scrap of crumpled tissue paper, the shoes tossed into a corner.

He felt nothing. As he wandered through the empty house, he felt nothing. The day had slipped away in what seemed like an instant, but it was nearly nine o'clock and he was hungry. This was the first feeling that returned: hunger, then all the others came flooding back, anger, longing, cold, pain, guilt, rage, despair, until he realised that once again he had only one place to go, and again it was not a path he had chosen.

*Never again*, he said to himself with every step as he walked to the rectory, *never again*, as he knocked on the door and nobody opened, *never again*, as he knocked again and heard footsteps, whispering, the rasp of the peephole opening, *never again*, as he greeted Sister Consuelo and told her he had come to fetch his father, *never again*, and there they were sitting in the basement around the radio, Father Pedro, the sacristan, the chemist, two men who had stopped greeting his mother when they met her in the street and his father, Benigno Carrión, miserable, old and bovine; never again would Julio Carrión González be on the losing side, he promised himself in that moment, never again.

It was a promise he would always keep, though he could not have known that then. Nor could he have known that he would make three mistakes before he would finally, permanently get it right. On 24 June 1941, he ducked down the narrow backstreets to dodge the flood of blue shirts trooping down the Gran Vía only to happen on another wave on the Calle Alcalá. His purpose was as firm as ever but he could no longer doubt his stupidity. Nor was he the only one. "You disgust me, Julio Carrion," Peluca's daughter Mari Carmen, had said to him some two years earlier, carefully enunciating his name and surname like a warning.

"I've been looking for you Julio, where have you been?" she had said that Sunday morning in May 1939, a morning when he had not thought to avoid her. When she had emerged from the church on her mother's arm, wearing a veil, she had appeared so demure that he had had to look twice to make sure it was her. "I called for you at the boarding house a couple of times."

It had been almost two months since Franco had marched into Madrid and he had been wrong in thinking that there was only one way to interpret so much interest. Not so insignificant now, am I, Mari Carmen? Just thinking this gave him a thrill of pleasure, but he was genuinely fond of her, and quickly decided not to give in to the temptation of hurting her. Instead, he gave a radiant smile and told her the truth.

"It's just... I'm out most of the day. I've been looking for work."

"Like everyone else," she smiled back at him before dashing his hopes with a cautious but firm whisper. "I wanted to talk to you because there's a meeting on Thursday at the Casa de Virtudes. We can't do much at the moment, we don't know how many of us are left, a lot of others are in jail and there are others we haven't been able to locate..." she paused and seeing that his expression had not changed, she smiled again, mistaking his impassiveness for quiet courage, "You know where the Casa de Virtudes is, don't you? The party will send someone to take charge. We don't know who it will be yet, but I'm sure whoever it is will know what to do, it's mostly a question of helping the people who've been arrested, that's the main priority..."

"What are you talking about, Mari Carmen?" He cut her short, a fear growing inside him unlike anything he had ever felt. "Are you mad?"

It was a solid, physical sensation, and all he could see was a reflection of his own fear in this beautiful madwoman whose long, gorgeous legs had taught him that, even in Madrid, the memory of Teresa González still lived on in her son because he, who believed only in what suited him, was only attracted to women who were brave to the point of being foolhardy.

"Well don't count on me," he said, in spite of the fact that Mari Carmen's eyelashes were just as thick, just as long, behind her veil of black lace. "Don't wait around for me, don't call me, don't ever come looking for me," he said although beneath her blouse buttoned to the throat, he could still feel the power of the most immaculate décolleté he had often seen. "Don't even mention my name, is that clear? Don't go telling people I know you or that I'm one of you. I don't want to get involved, all I want is a quiet life, but if you cause trouble for me, I can cause trouble for you. Don't say I didn't warn you."

He said this in a frantic, hurried whisper, as Peluca's daughter drew herself up to her full height, put her hands on her hips, and in five well-chosen words, spat her contempt:

"You disgust me, Julio Carrión."

This was what she said before she turned on her heel and walked away without looking back. She had carefully enunciated his name, his surname, and said nothing more. She did not need to. She knew he would understand. And he did, because he knew her. And there she was the *hija de puta*, he had not seen her for two months and it would only be three weeks until he saw her again, for the last time.

In the meantime, everyone had been arrested – those at the Casa de Virtudes were the first to go, but many more followed. "Mari Carmen and I escaped by the skin of our teeth, *macho*" Isidro told him shortly afterwards, "she wasn't there because the metro wasn't working, so she had to walk, I got away because I'd never been there before and had written down the address wrong. By the time we arrived, they'd all been taken away…" Someone – but not him - had informed the police, although the traitor, if he was still alive, could hardly have slept worse than Julio Carrión, who was torn between the fear that Mari Carmen might be arrested and the fear that he might go on running into her in the street. He could not decide which was worse – that she had been arrested and might at any moment choose to denounce him, might say his name, or that he might spend weeks, months, even years panicking over the thought that it would happen sooner of later. For the moment, they had not caught the loudest, bravest, wildest of them all and she was still free.

Many of the others had been killed, more than fifty had been executed at dawn on a single morning in August 1939, and if you were to calculate the ages of all those who died, they would not add up to a thousand years. He knew many of them, knew almost all of them by sight, the men and the women, because they were shooting women too, even those who were underage, everyone but her. It was unbelievable, impossible, but in the *barrio* everyone knew everything about everyone, and what they did not know he heard from Isidro, who never gave up hope of finding her. Isidro went on treating Julio as a friend until he too was arrested on the fourth or the fifth attempt - Julio could not remember any more – by those fools, those suicidal idiots to regroup and reorganise.

If it had been anyone else, Julio would have thought that she had sorted something out, found a Falangist lover who would protect her. Uglier women than she had done it, but not her. In the *barrio* everyone still knew everything about everyone, although it had been months since Isidro had shouted his last *Viva la República* in front of a firing squad. Everyone knew she still went to the prison every week to visit her husband, still lived in the same house with her mother and her sister and with a single sewing machine between them, lived with the heroic, useless memory of her dead father, and the uncertainty of not knowing how long Juan Ortega, a hairdresser who – no one knew how – had let off his gun on 6 November 1936 and the following day had held out in the Casa de Campo until he was shot just before sunset, would go on being the only useless hero in the family.

But for the moment, Mari Carmen, was free, he had glimpsed her himself that morning, and he had thought about leaving Madrid, going back to Torrelodones, the sheep, to a life that was not for him, but was better than prison, better than facing the *tribunal de las Salesas* and the blood-spattered walls of the eastern cemetery. His father would intercede for him, would talk to Father Pedro, and they would save him – or perhaps not, it was impossible to know – but he would then be forever branded, exiled from the world he had dreamed of, the world of those who, when choosing sides, never got it wrong. Mari Carmen was free, and for as long as she was, he was in danger. This was why he did not like the Falangists, why he despised them for no reason other than an instinctive shudder which forced him to remember himself in this world, this city in which he seemed to have spent a lifetime rather than just four years, since the day he had unpacked his suitcase in that little boarding house room he had once shared with his mother when Teresa had taken him to Madrid in a truck crammed with people to celebrate the triumph of the Frente Popular.

"Don't touch the rifle," on that second occasion, it had been Benigno Carrión, not his wife who had pointed to the bed where Julio was to sleep. "I'll look after the rifle."

And that afternoon, so as not to have to look at him, or listen to him, to suppress the contempt he felt for this old man who had spent three days in a drunken stupor, playing the role of the wronged husband, Julio had gone out for a walk.

As he had stepped out into the street, his cheeks still flushed with shame at the memory of the day before, when the young lieutenant, having heard why he was requesting a safe-conduct to Madrid, had invited Julio's father into his office. "Calm down and come with me," he had said, "There's no need to talk like that in front of your son…" Then he had turned to the duty officer, "Take the boy to the canteen and get him something." "What?" "I don't know, a hot chocolate, a glass of milk, anything…" As he spoke, the lieutenant had given him a look of pity that he could not bear to remember. And so, when he had finished hanging his clothes in the wardrobe, he had left his father at the boarding house and had followed those endless, glorious, magnificent legs, beneath a tight skirt and a military-style jacket, until they reached the Plaza Mayor where their soft, dark-skinned owner met up with a group of people her age, among them a friendly lad with a freckled face called Isidro who told jokes, He was the first person in Madrid to befriend Julio Carrión, and more than that, he was the one who told Julio where they went every day, the one who took him to the Unified Socialist Youth headquarters, the JSU.

"What about Mari Carmen?" Julio dared to ask the day he got his membership card and finally felt secure, like one of them.

"Mari Carmen…" Isidro smiled at him. "What about her?"

"I don't know…" he did not like his friend's smile, but there was no going back now. "Does she have a boyfriend?"

"Listen, I'm going to give you a bit of advice," Isidro was still smiling, "Forget about her, find someone else, seriously… Either that, or enlist and get yourself trained to fly anti-tank aircraft or fighter planes."

"Why?" Julio, who had always been lucky with girls masked his disappointment. "Does she only go for soldiers?"

"And not just any soldier. You should have seen her last November, when she used to go to la Moncloa with her mother, looking for deserters… 'You cowards! You bastards! You should be ashamed of yourselves. Is this what my father died for? Go back to the front and fight like men!' Fuck! You should have seen her, and that was before she made herself the uniform she wears now."

"What does it mean?"

"The uniform? Nothing, well, it's just something she designed. Didn't you know she was a dressmaker? Of course, last November, she didn't need it. She'd howl like an animal, or grab the deserters by the lapels, and whisper insults 'coward, *maricón*, go back to the front right now or give me your rifle and I'll go myself' And then, if they were young and good looking, she'd kiss them on the mouth."

"And did they go back to the front?"

"Fucking right they went back," Isidro burst out laughing, "they were more scared of her than the Falangists."

It had been only four years since that afternoon, and Isidro and the Juventudes Socialistas Unificadas no longer existed, but the streets were just as dangerous as they had always been, because Mari Carmen's legs still walked abroad. This was why he hated the Falangists, why he could not stand the sight of them, but that morning he had no choice.

They streamed down the Calle Alcalá, down the Gran Vía, stamping their boots, impervious to the heat, impervious to anxiety or fear because they had won the war, they were the lords of life and death, law and order, prison and the firing squads. They had picked the winning side, thought Julio, as all around him people ran alongside them, saluting, or disappeared into the dark alleys, looking for a few moments of precarious peace. Everyone was running in one direction or another, but there was nothing for him to do but stand still, because he was simply someone who worked for a garage on the Calle de la Montera, a customer at the bank that was just the other side of the Calle Alcalá, because he had two cheques to deposit, because he was nothing, no one, a fool incapable of working out what he believed in. This was why he stood waiting for the tide to ebb, for the stragglers to be absorbed into the heaving blue torrent that spilled down the major axes of Madrid. Where did they all come from? he wondered, realising that the people he had known for as long as he had lived in Madrid asked the opposite question – Where did they all go? At that moment, as the shops began to open again and a few courageous pedestrians attempted to cross the street, he spotted a lone Falangist, his face a rictus of pain, hobbling along the curb.

He was very young and skinny, and seemed delicate, less because of the thick glasses whose black frame emphasised the pallor of his skin, than because of the protruding breastbone which the arrogant brutishness of his uniform simply made even more pathetic. His face was slick with sweat, his mouth hung open, and his right leg was drawn up in pain. Julio stared at him. The man stared back for a moment before slumping to the ground.

"What happened to you?" Señor Turégano's right hand man approached him with the respect due to the colour of his shirt. "Do you need help?"

"I walked into a fire hydrant," said the Falangist, who was clearly no older than Julio. "I was marching with my brothers, but they didn't wait for me, I don't know if they even noticed."

"Is your ankle swollen?"

"I don't know. Let's have a look," the victim took off his shoe, pushed down his sock and stared at his red, raw ankle. "Fuck! It is swollen... And today of all days..."

"You need to bandage it," advised Julio, "If you like I'll get you a taxi, you should go home."

"No, I can't! Listen,...?" the boy raised an eyebrow questioningly.

"...Julio" he held out his hand, "Julio Carrión."

"Pleased to meet you." The boy shook his hand, "My name is Eugenio Sanchez Delgado, I'm the youngest son of Sánchez Delgado, you know." Julio did not know, but did not dare to say as much, "so I can't go home, not today... I have to support the others. You don't understand - this is our opportunity, our duty. Our fathers and older brothers won this war, and now it's down to us. Spain is just the beginning, we've got the whole world in front of us. Civilisation needs our youth, our strength. The

Western world is in danger and we must heed the call…"

This pallid, misshapen, who knew how to talk, who knew what he believed in, who was driven by a force Julio would never know, stared at him through his thick glasses and Julio recognised the glimmer in the boy's eyes. Mamá, he thought, Manuel, Mari Carmen, Isidro. He had seen this light before, the colour of conviction, the steely words that were worth dying for and he hesitated, only for a moment, but just long enough to remember Peluca's daughter. In the end, Julio thought, they're all the same. Julio Carrión González, who had made a promise to himself that never again would he choose the losing side had already been mistaken once. When Eugenio Sánchez Delgado got to his feet, wincing at the pain, gripping his shoulder then leaning against him for support, Julio did not realise that he was about to make a second mistake, one which would lead him to the third before he finally got it right.

"Come on, Julio. If you help me, we can make it. We'll defend Europe against the East. Don't you doubt it. Let's go…"

It mattered to me to know what kind of man my father was.

I didn't believe that Julio didn't care, but I did believe what he told me. His story had the same immediate, apparent improbability, the same fundamental truth, as his claim that I had been my father's favourite, something I had never even noticed. The whole is only equal to the sums of its parts when those parts are unaware of each other. For too long, the parts had been unaware of each other, I thought, and the whole was becoming too unwieldy, too contradictory, to escape the law of Complex Systems. My father was a complex system, one that comprised many components, and I remembered that disasters occur when the whole is greater than the sum of its parts.

I can't recall the exact date, I remember it was very hot, and that Miguelito was still a baby, so it must have been some night in June, or maybe July 2001, when we both woke up at the same time, my son tossing and turning in his cot, eyes closed, whimpering softly. Mai was still asleep, lying sprawled across me. Carefully I pushed her off, but it was so hot I felt no relief. Miguel was sweating too; when I picked him up I felt his smooth, white, velvety skin was damp. As I laid his head against my shoulder, he suddenly became calm, knowing that he was safe in my arms. It was 5.40am and he sucked furiously on his dummy as I heated a bottle for him in the kitchen. I didn't turn on the overhead light because I did not want to disturb him but also because I wanted to savour the unexpected joy of this easy, boundless intimacy between father and son, his skin against mine, this new, strange, heartbreaking contact he would not remember and which I was still unused to, since it was barely three months since he was born. Miguelito, so hungry, so tired, so helpless, utterly dependent on me, it was a terrifying responsibility and yet the solution was simple: take the bottle out of the microwave, attach the teat, sprinkle a couple of drops onto the inside of my wrist and bring the bottle to his mouth.

Having a son made a deep impression on me. I had never thought about having children as a purpose, a goal, or even a stage in my life. It was not that I didn't want children, but if Mai hadn't insisted, it would never have occurred to me to suggest it. For me, my wife's pregnancy was something strange, mysterious, almost frightening and yet I felt no surge of emotion when I felt him kick, or listened to his heartbeat, not even as I watched him grow with every scan, those grey smudges flecked with light and shadow the gynaecologist confidently identified as lungs, kidneys, arms, legs, because I couldn't see anything. Through it all, I felt disconnected, as though I were on the outside, but that all changed when Miguel was born.

I thought about that when he and I were alone. I carried him out onto the porch. Having a son made a deep impression on me, all the more so when I remembered how in a split-second, the very word 'son' had gone from meaning nothing to meaning everything, the split second when he took his first breath, and was suddenly himself, and I was suddenly his father. From that moment, in some sense, Mai ceased to matter. A second earlier the child we already knew was going to be called Miguel was her business. Not any more. She was still in the same place, but I was somewhere different, and I liked it.

When I took my son in my arms for the first time I suddenly experienced all the emotions I hadn't felt before. In time, the shock of these intense feelings, the surprises, the fears, the responsibilities, the indescribable joys, would become less intense, mutating into a constant, everyday love as Miguelito ceased to be like other children and began to be himself, with his own face, his own body, his own way of annoying me, the peculiar way in which he could be unbearable one minute and adorable the next, without ever ceasing to be Miguel Carrión, my son. But that night in 2001, when I took him out onto the porch, I found my father there, since he could not sleep.

I sat down next to him and, still busy with the baby and the bottle, I remarked that it was impossible to escape the sweltering heat even at six in the morning. But he didn't want to talk about the weather. "So where's Mai?" he asked point-blank, making no attempt to conceal his surprise. "Asleep," I said. He shook his head. "You must really love your wife, *hijo*," he continued after a moment. "Of course I love her," I said, "But I didn't get up for her sake, I did it for myself." "For yourself?" he insisted. "For myself." I insisted, "I like looking after the baby." He stared at me, incredulous, and then finally agreed that it really was too hot.

When my brother Julio left that evening "If we're not going whoring, I'd like to get home and see the kids while they're still up" – I decided to stay in the bar and take my time over the last drink. I still did not feel like going home, but the reason behind my hesitation was not at home, it was in the boot of my car. Before heading back to my quiet life, I had to go back to the apartment that did not belong to me on Calle Jorge Juan and undo the dirty work I had done only that afternoon. Although I had decided just to leave the two bin bags in the hallway, I still felt irritated, tired of taking responsibility for my father. Then, of course, there was

Raquel. I would have to phone her, call round, give her the key, see her, listen to her. I would have to curb the fierce excitement of the hunter she had awakened it in me, ignore the alarm signals that went off the moment she touched me, withstand the silences, the flawless performance of this role she had rehearsed; I would wonder what sort of game she was playing, ignore the fact that she was extremely clever, overlook that singular beauty that required you to look twice before seeing it, ignore the fact that she had been my father's last lover.

My father. Two words that had never been a problem for me, not even when things were difficult between us, when all the decisions I took were at odds with his plans, with the son he wanted me to be. My father. Words so easy to think, to say, to take for granted, that maybe the innate kudos of the concept blinded me to the man behind the words. A poor man, I reminded myself, a complete bastard, remembering what Julio had said. A father and his sons, new information to be fed into the experiment, Julio who had chosen to be a father though it meant giving up being a son, Miguelito who was barely three months old, a hungry, sleepy baby, on that night when his grandfather had stared at us in sheer disbelief, or perhaps not, perhaps it was disbelief mingled with contempt that I saw in his wide eyes.

"You're reading too much into it, Álvaro," Mai would have said, taking his side as she always did, "He's an old man, there are some things he doesn't understand, I'm sure it would never even have occurred to him to get up in the middle of the night to feed any of you, but that doesn't mean that he loved you any less." Mai never said these words to me, but I can hear them now, I can even refute them: "Maybe you're right, but lending money to your son so that he can sort things out with the mother of his children is not the same as getting up in the middle of the night to feed a baby, Mai." In the quiet of this half-empty bar it was no longer a matter of remembering every date, every action, every image of the man I could not bring back from the dead, but of finding new, hidden, meanings in the dates, the actions, the images of this man I thought I knew. Yet doing so made me a traitor, I thought, the scheming, treacherous son who listens to idle gossip, unsubstantiated rumours, put about by his enemies. But in this case the enemy was my brother and he was right. There was more at stake than memories of Julio Carrión González. What was at stake were my own memories. This is what I thought, and it did not make me feel any better, but it made me feel fair.

At that moment, it occurred to me that I could choose to do nothing. There was no solution; my father was dead. If he was not the man I'd loved and admired, then he would never be another. Nor would he have a chance to defend himself, to tell me what Mai had told me in his own words, persuade me I was reading too much into things. Yet if I was reading too much into things, I wouldn't have been able to understand Julio's anger. If I was reading too much into things I wouldn't instantly, involuntarily have remembered that sweltering summer night when my son, my father and I had not been able to sleep. If I was reading too much into things surely at some point I would have noticed some hint of the favouritism that had so riled Rafa.

As I paid the bill and walked back reluctantly to the car which contained the evidence of my problem, I found myself thinking about what Julio had said, the enormity of what he had said in those few words. "He was happy to give Rafa money for his businesses but when it came to my kids, nothing". What had struck me most about the conversation was his surprising insight that Papá was not one person but many, how our memories of him all differed as our conversation that afternoon had proved, which seemed all the more brutal, , more difficult to accept when I tried to square Julio's story with my own memories of our childhood.

"But Papá was always a good father," I protested, very sure of what I was saying, "he played with us, he was always there if we needed him, to help us, to comfort us…"

"You think?" my brother sounded sceptical. "That's what Rafa says too, but I don't remember it like that. Sure, he did magic tricks for us, especially if there were visitors, but only because he enjoyed it and he liked to show off. And, yes, he came to watch us play football, but as for the rest…" He shook his head and pulled a face. "I don't remember it like that. I think he was a good father when it suited him, when he could pencil it in, when he had nothing better to do, but I don't remember being able to count on him, the way we could with Mamá. We were talking about it one afternoon at Clara's and she reminded me that Papá never went to any of the concerts at her school, he never went to hear her play."

This was true, I thought, before admitting it aloud. I could still remember my sister's disappointment year after year, with Mamá, Angélica and I, sometimes Rafa, sometimes Julio, sometimes the whole family, everyone except Papá, sitting in the school theatre applauding. Clara didn't play particularly well, she was never going to be a concert pianist, but she was the best in her class and she always played in the end of term concerts, although Papá never attended a single one.

"She's right about that," I admitted, "But I think Papá didn't want to see her play the piano because it reminded him of his mother."

"His mother?" Julio asked, surprised.

"Yes, Grandma Teresa played the piano."

"He looked at me wide-eyed. "That's the first I've heard of it. I thought she was a teacher?"

"She was a teacher, but she also played the piano – badly, but she played it. I think I remember Papá telling me once that grandpa gave her a piano as a wedding present."

"Well, he never said anything to me." He thought for a moment. "There's something else weird about Papá, he never liked to talk about his family, his mother and his father."

"I suppose that's true. But even if we knew the whole story, that wouldn't excuse him for never going to see Clara play."

"No," Julio agreed, "Of course not."

The bin bags were lighter than I remembered, but even so, by the time I got them up to the flat, I was sweating. My brother had been right, it was difficult to agree on what my father had been like, on the details at least. It was something that should have occurred to me, I thought, after all I knew his secret, I was the one traipsing in and out of the apartment none of them even knew existed. And maybe, I thought, this was not his only secret.

Before Julio voiced the thought, I had often thought about our strange family structure. We were a tight-knit clan and yet we seemed to be floating in a void, with nothing behind us, nothing on either side, no grandparents, aunts, uncles, or cousins, no relatives of any kind. My father used to tell us that Mamá's father, grandpa Rafael had died very young, before the war, and grandma Mariana had died before my brother Julio could walk. I had seen a few photographs of her, holding my older brothers in her arms, a dark-skinned woman dressed in black who lived in some distant town in Galicia. She was not pretty, in fact she was a little frightening, like Papá's father Benigno, who was the spitting image of my father and of me. His wife was Grandma Teresa, the one who played the piano badly, although she looked more like his daughter in the only photograph I'd seen of her, a wedding photo in which she is smiling at the camera while her husband's face is sullen. She had died young, too, in the summer of 1937, during the war, and she'd never had any other children. Benigno had been over seventy when he died in the late 1950s. He never got to see my brother Rafa, the child his daughter-in-law was expecting at the time. I had never known grandparents, aunts, uncles, cousins, I had no ancestors, no old stories, just isolated facts, a few casual remarks, fragments that did not always correspond with what my brothers knew. This was why Julio had never known that grandma Teresa played the piano. Maybe this was why our memories of our father also did not concur, because there was no other version with which he could compare them, no source other the unreliable memories of one man who told us the same stories over and over, growing up in Torrelodones, the snows of Russia and Poland.

"Where happened, Álvaro?" Mai asked when I got home.

"Nothing," I said, "I went for a couple of drinks with Julio and I lost track of time."

"No, I didn't mean that. I was talking to Clara. I called her because I thought you might be there and she told me you'd had a bust up with Angélica at the solicitor's office."

"It was nothing, you know what she's like, she winds me up..." I paused and smiled. "But the good news is we're filthy rich!"

"I know, Clara told me."

My wife knew more about our inheritance than I did, because my sister had worked out what was coming to each of us with astonishing accuracy, as it turned out. At any other time, my sister's sudden fondness for mathematics would have seemed as surprising to me as Mai's happiness, although Mai did her best to hide it, as though she felt that being happy would be in bad taste, but I could still feel my father weighing on my shoulders.

It was all so intense, all happening so fast and I wasn't sure I could control it. This is why, when I talked to Raquel again, when I felt the bit between my teeth, it seemed incredible to me that I could have considered telling my wife about the meeting. In fact, I had spent the whole weekend thinking about telling her, ever since the night when our new-found wealth gave me the opportunity to take advantage of her joy at inheriting so much, at being the lawful spouse to an heir caught in a landslide.

"By the way..." I adopted my most innocent tone as she served the salad, "I don't suppose you know anyone who works at the Land Registry?"

"Me?" she looked surprised, "No, why would I?"

"I don't know, you're a civil servant..." Without giving her the opportunity to remind me that she worked for the Department of Health, I told her a long-winded story, noticing as I did so that with every passing day I was becoming a better liar. "It's something Rafa said, as we were coming out of the solicitor's office... He took me and Julio to one side and told us that one of Papá's properties – one of the apartments he showed us once, remember? – wasn't in the inventory. It looks as if Papá intended to give it as a wedding present to one of his partners' daughters, but the thing is, we don't know what's happened to the apartment, but we wouldn't want Mamá to think there was something funny going on. So...

I don't know… he thought that it would be more discreet if someone whose name isn't Carrión made enquiries."

"OK," my wife was very understanding, "Don't worry. I'll call from the office. I don't think there'll be any problem…"

There was no problem. On Friday afternoon, when she got home from work, Mai gave me a copy of the deed on which, in capital letters, was written the name Raquel Fernández Perea and next to it the word 'gift'. "Excellent," I said, "Rafa was right, problem solved," and Mai smiled, then said that the first thing we should do was change the living room furniture. But before that, we needed to paint the walls because they really weren't white any more. "Any colour you like," I said, feeling like a bastard for having lied to my wife simply because I was saddled with playing arbitrator, shuttling between the private and public faces of my father the hypocrite. At that moment, I was on the point of confessing, of telling Mai the whole story. Telling her that it had all been a coincidence, a chain of trivial events, a series of accidents unrelated to each other except for the fact that I was present at all of them. Neither Mai nor anybody else could have blamed me for what I had done on my own. Nothing would have been easier than telling Mai about it and then calling my brothers and sisters to share the burden of my father's secret. But I said nothing, not to her, not to anyone, and the following Monday I called Raquel. I said we had to meet.

"Really?" I could hear a playfulness in her voice that I was quick to defuse.

"Yes," I confirmed, "I've got news."

"News?" her voice had changed, "What kind of news?"

"Well…" I tried to find a way to sum things up, but couldn't think of one. "Look, it's not something we can talk about over the phone. We're going to have to meet anyway, so I'd prefer to wait until then, but I should tell you that the apartment on Calle Jorge Juan isn't ours, it's yours."

"Mine?" The news clearly came as a shock to her. "Are you sure?"

'Yes. Which means I have to give you back the key, though I'm not sure when we'll be able to meet, because I have an exhibition opening on Friday and as usual everything's running late…"

"An exhibition? Do you paint?"

"No," I smiled, "I don't paint, but that's a long story too. Look, why don't we meet up some afternoon…"

"Evening would be better…" she got in before I even had time to suggest a date, "That way we can have dinner - Japanese. And this time I promise I won't throw water over you."

"Dinner…" I was weighing up the suggestion, not yet ready to agree to it, when she pre-empted me again.

"Wednesday."

"No," I said, not realising that it was no longer a question of whether, but when, "I'm always busy on Wednesdays. Thursdays are better, but not too early."

"Ten o'clock?"

"Ten o'clock," I agreed, "But this time I get to choose the restaurant."

"Excellent," she said when I suggested the best restaurant I knew. "I suppose you know it's horribly expensive."

"I know, but don't worry about that, I'm paying. You know how much I like to get the better of economists…"

I was doing what I had to do, playing a part I had not chosen to play. I was shouldering the burden of my father's memory and nobody could blame me, not even Mai, and yet something like guilt took root inside me because that same night I lied to my wife again and felt all the worse when she simply accepted my story that my colleagues had decided to bring forward the end of term dinner by a month and a half.

When I got to the restaurant, it wasn't quite ten o'clock so I took a seat at the bar. I guessed that Raquel would arrive late, on purpose, and I was right. I guessed she would not come dressed in her business clothes, and again I was right, I guessed that nothing she could do or say could change me now, and I was wrong.

She arrived, wearing a strapless dress of a very pale, sparkling material that looked like an old-fashioned petticoat, the neckline and the hem trimmed with lace. It was a daring, almost dangerous dress, but the most harmful aspects were neutralised by a long-sleeved knitted jacket which she wore half-buttoned over the dress. The curious combination made her look like a little girl trying on her mother's lingerie who suddenly feels cold, or a mother hastily covering herself up with the first thing to hand. Clever girl, I thought, but I had been expecting that. What I had not been expecting was that, when she came over to me, she would press herself to me and kiss me on both cheeks, slowly, almost carefully, so that I would be completely aware that this was the first time Raquel Fernández Perea had kissed me.

"Hi," she said afterwards, and seeing my expression, she laughed. "What's the matter? In Spain, friends kiss each other all the time."

"And they have lunch at three o'clock when they get off work," I added.

"Exactly," she nodded and went on looking at me with an expression that was intended to be serious but failed. "OK, I'm sorry about the kiss,

166

really. I did it without thinking, I didn't mean to embarrass you."

She was wearing sling-backs with very high heels, which cut me down by a couple of inches, and she smelled wonderful. I realised this as she kissed me – slowly, carefully - on both cheeks, and I also realised that there was a small strip of plastic dangling from her jacket that had recently had a price-tag attached. It's the first time she's worn it, I thought, maybe she bought it because she was having dinner with me.

"You didn't embarrass me," I said. She was beautiful, extraordinarily beautiful now that I had learned to see it. "You have a plastic tag stuck to your jacket. Want me to take it off for you?"

"No, don't bother... It's new, I only bought it this afternoon," she said, as though she didn't care what I thought, "I can't bear hanging new clothes up in a wardrobe, I just have to wear them as soon as I've bought them. What about you?"

"No," I said, "Well... I don't really care, to tell you the truth."

"A real man."

"Maybe, what do I know?" Then I remembered the beer waiting for me on the bar. "Can I get you a drink?"

"Definitely a real man!" she laughed, "No, I'd prefer it if we went straight to the table. I'm hungry – for sushi and for news. You did reserve a table? The place is packed."

She set off down the aisle and I followed her. I no longer felt like a trained dog, or his master, the impatient hunter, licking his lips at the first sight of prey. With her, I felt like myself. The vast, almost cosmic, distance that separated me from Raquel when I was thinking about my father all but disappeared in her presence. As we walked to our table and sat down, as we looked at each other for a moment without finding anything to say, I remembered the apartment on the Calle Jorge Juan, the candles by the jacuzzi, the blue pills, the purple dildo, but at the same time I sensed that the woman sitting opposite me, her head tilted to one side, oblivious to the power of her face, the graceful beauty of her long neck, was not the same woman who slipped naked into a jacuzzi or lay back against a pile of pillows, her lips parted in a smile that showed the gap between her teeth. It was as though the Raquel who had known my father and the Raquel I knew were different, twin incarnations of the same person, identical twins, or two halves of the same woman. Maybe that was why I felt calm, why I was sure that I didn't need to be anybody except myself, ready to take control of the situation.

"Do you mind if we order before we start?" I suggested, unable to suppress a smile.

"What are we playing?" She smiled too. "Follow The Leader?"

167

"Yes, but you're not my leader..."

"Thankfully..."

"Anyway," I ignored her last comment, "This evening, I have a lot of things to tell you."

We both ordered sushi - Raquel pronouncing the Japanese for each dish, me prodding the menu and saying 'this one, this one, this one'. This was how I always ordered in Asian restaurants, but Raquel thought it was a joke and laughed, and she was much more beautiful when she laughed. So much so, that I was sorry when she listened seriously as I explained things to her in a calculated order, beginning with the will, the meeting with the solicitor, my surprise when I noticed that the apartment was not on the list of my father's assets, my discovery that she had been the owner for almost three months.

"He told me that once," she remarked, a mysterious longing in her voice, "But I didn't believe him. That's the truth, I really didn't believe him."

"Well, he was telling the truth. It's in your name at the Land Registry."

"How did you find out?"

"My wife told me." She frowned when she heard the word. "She works for Madrid City Council, in Department of Public Health.

"Your wife?" she repeated. "I didn't know you were married, you never mentioned her."

"Well..." I smiled, "Never is a big word – this is only the third time I've talked to you."

"I suppose that's true, still..." She struggled to find some other way to explain herself. "I don't know, you don't look like a married man. So, is she a doctor?"

"No, she's..." I paused, "She's an economist."

"You don't say!" she laughed, and then tossed her head as though she was no longer interested in my wife. "You know something, Álvaro? You remind me a lot of your father. Not just physically, although you're the spitting image of him. In other ways. A minute ago, when you were saying 'this one, this one' it was like a drum roll at the circus – do you do magic tricks too?"

"No, I'm too clumsy. I tried to learn once, but I gave up."

"The first time I saw your father," she looked at me intensely and I saw an excitement in her eyes I had never seen before, "He pulled lollipops from my ears. An orange one and a strawberry one. I'll never forget it."

"I believe you."

"Never…" She glanced away, as though she could not go on looking at me and talking at the same time. "I thought he was a charming man, extraordinary, a man I could trust, and he was so kind… I've never known anyone as charismatic as your father. He inspired affection, didn't he? He made you want to be with him. And when he hugged you, he made you feel safe. I don't know how to explain it, but he wasn't like other men."

She paused, silently doodling with her finger on the tablecloth. I didn't say anything. I was lost, navigating with no map, no compass through a voice that was at once heartbroken and fretful, gentle and brutal. She had drowned in her own words, in a flood of adjectives that were overstated, accurate, precise yet ambiguous; they were a fair description of the man she remembered, but unfair on me because I did not know how to interpret them. I could not see Raquel's eyes as she spoke, she would not let me see them, but I could see her mouth, those feminine lips so used to smiling, a slight emotionless smile underlining every point, every syllable, in every tribute she heaped upon a man who deserved them, but a man whose memory could not light up this beautiful face. Raquel Fernández Perea finally looked up from the tablecloth, and she knew what I had to ask.

"Did you love him?"

"No."

She said it straight away, without hesitating, looking me in the eyes, and her answer did not surprise me though I could not say why.

"It wasn't that exactly, it's not as simple as that…" she added, then paused. "Let's just say that when he wanted to be, your father could be irresistible. He only had to smile"

"That's true. It's the one thing we don't have in common."

"You're right, but I prefer the way you smile, it's more restrained, less aggressive… When he smiled, your father looked like a child's drawing of the sun, a big yellow ball with sunbeams streaming out of it. Oh, it was irresistible, but it was too much, almost brutal… No, brutal isn't the right word…" She thought for a moment. "Humiliating. Your father's smile was humiliating, Álvaro."

I nodded slowly, realising that I was seeing her for the first time. I had finally met Raquel Fernández Perea, peered behind the plastic veneer of the businesswoman accustomed to dealing with people then dismissing them, beyond the unvarnished bluntness tinged with a seductive irony, beyond the well-rehearsed roles, the pregnant pauses, to the woman herself, a person with no tricks, no trappings, no excuses. I could not know if she had consciously, even deliberately removed the last of the dark veils, or if she had simply been overcome by her own sincerity, but it didn't matter. I had seen her, was looking at her for the first time, and as was looking at me, she could see me, or perhaps there was some other reason why the spark of fierceness disappeared from her eyes and they were suddenly sad.

"I'm sorry, Álvaro,"

"What for?"

"I shouldn't have told you that I didn't love him." I held her gaze. She could have said "Take a knife and slash your wrists," and I wouldn't have thought it was a bad idea. "After all, he was your father."

I couldn't think of anything to say. For a moment, I felt the urge to run away. But then I remembered who she was, who I was, why we were having dinner together, the question that had brought us together and the answer to that question. I wasn't a child, a vulnerable teenager lost in the confusion of his own desire. From the first moment, I had known that something like this would happen and from the first moment, I had preferred not to know.

"You didn't offend me, Raquel," I said, my voice intact, "I have no right to criticise your feelings and besides... I'm grateful to you for telling me the truth."

"OK..." She looked at her plate and then at mine. "You haven't eaten anything."

"I'm not hungry."

"You should at least try..." she carefully examined the sushi on her plate and chose one she hadn't tasted yet, deftly picked it up with her chopsticks, dipped it in soy sauce and popped it into her mouth with a little sigh of pleasure, "...because this meal is going to cost you a fortune."

"It doesn't matter. I've just inherited a fortune, as you well know. Of course..." I took the key from my pocket and put it on the table, "...you've inherited too. There's something else... I went there."

"Oh... I'm sorry about that too, Álvaro. I'm afraid you have a lot to forgive me for. I suppose I should have gone over and collected my things before I gave you the keys, but, I don't know... It all happened so fast."

"It doesn't matter," I didn't want to imagine her in that apartment satiating my father's ruined lust. "I did it. That's what I wanted to tell you, I..."

"You?" she interrupted me, her eyes wide, smiling like a little girl. "You tidied the apartment, opened the wardrobes, emptied the drawers, got rid of all the stuff?"

170

"Yes, me... why, what's the matter" she closed her eyes, then opened them again. "It's hardly surprising, is it? I didn't want my mother or my brothers... I don't know, I just thought it was the right thing to do."

"Álvaro!" She looked at me as though I were a winning lottery ticket. "Of course it was the right thing to do, but I didn't expect... that's so sweet!" She started waving her hands as though to erase her infantile expression of joy. "No, no, I'm sorry, I didn't mean to say that... what I meant to say was thank you."

"Don't mention it. And don't get your hopes up, I'm not that sweet, I left the whole lot in two bin bags and dumped them in the hall." She raised her eyebrows in astonishment, so I tried to explain. "When you told me the apartment was ours, I put everything in two black bin bags. At first I thought I'd throw it all out, then I realised I should give you back your things, it was only fair, so you could decide what to do with them. Then, when I left the solicitor's office, convinced that the place must belong to you, it seemed stupid to cart the bags around until I next saw you, so I went back and left them there, in the hall. I did throw out a whole lot of stuff before I went to the meeting with the lawyer – the food, the half-empty bottles of shower gel and shampoo, the magazines, the candles in the bathroom... sorry. Everything else is there, I just hope I didn't break anything."

"It wouldn't really matter," her smile faded slowly, "Almost everything belonged to your father, or at least, he bought it..."

"Even the crockery?" I already knew the answer, but I missed the sound of her laughter.

"No!" she laughed, "The crockery was mine."

"Just as well, because if not, I could believe anything."

I took my plate, still almost full, and put it on her empty plate, but she barely noticed.

"Doesn't it scare you?" She asked, looking me in the eye with that intensity I had seen earlier when she was talking about the first time she met my father.

"What?" You scare me, I thought, I scare myself.

"Being able to believe anything."

Later, these words came back to haunt me, when they both helped and hurt me, when they sustained and crushed me, when I found myself alone among the living. 'To believe' is more ambiguous and more precise than any other verb, this was something I would learn, when I could believe and when I wanted to believe, when I found out what other people could and would believe, when that mattered more than anything. When I was left with nothing the words came back to haunt me, and that night, when

171

Raquel spoke them I sensed their importance, their transcendence, but I did not interpret them correctly. Although I did not want to recognise it, I wanted her too much to separate her question from my desire.

"Should it scare me?" I smiled, thinking we were flirting.

"I don't know. I'm not your father's daughter," I wasn't expecting this answer, and she realised it. "In any case, the truth is... The truth is I like you a lot, Álvaro. I like you the way you are, the way you think, what you do, what you say, the way you say it. I never expected your father to have a son like you."

"I think I'll have a drink now..."

She was a clever girl, I knew that, she was a clever, disconcerting girl, a complex, unpredictable woman, not two but lots of women rolled into one, but now I began to doubt my earlier confidence. I was still convinced that that night I had seen Raquel Fernández Perea for the first time, but that didn't mean anything, it was of no use to me if I didn't understand her, and I couldn't understand her, I couldn't decipher her words, fit the sound to the sense. "You know a lot about me and I know almost nothing about you", she had said the day we had lunch together. At the time I knew nothing about her, but I had learned, I had watched, I had studied, only to discover that everything I had learned was useless. The consummate professional, the stuttering little girl, the tank crushing the pavements of Calle Arenal beneath her caterpillar treads, the scatterbrain, the cunning weaver of fictitious intimacies, her naked body slipping into a jacuzzi surrounded by candles; I could touch her, I had to see her, I had to hear her, I had kissed her, but I did not know which of these people was her.

"Your older brother, on the other hand, I never liked.' She said after a moment, handing me back my plate on which a couple of rolls remained. "You won't believe this, but I can't eat any more."

"You are human," I crowed, raising my glass to toast her.

"Yes I am. Nobody's perfect..." she pointed at my glass, "I'll have one of those."

"Sure," I ordered another whisky and looked at her to see if she wanted to play again. "I can't say I'm all that keen myself."

"On what, whisky?"

"No, my brother Rafa."

"Oh yes, that's who we were talking about! He came to see me, you know," I could imagine, but simply nodded, "Last week. Of course he *did* make an appointment, and he was on time. The minute he walked in he told me he was in a hurry, said nothing I could say would change his mind, that the heirs had been unanimous in deciding to recoup the

172

capital, and then he closed the accounts. He treated me as if I were a shop assistant, I'm sure he'd address a girl in a bakery as 'hey you'. I thought he was arrogant and... predictable. The typical moron who looks at himself in the mirror every morning and says to himself, you're a rich and powerful man, never forget that."

"That's a fairly good description."

"But... I don't know. Your father was nothing like that, he was charming, he was nice, intelligent, he treated everyone with respect, he knew how to tell people exactly what they wanted to hear. But your brother didn't surprise me the way you have surprised me, because making a fortune and inheriting a fortune are two different things, and a man like your father usually winds up with sons like your brother. You probably don't understand what I getting at..."

"No, I understand," I assured her, "The trouble is that the first person you met from the family was the odd man out – me. You would get on well with my brother Julio, he's just as rich and powerful as Rafa, but he's a party animal, he's funny, a nice guy, almost as nice as my father. Plus..." my voice dropped all by itself as I let my imagination run riot, "Julio would have wheeled out his charm the minute he saw you."

"Really?" she smiled, and asked the question I was expecting, "Why?"

"To get you into bed. He never misses a trick."

"What about you?"

"What about me?" She didn't answer, but laughed. "I'm not much like either of them. But I have more in common with Julio..."

On one of the last days of school when I was eleven or twelve, the playground started to shrink before the bell rang for our first class, and by lunch time, it was half its original size. All morning, trucks kept coming and going, with men unloading bricks and bags of cement, to the amusement of the children sitting beside the windows - unfortunately, I wasn't one of them - and the despair of the teachers. Term was nearly over and the headmaster had finally decided to put up what he pompously called a sports complex - a far cry from the basketball court flanked by three miserable stands which we found when we got back after the holidays. I barely remembered the building itself, but what I did remember was the huge mountain of sand which grew bigger every day like some fantastical sand dune in the far corner of the playground. The idea of climbing it was Roberto's, my best friend since nursery school, but when we got to the top, I was the one who stood calmly at the edge of the precipice, head high, arms outstretched. "What are you doing Álvaro?" he asked. "Shut up," I said, "Wait and see..." The first time was the best, because the sand had only recently been piled up, it was hard, compacted and held my weight for a long time – a minute, maybe more. I felt it shifting under the soles of my feet a second before the landslide; I stood tall, head high, arms out and at first it seemed to slide slowly, almost imperceptibly, then faster, recklessly, vertiginously but I was not afraid, my feet tensed, my arms outstretched, my heart in my throat, exhilaration thrilling through every inch of my body. The first time was the best, but it lacked the excitement of the second, the third, the fourth, because something new was added to the experience every time, and sliding down the mountain was exhilarating, but standing on the edge, controlling your breathing, senses alert, savouring the moment when the ground would fall away under your feet was even more intense. I know, because that morning I did it over and over while the short-sighted, lenient playground monitor Father Sebas looked at me and smiled serenely. Later, when the workmen complained because they had to recompact the sand we had scattered all over the place, they told Father Sebas we could easily have broken a leg. After that, we were forbidden from playing there again – Roberto chickened out but I didn't. I liked doing it so much that on prize-giving day, I slipped away from my parents and brothers so I could do it one last time, and when I went up on stage to collect the first prize for mental arithmetic, I left a trail of sand behind me. My mother was furious but I didn't care, because it was one of the most exciting things I'd ever done in my life. But I soon forgot about that mountain, surfing down the sand, the ground opening up beneath my feet, forgot how exhilarating, how wonderful danger could be until almost thirty years later, when Raquel Fernández Perea, tired of clinking the ice around her glass, looked up at me and said:

"You come from an interesting family."

"You don't know the half of it…"

From that moment the countdown began. Ten, nine, eight, I'm falling, I'm going to fall. I wanted it, but she wasn't ready to give in, not yet. Just as I was about to suggest we go and get a drink somewhere else, she put her glass on the table with a decisive gesture and looked at her watch.

"Quarter to one, shit, and I've got to be up early tomorrow…" She gave me a nervous glance somewhere between relief and sadness, as though she was unsure. "I didn't notice the time."

"Yes," Maybe it's for the best, I thought, it is for the best, but I didn't believe it, "me neither."

My name is Álvaro Carrión Otero, in November I will be forty-one, I am the son of Julio Carrión González, a poor man addicted to the benign and possibly fatal trickery of chemicals, the woman sitting opposite me is

174

Raquel Fernández Perea, she is about thirty-five, an age which might easily make her my father's daughter or even his granddaughter, but she was his lover, the lover of an old man with a weakness for believing that the most important thing was not getting laid but knowing that the next time would not be the last - a battle so unequal, so clearly lost before it had begun that it could only end in a victory for death, and death had triumphed, my father was dead. But I am not, I am alive, I have a profession I love, a house I love, a son I love, a wife I love. My wife's name is Mai, she is thirty-seven though she doesn't look it, and her name isn't short for Maite, everyone seems to think, her real name is Inmaculada, but her little sister couldn't pronounce it and made up a nickname which she liked much more, I love my wife, I love my son, I love my job, I love my work, I love my life, and my life is not like this, clouds and guilt, surprises and lies, this is not my life, this is not for me, I am nothing like this angry, irritated, worn-out man scared by intense, fearsome, perverse desires, my name is Álvaro Carrión Otero, in November I will be forty-one, I am the son of Julio Carrión González...

I repeated this warning to myself as I asked for the bill, I repeated it over and over as I paid, followed Raquel to the door, asked whether she had come by car, as she asked me where I lived, as she told me that she lived opposite the Cuartel del Conde-Duque, as we discovered we were practically neighbours, as we decided to share a taxi, as I offered to drop her off at her place before going on to mine, as she refused my offer claiming my place was closer, as the taxi double parked, as I kissed her goodbye, even more carefully than before, as I opened the door and stepped into my apartment, as I took off my clothes, brushed my sharp teeth and got into bed, as I noticed the warmth beside me, Mai, asleep, her skin soft, and fragrant, as I lay there unable to sleep I was still repeating this little mantra, repeating the same warning over and over, but it was useless.

My name used to be Álvaro Carrión Otero, of course. Julio Carrión González was my father. To lust after Raquel Fernández Perea, who had been his lover, was utterly despicable, but I didn't care.

The following day, everything was clearer.

Everybody liked the exhibition. I had been fairly sure they would. Although I humbly accepted the praise lavished on me, making no distinctions as to the quality of the opinions – "It's incredible," said a bank manager's wife with diamond rings on every finger, "Even I can understand it." – the truth was that rarely in my life had the correlation between effort expended, which had been considerable, and the results,

175

which had been spectacular, been so gratifying. José Ignacio Carmona who, before he had taken the post as museum director and enlisted me as an advisor, had been my teacher, almost my guru and the chief influence during my years as a student, was thrilled. "Of course," I said as an aside, "we'll both get the credit for this," "Go fuck yourself," he answered and I realised that he felt a little bit proud of me. I was even more surprised by Fernando Cisneros's reaction. He showed up late, his burly frame squeezed into a suit that made him look like an excited bear.

"Congratulations, Álvaro, this is fucking incredible. Seriously."

Fernando had been José Ignacio's other pet pupil at university, and although all three of us were still good friends, from time to time Fernando almost seemed childishly jealous of the bond between our old professor and me. "No, no, you two are the disciples of science," he would say, "You're the real scientists, not me, I'm just a lowly civil servant..." I never took him seriously, but José Ignacio occasionally felt guilty and would offer Fernando a project that he would invariably refuse, though it would shut him up for a while. Black Holes had been the most recent offer, and I had ended up taking it on myself a couple of days after my father's second and fatal heart attack. At the time I would have been grateful for a hand to get it finished; Fernando didn't exactly say no, but wondered aloud how long we had before the upcoming elections for head of department. I told him to forget about it for the time being, that I'd get back to him if I thought I couldn't meet the deadline. I did make the deadline, but I knew Fernando Cisneros well, he was my best friend. I knew he felt guilty for not having helped out, but also that, on its own, no amount of guilt would have elicited a eulogy as warm and sincere for an exhibition which, by its very nature, did not belong to the kind of successes he valued.

"What the fuck were you thinking?" He had asked when I first told him I had accepted Carmona's job offer, "Having you gone fucking nuts as well?" I didn't answer, but he carried on regardless, "First José Ignacio loses the plot, now he's taking you down with him." "But what's so bad about it Fernando? I don't see what you're getting at..." "What's bad" he explained condescendingly, "is a physicist of José Ignacio's calibre giving up his career to put on exhibitions for ten-year-olds. It's bullshit," he said, "A waste of space." "No, it's not," I said, "First off, José Ignacio is not giving up anything for the museum, he'll be the director and curator, and when it's up and running all that will mean is he has to attend a couple of meetings a week. Secondly, a museum like this is not a waste of space, Fernando, I can't believe you'd even say that. You spend you whole life bleating about how difficult it is to be scientist in a society that's not interested in science…" "Listen, Álvaro," he shot back, "José Ignacio is one thing, he's already had his career, but you… you should be aiming for head of department, not pissing about with Physics as entertainment." At that point I laughed. The only major obstacle in Fernando Cisneros's political career was his utter disinterest in anything other than politics. It wasn't that he didn't do the research, publish the papers, he simply read less and less. Next to him, I was the Midas of research, the queen bee of publishing. "The one who needs to do more reading is you, Fernando, you're the one who wants to be head of department," I told him, "Anyway, my museum work counts towards academic credit." "Really?" "Of course," I assured him, although at that point I didn't know that this was true, nor that José Ignacio would manage to persuade the museum's board of trustees to sign a sponsorship deal to finance several research projects at the university.

"Hey you! I'm trying to congratulate you here," Fernando said, grabbing me by the shoulders when I responded to his initial congratulations with a shrug, "Con-gra-tu-late, get it? I am publicly admitting that I might have been wrong. If that's not enough to flatter your vanity, I don't know what is…"

"I know, and I'm grateful, honestly," I said, "How's the campaign going?"

"The campaign?" he frowned and stroked his chin. "The campaign's fine, we're bound to win, but you look like shit, Álvaro."

"Yeah, I know, things aren't going too well."

I looked around and saw Mai at the far end of the room, chatting to a group of people. She probably wouldn't miss me for a while, so I grabbed Fernando and dragged him into a corner behind the display.

"You're not going to believe this but…"

He looked at me, his face concerned, utterly unlike the mischievous grin he had given me when he had asked if I was having an affair a couple of weeks earlier. He was clearly expecting some dramatic revelation, a serious illness or a fuck-up at work. Over the years, Fernando had cultivated a systematic pessimism which overlaid his naturally feisty personality and would drag him down into bouts of depression so intense that sometimes he was forced to switch to automatic pilot and become his own doppelganger, a man who taught his classes with the mechanical reliability of a robot and spent his free time in his office doing nothing, a bitter taste in his mouth from constantly repeating that everything was shit. Until some departmental squabble emerged, at which point he would hurl himself into the breach with a passion, that astonished even me, a zeal more intense than he had been

177

capable of at the age of twenty. Back then, I had once joked with Fernando that his fundamental character trait was his need to plot and scheme, that he had been born a conspirator the way others are born artists and time had proved me right.

"OK, basically…" I leaped into the void without a parachute, "My father had a lover."

"Fucking hell - good for him. You bastard, you had me worried there…" He rubbed his face and shot me a wicked smile. "So your father had a lover, who would have thought… So was she around his whole life, or was she younger than him?"

"She's younger than me," I decided to repeat myself for emphasis, "Younger than both of us, Fernando."

"What!?" this piece of information stunned him. "Fucking hell, Julio, you old dog, there he was, going around all stiff and starched, and secretly he was a dirty bastard…"

"Yes," His reaction reminded me of my glee when I had first found out and I laughed with him, "But that's not the worst part."

He stared at me, astonished, "Do the others know about this? I mean does your mother know?"

"Nobody knows, not even Mai. I'm the only person who knows, and now you."

In as few words as possible, I told him everything that had happened, from the day of the funeral up to the night before, and I told him that none of what I was telling him was as important as it seemed.

"And that's not the worst part?" he asked when I had finished, bewildered.

"The worst part…", I took a deep breath and decided to see it through to the end, "is that last night I came this close to sleeping with her. Seriously, I mean *this close*. You know what this close means? It means she realised, and she looked at her watch and said it was getting late. If it wasn't for that… it's been a very long time since I've been this attracted to a girl, and it's not just that…" I paused, avoiding his eyes and I made another decision, without knowing whether it was for the best. "I don't know if I've *ever* been so attracted to a girl in my whole life. And yes, I know it's ridiculous, but it's the truth."

I looked up and his face was almost completely blank.

"Are you serious?"

"Yes."

"You're sure?" I nodded and he frowned. "You'd better not be taking the piss, this better not be a wind-up."

"It's not, I swear…"

"Fuck!" his voice rose until it was almost a howl as he put his face in his hands. "Jesus, fuck!" he took his hands away and burst out laughing. "So, what are you planning to do?"

I thought about it for a minute. "Nothing. I'll probably do nothing because I'll probably never see her again. Everything is sorted out now, we don't have any unfinished business."

"Apart from this."

"Yes, but that's just me."

"That's not true, Álvaro," he was thinking about something else now, "You can't know that."

Elena Galván had jet black hair, jet black eyes, her nose was too big, her lips were too thin, a sharp almost tragic face that she was the first to joke about. "With a face like mine," she would introduce herself, pointing a mocking finger, "You'd think they'd have come up with a better name than a Greek statue." By the time she had said it, a smile had softened her features so that she seemed like a different person. I never taught her myself, but by the time I came back from the States, her academic record was already legendary. And she went on outshining the other scholarship students because her remarkable intelligence did not stop her from being very clever, something that was not so paradoxical among the brilliant, ambitious young students. In addition she was charming, good-natured, funny and friendly. She was a pleasure to work with and was devoted to José Ignacio, so I wasn't surprised the following term when it became usual for there to be four of us in the bar, in the canteen, going for a drink after class. At first I thought Professor Carmona had decided to take this new chick under his wing, something he had done with students less worthy than Elena, but one day he couldn't come to lunch with us and when she got up to go to the bathroom I realised I had been wrong. "You never told me, you dog," I said to Fernando and he laughed. "There's nothing to tell," he said, "Nothing's happened yet. But it will," he predicted, his fingers crossed.

What happened lasted for two years and it was tremendous. If ever Elena Galván seemed genuinely Greek, it was on the morning she came into my office to say goodbye, her skin stretched taut and pale as parchment, her eyes ringed with dark circles. "Don't feel sorry for me," she said hugging me, "Look after your friend, he's in a worse state than I am and it will only get worse..." She was in love, a woman scorned but her words had the inexorable ring of prophesy.

"Go with her," I had said to Fernando the night before, one of many such nights, Elena nights, the same bar, the same drinks, the same conversation, the same ratio of doubt to certainty. "Go with her," I said

179

again after a moment, not that I had forgotten Nieves, who was a little like Mai, since they were cousins, who was nice, affectionate, and good in the best sense of the word, a good wife, a good friend. Nieves didn't deserve this, I had known her for years, we were still in school when she had started going out with Fernando and I'd always liked her. "You think I should go with Elena?" he asked me that night, after I had already told him twice that I thought he should. "What the hell's going on, Álvaro?" Mai had been asking me the same question every couple of days for some months now. "You must know..." While I still could, I told her I didn't know, that I hadn't the faintest idea, then afterwards, I told her to stop asking me. "Don't ask me, Mai, don't ask me tell you, because you know I can't."

We hadn't been living together for very long, and we weren't yet married. "So your friend is more important than me, is that it?" she said finally when we had reached breaking point. "No, that's not it, think about it." "I don't want to think about it." "Well that's your problem..."

"You think I should go with her, Álvaro?" Fernando asked me again, that last night, the same bar, the same drinks, the same conversation. Elena doesn't deserve this, I thought, and neither does he, it's two against one, and I knew that Nieves wouldn't win, that Fernando and Elena would either win or lose together, and yet I didn't dare tell him to go with her again. "What do I know?" I said, "If you're really not sure... Honestly, I don't know". But I did know.

From that moment, Fernando Cisneros began to believe that the biggest mistake of his life was not leaving with Elena Galván. "That's not true. You can't know that" It was a speech I repeated so often I knew it by heart. "You can't possibly know how things would be if you were living with Elena, you could just as easily be chucking saucepans at each other every night. The reason you think not going with her was the biggest mistake you've ever made is *because* you'll never know." He would listen to me patiently, nodding all the time, and when I was finished he'd repeat that not going off with Elena Galván was the biggest mistake of his life and eventually I didn't have the energy to keep arguing, although I never said I told you so.

From the first, Elena's prophesy was fulfilled, and continued to be fulfilled with each passing day. I saw her again many years later, on the Calle Preciados one afternoon in December. I'd taken Miguelito to see the Christmas lights, she was shopping with her husband, a good-looking man about her own age who was carrying a one-year-old girl. It was Elena who spotted me, and at first I barely recognised her because she'd put on weight, cut her hair and looked much better, prettier, with none of the dramatic tension about her, the bloodlessness that had characterised her last months with Fernando. I remembered José Ignacio on the morning she came to say goodbye, barging into my office screaming and shouting, "What the hell is going on round here? Has everyone gone mad?" "I don't know what you're talking about," I said, I didn't have the stomach for rhetorical questions. "Elena Galván has just told me she's leaving," he said, "She said she's accepted an offer from the Universidad de Castilla la Mancha. I don't get it… You think this department can afford to watch someone as exceptional as that walk away? We have to do something, offer her a contract, find her a permanent post, whatever it takes…" "That's not what this is about José Ignacio," I interrupted him, "It has nothing to do with that. Elena and Fernando have been having an affair for the past two years. It wasn't a couple of one night stands, it was serious. He couldn't bring himself to leave his wife so she's decided to go. She won't stay, no matter what you offer her." José Ignacio stared at me as though I'd just told him they were aliens. "But what about me? How come I didn't know about this? I'm going to tell you something, for what it's worth…" "No, don't say it," I pleaded. "Don't say it?" "No… please…" "We'll still have to take that fucking idiot to lunch."

For what it's worth, why doesn't he leave and let Elena stay here with us… This is what José Ignacio would have said if I had let him, and afterwards he would have regretted it, would have wanted to rip his tongue out by the root. I knew him too well, though not as well as I knew Fernando, who was remembering this very same event during the pause in my confession. It had been almost seven years since I had last seen her, almost six since he had last talked about her except to put her at the top of the list of the mistakes he had made in his life, he and Nieves got on as well as they always had done, and since then he had not been unfaithful to her as far as I knew, but Elena Galván was still part of his consciousness and always would be.

"I'm hardly the best person to give advice on this stuff, Álvaro, you know that."

"Nobody is…" I said.

"In any case…" He thought for a moment, then smacked his lips. "You were talking about what you might have done, weren't you – not even that, you were talking about something you felt might happen, but nothing did. And if it had? So what? It's not like it would be incest or anything, it would be… A peccadillo…" His definition made me smile, "An exotic interlude in your biography which, until now, has been pretty tame. The fact she slept with your father has something to do with it, you know…"

"No, Fernando, it's not that..." I interrupted him, "I'm not morbid. It's just the opposite, when I'm with her I feel..."

He interrupted me, like a judge about to pronounce sentence. "Look, this whole thing sounds pretty weird, Álvaro - not just the stuff about the woman, everything, the funeral, the letter, the meeting at the bank... I don't know how to explain it but... don't get involved. It doesn't fit with who you are, it's weird and you don't do weird. You're a guy who never does anything without planning it down to the last detail, you're always in control, we've talked about this before. OK, there are some things we can't control – falling in love, falling out of love, losing your wife, your parents, your job – these are twists of fate, but there are so many coincidences, all with you slap bang in the middle. If it were happening to someone else – someone less level-headed, someone weaker, more unpredictable... I wouldn't find it as strange if it were happening to me, Jesus every other week I'm sick to fucking death of my home, my wife, my job, my whole fucking life. But you? Don't get involved, do you see what I'm saying?"

"Yes, and you're right, nothing every happens to me."

"But this did," he nodded and smiled. "Is it good?"

"The best."

"What's her name?"

"Raquel."

"Really..." in a split second his whole manner changed, his expression, his posture, he raised his voice, and leaned towards me. "So anyway, I said to Raquel, don't even think about it, the guy's a fascist and the last thing we need is to wind up electing someone from Opus Dei to head of deanship!"

"So what did she say?" I didn't want to turn round, but I knew my wife was coming up behind me and that he had seen her coming.

"Raquel? Well..."

"What's this?" I heard Mai's voice, "It's late and you're still plotting?"

"What do you expect," Fernando shrugged, "It's who I am, you know that."

"Álvaro, your mother called," my wife slipped her arm round my waist. "Clara's gone into labour. Curro took her to the hospital and the kids are fretting. She doesn't want to miss the birth so she asked if they could sleep over at our place. I said they could, obviously."

"But I can't leave yet," I said, "I'm supposed to be taking some people to dinner."

"I know," she kissed me on the cheek, "I'll go ahead, but I have to take the car. Is the dinner in Madrid?"

"I'll drop him home, Mai," said Fernando, "Don't you worry."

That night, when I got home, everything seemed much clearer. It had felt good to tell someone my secret, and not just because I felt more relaxed now that I had told someone – and not just anyone, someone I trusted to take my side – but also because as I talked to Fernando, every incident that had been so hard to believe had suddenly felt more real, more solid. As I talked, I realised that words did not seem enough to describe how I felt, yet I carried on creating a narrative which - after his initial shock - Fernando had no trouble in accepting, perhaps because our own upheavals are never as upsetting to others, or perhaps because to him, my father's role was simply a taster, a backdrop against which the real drama played out – the anxiety of lust unfulfilled, the woman who had made me lose my self-control.

"The stuff about your father isn't so surprising, Álvaro. I know you don't think so," he said as he was driving me home after dinner, "every family has a closet stuffed full of skeletons."

His words reminded me of Raquel's – "human beings are boring and predictable, our lives are pretty much the same – two different ways of saying the same thing. But that night I had to accept that what I felt had opened up a new chapter, maybe a completely different story to the one that had been played out in that apartment on the Calle Jorge Juan.

Clara's labour went so smoothly that by Saturday afternoon, when we visited her, we found her sitting, smiling serenely, with the baby asleep in her arms. Íñigo and Fran, her other children, who had coped much better than Mai and I had expected, hurled themselves at her the moment they saw her which gave my mother, a little annoyed that she had no great tales of woe to relate the opportunity to make herself useful. But before she took the children to get something to eat, she beckoned me over.

"Listen, your brother Julio is completely tied up sorting out the death duties on the estate," she explained, "So he won't have time to check on the house at La Moraleja next week, and since your blasted exhibition has opened now, I told him that you wouldn't mind swapping."

"No problem," I smiled at my mother's display of authority.

"OK. Here, I've brought you the money and so on…" She slipped a hand into her handbag and fished out the usual sealed envelopes tied with an elastic band. "Call Lisette and tell her when you'll be over – any time except Wednesday afternoon, because she's started ballroom dancing lessons. She asked me if she could, obviously, and I told her of course, since she's out there on her own, the poor thing is bound to get bored…

I'm thinking of going back there at the end of May, but I can't leave Clara at the moment."

As she went on to tell me how happy she was to have a granddaughter named Angélica after her, I decided to go to La Moraleja on Wednesday afternoon. I'd intended to go through my father's study the next time I was there anyway, and with Lisette out of the house I would have free range. So I phoned Lisette and told her I would come over on Tuesday then phoned her on Tuesday afternoon to say I had an important meeting. I asked her not to mention it to Mamá since she would be furious, and said I would have to come over on Wednesday. "I'm up to my eyes on Thursday and Friday, Lisette, but don't worry, just put the post in my father's office and I'll pick it up and leave the money there for you, OK?" "But I get out of class at seven," she said, "I can be home by half past," "Fine," I agreed, "Let's say half seven, it's a bit late for me, but never mind... What time does your class start?" "At five," she said, "But if you want, I don't have to go to class... It's just, leaving all that money in the office with me not there..." "Don't worry," I reassured her, "You go to your class and I'll see you at half seven."

It was unlikely that she would be late leaving or back early, but even so I didn't open the door to my parents house until a quarter to five. I was no longer surprised by the cold premeditation, that was increasingly becoming a part of me; I was learning to lie, to tell half-truths, to hide what I knew which was simply a more rarefied form of lying, but as I stepped into my father's office, I remembered how I had felt the last time I had stood there, still whole, still shaking with unconditional grief over the memory of this man who was more extraordinary than we, his children, would ever be.

That afternoon, I did not doubt that my father had been an extraordinary man, I was simply no longer sure what the adjective meant. And I knew that I was doing what I had to do, but I didn't know whether I was looking for evidence that would acquit him or convict him. For a moment, I felt like a traitor, the scheming, treacherous son who had listened to rumours put about by his enemies and this feeling hurt so much that I stopped in the study doorway for a moment. And yet I knew that I could not simply do nothing. I was already involved.

I went to the living room, poured myself a drink and then headed back to the study, trying to remain detached, to stand back in order to focus on the problem. It was a technique I had used before and that afternoon it did not let me down. OK, I thought, there is the desk, four drawers on either side and a middle drawer. The middle one is probably locked, but the others will be open, they usually are. Two of the walls are lined with shelves – six in total – with cabinets beneath. The cabinets are probably locked, but the keys to the cabinets and to the middle desk drawer are usually kept with various other keys in a long silver box in front of the Enciclopedia Espasa.

There was nothing of interest in the desk drawers, but that did not surprise me. Some were empty, others were full of envelopes, writing paper, a box of recently printed business cards, pens, paper clips, a stapler, a few photos of his grandchildren and cheque stubs, each marked in his neat microscopic handwriting with the payee, the amount and the date. I went through it all carefully, systematically, putting everything back the way I had found it. I took down the silver box and I worked out which key opened the middle drawer, but there was nothing interesting or unexpected in there either. Current chequebooks for the business accounts, savings books for the accounts Papá had opened for my son and my nephews and nieces, my parents' passports and official letters from various places, from the Customs Office to the Department of Transport, mostly reminders of payments due. I didn't feel disappointed, I had expected as much.

I didn't hold much hope of finding anything concrete, but if my father had kept any trace of another life, I knew it wouldn't be found in the desk drawers he had casually opened and closed in front of his children. Nor would it be in the bedroom safe, since my mother always left it open whenever she took out her jewellery. But I had never seen the cupboards under the bookshelves open.

I decided to work from left to right. The first cupboard was empty, the second, which opened with the same key, was full of the many presents Julio Carrión González had received from his children when they were teenagers: dolls and certificates and miniature trophies emblazoned with the words "To the Best Dad in the World" I recognised some of these monstrosities as my own and smiled. That was why he never opened these cupboards in front of us, I thought, as I sorted through other gifts – fountain pens, desk clocks, commemorative plaques from his staff and the sort of odds and ends that only showed up at Christmas. Much of the third cupboard and all of the fourth was taken up with business gifts, since the two dozen or so coffee table books could hardly have come from anywhere else. There was a little of everything, from the flora and fauna of Spain to the treasures of cathedrals, reflecting the personal tastes of the person who had chosen them – probably some secretary doing a favour for her boss who could hardly be expected to know the tastes of the beneficiary. But between *Treasures of the Prado* and *The glories of Aigüestortes National Park*, I noticed something thick and blue with no spine.

I had to take out several of the books before I could get at the ordinary blue cardboard folder. It looked old and inside were a dozen letters sent from Zaragoza in Russia between 1941 and 1943 to a María Victoria Suárez Mena, a pile of old photos, what looked like a military record and some other documents. I closed the folder without studying the contents further, and put it on the floor next to me before returning the books to their original position. It's something, I thought, though it didn't look like much. The fifth cupboard was empty, as was the bottom half of the sixth but in the top half were five ring binders which my father had labelled with the past five years. I opened them one by one and found nothing more than tax returns with receipts attached, each in a transparent plastic folder. Behind the ring binders was a curiously shaped grey metal box. It was long and rectangular with bevelled edges and in the middle was a lock that none of the keys my father kept in the silver box would open.

I stopped for a moment and thought, then went back to the middle drawer of the desk. I'd noticed a small key-ring there with three little keys on it. Two were identical, and both opened the metal box, but none of them opened the tiny gold padlock on the small leather case I found inside. It was long and thick and looked as though it had originally been designed to hold chequebooks, but I had never seen my father use anything like it. There was nothing else in the box so I closed it and put it back where I had found it, making sure that nothing was out of place.

I was tinkering with the padlock, which was flimsy enough to be smashed using a screwdriver and a couple of blows of a hammer when I heard a door opening. It was only twenty-five past six, but all of my bothers and sisters had keys to the house. I put the case into the blue cardboard folder and quickly stuffed it between the books and notepads in my briefcase before calling out. When Lisette came into the study, my heart was still hammering, but I made a show of flicking through the post with the slow, deliberate movements of someone resigned to wasting his time.

"Álvaro!" she groaned in her sweet, singsong voice, "But your mother's right, you're completely impossible. I thought we said seven thirty?"

"We did," I got up from the desk and went over to greet her, "But by five o'clock I'd done everything I had to do. I was hardly going to hang around twiddling my thumbs in the university bar for two hours."

"It's just as well I didn't stay for the second hour, I knew it would be a bit late for you... Do you want a drink?"

"I've just had one," I said indicating the empty glass.

"Well another drink then? Go on."

"No, Lisette, thanks anyway. It's not that I don't want one, it's just that I have to drive," I started gathering the post together and nodded towards the corner of the desk. "The money's there."

She attempted a reproachful look, then smiled at me as she picked up the envelopes my mother had given me. "Well, I have to say, you're very sensible."

I followed her compact body, sweeter and svelter than ever in her tight-fitting black leotard and matching skirt that fluttered as she walked. As I said goodbye, I stared at the slit in her skirt which came up to her thigh. And suddenly the words were on the tip of my tongue.

"Hey, Lisette, I just wanted to know…" But then I came to my senses. "Nothing, it doesn't matter."

"What? She gave me an eloquent smile as though she could guess what kind of question it was that I dared not ask.

"Nothing, honestly," I kissed her on both cheeks and opened the door, "I was just being stupid."

I just wanted to know if my father ever came on to you, Lisette, if he looked at you, desired you, gave you presents for no apparent reason, whether he ever thought of inviting you to dinner, whether he actually did invite you to dinner. That's what I wanted to know, but I didn't dare ask you because I was Álvaro Carrión Otero, a good son, a good citizen, an ordinary guy with no idiosyncrasies aside from a morbid fear of funerals, a Physics professor who avoided problems, who could not even imagine doing something spontaneous, who would never ask his mother's maid an inappropriate question.

This was the man I used to be. I wasn't that man any more, I thought as I drove back into Madrid, but at least I still seemed like him, and I found that similarity comforting.

When he saw his brother Mateo for the last time, it had been several days since Ignacio Fernández Muñoz had seen himself in a mirror. In concentration camps there are no mirrors. Had he been able to see his reflection that morning he might not have faltered when he recognised his brother's eyes amidst a mask of taut, dry, ashen skin seemingly held in place by jutting cheekbones sharp as razorblades. Mateo had always had a round, doughy face – at home he had been called 'pancake face' - and he was very clever. Ignacio had never seen him with a beard either, which was why he hesitated when he saw those piercing blue eyes in an unfamiliar face, the face of an old man shuffling along, swinging his shoulders painfully with every step.

When he saw his brother Mateo for the last time, Ignacio Fernández Muñoz had renounced the human condition for a different, primal existence which was not life. He was no longer the man who, a month and half earlier, had stolen a truck to escape from Madrid, but a skeletal, primal version of that man, a body that existed only through and for what it needed, as though all other capacities – the ability to think, to believe, to feel - had melted into the brutal intensity of four elemental needs, the need to chew and swallow a hard crust of black bread whenever he could find one, to drink whenever he could without looking at what he was drinking, to clear the stones from a patch of ground so that he might sit or, if he was lucky, to sleep when he was tired, and to carry his blanket with him wherever he went so that it would not be stolen. In mid-May, in the camp at Albatera, it was hot, but no one knew where or how they would spend the next winter. Indeed no one knew if they would live to see another winter, but for as long as they clung to their blankets they did not have to think, did not have to feel. They talked a lot, there was nothing for them to do but talk and sometimes, when several of them gathered together to remember or invent stories aloud, they almost enjoyed it.

Ignacio was not aware of this, and would not be until he was alive again, when he had recovered his reason, his responsiveness, his faith and his true nature, and then it was difficult for him to accept it. Human beings are creatures of desire and desperation rips them from their very being. In the port of Alicante, where hope had guttered out, shots rang out one after another, day after day, bodies fell, sometimes in quick succession, sometimes separated by hours that seemed like eternity and he stared out to sea, at that great, still expanse of water, at the ships that would never arrive, towards the deliverance they no longer dared hope for, they who had not even had the opportunity to taste the bitterness of exile. They were the last of the faithful, betrayed by all, fodder for the firing squad, the victor's spoils of war.

In the port of Alicante thousands upon thousands were gathered, but no one wanted to speak. No one dared to say again, no, they will not betray us, they will not leave us here, they cannot do this to us, they will send ships, Blum failed, the French failed, and at the moment of truth, the English failed, the democracies of Europe cannot do this to us... Now, nobody spoke, not even the desperate, those who said no goodbyes as with secretive fingers they fumbled for their pistol, pressed the barrel to their temple and fired. Bodies fell like sacks, like trees felled before their time and he stared out to sea, at that great, still expanse of water, at the ships that would never arrive, listened to the shots, heard the bodies fall but he did not turn, did not see, he did not want to know. From time to time he heard screams, the sobs of children or of adults weeping like children, but he stared out at the sea so he would not have to look, so he would not have to know that one more Spaniard would rather die than live in Spain, in this land where he was born, where he had fallen in love and seen his children born, in the country he had fought for for three years, where he had known fear and cold and hunger and the unbearable loneliness of a long war, in his native land for which he had risked everything, for which he was about to die. Ignacio Fernández Muñoz looked out at the treacherous sea and did not turn his head. He was twenty-one years old, and he did not care if he died, nor did he care if he lived. He chose desolation over death and so became something else, something dry, dusty and inert, alive but barely human until the moment he recognised his brother Mateo's eyes and in that moment he wanted, with all the might he no longer had, to be mistaken.

He pushed his way as best he could through the crowd of solitary men silently watching the only thing that broke the monotony of life in the camp: a couple of soldiers with loaded guns leading the macabre procession of the condemned, the walking dead, who shuffled forward, hands shackled, linked to men as dead as themselves by a chain like some nightmarish umbilical cord. With all his might, Ignacio wanted to be mistaken, but he was not. It was Mateo, haggard, exhausted, so pale that it looked as though he did not have a single drop of blood left in the body, but it was his brother, the blue of his eyes still alive in the face of a man dead before his time.

"Where are they taking them?" "To Madrid, to face the firing squad." "But have they been sentenced?" "Have they been sentenced? What country do you think you're living in, lad?" Ignacio listened to the muttering voices, the whispering fear that leapt from mouth to mouth. "Why don't they just shoot them here?" "I don't know." "Franco is afraid to live in Madrid, he doesn't feel safe there, he's still in Burgos and apparently he wants to teach the madrileños a lesson before he moves in." "So what's he planning to do? Hang them from the lampposts along the Gran Vía?" "They don't care where it happens, the fuckers..." The defeated looked away as they said these words, hid their mouths from dangerous, prying eyes, everything was dangerous to them, the fuckers, Ignacio did not want to be like them, yet he scarcely dared call out his brother's name as he passed, although Mateo heard him, recognised his voice and, barely moving his head, his eyes flashed round looking for him. When his eyes met Ignacio's, he shook his head almost imperceptibly, an infinitesimal movement from one side to the other. He did it only once, but it was enough for Ignacio to know what he meant. Don't look at me, don't speak to me, don't say goodbye, don't tell anyone you know me, save yourself.

"Wow, when did they promote you to captain?"

Barely three months earlier, on 19 February 1939, when the Fernández family gathered in their house in Madrid for the last time, Ignacio had been the last to arrive. He had come from El Pardo and he was worn out. This was how Mateo had greeted him as he arrived, Mateo who collapsed rather than sat down on one of the armchairs in the living room. Ignacio hugged Casilda and Carlos and his sisters before answering.

"Day before yesterday."

"Fuck!" Mateo, who was still a sergeant first class, stretched out his legs, hooked his thumbs into his belt and in an ironic, almost philosophical tone carried on as though he were thinking aloud. "Of course, only communists get promoted in this army."

"Come on, Mateo, you've no right to say that, you know very well that Ignacio was promoted because he deserved it." María Fernández Muñoz, who had joined the Spanish Communist Party, the PCE, at the same time as her fiancé, and only a few months after Ignacio, snorted indignantly before looking up at her older brother. "Really, I don't know how anyone puts up with him."

Ignoring his sister's gesture of appeasement, Ignacio stepped forward.

"Maybe," he said, his tone as ironic as that used by his brother, "that is because communists devote themselves to killing fascists rather than inviting them for coffee to sue for peace, running away and leaving everyone else in the stockade."

190

Hearing this, Mateo got to his feet. He had deliberately hurt his brother, had known how much his words would hurt. Not being a communist himself, Mateo had been angry listening to Ignacio talk about anarchists and more recently about their own comrades. And had Mateo stopped a moment to think, he would have anticipated his brother's response, this accusation which had blown up in his face, because such rumours were now circulating in Madrid.

"Maybe I'll smash your face in."

"Maybe I'll smash yours."

"That's enough!" their brother-in-law stepped between them, warding Mateo off with his left arm and pressing his shoulder against Ignacio. "Have you both gone mad? That's all we need now…"

"Shut up, everyone, Mamá's coming."

Paloma's warning as she rushed towards her husband came too late for them to move away, and knowing nothing about the argument that had provoked the scene, tears welled in María Muñoz's eyes when she saw her sons standing together, embracing, a close-knit family there in her living room.

"What's going on here?"

"Nothing," Mateo slipped his arm around his brother's shoulder and the other around his wife's waist, "They've promoted your son to Captain and he's invited us all to dinner to celebrate."

"That's right," Ignacio allowed himself to be hugged, "I thought we might go to Lardy, but if you'd prefer somewhere else, just say the word."

"Are we really going to a restaurant!" chimed in his sister María, who, being the youngest, had rarely had the opportunity. Everyone laughed.

"We'll see…" her mother replied, "What a curious sense of humour you have *hijos.*"

María Muñoz, who had spent twenty years dieting with results so astonishing that she could now wear some of the skirts her daughters had worn before the war, kissed them quickly then rushed back into the kitchen so they would not see her cry. She thought that this was going to be the worst night of her life, but she was wrong. A few short months from now, she would look back on this memory as the best of times, a time of hunger, of danger, of worry and uncertainty and righteous anger, but also a time when her sons were young, strong and alive. Tonight, on the eve of her departure, the escape she and her husband had postponed until the last possible moment, she could not know that she would never see Mateo again, that she would never see Carlos nor Casilda, that she would agonize about Ignacio's fate for years in a foreign country where

Paloma, though she was not dead, would gradually give up on living.

Sometimes, when she looked back, the way her life had changed in these last years seemed impossible, incredible. She, too, had learned what it was to hate, and so she regretted nothing, but she did not quite understand what had happened to that solitary little girl who had seemed doomed to a very different fate, a calm, conventional future for one so educated. Her mother had died in childbirth and her father, of whom this child had only a vague, almost mythical memory had died during a typhus epidemic before the girl was seven years old. After that, María had lived with her father's two spinster sisters in a remote farmhouse in Jaén, an enormous old house as large as a palace surrounded by olive groves.

When they allowed her to climb up on to the terraced roof, all she could see was the rolling hills of olive trees flowing like water, like waves rising and falling as far as the horizon, an olive-green ocean flecked with silver and ochre on which the farmhouse sailed like an ark, closed off from the world. It was a magnificent sight, but its beauty frightened María, penned her into a terrifying loneliness.There were no houses to disrupt this sea of riches. There was no one to talk to, no one to play with. When she was small, she would spend her afternoons with the children of the caretakers, two boys a little older than she was, who were boorish but entertaining. They taught her to steal birds' nests, to cut the tails off small lizards, but all that ended on the day one of her aunts pronounced the momentous words: *young lady*. She was now a young lady and would have to learn to make something of herself. First she was taught by a governess, then another governess, then the convent boarding school in Jaén.

It was María's voice that saved her. When it seemed as though her luck had run out, as though all she might aspire to was a life in which every day was the same as the last, her voice with its extraordinary range, colour, and power opened the door to a new world. "María's voice is a gift from God," the Mother Superior told her aunts just before the girl turned fifteen, "We cannot teach her any more here. It would be a terrible shame not to nurture and hone such a voice, the girl should take singing lessons…" María's aunts looked at each other, perplexed. "What for?" asked Amparo, the elder of the two, who had remained single through choice when her father had refused to allow her to enter a convent, "She will inherit more than enough money to live on won't she?" She looked to her younger sister for support but did not find it. Margarita, who had still not recovered from her failure to find a husband and who lay awake at night worrying that her niece would run the risk of ending up like her if she did not escape from the social wilderness of the farm, gently contradicted her sister. "Of course," she admitted, "but you know a good singing voice is a valuable asset in polite society, and María has family in Madrid – our sister and her mother's brothers – and she will have to stay with them sooner or later, she can hardly be expected to spend her whole life with us. And even if she is rich, if she outshines others with her singing voice, she is all the more likely to make a good match. I think she should do it...

María had always thought that the features that would best serve her in finding a spouse were her pleasing face, the soft, velvety skin she had inherited from her mother, and most of all her strong, sleek, chestnut hair which she never wore up, not so much to show it off as to hide her ears which still stuck out despite years of fixing them down with sticking plaster every night before she went to sleep. She had never really liked her aunt María Pilar, nor her snobbish cousins Pili and Gloria, who could barely spend five minutes at the farmhouse in Jaén before they wanted to leave, but when Amparo finally asked if she would like to go and live with them, she could have kissed all three. And so she went to Madrid, she took singing lessons and she stopped thinking of her cousins as snobbish, she became good friends with Gloria, and she enjoyed herself more than she ever had. She learned that, though she was not a beauty, she was far from ugly, but she had never kissed a boy until that afternoon in June 1911 when, at the age of seventeen, she kissed a boy who had fallen in love with her as he listened to her sing the 'Drinking Song' from *La Traviata* in her aunt's living room. His name was Mateo Fernández Gómez de la Riva, he was from a very good family, was the best friend of her cousin's fiancé, and was seven years older than her.

"You know I'm a republican."

At which point, Gloria who knew one of the ladies-in-waiting to Princess Victoria Eugenia, burst out laughing.

"Come off it, Mateo, don't talk such nonsense – you a republican and your grandfather a count? You'll do anything to get attention..."

They were sipping drinks at a refreshment stand they stopped at on their daily walks down Castellana, one of the favoured haunts of the fashionable when the weather grew warm. It was certainly a strange place to make such an admission, but the incongruity was so obvious that he simply smiled while the others made fun of him. María, who had realised he was attracted to her, had watched him attentively and concluded that if he talked little and did not defend himself, it was because he felt superior to her cousins and his friends, so he did not bother to waste his breath. Mateo Fernández Gómez de la Riva was blonde and fair-skinned, his nose was large and his neck a little too long, but he was tall, slim and elegant after a fashion, and María had loved him from the first moment she raised Verdi's symbolic cup and her eyes met his and saw that they were filled with genuine passion which set him apart from the polite, almost indifferent applause of aunt María Pilar's other guests. That afternoon, as she watched him smile at the infantile jokes of people who suddenly seemed to be fools, she loved him all the more, because she found him interesting, mysterious, almost dangerous. And so, as they walked back, she stayed beside him and let her cousins walk on ahead.

"So you're a republican?" The rich little country girl who had grown up alone, surrounded by olive groves, felt a shiver run down her spine as she uttered this fiery, forbidden word.

"Yes," he answered artlessly.

"Really?" she persisted, making him smile. "Why?"

"Because I believe that all men are equal," she realised that he was being serious, though he was still grinning broadly, "Because I believe we should all have the same rights. Because I am ashamed of what is happening in Africa. Because it is unjust that poor men die like flies while rich men pay to avoid having to fight in a war that benefits only them. Because this country needs to be rebuilt from top to bottom."

"Is your grandfather really a count?" he nodded, "And you don't think that's good?"

"I think my grandfather is good, I've very fond of him. I think you'd like him too, he's a music lover, honest, generous, almost a free-thinker although he would never admit to it. What I don't like is the existence of Counts and Dukes and Marquises. But he's my mother's father so unfortunately, I won't inherit the title."

"But..." María frowned, "I don't understand, you're a republican, but you want to be a Count?"

"Yes, I'd love to be a Count. Because then, I could request an audience with the king, and I would go and see Alfonso and I'd say, here you bastard, take your Countship and shove it up your arse."

Without realising it, María blushed, clapped her hands to her face and burst out laughing, her feet making a few ridiculous little hops. With this instinctive, almost childlike series of actions she reawakened an old, almost forgotten memory, a lizard's tail wriggling on a rock as her blood sang in her veins, her body instinctively thirsting for dark, secret pleasures.

"I'm sorry," she said, her cheeks still blazing, "It's just... I've never heard anyone call the king Alfonso, or insult him... It sounds like blasphemy, doesn't it?" he smiled as though he liked what he was hearing. "And you're the first republican I've ever met."

"Do I scare you?"

"No, it's not that, just the opposite, it seems really..." she fell silent, weighed up the risk, weighed the word she had been about to utter, tried to think of a milder synonym but could not find one, "It's really romantic."

And then he kissed her, his lips barely grazing her cheek, like a foretaste, a pledge of true kisses, those that would not endanger the reputation of a young lady of good family on the most crowded boulevard in Madrid. And María was so reassured by that fleeting, chivalrous kiss – so conventional compared to the words that came from those same lips – that she recklessly put her arm through his as they walked back.

When they got home, her cousins rushed into the living room singing 'María has a boyfriend', and it was now her turn to endure their mockery with a stoic smile.

"Well, well... I shall write to my sister Margarita straight away," exclaimed her aunt María Pilar, as amused by the news as her daughters were, "I'll tell her she can stop taking eggs to the nuns at La Carolina... But seriously, I'm very happy for you María, I'm told he is a sensible and polite young man. He is an engineer, I believe. I would have been delighted..." she smiled at her eldest daughter, "if he had settled on one of my own girls."

"Well, at least my boyfriend isn't a republican," countered Pili, who was hopelessly in love with a dashing young army officer who her mother had heard had a wife in Alcalá de Henares.

"And Mateo is?" María Pilar looked at her niece, as though she had just heard a joke. "Really? What foolishness!"

"It comes from his mother's side, she is one of the Gómez de la Riva," commented her husband, who until that point had been ignoring the gaggle of women, "Almost everyone in that family is half-crazed. Oh, they're good people, amusing, cultivated, but a little odd. And to think that her father is a Count... I don't know how poor Fernández puts up with it. His wife is all right, but the brothers-in-law – the youngest one is trying to build one of those flying machines, and someone told me that one of the sisters is a spiritualist."

"Don't you worry, María," her aunt laughed, "It's nothing more than a childish whim, and in any case... Better a republican than a drinker or a gambler or a philanderer. I cannot tolerate fleshly vices, but childish caprices of the spirit, well, they will heal with time."

"And with his inheritance..."

This pronouncement by the head of the family settled the matter of Mateo Fernández's political ideas. They were not even mentioned when, in September 1912, Gloria achieved a long-held dream and was invited to attend a royal shooting party and told she could bring a close friend. María declined to accompany her. "Well really," her cousin said "stupidity is clearly contagious." By that time, Mateo was her fiancé, and she had kissed parts of his body even the most insolent officer in the Army had not seen. He had a good job at the Ministry of Public Works and was held in high regard by her family. Aside from this, María's life was much like that of her cousins, nor did this similarity diminish after her wedding. They were married in March 1913, a glittering affair with the Count de la Riva and his many children in attendance, though the one eccentric thing about the wedding was the groom's refusal to take communion. On 14 April 1931, the day the Republic was proclaimed, when she and her cousin Gloria argued for the first time, they shared the same pleasures and preoccupations, they cared for their children, they went to the opera and the theatre, they accompanied their husbands to dinners and receptions though the hosts of these events were not merely different, they were enemies. Gloria did good works, supported soup kitchens, schools for the underprivileged and charities distributing clothes to the poor, while María sat on committees campaigning for women's suffrage, compulsory education and public assistance for working mothers. Her children attended modern, secular, co-educational schools which were as exclusive as the religious, segregated, traditional schools their cousins attended, and so their lives were already radically different long before they found themselves fighting for opposing armies. But when she picked up the phone that day, María was not conscious that she had grown up to be so very different from her cousin.

"I can't believe it," Gloria was so incensed she did not even bother to say hello. "You've deposed the king. I hope you're happy."

"Not just happy, we're ecstatic," she felt so confident that she laughed as she said it, "Mateo says it's the happiest day of his life."

"So, what are you planning to do now?" Gloria enunciated each syllable carefully as though biting it off before spitting it out. "I mean, assuming the republicans have a plan for what they intend to do with this country - other than run it into the ground."

"Well, what we plan to do right now," María's voice had suddenly become so hard she barely recognised it, "is take to the streets and celebrate. I've already got my hat on."

"Take to the streets, with the rabble... Go on, that's all you're good for."

"The rabble?" At that moment, María Muñoz discovered that her indignation was both cold and hot, bitter on the palate. "No, Gloria, not with the rabble. With the people of Madrid. The rabble, as you call them, are the ones high-tailing it across the border. If you like them so much better than us, you know the way."

She hung up the phone and sat looking at it, unable to believe what she had just done. Meanwhile, her husband who had overheard the conversation from where he stood in the doorway with the children, all dressed up ready to go out, came over and hugged her, laughing.

But she was not laughing, and had left the house anxious, worried by the uncontrollable rage that had flared in her, and her cousin's reaction, every word, every pause like the sound of breaking glass, alarming, sinister, but most of all unjust. They have no right, thought María, no right to talk like that. And yet she wished she had not been at home, had not answered the phone. She loved Gloria, they had always been close, and although with the passing years they had seen less and less of each other and their husbands, who had once been inseparable, barely spoke, she still thought of Gloria as a friend. And it was true that her journey to political radicalism had been faster than Mateo's, for when she married him the republic had simply been a romantic dream, and while her husband had worked and plotted and met with people at the ministry, in cafés, in homes, addresses he did not confide even to her, María had continued to enjoy the comfortable life of a happily married woman. She had had to intuit the change, touch it with her fingertips to realise that the republic could be something more, a duty, a goal, an opportunity to live and raise her children in a different country. But she did not feel it as passionately as her husband, who needed no one on this, the happiest day of his life.

"Stop thinking about that nonsense," Mateo shook her gently as they arrived at the Puerto del Sol, "Look around you, look at what's happening - can you see it? It's amazing, and here you are worrying about your stupid cousin…"

It was amazing, but it changed her life forever, opening up an unexpected chink in her ordinary cares and pleasure; it forced her to choose a path she had never imagined and planted in her the seeds of a pride, a love, a pain that she had never known.

"We are what we are, María - for better or worse - and our place is here, with our own people."

Her husband was right, so much so that she felt ashamed to have argued in front of her daughters. But that was after her downstairs

197

neighbour had refused to open the door, when she had had time alone, to sit in her kitchen and think. They were hard, cruel days, more so than they appeared to be, more than she had thought when Mateo told her Paloma had arrived and had asked her to come into the dining room.

"Now, girls…"

In that last week of 1936, her elder daughter was twenty-one and had been married for more than two years, and her younger daughter was seventeen but their father still treated them the way he had done when they used to climb up on his lap, and they loved him for it. Both girls smiled as Mateo chose his words carefully.

"Your mother and I have been talking and… Well, you know that the government has set up an evacuation programme so that civilians who want to can go to Levante." As he was speaking, Paloma began to shake her head, and he began to nod as though agreeing with himself. "I won't lie to you, your mother and I are not leaving. If I asked the ministry for a transfer, I'm sure they'd refuse and with good reason, but it's also because I would rather work for the generals' Junta than for the government, because that's what I know and they need me here, not in Valencia. I didn't leave a month ago, I'm not leaving now, I don't think I'll ever leave, because this is my city, my sons are defending it and because I don't want to leave." His wife laid a hand on his arm but he did not lose his composure, "and no fucking General is going to make me leave Madrid. Whatever is going to happen to me, is going to happen here. But your mother has suggested that maybe the two of you…"

"No way," Paloma did not let him finish, "I'm not going. That's what I told my mother-in-law when she left for Almería and I told her I wanted to stay with my husband."

"Your husband is at the front, *hija*."

"But the front is in la Moncloa, Mamá. You can walk there from here. And the soldiers at the front get leave to come home. When Carlos is on furlough, I want to be at home to sleep with him."

"Paloma! Don't talk like that in front of your sister."

"But Mamá, all she said was sleep…"

Mateo Fernández laughed at his younger daughter's quip – though not as beautiful as her sister, she was quick and clever, and she was his favourite.

"Well, I'm telling you now, you're going to Valencia," his wife said, leaning over the table and wagging her finger.

"Me?" the girl leaned forward too until her nose and her mother's were almost touching.

"Yes, you María, running around, spending all day out in the streets, treating war like some kind of holiday, well you're wrong."

"I won't go. Besides I can't ..." she sat back in her chair. "I have a fiancé at the front too."

"He's not your fiancé, *hija,*" her mother declared, "he's a piece of foolishness."

"And you don't even like him, you always treat him like dirt."

"What would you know about it Paloma?" María turned on her sister, "How do you know whether I like him or not?"

"Of course I know!" Paloma Fernández Muñoz - the most beautiful girl in the whole building, in the Glorieta de Bilbao, in the Barrio de Maravillas, in all of Madrid – laughed. "Everyone knows! Don't you remember the day Papá told the maid you'd go down and fetch Esteban but the outside door was locked and the poor lad spent half an hour soaking wet and shivering, waiting for you? Remember what you said to us," she put on a whiny child's voice, "'You like him more than you like me, everyone in this house loves Esteban more than they love me...' Until the day he showed up in his uniform, and then he suddenly became the love of your life. It's true, isn't it, Mamá? What did I say to you that afternoon."

"You said, it's not Esteban she's in love with, it's his uniform," they both laughed.

"Leave her alone!" seeing his wife and his eldest daughter join forces, Mateo, as always, sided with his María, "She should know whether or not she has a boyfriend."

She did know. Her mother and her sister had preferred not to acknowledge the fact until one night in the autumn of 1938 when sergeant first-class Fernández, who should have been at the front, in the trenches at Usera, showed up unexpectedly. Panicked, they stood up, each with a single thought but for once, Ignacio, who collected bullet wounds the way he had collected lead soldiers as a boy, was unhurt.

"Ignacio is the one I worry about", Mateo Fernández said to his wife in the darkest hours of the darkest November of their lives. "I don't worry so much about the other lad, he's more sensible, but Ignacio has a reckless streak in him..." And yet Ignacio turned out to be a fine soldier. No one understood why, not even the boy himself, but he found out that first morning, a dog-day of cold and leaden skies as his boots sank into the mud and the icy drizzle lashed his face. They had been ordered to advance to take a hill, but the Sergeant commanding the detachment took a bullet early on. Looking behind him, Ignacio saw the enemy running towards them, howling like wild animals. And that was when it happened. As his comrades began to tremble, Ignacio Fernández Muñoz, with extraordinary calm, remembered his father, the look of stoic concentration on his face, the little speech her repeated over and over as he taught ten-year-old Ignacio to play chess. "You have to see the big picture, Ignacio. I know it's not easy, but you have to try, force yourself to see the whole picture – your pieces and mine – in that first glance before you even start to analyse it. If you can't do that, you'll never play well." His father was a fine chess player, and to prove that the other king – the real king – was just a man like everyone else, he always said the same thing "if you prick him, he bleeds". Ignacio remembered these things as suddenly, once more, he saw the big picture. These were not chessmen made of wood but men of flesh and blood, yet the thrill, the sense of revelation was the same. There are more of them, but we hold the high ground, they know how to fight, but they have to get up here and they can't run and shoot at the same time, because at the end of the day, they're just men, if you prick them, they bleed. The thought flashed through his mind in less time than it would take to say the words, and he felt his blood run cold, because suddenly he saw everything.

As he turned his rifle on his comrades, he looked at them one by one. Almost all of them were older than he was, but he did not need to raise his voice for them to realise that he was deadly serious.

"The first of you who tries to run, I'll take him down."

As he spoke, they stared at him as though he had gone mad, but their shock overtook their panic. With every second the enemy was closing in, but Ignacio continued speaking with a calmness he had never felt before.

"We're going to wait for them. We're going to take cover – because we can and they can't – and and we're going to wait for the fuckers, because although there are more of them, we hold the high ground, so we have the advantage. They have to climb the hill, and as they do, we'll pick them off one by one, got it?" He realised they were beginning to understand, "That's how easy it will be, because they can't run and fire at the same time, they're only men, if you prick them, they will bleed. But we have to stand firm. No one is to fire before I give the signal, clear?"

The enemy howled and ran, with every second they were closing in, but at the top of the hill no one moved, until the Sergeant, who had taken a bullet to the shoulder two minutes earlier, came to and dragging himself up onto one elbow said: "Listen to the kid, damn it! He knows what he's talking about…" before he passed out again.

Ignacio smiled and then another idea occurred to him, an idea which, before the day was out, would make him famous.

"One more thing… When you fire, you're going to scream, you're going to scream like someone is ripping your tooth out. If they can scream, so can we!"

Two of the detachment escaped but the others did as they were told, they screamed until they were hoarse, they fired as though they were shooting ducks at a fair, and the enemy retreated in panic.

That day, Ignacio Fernández Muñoz's detachment stopped calling him 'the kid'. In the afternoon, someone dressed his first bullet wound, a spectacular but superficial flesh wound on his left arm. His name was mentioned in dispatches the following day. He had not even been at war a week.

"Ignacio?"

"What..."

The first time they were given leave, when the worst was over though it had barely begun, his brother whispered to him in the darkness from his bed, as he had when they were children. The enemy had not passed. In the previous months, the two of them had thought of nothing else, there was nothing else to think about in Madrid in November and December 1936. Both found it strange that night to find themselves back in their parents' house, in the bedroom they had shared for so many years. Everything seemed strange, the beds, the pyjamas, the softness of the mattresses, the crispness of the sheets. Both felt vulnerable without the rifles which their mother had insisted they carefully place in the umbrella stand in the hall. Neither of them knew that this scene would never be played out again.

Mateo had already met a fiery, dark-skinned girl, who was very young, very passionate and dedicated her time to holding what the JSU called 'flash rallies' on the paseo del Prado. Her name was Casilda García Guerrero, and she prowled the tram stops, the exits to the metro, anywhere she was likely to find groups of people. Then she would approach them, try to persuade them to join the resistance, tell them where they could go, what they could do, where their skills might be useful if they chose to fight in their own way, to bury fascism by digging trenches or sewing uniforms. She was pretty, funny, a little plump, and the military trousers she wore fitted her well.

"You know I think what you're doing is really interesting," The second time he saw her, Mateo plucked up the courage to speak. "It's important to know that there are people motivating the rear-guard..."

Casilda smiled and thanked him.

"Do you mind if I walk with you a bit?" Mateo had ventured, and she nodded. "So what does your boyfriend think about all this...?"

"What is he supposed to think?" She answered him with mocking laugh.

"I don't know, you're too pretty to be out alone all day."

"I'm not alone. That guy over there, and that one there…" she pointed to a pair of innocuous boys younger than herself, barely more than children, "they're comrades. We come here together, but we split up so we can talk to more people."

Mateo frowned, though he was still smiling, "That's even worse… I'd be so worried, thinking about you out on the streets with your comrades, I'd probably forget to fire and the fascists would kill me."

"Would you?" Casilda's eyes met his in a proud, defiant look. "But I'm a free woman. Since my father enlisted, I've been getting on just as well living on my own. I don't have a boyfriend, and I don't need some man worrying about me."

Mateo nodded, as though he found what she had said commendable, then kissed her on the mouth which earned him a not very comradely slap in the face.

"Who the hell do you think you are? Cheeky bastard!"

"You've got a good right hook," he shouted after her as she stalked off.

But that had been some days before the Legión, the former monarchist forces, and the bombs from Italian and German planes crashing down on Madrid. Some months later, when fear stalked the streets of the city almost as much as at the front, and staying alive was a miracle on both sides of the trenches, Mateo ran into her one morning in Cuatro Calles.

"They still haven't killed you?" Casilda spoke first, smiling.

"No," Mateo returned her smile, "Because I wasn't out there worrying about you…"

This time, she was the one to slip her arms around his neck and kiss him on the lips with the same devotion, she brought to her impromptu meetings.

"Come on, let's go," she said taking his hand and he cursed his luck before refusing.

"I can't. Not right now, honestly. I have to get back to Usera, I have a dispatch for my commander – that car over there is waiting for me…" Casilda looked at the car and nodded.

"5, Calle de Espoz y Mina," she said simply, "third floor, left hand side. And try not to get yourself killed.

That day, Mateo Fernández Muñoz did everything in his power to get a furlough, a pass, a new assignment, a new posting as an intelligence officer, but in vain. The next day and the day after that he tried again with the same results until finally he went to see the Major, the only career officer fighting for the Republic, who found himself leading a rag bag of strays from the unions, locals, teachers, volunteers of all stripes and, among them, Mateo Fernández Muñoz who had joined the Spanish Socialist Workers Party in 1935 for purely ideological reasons and who was the only person under his command who actually knew what Marxism entailed. The Major had grown fond of this intelligent young man, so towards midnight when he saw Mateo, the commander smiled. For three days, while the bewildered Mateo had been trying to get a furlough at any cost, the Major had been waiting for him, and so he did not even let the lad finish the speech he had rehearsed.

"So you're telling me your mother is ill," he summed up and Mateo nodded.

"Yes, Major, I'm sorry."

"Tell me something, Fernández..." The wily authoritarian, who smoked continually, and could not speak without bellowing even when he was in a good mood, raised his finger and pointed at himself, "Do I look like an idiot?"

"No, Sir," Fernández smiled, against his better judgement.

"Ah, good! You had me worried..." he took a pad from the table, filled out a permission slip, and held it in the air, brandishing it like a toffee in front of a child. "OK. You go wherever you have to go and get laid – just once, got it? – twice if you're quick about it, and then get your arse back here pronto, by 5am. If you show up at one minute past five I'll have you court-martialled and shot as a deserter. Are we clear?"

"Yes, Sir. Thank you, Sir."

"And if we send these bastards packing and they ship us off to the godforsaken plains of Burgos, you'll see what war is really like, when the nearest town is fifty kilometres away, and I'll tell you something else..."

But Mateo had already taken to his heels and did not hear the end of the sentence. He did not know how he would manage to be back in time, but someone offered him a lift and after that, his luck held.

"At your service, Major."

At 4.45am, Mateo Fernández Muñoz stood to attention in front of his commanding officer who looked at him carefully, then slapped him on the back.

"Mother all better, Fernández?"

"Right as rain, sir."

"I'm glad to hear it. Just make sure she doesn't have a relapse."

After that, Mateo never again slept in the bedroom he had always shared with his brother, and Ignacio himself would move out a year and a half later. "So you're leaving me too," his mother never resigned herself to her children leaving, "But where will you sleep? Now I'll never get to see you or Mateo. I have no idea where you are or who you're with, well, it's a figure of speech, but listen to me, *hijo*, one of these days, the worry will kill me..." As he listened to her, Ignacio laughed. "You'll kill us first, Mamá," he said and kissed her forehead. "And as long as it's only worry, everything is all right." But by then nothing was all right. Things were going so badly that sometimes, in their separate beds, with different women, the brothers missed the whispered bedtime conversations, like this last one in which they told each other things they dared not say in the light of day.

"Are you awake?"

"No, Mateo, I'm asleep, you can tell by the fact that I'm talking to you."

"It's just, I wanted to ask you... Aren't you afraid?"

"No," But what he had said sounded so strange that he had to stop a moment and think, "I mean yes. Yes, of course I'm afraid, but never when it matters, never when I'm fighting. I'm afraid before, and afterwards... when I think that I could be dead, but when the commotion starts, I see things differently, it's as if I have eyes like a fly and can see everything at once. I don't know how to describe it, but I'm completely detached, calm and yet I have this rage burning inside me... Don't you feel that?"

"I feel the rage, but not the calm," Mateo smiled. "But I'm scared, all the time. I hold it together, so no one ever notices, and it's true that sometimes, at the worst moment, the rage takes over. But I'm still afraid."

"Good for you," Ignacio lied, "You'll live longer than me."

While his brother Mateo was fighting the war from inside a trench, Ignacio Fernández Muñoz was involved in the battles to defend Madrid and a number of other fronts. In almost every one, he received two different types of decoration: mentions, promotions, or medals, and wounds. He remembered every one, he could point them out and explain how he came by them in chronological order when he was seriously wounded for the first time, in Madrid, shortly before the end of the war. His parents went to visit him at San Carlos hospital and tears welled in María Muñoz's eyes when she saw him lying there naked, his skin a web of scars and stitches.

"In war, cowards die before the brave, Mamá," he told her, as though that might console her.

"Don't talk rubbish, Ignacio."

But his father smiled. He understood his wife's anxiety all too well and yet he was proud of this son he had once feared for. Mateo

Fernández Gómez de la Riva had always been a pacifist. To him, war had always seemed a terrible catastrophe and this war the worst calamity of his life, and yet every time he saw Ignacio's name in the newspapers, he felt a pride he could not hide.

"If your son were fighting with the rebels, the enemies would be falling over themselves to serve under his command." Even the Commander of the Armed Forces, for whom Mateo senior worked as an adviser, talked to him about Ignacio, "They're very superstitious, they believe that some soldiers are destined to survive, they even have a name for them... We're just as superstitious, but we explain things differently. We say war is unpredictable. How many times has your son been wounded? Quite a few. But always flesh-wounds, nothing serious enough to put him in hospital, a few stitches and he's off again... Honestly, I wouldn't worry about him. I've seen it many times, trust me. Ignacio has luck on his side."

And yet, although he would walk with his son down the Calle Fuencarral, watching as people threw their arms round him, listening to the whispers of admiration, Mateo Fernández had never trusted luck, nor had he ever forgotten that war is a terrible calamity. And he was thinking of Ignacio, as were his wife, his daughters and his son-in-law, when his first-born stepped into the living room on that autumn evening in 1938. But war is also unpredictable, and Mateo went straight over to María, pressed his forehead against hers, and asked her to forgive him.

Esteban Durán was not even twenty years old when a single, stray bullet pierced his skull. He was too young, and he was bored in this trench which seemed as deep as the moat of a derelict castle, bored of the stillness of these last days when it seemed as though the enemy had surrendered and forgotten to tell them, as though the fascists had deserted en masse out of sheer boredom. In the beginning, it had all been different. The trenches at Usera had been hell, then there had come glory, and finally exhaustion. The enemy had not passed, nor had they retreated, they had simply stopped and now they waited just across the rise, like a flock of vultures. Some days, there was sporadic gunfire to prove that the enemy was still there, other days there was nothing.

"Look at the head on that."

The corporals screamed like playground bullies, the sergeants scolded them like irritable aunts and the officers tried not to forget how young and hot-headed their charges were, though they no longer cursed their luck at having to leading a battalion of students who had never expected to be called up. After two years of war, the survivors had developed a maturity, except in their adolescent inability to cope with the inaction of a battle that had been fought to a standstill.

"Get your head down, you fool, or they'll blow it off!"

Behind him was Madrid, the streets, the buildings, the trams that no longer ran quite as often. Some afternoons, when she knew that all was quiet at the front because her brother Mateo was home on leave, María Fernández Muñoz would wash her hair, put on her high high-heels and take the tram to war. "I'm the sister of corporal (later sergeant, finally sergeant first-class) Fernández and I have an urgent communiqué for Ernesto Durán…" The duty officer would smile and she would giggle when she heard him shout, "Hey! Someone tell Esteban his girlfriend's here!" Towards the end, when the enemy seemed to have given up firing, Esteban would take María to one of the deserted buildings near the trenches and there, for half an hour, everything stopped: the fighting, the fear, the boredom, the bad news from other fronts, the screams that split the silent days.

"Get your head down, you fucking idiot!"

Esteban Durán, who had been in love with his sister's best friend ever since he went with his mother to pick up his sister at the school gates, enjoyed María's visits more than his furloughs, he remembered them as luminous, drops of intense, unadulterated happiness floating in the vast and desolate sea of days. He was not the only soldier to wake up every morning feeling as though his life depended on the tram, but many were unfortunate enough to be loved by cautious or reckless women, and every one of María's kisses seemed to hold him, bind him to the land of the living.

"I can still see heads!"

War was interminable, ugly, hard. María's visits were life, beauty, happiness; everything that war was not. And that afternoon, although Mateo Fernández Muñoz was on duty, he was lookout, Esteban sensed her presence. It was a sensation he had had on other afternoons, sometimes he was right, sometimes not. In the beginning, when the fear, the bombs, the hunger were new, María, who was mad but far from stupid, never came to see him if there was a chance she might encounter her brother. But in the autumn of 1938, the only reality was the war and now, María did not come to see him whenever she wanted to, but whenever she could, and every day he saved half of his rations in case he was lucky. "Esteban, you've got a visitor," In this topsy turvy world, the soldiers had more to eat than the civilians.

"For Christ's sake get your head down!"

Now, the baby of the family no longer tried to conceal her visits from her big brother, and he no longer felt it necessary to watch out for her, to ask, to worry. Not that they loved each other less, if anything they loved each other more, but it was different, because the only thing that existed now was the war, and they were losing the war. This was not the first afternoon that he heard the rumble and raised himself up to look for the tram, the truck, the car that might be bringing María. It was not the first time he had popped his head out of the trench and he had never suffered anything more serious than the ache of not being able to hold her in his arms. In the silence of this stagnant war, even the faint rumble of a vehicle in the distance brought the thrill of good news he had been waiting to hear.

"Esteban, get your hea…!"

Mateo Fernández Muñoz, who had promised his sister he would look after her boyfriend the moment he found out they were fighting on the same front, finished the sentence, but the man he was speaking to did not hear it.

By the last week of 1936, María was already in love with Esteban Durán. It had not been his uniform, but what it represented, the courage of a judge's son, of this timid well mannered medical student who had all but asked her permission before he kissed her, but who had won her over with a determination and a passion greater than others who had much less to lose. She did not know that this was the romantic longing that had led her mother to fall in love with her father, nor did she know that she would have to pay a terrible price for yielding to it.

"When they killed him, they killed my Esteban," she would say, and that possessive stuck in her mother's memory, in her sister Paloma's memory like a thorn they would never be able to remove. Mateo, who grieved with her for Esteban, never told his sister that his death has been a foolish accident. The first thing you learn in war, is that no death is foolish, all deaths are equally heroic, equally pointless, equally wretched. Seeing them cry, united in their grief, her mother remembered the respect she had felt for María on the afternoon she had seen her sitting on that same sofa, talking to Paloma as though she were the older sister, the afternoon she realised that her little girl was now a grown woman.

Carlos was still in hospital, though he was out of danger. At the beginning of 1937, he had been expected to die, but a month and a half later, Paloma was weeping as if she had forgotten that fact.

"The doctors have told me his right arm will be paralysed, and he'll be crippled, he'll be in pain for the rest of his life…"

"So…?" María tried to cheer her, taking Paloma's face in her hands and forcing her to look up. "He's alive, Paloma, he's going to live. So, he'll have a limp but he'll still be able to walk. He'll have only one arm, but he'll still have the other arm? And he doesn't need two arms to teach. He's twenty-six years old and the best thing is that next year he'll be twenty-seven, and then twenty-eight, twenty-nine. Don't you understand? Nothing can happen to him now." She went on stroking her sister's hands, squeezing them to let Paloma know she believed she would be happy. "They didn't kill him and now they won't get the chance to kill him, because he won't be sent back to the front. They'll give him a job in an office like Papá's, he'll be here in Madrid, he'll go to work in the morning and come home every night. Think about that, Paloma... Don't you see? You won't have to be afraid any more..."

As she listened, her mother realised how wrong she had been, and she felt sorry that she had doubted María, that she had doubted everything on that afternoon in that last week of 1936.

"Well, with your boyfriend or without him," she had said that afternoon, "I think you should still go to Levante. Believe me, I'd miss you more than anyone, but I would sleep easier knowing you were safe."

"No, Mamá, I'm not leaving," María had spoken slowly, without raising her voice, but with a determination her mother had never heard before, "It's not just Esteban. I've got a job in a government nursery. They need people, and I'm not just going to sit here twiddling my thumbs."

"I think that's a good idea," Mateo Fernández had unexpectedly agreed.

"But..." his mother turned towards her husband, "can we stop all this foolishness, please?" Then she turned to her daughter. "I won't hear of it, María. How can you have a job? You're still at school, you should be studying, you're only sixteen, *hija.*"

"I turned seventeen in October, Mamá. Ignacio is only fourteen months older than me and he's out in La Coruña with a rifle. The caretaker's niece, who's the same age as Ignacio is learning to be a tram driver. And you're telling me I can't go and tell stories to a few children who are all alone in the world because those bastards..." she lifted her arm and pointed towards the balcony as though German pilots were listening outside the window "... those bastards bombed their houses and murdered their mothers."

"María! I will not have you talking like that!"

"How do you want me to talk, Mamá?"

"All right," her father raised his palm, calmly interrupting her, "Your mother wants you to be polite. For example, say 'murderers' when you're talking about those evil fucking bastards."

"Very funny, Mateo," but although she did not join in her daughters' laughter, his wife smiled as she scolded him, "But that's exactly what I do mean, María. Because it could be dangerous…"

"Everything is dangerous, Mamá," María adopted a gentle, more persuasive tone, trying not to think of what would happen if her mother found out that she took the tram to the front to visit her boyfriend. "I don't know if you've noticed, but these days Madrid ends just down the street at the Glorieta de San Bernardo. They've already taken everything else. And since they're moving in a straight line from the sierra, we'll be next. The nursery I'll be working at is just past Cuatro Caminos, but I could just as easily be killed by a bomb on la Corredera when I go shopping. Those… murderers," she glanced at her father, "will only spare El Viso and the barrio de Salamanca. And anyway, I'm not going on my own. Charito will be working with me and Emilia is thinking about it. I was going to talk to Dorita about it too, even if she's a fascist, because she's good with children, but when I met her on the stairs we got into an terrible argument…" she paused and then continued in a voice very like the one her sister had used when mimicking her, "I'm so happy to see you María, I've got a little message for your brother Ignacio, and since I never see him now he's so busy killing people… 'Killing people?' I said, 'Yes, in the war,' she said. She asked me to tell Ignacio that she was dumping him and that when she agreed to go out with him, she didn't realise it meant being some Commie's girlfriend. You tell him, she said to me, that way he doesn't have to bother… You're right, I said, it's better if I tell him, that way my brother doesn't have to bother talking to a little bitch like you…" Her mother gave a sharp scream but María did not stop, "because there are hundreds of women throwing themselves at his feet. And do you know why? Because my brother is a real man, a hero, not like your brothers who are cowards, do you really think we don't know the bastards are hiding in a trunk in your house?!"

"You said that?" Paloma's eyes shone as her sister nodded, "Good for you!"

"Paloma! Really, what is going on in this house? Have you all gone mad?" María Muñoz slapped her hands on the table, got to her feet and looked at her family. "How could you do such a thing, María, how could you?"

"But I wasn't thinking of turning them in, what do you take me for?" her youngest daughter suddenly seemed as surprised as her mother. "I swear, I wouldn't have denounced them. It never even occurred to me, I promise."

"It doesn't matter! Don't you realise, it doesn't matter? They don't know that… Poor Doña Adoración, she'll be scared to death now, it's too awful to think about..."

"They'd do the same to us if they could, Mamá," Paloma said harshly.

"But we're not like them!"

"No, we're not!" Paloma vehemently agreed, "They were the ones who started it, they're the ones who wanted all this. We're only defending ourselves."

"That's not what I mean!" her mother suddenly felt terribly tired, and bitter tears welled in her eyes. "It's not that," she repeated, sitting down again, sadder now and calmer, "We've never been like them, we've never done the sort of things they do, everything we stand for is the exact opposite of what they stand for. Your father will tell you..."

Mateo Fernández loved his wife. He came close to her, hugged her and held her in his arms with the tenderness of a father cradling his newborn daughter, because suddenly he felt more sure of himself, more sure of the woman who loved him and their love, which could thrive even when times were hard.

"Your mother is right," he said, still holding her, "What is going on out there is shameful. And we cannot look the other way, because we are not like them. You know how I feel about this. I've said it often enough, but I'll say it again, I'd rather see your brothers dead than shooting people..." he looked gravely at his elder daughter, then his youngest, "...no matter how fascist, how dangerous or how guilty they are. That's something for a judge to decide, not people running around with guns. But, María, your daughters have a point..." He lifted his wife's head from his chest, brushed her hair from her face, "This is a war, and we didn't start it. They attacked us, we are defending ourselves, and you have sons at the front María, and your eldest daughter's husband and your youngest daughter's fiancé, and you should be proud of them, because all they are doing is their duty. Your sons are fighting everything you and I stand for, everything we have always stood for. Unfortunately this is not politics, this is war."

She got to her feet and straightened her dress, then without stopping to think, she kissed her husband and went out.

"I'm just going to talk to Doña Adoración for a minute..." When she reached the door, she turned back and looked at her daughters. "For the love of God..."

"Leave God out of this, Mamá," Paloma's voice echoed in the hallway, "He's not on our side."

Doña Adoración was reluctant to open the door to her. María heard the woman's footsteps, or maybe her daughters', as she rapped on the door, and tried to explain. Then she heard the footsteps walking away again quickly. She went back upstairs and sat on her own in the kitchen, until her husband came and found her there. He took her hands in his and said something she would never forget: "We are what we are, María, for good or bad, and our place is here with our own people". On 19 February1939, when she saw her children gathered in the Madrid house for the last time, this was perhaps another reason she believed that this would be the worst night of her life.

"What's all this?" Ignacio, who was exhausted, and who genuinely loved his brother and did not want to fight with him, had followed her into the kitchen. "That's some spread. If I'd known you had made all this, I wouldn't have invited everyone to Lhardy…"

María Muñoz smiled and looked at the feast she had prepared, a four-egg *tortilla de patatas*, fried sweet peppers, two quarters of a roast chicken torn into fine strips so that it would stretch a little farther, three onions cut into rings and seasoned with olive oil, salt and a little paprika and half a loaf of brown bread for the nine of them, ten if you counted her sister's niece, though she had bought some milk to make a little white sauce for her, because although poor little Angélica ate everything, she was only four.

"This is the last time we'll eat together for a long while," she said, "I was hardly going to serve lentils, we're all sick of eating lentils… But every day it's getting harder. This cost me a fortune, and even then, the onions are the last of the ones you sent us, the olive oil too…" María Muñoz paused and looked at her son, then finally said, "Are you still seeing that woman?" He nodded. "Be careful, *hijo*."

"Of course I'm careful, Mamá," Ignacio sighed and shook his head. "Careful not to get myself killed. That's all you need to worry about, not poor Edu. She's not going to hurt me."

Mateo had married Casilda some months earlier, after her father had been killed on the Ebro. "I don't want her to be all alone, and that way, if something happens to me too… It's always better to be married than single, isn't it, I think it will make things easier for her." It had been a brief, hurried wedding, there were no guests, and it lasted only as long as it took to fill out the form and sign their names. It had also been a sad wedding, but by then María Muñoz was accustomed to sadness, and Casilda, the eldest daughter of a typesetter and a seamstress whose father had set her to work in a printers before she was fourteen, was nothing like the sort of girl her first-born would have chosen as a wife if things had been different. But Mateo loved his wife and Casilda deserved his love, and things were not the same as before. She knew this, and yet even now she could not get used to the idea that her younger son was living with a married woman ten years older than he was. In spite of that, she regretted having mentioned her that evening, because Ignacio was right, he was still alive, and nothing else mattered.

"Do you know where tonight's dinner came from?" She went over to her son, hugged him and forced herself to smile, "Your father has been buying silver five-peseta coins, paying seven or even seven and a half pesetas for them... He's convinced that they are the only coins that won't lose value... We sold some things, and we converted everything we had into five-peseta pieces, he didn't want to mention it to you, because he didn't want you to think he was a defeatist... He's not a defeatist, you know that, he'll do whatever it takes... Anyway, I bought the ingredients for dinner tonight with all our loose change, piles and piles of *céntimos* – you should have seen me," she tried to smile again, but she could not, "I don't know when we'll all be together again, so don't fight with him, Ignacio, please, for my sake, please don't start arguing about the rights and wrongs of what's been done, and what shouldn't have been done, and whether it's all President Azaña's fault for not having that conspirator Sanjurjo shot. You need to cheer Papá up, build his confidence, tell him we can still win the war, promise me, because Papá is..." María Muñoz's voice faltered and her eyes filled with tears, "Your father's not well, Ignacio, he's ill, worse than ill, he's going out of his mind, he's going to die of a broken heart. You don't know, *hijo*. The Republic is everything to him, he has spent his whole life fighting for it. Sometimes I think he would rather die than... I have a bad feeling, María, he said me last night when we were in bed, I've a feeling that I'll never set foot in this shitty country again. That's what he said, and we cried, the two of us, and I thought about what my cousin Gloria said to me on April 14... It's terrible, Ignacio, it's so unfair..." She looked up and her eyes met his. "You can't know how much I hate them. I never hated anyone the way I hate them."

María Muñoz buried her face in her son's chest and Ignacio hugged her to him, experiencing a helplessness he had felt before, the same thick, black confusion, he had felt as his little sister had pleaded with him, shaking him, ordering him to do something. "Kill them, Ignacio, kill them, kill them all." María was screaming, hitting him, her eyes wide. "Kill them, Ignacio, kill them all." The day after Esteban Durán's funeral, his mother had clung to her, she had soothed her, held her in her arms until finally María broke down and wept. The day his mother fell to pieces, Ignacio needed help to react. It was enough for his cousin Mariana to appear in the kitchen.

"It's not over, Mamá, the war isn't over yet," he looked into his cousin's eyes and she held his gaze, "We still have half of Spain behind us, half a million men. It will be a long time before they kill us all."

Mariana Fernández Viu was the daughter of Lucas, his father's older brother, who at the age of twenty had had beautiful cards printed with the Ducal crown above his name and set himself up in what he called 'business'. He had never worked in his life other than to manage his inheritance with sufficient skill to marry a rich woman. The most fitting wife seemed to be a young lady from Pontevedra, who liked to show off as much as he did and as a result was less suitable than she had seemed. By the time his daughter, Mariana, was of marrying age, her parents were shut up in a country house in Galicia, the only house they had managed to hang on to. It was there that she met Rafael Otero, a delicate, ambitious young man with little education but many political contacts. He brought Mariana to Madrid in 1933 when his mentor, a right-wing member of parliament, offered him a ministerial job. The weather in Madrid did not agree with him and what he planned on being his rise to power resulted in a series of asthma attacks that finished him off him before the birth of his only daughter. Angélica was barely a year old when her father's enemies triumphed at the elections. From then on, Mariana lived with her daughter on limited means in a building on the Calle Blasco de Garay which survived the bombings only to crumble suddenly when the wooden buttresses that held it up collapsed. At that point, her uncle Mateo told her she could live with them. She would have given anything not to accept, but she had no choice. On that afternoon when her eyes met her cousin's in the kitchen, she had already been living with the enemy for a year.

Ignacio stared long and hard at Mariana as his mother sobbed silently, and he saw something in her eyes he had not seen before, a cold, metallic glitter. He saw patience, not resignation, and an easy calm. It was the calm of the farmer who pays no heed to the gentle rain slowly drenching his fields, the calm of the cook wringing the neck of a turkey, the calm of the gravedigger at his work, dreaming of the bean stew his wife has promised him for dinner.

Ignacio stared long and hard and Mariana held his gaze. He would never forget it, and there were many other things that night – words, gestures, silences – that he would always remember, his father's quavering voice as he said how ashamed he felt to be leaving, his mother's trembling fingers as she squeezed his sister-in-law's hand, pressing Casilda to take the bracelet, pleading, "Take it, please, I kept it for you, if things get worse, you can sell it. You might need the money when the baby's born…" He would never forget those words, nor would

213

he forget his sister María's strength, her smile as she said, "Don't be silly, Mamá, come on. You don't think we're leaving for good, do you? We'll all be together again soon, in France or in Mexico. And I bet you'll live to see a grandson born here in Madrid..."

Many things happened that night, words, gestures, silences. As they was going into the dining room, his brother grabbed his arm and looked into his eyes. "I apologise, Ignacio, I'm sorry. If anyone deserves to be promoted..." "No, Mateo, I'm the one who's sorry, I shouldn't have said that..." The brothers hugged each other and nothing more was said, and the brother who survived would remember that hug, would treasure it among his most precious memories, would relive it on the worst of days and the best, between the dizzy delight of love and the cold shock of death, between the rapid slide into poverty and the slow crawl towards prosperity, between the smell of fear, of carriages and trains, of nights spent in the open air, and the unconscious forgetting of that fear; later, he would relive it in his feelings and his desires, in the warmth of his wife's body on winter nights and the laughter of his children as they grew up without the weight of his brother's memory. Ignacio Fernández Muñoz would guard the memory of that hug like a priceless treasure, the safe-conduct that gave him leave to go on living, to be happy in a world in which his brother Mateo was dead. And yet, that night, as he walked outside, he could not forget the look in Mariana's eyes.

"Is she going with you?" he asked Paloma as they walked down Calle Fuencarral.

"Who? The Toad?"

"Paloma!" Carlos Rodríguez Arce stopped and looked at his wife but his outrage quickly dissolved into a smile.

"Is that what you call her?" Ignacio, for his part, made no attempt to hide his laughter, "It's a good nickname."

"You think so? María came up with it." It's just that she looks like a toad – you can't say she doesn't. She goes around all day grousing and grumbling, puffing her cheeks out and sucking them in, watching everything and never saying a word... She's disgusting!" She turned to her brother, "Of course she's not coming, though Papá did offer, more for the girl's sake than anything, the poor thing... But no... What could I say to her? 'Now that your lot are winning do you want to come with us?'"

"That I'd like to see," Ignacio raised his eyebrows.

"I'm sure it's true, I'm sure she spends all day down in that apartment listening to radio de Burgos, and then she comes up all smiles... and of course she's great friends with Dorita. She can't open her mouth without saying how charming she is and how it's such a pity that you two broke up..."

Ignacio glanced at Paloma, then at her husband, "If there one thing I don't miss, it's Dorita..."

Even if she had not been wearing that blouse, he would have noticed her, would have noticed the shock of red hair, the curvaceous hips, that look on her face that seemed to say she had seen everything but still wanted to see more, but the first thing he had noticed were her bare shoulders, pale and perfect sprinkled with just enough freckles. He liked what he saw so much that he leaned against a tree, lit a cigarette and stood watching her, watching the fabric as it swelled and fell with every breath. When he looked up he saw that she was smiling at him, a smile so shameless it would have terrified Dorita's fiancé and sent him scurrying away. But, luckily, he thought, I am not Dorita's fiancé any more. So he went up to the woman, took the basket she was carrying and said, "Give me your ration book and wait for me by the bank. I'll be right back..."

The women waiting in the queue for milk looked at him askance, and one or two grumbled – "every day it's the same thing... you should be ashamed..." because he would be served next, simply for being a lieutenant. "Here," he gave her back the basket with the milk in it. "Thank you," she said. "Don't mention it, in this heat, the kid would get sunstroke..." She lived nearby, in the Calle Viriato, and the basket was as empty as every other basket in Madrid, but he offered to walk her back. "So you don't have to carry all that," he said. She nodded and when she stood up, she adjusted the shawl in which she carried the sleeping boy, revealing the top of her pale breasts speckled with freckles.

She was a powerful woman, she had probably been fat before the war, now she simply had a rounded, fleshy figure. Hunger had been good to her, stripping away the unnecessary and leaving everything else in place. She said her name was Eduvigis and laughed as though it were a joke, she was thirty-one and had two children who were living in a village with her in-laws. "My husband took them with him last January, they're happy there, my brother-in-law told me, he comes up from Guadalajara sometimes. I'll just drop them off and come back, my husband said, but I'm still waiting for him. She looked after her neighbour's son, now that the woman had a job as a conductor on the trams. "That way we both get enough to eat," she said, "Well, when I say enough..." They were walking more slowly now. "I live here. On the top floor." "I'll come up with you," he suggested, "I can carry the basket." When they got upstairs she whispered, "I'll put him down," and slipped inside. Ignacio waited for less than two minutes. "Do you want to come in?" "Yes..." After that he spent more than a month away from Madrid. "When she saw him again she burst out laughing and, without a word, she let him in.

"The day Edu showed up," Paloma smiled, "The Toad was in the kitchen, and you can imagine… 'Terribly common, isn't she?' she said when Edu left, 'Really, I don't know how Ignacio could have sunk so low after Dorita."

"So low?" Carlos interrupted his wife with a laugh, "Edu is miles better than Dorita. And much prettier, too."

"Maybe," she gave him a gentle, jealous punch in the arm, "but I don't think the Toad is as degenerate as you, Carlitos… Anyway, Mamá said something that left her speechless. You know how Mamá can be when she wants… 'Two points, Mariana,' she said, "Number one: in this house no one speaks ill of my sons' partners. Two: I'd be curious to know if you find the food that Ignacio's wife brought as common as her, Because that girl has a mother, she has brothers, she has a family who are going hungry just like everyone else and she could have made a tidy sum selling this food on the black market. But she came here, common as she is, and brought us everything we need. If that seems vulgar to you, I am perfectly happy for you to give up your share."

"Good one!" Ignacio felt proud of his mother for a moment.

"Good?" Paloma raised her eyebrows, "It was better than good, the Toad didn't know where to put herself… You should have seen her, she turned seven shades of purple…"

"Poor Mamá!" Ignacio shook his head sadly, "Knowing the pair of them, it must have been terrible."

"I suppose it was, really," Paloma burst into giggles, setting off her husband, who knew the rest of the story. "What's her name, Eduarda?" Mamá asked me in a whisper, 'No, it's Eduvigis, Mamá," I said, 'a good Gothic name.' 'Your son raided a warehouse yesterday and ran into one of those thugs who've been hoarding food. He asked me to bring this over, he couldn't come himself,' she told us. And Mamá, I swear, she had tears in her eyes. That way we got to eat for a whole week without having to touch our ration books."

"Really?" Ignacio was astonished, "There wasn't that much food…"

"You think so?" his sister contradicted him, "Mamá collects recipes from "The Patriotic Cook" – mayonnaise with no eggs in it, béchamel with no flour in it, meat with no meat in it, she works miracles, honestly… That's why, when she opened that bag, you should have seen her 'Potatoes!' she shouted, 'Onions!' Of course the best thing was the *salchichón*. When María saw the sausage she said, 'why don't you hang it up in the pantry and we can worship it for a few days before we eat it?'

You wouldn't believe how much we laughed, I think it's the first time I had seen María laugh since Esteban died... 'What about you, *hija,*" Mamá said to Edu, 'Aren't you going to take anything for yourself?' Edu told her not to worry, there were only two of them and lots of us, but she asked Mamá how to cook 'Absent Partridge', because you missed it 'Oh, that's easy,' you know Mamá, she was thrilled to be able to help, 'It's just like making partridge stew, but without the partridge, wait a minute, I'll write down the recipe...' 'No, señora, don't trouble yourself,' Edu said, 'I wouldn't be able to follow it...' 'Don't you know how to read?' Mamá asked and Edu said 'No, I tried to learn from Ina, but I'm no good...' Paloma suppressed a giggle and Ignacio who had guessed what was coming laughed with her, '"Ina?' Mamá thought about this for a minute, 'What's Ina?', she was convinced it was some kind of government literacy scheme. Edu suddenly drew herself up, pushed out her chest, and said, 'Are you making fun of me, señora!' she said, 'What else would Ina be? He's your son!'"

"Ina?" Carlos laughed with them, "She calls you Ina?"

"Of course. Short for *Inacio*... What can you do? I'm very fond of her, but she is quite slow."

They had arrived at the corner of Hartzenbusch, and Ignacio was already running late. He put a hand on his sister's shoulder and smiled.

"Well, Paloma, at least you won't have to go hungry any more."

She looked at her husband and shook her head.

"I don't want to leave."

"Look Paloma," Carlos turned to her, tired and impatient, "We've talked about this already."

"Casilda is staying," she protested, "And she's pregnant."

"Casilda has just found out she's pregnant, and you know perfectly well that her mother and her brothers live in Cartagena, and she's leaving with them next week. Mateo has already arranged transport. You're leaving with your parents tomorrow because it's for the best, and that's all there is to it. We'll see how things go here, and when whatever happens, happens, you can come back or I'll go wherever I have to go."

For Carlos Rodríguez Arce it was difficult to say goodbye; he had been a teacher, role model and mentor to Ignacio before marrying his sister, but Ignacio was brief and not simply for Carlos' sake, but for his own. He hugged Paloma, and told her to eat well, then hugged his brother-in-law "I'll see you soon, all right?" Carlos placed his one good hand on Ignacio's arm.

"Be careful. Be very careful, and don't trust anybody..." he turned his head, looking around as though someone might be listening. "I've heard things… I don't know, there's something going on I don't like the sound of."

Ignacio smiled at his brother-in-law and thought how lucky he was not to have to fight this war from behind a desk, being constantly bombarded by news, alerts, rumours, predictions. Ignacio did not have time to pay attention to such things. Not that he did not listen to rumours, especially after the collapse of the eastern front and the fall of Cataluña. "We've lost the war", some said, "Bullshit," he'd say, the war would not be lost until the fascists marched into Madrid, something they would never do; and if they did march into Madrid he would not know about it, because they would have to kill him first. This was all that Ignacio Fernández Muñoz needed to know, the only thing more important to him than staying alive. Although he did still listen to news, rumours, alerts, especially now that President Azaña had fled to France, now that the political parties had disbanded, now that it was every man for himself, now that everyone blamed everyone else for the defeat they had not yet suffered or grumbled that only communists got promoted in the Republican Popular Army. For months, the anarchists had been whining like spoiled children over who got the most sweets; before they had hated the socialists, now they hated the Popular Army, it seemed as though they always needed someone to hate.

He had no time to waste on any hatred other than that of the real enemy, not the enemy within, the enemy that was still outside Madrid, because they had not passed, and would not pass. This was the only thing Ignacio Fernández Muñoz needed to know, the only thing more important to him than staying alive. Not that he did not listen to news, rumours, alerts, especially now that his parents were leaving and taking his sisters. His sisters had refused to leave when times were hard in the city and easy elsewhere, but now they too were leaving, by car, by boat, to Orán and from there to France. The friend who had organised everything was going on to Mexico, they were not. His father, Mateo Fernández Gómez de la Riva, had a good friend in Toulouse, a prominent republican who had offered to use his contacts with the French Left to help them find a place there. Mateo had accepted, deciding to stay in France so that he could be closer to his children, so that he could come back more easily.

Ignacio looked at his watch and hurried up the paso Fuencarral; he had to be at El Pardo by midnight, but he still had time to go to Edu's house, to spend a quarter of an hour there, half an hour if he hurried. As he came to the Calle Alburquerque, he turned and saw Carlos and Paloma kissing on the corner where he had left them; he could not know that this would be the last time he would see his brother-in-law. Nor would he remember Carlos's warning until 6 March 1939, when he was woken in the early hours by a sound he could not quite identify. He had arrived home, on leave, the night before, so exhausted that he lay down on the bed without even bothering to take off his clothes. Edu undressed him, took off his boots. "Wait for me, I'll be right back," she said, but by the time she got back he was already sleeping. But now, at 6am, she was sleeping while he was trying to identify the sound he had heard,' At first he thought it was a sniper, but then he heard shouts, orders, machine-gun fire. They have passed, he thought, no, like fuck they've passed, it's not possible. Less than eight hours ago, he had been at the front and everything had been normal. "What did you say?" Edu turned towards him and opened her eyes. "Nothing," said Ignacio, who had not even realised he had spoken aloud, "I have to go back to El Pardo." He got up, dressed hurriedly, grabbed his gun and rushed out into the early morning.

"Hands up!"

The shout exploded from behind him. Very slowly, Ignacio Fernández Muñoz raised his arms, very slowly he turned to stare at the four militiamen from the Iberian Anarchist Federation, their uniforms glittering with badges as they pointed their rifles at him. Ignacio smiled and lowered his hands.

"Jesus, you sacred me…"

"I said put your hands up!" The man giving orders said something to an older man who glared at the prisoner, his face a mask of hatred that was almost comical. "Take his weapons, Facundo."

"I don't understand…" but Ignacio had had enough experience of war to know that they were serious. "You guys are…"

"On your side? Oh, no…" and to underscore his words the man named Facundo pistol whipped him.

"Hands on top of your head where I can see them," said the other man.

"What's happened?" Ignacio Fernández Muñoz, a prisoner of his own side, marched down the Calle Bravo Murillo. He was not afraid, he was certain that this was a misunderstanding, an absurd mistake. "Aren't you even going to tell me why I'm being held?"

"As a communist. Better still, as an enemy of the people, a bourgeois, a counter-revolutionary and a queer, because that's all you communists are, a bunch of queers… Anyway, you're not in charge any more, all this shit about resistance and the Popular Front can wait, all that matters now is winning the war. The city has had enough of you, and it won't forgive your betrayal of the leader Negrín."

These words hurt Ignacio more than the pistol whipping he had received a moment before, so much so that he turned to challenge them.

"That's a lie!"

"I'll tell you what's a lie and what's not!" he felt the rap of Facundo's pistol butt against his skull again but he did not cry out.

"There's a new government defending Madrid now," the older one continued, "A genuinely revolutionary government of the people, with no communists, no bourgeois traitors and no cowards."

This can't be happening, thought Ignacio, not now, not today... They bundled him into a truck with half a dozen other men as bewildered and indignant as he was and locked them up in a cell at Puerta del Sol.

"What's going on?" "There's been a coup" "Who?" "Casado" "Casado?" "He had the anarchists and the socialists behind him." "Casado! ...a coup?" "Against the government." "Against us, they sold us out, it was just like the coup in '36." "But why?" "What do I know?" "They said that the communists were the only ones getting promoted in the army." "Then let them complain, but did they really need to stage a *coup d'état*!" "That's what they're saying." "Listen, I'm going to tell you something, if they'd put us in charge of the army at the beginning, I mean really in charge, it'd be a different story now." "And what's going to happen to us?" "I've heard they're going to court-martial us." "What for?" "I don't know, they're saying we are insurrectionaries." "Us?" "Like the fascists in '36?" "Exactly, but since I was in bed when I heard the shooting, I'd like to know how I could have been part of an insurrection, and an insurrection against who exactly?" "I thought they were the ones who'd organised the *coup*?" "I don't get it." "Me neither." "Of course Franco will be rubbing his hands with glee, they're going to hand us over to the fascists tied up with a red ribbon." "No, they're planning to execute us themselves." "What difference does it make? Franco still comes out the winner." "I don't understand, what the fuck went wrong?" "Nobody understands."

I'm glad my father isn't here to see this, thought Ignacio. At 11pm, the door opened and someone came in who did know what was going on. It was a journalist from the Communist newspaper, *Mundo Obrero*, and Ignacio knew him, they had played football together once or twice when they were children. I'm glad my father isn't here to see this.

"They came and arrested me at home a while ago," the man began, "but I had time to find out what's going on. Treason, fucking treason, a military coup just like the one in '36. Casado's taken charge, the socialist Besteiro is telling him what to do, and the head of the army Mera has fallen in with them, but apparently it's García Pradas, the head of the

220

National Confederation of Labour who's writing the speeches… They were all on the radio last night, they said that now that Azaña has resigned, Negrín has no right to govern, that Negrín is lying when he says he'll resist, that they're all running away like cowards…"

"Negrín a coward?" several angry, helpless voices protested.

"It's fucking unbelievable"

"Jesus, they've no shame."

"That's what they're saying," Ignacio's neighbour continued, "so they've set up what they call the 'Junta de Defensa'. Most of the counsellors are socialists, but there are anarchists involved, and they're all fired up. The socialists less so, and the ones who supported Negrín are opposed to it, then the rest of them are spilt. Most people don't know what's going on – I'm talking about the members, obviously. The leaders are the ones who organised the whole thing, and the anarchists seem to think that the coup is just the first stage in their stupid fucking revolution, but they're wrong, they hate us so much that can't see past the end of their noses, because what Casado is really doing is negotiating with Franco's government in Burgos. Even Mera said, yesterday, that his goal was to reach an honourable peace with no reprisals, or maybe they'll just surrender… Why would Franco negotiate peace with us now we're killing each other? You think that when he can smell victory he's going to negotiate? Did he negotiate in Asturias in '34, did he negotiate when he took Badajoz, did he negotiate when he got German planes to bomb the refugees on the road to Malaga and Almería? Like fuck! No one believes he will – and if they do believe that then they're stupid. That's why they have us locked up here. We'd never surrender, we'd never offer Franco half of Spain on a plate and they know it. They can call us cowards until they're blue in the face, but it doesn't change anything. They're going to throw open the city gates to Franco, you know they are, and the fascists will pass without having to fire a shot. Oh, I know they say they're trying to minimise the number of victims, but they've called up reinforcements to replace the men they've arrested. They're taking men from the front lines and posting them to Nuevos Ministerios, to Fuencarral and Chamartín where we were fighting. They're calling up rebels, but they haven't arrested them and why? Because to them, communists are cannon fodder, there's no other explanation. You'd better all get used to the idea, we are Casado's gift to Franco to keep him happy."

I'm glad you're not here to see this, Ignacio Fernández Muñoz thought, picturing his father, his gaunt, unshaven face, his lifeless eyes, refusing to eat, taking only small sips of water at that last family dinner when he had said that he was ashamed to leave. I'm glad you're not here to see our disgrace, our last humiliation… But the worst was yet to come. The worst they were spared until the following day. The worst turned up in the form of a lieutenant who had refused to go quietly, holding them off at his apartment on the Calle Ríos Rosas until he finally ran out of ammunition.

"We're fucked." He said by way of greeting, "we're completely fucked. The guys who arrested me at least had the balls to tell me that. Franco has given orders to his troops to let the anarchists from the XIV Division in Guadalajara through. Franco told his men not to fire so that they'd come running. The fuckers have got Mera's men to come and shoot us, all thanks to Franco of course."

"The bastards!"

"Traitors!"

After that no one said anything else. There was nothing else to say.

As the news sunk in, Ignacio Fernández Muñoz slumped back against the wall, slid slowly to the ground and beat his head against the stone once, twice, three times. Ignacio through about his father, his mother, the great joy they had shared for such a short time. I'm glad you don't know that we waged war on fascism for this, that we worked and slaved and screamed, dug trenches, choked back our fear, endured the bombings and the hunger, buried so many dead for this… Madrid, still holding out while others ate, others slept, others surrendered…

Ignacio closed his eyes, his ears against the clamour of a thousand silences. My family stopped fascism. What neither Rome nor Berlin could do, the Fernández Muñoz family had achieved. We stopped fascism at the front lines of Usera, at la Moncloa, in the University, in our dining room at home, "The Patriotic Cook"… In other cities, there was no need to fool your stomach. In other cities there was food, he'd seen it with his own eyes, fruit and lettuce and bread rolls. They said there was a football league at the front lines in Aragón, they said the soldiers were so bored they played football. Being at war and not fighting is boring, he knew that, but in Madrid, even the boredom was different, panicky, dark, dangerous. Because he was bored, my sister's fiancé was killed. Our wives endured the boredom of standing in the queue for milk, the queue for bread, for coal, but in Madrid it was simply one more part of the struggle, because we had to fight and fight hard, and all for this… I'm glad you're not here to see it, Papá, I'm glad you're not here to see it, Mamá, because none of us deserves this, Madrid doesn't deserve this ugly, heartbreaking humiliating defeat. But it was better to wind up here than to be out there, better to die a victim of treason than to live as a traitor.

He had joined the communists because he wanted to win the war, he had joined instinctively, intuitively, for very different reasons than Mateo, who had come to socialism through books. This was why he had volunteered for the Quinto Regimiento, why he was proud when they accepted him, because they did not take everyone. The Quinto Regimiento recruited only soldiers, real men, men like Ignacio Fernández Muñoz who knew what they wanted. And when he joined the Quinto Regimiento he felt at home. Other regiments discussed orders, voted on them, refused to submit to army discipline, but not the Quinto Regimiento. He served under Modesto and was so dazzled by the man's courage, his authority, his sangfroid that he became a communist so he could be like him, and serve under men like him, men who prepared to do anything to win the war, who never stopped, never tired, never complained. And he fought when he was eighteen, when he was nineteen, twenty, twenty-one, he fought to win, with those determined to win, men who screamed as he did, in silence, in that dank prison cell in Puerta del Sol.

When he heard his name, he thought he was about to die, but he did not care.

"Your brother-in-law's got balls, you know, for a guy who works behind a desk..." said the soldier who dragged him from the cell, "From what I heard, he's got that general he works for wrapped around his little finger. And he's been asking about you..." he looked round at his comrades and winked. "Maybe it's because you look like his wife, is that it?

They laughed at him, but he did not care.

"So I'm free to go?" he asked, though he did not care.

"No way. You think you're free? You were a captain by the time you were twenty. You like giving orders, getting promoted, bossing other people about."

They put him in another cell 'with the big shots', they told him. But there were no big shots in the cell, only his friend Vicente Dalmases, who had recently been promoted to captain and posted to El Pardo, and a couple of men he didn't know, lone men who were shattered, crushed, empty inside. The officer who worked the morning shift did not speak to them. The night guard, Rogelio, was a union man and gave them cigarettes because, Ignacio realised, he could not bear to see them locked up.

"They're transferring you all to the jail in Polier tomorrow," he said one night.

"Don't do this to me, Rogelio," Ignacio clutched the bars and looked into the man's eyes, "You kill me. I'd rather be killed by you than Franco. Shoot me or get one of your comrades to do it, but not Franco, Rogelio. Don't hand us over to them, don't let them take us alive. You do it, or give me your gun and I'll shoot myself right now."

He would happily have killed himself, he didn't care, but Rogelio was staring at him in silence, his eyes filled with tears. He walked away and came back almost immediately, quietly opened the door to the cell, then closed it over so that it looked as though it was still locked.

"Wait twenty minutes," he said, "Then make a run for it. There are guns in the cabinet in the hall, I've left it unlocked. Get rid of your badges, and don't let anyone know you're communists," he dropped his voice to a whisper, his face close to Ignacio's, "There are usually trucks in las Vistillas about this time…"

Ignacio didn't thank him. It was something he would never forgive himself for, but it was all so fast, so sad, so sombre and he was no longer himself, no longer capable of feeling anything, caring about anything, believing in anything. But he was capable of stealing a truck, capable of creeping up on the driver like some furtive, vicious predator, some animal with no scruples. "Hands up" It was his turn to say the words, and he remembered Facundo and his captain. The truck driver made a sudden movement and Ignacio killed him, but he did not care, because he was not a man any more, he did not think, did not believe, did not feel.

Three years later, in the pantry in a house in Toulouse, there was a bed and in it, by his side, a slight woman with black hair and large black eyes as beautiful as her hands, as her body, as the face she now lifted from his chest.

"What's the matter, Ignacio? Why are you crying?"

He gazed at her with a love he had never felt before, a love that had budded inside that stone that rolled among other stones, a stone that did not think, did not feel, did not believe in anything, until it found a love that made it possible for him to be reborn, to be a man again.

"I killed a man, Anita."

"Just one?" she smiled, "You killed a lot of men, didn't you?"

"No. The war killed the rest of them, but I was the one who killed that anarchist… I killed him because I wanted to. My life had been saved twice, first by Carlos, my brother-in-law, then by a socialist named Rogelio. They saved my life and I never thanked them, and I couldn't bring myself to forgive that man… Maybe that's the only reason I'm here. Maybe he would have killed me, he did something with his hands, I didn't know if he was armed – he had a pistol inside his jacket, I saw it when he fell. Maybe he would have killed me, but I'll never know because I shot him. They had betrayed us, they were murdering us, so I hated him, even though I didn't know him. I aimed at his head and I killed him, I couldn't bring myself to spare his life..."

"Don't cry, Ignacio," Anita pressed herself against him, comforted him, using the same words his granddaughter Raquel would use many years later before promising never to tell her grandmother. "Don't cry, please, don't cry."

It was warm in that field in Albatera in mid-May, but Ignacio's blood froze in his veins as he watched his brother Mateo climb into a truck, turn and look for him, then seeing him, bring the hand that was not handcuffed to his lips, kiss the palm gently and turn it towards him to say goodbye.

At that moment, Ignacio Fernández Muñoz realised that his heart was broken.

And that it was no longer a human heart.

The first thing I found out that morning was that María Victoria Suárez Mena, a girl from Zaragoza and a member of the Women's branch of the Falange, had offered to be my father's 'war godmother' after seeing his picture in the paper. A thin, lanky thing with a nose like a hawk's beak and a shock of red hair, she had enclosed a photo with the first letter she sent to him at the Grafenwöhr camp in Bavaria. It was a stupendous, deeply patriotic picture, framed by a wide clear sky, with a handful of decorative clouds, and a thin strip of bare, arid earth at the bottom. In the foreground stood a flagpole and next to it, there she was in a blue shirt, a shapeless skirt, and bare legs. Although her nose was a little too big, she wasn't ugly, though she had no breasts to speak of. In any case her looks were much less inspiring than her prose, a heady mix of inane bloodthirsty rhetoric which – in the name of the mothers of Spain, those kindly old women who sit around an open fire sewing with never a word about the terrible worry they feel for the sons they have given up for their country – encouraged him to crush, exterminate, eradicate, destroy, thrash and kill the culpable rabble of Russia.

Jesus, what a country! I thought, bored by the endless repetition, how can they be so fascist and so pompous - the loving arms, the puffed out chests, the smell of home-made bread, the tots clinging to the apron strings of Mamá as she bids her son farewell with a heroic smile that is sensitive yet strong, not to mention the Virgin Mary, I thought, remembering Father Aizpuru, our mother in Heaven, who might not wear an apron, but is determined to drape her protective mantle over the German tanks, all hail Europe, hail to the Führer, to his iron fist, to the defenders of civilisation, death to Marxism, to the tyrannical beast...

My father's 'godmother', like most of them, was barely seventeen years old, her spelling was shaky and utterly at odds with the limpid, extravagant passages she carefully copied out in handwriting as naïve as her parting advice: don't forget to wrap up warm, from what I hear it's cold out there in Russia. Until she got annoyed and her letters became more entertaining: Dear Julio, I haven't had a reply from you in some time, Dear Julio I'm scared because I haven't heard from you for so long, Dear Julio I know you are fine, but I haven't heard anything for months now, Dear Julio, if you didn't want me to write to you, you could have told me, this is the last time I'm going to write, Julio, and it was.

That peaceful morning, I had no classes so I began my day with María Victoria Suárez Mena's letters. I was alone in the house and sunlight streamed into the room my son called "the room with daddy's books", a study lined with bookshelves that was bigger than the living room, but so oddly shaped that Mai could not think what to do with it. I liked it, because it was a corner room with two windows opening onto a quiet terrace from which I could see the sky, and it was at the end of a long hallway, far from the living room, Miguelito's bedroom and the kitchen. I also liked it because it had two desks, something that intrigued the cleaner, though she never dared come in if I was there. Ignoring the desk with the computer on it, I cleared the books and papers from the other one and set down the blue cardboard folder and the small brown leather folder whose lock I had been trying to pick the previous afternoon.

The cardboard folder contained papers relating to Julio Carrión González: his military record bearing the date that he enlisted, noting that he was a minor but had his parents' approval, a physical description, height, weight, colour of eyes, vaccinations, date and place of birth, and his profession, listed as mechanic – all in duplicate – a German document corresponding to each document in Spanish, medicals, pay slips, a form detailing his admission to the Spanish hospital in Riga and a form discharging him when he left. There were photos too, lots of photos: my father wearing a Spanish army uniform, a German uniform, at attention, at ease, my father with snow up to his knees, mud up to his knees, fooling around next to a signpost with arrows pointing in opposite directions – Berlin 1485 km, Saint Petersburg 70 km – partying in a bar somewhere, flanked by two beautiful blonde women who seemed to be doing a lot more for his patriotism than poor señorita Suárez ever could, and later, when the fun was over, wrapped in a greatcoat, blankets, the only thing visible a pair of eyes that might have been his, might have been anybody's, standing guard beside a trench as the snow fell. His friend Eugenio was in many of the photos, the skinny lad who wore glasses and looked like an intellectual; my father told me that he had failed his physical but his family – all Falangists apart from his father – had pulled strings so that Eugenio could enlist.

I hadn't seen Eugenio at the burial, but he had been at the funeral, as skinny as ever, formal, elegant and exquisitely polite as he offered his condolences, first to my mother, then to his goddaughter Angélica, and then to the rest of us, whispering precisely the right words to each of us. I'd always liked him, and I couldn't imagine him bellowing out the advice my father's war godmother had appended to her letters, but he did, he must have done, because he wore the Falangist Yoke and Arrows on his lapel, until one winter night in the year that I was born. It was a night like any other until the phone rang and he heard his brother

Romualdo's voice. It was his brother who, in less than five minutes, told him that his daughter was a communist, that she had been arrested in a dawn raid at Moncloa and taken for questioning, that an officer whose name he would never discover had ruptured her spleen with a kick and dragged her out of there naked, that she was currently undergoing surgery at el Clínico and that the prognosis was bad. She ran away, so did he.

"Poor bastard," was all my father would say, "his children destroyed him. If ever this country produced an honourable man it was Eugenio Sánchez Delgado. If ever there was a man who could have exploited people but never did, could have robbed but never did, a man who genuinely believed in what he did, it was Eugenio, and for what? So that a couple of ungrateful brats could ruin his life…"

Anyone listening to him might have thought that his children's clandestine militancy had ruined him financially, but he was the one who walked away, he was the one who could not bear the fact that the regime in which he had invested such faith could arrest a defenceless eighteen year old girl, strip her naked and rupture her spleen.

The Sunday after the Communist Party was legalised, he and his wife came to lunch at our house. We all lived on the Calle Argensola, I was twelve, but I still remember the look on his face, the patience with which he handled the protestations of my father to whom the recent events in Spain seemed acceptable, even desirable – everything except this.

"Democracy?" he voiced the question only to answer it himself, "OK. Elections? Fine, I'm all in favour. Unions? If we have to. Socialists? Well, I suppose there has to be a left wing… But this? No, damn it! No Communist Party. Anything but that… Fucking hell. They've got democracy in the United States, haven't they? And what about England, that's a democracy, isn't it?" his tone grew louder, more passionate, more dramatic as he stared into his friend's eyes, looking for an approval he did not find. "But do they have a Communist Party? No, of course they don't! I can't believe it…" he eventually gave up, tired of asking questions that only he seemed to want to answer, "it's as if you don't care."

"That's because I don't care, Julio," his old comrade answered, his voice unruffled. "I don't like communism, but two of my children are communists, and I love them. They're young, they're passionate, and they fervently believe in what they say. Maybe they're making a mistake, but I made mistakes too when I was their age. So while I'm not happy about it, I'm not worried about it. I don't owe anyone anything as you well know."

My father fell silent and my mother changed the subject, and there was no mention of politics again until after they left when father said how much he pitied them. "Poor Eugenio," he told us, "his children have ruined his life." He concluded with his usual threat "if one of you gets involved in politics, I'll put you out on the street."

My two eldest siblings had experienced the last rounds of resistance against the dictatorship since Rafa went to university a few months before Franco died and Angélica one year later, but Rafa talked as if nothing had happened there and in the years before she left her first husband, the only thing Angélica remembered was the fact that until the day she finished her studies, she was paralysed with fear every time she saw a poster or an advertisement for the Youth Movement run by a young militant named Adolfo Cerezo. My brother Julio, who was born in 1961, was much more interested in politics, but he was drawn to the other side. He was the one who was the most eager to find out more about Papá's adventures in Russia.

"Were you in Possad, Papá? Did you cross the Voljov? Did you swim across lake Ilmen?"

"I was there, yes, I crossed the river Voljov more than once, but I wasn't at Ilmen, thankfully..."

Julio, who had learned German military vocabulary by heart, would take any opportunity to toss out battalions of words - Komandaturs, Oberkommandos, Luftwaffe, Wermacht, Sturnbannführers and Stablieters, his extravagant pronunciation mangling the words so they were incomprehensible.

"Did you get frostbite, Papá? Did they give you a medal?"

"Will you shut up, for God's sake! You're such a pest..."

Being four years younger than Julio, I sat in silence and observed their bickering, and every time Julio would come away convinced that our father had been a hero, but one Saturday night, after watching a film about the war in the Pacific on television, I dared to ask a question of my own.

"Why were you fighting for the bad guys, Papá?"

He glanced at me with a look of fear that resolved itself into a smile when he remembered I was only ten years old.

"And who told you they were the bad guys?"

"In the films, they're always the bad guys, aren't they? Besides, they lost the war. The good guys always win in the end, don't they?"

"No," he answered, "In the end, the strongest always win, but they're not always good. And after they win, they have lots of money and they spend it making films, and in the films the bad guys are always the ones

229

who lose."

"Maybe, but what about the Jews?" I persisted.

"You're right," he nodded, "But we had nothing to do with that. And a lot of the Germans we fought with had nothing to do with it either."

"So the Nazis weren't bad guys?"

"Of course there were bad guys. But the other side had bad guys too. And there were good guys on both sides, and sometimes it was hard to know who the bad guys were and which ones were less bad, do you see what I mean?"

"No," I said honestly, "I don't think so."

"You're only little, Álvaro, you'll understand when you grow up."

Time passed. One day Julio took down all the swastikas from the walls of the bedroom we shared and never mentioned them again. For several years, I had to study German and I learned to pronounce words that I had never felt tempted to say out loud, so I felt a shudder when I read – first in German, then in Spanish – the oath I found in the blue cardboard folder. "Do you, before God and upon your honour as Spanish citizens, swear obedience to Adolf Hitler, Führer of the German armed forces, in his fight against communism, and do you swear to fight as valiant soldiers, prepared at any moment to give your lives to fulfil this oath?" Underneath, first in Spanish, then in German, was the reply that my father, along with thousands upon thousands of Spanish men bellowed in 1941 at the moment they became German soldiers: "I swear!" On that sunny, peaceful morning in April 2005, I still did not understand.

"You know Álvaro's father was in the Blue Division?"

Fernando Cisneros understood better than I did. When I first went to university and met this tall, bearded, bear of a man, talking about the Civil War in the first person plural, I began to understand some things, although there were others I would never understand, and I made the mistake of admitting to him that my father had been in the Blue Division.

"Álvaro's father fought alongside the Nazis in Russia…"

This was at the beginning of the 1980s, while the dust of the dictatorship still clung to our shoes and whichever girl he was talking to would stop talking and shoot me a look of amazement mingled with compassion, if I was lucky, or disgust if I wasn't. Then he would invariably seize the opportunity to tell the story of his own fearless grandfather.

"OK, Fernando, that's enough now," I grumbled from time to time.

"Enough of what?" he would counter, "What are you saying? That it's a lie?"

"No, it's not a lie, but I don't want every girl on campus finding out. I'd like to get laid too, you know, and you're not making it easy…"

"I don't see why?" He shot me a look of smiling wonderment, "You've still got the Falangists. They're pretty hot, or so I'm told."

"Maybe, but aside from the fact that we don't know any Falangists, they're not my type. I get enough of that shit from my sister Angélica."

"It's your own fault," he said, laughing, "You shouldn't have had a Nazi for a father."

On the day his grandson presented his doctoral thesis, I met the fearless Máximo Cisneros and his equally admirable wife Paula. I had presented my own thesis some months earlier, though it did not even occur to my family to attend, although my father paid for dinner afterwards at a restaurant so overpriced it was beyond the means of anyone other than him. The whole Cisneros family came to the presentation of Fernando's thesis. His grandparents on his father's side were almost eighty, his mother's father was older still, but all three climbed the stairs to the hall and sat through the ceremony although it was unlikely they understood a word of what their grandson said during his presentation. When Fernando finally introduced me to Máximo, whose courageous story I knew by heart, I realised it had been worth postponing my return trip to Boston by five days. Changing my flight had cost me a fortune, but it had cost him much more to come here to see his grandson graduate *cum laude*, something that clearly made him happier than it made Fernando himself. I was excited to meet him, and I told him so, so much so that I didn't mention how many times his grandson had used the story of his suffering to get laid.

The last time he told the story we were both already over thirty. I'd just come back from the States, Fernando had got married, and his grandfather had died. We had gone for dinner, José Ignacio Carmona hadn't been able to come with us, and Elena Galván was complaining about having to shell out a third of her salary renting a place in Tres Cantos because her parents lived in Getafe on the other side of Madrid. She had casually added that she was from a military family. I had long since realised that Fernando was a law unto himself, but this time he caught me completely off guard.

"Really? You have something in common with Álvaro then… His father was in the Blue Division. I suppose your grandparents were too?"

"No," said Professor Galván, completely unaware of where he was heading, "my grandparents stayed here in Spain. They'd had enough of war."

"Yes," Fernando smiled back at her, "I suppose that's why they started it. Because if your father made it to colonel, that must mean both your parents were part of the revolution." She nodded, still smiling, "Where?"

"My father's father fought in Morocco, my mother's in Santander."

"Did we shoot him?"

Elena laughed. "No, you didn't shoot him. But he spent nearly a year in prison."

Fernando paused for dramatic effect, looked down at the table, then looked up into Elena's eyes and shook his head, his smiling fading until it was just a memory. I'd seen him do it so many times that I knew every gesture, every sigh. "Mine spent sixteen"

"Sixteen..." Elena looked serious all of a sudden, while Fernando was laying it on thick. "You mean your grandfather spent sixteen years in prison?"

"Fifteen, actually. Fifteen years nine months and three days." He paused again, then took a deep breath before making his final play, like a centre forward eyeing the wide expanse of the goal. "He could have got out any time, you know. All he had to do was apologise. He was a journalist, self-taught, his father worked in the printworks for a newspaper and got him a job as a runner, but he learned fast and was good with words. He was editor in chief of *Abc*, the republican newspaper in Madrid, during the war. He was sentenced to death, but the sentence was commuted to thirty years in prison, and he was moved from one prison to another until finally he ended up back here in Madrid. Then it occurred to him to set up his own paper in prison – a magazine, really. He did it pretty much all by himself and managed to publish an issue every month. It wasn't much - you can imagine - but he was happy. And the magazine had a good reputation among other journalists. So the governor of the prison offered him a deal. If he apologised – meaning, if he was prepared to write a series of editorials in which he admitted he was wrong, and flattered Franco – the governor guaranteed he'd be out within the year. My grandfather had been banged up for nine years by then. He said he needed time to think about it. He wrote to his wife and told her everything and my grandmother, who was on her own with two children, wrote back just sixteen words: "Dear Maximo, don't do anything for me you wouldn't do for yourself, I love you, Paula." He served seven more years in prison because he wouldn't apologise.

"Fuck..."

Elena Galván, a genuinely liberal girl from a genuinely fascist family – an ideal subject, in other words, for what we called the "Cisneros experiment" – was so shocked that she began to call us by our first

232

names.

After that, they took his newspaper away from him and gave it to another prisoner, someone who was prepared to write the sort of editorials they wanted, but they left his name on the byline." Elena closed her eyes, and when she opened them again, they seemed bigger. "They did it to humiliate him, obviously, but he didn't give in, they couldn't break him. Nobody could, until he finally got out of jail and had a breakdown. 'I can't do anything else, Paula,' he said to my grandmother, 'the only thing I know how to do is write,'" Fernando spoke as though it was something that had happened to him, every syllable causing him pain. "He was blacklisted everywhere and was never able to publish in a newspaper again. Of course, he wrote articles for the underground press but under a pseudonym. He took a job in a hardware shop and that's where he worked for the rest of his life, selling screws and nails…"

Elena gazed at him as though there was nothing else, no one else, but Fernando's eyes, his hands, his voice, and I – because I was there – I could think only of one thing: he's going to fuck her, the bastard's going to fuck her…

"Why don't you tell her the story of your other grandfather," I suggested, kicking him under the table "He was in prison too."

"Don't interrupt me, Álvarito" he stamped down hard on my foot.

A couple of years earlier, in a moment of weakness that he would always regret, Fernando had let slip that his other grandfather, Pepe, wasn't his mother's real father. "Unfortunately, my real grandfather's name was Florencio Jiménez," he admitted, "and he wasn't a fascist, he wasn't anything, he was a shit… He had a grocery shop in Legazpi and made a fortune on the black market during the war. His brothers were unimpeachable socialists," Fernando added, trying to salvage the family's reputation, "and they never suspected a thing, because he was always careful to do his black market business outside the neighbourhood, but everyone in Legazpi knew him so, instead of keeping his head down, on the first of April 1939 he stepped out on the balcony of his house wearing a blue shirt and singing the anthem of the Falangists, *Cara al sol*. When the Falangists arrested him, he bought his freedom by giving them the names of every communist he knew, and a few that he made up. The day he was released, he went back to his shop and waited for it to get dark. This was where he had stashed the jewellery, the silver, the watches he had accepted as payment for food and medicine. He didn't even go home to say goodbye, he just took off and no one ever heard from him again, until his wife, who had been

233

living in sin for thirty years with her brother-in-law Pepe applied for a divorce. That's when they found out that Florencio was in Mallorca, that he owned two hotels and a villa with a swimming pool and was living with a girl half his age. He said she could have a divorce as long as it didn't cost him a penny."

The story of Florencio Jiménez was much worse than my father's, but maybe even that would not have put off Professor Galván who, by the time the coffees arrived, looked as though she were about to fall to the floor and cling to Fernando Cisneros' knees, offering herself in reparation for the sins of her ancestors. Which is what she did, more or less. "Do you fancy coming back to my place for a drink?" she said as we got up to leave. Fernando got in before I had time to make up an excuse. "Álvaro can't..." he said simply, "but I'd love to."

I thought about that story and the other stories I had heard about Fernando's grandparents as I read the letters that my own grandfather Benito Carrión, had sent his son Julio from Torrelodones. There were only five of them, and they were dreary, full of spelling mistakes and clumsy syntax, 'Dear son, I hope that this letter finds you well, I am fine, thank God' but these did not surprise me as much as the fact that there was no mention of politics, no reference to murderous Marxism, or the bestial tyranny of Russia. Instead, every line was steeped in the profound faith of a man more worried about his son's soul than his survival. "remember to go to mass every day, do not lust after women, don't be ashamed to pray because to pray is to talk to God, remember that death lies in wait and you can never know when it will come, so prepare your soul so that you may die in a state of grace." That's cheerful, I thought, poor Papá, you go off to war and your father sends you stuff like this...

I hadn't realised that my grandfather had been quite so religious, although it was always the first thing my father mentioned about him. It was not a trait his son had inherited, just as – at least in my presence - he had never paid lip service to the ideals that had had him posted to Russia. My father was not a fascist, because his politics had more to do with fighting the things he despised than with trying to mould the world. He was anticommunist, yes, but more than anything he despised politics and politicians – the women more than the men. "Look at her!" he'd say when some election candidate appeared on television, "She should be at home cooking the dinner and looking after her children instead of mouthing off on television." Still, he managed to get on famously with them.

Although things had been going well for him for a long time, my father only truly grew rich during the last years of Franco's regime, especially after he rode out the storm of the energy crisis in the first years of democracy. For a man as charming as he was, the teams of military and the technocrats of the Opus Dei, who were unimpressed by magic tricks and silly jokes, had been difficult customers. The young, inexperienced democrats who had just come to power were much easier. He told them what they wanted to hear, presented himself as anti-Franco to a greater or lesser extent, hand-picked anecdotes from his repertoire that he thought they would like and effortlessly turned himself into the star of whatever event he was attending. Every morning when I came down to breakfast I'd find him in the kitchen with a glass and a couple of Alka-Seltzers. "Jesus, I've never gone out so much in my life, from what I can tell democracy means staying up all night..." My mother, who would go back to bed after Clara and I had taken the bus to school, was thrilled. And yet when Antonio Tejero Molino stormed the Congress with all guns blazing in 1981, she seemed much less worried than he was – he paced up and down the living room with his hands on his head repeating "this can't be happening, those bastards are going to fuck me over now, fuck, fuck..." He was so devastated and so furious that Mamá didn't dare tell him not to swear in front of us. That was how we found out, during the six long hours it took the king to prepare his speech for the television cameras, that the reason he was so upset was on account of some fantastic contract he'd been offered that hadn't yet been signed.

I was very young at the time, and I found my father's cynicism amusing. His manner made him an ideal parent: accommodating, patient, generous and beneficent – anything for a quiet life as long as none of his children thought him a fool. There were few things my father forbade us, because he usually managed to dissuade us in advance. He was a brilliant man, and even though it was impossible not to love him, the cold, calculating cynicism I had found so amusing as a teenager was what kept me from being truly close to him. It also confirmed my suspicion that Julio Ignacio Carrión could never have been a fascist, in spite of all the evidence to the contrary.

The evidence was spread out on the desk in front of me, but I was less surprised by what was in the documents than by the simple fact that they existed at all. The fact that my father hadn't destroyed them, had filed them away in a cardboard folder and had not even bothered to hide them seemed unbelievable at first. A fraction of a second later it seemed perfectly reasonable since it simply served to underline the implausibility of the life of Julio Carrión González. I was certain that he had felt no nostalgia for that time, that he had not thought about it for thirty years. I had often seen him fob off my brother Julio, parrying his questions with

235

monosyllabic replies. We knew he did not like talking about the Blue Division, yet he had not destroyed the evidence, hadn't locked it up in a safe deposit box. His silence on the subject, which had always seemed understandable to me, made what I had found all the more implausible, as though the papers belonged to someone else. Then I understood that if Julio Carrión González had not bothered to get rid of them, it had nothing to do with nostalgia or carelessness, it was simple laziness. Because these documents weren't dangerous.

"As all of you probably know, once upon a time, this country had an opportunity…" So began the first class I ever had with José Ignacio Carmona, "…and this country was robbed of that opportunity. It was not just the poets who went into exile, but the scientists, the physicists, the chemists, the biologists, the doctors, the mathematicians… So what? you might say, that was a long time ago, and you'd be right, but we still have the dust of the dictatorship clinging to our shoes, even you, though you might not think so. It takes a long time for plants in a desert to grow back, and unfortunately, the sciences do not recover as quickly as literature. That's why I would rather tell you this now so that you don't come back to me later and say I didn't warn you how difficult it is to be a physicist in Spain. Bear that in mind if you're having doubts about studying it, because there's still time."

When he had finished his speech, he stared at us, frowning, then he turned, picked up the chalk and started outlining the course on the blackboard. Nobody walked out, no one asked questions though a couple of people laughed quietly at this young professor who seemed so old-fashioned, so out of touch with the joy, the euphoria in the air now that the left was coming to power. But José Ignacio Carmona was right, as we would quickly come to realise, when we peered into the abyss to which all progress had been consigned. "Do you still give the same speech to the first years?" I asked him at the beginning of the year. "No," he said, "I'm more optimistic these days, but I still do the whole spiel about opportunity and deserts. The funny thing is, these days, when I finish the speech, they clap," he smiled. "It means they're more intelligent than we were," I said. "No, they're not," he replied, "it's just that they're looking at it from a greater distant. Optics is a paradoxical science."

By one of the paradoxes of optics, my eyes were focussed on a point somewhere beyond the edges of the blue folder, toward a horizon that had never come so clearly into focus. Once upon a time, this country had an opportunity, I remembered, once upon a time, this was a country of honourable men and women who did not keep documents in folders to justify themselves, they burned them. To such men and women these

236

documents were dangerous, but not to my father. Because there were no longer honourable men and women, only little men and women in a poor, pitiful, backward country doing whatever it took to survive, so that one day they might live in a great country, in a rich, first-world country in which everything happens by magic.

The hand is quicker than the eye, my father used to say, and he should know. One day, there was a war, then one day it was over, one day, slowly, thanks to the work and effort of a few, grass began to grow again in one small corner of the desert, but everyone got the credit, and how could you not understand, how could you not admit the benefit of understanding to so many little people struggling to survive, where the laws of arithmetic did not apply, where the credit due to a few could be divided among everyone, and the guilt of a few could be multiplied to everyone so that no one took any credit and no one accepted any blame. It was something my father always counted on, that Spain was a country where the laws of gravity, the laws of cause and effect did not apply, a country where no one had ever seen an apple fall from a tree, because the apples had always been on the ground, it was more practical that way, more convenient.

It was because they were not dangerous that my father hadn't bothered to destroy these documents, why he hadn't bothered to sort through them. But optics is a paradoxical science and magic an inconsistent art, an artifice that sooner or later crumbles under the inexorable force of the laws of physics. Lenses stick, they hide things, they get dirty. The bare branches of the apple tree, and the fruit carefully arranged on the ground are a clever trick staged by a set designer when there's no one around. It takes time for a desert to grow back, because the grass must push up through the earth before the eye can see it, which is why time, a lot of time has to pass before the day comes when someone remembers that apples don't grown on the ground, they must fall from trees, and first-year students applaud José Ignacio Carmona.

I closed the cardboard folder and set it aside. I had planned to track Raquel Fernández Perea through her lover's secret files, but what I had found here did not make me want to carry on. Suddenly, I needed fresh air, I needed to get out, away from the uniforms, the letters, the oath written in two different languages, away from my own suspicions. I was about to leave when I remembered that I didn't have another free morning until the following Tuesday and the lock on the leather folder needed only two taps with a hammer to get it open.

There were no cheque stubs inside, just a pouch filled with tissue paper, a single handwritten sheet of paper that had been torn up and stuck

237

back together with sellotape and a photograph of me standing behind the most beautiful woman I've ever seen, in front of a crowded café that looked strange for some obscure reason. On the back of the photograph, in an elegant, feminine hand, it read: "So you won't forget me. Paloma." and underneath, "Paris, May, 1947." Reading this, I worked out that the man in the photo wasn't me, and that the terrace had seemed strange because the tables – unlike those on the terraces of Madrid – were round.

Paloma, I thought, Paris. "You ought to have been in Russia, or Poland, now that was cold" my father had always said when we complained about the cold. He had been in Russia and in Poland, he'd been to Latvia twice, the first time when he was wounded, and the second just before he flew back to Spain, but Riga had been the last stop on his journey and he didn't fly back via Paris, nor had his journey home taken three years. I got up and scanned the bookshelves for an encyclopaedia but sat down again before I found one. Idiot! I said to myself, you know that the last troops from the Blue Division were back in Spain over a year before the Second World War ended. That wasn't the problem.

The problem had pale eyes and dark, glossy hair that framed her face like a ring of dark water. Her face was so beautiful that it was difficult to describe, to pick out a single crucial detail between the high cheekbones and the gentle curve of the lips, between the softness of her eyes and the stark purity of her jawline; between the elegant perfection of her nose and the perfect curve of her eyebrows. She looked directly into the camera with the trace of a smile, but it was her eyes, the cruel, enthralling flames that burn in the eyes of the huntress, that lit up the photograph. Her dress, made of some shimmering weightless fabric, hugged her body, marking out the perfect curve of her hips. She was as dazzling as the goddesses of the silver screen, the sort of woman they didn't make any more. But even that did not shock me as much as that first glimpse of myself standing beside her until I realised that this man who had my face was not me, but my father.

My father had been in Paris in 1947 with a Spanish girl named Paloma, the most beautiful woman I had ever seen, so that next to her he looked ordinary, shorter, weaker, smaller than he really was. Maybe because he was younger than she was. It can be hard to guess the age of a beautiful woman, but she looked as though she was over thirty, while he had just turned twenty-five. He was wearing dark trousers and a white shirt with a couple of buttons open and the sleeves rolled up. He looked curiously scruffy, this young man I had seen so often in uniform, let alone compared to the elegant gentleman he would become. Standing

238

behind her, he looked like an errand boy, while she sat on a high stool, her body turned towards the camera, her legs to the side, her head thrown back a little, resting against her companion's chest. And it was not just the way he was dressed. There was something curious in the man's bearing, in the arrogant, defiant curl of his lips, the determination in his dark eyes, a ferocity or perhaps a flicker of emotion, love, I thought, or desire or perhaps simply pride at having been chosen from so many.

The Spaniards living in Paris in 1947 had not gone there in the spirit of adventure, but I didn't know who she was, where she lived, nor which side she was on. All I knew was that this photo had been important to my father, since he had not destroyed it, and that it was dangerous, because he had taken the trouble to hide it. If I'd stumbled on this photograph among a stranger's papers, I would have thought he had a twin brother, someone identical but different to the smiling soldier in the German uniform posing at the crossroads, Berlin 1485km, Petersburg 70km. I was certain that they were the same person and yet I leafed through the cardboard folder again and took out one or two photos to compare them. I could find no document that might explain what my father was doing in a hostile country at such a difficult time. Nor were there any other photos of this woman. So I took out the letter that had been in the same pocket of the leather folder and placed it carefully on the desk.

*My dearest, darling son,* but this letter – from the familiar old-fashioned handwriting – seemed to be from my grandmother Teresa, *please forgive me for the pain I have caused you, I did not do so deliberately for I love you with all my heart.* At first I was disappointed, because Paloma's beauty deserved more. *And I will love you until the day I die.* And it was Paloma I was still thinking about, trying to work out her age, where she was from, why he had kept the picture all these years. *please try to understand me. And some day, when you are a man, when you have been in love,* until I realised that this was a letter of goodbye, *when you have suffered for love and you know the pain of heartbreak, maybe you will understand. If you can find it in your heart, forgive me. I made a mistake in marrying the man I married,* but I thought grandma Teresa died of tuberculosis, *but not in having two children whom I love more than anything in the world,* but you didn't have any other children, only Papá *you don't understand it now,* how can this letter be dated 2 June 1937, the day you died Grandma *but you'll grow up, you'll get older and you'll have principles of your own, maybe mine, maybe your father's, and you'll realise that there is more to principles than it seems, you'll realise that your principles determine how you live your life, how you fall in love, how you see the world, people, everything,* but the only thing he ever told me about his mother was that she played the piano badly, *never be afraid of ideals, Julio, because a man with no principles is not a man,* that she was good, that she was a teacher, that she loved her husband, *men who have no principles are puppets, or worse,* that she was a tart, like so many women, *they become immoral, dishonourable, heartless,* but this is not the voice of a tart, *do not be like them; be a good man, a brave man, an honourable man,* my grandmother was not a tart, and my father stole her from me, *be brave, Julio, and forgive me, we were unlucky, hijo, but one day the war will be over, reason and justice and liberty will win through, and when all of this is over, I will come and find you; we'll talk, and maybe by then you will think differently,* I never knew what my father thought, *and you'll understand me, I hope you'll understand,* all I knew was that he couldn't abide politics, *maybe I am wrong, but I am doing what I feel I have to do, and I am doing it out of love, out of love for Manuel, for myself, for my country, out of love for my principles and out of love for both of you, so that you might have a better life,* there's nothing worse than politics, nothing more sordid, more disgusting, *so that in your life you might know more freedom, happiness, justice,* if you want to ruin your life, you want to throw your life away, then go into politics, *I know you don't understand that now,* that was what my father used to tell us, the son of a woman capable of writing this letter, *but I love you, I have faith in you, I know you will grow up to be a good man, a brave and honourable man,* were you a good man, Papá? I wondered, were you brave and honourable? *Brave enough to forgive your mother* as brave and good as she was? This woman you never mentioned, this woman *who will always love you and who will therefore never completely forgive herself, yours, in Socialism, Mamá,* she was your mother, Papá, for fuck's sake, she was your mother, *My dearest, darling son,* as I started reading again from the beginning, my hands were shaking. I would have loved you grandma, I would have been a better man if I'd known you earlier, if I'd been allowed to read this letter instead of having to steal it, but you left the man you married for a better man and your son buried you alive, invented a life for you that you would not have wanted to live, and obliterated his sibling because he went with you or because you took him with you. My father had ripped up this letter and stuck it back together, long ago, the sellotape was yellow and peeling away from the paper, as though at fourteen he had already decided how to live his life, how to fall in love, how to see the people, the world, everything, maybe that's why he didn't go with you, but he grew up to be more than a man, he grew up to be a magician, a wizard, a snake-charmer, the most irresistible man in the world. He was lucky, grandma, he got to be rich, important, powerful, but we were not lucky, this country was not lucky, reason and justice and liberty did not prevail. Could you have come to find him, grandma, did you wind up in prison, in a mass grave, in a ditch by the roadside? You can't begin to know what your love means to me, you can't know how proud I am to be your grandson, your son's son, I loved you long before I knew you Teresa, I have always admired people like you. And I know it has come too late, I know it is a pyrrhic victory, that it cannot make up for that defeat, but you have won the war now, grandma, a victory that is of no value to you, but it is important to me.

*My dearest, darling son,* I read the letter again, *please forgive me for the pain I have caused you, I did not do so deliberately for I love you with all me heart,* I read it over and over, learned it by heart, read it until I was sure I would never forget it, until I cried myself out, forced myself to see it though my father's eyes, *when have suffered for love you might understand,* tried to see it through the eyes of a fourteen-year-old boy whose mother had just abandoned him, *If you can find it in you heart, forgive me, I made a mistake in marrying the man I married,* and to be fair to that boy, I repeated that word, abandoned, that squalid, ugly word over and over, *but you'll grow up, you'll get older and you'll have principles of your own,* and I had grown up, I had formed my own principles, and they were very similar to what I was reading. Now I didn't feel like the treacherous son who listens to rumours put about by his father's enemies, because this voice called out to me, spoke directly to me, because it was my grandma's voice and she was right, *do not be like them; be a good man, a brave man, an honourable man.*

"What's all this?"

I hadn't heard Mai come in. Nor had I been expecting her so early, but when I looked up and found her beside me, pointing at the papers on the desk, I remembered that Miguelito had a birthday party that afternoon and didn't need to be collected until eight o'clock.

"They're some of my father's papers," I said with a vague wave of my hand, "When I took the money round to Lisette yesterday, I found this folder. Look…"

"No, I was talking about the photo…"

My grandmother Teresa, youthful and serene, wearing a simple hat, tiny pearl earrings and a jacket buttoned to the throat, the very picture of a bland, bourgeois housewife, smiled out at us from the silver picture frame – it had been a wedding present but we'd never used it because we thought it looked too solemn. I'd spent half an hour searching through every drawer in the house for it as soon as I'd happened on the portrait in the blue folder among several photos of her with her husband and a photo of the two of them with father aged four or five posing in front of the pond in the Retiro. Benigno wearing a dark suit, a white shirt, no tie, but with a thick belt, ill at ease in his Sunday best, his cap in hand, blinking as though the sunlight bothered him. He looked older than he did in his wedding photo, but it was less the age difference that distinguished him from his wife and more his sullen, contemptuous, almost neurotic expression. Not only was Teresa better dressed, she looked happier, more comfortable in the city, with her son in her arms. She was clearly more sophisticated than her husband, more confident, more worldly.

"It's my grandmother Teresa," I said to Mai, "My father's mother."

"I know that," she nodded, "What I don't know is why you've framed the photo. Wouldn't a photo of your grandfather be better? Look…" She picked up a photograph of Benigno Carrión from the desk and showed it to me, as though I hadn't seen that face every day for years when I looked at my father, as though I hadn't seen it every time I looked in the mirror. "You're the spitting image of him, and he's a lot more handsome than your grandmother."

"No," I said with a brusqueness she didn't understand.

"Well, I think…" she insisted.

"Anyway they're not your grandparents, they're mine - the frame has been lying around in a box for the last seven years, and I'm going to leave it here in the study, so I'm the only one who'll be looking at it."

"OK, OK…" Mai tossed the photo onto the desk and stared at me, shocked and upset. "What the hell is wrong with you, Álvaro? Your mother's right… you've changed."

"No, it's not that…" I got up, hugged my wife and kissed her face. "I'm just worked up. I've spent all day going through this stuff, it's amazing. Here, let me show you…"

I showed her the photos of my father in his German uniform, in his Spanish uniform, saluting, showed her the most cheerful of María Victoria Suárez Mena's letters, grandpa Benigno's sanctimonious letters to his son, the oath of loyalty to Hitler and watched as she read in silence, as she began to frown, and her face soured.

"Gives you the creeps?" I said at last and she looked at me, her expression almost frightened.

"Yes, it gives me the creeps. Seriously" she said, but I noticed a little click of her tongue before she spoke, something like a switch turning on, the tremor of a chord breaking. "But you can't help feeling sorry for him, no? I mean the poor thing, what else could he do back then, with the

242

country in the state it was, life was tough, people were starving…"

"Of course," I didn't like hearing her make excuses for him, and she realised as much.

"You don't think it's understandable?"

"He was my father, so my opinion doesn't really count," I sat down again and looked up at her, "What's important is that you empathize with him, don't you?"

"Well, yes… because I'm in no position to judge. I have no right to decide whether he's guilty or…" she glanced at me and saw something in my face that convinced her to change tack. "We didn't live through it, Álvaro, who knows how we might have reacted to such a difficult situation, to all that violence, the hatred, and the deaths. It's not part of who we are. I suppose you and I would have been pacifists in '36."

"Well I know I wouldn't have been, Mai," I countered, "and neither would you. Because there were no real pacifists."

"But there were decent people."

"Of course there were, they were all Republicans."

"Don't be ridiculous Álvaro! Really, it's impossible to talk to you, you're starting to sound like Fernando Cisneros…"

Mai was right, I did suddenly sound like Fernando, I was saying things he might have said, and if what I was saying wasn't exactly bullshit, it was hardly a dispassionate statement of fact, but I didn't care that I was being unfair. Mai hadn't said 'good people', she had said 'decent', and looking into her eyes I felt that between these two adjectives, something had shattered. But if I did not show her my grandmother's letter, it was not because I was trying to put the pieces back together again. If I didn't tell her what had happened to me that morning it was because, just in time, I remembered her grandfather Herminio. I knew only that his surname was López, that he'd been a labourer in Cáceres and had enlisted as a volunteer only to be killed three days before he got to the front, that he had died too soon, too young, too close to his home town.

I didn't know what he looked like and neither did Mai. In her parents' house, there were no photos of him, his name was never even mentioned except when they were extolling the virtues of his widow – as though he'd decided to get himself killed, and it was his fault that his wife had to carry on alone. No one had any sympathy for Herminio. Mai, who was so liberal, so pacifist, so wrong-headed, sympathised with her own father, who had chosen to expunge all trace of militiaman López when he became engaged to the youngest daughter of a second lieutenant who never found out that his son-in-law was the son of a communist.

243

"Imagine, the poor man, what he must have been through..." she said when I first met her, and when I heard those words I sympathised with her father too. And if I hadn't read my grandmother's letter, these words that had weighed so heavily on me, calling out to me after so many years, I might never have remembered that Mai also had a secret, dangerous grandfather. A grandfather who had been quickly, untidily buried by his son, just as my father had buried his mother. This was why, before apologising, I thought of her grandfather Herminio López, a man without a face, a man without a history. Maybe it wasn't Mai's fault, but it had to be someone's fault, because apples don't grow on the ground. Apples have to fall from trees.

"You're right," and in conceding to her, I altered the phrase that had triggered the argument, "I shouldn't have said that. Obviously there were good people on both sides. It's just that..." I gestured towards my father's papers, "... this makes me feel sick."

"I can understand that," just as well, I thought. "I'm popping out to buy a few things, do you want anything?"

"If you were to bring me back some pastries from La Duquesita, I'd be eternally grateful," she smiled and kissed me.

After that, things happened quickly: my mobile ringing, Fernando's voice, out of breath as he asked me a question I didn't understand. "It says I have a missed call from you," he said, and he was right, because a couple of hours earlier I had given in to temptation and called to tell him everything, but I'd rung off as soon as I imagined how the conversation might start "Hey, I've just found out, I have a heroic grandparent too..." Fernando had his own ideas. "So did she call?" "Did who call?" "Your father's mistress." "No, nothing like that." "Well that's a let-down!" he said after a long pause, "I was in the middle of a tedious budget planning committee and I thought it must be that so I rang you straight back," "Well you can go back to your meeting then, because there's nothing to tell..." As I was about to hang up, I picked up the leather folder to put it back inside the blue one and I thought I felt something else in there. I emptied it out as I said goodbye to Fernando, but the phone rang again immediately.

I found myself with two identity cards in my hand, both bearing the name Julio Carrión González, both issued in Madrid, the first issued in July 1937, the second in June 1941.

The first was for the Unified Socialist Youth.

The second for the Falange Española de las JONS.

The call was from Raquel.

I was about to tell her I needed time to take in what I had just seen, to make sense of what I had remembered, to reformulate the most complex and serious problem I had ever faced in my life. I needed breathing space to work out a hypothesis in order to redefine my concept of probability, redefine my father, redefine myself. I'm here, I was about to say, I'm a physicist, probability is something I can rely on, something I need. I need to feel that there is some cosmic order that holds up my small, insignificant shoulders. But right now I don't know who I am, don't know what I signify. I need time to think about it, about the chaotic structure of a reality that seems to be crumbling and its repercussions on my fragile, inadequate mind.

I felt exhausted because, to me, curiosity had never been like this. For me, curiosity is a methodical process, a linear sequence of data, a precise number of formulae requiring a precise number of solutions, which make it possible to formulate new questions and so on ad infinitum. I know it doesn't sound like much, it's not very original or exciting, but I'm not a detective, I'm a physicist and I need to be able to predict things. And right then, Raquel was the least of my problems. At the end of the day, an eighty-three year old man with a thirty-five year old mistress is biblical, an age-old premise, and therefore it is entirely plausible, it respects the relationship between order and chaos. I was about to say all of this, and I would have were it not for the fact that the moment I heard her voice the cards burning my fingers were transformed into two ordinary bits of cardboard, the sort of useless thing I might find in my pocket.

"Hi, it's Raquel, we have to meet up," she said in a single breath, as though she was about to tell me not to get any ideas. "I need to give you a couple of things that belonged to your father, and I'm guessing you haven't got much on right now."

"Um… I don't know…" her last comment disconcerted me, "Why do you say that?"

"Your exhibition," the tank woman, on the other hand, was very sure of her own power. "The private view was last Friday, wasn't it?"

"Yes… it was."

"How did it go? Did you sell much?"

"No, I didn't sell anything." I laughed and recovered some of my composure. "It's not that kind of exhibition, it's an exhibition in a museum."

"About what?"

"Black holes."

"Wow." She paused and I could hear the smile I couldn't see. "Sounds terrifying and mysterious."

"Well, that's precisely why I put on the exhibition," the physics professor took over, "To show that blacks holes are neither terrifying nor mysterious."

"Really? That's a shame."

"Why?" I smiled, "Are you a fan of mystery and terror?"

"More than you might think. I still haven't got over people saying there's no such thing as extraterrestrials..." just as I was about to contradict her, she cut me off. "No, please don't explain it to me. I'd rather go on believing in Close Encounters of the Third Kind."

"Typical woman," I said.

"I'm not quite sure how to take that..." she paused, "Well you can try to make a man of me if you like."

"What? I would never do something so stupid."

"No?" she stifled a giggle, "Why not?" she paused again, hoping that I would answer, but I held firm. "What I meant was, you could take me to see your exhibition."

"Would you be interested?" I had expected anything but this, and was even more surprised to note the thrill of excitement her suggestion gave me. "Would you really like to see it?"

"I suppose..." she adopted a comic, slightly condescending tone that did nothing to discourage me. "I mean, we've already been for Japanese, and the only other thing I know about you is that you're into Physics. I mean, we could meet at La Cúpula del Palace, but that's the sort of place I'd suggest if I were meeting your mother. I'd rather deal with you, even though you are the black sheep of the family. I suppose I could suggest a bar, somewhere quiet, elegant, expensive with soft lighting and designer furniture, the sort of place I'd never invite your brothers, but I find bars like that tacky. Or maybe a café – the Commercial or the Gijón – I'd feel more comfortable there. If I were free in the mornings, I could go to the university and sit in one of your lectures, but as you know I'm a busy woman. Busy, but curious. The other evening you said you didn't paint so I thought maybe you spent the weekends sculpting or woodcarving or restoring furniture, but black holes are a lot more interesting. More in keeping with your foibles."

"Of course," I said, "I only hope they're in keeping with yours."

"So..." she said, laughing, "shall we meet up there?"

"No, it's probably easier if I pick you up and we drive there. The museum is in Acobendas."

"As far as that?" she sounded surprised.

"Far?" I said, "That's not far, it's just round the corner... Anyway, it's worth the trip. As you know, I'm a very good teacher."

"We'll see about that," she laughed again, "So how does tomorrow sound?"

"Tomorrow?" I said tentatively. Tomorrow I thought to myself, tomorrow fuck, fuck, fucking hell, why so soon? Why tomorrow? Why does everything have to happen at once?

"I say that because it's Friday, and that way if we're having a good time, at least we don't have to get up early the next morning... Obviously if you've got a wedding reception or something on Saturday we can leave it for another time."

"No, no, I mean, yes, if you like..." You're a complete bitch, Raquel, this is dangerous. "I don't have anything on tomorrow."

This was a lie. I was supposed to be looking after Miguelito. Mai was going out to dinner with her girlfriends. She'd let me know well in advance. So, before she reappeared with half a kilo of pastries from my favourite bakery, I remembered that Clara, who owed me a favour, had already agreed to have Miguel for a sleepover – pizza, popcorn, films and karaoke - the sort of thing Miguelito couldn't resist and his mother couldn't object to.

Once I had got them both to agree, I thought about Raquel. Not about my grandmother, nor the letter, not about my father, nor the two membership cards, his uniforms, or the oath of loyalty, just about Raquel. Everything else could wait, because all I could think about was Raquel Fernandez Perea, the only woman who had ever made me lose control, who, without trying, had disturbed my lush peaceful garden where nothing happened unless I wanted it to happen, unless it was consistent with who I was, with my life, the life of a man to whom random things simply didn't happen.

I couldn't stop thinking about Raquel. I couldn't. And when I saw her, as I ran my tongue along my razor-sharp teeth. I felt that same thirst, that same perfect, pure desire I had felt that first night when she'd arrived dressed to kill. Ten, nine, eight, I'm falling. My heart leapt into my mouth with the agility of a well-trained pet and the shock was so great that I didn't even notice she was not alone.

"Hi," she leaned towards the car window, her breasts taut against her low-cut dress, "Get out for a minute, I want to introduce you to a friend of mine."

The other girl had short hair that was dyed pink with mauve highlights, a bit over-the-top, but it suited her. She was tall, big boned, good-looking at first glance, though less so when I looked closely at her – the opposite effect that Raquel had had on me.

"This is my friend Berta." She gestured towards me, "This is Álvaro," she looked at me, "Berta wanted to meet you, she's heard so much about you."

"She's right," Berta came up to me and kissed me on both cheeks.

They both smiled at me separately before smiling at each other; I tried hard not to blush and realised that I had failed. I should have expected something like this, but I hadn't thought Raquel was capable of improving on her previous military campaigns. To get her back, and because I couldn't think of anything else to do, I stared at her friend. Berta's skin was a little rough, but she had a good body, and she was wearing green combat trousers with dozens of pockets and a pink spaghetti-strap top.

"So are you interested in black holes too?" I asked.

"That depends..." Berta laughed, "Not as much as I am in other holes..."

"Do you want to come with us?" I suggested, and regretted it even before I had finished the sentence, though I was pleased to see that my suggestion made Raquel nervous. "Up close and personal, I guarantee, they're more interesting."

"No, she can't..." So nervous that she was the one who answered. "It's a pity, but Berta has a rehearsal. Actually, she's going to be late..."

Berta quickly backed her up, kissed us goodbye and walked away slowly as though she didn't care if she was late.

"Is she an actress?" I asked Raquel when she was sitting in the car next to me.

"Yes. Theatre. She's good too," she smiled at me, "She's rehearsing, Valle-Inclán's *Barbaric Comedies*, they're doing all three. You should come to the opening night."

"She's not much like you," I said, as I tried to start the car and keep my eyes off her body.

"Who, Berta?" she seemed surprised.

"Investment advisors don't normally have friends with pink hair and diamond studs through their nose."

"We're best friends. We've known each other for years," she looked at me and paused, "You know, I tried to be an actress too. Or at least I was in the drama society at university. That's where we met. Berta was talented, I was terrible."

"I don't believe that," I said.

"Well it's true, honestly..." she turned to look at me as she spoke, "I liked the theatre, I loved acting, but it didn't come to anything. It's not that I couldn't do it, it's just that even I didn't believe in what I was saying, and after a while I couldn't get the lines out. I'd dry up halfway through. We put on Strindberg's *Miss Julie* once, do you know it?"

"No," as I shifted gear, my hand grazed her knee but she didn't move away. "Should I?"

"Of course you should!" But she smiled as she said it, forgiving my theatrical ignorance. "It's a masterpiece! A story of impossible love... there are only three characters, Julie, the daughter of a Count, her footman Jean, and Kristin the cook. The director, who was playing Jean, was interested in me so he offered me the part of Julie, she's young, beautiful, rich and aristocratic but in truth she's unhappy because she feels trapped by social mores, she hates it, it's like a prison, but she doesn't dare to escape. Julie despises men, she feels being attracted to them is a weakness, but she's in love with Jean. She knows she can never marry him, that he'll marry the cook even though he's in love with her."

"What a tragedy!"

"Well it is! What do you expect?" she accepted my sarcasm good-naturedly. "The play takes place on the Feast of Saint John when the footman and Miss Julie meet. She flirts with him, he seduces her and they decide to run away together. It ends at dawn when Miss Julie's father, the Count, rings the bell which is the symbol of his power. It's the sound that brings them back to the real world, returns each of them to their allotted place. It's one of the best parts ever written for a young actress, a gift... I did my best, honestly, I rehearsed and rehearsed, but every time I said the lines I couldn't bring myself to believe them, I couldn't believe in Julia's suffering, her hysteria, her rage... So I gave up, I stopped going to rehearsals, and quit the drama society for good. In the end Berta played Miss Julie and she was so good they extended the run."

She paused, as though she was expecting some response from me. I felt disconcerted, not simply because it would never have occurred to me that she had wanted to be an actress, but also, maybe particularly, because of the artlessness with which she'd told me this story, as though she didn't care what conclusions I might draw from it. I had never been certain of her behaviour and now, though it seemed childish, I had another reason to distrust her, this skill, this self-assurance which from the start had seemed artificial and rehearsed. Yet her revelation didn't put me off, for I had become a guinea pig, a lab rat, that knows what is waiting at the other end of the tunnel but can't resist going through it, the same way the bull can't resist charging a matador's cape.

"What's the matter?" she asked. I remembered that she was an intelligent girl, and I knew that she knew what I was thinking.

"Nothing." I realised there was no need to explain further.

"I'm a really terrible actress, Álvaro, believe me, I am."

"Can I ask you a question?" She nodded. "It's a bit personal, you might be offended."

"If I don't like it, I won't answer."

"Did you sleep with the director?"

"Álvaro!" she burst out laughing and I did too, we laughed so hard that I veered onto the hard shoulder and didn't even realise it until I heard the noise, the tat-tat-tat you get when you the car crosses the white line. "I don't know how a nice boy like you could ask such a question!"

"Just curious," I replied, "Anyway, you don't know what kind of a boy I am yet."

"Seriously?" She laughed again, but I didn't look at her this time. "I suppose you're right… And yes, I did sleep with him. I was nineteen and he was thirty, I was a terrible actress and he was a very good actor…"

"And you believed in him."

"Of course. We were together for a while, but he never forgave for walking out. First I left the theatre, then he left me. It didn't really mean that much to me. Oh, I cried my eyes out at the time, but I was grateful afterwards. I've never met anyone who so attracted and infuriated me at the same time. He was handsome, intelligent and sexy, but he was also neurotic, a perfectionist to the point of mania, he was the most neurotic man I've ever met."

"That's the theatre."

"Yes," she smiled, "But it can be wonderful too – and nothing wonderful comes for free."

That's why we're in this mess, I was about to add, but I didn't say anything because I was having fun, and I almost felt disappointed when we arrived in Alcobendas.

Stepping into the foyer, I glanced at the pendulum and congratulated myself on my ingenuity and the synchronicity of time, space, chance, the traffic in the city, and the planet. Two and half minutes, I calculated, three at most. I looked at my watch, and explained the structure of the museum to Raquel, leading her slowly towards the circle of vertical rods between which a large sphere oscillated. A moment before the impact, I fell silent. Raquel looked at me, surprised and I pointed towards the pendulum.

"One," I counted aloud, "Two," I paused, "Three."

The ball knocked over one of the rods. She looked at me and smiled.

"What happened?" she asked.

"What happened?" I asked.

"The ball is spinning?" she guessed.

"No, The ball doesn't spin. The pendulum moves continually between the same two points, first one way then the other, always with the same force, the same inertia, the same reassuring stability," she frowned, thinking, "What's moving is the earth, Raquel. It's moving right now beneath your feet, turning on itself, that's why the ball hit the bar and knocked it over. In twenty four hours it knocks them all down. Don't tell me that's not wonderful."

"It is," she finally admitted, her eyes on the pendulum, "It really is."

"Better than the theatre?" She laughed. I loved it so much when she laughed. "And better still, it's free."

She turned towards me and her laughter resolved into a deep, radiant smile, the small expression of a private joy that I would later come to know well. It was her way of saying that she was happy with me, that she was delighted to see me. It would not be long before I learned to live hanging from that thread, that smile which, that afternoon, I did not yet understand.

"I really like it," she looked at the pendulum one last time. "Come on, teach me some more."

I gestured in one direction and slowly began walking. For better or worse, I was still the same, the son of my father, the magician, the playboy, the wizard, the snake charmer, a more extraordinary man than any of his children would ever be, the lover of the woman who was walking by my side. He would not have hesitated, and I did not hesitate. I had a few more things up my sleeve as spectacular as Foucault's pendulum, but I tried to eke them out carefully, planning the tour as though it were a performance, setting traps, altering the logic, the immutable laws of the universe. All that mattered was her, impressing her, making her happy, softening her up, winning her admiration the way a magician might, if he wanted to save the best trick for last. Raquel allowed herself to be led, adopting the curious, reverent, rapt attitude I had often noticed in intelligent adults and in most of the children who visited the museum. But what most impressed her was something that happened right at the end, as she was staring into a spiral that I could stare into for hours…

"Hey, mister…"

It was a girl of about twelve. She had been watching from a distance as I encouraged Raquel to push the red button, as I told her to be patient, as inside the vast bowl something began to move, began to change, began to take on a surprising, ethereal form… Raquel let out a shrill, excited gasp.

"It looks like… a miniature tornado," she said almost fearfully, as though she was afraid of saying something stupid.

"It doesn't look like a tornado..." I said, "It is one. You're looking at a tornado, a small one but a tornado just the same. It's the closest thing on this planet to a black hole because it even absorbs light."

"But," her eyes shone with such intensity that for a moment her face reminded me of that beautiful unknown woman Paloma, I thought I could see a similarity – in the shape of her face, the angle formed by the chin and the neck, the high cheekbones. "How do you do it?"

"I can't tell you that. We Magicians never reveal our secrets."

I expected a wink, some spark of recognition, but she must not have heard me repeat the mysterious, frustrating phrase with which my father had invariably concluded his performances when I was a child, because she was still smiling into the tornado, absorbed by it, her eyes shining with childlike enthusiasm. My own eyes were drawn to her beauty, dazzled by it, blinded by it; it seemed to exert some tyrannical power over them, as though forbidding them ever to look at another woman. It was at that moment that the little girl shattered the illusion.

"Excuse me, mister... Do you understand this stuff?" She gestured around her at the exhibits. I nodded. "Could you explain something to me? There's something I don't understand..."

I walked with the girl to the exhibit demonstrating the Coriolis effect while she explained that she'd come with her school, all her friends were in the shop and her teacher was no use because she only taught maths and was never very good at science. What I don't get is, when I look at it, it looks weird, and I know that something weird is happening, but I can't work out what it is." I was amused by the way she talked, her forcefulness, the brusque way she interrupted me in mid-sentence before I'd finished explaining the effect.

"Of course, that's it," she yelped, "the water isn't flowing the right way, it's going down the drain the wrong way..."

"That's right," I said, "so do you understand it now? That's why, when you turn on a tap in the Southern Hemisphere, the water drains in the opposite direction to what we expect in the Northern hemisphere."

"I get it now," she nodded emphatically as though someone had wound her up.

"Actually," I said, "What I've just explained is written on the sign. I should know, I wrote it. Next time, even if it seems a bit long, it's best to read right to the end before asking questions."

"I know," she started to blush, "But I was listening to you telling her stuff, and she wasn't reading the signs either..." she pointed over my shoulder to Raquel, who was now standing next to me. "Anyway, sorry..."

"No, don't be sorry, it's not a problem. It's just that I'm not always here."

She thanked me again and ran off.

"Clever girl, isn't she," I said to Raquel, "That's the best thing about working here."

She gave me a strange look, though not as strange as the words she said next.

"I think I was wrong about you, Álvaro."

"What do you mean?"

Raquel Fernández Perea couldn't have known about the documents I'd found in my fathers study, nor what had happened the previous day. She couldn't possibly have known about the existence of the little leather folder with the flimsy lock, she couldn't have read my grandmother's letter, though she might have seen the photos of her lover wearing his Spanish uniform, his German uniform, and some night when she was foolish enough to complain about the cold, she almost certainly would have heard him talk about the weather in Russia and Poland. I was fairly sure she couldn't know anything more, it wasn't logical, it made no sense that Julio Carrión González would brag to some young girl about a past he did not want even his children to know about. And yet, as we walked slowly towards the exit, her words hit me like a volley of sharp, judiciously aimed arrows.

"Because you're not like your father."

"That's what you said the other night."

"I know, but… then it was just a hunch. Now, it's a certainty."

I stopped and looked at her, her serious, almost solemn expression belied by her tender, half-closed eyes.

"Is this about the girl…?" I wondered aloud and she nodded. "I was happy to talk to her, explain things, because then I know I'm not wasting my time…" she nodded again and I slipped into the warmth of memory, "Papá would have criticised me for wasting my time on things like this. He did it often enough – my mother still does. The only time she ever came here she said it was more like a children's playroom than a museum. It wouldn't even have occurred to my father to come, but if he had he would have agreed with Mamá. Neither of them ever really understood what it is that I do, they've never really tried…" Raquel Fernández Perea was still staring at me with the same solemn expression, the same tender eyes. "My father was handsome, rich, powerful and ignorant, the way only rich and powerful men can be ignorant: not because they don't know much – my father knew a lot of things – but because they behave as though whatever it is they don't know about

253

doesn't exist, as though it's trivial or worthless. You know that, or at least you must have suspected it, I mean you knew him, and yet…"

"And yet I slept with him," she finished the sentence for me, "that what you were going to say, wasn't it?"

"Yes," I was afraid I'd done something stupid, but she didn't seem offended or angry with me. "Sorry."

"What for?" she smiled again, "Don't worry. It's just I don't feel like talking about your father."

"Me neither. Fancy going for a drink?"

"Don't tell me there's a bar here too?"

"Oh yes, and you're even allowed to smoke in it."

"You know what?" she took my arm, pressed against me for an instant, but it was enough to dispel the awkwardness of the conversation, the insinuations, "I'm going to tell you something I've never told anybody. It's stupid, but, I don't know, I just thought of it… In my final year at secondary school, they gave me a test, like an IQ test – I'm sure you know the kind of thing."

"No, I went to Marist Brothers School…"

"What, and everyone there was clever?" I shrugged my shoulders and she laughed. "Well, anyway, we all had to do them. There was a rumour that a lot of the questions were trick questions, and you had to read every question twice so as not to fall for them, and it was true. In the Maths test, there was data missing in the problem, and in the Language test some of the answers were identical. Then later, on a different sheet, there were two almost identical drawings of a housewife hoovering. They looked the same, with headscarves and pleated aprons and faces like something out of a 1950s advertisement, but one of them was hunched over more than the other because although they both had their left hand on the handle, the first woman had her right hand halfway down the extension, while the other woman had hers much farther up, near the handle. Do you see what I'm saying?"

"Yes," I smiled, "I've seen that sort of drawing."

"I'm sure you have. So, the question was 'Which of these women will end up feeling more tired and why?' So, there I was, I'd always got good marks, was one of the best in the class, and I put neither of them because the vacuum cleaner engine does all the work… Can you believe it, I was the only one who got it wrong? The only one, honestly, the teachers couldn't understand it. Even my friend Marga, a moron who got herself suspended from school at least three times a year got it right. And she said, 'Have you never used the vacuum cleaner at home?' so I said, 'of course I have, lots of times' and she said 'how could you get it wrong, then?' I didn't know what to say. Afterwards it occurred to me to argue that it was outrageous, in a girl's school to have a picture of a woman pushing a vacuum cleaner as an intelligence test designed to test your aptitude for university, it was sexist, and that that was why I'd answered the way I had."

"Very clever," I admitted.

"Maybe, but I still didn't get the marks. That damn Hoover lowered my average in science. In the final examination they recommended I study humanities... And that's not the worst of it... The worst thing is I still don't understand."

"Well, I can explain it to you if you like."

"OK."

She grinned and went on smiling as though walking through the cafeteria, the light, the commotion, the catcalls of the children pressed against the railing had changed something until we found ourselves somewhere else, somewhere unfamiliar yet comfortable, not simply because Julio Carrión González had disappeared but because the intimacy Raquel had instigated when she took my arm had been reinforced by a flurry of little gestures. It fascinated me to watch her movements, analyse and interpret them every time she leaned forward and brought her face close to mine, every time she brushed my fingers with hers then quickly pulled them away, every time she folded her arms on the table and leaned on them, carelessly or deliberately, pushing her breasts together, but what I found even more compelling was the lightness of her voice, weaving a commonplace story and yet one which was strange to her and precious to me.

"Well, I think I should phone Marga and tell her I finally know the answer to the vacuum cleaner question."

"Do you still see her?"

"Not much, but I still see her from time to time. She was my best friend in secondary school and when we started university, but she studied to be a teacher, then she gave it up, got married, had a kid, then I got married, both our husbands were assholes, I got divorced, she didn't, she had a daughter, I didn't, and now... We just don't see much of each otherus... I love her, but I can't understand how she can live like that. Obviously she thinks exactly the same thing about me, but anyway, she's not nearly as stunning as Berta, so you got a good deal."

" I didn't think Berta was all that stunning," I objected.

"That's because you haven't seen her naked," she raised one eyebrow and laughed. "It's not that big a deal – it's obvious you don't go to the theatre much! Directors are always getting her to take her clothes off..."

I'd never heard her talk like this. I was so caught up listening to this ordinary, funny, ironic, intelligent, bitchy woman I had just discovered that I didn't notice the waiter arrive.

"Álvaro, *darling*, it's a quarter to nine," the waiter said and I realised then that we were the only customers left in the bar, "It's not that we're closing up - we should have closed fifteen minutes ago."

"Sorry, Pierre," I said, putting some money on the table. "I didn't realise."

Pierre was tall, heavy-set, muscular with sideburns like a bandit and a long thin moustache which seemed entirely incompatible with his style.

"No problem, honey, it's just that today is Friday," he said as he headed towards the cash register. "And you know what happens on Fridays."

"Well I don't know," Raquel protested, "What does happen on Fridays?"

"His boyfriend comes home, I explained, "he's in the army or rather he's a professional in the Armed Forces, as he says. You should see him on Mondays, he spends all day sighing and complaining about how he aches all over."

"Why do you call him Pierre? Is he French?"

"No, he's from Talavera de la Reina, It's just that he thinks Pablo sounds too butch," Raquel was laughing so hard, enjoying herself so much, that only then did I think of something that I should have thought of earlier. "Do you want to hang on here for the change. There's something I forgot to do. I'll meet you at the front door in a couple of minutes…"

The shop was closed, but one of the assistants came over and opened the door, tapping his watch as he did so. When I came out, Raquel didn't ask why I'd kept her waiting or what was in the plastic bag. The motorway was clear and we were back in Madrid before we realised it. At the first light on the Paseo de la Castellana I turned to look at her.

"What are you looking at me like that for?" she said, nipping her lower lip with her teeth.

"Where are we going?"

"I don't know," she shrugged her shoulders.

"Of course you know Raquel, you always know everything. You always have done."

"Which would you prefer, a plan including dinner or not including dinner?"

"Depends what the alternative to dinner is," she laughed, but quickly recovered herself.

"Well, I don't know," she shrugged again, "How about another drink?"

"Where?"

"What do I know" she smiled, then turned to the window for a moment, as though she needed time to think, but I wasn't going to let her off that easily. "That way, I suppose."

"In that case, I'd prefer to eat first."

She'd reserved a table at a restaurant close to where she lived and where everyone seemed to know her, just as they had in the first restaurant she'd taken me to, but this time I didn't need her to explain the menu to me.

"Here," I took a gift-wrapped box out of the plastic bag and put it on the table.

"For me?" she picked it up, brought it to her ear and shook it, "Is it a present?"

"Yes, but it's not a present *for* you … It is you, it's like a metaphor, something that defines you."

She frowned at me, carefully took off the wrapping paper and took out a cardboard box. She seemed disappointed.

"This is me?, she said, "a board game?"

"It's not a board game," I said taking the box, "Don't go all economist on me Raquel."

I took out the contents of the box. I set the base – a black plastic circle with two grooves in it – on the table and slotted the two transparent side pieces into the grooves. Then I took out the most important piece. The external pendulum was crossed vertically by an oval piece of metal which held the inner pendulum – a rod with two plastic balls attached, one red, one black that spun freely. A couple of small horizontal rods stuck out from both sides of the metal oval a few centimetres beneath its centre of gravity. I slotted them into the Perspex walls so they would support the double pendulum which now swung in the air.

"This device, which you so disparagingly dismissed as a executive toy, has two pendulums – see?" I said, holding them tightly so as to give nothing away, "The outer one is an ordinary pendulum, it swings over and back, over and back, over and back, always the same. But the internal rod is a chaos pendulum, it's like you." I set the first pendulum in motion, waited a few moments and then the second began to swing wildly. "It's impossible to predict which way it will swing at any point - see? It speeds up, slows down, stops, starts, changes direction, changes its mind, seems to be mocking us... It's unpredictable, unknowable, fascinating, but it's never the same, because it moves according to a

257

mysterious force, but you'd never guess that if I hadn't told you, it's funny, brilliant, strange... just like you."

She stopped the pendulum and set it going again. Then she looked deep into my eyes.

"I'm all those things?"

"And more..." I said, captivated. "I forgot to mention that watching it is addictive. Like the sea. You never tire of looking at it."

Raquel Fernández Perea closed her eyes, covered them with her hands, smiled and sat motionless for a moment. Then she began to shake her head.

"This is madness..." she whispered before picking up the menu and saying at a more normal volume. "Would you like to share something?"

"Yes," I paused, waiting until she looked up at me questioningly, "Madness."

She closed her eyes again and blushed.

"Apart from that?" maybe she'd been telling the truth, maybe she was a lousy actress, because her voice was shaking.

"Apart from that, I don't care, so why don't you order for us both? I mean, that's what you would have done anyway..."

And yet she gave me the option of staying sane.

Dinner was hurried, awkward and confused. Raquel didn't eat much and I didn't eat anything, but we both drank a fair bit. The wine she chose soothed my palate without eliminating the tingling sensation I could feel on my tongue. It was fear, but it was delicious, the thrill of being overwhelmed by her every gesture, by every movement of her body as it tensed, relaxed, shifted.

I tried to anticipate how she would feel, the taste, the smell of her, everything I might sense through my hands, my fingers, my lips. I wanted her so much that I didn't even remember that I had forbidden myself from thinking about my father.

She had decided to behave as though nothing was happening, offered me a way out when we both simultaneously said "no" to dessert.

"Shall we go?"

"Please," I choked on the word as though I really was drowning.

Leaving the restaurant, we walked at some distance from each other in the direction she had chosen, as men and women do on the brink of their first time. We came to the doorway of an old house. The façade had recently been painted a daring blue which contrasted with the creamy white of the antique mouldings. She leaned against the wall and from her bag she took the stainless steel propelling pencil and the silver pillbox I had found in the bedroom she had shared with my father. She placed both in the palm of one hand and looked at me. She didn't say anything, she didn't need to. She was offering me a way out and I rejected it, kept it in my pocket with the final excuse, the final pretext. Then I kissed her, and as I was kissing her, for the first time in my life I was perfectly aware of the earth turning on itself, wheeling about the sun, just beneath my feet.

On 25 April 1944 a young, silent, dark-skinned man, with a military crop but civilian clothes stepped off the Berlin train at Orleans. In the inside pocket of his jacket he carried a card issued in Madrid in 1937 by the Unified Socialist Youth and bearing the name Julio Carrión González. In the right-hand pocket of the same jacket, he had another card, issued in 1941, also in Madrid, also in the name of Julio Carrión González, this one for the Falange Española de las JONS. Somewhere in his bag, carefully folded, were a German uniform, a Spanish uniform and between them his military record and a safe-conduct in the name of Julio Carrión González issued in Riga some four months earlier by the Commander in chief of the Spanische Freiwilligendivision or the Blue Division.

The man should not have been on this train. Members of the Blue Division had been repatriated in autumn 1943, except for some 3,000 volunteers who elected to serve under German command. But even these men – the Blue Legion – returned to Spain in April 1944 as Hitler's armies were preparing to retreat from the Eastern Front. There was no reason why Julio Carrión should have been in this place on this date, and yet all of his documents were authentic.

The solider with multiple identities was travelling alone, carrying only one light bag, but ten minutes before the train was due to arrive at the next station he would make take it from the luggage compartment, put on his scarf and his hat and nod goodbye to the other passengers with whom he had not exchanged a single word. If any of them remembered him, they would only remember him leaving the train just as, when he climbed into the next compartment, the passengers seeing him struggling to put his bag into the luggage rack, before taking off his scarf and hat, would assume he had just boarded the train.

As they came into Orleans station, he repeated the same obvious, exaggerated actions as he had every other station. And as before, he stood away from the carriage door, his hat tilted forward, hiding his face, politely allowing ladies, old men, couples with children and – especially – German soldiers on first, always taking the last place. In Orleans too he waited until all the passengers joining the train had boarded, but he did not follow them into the carriage itself. Instead he stood by the door until the train started to move and as the engine slowly pulled out of the station, he jumped down ending up far down the platform, a long way from the other passengers who had just disembarked and were greeting people who had come to meet them, or dragging their suitcases towards the exit. He began to walk towards them quickly, purposefully, fingers crossed, as though he had nothing to hide. As he turned the first corner he pulled off his tie and tossed it into a rubbish bin, and as he rounded the second corner, he took off his hat.

This young, silent, dark-skinned man who had genuine documents of every sort was in fact Spanish, but he had no desire to go back to Spain because he was convinced that Hitler was going to lose the war. This was why he had just deserted.

The choice of Orleans had not been an accident. At the beginning of the campaign, he, like everyone else, had been surprised that the train taking them to Germany, which had stopped in every station until they reached the border at Irún, was scheduled to go from one end of France to the other without stopping. As they crossed the border, the volunteers in this glorious European campaign to wipe Russian barbarism from the face of the earth were wreathed in honours. In every Spanish city, large or small, there had been celebrations, banquets, receptions, girls laden with flowers. It seemed strange that nothing similar was happening in France, nor did logic help him to work out the origin of the harsh, sharp metallic sounds he heard two or three times as the train slowed down to go through the first station.

"What was that?" Eugenio, who had not taken his head out of his book since they left Madrid, looked up at Julio puzzled.

"I don't know..." Julio, who was sitting by the window, looked out and saw a figure in the distance, his arm raised.

"They're throwing stones!" someone shouted, "The French bastards are throwing stones at us!"

At first no one know who they were or why they were doing it, but it quickly became apparent. As the train passed through the next station, Eugenio and Julio ran out into the corridor and carefully slid open the window.

"They're yelling 'sons of bitches'," Eugenio glanced at Julio, "In Spanish."

"They don't have an accent."

"They're not French, then."

"No, I'd say they're Spanish."

"Jesus," Eugenio closed the window, shaking his head slowly.

"What did you expect," Julio thought. It was not the first time Eugenio's reactions had surprised him, but he said nothing, because he had not yet dared broach the subject of politics with him. He was too afraid of putting his foot in it, of not getting the terms, the vocabulary, right, of saying something suspicious though he knew he was being overly cautious since his friend had a prodigious ability to hear only what he wanted to hear. Eugenio went about as though he floated a couple of metres above the ground. He had his own version of the world, he didn't notice what was going on around him, and he took ingenuousness to new heights with a unique combination of naïveté and fanaticism which denied any reality that refused to bend to the fierce will of his gaze. It was not simply that Eugenio Sánchez Delgado was convinced that he was right, it was unthinkable to him that anyone could possibly make the mistake of believing the contrary.

"It incredible," he said after a moment, "After all the effort we've put in, all the deaths, the blood, now that we're finally rebuilding a free country, they come and start throwing stones at us. At *us*! Does anyone here understand?

His glasses would slowly slide down his nose, underscoring the theatrical fervour of these diatribes, until they were perched on the tip and he would push them back up with his forefinger. The first time Julio had heard him talk like this he had been surprised at his fervour, at such an utter lack of cynicism; in vain he waited for a wink, a nudge, to which he might respond with a loud complicit chuckle. It took him some time to comprehend that his friend was utterly serious. Now, when he spoke, Julio did not doubt his sincerity, though he still thought that what Eugenio had said bordered on perversity or stupidity.

"*Hombre*," he ventured to suggest, "they lost the war."

"So what?" Eugenio turned brusquely, his glasses already halfway down his nose, "We could have lost it, couldn't we? And you think if we had done we'd be in France attacking out own countrymen? No, sir. We'd be in Spain helping to rebuild the country, we'd be doing our duty as Spanish men.

Eugenio Sánchez Delgado was unique, or at least Julio had never met another Falangist as pure, stupid, honourable, idealistic or as innocent as he was. At Orleans station, his friend was on the verge of tears at the sight of a small gang of rabid, Republican Spanish exiles who, when they ran out of stones to throw, slashed their thumbs symbolically across their throats.

"It looks as if they're…" *organised*, was what Julio had been about to say, but he changed his mind "…worse in Orleans than anywhere else."

"It's a shame…" Eugenio shook his head, not really listening, as the whistle went and the train pulled away.

"There was this guy, Casimiro, from Seville, " Romualdo, Eugenio's brother, came to let them know what had happened. "He told the captain that some communist told him to go fuck his mother, but that's a lie. I was there and what happened was that the communist does this ..." Romulado drew his thumb across his throat, "and shouted 'Go on! Run away! Cousin Pepe will slit your throats for you, *hijos de puta*!'"

"Cousin Pepe?" Eugenio looked at them both, surprised, "Who's cousin Pepe?"

"Stalin," Julio, who had been careful to think about every word he spoke since leaving Madrid, didn't stop to think before he said this.

"And how do you know that?" Romualdo shot him a malicious smile.

"I just worked it out," Julio looked at the brothers, and adopted a cheery, offhand tone, "It's common sense, isn't it?

"Really?" the elder of the Sánchez Delgado brothers laughed "And what would you know about common sense, Julito?"

Romualdo was like a broader, taller, more muscular version of his brother. Dark-haired, pale skinned, with a hooked nose and thin lips, they looked like two loaves from the same oven, one with too much yeast, one with too little. This was why, when Julio saw Romualdo in the sea of blue shirts he had been trying to escape from until fate had turned up in the form of a weak, wounded Falangist, he recognised the perfect image of danger.

"Where have you been you little fool?" Romualdo greeted his brother, not bothering to look at the boy's ankle. "And who's this?" he asked, pointing to Julio.

"He helped me get here. I sprained my ankle - I'm limping in case you didn't notice..."

"Honestly! You're the cross I have to bear..."

Then, without saying another word, he turned his back on them and looked up at the balcony where Serrano Súñer, Franco's brother-in-law, was due to appear.

"Right, well, I should go," Julio said, his voice tremulous and shy. "I'm working in a garage on the Calle Montero, and I only came out to get some change. I can't hang around, my boss..."

"Of course..." Eugenio smiled and clapped him on the back, "Thanks for everything, Julio. See you around."

"Sure," mumbled Julio, "see you around." And off he dashed.

Julio didn't take another breath until he was safely away from the crowd, and then he broke into a run, he ran up the Calle de Alcalá, crossed the street and went into the bank, where he found he was the only customer. The stone-faced tellers were all seated at their windows, not even pretending to be busy, and Señor Gutiérrez, usually so talkative and happy to waste time, served him so quickly that he barely opened his mouth to say hello and goodbye. Julio realised that he still didn't know what this demonstration was about. It was 24 June 1941 and in Madrid the only thing that was certain was that it was better not to know, not to know anything or anyone.

"What happened to you?" Señor Turégano didn't reprimand him when he got back. "You look very pale, Julio. Are you sick or something?

"No, it's not that... It's just... there was a Falangist march at Alcalá and Gran Via, there were thousands of them, and a lot of them were carrying guns, so a lot of the shops closed for a while, and so did the bank, I had to wait until they opened again," as he spoke he took the deposit slip and the change out of his pocket, then he remembered something else, "With all that going on, I forgot to buy the beers. If you like I can go for them now."

"No, no... don't worry about it, I think the best thing to do today is stay inside."

Julio had always assumed that his boss had celebrated Franco's victory two years earlier but his assumption was based on nothing more than Señor Turégano's current circumstances. In Madrid at that time Republicans owned nothing. Not even their own future. But although the period between spring 1936 and spring 1939 never came up in the conversations at the garage, it was likely that some of his co-workers had just as dangerous a past as he had. This was why no one ever dared to ask, and that day, everyone in the garage worked harder and more diligently than ever, as though being shut off from the outside world in this cool, foul-smelling basement, was a blessing, a privilege worth working hard for. There were no visitors that day, no one came by to drop off or pick up a car, no one came in to ask for a quote, until finally, at nightfall, as they were closing up, Eugenio Sánchez Delgado appeared and asked for Julio.

"I came by to say thanks for this morning," he had changed his blue shirt for a white one, wore a bandage round his ankle, had showered and was looking a lot better. "I wanted to buy you a beer, if you're free..."

"Sure," Julio smiled, "Hang on a minute, I'll just change."

Eugenio insisted on walking to his favourite bar on the Plaza Santa Ana, his foot was fine, he explained, it was nothing serious, just a sprain. His mother, who had been a nurse during the war, had given him an injection, put on a tensile bandage and told him not to walk on it too much, but he wasn't paying much attention, because, well, you know how mothers are.

"It was a stroke of luck," he said when they were finally sitting at a table with a beer in front of each of them, "Because I've decided to enlist. Tomorrow or the day after. My brother Romualdo says that the Falange has decided, they're just waiting for Franco to give the nod, and he'll have to, won't he, I mean, after all the Germans did for us... My brother says it's best to sign up as soon as possible because the Russians won't hold out more than a month and if you don't sign up now, you probably won't get to fight at all..."

Eugenio was the same age as Julio and had been born in Madrid, but he had spent the war in the rebel zone – the Nationalist zone Julio corrected himself silently as he listened – because his mother's family was from Salamanca and they had been spending the summer with his grandmother when the rebellion broke out. His oldest brother Fernando, who was a cadet at the Military Academy in Zaragoza, had decided not to go with them even though he was on holiday, and had died in Cuartel de la Montaña. Arturo, the second oldest, had also been a Falangist since before the war, and had lost both legs at Brunete. Romualdo who was two years younger had enlisted in the Youth Movement, but he had not been allowed to join the ranks until the autumn of 1938 and had marched into Madrid without sustaining any serious injuries. Eugenio had another brother, Manolo, who was alive and living in exile in Mexico, but he did not mention him that evening.

"And what do your parents think?" Eugenio raised his eyebrows as though he didn't know what to make of the question, "Because, I don't know, one of their sons is dead, one is in a wheelchair and now the two of you are heading off to war..."

"They don't like the idea, obviously, but they understand. It's like Serrano said, history and the future of Europe demand the extermination of Russia. Russia is to blame for Fernando's death, and for Arturo being crippled, and our parents know that. My family has a score to settle with Stalin, and Romualdo and I are the only ones who can do it..."

That night, after they had gone their separate ways, Julio walked back to his boarding house. He was still trying to understand Eugenio. In his situation, to have a friend like this was both an asset and a ticking bomb, an advantage and a risk, a promise and a threat. Julio did not know Eugenio well, but he had sensed something he could easily exploit, the same unconscious, smiling, submissiveness he got from Manuel, from Isidro, from Señor Turégano, from the girls who had hung around the door of the Casa del Pueblo when he did his magic routine. Today, he had not even needed to resort to tricks or jokes to discover Eugenio's weakness, that inexplicable tendency to confide in him, to seek out his company. Some are born handsome, rich, are born princes. Julio had been born charming and he knew it, but he had good reason to distrust casual meetings.

Some years ago, the prettiest legs he had ever seen had played the same role that Eugenio's sprained ankle had today. But Mari Carmen Ortega, Peluca's daughter, who had just turned seventeen in June 1937, had been too much of a woman for him at the time. So much so that when he had decided to accept the challenge of her smouldering glances, her mocking smiles, he chose a circuitous route.

"Watch carefully..." he said, standing in the centre of a group, "The hand is quicker than the eye." And as he said it, he unfolded the sheet of newspaper he had torn to shreds as soon as he had seen her step from beneath the arches. She laughed and clapped three or four times, less enthusiastically than the others, but she looked him in the eye, and for him, that was enough.

"All right..." he said then, considering the show over, "Shall we go?"

"Wait a minute..." Vida, a slim, graceful girl with small, bright eyes put up her hand. "You said you were going to show us a coin trick, Julio."

"I can do it on the way," he said, "It's easy."

"What!" Mari Carmen made no attempt to hide her surprise. "You mean he's coming?"

"Yes he is. Come on," Isidro put a hand on his shoulder as his beautiful comrade in her homemade military jacket shrugged her shoulders.

That very afternoon, Julio had worked out that Isidro and Mari Carmen were vying to be leader of the group using the same techniques. Isidro was theoretically the leader, as he was head of the local Youth Cell. He was physically unimpressive, serious, bookish, he looked much younger than he was, spoke little and never danced. She was the eldest daughter of one of the heroes of 7 November 1936, the glorious day on which the people of Madrid had driven the fascists out of Madrid, but more importantly, she was a grown woman, determined, brave and stubborn with a magnificent body and an attractive face. She had a big nose and a broad mouth – too broad for the fashion of the time, but the moment they saw her, men forgot that she wasn't their type.

That very afternoon, Julio also found out that his sudden infatuation was contagious. There were few men on the streets of Madrid in the summer of 1937, and most of them were in uniforms, but three out of four of them would stop and brazenly look Mari Carmen up and down. And Mari Carmen always looked back at them and smiled. It was another string to her bow and one that Isidro could not possibly match. When Julio met her, she was semi-engaged to one of the Russian pilots who performed aerial acrobatics above the city now that they had driven off the German planes, as if they had become infected with the audacity of the people of Madrid, who paid no attention to the air-raid sirens, but stood in the middle of the street so they could watch the bombs drop and applaud when it was over.

"What about your boyfriend?" Isidro would ask her from time to time, "Did he write to you today?"

"Of course he did!" she said "An M and a C, clear as day up there... You can ask her..."

Then she would elbow whoever's turn it was to back her up and the girl would nod as though her life depended on it while Isidro choked back his frustration that there was nothing explicitly or implicitly heroic about his life.

"You can't understand a word he says, you can't even communicate with him."

"Who says I can't?" Now it was her turn to laugh, "Some day I'll show you how well I communicate with him, idiot"

At such moments, Julio realized that there were other means by which Mari Carmen and the Russian pilot could understand each other and he felt a terrible spasm of jealousy, not so much for the fictitious pilot, but because it made him pity himself and he could not bear to be pitied. This sudden, unaccustomed feeling of inferiority, of weakness pained him more than the fact that he had no right to be jealous of someone else's fiancée. But he never gave up hope, not even when Mari Carmen showed up one day at the headquarters of the Socialist Youth Movement, the JSU, with her pilot. He was very young, barely more than a boy, with a shock of white-blonde hair and impossibly pale velvety skin.

Julio never gave up hope, because he had discovered that Mari Carmen was like him, she had the same innate ability to seduce, to persuade, to get along with people. It was easy for him to be popular in the JSU. He was clever, he learned fast and most of all he quickly mastered the language, the ideology, the repertoire of myths and expressions adopted by the Left. He was his mother's son, whether he liked it or not. Otherwise, he liked this new life better than the old one. He liked the city, liked to wander the streets, meeting new people every day, moving from one meeting to the next, one bar to the next, one cinema to the next. Julio Carrión's life had never been so intense, so full of dates, plans, things to do. Little by little, he frittered away his father's savings while the old man, constantly drunk, stayed shut up in his room at the boarding house, praying and weeping and cleaning his shotgun. Benigno Carrión never found out that his son was an enemy activist, because in truth Julio was no activist. He was content simply to be led, to feel wanted, to hang out with those who gave orders, all the while discovering in himself a talent for imposture.

Mari Carmen Ortega never did fall into the arms of Julio Carrión. She had ditched her Russian boyfriend long before he went home, trading him for a sergeant in the Fifth Regiment who, though not as tall, was twice as heavy. His name was Antonio and he was from Vicálvaro. She had no trouble communicating with Antonio and they were married in July 1938 at which point Julio, who had never stopped loving her from a distance, did not dare to carry on.

"I don't believe it..." Isidro would joke, "I don't know which is scarier, Vicálvaro or the Soviet Union.

Vida, who had been in love with him since that first day and with whom he had a informal, erratic relationship was the only one who did well out of the situation, until the war ended and Julio abandoned her as quickly as he did the others. Julio Carrión was thinking about all this on 24 June 1941 as he slowly walked back towards the boarding house. Vida was in jail, but she had not informed on him. Mari Carmen was still free and might denounce him at any moment. Fortune favours those who know when to back a winner, and he had not known. Meanwhile, his life had changed. It was dreary now, squalid and monotonous, but it could be worse. Much worse.

That night, as he went to bed, Julio Carrión did not know what to do. When he woke the following morning, not only did he see things more clearly, he felt a cold shudder run through him when he remembered the foolish ideas he had been toying with the night before. I've done enough stupid things in my life, he thought, and yet he walked out of the building, not bothering to stop in the doorway to make sure he did not run into Mari Carmen, as though he knew that two days later he would enlist.

The newspapers were to blame, the bulletins he heard on the radio, the comments on the streets. The Germans had destroyed two thousand Russian planes, he heard one of Señor Turégano's customers say that morning, bombed them right there on the landing strip, I tell you, they'll be in Moscow before you know it... His boss smiled and repeated the story to later customers. In the street, in the queues in front of the newsstands, on the corners, everyone was saying it. Stalin isn't likely to hold out as long as the fucking Maginot line. No way. I'm telling you. No one can stop them, look at France, Belgium, Poland...

The following day, things had moved on, the newspapers were talking about a German victory, announcing the imminent fall of Minsk, Kiev and Odessa. Julio remembered the four-and-a-half peseta taxi ride that had separated Franco from Puerta del Sol in 1936. The Germans were stronger, richer and more powerful, they were better armed than Franco, a weak general whose troops had mostly been foreign mercenaries, and who had had the majority of his own country against him, yet Franco had won the war. And Julio Carrión González, who had promised himself that never again would he be on the losing side, had lost. This time, it was easier to be certain.

Eugenio had given him his telephone number, but Julio did not dare to call him. However when he left work on 26 June, he went straight to the Cervecería Alemana in Plaza Santa Ana and found Eugenio there with a group of uniformed Falangists. They were gathered around Arturo who sat in his wheelchair, two medals pinned to his shirt, a blanket thrown over the empty space where his legs had been, and a burning envy in his eyes.

"Hey!" Eugenio was happy to see him, "Have you decided to come with us?"

"Well... Yes... I think so."

Afterwards, Julio Carrión González would often remember the night of 26 June 1941 as though it had happened to someone else, as though he had been a spectator watching this passionate impromptu display of camaraderie, as half a dozen strangers gave him a brief, bone-crushing hug.

The other men were older, friends of Arturo and Romualdo. They knew what war was, or at least they knew how to drink and to pretend. Later, when he came to learn for himself, rejected everything he knew, and began giving new names to everything in this world of black and white, this world in which the only men who survived were those who could renounce logic in favour of animal instincts, he no longer recognised himself in his memory of that night of drunken revelry. And yet it was him, he had done these things, when he did not yet know that the engines of friendly planes sound just like those of enemy planes, when he did not yet know that the cold can drive you mad, that snow can blind you, when he did not know that fear is a form of caution, sleep the promise of death, and he got drunk with Eugenio Sánchez Delgado who was just as ignorant as he was, who knew nothing about Julio and yet that night invited him home for dinner, introduced him to his father, his mother, treated him like an old friend, an accomplice.

None of this surprised Julio, because his true friends, his true comrades on the other side had also never asked anything of him before accepting him. They were so sure of the rightness of their cause, so persuaded by the incontrovertible, universal value of the ideas they promoted that they welcomed newcomers with almost evangelical warmth, confident that their desire to join was sincere. That night, in the house of the Sánchez Delgado family, Julio Carrión believed he had found the flipside of that zeal, that innocence, and he felt at home, safe in this dining room with its dark wood furniture, its walls hung with copper engravings of religious scenes, where grace was said before dinner and afterwards they had cakes and a bottle of their best brandy to toast the war as though it were a party. Eugenio's parents – his father, short and slight with a little moustache that made him look like a rat, his mother more handsome, blonde and heavy-set – were not simply friendly, they were affectionate, almost paternal towards him. Both took it for granted that their sons were not going to war, they were headed for victory, and Julio found that he was infected by their utter confidence, convinced him that he might not even see combat.

His own father did not share their optimism. The following day, before he signed up to his new comrades' party, with Eugenio as his only character reference, Julio went to see his father in Torrelodones since he needed his signature to enlist. He was sorry that Eugenio had insisted on coming with him, since Benigno was cold, silent and disconsolate. A week earlier he had discovered that his wife had died of pneumonia in the penal colony at Ocaña. He had not even known she was in prison, because he had made no enquiries about her nor about his daughter since they left. If he said nothing of this to Julio, it was not to spare him anxiety, but because he would have been ashamed to go into embarrassing explanations in front of this stranger in the blue shirt.

By this time, Julio Carrión González did not think about his mother every day, but the brief, intense flashes of memory, of lost tenderness and affection, still hurt him deeply. Although the world was so warped it made him forget the unforgettable, banishing the recent past to some vague frontier where with every passing day the colours faded, against his will, he would still happen on Teresa Gonzalez, see her in the eyes, the hands, the gestures, of other women; women walking with their teenage sons who could not know that the mere sight of them, the difference in their height, or perhaps simply a fleeting caress, could suddenly make him feel unbearably alone. At such times, Julio Carrión, who had never stopped loving his mother, despised himself for his weakness, for he lived in a world in which she had never existed, had not been the woman she was nor he her son. But Teresa González had existed. And Julio would soon discover that he was not the only one who knew it.

"How's things?"

"Fucking great," Julio returned Romualdo's smile, "You?"

"Great."

They both laughed as Casi, the Sevillian who had shot at one of Pepe Stalin's Andalusian cousins in Orleans, told everyone to be quiet in a hysterical, terrified whisper.

"Shut the fuck up." He did not say another word until they had covered half the distance between the Polish prison camp and their own, "If we get caught, we're dead."

"To say nothing of the bollocking I'll get from your brother," Julio said to Romualdo who was walking beside him.

Only when they were close enough to the camp, did Casi dare to laugh along with them.

"How did it go?" asked the sentry they had bribed to get out as he pocketed the other half of his money, "What are the Polish women like?"

"What Polish women?" Julio stared at him as though he didn't understand, "We just went out for some fresh air."

"Yeah, yeah…" the sentry gave him an sardonic smile, "I'm sure."

"You'd better be sure," Romualdo's tone was categorical.

Julio's girl had not been very young, but she had been pretty enough. She had auburn, almost red hair, pale eyes and she was big-boned, which did much to disguise her skeletal thinness. This alone was enough to make her attractive compared to the shorter, more delicate women who had no way of concealing their emaciated bodies, their desiccated hands stretched out imploringly to new recruits, who, gave them whatever they had, sweets, fruit, bread, sometimes even cigarettes.

"They have women here!" the rumour spread the day they arrived in Grafenwöhr, "Thousands of them, a whole camp full."

That afternoon, they had unpacked their German issue kitbags, laughing as they tried on the uniforms, the flannel undershirts that came down to their knees and the long socks that all but came up to their armpits. "What the hell is this?" "What do we need so many brushes for?" "What about these strips of fabric?" "They're ribbons for your long hair." They found out that the women were Polish prisoners and that German High Command forbade any contact with them. The penalty for infraction was harsh, something they did not really understand, any more than they understood why they had been issued with so many brushes. So, in spite of the fact that simply going near the Polish camp was considered an offence, from their first day they had flouted the rules, making the most of the few hours they had after afternoon drill to wander over, taking the most circuitous route, to the wire fences through which a

271

thousand arms snaked out towards them. The Spanish officers chose to consider this breach of discipline a harmless prank, although Julio and Eugenio did not know it would be the cause of the first rift between them.

"What did she say?" El Casi asked the elder of the Sánchez Delgado brothers anxiously as he watched him walk back from the wire fence where he had spent some time talking to one of the prisoners.

"I don't know what to tell you..." Romualdo scratched his head, "Given that she doesn't speak much French and neither do I... Now, if that swot over there would just help us..."

Julio realised Romualdo was talking about Eugenio, but his friend did not even turn his head, but carried on walking beside Francisco Serrano Romano, nicknamed Pancho a quiet lad from Estremadura who looked much younger than his nineteen years, and of all the soldiers was the most generous to the Polish women.

"What's with you? Don't you eat?" Romualdo had asked him one day as he watched Pancho stuff bread and fruit into his pockets.

"Not much," Pancho shrugged. "It's just that where I come from, we're not used to eating much."

Everybody, including Pancho laughed at this.

Julio and Eugenio had grown accustomed to this precocious lad who had no interest in talking about anything but the war, about the regiments, the number of soldiers in each, their history, battle plans, and consequently rarely said anything on the walk to and from the Polish camp. That afternoon, Eugenio was almost as silent while his brother and el Casi walked behind whispering in low voices.

"What are you two talking about ?" Julio finally went over to Romualdo, "Is somebody going to tell me what's going on?"

"No, because there's nothing going on," Romualdo said, then looked stroked his chin, "Say, Julito, do you speak French?"

"A little..."

"How little?"

Although it had been a long time since he had spoken French, as long, in fact as it had been since he had seen his mother, he spoke it fairly well, so he was the one who handled the more delicate negotiations, those things that could not be communicated in the universal language of gesture and mime. It was not very complicated. The Polish women did not want money – money was useless to them in the camp – but it was easy for the soldiers to buy soap, cologne and especially food. Aside from paying whichever woman they had chosen, they would also have to bribe the prisoners who had been entrusted with patrolling the camp at night and the women who kept the German guards occupied while they crawled into the camp through a sort of supply hatch. But in the end it was cheap. In all, the Polish women would cost them less than half of what they had to pay the Spanish guard to keep quiet about their nocturnal sortie.

"Right, there's only one thing missing now..." Julio handed Romualdo a piece of paper with a list of what the prisoners had asked for and the date of the next new moon.

Eugenio had not heard the bear hugs, nor the belly laughs of his brother and El Casi as they welcomed Julio Carrión into the brotherhood, but he sensed it, and by the time they returned from their afternoon visit some days later, everyone knew.

"So you're all going to do this?" he looked at each of them in turn. "Even you, Julio? When is it happening? Tomorrow, when there's no moon? Big fucking men, aren't you!"

"Shut up, Eugenio."

"I will not shut up, Romualdo. I'm don't take orders from you. Certainly not after this..."

"Here we go," Romualdo gave a contemptuous laugh, "from the man who goes to communion every day..."

"A man doesn't need to go to communion every day to be disgusted by what you're doing to a bunch of poor Polish women, dying of starvation..."

'Wait a minute, little brother" Romualdo took a step towards his brother, "Those poor women are enemies of the German people, remember? Be careful, or you'll get yourself locked up as an enemy sympathiser..." At this, El Casi laughed, and turning to look, Romualdo noticed Pancho. "And what's the matter with you?"

"Nothing's the matter," Pancho said calmly, "But I think your brother is right."

"Well, well..." Romualdo laughed, "Looks like we've got ourselves another member of the God Squad!"

"No surprise there - he's permanently fasting!" El Casi joked.

Things went no further that afternoon. Julio, who agreed with Romualdo, avoided Eugenio that night, and made sure that they were not alone together the next day. Later, when it was all over and he slipped into bed with the scent of the woman still on his skin, he felt so powerful, so sated, that he stopped worrying about anything except the winks, the complicit smiles, the clever comments of his comrades. By dinner time the following day, the news had reached some of the officers, who shook their heads in a mixture of indignation and indulgence while insisting that the escapade was not to be repeated. In the meantime, Eugenio acted as though they did not know each other until Julio, finally worn down, spoke to him on the train that took them to Nuremberg every Sunday on their afternoons off.

"Tell me something, Eugenio," he said, sliding into the seat next to him before Pancho could do so. "Are you never going to speak to me again?"

"I don't know..." Eugenio stared at him for a moment as though they had just met, and then turned to look out the window. "To tell you the truth, I don't much feel like talking to you..."

"But why?" That's what I don't understand. What do you think? You think I behaved badly? Well you're wrong... I took her soap, potatoes, apples, chocolate, I even brought her a bottle of perfume. She's probably the happiest woman in the camp right now."

"What about you?" Eugenio turned round so quickly his glasses almost flew off his nose, "What kind of person are you, Julio? That woman risked her life, don't you understand that? She risked her life for your apples and potatoes..."

"Nobody forced her to..."

"Nobody? You forced her to, you and my fucking brother, and that other idiot. You forced them because they were desperate, so desperate that they were willing to risk their lives for a couple of fucking apples. If you were caught, you'd have got a telling off and a couple of days in a cell, but they would have been killed, they would have been *executed* because they're prisoners of war, don't you get it?" Eugenio fell silent, then shook his head. "I don't understand you, Julio. Romualdo, yes, because Romualdo is an animal, but you..."

"For goodness sake, Eugenio," Julio Carrión was more surprised than offended, "What is this? I just don't think it's that serious. We're not Germans, we don't have to be like them. All we did was get laid, nobody was hurt. It might be a sin, I won't argue with that, but it was good for us and it was good for them too... I'm beginning to think your brother was right, I mean, which side are you on?"

"Listen you bastard!" Eugenio shouted, jabbing his finger at his friend. "I'm going to tell you something, and I'm only going to tell you once. Don't you *ever* doubt me, because I know exactly which side I'm on. Better than you do, better than anyone, got that? I'm on the side of civilization, the real socialist revolution, I'm against communism because it's inhuman, criminal, it's madness and has no respect for God or man." He paused a moment and pushed his glasses back up his nose, then carried on, "I know that they are making mistakes and they will go

274

on making mistakes, because our task is not an easy one and the enemy is powerful. The women you slept with may or may not have been communists, but whatever they were before the camp doesn't matter. And I'm not saying they shouldn't have been locked up. All I'm saying is that now they are just a bunch of poor, lonely, desperate women, and you have no right to abuse them the way you did."

Julio Carrión González got up from his seat, convinced that he had lost a friend, an ally, that Eugenio would never trust him again. He could not understand this overblown, puritanical tirade, which did not raise the slightest doubt nor the first hint of regret in his mind. The reason he was worried about losing Eugenio's friendship was very different. Julio was not yet sure of himself, and the company of this god-fearing, loyal, honest lad whose only friends were Julio and Pancho, had offered him some kind of guarantee. That afternoon, on the train to Nuremberg, he was certain he had lost that friendship, but for them the war had not yet even begun.

At the end of August, when they began the bizarre, exhausting journey towards the Front – nine days by train and more than thirty marching, covering almost forty kilometres a day, the incident with the Polish prisoners began to fade, the happy, golden days spent in Grafenwöhr unravelling like the threads of a dream. Exhaustion quickly overcame physical pain, dulling their senses, then weighing on them like a millstone on the heroic expectations of those who had enlisted in the most powerful army in the world only to discover that trains and trucks did not cover even half of their path to glory.

Eugenio could not comprehend it, just as he could not comprehend that they were to be robbed of the glory of marching into Moscow being instead despatched to the north, while Latvian volunteers, better adapted to the cold, had been dispatched to the Ukraine. In his struggle to endure this unending series of disappointments, the exhaustion sapped the strength from his delicate body more cruelly than it did the others. The younger of the Sánchez Delgado brothers armed himself with dogma. His eyes burned once more with the simple, unadulterated fervour Julio had first witnessed in Madrid; these eyes did not see the yellow stars, like cattle brands, on the chests of the thousands of Jews they passed in Grodno, Vilna, and Minsk. Julio silently watched over him for some sign of mutiny or dissent, he knew that Eugenio did not like to see such things, no one liked to see them, not even him, but no more was said about the 'mistakes' which great causes necessitate.

However it was at this point that Julio discovered just how honest Eugenio Sánchez Delgado was, because when he began to feel contempt for himself, he once more treated Julio as a friend, mistakenly believing that he was no better than Julio. Finally, at the end of October, as they were camped out on the banks of the Voljov, Julio realised that the precautions he had imposed on himself since leaving Madrid, the permanent state of watchfulness that made him think twice before saying a word, were as extreme as Eugenio's sackcloth morality.

"It's beautiful here, isn't it?"

The comment caught him unawares during their first shared sentry duty. He would never have suspected that Romualdo was sensitive to the landscape, but it was true, it was beautiful here with the leafy bank of trees and the shifting light of a late autumn sunset.

'Yes, it is..." Julio replied, "Especially now when nothing's moving."

Neither of them could imagine how much they would come to hate this placid river which would soon become their own stretch of hell.

On the far side of the river were the Russians, who until now had been retreating, leaving cities and villages at the mercy of the German army, leaving the slender, graceful towers of Novgorod as defenceless as the crude wooden houses with their pitched roofs. They had marched through countless villages and no one had spoken to them as they passed, and so they had come to the Voljov, this calm river whose verdant banks and tall trees made it a beautiful place to rest, but it was just one more river, it could have been any river except for the fact that it was here that the Russians had decided to stop.

That afternoon, as they gazed at the scene, that both men were convinced that this front was also temporary, contingent. If the Russians had retreated this far before their arrival, it seemed logical that they would now retreat even further. This was the opinion of most of Julio's comrades, and he did not argue with them, though from time to time he thought of the taxi meter running, the four-and-a-half peseta fare that separated Franco from Puerto del Sol.

"God knows where they're going to send us," said Romualdo, looking up at the leaves on the trees, "once we cross the river..."

"Probably to Leningrad," Julio suggested, "It's close."

"I think I'd rather go to Moscow."

"Your brother said the same thing."

Romualdo went back to looking at the river, but a moment later, he smiled, then turned to Julio and stared at him.

"You said Leningrad..."

"Well, that's what it's called, isn't it?"

"No. The Germans call it *Sankt Petersburg*, so I guess we should too."

"I suppose so..." Julio felt a lump rise in his throat, a great hole open in the pit of his stomach, but then his comrade burst into laughter and clapped him on the back.

"Don't worry, comrade. Of course I know... I know the whole story." Julio simply smiled, his heart still in his mouth. "Did you think I was going to trust my idiot brother? It's all right, everything's fine... I'm not like Eugenio, I'm no saint. I asked around, and I found out that your mother was a communist, but the comrades in Torrelodones told me that your father was one of us and that you stayed with him instead of leaving with her. So you see, I know the whole story. Don't think I'm shocked. We have a Commie in the family too, my brother Manolo - didn't Eugenio tell you?"

"No," Julio smiled again, calmer now, "I had no idea."

"Well we have, Manolo is an unrepentant Red... As a kid, he was always good at drawing, and he wanted to be a painter. He studied at the art school, and became friends with every queer in Madrid, then he found himself a girlfriend and cleared off to Peguerinos at the first opportunity. He's in México now and from what I've heard, he's fighting over there..." Romualdo laughed again, as if the whole thing were funny. "Fuck it! That's life. I don't know why, but it happens even in the best of families. So, if you want to call Saint Petersburg Leningrad, go ahead. I know I can trust you, and I'm not about to tell anyone your secret. Now, come on, get out the deck of cards and lets see if I can work out how you do that trick with the seven of clubs..."

As he began to shuffle the cards, Julio Carrión González felt a wave of relief so profound that he had not had such a sense of peace since he was eleven years old. But this feeling of wellbeing that filtered through his body like a drug, like a warm intoxicating drink, did not prevent him from learning a number of things that would prove useful for the rest of his life.

The first thing he learned was that he was lucky, that capricious Lady Luck, was on his side, as biased in his favour as a mother. It was something he had sensed on many other occasions, but now he was certain. The rest, he could guess: Romualdo Sánchez Delgado had suspected him, had found out from his brother that Julio was from Torrelodones, and there in his village, which had held out to the last, when Falangists had spent three years hiding out in wardrobes, don Pedro, the priest, had told him the story of Teresa González, adulteress and communist who had run away with the teacher from Las Rozas while her eldest son, out of loyalty to his father, had stayed behind. And Romualdo had been satisfied with the story. This was the second thing that Julio Carrión learned: even the most intelligent people were fools, or could be fools when confronted with someone more intelligent than they were. He was intelligent, and because of this, he did not relax but simply added to his understanding of the world the fact that nothing comes for free, and that for every Eugenio Sánchez Delgado, there was an older brother like Romualdo. Neither luck nor intelligence would be useful to him if he simply trusted to them, because the only truly intelligent decision was to trust no one, not even oneself.

From that moment on, Julio Carrión González allowed himself to think about his future, to plan out the life he hoped for, one worthy of a conquering hero with nothing to hide. Every month, his father received his son's twin salaries - one Spanish, one German – a standard practice the divisions could not avoid. Benigno had promised to save the money for him and Julio was sure that his father would keep his promise since he had more than enough to live on. So, on the few good days of that short, traitorous autumn, Julio could picture himself walking down the Gran Vía with an imposing woman whose clattering heels threatened to crack the pavement.

The daydream fell to pieces quite suddenly, tumbled like a house of cards. By mid-October, the mercury in the thermometers never rose above zero, their winter provisions were insufficient, the Germans had ceased to advance, the Russians did not give another inch of ground, and any attempt to cross the Voljov was a return journey.

On one of the many offensives that began only moments before the order came to retreat, El Casi was killed. It was not yet November. That day, faced with his first corpse, Julio realised what war really meant as Eugenio wept silently and Romualdo howled obscenities. "Those fucking bastards! It's as if they knew we were coming, like they were waiting for us!" Every night was colder, every day they were more depressed, and every morning more and more of them woke up from their dreams of glory realising that they were lost and far from home. Surely the Germans, realised just how cold it would be here in December? What about Napoleon? Surely even an idiot knew about Napoleon's Russian campaign? Every night was colder, every day they were more depressed, and less cautious about what they said. Most of them tried hard not to die, not to get wounded, not to fall asleep – that was enough for them, that was what war had become.

"Promise me one thing, Julio," Eugenio's voice cracked and his eyes welled with tears, "If I get frostbite, don't let them cut off my legs, please, swear you won't let them. Even if I get gangrene, even if the Germans promise to give me those metal things to help me walk, don't let them persuade you. My mother couldn't cope having another son with

278

no legs, Romualdo and I have talked about it, and we'd both rather die than that…"

"I'll promise you something Eugenio," it had been a long time since Julio Carrión González had cried and yet his eyes welled with tears, "I won't let you get frostbite. Neither of us is going to get frostbite, I swear."

It was coming up to Christmas and cold was gnawing at the thermometers. At fifty degrees below zero, the last defenders of the village of Possad, the farthest position Julio had reached on the other side of the Voljov, retraced their steps to the western bank of the river. This failure wounded them more than any other, because they had managed to go farther, to hold out longer, they had endured the cold and the despair, and all for nothing.

There, in the hell that was the eastern shore, December had begun to pick off its victims. These strangers, these men from a distant land of grapevines and almonds, of olives and oranges, were dying of exhaustion. They were fighting two enemies: one brutal but visible, the second more cunning, more cruel. To sleep was to die, a traitorous death, silent and gentle like the enfolding arms of a beautiful woman. As the snow fell, its immaculate whiteness permeating the maddening silence of Russian winter, the strangers marched on, advancing through the frozen wasteland. It would be so easy now to surrender, to stop, to give in; to yield for a brief moment to sleep, to remember the crisp sheets of a warm bed from childhood, to close your eyes so as not to look upon this monstrous, deadly beauty. And in that moment, came death. The lucky ones whose friends noticed they were missing and woke them in time, paid for that moment of sleep in their feet and their legs or with a sudden blindness that made them scream though they knew they would not be blind forever.

It was their morbid fear of freezing to death on the coldest days of that terrible winter that brought Julio and Eugenio back together. For January, which they spent languishing in trenches on the western banks of the Voljov, was colder than December, and the frostbite and gangrene it exacted frightened them more than the enemy bullets that whistled over their heads. People said it was the worst winter for a century, but that was no consolation. They were comforted only by their trust in each other, their pact to watch over each other, a pact which Pancho quickly joined making it easier for someone to check regularly that whoever was on guard had not fallen asleep. The cold abated in February and the number of those who froze to death grew as the more careless of them thought that, with the temperature now only minus twenty, they had nothing more to fear. Julio, Eugenio and Pancho remained vigilant until finally the thaw came. It was then that the lice once more became their principal preoccupation.

"I can't believe it!" Eugenio complained, "It's cold enough for us to freeze to death but it doesn't kill these little bastards."

Pancho, who was very good with his hands, made a pair of tweezers from two thin metal shafts and a spring which they used to pick lice from the seams of their clothes once they had deloused themselves, but the battle was as hopeless as their attempts to cross the Voljov.

"It's like we came to wage war on lice rather than Stalin…"

When the first signs of spring appeared, Julio Carrión González was no longer sure that he had chosen the winning side, though he still had no doubt that they would be victorious. The winter had been disastrous for the Germans, but the Russians had lost their allies.

He repeated what he had heard and fed on the fervour with which his comrades greeted his words. At any other point in his life, Julio Carrión would have laughed at the wilful credulity that spawned this epidemic of euphoria, but war had stripped him of his cynicism. It pained him to remember his own gullibility, how he had greedily swallowed the idea of a blitzkrieg hook, line and sinker, his faith that the Germans would do all the work and that he would march into Russia on clouds of glory. He still remembered the words of Eugenio's mother: "You're not going to war boys, you're heading for victory," and his father's troubled expression as he had repeated this word for word. Now, with Madrid, Mari Carmen and his job as a mechanic so far away, and death so close at hand, he could not understand how he could have so misjudged the extent of the danger that lay in wait for him.

In the spring of 1942, Julio Carrión still believed that his side would win, but he was not thinking about victory, he was thinking about his own survival. He hated the war, hated the soldier's life, but when he was given orders he obeyed, never truly slacking but never too eager, realising that insubordination might be as costly to him as heroism. When they advanced, he was never in the front line, but he never straggled behind, when they retreated he was never the first nor the last to take to his heels, and when "Stalin's Organs", those artillery trucks carrying rocket launchers, simultaneously boomed out their war music, he hit the ground a few seconds before the order was given, but only a few. He pretended to blend into the mediocrity of the troop, just another soldier with no distinguishing marks, and yet at Possad he fought like a wild animal, like the hero he had never claimed to be. He was fighting for himself, for his life, because every minute he survived he was one minute closer to emerging alive, because they were few, because there was no one at hand in whom he could entrust his survival. Afterwards, he was decorated for bravery, but as he stood feigning the pride and excitement he could see in Eugenio's eyes, all he was thinking was that for two, perhaps three months, he would not be expected to volunteer for a mission.

Nor did he, but the thaw proved as difficult for him as it was for the others and he missed the snow when he stumbled into another patch of swamp where and his legs felt like lead. Even the briefest of *sorties* was torture, since every time they pushed the wheels of the trucks, they jerked forward only to sink back into the mud again. Now that they had no time to pour scorn on their allies, since the German High Command had turned them into lumberjacks, carpenters, labourers lashing tree trunks together to make the marshy roads passable, even Eugenio Sánchez Delgado began to lose faith.

"I don't get it," he would say, "Why won't they help us? The people living in the log cabins over there, or even people from the village... I mean, surely they approve of what we're doing? They're going to use the roads too."

"They're doing it to piss us off, Eugenio."

"To piss us off?" he looked at Julio with utter astonishment, "Why would they piss us off? We've come to liberate them, we're freeing them from a tyrant, dragging them out of the Middle Ages..."

"Come on, don't be so fucking stupid!" The strain of everything had eroded Julio Carrión's patience. "Think about it, we're a foreign army and we're invading their country. Because that's what we're doing, conquering them, requisitioning their livestock, eating their food, destroying their harvests... and you think they should be out here helping us?"

"That's why we can't cross the river."

Pancho, who had listened to the daily variations on the subject unexpectedly interrupted one afternoon.

"What?" Julio and Eugenio asked simultaneously.

"That's why we can't cross the river," Pancho said again, his voice calm and clear, "Because everyone on the other side is Russian, and occupying a country and defending it are two different things. It's much easier to fight alongside your family than it is to be thousands of miles from home. It doesn't matter whether we're better or braver or have better weapons, they have something we'll never have."

"Righteous anger," said Julio thinking of Madrid, "Because we're turning them out of their own homes."

Pancho did not waste his breath agreeing, he simply nodded as Eugenio hurled himself against the truck they had been pushing with such fury that he managed to shift it by himself. Julio went to help him, but said nothing more because he realised that for all his zeal, his unshakeable principles, it had just occurred to Eugenio that the Russians might win this war.

Pancho had put his finger on something Julio had unconsciously intuited the first time Eugenio complained that the Russians refused to help them; he had often railed against his friend's foolishness, but until Pancho's comment, it had never occurred to him to connect the enemy's strength with the reluctance of the Russians to help. From that moment, he no longer felt so compassionate towards the local populace whose apparent laziness bolstered the morale of their countrymen on the far side of the river.

And yet Pancho, whose real name was Luis Serrano Romero, did cross the Voljov. He did so at sunset one summer evening when the river was at low ebb, and he did so alone, though his friends recognised the furtive figure slinking toward the narrow, stony bend where the water was shallow. Later, they realised that he had counted on them seeing him because that night, sentry duty fell to Eugenio Sánchez Delgado.

"Over there... doesn't that look like Pancho?" Recognising the figure on the river bank, Eugenio turned to Julio with his usual expression of disbelief, "Where the hell is he going? Has he gone mad?"

Pancho was moving quickly, soundlessly, not looking back, and they did not dare call out his name because he was their friend, and although they did not know where he was going, they knew he had no business being there, he should have been in the trench, sleeping in his dugout. To call out would have been tantamount to turning him in, and yet they couldn't simply stand there with their arms folded while Pancho waged war on his own.

"What's he up to?" Eugenio voiced his worst fears, "You think he's deserting?"

"No," Julio suddenly understood what was happening, "He's going over."

"What?" Eugenio stared at him, wide-eyed, his lower lip quivering.

"He's going over to the Russian side. Come on!"

Julio started to run and Eugenio followed, trusting to a plan that did not exist, for there was only one thought in Julio Carrión González's mind, something that Romualdo had said which came back to him now, that even the cleverest people could be fools. He was the biggest fool in the Division, because he should have known, should have guessed, should have been able to read the signs – signs he knew only too well: Pancho's silence, his stoicism, his willingness to eat only half his food and give the rest to the Polish women at Grafenwöhr, his comment about the people in his village not being accustomed to eating much, and his eloquent explanation of the Russian resistance. He should have realised why Pancho knew by heart the number of soldiers in every regiment, the number of officers and their ranks, but he had been a fool, he, Julio Carrión González who had thought himself the cleverest of them all. It was impossible to know how many traitors figured among the number of deserters the High Command reluctantly admitted to. Among those who had been court-martialled and sentenced to death were many who had been captured while trying to defect to the enemy, he knew that, but Pancho had been more intelligent than all of them. This was what Julio Carrión González was thinking as they reached the river bank and found themselves looking down the barrel of Pancho's sub-machine gun.

"Not another step," he said, his voice as composed as always, "Not another step or I'll shoot you."

"Don't do anything stupid, Pancho," Eugenio raised his rifle, his hands shaking as Julio held up the lantern to illuminate the scene. "Come back with us and we'll say no more about it."

"No," hearing him speak, Julio realised that he would rather die than come back, "First of all, my name isn't even Pancho. Pancho is my little brother. I used his name when I enlisted, because they would never have taken me under my own name. My name is Luis Serrano Romero, Private First-Class, Seventh brigade, the Zapadores Battalion. And I'm not twenty, I'm twenty-four," then still holding his gun in his right hand, he slipped his left into his pocket and took out a small red cardboard folder that Julio immediately recognised. "See this? It's right here in black and white: Luis Serrano Romero, membership number 93, Socialist Youth Movement, 16 September 1936, Villanueva de la Serena, Badajoz."

He put the card back into his pocket, and Julio realised that he had never heard the man string so many words together.

"I set out from Villanueva de la Serena with this card tucked in my boot, survived the freezing cold and the thaw, the dust and mud and sand... And here I am - here we are, both of us."

"You're crazy."

"No, Eugenio, I'm completely sane. So sane I gave the Nazi salute every day, sang your fucking anthem, knelt during your masses, swore your fucking oaths and I cursed every one of you every day, just so I could get here, and do what I'm going to do."

"You're crazy..."

Eugenio repeated dully, his eyes wide.

"No. I'm not," he almost smiled, "You're the one who doesn't get it. Well, right now I'm going to join my comrades. Dead or alive. But if you try to kill me, I'll shoot one of you first. Maybe both. I'm a better shot than either of you, I've been to war before, you know."

That moment seemed to last a lifetime. All three knew what Eugenio and Julio should do, and all three knew that they would not do it. Julio and Eugenio knew that Pancho was not the first nor would he be the last, that one more desertion does not change the course of a war. Julio and Pancho knew that Eugenio would never kill a friend. Eugenio and Pancho did not know that Julio would never kill someone who might be useful to him at some point.

"Go," Eugenio said, lowering his rifle, "Go on you fucking traitor!"

Pancho started sideways across the river, turning back at every step, still pointing his gun until he knew he was safe. Then, standing on a boulder halfway across he stopped, tied a white handkerchief to the barrel of his gun and took out his identity card.

"I'm not the traitor, Eugenio," he yelled, "You're the traitors. Traitors to your country, to your independence, to the law your generals swore to uphold. Long Live the Spanish Republic! Long Live the People's Glorious Struggle!"

"Fuck you, you bloody Red!" Eugenio raised his rifle and was about to fire when Julio stopped him with a furious swipe.

"What are you doing, you idiot?" He took Eugenio's gun, "Now you decide to fire? If you were going to shoot him you should have done it before, moron. What are you trying to do, wake everyone up so they can all come down here and see that we let him escape? You want the both of us to end up in front of a firing squad?"

Eugenio shook his head, then he started to cry, and there was so much grief, and despair, and loneliness in those tears that for an instant Julio Carrión González was a child again and he hugged his friend until Pancho was on the other side of the river, until Pancho's cry *"tovarich spanski tovarich!* Don't shoot, I'm coming over!" faded into the distance.

"I'm going back, Julio." For Eugenio Sánchez Delgado, who would go on to fight for months at the Leningrad front before his battalion was repatriated, the war ended that night. "Hitler can go screw himself, I'm going home, I don't understand this war… You saw him, didn't you? You saw how much he hated us. But still has was able befriend us, march with us for thousands of kilometres, fight alongside us, save our men when they were wounded, shoot his own comrades…" His last remark seemed incomprehensible so Eugenio felt compelled to explain it, "The people he thought of as his own – Russians – people from a different country, who speak a language he doesn't even understand, 'my comrades' he called them. How much hatred does it take not to break down, to be a Spanish soldier fighting for the Russians against his own people?"

Julio Carrión did not answer straight away. "I don't think he's fighting for the Russians, Eugenio," he spoke slowly because he needed to be certain of what he was saying, "And I don't think he hates us personally, or that he hates the Spanish. I think that what he hates is Franco, the Falangists, the Nazis... He's fighting with the Russians, but not *for* the Russians. I think he's fighting for Spain."

"For Spain?" Eugenio attempted a sardonic laugh, "But Spain isn't even involved in this war!"

"Really?" Julio smiled, "Then what are we doing here? We're allies with the Germans, and they don't have many allies. And if Germany loses the war..."

"Then we lose too..."

"That's what he must be thinking. And if that happens, then his comrades – his real comrades, the Spanish republicans – will have won. That's why he's on their side."

Eugenio squeezed his eyes shut and when he opened them again, there were no tears.

"I'm going back, Julio," he said simply, "I'm going back."

Well, I'm not, thought Julio Carrión González. Pancho's desertion had triggered something in his mind. He had just discovered that, although it was still a threat, his past might well turn out to offer him security against the future, because regardless of who lost the war, he could win, and being on the winning side was all he cared about.

"Eugenio, can I ask you a favour?" A couple of days later, while they were resting in their dugout, he had already begun to fashion a plan. "The other night, that thing with Pancho... I've always thought I wouldn't be wounded, that nothing would happen to me, but if something does happen... In the bottom of my kitbag there's a leather bound Bible, it's quite beaten up, you can hardly make out what it says on the spine. It was my father's Bible, he gave it to me when we went to see him the day before we enlisted, I don't know if you remember..." Eugenio nodded. "Well, it occurred to me... I don't have any brothers here, not like you, so if anything does happen to me... I don't know why I'm asking, I'm not really religious or anything, but... would you bring that Bible to me?"

The subject was never mentioned again, the war went on, ever the same, ever worse, the interminable marching, the cold, the frost, the corpses, the blood, the lice, orders to advance, orders to retreat, major offensives that melted into nothing, resounding victories that never came. It was brutal, monotonous, mind-numbing, but its cruelty did not prevent them from fulfilling their promises. The day Julio found out that Romualdo had woken at dawn with frostbite, he did not waste time finding Eugenio. There was only one thing to do, and he knew it, others in his division had done it before: he loaded his pistol, headed straight for the small field hospital and screamed that he would gun down anyone who amputated so much as one of Romualdo Sánchez Delgado's toes.

When Eugenio found him, he still had the pistol trained on the puzzled German doctor who, through an interpreter, repeated over and over that the Führer's army would provide Romualdo with first-class prosthetics free of charge.

"Tell him I'll kill him," Julio said to the interpreter, his eyes still locked on the doctor's face.

In the end, the doctor shook his head, disappeared and came back with two ampoules of yellowish liquid which the Spanish nurse recognised immediately.

"It's to stop him getting gangrene," she explained as she injected Romualdo first in one leg, then the other, "But I'm not promising anything."

Some days later, Julio Carrión guessed where he was when he saw the same woman's face, but the first thing that he saw when he woke in pain was his father's Bible.

"That lunatic friend of yours brought it in the day before yesterday, the one who was with you when you were raising hell," the nurse said, smiling, "He said it meant a lot to you. There's a letter from him inside, I guess because he is one of the ones on his way home."

"What happened to me?"

"You have a head injury. It didn't seem serious, but then you lost consciousness and it's taken you quite a while to come round. How do you feel?"

"My head hurts. A lot."

"Take it easy, I'll give you something for the pain. And don't worry, I'll send you to Riga with the next convoy. Your brother's friend will be going with you – the one who came in with frostbite."

"Romualdo?"

Nine months later, in the Spanish War Hospital in Riga, Julio Carrión said the name again when he recognised the back of the head of a lieutenant who was moving an armchair to the window to enjoy the illusory October sun.

"Julito!" Romualdo recognised the voice before he'd even got to his feet, "It's good to see you, *macho!*"

"What are you doing here?" Romualdo had a spectacular bandage around his neck and a smaller one on his left hand, "When I heard, I couldn't believe it. You do know that if you stop getting yourself wounded, they'll discharge you and send you home. Or maybe you've fallen in love with Riga…?"

Romualdo laughed, "Don't tell me you're not enjoying life here in the rearguard…"

Julio smiled. His friend was right, his life was better than it had ever been.

"Well," he said, "in my case, the neurologist let me go home."

"Yeah, I know…"

Julio gestured to the stripes on Romualdo's uniform, "They've promoted you again?"

"Yeah, at this rate, by the time the *russkis* kill me, I'll be a colonel…"

They had been injured at much the same time, on a front even harder and crueller than the hell of Voljov. Romualdo had originally contracted frostbite in the last week of December 1942, Julio had been wounded on 1 January 1943. Their twin misfortunes had spared them certain death in the slaughterhouse of Krasny Bor but now they found themselves once more in the very same hospital to which Romualdo, having been discharged six months earlier, had just returned.

"La Luna?" Julio suggested as they stepped outside

"La Luna" Romualdo happily agreed.

"Have you had any news of Eugenio?"

"He's got a girlfriend apparently. A student, pretty ugly too, from what Arturo said in his letter… Otherwise everything's fine, he's back at university and it looks like they're going to appoint him head of the Spanish University Syndicate, because obviously he's a hero these days, but I don't know… My mother is the one who usually writes, and she makes everything sound wonderful because she wants me to come home too.

The Luna bar, which was owned by a disabled Spanish veteran who had married a Latvian girl, was almost full, but the Spanish soldiers at the tables were in no mood to sing or call for a guitar. Almost all of them were drinking alone and in silence, neither talking to their comrades, nor paying attention to the few painted ladies who would get up from the bar and wander slowly round the room.

"Well this looks cheerful," grumbled Romualdo, thinking back to the cheering and excitement of the previous winter.

"What do you expect?" asked Julio.

"I don't know…" his friend fell silent as they were served the drinks. "Apparently the Germans are developing some secret weapon, some kind of paint, well not paint exactly but some kind of coating that makes tanks invisible."

"Invisible tanks?"

"Well something like that, I don't know…" Romualdo stared at his glass. "I don't know how it works exactly, but apparently the paint or whatever surrounds the tanks with a kind of mist, that makes them invisible. One of the captains told me, and he's on good terms with the Germans…"

Julio looked at him and lifted his glass; he knew what he was hearing. Secret weapons, miraculous bombs, magic aeroplanes, uniforms made from bullet-proof fabric. He had been away form the front line for a long time but even he had heard stories like this, the old wives' tales that had proliferated since Stalingrad, the battle that was to have secured them victory but which had ended in disaster and defeat. But he simply smiled and sipped his drink. War reveals another side of a man, and Julio Carrión González had come to respect Romualdo Sánchez Delgado, a man he would never have trusted in peacetime.

"Apparently we're being shipped out," his colonel had whispered to him in that same bar less than twenty-four hours earlier, "It's not official yet, but they're about to give the order. We've known for a long time that Madrid doesn't want us here any more, since things started turning ugly back there."

Colonel Arenas glanced around to make sure no one was listening.

"I think it's disgraceful, but then they didn't ask for my opinion."

"I think so too, Colonel, you know that," Julio leaned forward placing both fists on the table, and his superior officer gave a satisfied smile.

"Even the generals in Madrid realise that they can't ship us all home at the same time, because obviously that wouldn't look good. So they're thinking about leaving a couple of battalions of volunteers who will work directly with the Wehrmacht… The Blue Legion, they want to call it, have you heard about it?"

"No, sir." This was the truth.

"The thing is, if they disband the Division, that means disbanding General Headquarters, which is tantamount to leaving thousands of soldiers on their own in the arse end of nowhere. Anyone who joins the Blue Legion will be considered a German solider so officially Spain won't be involved in the war. They're intending to leave a detachment of the Guardia Civil in place, but they're just here as Military Police – they never do anything that isn't in the rule book..." Arenas was studying Julio as though seeing him for the first time, "And the way things are going now, we might have to bend a few rules, know what I mean?" Knowing what was at stake in this comment, Julio did not blink, but held the man's gaze. "That's why I thought I'd suggest to high command that they create a new posting, and I thought you would be good, because it's a job that would suit you down to the ground."

Twenty-four hours later, sitting at a table in the same bar, Julio was replaying every word.

"OK..." as Romualdo raised his glass, he decided what he would tell his colonel, "let's drink to invisible tanks."

Julio Carrión González was not on board any of the three trains that repatriated the Blue Division in the last months of 1943. At the beginning of 1944, he was the most mysterious Spaniard in Riga. He had a small but comfortable apartment in a magnificent building in the most elegant part of the city, a sizeable income to judge from the way he squandered money, but no job, no responsibilities and no position that anyone knew of. He wore civilian clothes, though both his Spanish and his German uniforms still hung in his wardrobe, he enjoyed no particular diplomatic immunity or protection, but he was well known to the Guardia Civil responsible for order among the volunteers who had decided to stay, and was also familiar in a number of the offices at Wehrmacht headquarters.

"What I'm offering is not a cushy job, believe me..." Colonel Arenas had detailed the disadvantages of the post after Julio had accepted the position, "Or maybe it is, it certainly could be, but it's also very dangerous. After I leave, the Spanish army will officially have no presence in Riga. So you will cease to exist. I'll give you a safe conduct before I leave, but I don't know how long it will be valid if the war drags on. By the time I get back to Madrid, the pansies from the ministry may well have cancelled the operation, so I can't give you any guarantees. At worst, you might find yourself completely isolated here a couple of months from now. If that happens, it'll be up to you to make your own way back. And I don't know if the Germans will be much help, if we double-cross them."

"At your service, Colonel, don't worry about me."

Julio Carrión González was one of the few Spanish soldiers in Russia who had no wish to go home, and the only man wounded in combat who was prepared to lend a hand at General Headquarters in Riga instead of making the most of his convalescence, getting drunk every night in La

Luna. "I can't just stand by and do nothing, Colonel, while my comrades at the front..." Arenas had been so impressed by this display of gallantry when he first met Julio, that he had offered him a job as an aide-de-camp until the doctors pronounced him fit to go back to the front. Julio Carrión González knew that this would never happen, since the doctor had advised him that if he continued to suffer the savage migraines resistant to all painkillers, he would have to be sent home, and Julio had had every intention of continuing to pretend to suffer from them.

Working with Colonel Arenas, Julio discovered that life in the rearguard was tailor-made for someone like him. After a year and a half at the front, he was as dazzled by Riga as he had been by Madrid when he had first arrived there from Torrelodones. War seemed remote in the streets and the boulevards, the cafes and the restaurants of this picturesque city which, though small, had cosmopolitan ambitions and which boasted a flourishing black market. In Riga there were ample opportunities to grow rich.

And so, when his convalescence was finally over and he was definitively refused permission to return to the front, Julio quickly auctioned off his seat on the train home. Colonel Arenas, who knew nothing of Julio's financial motives for staying, interpreted his reluctance to return as proof of his devotion to the cause and authorised the change which his assistant had requested: "Don't make me go back now, Colonel, let me stay here, let me do what I can to help my comrades..."

Arenas never regretted having acceded to his aide's request. He liked Carrión, he was funny and immensely likeable, constantly telling jokes, making strings of coloured handkerchiefs appear from his pockets. Carrión knew all the best places, the liveliest bars, the finest restaurants, the most discreet brothels, he knew where to get cigarettes, brandy, perfume, even morphine. It was a pleasure to take him to the receptions and tourist excursions organised to entertain high-ranking officers, since all were charmed by the young man. But Colonel Arenas, an upright, generous, almost gentle man was no fool. It was because of this, and because he suspected that his protégé might well be capable of doing anything to get ahead, that it occurred to the colonel to leave a man behind in Riga, a covert link between the volunteers of the Blue Legion and himself and in turn a link with the Spanish High Command. If Carrión had refused the position, he would have abandoned the whole idea. But he had known that Carrión would accept.

What Colonel Arenas would never know was that Julio Carrión González would step off a train at Orleans on 25 April 1944. The retreat of the German army from the Eastern Front was so sudden that it put an end to Julio's plans of getting rich, and robbed him of the almost limitless funds in the account maintained by the War Office in Madrid. But in the hotel where he found a room for the night, no one asked for explanations.

At the time, Europe was teeming with Spaniards – civilians and soldiers, exiles and volunteers, men and women fighting for one side or another. There were so many of them in Orleans that it did not take him long to find them. By the time he did, he had bought himself some cheap French clothes and in his pocket was the JSU card which he had hidden between the flyleaf and the cover of his father's Bible three years earlier, on his last night in Madrid. At the time, he had thought it might prove useful if he was captured by the Russians. Now, he had other plans.

He did not like the look of the bitter, surly regulars he found in the first Spanish-speaking bar so decided to try his luck next door. There, at the back of the bar, he found three men some years his senior, hard-working family men who were chatting in low voices as they polished off half a bottle of wine. He moved closer so that he could hear snatches of their conversation. The tall, grey-haired man with the easy smile who was sitting in the middle gestured theatrically as he made fun of one of his friends, Julio recognised the Madrid accent as he said: "Come on, don't fuck around…" That was why Julio chose him.

"*Perdone…*" the men did not seemed surprised to be addressed in Spanish, "Could I have a light?"

"Of course, *hijo,*" said the man, "Here."

Julio lit his cigarette, looked at the men and decided they didn't look much like anarchists. So, with a sly movement, hiding his arm with his body, he raised a clenched right fist in case they were communists, but did not call them comrades, in case they were socialists.

"Cheers, *compañeros,*" he finally ventured to say in a whisper.

"Put down your fist, you little fool," the madrileño who had given him a light was shaking his head with a benevolent, almost paternal smile, "Well, aren't you just what we needed…"

The whole is equal to the sum of its parts only when the parts do not interact.

This is how it was, how it had always been before that night which altered the laws of Physics, which refuted the eternal and sacred laws of the universe, leaving my tiny insignificant shoulders unprotected.

When I left Raquel's, dawn was breaking, and on the dirty pavements between the badly parked cars, beneath the pale curtain of last laughs, I found not a shard, not a splinter, of that vital axiom which had been shattered, painlessly and without the least resistance on my part, into a million tiny, subatomic particles.

This was not me, my life was not like this, and yet never had I felt more alive than I did at that moment when I found myself alone – not free, because my freedom no longer belonged to me. The hand is quicker than the eye, and even as I walked away, I felt Raquel's hand holding me back though she did not touch me, her voice dictate my movements though she did not speak to me, and her beauty, all-powerful even in her absence, fetter my eyes completely. And I was happy, I missed nothing and no one. Not even my father, or my longing not to be his son.

I had resolved not to think about him any more, and I managed to unplug the cable, but he was still there, in some corner of my mind. I was alive, he was not. This was significant, yet it did not answer the one mystery I did not need answered, for the most mysterious thing about that night was that I did not feel the expected surprise, the awkwardness while I lay in bed with my father's mistress.

I was in bed with Julio Carrión González's lover; this was the first time I had touched her, the first time I had caressed her, kissed her, slipped my tongue, my fingers and my cock inside her. The first time that my body felt the fingers, the tongue, the mouth of this woman who was no longer my father's mistress, but mine, as though my freedom now resided in some obscure nook of her body. My freedom lay sleeping with her in a bed which felt like a new world, then like a newborn universe, impervious to the laws of physics, like a part of me that did not know how to and did not want to be reclaimed. I can't say that I did not realise what was happening, I simply didn't care, because this was the first time, and yet as I left her place, I felt as though I had done nothing, learned nothing, experienced nothing except the right to hope for the moment in which I touched, kissed, caressed Raquel Fernández Perea so that my hands, my tongue, my cock might recognise in her some unfamiliar part of myself.

"The bottom line…" said Fernando Cisneros the next day sitting at a bar halfway between his place and mine, "… is you've got it bad."

"*Hombre…*" his distillation of events was so crushing that I faltered, "I… I don't know. I suppose that's one way of putting it."

"One way?" he laughed, "Oh, no – it's the only way. I saw this coming, anyone could have seen it coming from the very beginning."

He was right. Even I had seen it coming, though I did not want to, didn't want to think about it, or even imagine it. But it was true. Anyone could have seen it coming from the very beginning, from that cold March morning when that mysterious woman had stared at me, patiently, determinedly, like someone with a mission, captivating my eyes, the useless lenses that now saw her everywhere they looked. So I did not disagree with Fernando, I simply asked for the bill.

"I assume you're paying, you dirty little fucker?" he chided me before I could take it, "It's the least you can do."

He smiled, and I saw Raquel's smile superimposed on his, floating in the warm, boisterous air of the bar as we stepped out into the street, but it was there too, on the billboards, in the shop windows, in every woman I passed… Every woman was Raquel, was on the verge of becoming her, or had already been her, it was this that defined them. I walked along the pavement, aware of the time, of Fernando waiting to cross at the zebra crossing, which was the easiest way to get to the restaurant where we'd arranged to have lunch with my wife, and I smiled, I smiled every time I remembered some detail, a gesture, an image in my short-term memory, the only memory that mattered to me now. I finally had all the variables in the equation, but now I did not feel able to solve it, and my wistful longing for my warm and safe, tender and loving home, dissipated with every step, with every thought.

"Álvaro…" Fernando put a hand on my shoulder as we waited for the light to go green.

"What?"

"Get that smirk off your face."

Afterwards, I had studied her slowly, for a long time, from her toenails with their bright red nail polish, to her long brown hair, its tousled shock of curls. I stared as if my eyes might see beyond what was in front of me, might sense the outline of the bones, the colour of the blood, the obedient ranks of muscle under her skin and still I could not understand her. She let me look, saw herself through my eyes, and waited for my eyes to meet hers. I didn't now what to say. I watched her lips curl into a lazy smile and I kissed her slowly, patiently, kissed her for a long time and the Earth began to turn again.

"You have a nice place," I said finally.

"You haven't even seen it yet!" she said, laughing.

she had led me by the hand through the foyer to a lift that was so small, so cramped, so slow, that it had seemed complicit in our fate.

"If you don't let me go, I won't be able to get the door open …"

The straps of her top had slipped from her shoulders, her skirt was rucked up to her waist and her cheeks were flushed. I kissed her before releasing her, the skirt slipped back down into place but she did not readjust her top.

"Do you want a drink?" She laughed as she held the door open for me. "No."

Her room was at the far end of a narrow corridor which had doors on either side. I bumped into scattered pieces of furniture, stumbling like a blind man, led by her lips, her eyes, allowing myself to be guided by her into the spacious room. It was curiously shaped but comfortable, a cast iron pillar with a capital of leaves and tendrils painted black stood to one side of the bed and a row of windows framed the night sky as though it were a photograph, an imagined image of itself.

"But the room is really pretty," I insisted.

By now I had had time to examine it, to study the elegant antique wooden writing desk, it's finely turned legs gracefully counterpointing a severe armchair upholstered in black leather which I also liked. The carpet was beautiful, a grid of brightly coloured geometric patterns – Turkish, I decided, or maybe Moroccan; and I liked the nineteenth-century porcelain lamp with coloured crystals dangling from white enamel arms artlessly painted with blossoms. The easy chair was upholstered in a sort of cut velvet I could never remember the name of, and ornaments were dotted here and there. I liked everything but not as much as I liked the complete incongruity of this room and that other bedroom – large, semicircular, with walls of terracotta stucco and white alcoves, that temple to a kind of bad taste only the truly rich are capable of.

"Yes, it is beautiful…" she said, "especially during the day. The view is magnificent, because we're so high up. I love this house," she smiled, "I've always loved it. I was very lucky to get it."

"Did you inherited it? I'd love to have inherited the house I lived in as a child, but one of my sisters got there first."

"I didn't live here as a child, but it was a sort of inheritance, even if I'm paying for it… What happened is that they were knocking down my old place – well, mine and my ex-husband's really, but in the divorce settlement I got the flat, and the mortgage."

"You didn't tell me you were divorced," I protested, but she laughed, and went on talking.

"Anyway, the whole street where I lived was being knocked down as part of an urban regeneration project, and instead of buying somewhere else with the money, I got another mortgage and took this place. It used to belong to my grandparents, but it was empty then. When my grandfather died, my grandmother decided to go and live with her daughter Olga whose own husband had died a couple of years earlier and who lived close to where my parents were on the Carretera de Canillejas. But she still thought of this place as home and didn't want to rent it out. She didn't even want to sell it to me. 'How can I do business with you, *hija mía*,' she'd say, but a couple of months ago, I finally managed to convince her. The truth is, no one else was interested in this apartment. Both my brothers are married and have their own place, I'm the only one who wanted to live in the centre of town, and of course I can walk to work from here. San Bernardo, Santo Domingo, Ópera... It's more or less a straight line..."

You have another place now, I thought, a much more expensive apartment than this one. I thought this, but I did not say it. She looked at me and kissed me on the lips as though to reward my silence. Then she turned and took something from the bedside table.

"This is them."

"Who?"

"My grandfathers – both of them."

It was an old crystal frame with carved corners. The photograph was of a tank, with four men leaning against it, two on either side so as not to block the driver who smiled radiantly into the camera. On his left stood two young men, one tall and blonde, the other shorter and dark-haired. They looked happy, as did the man crouching on the ground on the right, and the fourth man, also on the right who was so young he looked like a boy.

"The one pretending to drive the tank is my grandfather Aurelio Perea, my mother's father. He was a tank driver in the Rupublican army during the civil war, that's why he's sitting up there. He wanted to drive across the border in that thing..." she looked at the photo and smiled with an almost childlike innocence, stroking the crystal frame with her fingertips. "The one crouching over here," she moved her finger, "his name was Nicolás, he was Catalan, from Reus. They called him The Confectioner because before the war he used to go around the villages selling sweets. This guy here was from a village in Alicante, but I can't

295

remember his name, all I remember is that they nicknamed him The Kid because he was seventeen. I met this dark one when I was young. His name was Amadeo, known as Salmones, and he was from Asturias, he was friends with my grandfathers right up to the end. This tall, blond guy," her fingers moved to stroke the last face, is Ignacio Fernández, my father's father. He was a Capitan in the Popular Army and head of his section. When he saw the tank, he started yelling Hey, Sardine, come here, I've found a donkey you can ride back to your village…" she looked at me and smiled. "That's what they called my grandfather Aurelio, because he was from Málaga. Ignacio, my other grandfather, was from Madrid, and they called him the Lawyer, because, well, he was a lawyer. He and his wife, my grandmother Anita, were the ones who used to own this place."

I looked at the men carefully, but it was difficult to make out their faces, not so much because it was a bad photograph, though it was, nor because the photographer had taken the picture from a distance to fit in the tank, but because their smiles were so broad, so ruthless, so wild that they seemed to have taken over their faces.

"Where was this?"

"I don't really know, I can't tell you exactly… It was in one of the camps, in the woods somewhere in Ariège," she looked at me and realised I didn't understand, "a region in the French Pyrenees on the border with Spain, somewhere between Toulouse and Huesca. The photo wasn't taken during the civil war, it was the Second World War."

"I get that, but I don't understand…" and although I had resolved not to do so, I thought about my own father, his military record, the two uniforms so neat, so pristine, so utterly different from those of the smiling men who were dressed any old how. "They were soldiers?"

"Yes… well, they were guerrillas."

"They were Spanish?"

"Of course."

"But they were fighting in France."

"Yes."

"Against…" I couldn't bring myself to finish the sentence. Raquel laughed.

"Against the Nazis, obviously. The tank is a German one – they captured it along with eleven members of the SS, including two officers. They loved to tell us about it, 'You should have seen us, five poor bastards, that's what we were, a bunch of raggedy, scruffy, badly armed kids, but we captured those Ayran bastards…'" she moved closer to me and kissed me, but the glow in her face gradually faded, "They were

296

Spanish communists, exiles. They kicked the Nazis out of France, they won the Second World War, and what good did it do them? But don't worry, it's normal not to know about them. Nobody knows about them – there were thousands of them, nearly thirty thousand, but there are no Hollywood movies about them, no documentaries on the BBC. There are films about the French prostitutes who put cyanide in their vaginas, about the bakers who put poison in their *baguettes*, but never about them. If there had been a film, the audience would have wondered what happened, why they fought, what they got out of there… And in Spain we don't talk about them, we pretend they never existed… Anyway, its an ugly, unjust story. One of those Spanish stories that spoils everything"

Then she smiled again, but she could not disguise the rictus of bitterness, the trace of a terrible ache, a deep-rooted pain that she bore with modesty but also with pride. I thought it was the saddest smile I had ever seen, and I did not know what to do, what to say. She kissed the photo, put it back on the little table, then turned and hugged me; I took her in my arms and kissed her again and my body discovered in hers a warm and safe, tender and loving home with no dark attic rooms, no locked doors, no secret corners, no basements boarded up against time's humiliation.

"My father fought in World War Two," I whispered into her ear, in deference to the gentle bitterness of her smile.

"I know," she said.

"But he fought on the side of the Nazis," I went on, my lips grazing hers as I spoke, "He was in Russia with the Blue Division."

"I know," she drew away for a moment, ran her fingers through my hair and stroked my face, "But he was never here, he was never in this bed."

She said this and everything resumed it course, running gently, like water, eroding the importance of words, which suddenly seemed futile, awkward, pompous. Raquel Fernández Perea opened her eyes, and suddenly every pendulum in the world began to move in harmonic motion which brought time to a standstill, anihilated space, Raquel Fernández Perea closed her eyes making every pendulum in the world reverse its arc, taking reality to a fresh universe, tender and newly born. Raquel Fernández Perea breathed, and an invisible thread made her breasts rise, and I wanted to die…

"Álvaro…"

He wanted to die right there, to end on this moment of abundance, to give up hoarding trivial moments that were unworthy of a man who might have elected the devastating beauty of such a death. Raquel smiled, letting herself go, "Álvaro…"

A half-formed, involuntary, delicate smile, because she smiled with her whole being, with every inch of the flawless skin that quivered beneath my hands. Raquel Fernández Perea surrendered, lost control, dissolved before me, with me, only to regain control of her body, her movements suddenly more precise, more regular, and I listened to her voice, and I obeyed, I followed the voice, and I wondered what would become of me, wondered how I could ever wake up in another bed…

"Álvaro…" the third time, Fernando did not simply say my name. He stopped in the middle of the pavement and shook me by the shoulders.

"What?"

"What?" he paused for breath, but did not let go of me. "I'll tell you what. You've got this girl's cunt plastered all over your face – Jesus, I can practically see it."

"Really?" I grinned, "You can see it?"

"Pubes and all," he laughed. "Not that it bothers me, don't get me wrong, but I don't think your wife in there…" he nodded to the door of the restaurant, "is going to appreciate it the way I do."

"She didn't say anything to me this morning."

"That's because she doesn't know the signs. She's not used to it," he said, "But, believe me, my wife will spot it in a heartbeat."

"I don't care," I said without thinking, but I suppose I was telling the truth.

"Don't be such a prick, Álvarito," he shook me by the shoulders again, "Now listen up. You do care, got it? You do fucking care. And I care. So get that smirk off your face, because I'm not going to get an earful about my past sins given how virtuous I am these days."

The whole was no longer equal to the sum of its parts, even when those parts did not interact. But I tried to pretend that I still believed that, and I offered to sit with the children, between Miguelito and Max, Fernando's younger son and the peace-offering he had made his wife when he still wasn't sure if he was making the biggest mistake of his life. Max, named after Máximo his admirable great-grandfather, was a year older than Miguel, but they got on well together. That day, Miguel had brought a Spiderman doll that shot a web when you pressed a button and had a whole arsenal of guns and bombs hidden inside his body and Max had brought a Tyrannosaurus Rex with retractable claws that made realistic sounds, according to him, as though anyone had ever heard the roar of bloodthirsty dinosaur. He'd also brought a plastic Smurf to be the victim, so Spiderman dodged between the plates and napkins trying to save the Smurf until the food arrived. Mai, facing the other end of the table, listened with an attention bordering on enthusiasm to the story of her cousin Pilar, Nieves' little sister, a recent but fanatical convert to the concept of the urban spa.

From a distance, I could hear the murmur of superlatives – amazing, fantastic, fabulous, wild – as I cut up the kids' steaks for them and glanced occasionally at Fernando who would shake his head and raise his eyebrows, but he could not distract me from my task. I was thinking about Raquel, about how she had looked when I last saw her, at half-past six that same morning, when she had walked me to the door and stood there, naked, smiling, staring after me as I started down the stairs.

I was thinking about the warm, rumpled sheets on her bed, and I could picture her alone, sleeping on her side, could make out the outline of her body as she slept. She must have got up later, had breakfast in the clean, cool of the kitchen next to a window so that the sunshine could warm her body, she must be there still, maybe she went back to bed, maybe not. Maybe she is having lunch out, maybe she's meeting her actress friend, maybe she needs to tell someone, maybe not, she might be having lunch with her parents, then she will come back home, to the same warm sheets, this bed which is a new-born universe, exempt from the laws of physics which became a part of me even before I knew it.

I dreamed about these things as I thought about Raquel, my mobile phone was burning a hole in my pocket, burned and my head hummed with impatience at the gruelling effort of keeping myself under control, until during one of the abrupt silences so noticeable in noisy conversation, I head the last phrase of one my wife's recurring complaints.

"Well of course you can go but it's difficult for me, especially on Saturdays, because we have to make plans for the boy…"

"Go ahead…" I interrupted her.

"Go where?"

"To the spa – that is what you are talking about isn't it?"

"Álvaro…" my wife said, adopting a weary expression I knew all too well, the expression she always resorted to to let me know how impossible I was, "you know perfectly well we've got tickets to take the kids to the theatre this afternoon."

"Of course I remember…" I said, smiling, "But Fernando and I can take them, can't we? I mean there are no names on the tickets.

"Huh?" Fernando looked at me with an expression of panic I preferred to ignore. "What are you talking about?"

"Álvaro!" Mai shot me such a grateful smile it almost made me feel like a bastard, almost… "You'd do that for me?"

299

"Of course. I love Anderson's fairy tales, and I'm sure Fernando does too."

"Sure, I love them – and a musical too, I mean..." He kicked me under the table and lowered his voice. "Álvaro, you can't be serious."

"Fernando darling," Nieves leaned over and kissed him, definitively signing his death warrant, "You can't believe how grateful I am."

"But *The Searchers* is on TV this afternoon," he grumbled.

"You've seen it a hundred times."

"I know, but I'd like to see it a hundred and one..."

I don't know why I did it. "You scratch my back, I'll scratch yours..." I whispered to him as we left the restaurant, but he just told me to fuck off, convinced that I was going to leave him to look after Miguelito while I took off. I was tempted to, but in the end I went to the theatre with him and his kids, because I was afraid to be on my own. Because I knew that if I went home on my own I wouldn't last five minutes, I might not even make it home, because the first corner I came to, I'd turn and wind up at her place, because I didn't know what was happening to me, nothing like this had ever happened to me before.

Not used to it, Fernando had said, and it was true. For most of my life I had been an ordinary, maybe even unexceptional guy living in the little patch of garden that was my life, where there was nothing to trouble my eyes or my conscience. I had built up this patch of land, because I loved it, I loved my life, my work, Mai, and that was why I had only ever been unfaithful to her when I was away from Madrid, meaningless one night stands with women I met by chance, women who meant nothing to me. If ever I thought I might like a woman more than that, I armed myself to the teeth, that's they way I was, that's the way I'd always been, and yet now I barely recognised myself, for that man had never felt as truly alive as I did now, now that Raquel Fernández Perea had happened to me, like a twist of fate that changes the lives of those it touches forever. Yet everything seemed as simple, as elementary as hunger, thirst, asleep, this strange new definition of need which I found difficult to reconcile with the cautious man I had been. I needed to see Raquel, needed to kiss her, caress her, to possess her, I needed to hear her voice, to breathe her in, but most of all I needed to know that tomorrow, this urgent, brutal need would burn in me still. I needed to need Raquel. This was what sustained me in my resolve not to move too fast, not to overwhelm her as long as I could feel her on my face, between my hands, under my skin just by closing my eyes.

"It was good, wasn't it?" I said to Fernando as we came out of the theatre with the kids, still excited, their hands red from clapping. "I

300

enjoyed it."

"What?" he raised an eyebrow.

"What do you think – the musical."

"Will you buy us the CD, Papá, please!"

"No way, we've spent far too much money already." Fernando dismissed his daughter's request with the same brusqueness I would have used on any other day.

"I'll buy it for you, Lara." I said before turning to the boys, "What about you boys, do you want a tee-shirt?"

"It's a terrible age," my best friend looked at me worriedly and patted me on the back, " a terrible age to go losing your head..."

In the end, I held out for forty-eight hours.

I had my head screwed on more tightly than ever and I held out for forty-eight hours, an agonising ocean of seconds, although they dissipated the moment I saw her again, when she looked at me and decreed the non-existence of every living thing beyond the compass of her encircling arms.

I had held out for forty-eight hours and during that time nothing had happened, yet a lot of things had happened.

"Your grandmother was a strong-willed woman, Julio."

"Álvaro," I gently reminded her.

"Yes, of course ..." She thought for a moment, and her small, deep eyes glittered like pin heads. "A strong-willed woman. Too strong-willed, perhaps."

On Saturday evening, after the musical and half a pizza, Miguelito had fallen asleep in the back of the taxi and I'd had to carry him up to his room. Mai wasn't much more awake, but she opened her eyes and gave me a radiant smile.

"You OK?"

"Wonderful. You can't imagine, you should try it. Come here... smell me." she was lying on her back on the bed, naked, half covered by the sheet, her arms flung wide.

I sat on the edge of the bed and inhaled deeply. She smelled of vanilla and cinnamon and something like mint.

"It's amazing, you smell like an ice-cream parlour."

"Really?" she chuckled, "It's a relaxing body treatment. You shower in cold water then hot water then cold, then you put the cream on. The masseuse recommended it, I'm floating on a cloud right now, honestly. It contains hashish extract, that's why they have to put in so much perfume."

301

"It must be wonderful." I leaned over and kissed her on the lips, "Do you want me to pull the sheet over you?" She nodded. "OK, I'm just going on the computer for a bit, I'm not tired."

"But you didn't sleep at all last night."

It was true, but I hadn't been tired then either. I sat in front of the computer but I didn't manage to switch it on. Teresa González, young and serene, in her little hat and pearl earrings, stared out at me from the silver frame, the very picture of a smiling, harmless middle-class wife. Her picture sent a sudden wave of love surging through me, as deep as it was ambiguous, since it related to everything I had gained and everything I had lost in losing my father. I had gained a grandmother, and found a rare fierce happiness. Everything had changed so much, so quickly, that I could not analyse what was happening to me and experience it simultaneously. I had decided to experience it, and yet when I picked up the photo of Teresa González and touched the glass with my fingers, as I had seen Raquel do with the photograph of her grandfathers, I wondered whether it was not more commonplace for people to have photos of their father or their mother on their bedside table.

I should have continued in that vein, gone on probing the differences, the coincidences, the real meaning of the old words that weighed so heavily on us, kept us obligated after so many years, but Spanish stories ruin everything, and I had fallen in love, and I had decided not to analyse that love but to experience it, to serve it loyally and selflessly, with the noble spirit of a medieval knight or the terrible desperation of a treacherous son rebelling against his father. My father. Two words that had never been a problem for me, before I knew Raquel, before I knew Teresa, the young beatific smile of a woman whose luck had run out, for whom reason and justice and liberty did not win through. My grandmother, a sudden wave of love and an intensity, a purity difficult to explain, would have made me a better man if I had known her earlier, if I had known her in time. Her memory would have stayed with me for years, would have given meaning to my name, but she had turned up now, when I was wrapped up in a complex and contradictory confusion, a fervour that simultaneously included and excluded her.

Bad luck hounded you your whole life, grandma. I would have loved you so much, would have boasted about you to the girls I fancied at university... I would have learned your letter by heart and recited it over and over, to the girls, to myself, so that I could feel your presence, feel your support when I decided to be different, decided to be the son my father never wanted, the only son who did not want to be like him. I needed you so much, grandma, you were here and I didn't know you, but

302

now I see Raquel Fernández Perea everywhere I look, I am bound by the need to need her.

I pressed my lips through the glass before setting the frame down again next to the monitor, and the memory of Raquel's lips came to me with sudden excitement that made my hair stand on end. Afterwards I went to bed, calmly, as though my life had not been turned upside down in the past three days, as though I felt able to cope with my confusion. But before I fell asleep, I wondered what sort of secrets forty-year-old sons might discover about their recently deceased fathers at the beginning of the 21st century, and it occurred to me that there was a detail that eluded me.

I did not realise what it was the next morning when I woke up, late, less good-humoured than Mai who floated around the house as though her body weighed nothing. But much later, as I was sitting at the lunch table with my in-laws, I realised what I had not noticed. Sunday afternoon was heavy and slow and favourable to contemplation, but as Mai allowed herself to be crushed under the weight of the hours that separated her from the bliss of the previous afternoon and I sat in front of the television with Miguelito, seeing the beauty of Raquel's body in every frame of Disney's *Peter Pan,* my mind came back again and again to a nagging, insoluble detail to which I could find no explanation. My grandmother Teresa had walked out on her husband on 2 June 1937. Her son was had joined Unified Socialist Youth 52 days later. The discovery of Julio Carrión González two membership cards had so shocked me that I had memorised the date of the first – 23 July 1937 – without realising what it meant. Now, the discrepancy between these two dates seemed more despicable, more painful, than the existence of the membership card for the Falange Española from 1941.

To be a traitor is first and foremost to betray yourself. Maybe it is this lack of self-respect at the root of all betrayal that makes traitors so contemptible. At the time when my father changed sides, ideological treason was much more than a theoretical shift. He had often told us about his friend Eugenio, the only honest man this country had ever produced, the only one who could have used people, but never used people, could have stolen, but never stole, who could have informed, but never did. I remembered his words, had filed them away as though they were the words to a banal, repetitive song the chorus of which was "Cold? You think this is cold? You should have been in Russia, in Poland, now that was cold!" Traitors first and foremost, betrayed themselves, and stick to his ideals, regardless of what it was had come between my father and my grandmother, would have been more honest, more loyal, more respectful of her than to join the Youth Movement of her party and then jump ship when the die were cast, only to bury her alive later on.

It was no use thinking that I was getting things out of proportion, or reminding myself that I knew a lot less than I thought I did. "Maybe I am wrong, but I am doing what I feel I have to do, and I am doing it for love." This was what my grandmother had done, and that was what I did on Monday morning. I gave a first-rate lecture, though I wasn't sure why, though I was shorn of my freedom, though Teresa González was lodged in my heart and my father was weighing on me like some crippling debt I owed or was owed – all I knew was that it was long overdue. But even so, I gave a first-rate lecture which finally put paid to the prestige of that little patch of garden that had been my life.

At 12.40pm, the registry office in Torrelodones was deserted. I thought my luck had finally failed me, but I cleared my throat, banged on the reception desk, and a skinny, young man in glasses appeared, looking at me nervously with the terrified air of a trainee. He could have been one of my students, and that thought reassured me.

"OK. Can you fill out these forms please..." he said when I explained the purpose of my visit.

"Listen," I cut him off, "I can't hang around. This is really important to me. I'm a professor, I teach at U.A.M., and I don't have much time..."

"You don't have to come back," he replied. "We can post the information to you in Madrid."

"I know, but I'm guessing everything is on computer, isn't it?" He nodded warily, "So even if you're going to send me the information later, couldn't you look it up quickly right now and just tell me. It'll only take five minutes."

'That's not procedure. Standard practice is to send the information by post, my boss isn't here right now, and I'm just a student, I'm only here for ten days, and..." He looked at me, clicked his tongue then nodded. "What was your grandmother's name?"

"Teresa González."

"Teresa González what?"

"I don't know." He looked at me, his eyes wide. "Honestly, I don't know, as I said before, no one ever talked about her at home, I didn't even know she had had another child, and I've only just found out that she didn't die of tuberculosis in 1937. I think she might have been a victim of the reprisals after the war, but I don't know. Maybe she left the country, I've no idea. All I know is that my father was born here in Torrelodones on 17 January 1922."

"That should be enough…" he mumbled, more to himself than to me, before disappearing through a glass door.

It took longer than five minutes, but he was back within ten.

"Puerto," he said handing me three sheets of paper. "Teresa González Puerto, daughter of Julio and María Luisa, born on 3 August 1900 in Villanueva de los Infantes, a village in Ciudad Real. I've found only three documents relating to her. A marriage certificate dating from 1920 when she married Benigno Carrión Moreno, a birth certificate dated 1922 for her first child, Julio Carrión González, and a second birth certificate dated 1925 for Teresa Carrión González. That's all there is. She certainly didn't die in this district. Are you registered as living in Madrid?" I nodded, "In that case, you can go to the registry office there and put in a request. It make take them a while, because they'll have to circulate it to all the sub-offices in Spain, but they'll track her down, unless her death was…" He stopped, groping for a word. "Unless her death was, let's say… unofficial. There were thousands of men and women whose deaths were never officially registered. Some of them were declared dead later on, when their families brought pressure to bear, but if you say that your father didn't want anything to do with her, I'm not so sure…"

"Because he was a Spanish Communist not a Polish Jew, my father wasn't lucky enough to be sent to the gas chambers by the Nazis."

Adolfo Cerezo, a man Angélica introduced us to that evening, said these words in my living room with a drink in his hand and a serene smile on his face.

Later, while Mai, who had been involved in organising the dinner party, disappeared to find a box of chocolates, get more ice from the kitchen, check on Miguel, open the French windows, and show my sister the new dress she'd just bought, I listened as he told me about his mother's family who were from a village on Gran Canaria named Arucas.

"The war never got that far," he said in the same sociable, seemingly offhand tone, "The rebels dispatched the whole African army to the islands and there was no way anyone could resist, there was no revolution, the people had no guns, there were no priests shot, no nuns raped, no riots, no propaganda, nothing. Arucas held out longer than anywhere else, and that was only for a day and a half. I'm sure you've never heard about this before …"

"No," I admitted, "But the name sounds familiar."

"Oh, it's a big place. That's probably why the Falangists thought it would cost them a fortune in bullets. So they caught my grandfather and about sixty other Republicans, threw them down a well and tipped in quicklime - not too much, you understand, just enough so the ones at the top couldn't get out, they were famously stingey..." He paused before explaining, "Auschwitz was more compassionate, you know, because the men at Arucas took a long time to die. Nearly a week. And they cried and pleaded, and the quicklime glowed in the night, and the people in the village called it the well of wailing witches, because what happened was like witchcraft. But they went on sleeping the sleep of the just all the same. That's why my grandmother moved out to the peninsula, because she couldn't bear to hear that name, and she never set foot in Arucas again. My mother was seven years old when they left the village and she never went back either. But it's a nice place – that's almost the worst of it – Arucas is pretty..."

"You've been there?" I said. He nodded.

"Many times. And I went to the well. I saw where it had happened, I even took flowers, there are always flowers there, some dried and withered, others fresh, piled on top of the well cover."

"That's terrifying. What an appalling story," I said at length.

"Yes, it is appalling," Adolfo agreed, "Because he was a Spanish Communist not a Polish Jew, my father wasn't lucky enough to be sent to the gas chambers by the Nazis."

"I know it's a terrible thing, and it must be terrible to have to live with such a story, but I have to say the whole thing gives me the creeps," said Mai after my sister and her boyfriend had left, "to still be dwelling on it all these years later..."

"If we'd dealt with these things earlier, we wouldn't need to do it now..." I said, though at the time I didn't really know what I was saying, I didn't fully realise the significance until that morning at the hall of records in Torrelodones as I looked into the eyes of the strange boy who was trying to prepare me for the worst.

"If we'd dealt with these things earlier, we wouldn't need to do it now," this was what I had said, but at the time I didn't know what it was to imagine the terror, the suffering, the desperation, the fear and the pain which might contort a face – the face of a man, a woman, that a child has seen every day of his life, smiling out of a photograph on the sideboard, hanging in the hallway of the house where he grew up. "Your grandfather, your grandmother, my mother," just a name and a face and if you're lucky a sentence or two, maybe some beautiful or valuable object that had once belonged to them, but nothing more, no living memory to connect you to the frozen smile of the past. Then the darkness comes, the ground opens up, a lock slides home, a firing squad assembles or the barrel of a gun is pressed to the nape of a neck, and then we sense what we have never seen: the terror, the suffering, the desperation, the fear and the pain, we feel this body we have never held, the hands we have never touched, the tears that the photograph can never shed, and the acrid taste of lead in our mouths.

I felt these things as I imagined Teresa González Puerto tumbling into a well, collapsing in a ditch, dying in a mass grave, her eyes slowly closing as she waited for death. "Your grandmother was a good woman, she loved her husband and she loved to play the piano…" I felt all these things and my face distorted with rage. "I go to Arucas from time to time, I don't know why, but I feel I need to go, it makes me feel better. I look at the well, I take flowers, that's all, it sounds stupid, but I need to do it…" Adolfo had told me that night. Yet there are others – the grandchildren of the rebels, of the fascists, of the Arucas butchers whose version of the story would be different, whose rage and tears would be different from Adolfo's, from Fernando's or my own. I thought about this, but my grandmother's name had been Teresa González Puerto, and she had lost the war but had never lost her reason, she deserved me to win on her behalf.

"I'm really sorry," the boy had looked at me, his face concerned, almost afraid. "I shouldn't have said that, I've got no reason to think… I'm really sorry."

"You've nothing to be sorry for, just the opposite," I forced myself to remain calm, took his hand and he shook it firmly. "I'm very grateful to you."

I took the official version of my grandmother's life, three meagre sheets of paper, and walked towards the main square. The café terraces were almost empty, it was early, it was Monday. I picked a table in the sunshine and ordered a beer from a short, engaging, dark-haired waitress who looked like she might be from Ecuador or maybe Peru. I drank the beer and ordered another as I read and re-read the documents, the summary printed in ten-point Arial at the top of the photocopy. Then I paid the bill, left a generous tip and went into the bar.

"Excuse me, I don't know if you can help me, I'm looking for someone…" It was the appearance of the woman behind the bar – fifty-something, sturdy, self-possessed – that persuaded me to talk to her. "Are you from here?"

"No, but I've been living here for thirty years," she said, smiling.

"I see…" I smiled back. "Its, well… I'm looking for some friends of my father, he was born here in Torrelodones but he left for Madrid when he was young. I thought maybe you might know them… On of them is called Anselmo, he'd be quite old, the same age as my father was when he died at eighty-three…"

"No…" she shook her head. "I don't know anyone called Anselmo."

"And a woman everybody always called Encarnita?"

"A tall woman with short grey curly hair, very tall and old…"

It was her. No only did the woman know Encarnita, she knew where she lived. I got lost more than once, taking the wrong turning at ridiculous roundabouts that looked as though they had been deliberately designed to disorient drivers who weren't local, before finally finding the place, a stone cottage set in an overgrown garden with tall trees surrounded by a hedge of rose-laurel. Next to the gate there was an entry phone. I pushed the button and said I had come to see Encarnita. Someone buzzed me in. A blonde woman of about thirty with short hair and pale white skin stood at the door waiting for me.

"Good morning."

"Good morning," she replied, and from her accent I realised that she was foreign.

"My name is Álvaro Carrión, I'm the son of an old friend of Encarnita," I articulated slowly, "I'd like to talk to her for a minute, if that's all right."

"La Señora no here."

"What time will she be back?" The woman didn't answer. "I don't mind waiting."

"Señora Encarnita here, Señora Encarna no here."

"OK, but…" The coincidence of the names made me wonder. "I don't know… I'm looking for the older lady."

"Ay!"

That was all she said, her nervous expression looking almost like grief. She disappeared, leaving the door open. Some minutes later she came back with a young girl wearing tight jeans, a cropped tee-shirt and a blue stud in her bellybutton.

"Hi," she stuffed her hands into her pockets and smiled, "Jovanka said something about my grandmother, but I didn't really understand what she was saying. She's from Croatia."

"That's probably why she didn't understand me. The thing is…"

I introduced myself, explained who my father was, told her I had seen her grandmother at the funeral and that I wanted to talk to her because I thought she might have known my grandmother.

"Oh, OK… I'm sure she'd love to, she loves talking to people, but she gets tired easily…" Just then, we heard a car and she craned her neck to look. "Look, there's my mother now."

I repeated my story for the third time to a graceful, friendly woman a little older than me, who listened and nodded until she felt she didn't need to hear any more.

"Come with me," she stepped into the hall, then turned to her daughter. "Cecilia, go and tell Jolanka your father phoned to say he won't have time to come back for lunch…"

"OK, but after that I'm coming back to listen."

Her mother smiled and walked down the hall to a glass door through which the sun streamed. There, in a semi-circular living room that opened onto a back porch which revealed how old the house truly was, Encarnita was sitting in front of the television, ramrod straight in a wicker chair stuffed with cushions. She did not seem particularly interested in the programme because she turned and looked at us, then switched off the television.

"Hello Mamá…" her daughter bent down, kissed her forehead and stroked the woman's cheek. "How are you feeling? Look, you've a visitor. This young man is…"

"I know," Encarnita cut her daughter short, looking at me, "I recognise you."

"Yes, we met recently at my father's funeral," I said, "My name is…"

"Julio Carrión."

"No," I smiled, "That was my father's name, and I have a brother named Julio, but my name is Álvaro. Álvaro Carrión."

She was a little taken aback, and I realised she had mistaken me for my father. Her daughter asked if we would like something to drink then headed towards the kitchen. The teenager with the pierced bellybutton showed up and sat next to her grandmother who gazed at her for a moment, as though she didn't recognise the girl.

"Of course…" she said after a moment, "You're Julio's son. So you're Benigno's grandson, then…"

"That's right." I nodded, smiling, trying hard to mask my disappointment, but it was as if she could tell what I was thinking.

"I've still got all my marbles, you know, but sometimes I forget, I get lost in the past and it takes me a minute to get my bearings. Apparently it has something to do with my circulation, at least that's what the doctor tells me, but once I get my bearings, I'm fine," she smiled and turned to her granddaughter, "Isn't that right Cecilia?"

"You're in great form," Cecilia took the woman's hand and squeezed it, "I wish my memory was as good."

"The thing is, the reason I've come…" But after what she had said, I felt it would be insulting to beat around the bush. "Encarnita, did you

309

know my grandmother, Teresa?"

"Your grandmother?" She opened her eyes wide. "Of course I knew her! Everyone in the village knew your grandmother. And not just this village – she was well know in these parts, your grandma…"

"And do you remember… Do you remember if she was a socialist?"

"A socialist?" Encarnita burst out laughing, then slapped her thighs and looked at me as though this was the stupidest thing anyone had ever asked her. "Of course she was! Although saying she was a socialist is putting it mildly, she was more than that… your grandmother all but invented socialism in these parts. No one in the village had ever heard of socialism until your grandmother got it into her head to get involved in politics…" She raised her finger, suddenly serious.

"Now let me tell you something. She might have been a socialist, in fact she was a dyed-in-the-wool Red, but she was a good woman, I'll say that for her. She was intelligent and she was brave. Maybe too brave, but I never met a better woman. I was very fond of your grandmother, because Teresita… she'd be your aunt wouldn't she?" I nodded at the name of this woman I had never seen, even in photos.. "Well, now, Teresita and me, we were the same age and the best of friends, so I'd go round to your grandparents house nearly every day, for tea, or to play with Teresita, and of course she'd come over to my house too… Later, my parents forbade me from going to her house, after your grandmother became a teacher, but I still saw her at school every day."

"Why exactly did your parents forbid you from going to my grandparent's house?"

"On account of your grandmother, of course. She was a militant, she was very active politically – you can't imagine – and my family were monarchists, one of my mother's brothers had been executed by communists in Madrid. Now here was your grandmother, holding rallies in the street… as you can imagine, they didn't approve."

"But my grandfather was right-wing?

"Your grandfather was… I suppose he was right wing. More than anything he was a Holy Joe, but he was never very comfortable at home because…" She shook her head. "I don't like to speak ill of the dead, but your grandfather was spineless, and that's the truth, he was always a weak man, even my mother said it, and his wife was worth ten of him. I think that worried my own father, you know? Because my mother… Well, she was a Nationalist, I'm not saying she wasn't, but back then, women suddenly had a lot more freedom, the could come and go as they pleased, they had the vote, they had the right to get married without their parent's consent, they could divorce and keep custody of their children, they could go out to work, live on their own, they could be leaders of political parties, they could be elected, become ministers... Just imagine it!"

She looked at me as though waiting for me to draw my own conclusions.

"And your mother was happy about that?"

"Of course she was happy! Why wouldn't she be?" Encarnita laughed "I was only a little girl back then, I didn't understand, but looking back on it now, well... I think my mother was very fond of your grandmother, if only because she felt grateful for what she had done for women. And my father couldn't bear that, he couldn't stomach all this talk of women's rights. I was the one he took it out on, because I was terribly fond of Teresita... Not that I did as I was told, of course. I didn't go to your grandparents house any more, but I still played with your aunt at school, or out in the street, or down by the river. That's the way things were back then I could only have been eleven or twelve at the time, but I defied my father. Some of your grandmother must have rubbed off on me..."

She smiled again, and I smiled too as the ghost of Teresa González hovered over us like a good fairy, a gentle, munificent presence untroubled by the arrival of a lanky teenage boy, his face scarred with acne. His name was Jorge, and as he sat eating all the crisps his mother had brought, I realised that there was a question I would have to ask sooner or later.

"Encarnita... do you know how my grandmother died?"

"Well, I..." She looked at me, as though realising how strange the question was. "Surely you know... I mean your father must know?"

"I don't," I clasped my hands together, squeezing them hard, suddenly ashamed of the extent of my ignorance. "I suppose he must have known, but I don't. He never talked to us about his mother. Never. A couple of days ago, among his papers, I found the letter she wrote to him when she left. It wasn't until then that I found out she was a socialist, that she'd left her husband, and that she had a daughter. Before I read that letter, I believed my father was an only child and that my grandmother had died of tuberculosis in 1937."

"God preserve us!" Encarnita shook her head, "That's... it's shameful!"

"Yes," I looked her in the eye, I couldn't turn away. "It is."

"I mean I can understand... in those days, it was difficult being the child of certain people, it could even be dangerous... But afterwards... for him to say nothing to you, her grandchildren."

She gave a long pause. "I don't know, maybe... In any case, your grandmother did not die of tuberculosis. *He* was the one with the disease."

"Her lover?"

"I wouldn't call him her lover..." She took a moment to consider the word before rejecting it. "The man she lived with."

"Manuel," I said.

"That's right, Manuel Castro. He was a teacher, too, and a socialist, he was a good man. He was a great orator, from what people said. Your grandmother was a fine public speaker, but he... I was only a child, but even I could tell, because back then a politician needed to be imposing. They were statesmen, you understand? Not like the politicians nowadays, changing their minds every other day, they were leaders, and they knew what they were talking about. "Don Manuel was held in high regard in the party, like your grandmother in her own way, she was one of the leading lights too... Anyway, they were made for each other, truly they were. He was the one who had had tuberculosis, but by the time he came to Torrelodones, he was cured. He was tall and slim, but he was a strapping man. All the children loved him, because he was a magician."

"He was a magician?" Suddenly my heart was pounding, "You mean he did magic tricks?"

"Of course. He was the one who taught your father." I nodded. "If we were well-behaved in school, and we'd done all our homework, Don Manuel would make things appear out of his pockets, from behind his ears, and then make them disappear again." Her eyes lit up. "It was marvellous... and what with that, and the fact that he lived with your grandparents, on account of he'd been evacuated from Las Rozas, well anyway... What happened, happened. Now I'm going to tell you something else..." She raised her index finger again. "It was an awful scandal, everyone was shocked because, you see, he was married too, he even had children, but they weren't thinking about that, they didn't worry about such things. Your grandmother didn't hide herself away, she wasn't ashamed – quite the opposite, she looked radiant, it did your heart good to see her, because she was convinced that she had every right to do what she was doing. That's how she was, and I have to say, I think she was right, I envy her, because I..."

She stopped suddenly, as though she'd bitten her tongue, and shot me a look of panic that I didn't know how to interpret.

"Well now, where was I?" she said quickly, "They left the village, taking Teresita with them, or maybe Teresita decided she wanted to go. Your father, he didn't want to leave, so he stayed her with your grandfather. It's strange because Julito adored Don Manuel, they were always together, Julio was even his assistant when he did magic shows for the soldiers.. Afterwards, they were both put in prison, separately of course. Don Manuel was released years later, I know that much, even if I can't remember now who told me…"

"What about my grandmother?"

"Your grandmother… Yes…" She looked me in the eye. "Your grandmother died in prison somewhere, but I don't remember where. There were a lot more prisons back then, but it was one of the famous ones… All I know is that, like all the other teachers, she was given a long sentence. But she died soon afterwards, two or three years later, I think. It might have been tuberculosis, but I don't remember now… The only thing I remember is that your grandfather mentioned it to my father, and that's how I know."

I felt a great wave of relief and a surge of grief at the cruel way things had turned out. It was a relief to know that she had not been executed, that she had not left home alone, but it was terrible to know that like so many others she had not survived. I was a comfort to know she hadn't been tossed into a well, that she hadn't been dragged from her bed at dawn and shot dead by the side of a road, but it was horrifying to think of where and how she might have died. It was better that she had not lived to see what her enemies had done to this country and terrible that she had not lived despite what her enemies had done to this country.

Encarnita stared at me as I chided myself for my naïveté, for my weakness in thinking that somehow Teresa might have survived. Many people had survived, but in my heart I had always known that she was not one of them, because had she still been alive, her son would not have been able to erase her so completely.

"She was a strong willed woman, Julio."

"Álvaro…" I reminded her gently.

"Yes, yes…" she was deep in thought, "A strong willed woman. Too strong-willed, perhaps."

She was a strong-willed woman, I thought, Teresa González Puerto, a good woman, a very good woman, a fact worth mentioning since to be a good mother is not a given when a woman is strong, intelligent and brave in a land where the laws of gravity do not apply. Teresa González Puerto had married the wrong man, had tried to be a meek middle-class wife but could not bear it. She had believed in the dream of her own freedom, had risked everything only to lose everything, even her life. And so, although it grieved me to see my grandmother's smile, the memory of her urged me on to another strong woman.

"What about this photograph?" I handed it to Encarnita and she brought it close to her face. "Do you know who this woman is?"

"She's extraordinarily beautiful," she said with a smile.

"Extraordinarily beautiful," I agreed.

"But I'm afraid I don't know who she is. If I'd seen her, I would remember." She paused a moment then peered at the photo again. "The man is your father, of course, it would have been around the time he came back."

"The photo was taken in 1947," I said, "There's a inscription on the back."

She turned it over and thought for a moment: "Paloma, Paloma... I don't know. There are so many girls called Paloma. But he didn't bring her back here, that much I can tell you. 1947, that's right... He'd been gone for years by then, I never thought he'd come back, there were three of them from Torrelodones who shipped out to Russia, one of them was killed, and the other one came home three or four years before your father."

"What did he do?" I asked, suspicious now of everything I thought I knew. "Did he go back to live with my grandfather."

"Certainly not! Your father never liked the village..." She laughed, before going on to confirm what we as his family had always known, "Or to be precise, he liked to come here to be seen, to strut around and boast, and that he did, because he came back a gentleman, with money and fine clothes, not at all like your grandfather, who was always a country bumpkin... Your father was a real ladykiller, he had a way with women. I never saw it myself, but there was many a girl in the village who made cow-eyes at him, and then of course there was Señorita María."

"Señorita María?" The name meant nothing to me.

"Mariana, her name was, she was the niece of Don Mateo Fernández who owned the Casa Rosa." she said, taking it for granted that I knew what she was talking about.

"It's a big mansion up on the hill," her daughter interrupted, "You can get there from a path at the end of the street. You can't really see it from here, but it's a beautiful old house, with ivy on the walls. You should take a look at it before you leave... Nowadays, there are several modern houses around it, three of them, I think, but back then it was all part of the Casa Rosa gardens."

"So what did my father have to do with the house?"

"Well..." Encarnita frowned, "To be honest, no one ever quite knew. Your father would come back, and obviously everyone in the village knew him, but apart from visiting your grandfather, he would go up to see Señorita Mariana. I can still see him walking up that hill… People used to say they were having an affair, but who knows? People like to talk and more often than not, they haven't the first idea. And besides, aside from the fact that Señorita Mariana was quite a bit older than your father, she always struck me as a cold, serious, rather bitter woman, maybe because her husband died early on, leaving her with a little girl – a pretty little thing, with blue eyes and blonde hair… I have to say, blonde hair did run in the family – most of the Fernándezs were blonde and blue-eyed. I don't remember the little girl's name. Her mother didn't allow her to come down to the village, they never had any dealings with us, you know the kind… thought they were better than us. They'd turn up every June in a taxi, and we wouldn't see hide nor hair of them, except at mass on Sundays, until a taxi came to collect them in September. Fermina, who used to be Don Mateo's housekeeper, would do their shopping for them, but apart from her and her husband and kids, your father was the only one Señorita Mariana ever talked to. But she wasn't the kind of woman to have an affair with a man like him."

"Why not?" I asked, "If he was such a ladykiller…"

"Ladykiller he might have been, but back then things weren't the same as they are now. People were very correct, Señorita Mariana was a lady and he was… well, he was no one, even if… I don't know, you can never tell. But there was some link between them, that much I do know, because every time he came to Torrelodones, he'd go up to see her. And later, when the house was sold, she wrote to the mayor, to her lawyer, she even wrote to the Civil Guard saying he was the one who had put her out on the street, said that he'd stolen the place from her even though that house had never really belonged to her. To Señorita Mariana, I mean… It belonged to her uncle Mateo though I'll grant you that before that it had belonged to her grandfather, her father's father. But it was Don Mateo who inherited it when the estate was divided up. Don Mateo got the house, and Señorita Mariana's father, Mateo's older brother, must have got something else. The family had a lot of money."

"But then…" I was completely lost by now, "Why was she living in the house if it wasn't hers and she had money of her own? And how could my father have been responsible for putting her out on the street?"

"Ah, *hijo*, that I don't know… Nobody knows, or at least nobody in the village does, it was always a curious business. Señorita Mariana spent the summers at the house because the people who owned it weren't here, in Spain I mean. I think they moved to France after the war."

"So they were Republicans?"

"Pah!" she smiled, waving her hands emphatically, "Atheists, that's

315

what they were, wouldn't let me near the house, wouldn't even let me up the hill... The children – though they weren't really children, you understand, the youngest of them would have been ten years older than me – well, the children never made their communion, they weren't even baptised. Their parents wouldn't give my parents the time of day by then, whereas before the war, they had all got on well together. But that wasn't unusual in those days... After the war, they left and went to France and they left the keys to the house and to their place in Madrid with their niece Señorita Mariana, she was the only one who stayed behind."

"And she got to keep everything?" I guessed, and Encarnita nodded vehemently, "Because if she stayed here in Spain, she must have been in with the new regime."

"That's what everyone round here thought... No one was surprised and it wasn't a time to grumble or ask awkward questions... Don Mateo didn't come here for three summers during the war, it wouldn't have been possible, not with the front at Moncloa. And then one day his niece shows up as lady of the manor – she liked to put on airs, and was prickly with it, because she was flat broke. I don't know what her father had done with all his money, but it was gone. After that, well I expect it's as you say..." she shook her head sadly, "When her family left, she must have thought she'd won the lottery and was set up for life. Then one day your father shows up in the village and he's a Falangist. About a year later, the house was sold and we never saw Señorita Mariana or the little girl again, it was as if the ground had opened up and swallowed them. It was almost the same with your father, it was a long, long time before he came back to the village – ten years, I think. Well, he'd come to see your grandfather, but he'd park the car right outside the front door, and he'd leave without saying a word to anyone. By the time I next talked to him, he'd married a foreign girl and they had two or three children – you're a big family aren't you?"

"There are five of us. But my mother isn't foreign."

"I know, I know," she smiled, "But we always called her that because she looked a bit foreign, and because your father had been all over the world... she turned up here one day, slim and elegant and wearing sunglasses that covered half her face, and she was always so quiet, it was as if she didn't understand what was being said. Someone said, 'She must be foreign', and that's what we all thought. Later on... well, I never did talk to her much, but when she stopped and said hello I realised she wasn't foreign."

The whole story sounded so bizarre that I was convinced there had to be a simple explanation. "But maybe my father was working for an estate agent who wanted to buy the property, and maybe they did the deal directly with the owners. As far as I know, he always worked in the property business, and he started out buying places that were falling down, doing them up and selling them on."

"That would make sense," Encarnita's daughter said.

"Maybe, I'm don't know..." Encarnita was clearly not convinced, "As I said, it was all very mysterious."

She handed me back the photograph and I slipped it into my wallet, checked my watch and realised it was half past two. I took Encarnita's hands in mine, and apologised for taking up so much of her time.

"You can't imagine how grateful I am for everything you've told me about my grandmother. Honestly, I can't thank you enough."

"Are you leaving already?" she said, clearly surprised.

"Mamá," her daughter said gently, "I'm sure he wants to have his lunch, and we should be having ours."

"All right, but first... Can someone bring me the photo from the dressing table in my room?" Her granddaughter got to her feet, "I want you to see this before you go."

It was an ordinary class photograph, fifty pupils – boys and girls – lined up by age and height on the steps of a large building. There were four adults in the picture – three men and a woman – two on the bottom step, flanking the children in the front row, the other two standing together one step higher than the back row. The woman looked like a younger, sultry, stylised version of my grandmother, her hair loose, her eyes shining. Next to her was a thin, dark-haired man, his long face seen in profile, and he was gazing at her, smiling, as though they were alone.

"That's my grandmother, isn't it?" Encarnita nodded at my redundant question, "And that must be Manuel."

"Yes. See the way he's looking at her? That's why there was such a scandal when it all came out... That little girl there, that's Teresita. And there, that's me, and that girl there is Amada..."

Teresa Carrión González looked like her mother and her brother. Dark-haired with dark eyes her hair was parted in the middle and braided into two pigtails each tied with a ribbon. Her nose was smaller than my father's had been, but her mouth, with its thick lips, could have been my own. Posing stiffly but happily, wearing a clean smock, her hands tucked into the pockets, her chin tilted upwards just like her mother. I gazed at her for a long time.

"Would you mind lending it to me? I'd like to have a copy made..."

"No!" she snatched the photograph away with a strength I would not have suspected. "It's out of the question."

"But Mamá…" By the time her daughter intervened, she was clutching the frame to her chest. "He's not going to keep it, he just wants to have a copy made and then he'll bring it back. Surely you don't mind…"

"Well, I do mind! I mind very much."

"But it's his grandmother, Mamá! How can it hurt…"

"It can hurt! It hurts me…" Now Encarnita had lost her composure, she was wailing like a little girl; and I suddenly felt sorry that I had upset her. Then she said something which was even more surprising. "To me, it's a photograph of your mother, and I don't want him having it, I don't want him borrowing it. It's mine and I want to keep it."

"All right, Mamá…" Encarna put her arms around the old woman, "It's all right, you don't have to give him the photo. He doesn't mind, do you?" She glanced at me, signalling that we would talk about it later.

"No, of course not," I said quickly, "I'm terribly sorry I upset you."

"Don't worry about it," Encarna reassured me, "It's all right. Cecilia, take grandma back to her room. Go on, she can put the photo back in its place and then we'll have lunch."

She transferred her mother into the arms of her daughter and waited for them to leave.

"She's eighty years old, you know," she smiled. "She's in good health, as you can see, but she gets these little turns from time to time. I'll have a copy made for you. I'll take the photo down to the village some afternoon and tell her I want one to hang in the chemist where I work. I've already got one, but I'm sure she won't remember. Give me your address, that way I can sent it to you…"

Encarna showed me to the door and pointed up the hill to the house we had talked about earlier, then waited at the door, but I was only halfway down the steps when she called me back.

"Álvaro!" As I turned back, she came down the steps to where I was standing. "I was thinking… There's something I want to tell you. I'm not really Encarnita's daughter… Well, I am, she is my mother, but not my biological mother."

She looked at me for a moment as though giving me permission to ask the question.

"My mother's name was Amada," she continued, "the other little girl you saw in the photo. She died three years ago. She and Encarnita lived together for more than fifty years, they were only ever apart for two years. Amada was younger than Encarnita, and she was never strong. When she was twenty-one she panicked and confessed, she was so terrified she ran away to Madrid to work as a maid. She had a boyfriend while she was there, he was doing his military service, he got her pregnant and then he disappeared. So she came back to the village, alone, and more frightened than ever. Her father was in the Civil Guard and her parents didn't welcome her back with open arms. But Encarnita forgave her for leaving. Her father, who owned the village chemist's shop – it's mine now – had just died. Encarnita was an only child, and she was well off so she took my mother in. I was born and grew up in this house... And I live here now with my husband and my children. Encarnita's mother the only grandmother I ever had, set up a room for herself on the ground floor, and as to what went on in the rest of the house, she preferred not to know. My mothers slept in the master bedroom upstairs. They always swore they weren't lesbians. They were friends. They slept together, they were jealous, they were unfaithful, they'd have knock-down fights in the kitchen, but they weren't lesbians."

"Maybe they didn't know..." I suggested, trying to be pleasant, though I didn't quite know why she was telling me this story.

"Of course they knew! How could they not know? They knew perfectly well, they just refused to admit it... They only time I ever dared to talk to them about it, they were furious, wanted to know how I could say such things." She smiled and I smiled with her, "And they went on going to mass arm in arm every Sunday, they even went to confession, but they didn't mention what they got up to in bed. Encarnita managed to convince my mother that this was something friends did, and that it's only a sin if you do it with a man. And they went right on gossiping about other people, telling me not to trust boys because they're only after one thing. They were very much in love with each other and I think they were happy together, but it was never mentioned. I just wanted to tell you because you came here to ask about your grandmother, nobody had told you anything and I just thought... well, it's not so rare – in this country at least."

"Thank you, Encarna," she shook her head, smiling still, "Thank you for telling me."

I kissed her on both cheeks and said goodbye. As I got into the car, I felt the gentle, benevolent presence of my grandmother Teresa still hovering over me, protecting me. I was glad to have learned so much although I felt incapable of evaluating all the new information swirling round my mind – the image of my grandmother, so pretty, so young, so proud, this little miracle of history which had brought her to life, then killed her. There was something heroic and yet familiar, something small yet exemplary, something larger-than-life yet real, something Spanish yet universal about Teresa González Puerto, and all of those qualities converged on a single point. Me.

I would have fallen in love with you, grandmother. Had I been your age, had I known you in 1936, had I not been your grandson. And this thought made me happy, because it was a wonderful thought and because it freed me of the suspicion of being unfair to this love which at any other time would have been enough to give meaning to my name, and which had come to me only now, that I was no longer free, when I no longer wanted to be free.

So, at 4pm, I closed my eyes and pressed the button on Raquel's entry phone.

"Yes?"

"Hi, it's me."

"Álvaro." It was not a question but a statement.

"Yes, it's just... I went down to Torrelodones to sort out some of my father's papers and..."

"...and you just happened to be in the area."

"No, I came specially."

"Come up."

When I got a taste for jumping off the huge mound of damp, compacted, sand which had appeared overnight in the corner of the school playground, I still thought the first time had been the best, but it lacked the excitement of the second, the third, of the fourth, because something new was added to the experience every time. Slipping into Raquel's bed for the second time, I was more moved than I had been the first time; it was a good thing, because the amazement of the first time settled into something more certain and more amazing, and the only worthwhile miracles are those which can be repeated. Therefore, as I looked at her, as I watched the regular rhythm of her breathing, I found I was able to speak, to do more than just babble.

"I'm going to tell you a story," I turned towards her, kissed her and took her in my arms. "I hope you'll like it..."

I didn't tell her about my grandmother, I couldn't bring myself to, I hadn't even told Fernando Cisneros yet. It was not simply that I liked to think that Teresa belonged to me, nor was it a sense of propriety. There was something else, something hazy and romantic about my reticence. It was all happening at once, too fast. I needed time to grow accustomed to the memory of my grandmother, to allow this sudden, intense, innocent passion to settle until they became familiar images, old stories. Only then would I be able to tell the truth, this secret, suppressed truth, without seeing myself as an interloper, an opportunist, a secondhand grandson. Teresa González Puerto deserved better than that. So I told Raquel the story of Amada and Encarnita without even mentioning my grandmother, as if I'd run into an old friend of the family in Torrelodones, the local chemist who had insisted I come back to her house because her mother wanted to offer her condolences over my father's death, not realising that the glass of wine she'd drunk on an empty stomach would loosen her tongue.

"So, did you like the story?"

"I loved it," Raquel said, laughing, "It's unbelievable, don't you think? Two women living together for fifty years, doggedly oblivious. But didn't you realise? Surely you suspected something?"

"I don't know." I kissed her again, "You know I don't know anything about what you women get up to. Like you, for instance... What do you and your friends get up to?"

"God, you men can be so boring," she said, still laughing. "You're only after one thing."

And at that moment, as I was looking at her, everything clicked into place.

"Fuck!" I pushed her away gently, sat on the edge of the bed and put my head in my hands, "Fuck, fuck, fuck, fuck!"

"What's the matter?" Raquel sat next to me, "Álvaro?"

It had been my fault too, I thought as I looked at her. Because if I hadn't been wandering around like an idiot for two days dreaming of this bed and wondering how to get back here, I might have been quicker, more intelligent. But Encarnita's story only vaguely tied in with something I remembered from family stories: something about a little house near a train station, a little girl of seven or eight who had never spoken to the schoolmistress' son but who met him, years later, walking down the Gran Vía, now a grown man. It was mostly Raquel's fault, I said to myself. But neither of us was to blame and I had no intention of letting my father spoil this afternoon for me. Not entirely sure what this connection might mean, I let myself fall back slowly onto the bed, drew Raquel to me, and made up an excuse.

"It's nothing. I just remembered I was supposed to be at the university, I had an important meeting, but then I remembered I arranged to vote by proxy, so... It's nothing." I drew her closer, until my nose was touching hers. "I don't know where my head is these days."

She drew back slightly and smiled, and everything resumed it course, running gently like water, as though Señorita Mariana's pretty, blonde, blue-eyed daughter, whom many years later Encarnita would not recognise, having seen her only once or twice, was not called Angélica.

As though that same little girl would not grow up to be my mother.

321

The first time Ignacio Fernández Muñoz saw Anita Salgado Pérez, he thought she was beautiful. He also thought she was Spanish. Not simply because she was slight, or because of her dark hair and her huge dark, melancholic eyes. The stranger who was walking along the footpath towards him had pale skin, her body was slight but curvaceous, proportioned and graceful as a doll, she might easily have been French, but she was Spanish, he was certain of it. It was something about the way she walked, about the way she did her hair, but most of all it was her face – her expression, cautious, somehow fearful and yet defiant. It was an expression Ignacio Fernández had seen often in the past three years, on the faces of men and woman, the old and the young, even on the faces of Spanish children. So, when he saw her slacken her pace as she came to the doorway he had been fruitlessly watching for half an hour, hiding awkwardly behind his newspaper, he almost spoke to her, to explain his predicament and ask her to let him in, but he did not.

"¡*Perdón*!" she said in Spanish and looked up at him

"*No ha sido nada*," he replied, and she smiled before slipping the key into the lock.

At that moment, Ignacio Fernández Muñoz realised that he could dispense with explanations, which in this case was extremely convenient. He went back to his newspaper, stared at the headline he had been staring at without reading, heard the creak of the hinges, watched from the corner of his eye as she stepped inside and simply shifted his foot to stop the door from closing completely. Then, his heart pounding in his chest, he glanced to his left. An elderly couple, shuffling slowly, had just rounded the corner of a distant street. He could see no one else, so he turned and looked in the other direction. A teenager on the pavement opposite was oblivious to his presence. Ignacio slipped inside. The hallway was damp and cold. He waited a moment before climbing the stairs, listening for the least sound, but none of the residents chose that moment to pop their heads round the door. Ignacio had deliberately chosen a time when they would be having lunch.

When he got to the second floor, he glanced around and found the door he was looking for, rang the bell and promptly heard the familiar clattering of heels. He was touched to hear the sound of his mother's footsteps, he recognised it still. But when the door opened, she did not recognise him. Shrouded in the half-light, Ignacio saw a look of fear steal across her face, her eyes wide. He stepped forward, pushed her back into the apartment, then stood behind her, his arm around her waist, his right hand covering her mouth as he kicked the door closed behind him. He moved quickly, cleanly, as though this woman were an enemy solider.

"Don't shout, Mamá, please, don't shout." Slowly, he let her go. "It's me, Ignacio. I've escaped."

María Muñoz slowly turned and stared at him. She could not believe that this filthy, emaciated, bearded man was her son Ignacio. Three years of incarceration and forced labour had transformed the only son she had now into an ageless man so gaunt she could see his ribs through the dark fabric of his shirt. He seemed shorn of his humanity, of physical and spiritual dignity, like the desolate souls left to die alone in the filthy sheets of the charity hospitals. This was what María saw when she looked at Ignacio. He saw it and he felt so alone, so lost without her that he broke down and slumped against the wall. Seeing his pain, her detachment unravelled.

"Ignacio!"

Mother embraced son. She did not put her arms around him, did not hold him up, but she stroked his face until she could no longer see him through her tears, then she closed her eyes and pressed her face against his chest, seeking succour, just as she had done in Madrid on the last night they had dinner together.

In Ignacio Fernández Muñoz's memory, the hot, silent tears with which she mourned his life and Mateo's death, grieved for the inevitable devastation and the improbable salvation of her family, fused with other tears that were different, remote yet familiar. It seemed to him that his mother's eyes and those of thousands of men and women with very different stories formed a vicious, unbreakable circle that would last until the end of the world.

This was how he remembered the scene years later; as though nothing had happened since that day when his brother's eyes met his as Mateo stood in the truck that would take him away. That day when he had brought his one free hand to his lips to let his brother know that his heart was breaking. And yet things happened, many things had happened since that day, the most important of which was that he was still alive. He would not have cared if he had died, but he was fated to live and so he did. He went on seeing, hearing, sleeping and breathing ever since that day in the camp at Albatera when he had collapsed only to feel a friendly, complicit kick which made him open his eyes just in time to see the guard's boots marching towards him.

He heard a urgent whisper in an Aragonese accent. "Come on, man, get up, don't be fool..."

When he turned his head he saw a short, swarthy *miliciano* looking at him anxiously.

"What's the matter with you?" the guard gave him a less friendly kick.

"Nothing," the miliciano answered for him, "he just twisted his ankle."

"And that's got you rolling on the ground?" the officer greeted the news with a vicious grin, "You call yourselves "men of steel", but you're just a bunch of sissies."

"I know… but it really hurt," the miliciano yanked his left arm and got him back on his feet, "You're alright now?"

Ignacio simply nodded, eyes fixed on the ground, and went back to marching alongside the man who had saved his life.

"Who was it? Your brother?" the man asked after a moment.

"Yes," Ignacio answered eventually, "My older brother."

"Yes…" he nodded his head as though pleased with his intuition. "That's what I thought, you don't look much like queers."

Ignacio Fernández Muñoz smiled, because to survive meant to keep smiling, and he looked at this skinny, nervous little man walking alongside him, with his big, knotty hands, his cropped hair balding in patches, a typical farmer's son raised in the great outdoors.

"Thanks for what you did earlier," Ignacio said holding out his hand as he introduced himself.

"Jesus, you're lucky!" the man shook his hand.

"Lucky?"

"Of course…" he looked as surprised as Ignacio. "D'you know how many people in Spain are called Ignacio Fernández Muñoz? Hundreds – thousands probably – which means you won't get into trouble if they decide to shoot your brother. Where are you from?"

"Madrid."

"Some people have all the luck!" and in a curious, morose tone that Ignacio would quickly grow accustomed to, the man told his story. "My name is Roque Ansó Ansó. There's only about three hundred of us in our village and we're all related, the fascists and the rest of us, so neither peace nor justice is going to get me out of here as my grandmother would say… My older brother was killed too. He was posted to the front over in Castellón. I think it's better to die that way, with a bullet to the head, but maybe my mother's luck will hold…"

They became good friends. The sort of friend a man might make in a concentration camp, on a working party, in a prison, in war. Roque was twenty-five years old and the two men had nothing in common, but they could sit side by side in silence for hours at a time. This facility, so rare in a place where there was nothing to do but walk and talk, would have been enough to bring them together even if Ignacio had not been taken with Roque's deadpan humour in the face of adversity, the indolent yet somehow elegant fatalism common to those who are destined from birth to a life of poverty and struggle. Roque's stoicism compensated for the brutal, black rage that overwhelmed Ignacio every time he looked around him and his mind went over all the things he had once had, the things that had been snatched from him, above all his faith. At such times the blood would drain from his cheeks and he would clench his fists, beat the air, then suddenly he would feel Roque's hand on his shoulder, hear his gravelly voice saying "Keep it up - just as long as you don't take it out on me" and they would both burst out laughing.

They became good friends, and this elemental yet complex friendship saved them both, for if Roque had not told him he was lucky, had not reminded him how many Spanish communists shared the same name, Ignacio would not have been able to interpret the look of disappointment on the face of the lieutenant in the office to which he found himself summoned to make a statement in mid-June.

"How nice – someone else with an unusual name!" the man muttered, licking his finger and leafing through one of the box files that had spilled onto the floor.

That alone might not have been enough, because when Ignacio Fernández Muñoz looked into the colonel's eyes, he had only one thought: pity I wasted that bullet on the poor bastard in Vistillas when I could have put it between your eyes you little cunt. But, in spite of his homicidal fantasies, he realised that Roque was right, and he could take advantage of this man and hide himself among the thousands of Spaniards who shared his name, so that he might live to put a bullet between the eyes of men like him. This prospect seemed more felicitous, more heroic, than the arrogant posturing Republican officers resorted to, which perhaps his brother Mateo had resorted to. If they shoot me, they win and I lose, he thought. If they don't shoot me, I win and my side wins. Prison extended the time and lessened the intensity, but it did not alter the outcome of that future. And so he stepped into the office, his arms limply by his sides, shoulders hunched with a respectful air of fear he did not drop in the presence of the enemy.

"Fernández Muñoz, that's your name, isn't it?" the chief officer asked the question.

"Yes, sir. Ignacio. I don't have any papers, they were stolen."

"OK... Seems to happen to all of you." This remark, rather than

325

irritating him seemed to amuse him for this, after all, was why they had won the war. "Ignacio Fernández Muñoz. Peláez, you heard him...?"

"Yes, but with a name like that," the lieutenant confirmed what the prisoner already knew. "I've got volumes of them here, colonel."

"Where are you from?"

"Madrid, Sir!" The colonel smiled at his subordinate.

"No exactly helpful..." he allowed himself a little laugh, "...is it Peláez?"

The latter did not respond and the colonel turned back to the prisoner.

"You're very young, aren't you lad? How old are you?"

"Twenty-one, Sir." He ventured some information he had not been asked for. "I didn't do anything, I'm just a conscript, I was drafted at 18. When I was called up... well, I had to go, what else could I do? But I didn't volunteer or anything..."

A moment later he could heard the quiver of a doubt in Peláez's voice. "So far I've found three soldiers named Ignacio Fernández Muñoz from Madrid who are twenty-one, but the only one who fits is a Captain."

"A Captain? At that age?"

"Yes," said Peláez, who was no longer surprised by anything. "The Communists went round promoting people without rhyme or reason..."

"Pff..." Ignacio gave a sigh and murmured. "Me a Captain? Heaven forbid!"

"The aforementioned Captain Fernández Muñoz..." The lieutenant glared at him as though he could read the truth in his eyes. "...was a communist. He was arrested in Casado and sent to Porlier, but he never arrived there, so I have no further information."

Ignacio looked at the lieutenant, then at the colonel, and realised they were trying to decide whether the man before them could have been a communist Captain. The Albatera camp was so vast and so crowded that he had not even managed to find his own brother and he realized that what everyone said was true: the fascists had too many prisoners to cope with, they didn't know what to do with them. In his case, this could mean only one thing: if he stood his ground, they would end up sending him back to Madrid to be identified there.

"I'm not a communist, Sir," he said, whimpering like a frightened child, "I swear to you, I've never belonged to any party..."

When the colonel informed him that the most likely outcome would be that he would be dispatched to Madrid on the next possible train, where he should present himself at the recruiting office where he had enlisted with witnesses or documents that could corroborate his identity, Ignacio smiled and thanked the man. You think I'm going to let them

326

identify me? He thought as he walked out of the office.

He had not gone a hundred yards before he remembered that he was tall and blonde. His looks counterbalanced his good fortune in having a common name, making it easy to identify him in a crowd whilst Roque would go unnoticed. For a moment, panic seized him, but then he realised that the socialist gaoler, the man called Rogelio, had saved his life twice over, because if he had not escaped, if he had been arrested and released in 1939, as most of his communists brothers had been, there would have been a physical description – height, weight, colour of hair and eyes – in Peláez's files. The Republican gaolers in Madrid had not destroyed the lists of communist prisoners arrested in 1939. It had been one of their gifts to Franco, and it had taken Franco's men only two days to round them all up again. How many of them are still alive? wondered Ignacio, and he felt ashamed that he had been so weak, had almost panicked. What did it matter, he thought, he had nothing to lose. He had already lost everything, and yet he was planning to escape with Roque.

"It's impossible," Rufino, a Catalan railwayman his father's age, interrupted Ignacio, shaking his head vehemently. "You can't throw yourself from a moving train like that. You'll kill yourself."

"Clever isn't it?" Roque gave Ignacio an admiring glance.

He had liked the idea from the outset, so much so that, when he was summoned, he had taken the risk of assuming a false identity, adopting the name of one the soldiers who had served under Ignacio, a lad his own age who might be alive or dead, might even be here in the Albatera camp. It was a dangerous ploy, and he knew it, but his name was Roque Ansó Ansó, and neither peace nor justice was going to get him out of here, so Roque trusted to luck.

"I was thinking..." Rufino came to see them some days later, "It's not going to be easy, because they're probably going to put you in freight cars, but if you pay attention to the light, you can count the tunnels. After the ninth tunnel, you'll notice that the train slows down. That's where you should jump. It's flat land, but there are trees, you'll be easy to spot, but at least you won't kill yourselves jumping. You'll need to hide out until it gets dark, and then if you follow the tracks for a couple of kilometres you'll come to Tarancón. If the same station master still works there – a pot-bellied man of about sixty with grey hair, though he's almost bald – you can trust him. His name's Alfredo, tell him I sent you and he'll put you on a goods train to Barcelona."

"What if this Alfredo isn't there?" asked Roque anxiously.

"If he's not there, then we'll get onto the Barcelona train ourselves. And from Barcelona, we can get to your village and from there we can get across the border," said Ignacio.

"Sure..." Rufino smiled, "I swear, you lads from Madrid, you're unbelievable, you don't know the first thing – have you even seen the Pyrenees?"

"I've seen a photo," Ignacio laughed.

"That's what I thought. How do you intend to cross the Pyrenees without a guide?"

"What would you do, Rufino?" Ignacio asked.

"Me? I'd stay in Barcelona," Rufino paused a moment and studied the two men carefully, then continued, his voice hesitant and serious. "I'm from the city and my wife still lives there, but I couldn't give you her address. If you were followed... It's too dangerous, and she already has enough on her plate with three kids and me locked up here."

"Of course, Rufino, don't worry about it," Roque reassured the man.

"As far as we're concerned, you don't have a wife," said Ignacio, "All right, so, there we are in Barcelona, we don't know anyone, what do we do?"

"You go to the market at la Boquería," Rufino said, calmer now, "I used to go there all the time when I was your age. Hang around, give a hand unloading the trucks, get yourself known, and wait until you find someone who's going to Gerona and is prepared to take you along. It used to be easy to get work there, though nowadays I imagine there's thousands of people willing to turn their hand to whatever they can get, but I can give you a couple of names." He fell silent for a moment. "It's not dangerous, and from Gerona, find some way of getting to Puigcerdá. The women there cross the border all the time to go shopping in France. They follow the train tracks, carrying a basket. Obviously you two can't do that, but you can go across the fields, it's much easier to cross there than at Huesca because the pass is wider and the terrain is flat. That's what I'd do."

"Then that's what we'll do," Ignacio looked at Roque.

Ignacio thought of Rufino as he jumped from the train, thought of him when they said goodbye to Alfredo who gave them civilian clothes, a bottle of Valdepeñas and a ham sandwich from a pig he'd slaughtered himself before putting them on a goods train to Barcelona. When they tried to give him some money, he laughed.

"The money you've got is worthless," he said.

"I know, but you could change it at a bank, couldn't you? At least some of it?"

"No, you can't even change a céntimo..."

"But what about everyone else? What about all the people from our zone, how do they manage?"

"They don't," said Alfredo, "They're fucked."

As he heard the words, Ignacio remembered his cousin Mariana, the placid, metallic glitter in her eyes, the impassive, implacable gaze of a farmer who does not see the rain that falls gently on the meadows. He consoled himself with the thought that at least he had been able to say thank you the night before they left to Rufino who, in his way, had saved Ignacio's life. Even Roque admitted as much, and stopped insisting that they would be better off in his village when things in Barcelona began to go to plan. Barely had they helped to unload three trucks in the market when they found what they were looking for, and from Gerona they made their way to Puigcerdá, through the fields by day, along the road by night, by cart and by truck. Without Rufino they would not have got far, nor without the help of the shepherd they ambushed near Puigcerdá only to discover that he would have shown them the way even if they had not knocked him to the ground and put the man's own knife to his throat. When they realised that they had finally arrived in France, the two men hugged, they laughed, they screamed, then they walked on towards lights in the distance that seemed to be a village and spent the night in a barn, each under his own blanket, the only thing they still possessed. They were exhausted, but still Ignacio found the time to think of Rufino. "If you make it to France, write to me and let me know," he had said, hugging them hard. "Where will I write to, Rufino?" He had looked at Ignacio and hugged him harder still. Before he fell asleep on that penultimate night of June 1939, Ignacio Fernández Muñoz's thought of the people to whom he owed his life and the fact that he needed to find some means of repaying that debt.

"*Bonjour messieurs,*" he opened his eyes the following morning and found two gendarmes staring down at him. "*Vos papiers s'il vous plaît.*"

"*Bonjour,*" Ignacio said, bounding to his feet, trying to convince himself that he saw no malice in the faces of these officers. "*Mais nous n'avons pas de papiers, parce que nous sommes des réfugiés espagnols, républicains, vous savez... Nous sommes arrivés hier, très tard.*"

"Huh?" Woken by the voices, Roque stared at Ignacio in astonishment, "You speak French!"

"*Alors,*" the gendarme gestured for them to follow him, "*Venez avec nous.*"

Roque got to his feet ready to go. So began the second part of their journey which was easier than the first and more difficult for there was no Rufino, no Alfredo, to help them.

The gendarmes loaded them into a truck in which there were a number of other Spanish people – a short, bald man of about forty wearing glasses and a suit and tie, clutching the briefcase containing his papers, a grey-haired woman who did not speak, but wept quietly throughout the whole journey and two *milicianos* who looked quite like Roque, one from Galicia, the other from Valencia. They explained what would happen next but Ignacio could not believe it was true. Not in France, in spite of the non-intervention policy, the closing of the border, the guns legally bought with Spanish Republican currency that were still rotting in a customs house somewhere, having never reached the border. He did not want to believe it, but he thought back to the crack of bullets in Alicante, to the Spanish men and women who took their own lives rather than live in Spain when they discovered that the whole world had abandoned them, when they realised that neither the French nor the English nor the Americans, none of the countries who claimed to be the enemies of fascism, would send a ship for them. No one had wanted to help them, even if it was only so that they might taste the bitterness of exile; they were left to be cannon fodder, to be the spoils of war to the victors, the last of the faithful, betrayed by everyone. He knew what had happened, he had been there, and still he could not bring himself to believe it. Back then, perhaps, but surely not now that they had been defeated, surely France had always opened its doors to exiles…

Ignacio Fernández Muñoz did not want to believe what the men told him. He would quickly learn that whenever anyone, anywhere, in any language sang the anthem that urged to wretched of the earth to rise up, it would be about them, about the Republicans, about the Spanish communists, for there were perhaps others in the world as wretched as they were, but none more wretched.

It was something he learned quickly, when he got up from the long bench where dark-skinned men clung to their blankets, where women with children sat carrying wicker baskets, and went over to the officer sitting at a table with a sign marked *Information.*

"Excuse me, Monsieur, I'd like to know why I was arrested," he asked with exquisite deference in French.

The man dropped the pen he had using to fill in a form and studied Ignacio.

"If I'm not mistaken, you're Spanish, yes? A Republican soldier? And you crossed the border illegally." Ignacio nodded and got a mocking smile for his pains, "In which case we have an excellent reason for arresting you, since we do not want our country overrun with murderers."

"Murderers?" Ignacio repeated feeling the blood freeze in his veins, "I am not a murderer, Monsieur, I am an antifascist who fought for the freedom of my people."

"Killing priests and nuns."

"Priests and nuns?" Ignacio Fernández Muñoz paused for a moment to suppress the righteous anger boiling in him, "I never killed a priest or a nun. I fought for three years in defence of the elected government of my country. I fought a war, and we lost. We lost because the French, like the English and the Americans, did nothing and allowed fascism to triumph…"

"Get back to you seat! At once!" the gendarme shouted. And yet, when it was his turn to be questioned, the civil servant behind the desk treated him with greater respect.

"You speak very good French." He smiled before continuing, "Have you family here in France?"

"Yes, my parents and my sisters live in Toulouse. I crossed the border hoping to find them," he explained.

"Are they Spanish refugees like you?" Ignacio nodded silently, though he could sense that the conversation was not going well, "You're not Basque are you?"

"No, I'm from Madrid," the answer seemed to do little to cheer the official. "Why? Are there different rules for Basques?"

"Not exactly, but the government is negotiating on their behalf, they're counting on the support of the church, of the French bishops. They say the Basques are a very devout people, conservative, respectful of tradition, not at all like you lot."

"Like who?"

"Like the rest of you!" The man took off his glasses, then went on in an amiable, seemingly well-meaning tone. "The ones who burn down churches."

"I've never burned down a church in my life…" Ignacio protested, his voice a whisper.

"Well, I'm afraid even so, it's not possible… Are you married?"

"No."

"Then there's no possibility of you meeting up with your family. If you had a wife and children here in France, you could request a transfer to a camp for families but…"

"A camp…" Ignacio repeated the word as though he did not understand it.

"Yes. For the time being, Republican combatants are being housed in camps, although in your case… You're not like the people over there, you're an educated man. Now, if your family's financial circumstances were… You take my point. What I mean is that in certain circumstances,

331

I might be able to do something. If you'd like to take a seat over there, until I finish interviewing the others…'

Ignacio Fernández Muñoz accepted the suggestion and got to his feet. The next interviewee was Roque, who was so short, so dark-skinned, a typical farmer's son raised in the great outdoors. Roque Ansó Ansó who had risked his life to get to the promised land and who now, in the face of a French uniform, visibly shrank, as he had when faced with Spanish uniforms, as though aware of the inferiority that flowed in his veins, as though before he learned to speak, to walk, to laugh, he had learned that people like him could not expect any favours, or even impartiality from any authorities anywhere.

Ignacio heard him stammer "*es que no le entiendo, lo siento pero no le entiendo,*" He remembered his father saying those same words "I'm sorry, I don't understand" on the days when the terror, the shame were at their worst, "We are what we are, no matter what, and we belong here with our own people." I am who I am, thought Ignacio as the official said again "*Nom, prénom,*" in an arrogant, scornful tone very different from the one he had used with Ignacio, a tone reserved for those without the wherewithal to pay backhanders. "I am what I am", and only when he thought of the prospect of living in Toulouse, sleeping in a bed again, finding a job and maybe a wife, sleeping in on Sundays, did Ignacio understand what his father had meant when he said "I am who I am, no matter what, and I belong here with my own people."

Faced with this burning chasm, the son of Mateo Fernández Gómez de la Riva learned also that his righteous anger could grow and change, could become tinged with tenderness and pride, the basic ingredients of a nebulous yet universal love for humankind. If only for that love, it was worth trying. This is what Ignacio was thinking when he got up from the chair to interrupt the tableau. He went over, put his arm around Roque's shoulder, and acted as his interpreter until the interview was over.

"I'll see you later," he said, patting Roque on the back as he watched the official finish his report with a single, damning word: *indésirable.* "I think they're sending us all to the same place."

"Excuse me …" The next person in line, the short bald man with the glasses, still clutching his briefcase, said to Ignacio in his thick Majorcan accent. "Would you mind interpreting for me too?"

"You're the one from Madrid, the one who speaks French, the one they call The Lawyer?" At the Barcarès camp, Ignacio Fernández Muñoz quickly became famous, although most people did not know his real name, only his nickname. "Wait a minute, we need to talk about your case…" the official had said to him that morning when he had finished interpreting for those being interrogated that day. "I don't think so. I have nothing to say to you. I'm a Spanish communist just like them and just as *indésirable*. The man looked at him, irritated to lose a backhander, but simply scribbled the word on Ignacio's form and stamped it, "fine, have it your way..." Then they were all boarded on to a truck and driven to a forbidding stretch of beach enclosed by barbed wire fences.

"Fuck," Roque said when they arrived, "We've gone halfway round the world to wind up somewhere just like Albatera..."

"True, but the ground is softer here, and there's no shooting." Ignacio comforted him.

"You're the one from Madrid, the one who speaks French, the one they call The Lawyer?" His clients from the commissariat, some twenty of them, though the women had been taken to a different camp, had spread the word, and now everyone called him The Lawyer. He liked it, it made him sound like a bullfighter. "That's me." "Could you tell them my wife is here, I don't know where she is, but she's got my two with her, I have to find her", "Tell them I didn't do anything, tell them I'm from a village near Sevilla and that I fought in Santander, but we didn't kill anyone", "My brother's in France and I want to find out where he is, that's all, can you tell them that? And my fiancée, she's all alone, I don't know where she is, but I've got to find her, but they don't understand", "I think my wife is dead, and my children are only young, they won't listen to me, I don't know what to do", "I have two daughters, one seven, the other one's eleven, they're supposed to be with the older sister and their mother is worrying herself to death because she can't find them, go on, tell them, tell them..."

They came from all walks of life, young and old, tall and short, educated and illiterate, they came from the city and from the country, from the coast and the interior, from the mainland and the islands. "You're the one from Madrid, the one who speaks French, the one they call The Lawyer?" He heard the same question in every imaginable accent and his answer, was always the same: "That's me", "The thing is, I have got this problem and these people don't give a fuck..." They came from all walks of life, and each of them had a problem, and the problems were all the same – a wife, a fiancé, a mother, a father, a brother, a sister, children. He listened to them and did what he could for them even though he knew that it was pointless.

"Hey, Lawyer. I did burn down the church in my village..." a boy from Zamora told him one day, "No one died, but only because the priest had already done a runner, if he hadn't, who knows, I mean there's no point lying to you... So anyway, we took all the statues out and put the boy saints on top of the girl saints, and it was laugh." Ignacio smiled but the boy went on, his voice serious, "I just wanted to tell you in case someone said something, but don't go telling the French, OK?"

"They don't care," Ignacio said to the boy "It's just an excuse, a way to justify what they're doing to us, it's completely cynical."

"What does that mean?"

"Cynical?"

He went over, put his hands on the boys shoulders and looked him in the eye. "It means they don't give a fuck if you burned down the church. If you were a republican, you're fucked. That's what it means."

Then he went to the commanding officer, ignoring the bored expression on the man's face and pleaded the case of a Spanish lad, recently married, whose friend had said he'd seen his wife sitting in a ditch just across the border. He got the same answer he always did: "No."

"Why do you do it?" the French officer asked him later in a genial, almost friendly tone. "Why do you come and see me over and over, when you know I'm going to say no."

"Because they have the right to be heard," Ignacio replied, "Because they're not criminals or murderers. All they did was fight for their country, they did nothing to deserve being locked up like this." He thought about turning on his heel, but realised that the time had come to say something more. "I didn't do anything either, but I'll tell you now, I wish I had burned down a church. If I'd known that things were going to turn out like this, I would have done, believe me."

"You're the one from Madrid, the one who speaks French, the one they call The Lawyer?" "That's me." And the next time he saw him, the officer in charge of the camp took his hand, shook it and said goodbye.

In Bacarès, everyone knew Ignacio Fernández Muñoz, but the only people who addressed him by name were Roque and Lieutenant Huguet, with whom he had a glass of wine every night. And, one Sunday in October, when he heard a woman's voice say his name, he realised that his efforts had been rewarded. It had taken three months for his family to find him through Donato, a prisoner who was working in Perpignan and came back to the camp every night, and who put out the word to the network of Republican exiles in the south of France for anyone who asked. Finding a familiar face among the sea of French people in their Sunday best who came every week to gawp at the communists in their cages was not easy, especially because on that particular Sunday there were a number of foreign photographers, Americans mostly, perched on ladders trying to get an aerial shot of the prisoners - an image that was clearly popular in the Western newspapers since they kept coming, week

334

after week.

This was the one thing the West had done for them: take photos. Thousands of photos, portraits and group shots of Spanish people locked in cages like monkeys in a zoo. The men in Barcarès despised the photographers and yet they continued to indulge them. When one of them spotted a camera, he would yell "Photo!" and everyone would get to their feet, raise their fists, tilt their chins in salute. From outside, it might have seemed a vain, futile gesture, but for the men it was a fervent affirmation of their identity, of their determination, it told the world that they were still alive, they were still the same men they had been. So, although they despised the photographers, they all got to their feet that Sunday, stared into the lenses, and among those on the far side of the fence saluting with them, he saw his little sister and called out her name.

"Ignacio, Ignacio... You don't know..." María babbled, starting sentences she could not finish, as they reached through the fence to touch each other. "You can't possibly know... When we found out... Paloma wasn't there that day, but one of my friends was with me... I was in a café and then... Ignacio..."

"María..." He cupped his sister's face as best he could, "Slow down, María. I don't understand a word you're saying."

"It's true." She withdrew a fraction and closed her eyes for a moment, "I'm just nervous. We thought you were dead too, I... I thought I'd never see you again. That's what I was trying to say, and then this man came into the boulangerie where Paloma and I work. They put Paloma out front serving. I work at the back at the ovens. I don't mind, but..."

At that moment, a Senegalese soldier stepped up and reminded Ignacio that communicating with the outside world was forbidden. Ignacio nodded and, in French, told the man that he was just saying goodbye.

"We can't stay here," he whispered in Spanish, "Move down the fence to where all those people are standing, find a space and wait for me." It was a respite which they both needed, an interlude in which they had time to take in the fact that they had found each other, that they could once more talk and touch, even if it was through the barbed wire.

"Anyway..." She picked up where she had left off. "This man came into the boulangerie and Paloma had finished her shift, but there was another girl there, her name is Anita, she lives with us now, and she took the message – it was a note to arrange a meeting, it said it was about you – so she gave it to me, she knows how things have been at home, ever since Mateo and then what happened to Carlos..."

"What happened to Carlos?" His voice sounded alien and hoarse in his ears.

"Yes," María looked down at the ground, then back at Ignacio, "Carlos is in prison. He's been sentenced to death, for military insurrection. It's so ridiculous it would be laughable, if it wasn't so tragic. But the worst of it is, it was the Toad who turned him in."

"The Toad?" Ignacio remembered the hard cold glow, patient and pitiless, in Mariana's eyes as they followed him.

"The Toad," his sister confirmed, "That bitch. It was different for Mateo, there was nothing we could do, someone in the camp at Alicante recognised him. He never found out who, but it was someone who knew him well, who knew the whole family. Mateo was killed not just for being who he was, but for being Papá's son, Mamá's son, for being your brother, Ignacio, for being Carlos's brother-in-law. Just imagine it: a little rich boy, a philosophy student and a socialist, the son of a Republican engineer, the grandson of a Count and an Andalusian landowner, his brother a communist promoted to Captain and his brother-in-law an officer. He was the perfect scapegoat, he represented everything they despised: philosophy, law, university. They must have be thrilled, those murdering bastards... Anyway, Mateo got angry, called them every name under the sun, and they didn't dare beat him up. They were too worried that he might die ahead of time."

"Of course... they wanted him executed in Madrid..." Ignacio remembered the rumours he had heard in Albatera, the whispered stories that at the time had seemed outlandish in their cruelty rather than real and tragic.

"And that's what happened. He was shot by firing squad on 29 May. They published his name and our names in the papers the following day."

"Nice of them," Ignacio thought about Casilda, his sister-in-law.

"Charming," María tried to smile and failed. "Of course, now we're the cancer of Spain... you know, the people who destroyed our country, the soulless liberal mob, the traitors who sold the country to Stalin..." She paused, then shook her head, "They're bastards but I still can't believe that they could be so brutish, so stupid. And they're the ones who are ruling Spain now. It breaks my heart... Anyway, before they shot him, on the journey to Madrid, Mateo was able to tell one of the other prisoners everything. He's still in prison, but he told his wife, who found Casilda when she went back."

"How is she?" For a second, he felt his throat close. "Is she in prison?"

"No, she's free..." her smile reassured him. "Though she went through hell, too. She was locked up in a convent in Cartagena after the war, so she never got the chance to go and see Mateo. By the time they let her go, he was dead. At least now she's at home, and she has her baby. She named him after Mateo, but he has his mother's surname, because after the war civil marriages were declared null and void. But you know, although the baby was premature, they're both fine, they're thin, but they're healthy. So you're an uncle."

Ignacio remembered his brother's wedding, a quick, impersonal ceremony so brief that he did not even arrive in time to be a witness, or to see the civil-servant who had taken his place. He had been so surprised that Mateo had decided to get married, it seemed so absurd, so unseemly in the icy autumn of 1938, that he had paid scant attention to his brother's reasons. At the time, he had thought it was some whim of his sister-in-law, and now that it was too late to regret it, he shuddered to think that, far from protecting Casilda, the marriage had made her life more difficult.

"It was Casilda who told us that Mateo had seen you in the camp in Alicante, that you were alive." María looked at him, tried to smile and this time she succeeded "But we didn't hold out much hope. We found out that ordinary soldiers had been released as long as they had never belonged to a political party, but officers... Papá was devastated, he kept saying that the one thing he regretted was telling Mamá that at least you and Mateo and Carlos had finished your studies, so you'd move up the ranks quickly, that you were destined to be officers not cannon fodder. Now he thinks it's a miracle that they didn't make the connection between you and Mateo."

"And he's right." Ignacio smiled at her.

"When I went home and told him you were here... it was like he came back to life, honestly, and Mamá, well... you can imagine." Then tears welled in the eyes of María Fernández Muñoz, the youngest, the most resilient, the strongest of them all. "They wanted to come, but I wouldn't let them, it's a long way, and they need to look after Paloma... We all need to look after Paloma, she's beside herself... She keeps saying she should never have come, that she always knew she should have stayed behind in Madrid, that it's our fault, we forced her to leave Carlos behind, that she could have hidden him, helped him escape... It's stupid. We've told her that the minute he was arrested she would have been put in prison too, but she won't listen..."

Ignacio had never recovered from the shock of realising what Mateo's studied indifference had meant that morning in Alicante, when Mateo's eyes met his, and he shook his head almost imperceptibly: "Don't look at me, don't speak to me, don't say goodbye, don't tell anyone that you're my brother, save yourself." Now, Ignacio Fernández Muñoz was reeling from the shock of what had happened, a fate that might just as easily have been his. He was thinking of José María Heredero, too, about that night in March, when there was still time to save the only man he had ever killed. José María Heredero, a professor of criminal law, the son and grandson of right-wing lawyers, the black sheep of the family, was safe, he could have hidden him, he would have known what to do... Ignacio was still thinking that the best thing to do would be to find him when he reached Vistillas, even when he was looking for a truck, watching the driver. If he hadn't done this, it was not because he was afraid of the fascists, but because he was afraid of his own people. But he was fit and healthy, he had had two legs that would carry him wherever he wanted to go. Carlos didn't.

"Casilda found out he was in prison and went to see him, she pretended to be his wife. She took him a parcel and smuggled out a letter for Paloma in her bra. Since she was heavily pregnant at the time, and had milk stains on her dress, they didn't really search her when she was leaving. She forwarded the letter to us, I don't know how she did it because it had a French stamp, but she promised Carlos she would get it to us, and she did, even though it took two months. That's why we don't know if he's still alive... He was all on his own in Madrid when it happened, nobody warned him, but he hadn't been involved in the *coup* so maybe... Well, I hardly need to tell you." María looked at him bitterly. "He remembered José María Heredero, he thought if anyone could help him, he could. They'd been best friends ever since university... He went to his apartment on the Calle Torrijos but there was no one there. He set off for Aranjuez on foot, the poor thing, limping, with his gamy leg, God knows how long it took or what state he was in when he arrived. But he knew José's parents had a house there, and he found it, and there was José, spending the Spring in the country, wearing tennis whites and carrying a racket, the bastard, this is the same man who used to argue with Carlos because he wore a hat, the guy who bought workman's overalls in the summer of '36 and didn't even take them off when he went to bed..."

Don't say any more, María, Ignacio wanted to beg her, please, don't tell me any more, I don't want to know... This was what Ignacio thought, and what he could not bring himself to say because the most important thing was not what he wanted but what he needed, and he needed to know the truth, he needed to grieve for Carlos Rodríguez Arce, his teacher, his brother-in-law, his saviour, his friend.

"'Carlitos, what brings you here?' José said when he saw him, the... I can't think of a name for him. Anyway, he invited him into the kitchen, gave him coffee and biscuits, and told him to stay there. Carlos didn't know what to do, so... You know who helped him in the end? José María's sister."

"She was always in love with him," Ignacio remembered the brash, shameless girl who used to wait for his brother-in-law outside the classroom door even after he and Paloma were engaged.

"No, not her." María smiled, "Not Mercedes, she ended up marrying one of them. No, it was Isabelita, the youngest, you remember, the one who was always so holier-than-thou... Anyway, she came into the kitchen and said, get out of here Rodríguez, it's not safe. 'But I'm waiting for your brother,' Carlos said. 'I know, that's why I'm saying you should go, as quickly as possible...' She even gave him money for the train back to Madrid. You see, Mamá was right, you never know who to trust, your friends or your enemies. So Carlos went back to Madrid, but where could he go? He could go home, obviously, but he had a key to our place and he was exhausted, so he waited until it was dark and headed for our apartment on the glorieta de Bilbao. And who do you think he ran into?"

"The Toad, of course," said Ignacio.

"Of course. And what do you think she told him?" María raised her eyebrows, waiting for the answer Ignacio did not dare give. "She told him he had no right to be there. Can you believe it? It's..." María pressed her lips together, her face a rictus of anger. "The nerve of that cow! Papá took her in when she was about to be thrown out on the street... So, when she said that, Carlos laughed, you know what he was like. 'I've got more right to be here than you, Mariana, but let's not argue,' he said 'I need somewhere to spend the night, I need to sleep, and I need something to eat. After that, I'll be on my way, don't worry. I've no intention of staying in this shitty country.' 'All right,' the Toad said, 'on one condition. I get to sleep in my uncle and aunt's room.'"

Now it was Ignacio's turn to clench his fists, press his lips together, a fleeting, hopeless look of anger that flashed across his face at his sister's words.

"We should have killed her, I'm mean it, I thought about it more than once, when she used to come up from Dorita's apartment, we should have grabbed her and... Carlos would still be here with us now."

Ignacio felt tears sting his eyes and let them trickle down, María too was weeping.

"Anyway," she dried her eyes with two deft swipes. "She gave him some bread and a bit of cheese and Papá's bottle of brandy... Carlos slept in Paloma's room. He'd already decided to leave the next morning, he didn't trust the Toad, but he was exhausted. At eight o'clock, a Falangist brigade dragged him out of bed. She stood there, calmly watching the whole thing, she even waved the soldiers goodbye. 'Your cousin was right,' Carlos spat at her, ' You're nothing but a toad.' She slapped him, on top of everything else..."

They went on crying, on either side of the barbed wire fence, united by heartache and by everything they had lost.

María was the first to break the silence.

"I've brought you cigarettes, some croissants, some chocolate and some pencils so you can write to us... Stand back, I'll see if I can throw the packet over the fence."

"No," he said, "It's easier to push it under the fence, it's only sand, you dig on your side and I'll dig on mine. Oh, one more thing... I was going to ask the camp commander, but it's better if I ask you... Can you see if you can get copies of the French Civil and Penal codes, and a copy of the asylum laws, that's the most important thing. Do you have any way of getting in touch with the man who came to see you? All right, well give the books to him and he'll try to get them to Donato, the guy from Lugo, remember his name."

After María's visit, Ignacio Fernández Muñoz's life at the Barcarès camp changed. The grubby, well-thumbed books arrived, notes scribbled in the margins of every page and he began to study, happy to have something to do to relieve the crippling boredom of the days. The books allowed him to prepare for the difficult times ahead. The autumn of 1939 was hard and the winter of 1940 harder still. The last days of summer took with them the innocent joy of those who believed they were no longer destined to be victims and the first rains washed away the last traces of optimistic excitement with the knowledge that only their location had changed. They were no longer in a Spanish prison, but a French prison camp. They could no longer lie in the sun, play football, go swimming without catching pneumonia or even pose for the photographers, who no longer came. The rain filtered through the roofs of the huts, the tides rose higher, the beach shrank, everything was wet and miserable, every night colder, every day shorter.

All the while, Ignacio Fernández Muñoz studied. Ignacio, who, as a soldier had despised the pedantic nitpicking of the Republican authorities, now took a refined almost morbid pleasure in enumerating for lieutenant Huguet every article, principle, doctrine and provision of French law which was breached by his incarceration.

"What do you want me to do, Ignacio? You think I want to be here?"

Huguet said defensively.

Ignacio did not answer, but went on studying. Every morning, he reopened his books so he would not have to see, so he would not have to hear, and yet he knew, just as he had in Alicante when he had stared out to sea. Men as tall as towers wept like children, waded into the sea until they disappeared from view. There were those who took off their clothes and lay on the freezing sand; those who ceased to speak, eat, move and those who would get up all of a sudden and say: "Goodbye. I'm going home now." Some madder than others, but for the most part they did go back, because they were too young, too strong, had too much life left ahead of them to remain here, incarcerated for no reason, with their bellies full of sand.

Sometimes, the whole day long, loudspeakers would repeat: "People of Spain, go back to your own country. Your families, your people, your homes are waiting for you. Your country needs you if it is to recover. Those of you who have committed no crime have nothing to fear from Franco. No one believes the wild stories about repression any more..." Huguet introduced Ignacio to the owner of one of these voices one afternoon, though he did not mention the man's name, nor Ignacio's.

"The is the Lawyer, one of the prisoners' spokesmen. He is highly respected by everyone here and has considerable authority especially over the communists," he said by way of introduction.

The plump, well-groomed, one-armed man stepped confidently towards him.

"I used to be one of you. I fought with the Reds against the Nationalists," he held out his remaining hand.

"Fuck off, you bastard," said Ignacio, stuffing his hand into his pocket.

Huguet never quite believed Ignacio's interpretation of this encounter, and Ignacio could understand why, because the carelessness of Franco's men, who did not even bother to learn the terminology of those they pretended to be, was unbelievable. What was more shocking still was that they succeeded in duping some of the prisoners.

Some men decided to go home, although they realised it was a trap, that they would be doing forced labour, and every day the gendarmes brought in more undocumented men who had crossed the border without the least idea of what awaited them. The newcomers upset him most, because in their vulnerability they were a mirror-image of Roque, of himself. "Have you got any money?" the old hands would ask them with a mocking smile. "Of course," they would say, "We didn't have time to spend it," and for an instant, hope would dance in their eyes, "Why? can we change it here?" "Of course, you can change anything here. We use Republican pesetas to wipe our arses, and yours will come in handy because we haven't a peseta left..." And everyone would laugh, everyone except the newcomers who would glance around them with a look of utter despair.

Every day, new recruits joined this desolate army and all the while Ignacio Fernández Muñoz went on studying. Things in the camp were going from bad to worse, even for the communists, the only prisoners who, from the moment they arrived, had set about organising things and had managed to create a stable, efficient infrastructure connected to their French comrades. Only this had made it possible for them to survive the humiliating blow Stalin had dealt them in his perverse alliance with Hitler.

For those who were free, it was terrible; for those in prison, it was a catastrophe. For Ignacio Fernández Muñoz, newly arrived in Barcarès and still the butt of jokes by the camp veterans, it was a bitter starting point, one more sign of his infinite misfortune. Betrayal is the rule, he thought, betrayal is our fate, it is the norm in our lives. I live, I survive, I breath only to be betrayed, in Spain and beyond, by friends and by enemies, to my face and behind my back. Betrayal is the one constant in my life, he thought.

"This war is not our war, it is an imperial war between capitalist powers, it does not concern us," this was the opinion of their leaders, announced with the serenity of someone enjoying life in Paris with false identity papers, someone living in a *dacha* on the outskirts of Moscow with his wife and children, who slept in a warm bed every night, and ate well every day. This they proclaimed with a joy born of prosperity, and the French and the English – the supreme traitors to the Spanish cause – deserved nothing more. Ignacio agreed with them on this last point, though not on the rest, and he loudly said as much. He had just arrived in Barcarès and had not yet met lieutenant Huguet, he had not yet been given his *nom de guerre*, but he dared to speak out because he had nothing to lose. This was why he spoke out, why he said that for him the Nazis were and would always be the real enemy.

Had he been free, he might have been expelled from the party, but he was imprisoned and so were those he spoke to. These men did not sleep in warm beds at night, did not enjoy several meals a day, they were far from Paris and this was what they wanted to hear. They needed to hear something like this from someone like him, someone who been raised in a prosperous family, who had studied, who had been trained to lead, but who found himself here, just as fucked as everyone else. Outside, he

342

might have been expelled from the party, in here he quickly rose through the ranks. He never asked questions, never asked to see any identification from those prisoners who came to him and asked if he was the guy Madrid, the one they called 'the Lawyer', and this helped to restore a tacit reconciliation between his comrades and the other Republicans in the camp, although it did not make him feel any happier.

In his eighteen months of clandestine politics, the only thing that comforted Ignacio Fernández Muñoz were the escapes. He had no personal ambition, and never thought about his future since he was utterly convinced that he did not have one. For him, the word future extended only to the next twenty-four hours, but if one day he were able to choose a life for himself, he knew he it would not be in politics. Only two or three years earlier, it had occurred to him that he might stay in the army, become a professional soldier after the Republicans won the war. Now, although all was lost, he realised that this reflex had become more deeply rooted in him. This was why he revelled in the escapes, organising them, conceiving them. Given the responsibilities he had taken on, he could not escape himself, but he enthusiastically planned every one.

"Where will I go without you?" The night he left, Roque hugged him as hard as he had on the day they realised they had arrived in France. "How will I work out what they're saying?"

Ignacio looked at him and felt proud. Roque could have left the camp months earlier, he had papers, he would be running no risk, but he had not wanted to leave. At the beginning of 1940, with the prospect of a war with Germany, the French government had begun to consider the waste of resources represented by tens of thousands of idle Spanish prisoners. Their initial ideas foundered with men like Ignacio. Few Republicans were prepared to join the French Foreign Legion, considering it an insult given the parallels with the Spanish Legion, and many more chose to stay in the camp rather than sign up for forced labour details which did not even guarantee them the right to visit their families. But this was one thing, escaping was very different. Ignacio laughed before responding to Roque's question.

"You'll manage, take my word for it... and let's face it you'll be better off away from here, Roque."

The Perpignan comrades arrived and began to dig on the other side of the fence. Ignacio saw them only in fits and starts, when a flash of light imprinted on his memory an image of this perfect digging machine, the French on one side, the Spanish on the other, arms working tirelessly, sinewy and powerful, two perfectly synchronised halves of a whole. They did not take this much trouble with individual escapes, but more than fifteen of them were planning to escape that night, so they had carefully studied the storm clouds. The Senegalese guards were afraid of electrical storms and hunched their shoulders at the first peal of thunder, making a dash for the barracks, and they did not reappear until the rain had stopped by which time the escapees would be home and dry, perhaps even sleeping in a real bed in a house with a roof that did not leak, sheltered by some French citizen with a heart and a conscience. Ignacio Fernández Muñoz was moved at the thought. With every escape, he felt the same thing, but this was one time he would not forget. Not simply because he knew that it was probably the last time he would ever see Roque, but also because this night brought him closer to Aurelio Perea, alias The Bigmouth, who in time would become something more than a friend, almost a brother.

"Which one of you is the Lawyer?"

A young Frenchman peered through the fence, a sheaf of papers in his right hand.

"That's me." said Ignacio, stepping towards the fence.

It began to rain, but the boy, unperturbed, opened the umbrella he had hanging on his arm, and began to read:

"Yesterday, 16 May 1940, the Antifascist Committee of the Departement of Roussilon, made up of the French Communist Party, the French Socialist Party and the General Confederation..."

"Listen, why don't we skip all that," Ignacio interrupted, both moved and bewildered that the boy had actually brought the minutes of a meeting and was fully intending to read them here, in the dark, in the rain, in the middle of an escape.

"*Comme vous voulez,*" the young man looked at him, then carried on reading. "The members of the committee salute their Spanish brothers – in the first draft it said 'comrades' but I suggested changing it to 'brothers'. Anyway – their Spanish brothers in the struggle against fascism, unlawfully incarcerated at the Barcarès camp as a result of inexcusable cowardice on the part of the current government..."

"Perea!"

Domingo, the lad from Seville started yelling in Spanish, but this did not deter the adolescent spokesman.

"...and offer them their unconditional support, just as they supported the cause of Spanish Republicanism against the criminal weakness of the League of Nations Non-Intervention Committee in London..."

Roque looked at Ignacio before slipping under the fence and smiled at him from the other side. Domingo, who was leading the escape, started shouting again while the young man went on reading as if there were an absurd dream.

"...the victory of fascism, as embodied by the figure of General Franco."

"Perea! I'm going, if you don't come now, you'll be left behind."

"...aided and abetted by the Axis powers..."

"Come on, lad," Ignacio realised he had to do something, "just give me the papers. Tell everyone involved in the meeting that we're very grateful. I'll read it to our comrades here later, but there's too much going on at the moment." He turned and switched into Spanish "And Domingo, could you shut up? You'll have the Senegalese out here, storm or no storm..." He turned back and saw a lone man heading towards him. "What's the matter, Perea?"

"It's just..." The Malagueño spoke in a whisper. "When I was little, my grandmother used to say to me 'Don't get hit by lightning, lad, Don't get hit by lightning', because where I lived, there was a man walking through the fields during a storm, and he was hit by a bolt of lighting and burned to ashes, and now every time I see that fence..."

Perea seemed paler, his eyes darker than Ignacio remembered. He knew the man vaguely, had talked to him only once or twice, but Ignacio had not forgotten him: "How come your wife is in Nîmes? I thought there weren't any refugees there..." He had once asked. "Because her father is a bullfighter" Perea had answered, clearly thinking this explained matters. "What has that got to do with it?" Ignacio asked. "Isn't it obvious?" Perea said condescendingly, "The Arena of Nîmes! The biggest bullring in the south of France. My father-in-law knows the owner, so..." Ignacio thought of the conversation now as he saw the abject terror on the face of the bullfighter's son-in-law.

"You're afraid of thunderstorms?" said Ignacio in a whisper.

"No," Perea protested, "I'm not afraid of thunderstorms, I'm afraid lightning will strike just as I'm crawling under the fence..."

"Well, what are you going to do, *macho*, go or stay?"

"I want to go to Nîmes, I want to see my wife."

"Well then go, Perea!" He took the man by the arm and dragged him to the fence, "Stop fucking around and go!"

As he watched Perea slither under the fence, he heard the French boy's voice from the other side.

"The French people do not share the views of their government, we do not support this policy, this betrayal. We share a common fate, that is what we wanted to say."

"Thank you, comrade." He found the fervour of this young man so

345

moving that he almost crawled under the fence to embrace him. "Thank you, from the bottom of my heart."

Perea was not struck by lightning and the escape went off without any problems. The Lawyer went back to work, filling in the hole, getting rid of every trace of the tunnel. Afterwards, he waited for a few minutes to make sure there were no problems, and then headed back to sleep, drenched, sneezing and happy. He felt happier still when, early in 1943, he met Perea again in the last place he would have expected: a remote sawmill in the mountains near Ariège that served as a cover for a brigade of Spanish guerrillas who had joined the French resistance.

"Hey, Lawyer!"

He looked around but could see no one he recognised among the men scattered on either side of the path.

"Someone's calling you," said Amadeo.

"I know, I just don't know who's..."

"Lawyer!" the voice came again. He turned to his left and finally he saw him.

"Perea!" Aurelio ran up and they hugged each other. "Am I glad to see you! But what are you doing here? I thought you were in Nîmes?"

"I spent four months there, living like a king... My wife is staying with a doctor, a friend of hers, he helped her get her *carte de séjour*. I didn't set foot outside, obviously, I just curled up in a warm bed next to her and had three hot meals a day, it was great... Until the local chemist turned up unannounced one night and caught us in the middle of dinner. The little bastard stood there staring at me. He asked the doctor who I was, but he obviously didn't believe I was a deaf-mute... I couldn't stay there any more, it was too dangerous for everyone, so I left. I hid out for a couple of weeks, stealing food, sleeping anywhere I could, until finally I thought, I have to decide. Either I go back to the camp, or I go back to Spain and they throw me in prison or send me off to build roads for a couple of years. I nearly did go back, but when I got to the border, I saw the Civil Guard at the checkpoint in the distance and I thought: no, I'm not going there... So I turned back and this time the French sent me to Saint-Cyprien, just for a change, then they sent me out on a work detail, building roads, the same as if I had gone back to Spain. So the first I heard of an escape plan, I got out of there. So here I am, back at war, sleeping on the ground, eating sardines out of a tin, this is my world..."

"Our world, Perea," Ignacio said, smiling at his old friend. He looked much better, Ignacio thought, he had put on weight and was tanned. Ignacio thought about the cruel fate they shared, a fate in which war was something to be desired, almost a blessing compared to the intolerable life of the camps. But the joy of seeing Perea again, the first connection he had made with his recent past after a series of goodbyes was stronger than all that, and so he hugged Aurelio.

"What about you?" Perea asked, "What have you been doing?"

"Oh, I've had a rough time, although..." Ignacio smiled, "Same as you I suppose."

"Same as everyone," he thought, although this was only true in part, the part that did not include having met Anita.

As for the rest, he too had been sent out on work detail, and although he had been moved three times, he had managed to stay in the south. At first he had worked in a pot factory, then in a mine, then in a tyre factory which, under the Vichy regime had been turned into a warehouse supplying parts to the German army. He had arrived here in December 1941, but had been planning his escape for some time, ever since he heard that they were being sent to Toulouse. It had taken him three months to concoct the perfect escape, a plan so simple that it entailed ducking down a side street on one of the weekly trips to the public baths while his companions staged a protest about working conditions.

That night, Ignacio Fernández Muñoz had bathed like a king, in the bathroom of his parents house, but the pleasure he felt could not allay his heart or calm his thoughts.

On meeting his family again he had had similar feelings. His mother was worn out with tears and she went on stroking him, repeating his name, whispering the sort of things she had written to him during the war, the sort of things Ignacio had not heard since he was a child. María, curious at all the noise, had come out into the hallway and screamed. His sister's hug was different, hearty, triumphant. She was still rocking him in her arms when his father appeared and with him a lean, gaunt figure, her eyes larger than he had ever seen them, her face a mask of tragedy that transformed but did not destroy her beauty. It was Paloma, the new Paloma, melancholy and frail, as beautiful as ever, but no longer the lively, rosy-cheeked girl she had once been. This transformation shocked him more than the haggard appearance of his father, an old man at 54 though he still managed to smile.

"Thank you, *hijo*," he said afterward, stepping back, but not quite letting go.

"For what?"

"For being here." Tears brimmed in his father's eyes.

"I've thought about you so much, Papá..." Ignacio's voice quavered, "After I was arrested in Madrid, when they put me in a cell, I thought about you all the time, I was so happy that you weren't there to see it, to see how we were betrayed, Papá…"

"We have nothing to be sorry for, Ignacio." His father's lips quivered beneath the weight of his words, "I have no regrets, *hijo*."

"Well, I don't know what we're all doing standing here with the dinner getting cold. Ignacio must be starving, aren't you?" said his mother after a moment.

"Of course I'm starving," he said, laughing, "You can't imagine…"

He followed his family into a small gloomy dining room with cheap furniture and mismatched chairs. But his parents' obvious hardship troubled him less than the pair of large dark eyes, which grew deeper and more brilliant as he moved towards them, the eyes of the strange girl he had seen earlier in the doorway. Seeing him, she got to her feet, and in spite of his excitement, his exhaustion, the joy he felt at being with his family once more, Ignacio Fernández Muñoz noticed the perfect curves of her body, the gracefulness of the hand she extended to shake his.

"Hello," the word tumbled from her generous lips.

"Hello," he said, gently shaking her warm, soft hand.

"Of course, you haven't met…" María Muñoz introduced them, "Anita, this is my youngest son…" She hugged him again, unaccustomed to having him by her side. "Anita is a friend of your sisters, she's like another daughter to us…"

On that afternoon in August 1939, when Paloma Fernández Muñoz had found Anita crying on the curb outside the boulangerie where they both worked, she barely knew her. And yet, that afternoon, she sat down beside her, put her arms around her, and comforted her like the little girl she still was. It seemed to Paloma that she had never seen anyone cry with such abandon, had never seen anyone so utterly vulnerable. Paloma had not yet received Carlos's letter, she had had no news of him, and every evening as she stepped into the building, she closed her eyes for a moment to calm herself even as she savoured the thought of stepping into the apartment and finding him sitting on the sofa chatting to her parents, telling them all the details of his escape.

And so she comforted Anita, took her into the boulangerie and suggested that the girl tell her, slowly, what was the matter. Anita did as she was told, she told Paloma everything. She was fifteen years old and from a village near Teruel. The fascists had murdered her father before the Republicans routed them. She and her older sister had fled with their mother to Barcelona as soon as the army retreated. They had been forced to leave her sister behind in a village near Gerona because she was suffering from tuberculosis and could not walk any more. Broken-hearted at having abandoned her daughter, her mother sickened. After they crossed the French border, they spent four months in a refugee camp, but by June, her mother was so ill that permission was given for her to be transferred to the hospital here in Toulouse. Now the doctors said there was nothing more they could do and that her mother had to leave because they needed the bed, but she couldn't bring her mother back to the hostel where she was staying, because they slept eight to a room and Anita didn't make enough money to pay for a room somewhere else and now she didn't know what to do, her mother was dying, she couldn't leave her out on the street.

"The only thing I can think of is to kill her. Kill her and then kill myself," she said with such determination that it was frightening.

Paloma sat in silence, looking at the girl, finding it hard to accept this story which seemed too cruel, too strange, too pitiful to be true, especially for a girl of fifteen. Paloma did not doubt the girl for an instant, but simply thought: "What have we done? What have we done to deserve tragedies such as this? What did she ever do to deserve a fate so cruel, so overwhelming?" Back then, she still had the courage to ask herself such questions, but she never found an answer.

"I have to go to the hospital," Anita said, "It's visiting hours."

"OK, you go, but come back here and find me afterwards."

Paloma already knew what she had to do. That night, she took Anita home with her and coaxed her into telling her story again. She saw her mother glance at her father. He nodded.

"Listen," said María, "We don't have much room here, there are four of us and only two small bedrooms, but there's a long narrow room next to the kitchen, a pantry, with a window onto the courtyard. If you like, we can clear it out, and put a bed in there. There won't be room for much more than that, but at least your mother will get a bit of peace, and we can help you take care of her. I give singing lessons here, so I don't need to go out, that way if anything happens while you're at work... What I don't know is where you're going to sleep, although..."

María Muñoz did not manage to finish the sentence. Before she could give the girl the choice between the small sofa in the tiny space they called the living room or a mattress on the kitchen floor next to the cooker, Anita Salgado grasped her hands and tried to kiss them.

"No, *hija*, no, there's no need... We're all in the same boat. This time we're helping you out, but maybe later you'll be the one helping us."

Long before the day Ignacio came home, Anita had become another daughter to Mateo Fernández and María Muñoz and she lived with them after her mother died. Two days after the funeral, as she was cleaning the kitchen, she heard a howl of pain and a dull thud as though something

349

had fallen out of a cupboard. She dashed out and found Paloma kneeling in the hallway amid a crumpled mass of pages, beating the tiled floor with her fists.

Paloma's parents were out that night and María was visiting a friend, so the two girls were alone in the apartment. Anita guessed what had happened, she had been expecting it, and she stood there, paralysed, not knowing what to do. She knew that the first thing was to help Paloma to her feet, and this she did. She dragged her to the nearest chair, then picked up the pages which were still scattered on the floor, long paragraphs in small, elegant handwriting, a man's handwriting, Anita thought, though she did not know how to read. María explained to her later that it was a letter from Paloma's husband, and did not begin, *Dear Paloma* as she had expected, but *My Love*, and then *The Toad has turned me in.* But this she discovered only after she had tended to Paloma, had comforted and supported her until the others came home. And that night, without asking permission, she took the mattress on which her mother had died from the pantry and put her own mattress in its place. It was her way of drawing a line under her own grief to make space for the grieving widow.

Anita Salgado Pérez may not have known how to read or write, but in September 1939, at almost sixteen, she was an intelligent girl. So when María read the letter aloud for the first time, she learned by heart many of the passages Carlos Rodríguez Arce had written from his prison cell. *When they shoot me, I'll shout ¡Viva la República! like everyone else, but that will not be what I am thinking, when they kill me I will be thinking 'I love Paloma'...* It's so beautiful, Anita thought, and she felt like crying, *I have loved you with all my strength, I love you still with everything I am, that is how much I love you, remember that and forget me...* Oh my God, she thought, what it must be like to have someone write such things, how terrible and sad but how wonderful... The condemned man begged his wife to live on without him, to meet someone else; *if he can offer you only a tenth of the love I have for you, my darling, and half the happiness that I have known with you...* and Anita would fall asleep, still thinking of the exquisite gentleness of his words and the appalling death that had put an end to such a passion.

Some three years later, in the first days of the summer of 1942, she would receive her own love letter, a provisional goodbye, less dramatic and much briefer, but one that she would be able to read for herself. *Before* p *and* b *there is always an* m... A Spanish refrain used to teach children spelling, it said at the top of the page and underneath, hurriedly scrawled, "I love you, Anita". Then she would be the one to cry, to despair, to learn for herself the true cost of beautiful things.

"If you want, you can sleep in my bed," she said to him, that first night, when he was still a stranger. "Honestly. I'm only little, I can easily sleep on the sofa."

"No, that's all right," Ignacio smiled. He had just washed and shaved and was wearing a pair of his old pyjamas. "I'm used to sleeping on the ground, so I'll be happy with a mattress. Mamá told me you know where there might be one."

"Of course, I'll get it for you. Where do you want me to put it?"

Ignacio Fernández Muñoz looked at Anita Salgado Pérez and was astonished to discover how much he enjoyed looking at her, as she stood there, barefoot, in a plain white nightgown and María's old silk dressing gown embroidered with Chinese dragons. Trying to understand his gaze, she brought her hand up and took the last pin from her chignon so that her dark, wavy hair fell in elegant confusion about her shoulders.

"Where would you put it?" he asked, revelling in the sight which warmed him.

"I'd put it here, it's warmer," she glanced toward the stove.

He simply nodded, and Anita made up his bed where she had once slept herself. Then she watched him get into bed and smiled to see him wriggle against the coarse wool mattress.

"Are you comfortable?"

"Yes," he said, then he laughed, "Actually, no. I'm not. It's been years since I've slept on a mattress, or washed with hot water or worn pyjamas... You can't imagine how many times I've dreamed of sleeping in a real bed, with clean sheets and a pillow, but now I'm here, the bed feels too soft. That's life, I suppose..."

The next morning, when Anita got up, Ignacio was sleeping with the placid abandon of a child while his younger sister, the other early riser in the family, watched him with a childlike smile. They ate breakfast quietly, standing up, so as not to wake him while María told Anita stories about her brother. Anita thought of them all day, could still hear them in her head that night when they were alone together in the kitchen and he told her he was not tired.

"Oh, all right..." She thought a moment, "Well, if you're not tired, would it bother you if I washed my hair? It's just that it's so long, I can't do it in the washbasin, and the sink here is much bigger."

He shook his head. It did not bother him, because he did not yet know how much it would bother him. He sat on one of the chairs, poured himself a glass of his father's terrible wine, lit a cigarette and watched her.

"Jesus, it's been years since I've had a glass of wine…" he said, as though to himself, but he saw her turn and noticed the flash of pity in her expression; he yielded to the playful urge to carry on. "It's been years since I've had two cigarettes one after the other."

Anita, for her part, slowly took out her hairpins, her arms stretched above her head, until her curls tumbled down onto her shoulders. Then, without saying anything, she poured the pan of hot water she had waiting into the sink, turned on the tap so it would not be too hot and tested the temperature with her hand. When she was happy with it, she tossed her hair forward and plunged her face into the water, leaving her neck bare.

Ignacio said nothing as he watched her; he would not have known what to say, other than it had been years since he had seen anything so beautiful. He could have stood watching this scene for the rest of his life, for it would have taken a lifetime to truly appreciate her grace, the harmony of her movements, the quiet beauty that belonged to a time of peace and joy, of serenity and pleasure, that spoke of a time when happiness and reason, faith and love were possible. It was an image that distilled everything he had lost, everything that he found again in that instant.

Ignacio Fernández Muñoz realised the transformation. He felt a strange burning in his eyelids, the pale throbbing of his new skin, he relived the colours and the smells, the dizzying sounds of Madrid, which he thought he would never know again and he suddenly felt alive once more, alive and aware. Then Anita wrung out her hair, piled it on top of her head, twisted the towel into a makeshift turban and turned to look at him. He gazed at her glistening skin, the white fabric like a translucent veil against her taut, firm breasts, the dark nipples, and for the first time in many years he felt capable of suffering.

"All right, well… I'll leave you in peace…" she saw the deep, intense, almost fierce look in Ignacio's eyes and suddenly she plucked her nightdress away from her skin as though only now aware how naked she seemed, or as though she regretted her innocent, but not entirely unconscious flirtation.

"Good night."

He nodded, but as she passed him, he could not stop himself from reaching out and grasping her nightdress. His right hand clutched it for only an instant, and she simply stood, motionless beside him. She was trembling. When he noticed this, he let go.

"Good night," he said at length.

Anita went into the pantry and closed the door without looking back, and when they saw each other the next day, they said good morning as though nothing had happened.

"How are you?"

"Fine. It's been years since I've had a lie in."

She laughed, and after that it became a game between them. It's been years since I read a book, it's been years since I've eaten so well, used a fountain pen, played chess, done a crossword. Anita listened and smiled at him, she woke up and went to bed with these words in her head and no longer thought about Carlos Rodríguez Arce's letter.

"There's one thing you never talk about, Ignacio…"

It was she who dared, hoping to draw the one confession which, calculatedly, he had withheld.

"What's that?" Sitting on the mattress, his back pressed against the warm stove, he saw her cheeks flush."

"How many years has it been since…? You know"

"No," he said, laughing, "I don't know."

"Well…" Blushing furiously now, Anita lowered her eyes. "Your mother told me that you had an affair, back in Madrid, with an old married woman…"

"My mother didn't like her, but she was wonderful, she had red hair and she was very beautiful. And very generous, too." He glanced at her. "She taught me a lot of things. And she was thirty, she wasn't old."

"Maybe, but she's still older, I mean you're only twenty-four now, aren't you?" He nodded. "That's the one thing you never talk about… It."

"It?"

"For God's sake, Ignacio" she pounded her fists against the mattress, then squeezed the words out in a rush of breath: "How many years has it been since you've been with a woman?"

He put a finger under her chin, lifted her head and looked into her eyes, and he found her so beautiful, so young, so genuine, so worthy of being loved and protected that he realised he would not lie to her, even if he did not tell her the truth. Because if Anita was a lady, the prostitutes in the brothel at Barcarès were not. Twice, Ignacio had turned on his heel at the very sight of them, until on the third and last time he allowed himself to be dragged along, Roque had pushed him through the doorway. These scrawny creatures were paid with the coal they had managed to filch over the course of a month while working in the mines. Now that he was alive again, these creatures did not count, because the man who had been with them was not him, but a corpse. That man no longer existed, had never been more than an empty shell. And so he did not mention this, he wiped it from his memory and confidently gave her a genuine response, the only response that Anita Salgado Pérez wanted to hear.

"Three years. Not since 27 February 1939. Three years, one month and two days..." He glanced at the clock on the wall opposite. "...three days, now."

"That's a long time," she whispered.

"Yes," he pressed his index finger to her forehead, gently drew it along her face as though to brush away a lock of hair, then stroked her earlobe. "A very long time."

Anita lowered her face again, relaxed her shoulders, curled up as though she needed time to think. He withdrew his hand and watched her from a distance, but she straightened up, closing the distance between them.

"I've never been with a man... But I have a fiancé here in France." Ignacio nodded wordlessly. "Well, he's not my fiancé exactly, more of a boyfriend..." They were now so close that Ignacio's nose was almost touching hers, "I don't know... French woman aren't like us, they're much more brazen, and I don't want him to think..."

"What?"

She did not answer, but when he kissed her, she parted her lips.

"And that night, Samson fell and with him all the Philistines" was how, years later, Anita summed it up. "Why do you say that?" her husband laughed. "I don't know, it's something my grandmother used to say..." And yet that was what that magnificent night had been for her, Samson falling with all the Philistines, and Anita Salgado Pérez, as much a dreamer at eighteen as she had been at fifteen, would not have settled for less, a soldier, a fugitive who had been waiting three years for her, on a cramped, narrow bed in the pantry, in an alien city in an alien land.

Anita, who had been so jealous of the words of love sent to another woman by a man she would never know would not have settled for less, still less would she have settled for Paul, her fiancé, who worked in a butcher's shop and was older than Captain Fernández Muñoz though he seemed younger than this man who, from time to time, would draw back and gaze at her as though he had never seen a woman. A fugitive's love is passionate and precarious, intense and fleeting. This is what Anita thought, and she tried to commit to memory each instant of this miracle, to understand every nuance, the troubled logic of its beauty. "What are you waiting for?" she whispered in his ear, and he, who had been moving slowly to allow his mind time to adjust to the reality that quivered beneath his fingertips, paused for a moment. Then he looked at her, her wet silken lips, the glimmer in her dark eyes, and the pillars of the temple began to shake.

In that moment, Ignacio felt every single day of those three long years. From this heaven, he looked down on hell, remembered the constant dull ache of his life as it had been, the humiliation, the cold and the exhaustion. And he had faith in Anita, as though her body could make the world right again, as though he knew that the happiness he felt at that moment could change everything and keep him from tumbling back into the pit of despair. And in that moment, he fell in love with her, loved her as he would never love anyone else. For the rest of his life, long after she had shown him that he had the right to live a life as normal, as mundane as the lives of those who have never know any other, he still felt that she had saved him, that in this cramped pantry, Anita had saved him from a death worse than death itself.

The interlude would not even last three months, but every moment of this extraordinary time expanded such that every incident, every minute was imprinted on their memories. Ignacio would never forget Anita's tears on the night she dared to confess something she had never told anyone, how she had stolen the petticoats of a dying woman when she was fifteen, because that day she had just arrived in the refugee camp with nothing other than the dress she was wearing, because she was having her first period and there was no one to help her, she did not know what to do. Anita would never forget the wordless grace with which Ignacio had taken one of the big books he was constantly reading out of her hands – she had picked it up out of curiosity and was holding it upside down.

"Tomorrow, I want you to buy me four exercise books. Two ruled, and two with little squares, the ones the French children use at school. Ask one of my sisters to go with you, they'll know." He waited a moment for a question that did not come. "I'm going to teach you to read and write."

"No," She looked away as she spoke, as though offended by his words.

"Yes," he insisted gently.

"No. What for? I can read a bit already. Your mother is teaching me, and anyway, I can get by…"

"You can't get by, Anita." Ignacio did not let her go on. "Nobody can. You have to learn and I can teach you, I taught so many soldiers that I know the lessons by heart. Mamá is very busy but I don't have anything to do in the mornings. It's much easier than you think, and besides…" he put his arms around her and hugged her to his chest as though he did not want to look at her, "I don't know how much longer I can stay around

here. Sooner or later, someone is bound to see me, to ask questions...
That's how it goes. We're in an occupied country in the middle of a war,
everyone has their own problems, something they need in exchange for
informing on a fugitive. I don't know what's going to happened to me,
Anita. If you don't want to learn for your own sake, do it for mine. That
way, when I have to leave, at least I'll know I've done something for
you."

"You've done so much already!" she protested, breaking free of his
embrace.

The next day, she came back with four exercise books.

"What about your homework?" Ignacio would ask her the same
question every night and Anita would shrug and smile: "I didn't have
time to do it." "Really? And why not?" he would feign surprise. "It's just
that I have this boyfriend who takes up all my time," she would say and
they would both laugh. Then they would sit together at the kitchen table,
the pupil tracing lines and curves, the teacher watching her, a smile
playing on his lips.

She learned quickly, because she was learning from Ignacio, for
Ignacio. She did her best to please him, especially now that he had
marked out their future with the terrible words "I don't know how much
longer I can stay around here", words that exploded in her mind like
gunshots. So began the countdown, and as it slipped away time became
something precious, the most valuable thing that Anita Salgado Pérez
had ever possessed. Never, not even on the day she had robbed the dying
woman, had Anita felt anything like the terrible dread that choked her
every evening as she slipped her key into the lock. Never, not even when
she was a child living in a village surrounded by mountains, had Anita
felt anything like the joy that melted her heart when she saw him leaning
against the stove and he said: "What about your homework?"

She no longer spoke to him in words. If they were alone in the
kitchen, she would throw herself into his arms, and if they were not
alone, she would find some excuse to push him into the pantry so that she
could hug him until her arms were tired. Then she would sit next to him
at the kitchen table, reading the words aloud as he ran his finger
underneath: "A −ni-ta is a lit-tle ap-ple,". She had never been so happy,
and it hurt her, because her happiness no longer had anything to do love
letters, fine words or romantic notions about renegade soldiers. It was
something bigger, something deeper than that, so powerful, so painful
that it would wake her in the night with a jolt like a premonition of death.
And when she saw him sleeping next to her, she would think:
"Tomorrow, he might not be here, tomorrow I might be all alone in this

bed..."

Until one fine evening in June, she did not find him waiting in the kitchen. No one asked about her homework, no one was waiting for her, only the exercise books lying open on the kitchen table with the words *"Before* p *and* b *there is always an* m..." and beneath it, in the space where in awkward, hesitant pencil she was to write an example, was an unexpected phrase in an elegant, cursive script, "I love you, Anita" and his signature, just his first name, Ignacio. Then, before she had managed to decipher the phrase, the fugitive's mother came in from the dining room and told what had happened:

"He's gone. He had to go... The downstairs neighbour, Madame Larronde, well, she came to see me this morning to warn me that her brother-in-law was planning to turn him in. With these windows onto the courtyard, everyone sees everything that goes on...

"Oh God," Anita's eyes widened and she brought her hand to her mouth.

"I told him not to go, I said we would go and see this man together, offer him money, but he wouldn't stay, he said he wasn't prepared to put us at risk..."

María Muñoz said no more, preferring to spare Anita her son's actual words, the dread that she would carry alone until the war was over. "It's too dangerous, Mamá, for you but for me too," was what Ignacio had said, "If I go now, I can turn myself in voluntarily. I'll be arrested, they'll put me in solitary for a while, and then they'll send me back to work. But if I'm caught by the Vichy regime, they'll deport me to Germany and the Nazis will put me in a concentration camp. Don't worry, Mamá, I knew this would happen some day and I know what I have to do..."

María Muñoz did not tell Anita this part of the story because she had stayed with him until the last, had seen him go into the pantry and reappear with the exercise book, seen him write something in it and place it on the table before leaving. He had barely reached the stairs when he came back to ask her one last favour: "Look after Anita for me, Mamá," he said, taking her in his arms and kissing her. This was why María Muñoz said no more but simply watched Anita silently, helplessly, realising she could do nothing to help her. Only Paloma knew what to do; something of her old compassion came back to her that night. Everyone was asleep except Anita. She had refused to leave the kitchen table, and was still sitting there, the exercise book in front of her, staring lifelessly ahead, when Paloma came and, over Ignacio's words, placed a photograph that Anita had never seen.

"Look," she nodded to the golden image, "It's a picture of the family

357

on my wedding day. In those days - eight years ago now – there were three young men, see them? This one…" she stroked her husband's face with her finger. "…they took from me, they murdered him. This one…" she pointed to her brother Mateo, almost as elegant as the groom in a tailcoat, a white gardenia in his buttonhole, "…they murdered him too. This one…" her finger stopped over Ignacio, a gangling boy, his legs disproportionately long for his height, "This one is not going to die. This one is going to live. Because they can't kill all three of them. It's what in mathematics they call the balance of probabilities." At last, Anita raised her head and looked at Paloma. "When you've finished this book, ask my brother to teach you maths."

Anita smiled at Paloma, then gazed at the faces of the Fernández Muñoz family, happy and flourishing, a side of the family she had never seen – the  parents much younger than she could ever imagine, Mateo with his long hair and his moustache, María, elegant, wearing rings on her fingers, bracelets and necklaces. She smiled at the bride and groom, Paloma, startlingly beautiful, and her husband, happy, as though no one knew better than he how lucky he was.

"Can I keep the photo?" she asked Paloma.

"OK, but just for tonight, you can give it back tomorrow," Paloma said, kissing the top of Anita's head.

Anita waited until she was alone again before looking down once more at this boy of sixteen who looked so young that it felt as though she remembered him at that age. "I wonder where you are now" she felt a spasm of loneliness, "Where are you Ignacio, where are you?"

Ignacio was in the basement of a barracks, in a makeshift cell, and he was reasonably happy, for everything had gone according to plan. He had made his way back to the tyre factory without incident, checked that his work detail was still there, he even had time to hug Amadeo, the Asturian labourer he had entrusted his political responsibilities to, before turning himself in to the manager.

"Where the hell have you been, *macho*?" Amadeo asked in his singsong voice, "You look like you've spent two years in a spa…"

"I'll tell you later," Ignacio smiled. "How are things here?"

"Obviously not as good as wherever you've been, but they're much the same as ever." Amadeo laughed.

This meant that the boss was still the same commandant who was prepared to do anything for a quiet life and who, although he was part of the regime, felt no undue affinity with the policies of the Vichy government. This, perhaps, was why he had never sent a prisoner in his charge to almost certain death in the German concentration camps, and

Ignacio proved no exception. "Ah, the Spanish!" he marvelled, having heard Ignacio out, "What did the French ever do to deserve such neighbours?" Ignacio could have answered the question, but did not, and was rewarded for his silence by being sent to the makeshift cell in the basement. And here, where once he had felt helpless, he realised that Anita was still with him, and never again would he feel as lonely as before.

He had an advantage over her in that he knew her daily routine, could picture her in specific places surrounded by faces he knew. He knew the cup she always used at breakfast, the order in which she took off her clothes, the foods she liked, the way she washed her hair in the kitchen sink. Each day in the cell was the same for him, but he would wake up and think of Anita waking up, before he fell asleep he imagined Anita sleeping, and this image gave his time purpose and meaning.

Had he been able to see Anita, Ignacio would have been happier still, and intensely proud of her. She flushed the toxin of self-pity from her system so quickly that the day after Ignacio's departure, she got out her exercise books, sat at the kitchen table and announced: "I'm doing my homework". Then she drew a box around the last sentence he had written, and in the space remaining she wrote copied out five times *"Before* p *and* b *there is always an* m..." then on the facing page, she copied out the words: empire, combat, embolism, compass, camp, tombs, sombre. ""*Before* p *and* b *there is always an* m... I love you, Anita."* This was the first sentence that she wrote when she finally reached the blank pages at the back of the exercise book, before copying out the simple sentences he had written to help her learn to read: "Anita is a little apple, Anita is as stubborn as a mule, I am mad about Anita, I am going to eat you up with kisses. Time to stop reading and come to bed." By the time she had copied out all the sentences, she realised she was getting fat.

She was getting fat, but she tried not to think about it. At first, she did not worry because she felt fine, she had a good appetite, she slept well, never felt like vomiting. Her older sister had always realised she was pregnant when her morning coffee made her feel nauseous. Anita could not remember the last time she had drunk coffee, but the repulsive cereal she had with milk every morning still tasted the same. As for her periods, everyone knows girls sometimes miss their periods when they're worried or upset. But her waistline refused to accept this, it ballooned, and her breasts ballooned and Anita found it increasingly difficult to button her shirt in the morning until one day it would not close at all. That afternoon, Anita sat on the bed in the little pantry and cried.

"What's the matter, *hija mía*?" María Muñoz asked, stepping into the little room, her voice tremulous with panic. "Have you had bad news, have you heard something?"

"No, it's not that."

"Thank God," María ran her hands over her face. "Thank God... But, then, what's the matter?"

"Nothing." Anita managed to go on talking, though she could not bring herself to look at María "I was thinking... Well, you've always had bad luck with Ignacio, haven't you?"

"Bad luck? No, I wouldn't say that... what do you mean?"

"I don't know... Back in Madrid, with that woman he was seeing, the one who was always so rude..." Out of the corner of her eye, she glanced at Ignacio's mother who still seemed puzzled. "And now, here, with me."

"With you?" María Muñoz thought Anita was trying to tell her about a relationship which everyone in the house had known about since the beginning; "But I love you very much, Anita, truly I do. Don't worry, I never thought you were anything like that woman."

"But I am like her, María... I am, because... But don't worry, I'll leave.... I'll take my things and go back to the boarding house..." Seeing María's worried expression, the same look she might have given her own daughters, Anita realised the woman still did not understand. "After the baby is born, I mean..."

María Muñoz stared at the girl, then buried her face in her hands and rocked back and forward on the bed.

"I'm really sorry," said Anita, not quite sure what was happening, "Honestly, I'll leave, I can't stay here, I'd die of shame..."

"Dear oh dear," her future mother-in-law took her hands from her face and Anita saw that she was smiling through her tears. She took Anita in her arms and said the only words the Anita had not expected to hear: "What do you mean you'll leave? Don't be silly, you can't leave, you have other things to think about – you need to eat properly, get lots of sleep, a little exercise... Oh, Anita!" María held the girl at arms length, then hugged her again, "I'm so happy, honestly, I'm so happy."

When Ignacio's mother emerged from the pantry, she wanted to believe that this news could mean only one thing. Things were beginning to change. They were finally beginning to improve. She was so sure, so happy, that when her husband put his head in his hands when she told him the wonderful news, it did not trouble her.

"Have you gone mad, woman?" he stared at her like a father scolding a child, "What's done is done, I accept that, but for you to be happy about it... I mean, honestly, María, this is all we need!"

"Yes, Mateo, you're right," María said. "This is exactly what we need. You're right, I'm mad. They murdered my twenty-three year old son, my daughter is a widow at the age of twenty-four, I have a grandson in Madrid I've never seen, a grandson I might die without seeing..." At this thought, she paused, saddened, then went on: "Of course I'm mad, what woman would not be in my place? But if you want to know the truth, I don't care... So what if they're not married? So what if Ignacio doesn't know he's going to be a father? It's hardly our fault, and besides... So what if Anita's father is a forester and the girl is illiterate..."

"No, I'm not saying that, but..." her husband tried to interrupt her.

"But what?" she cut him off, before realising that it was not her husband she was arguing with. "I'm not the same woman I was, Mateo. I'm not wrong as often as I used to be. The only thing that matters to me right now is my grandson, your grandson, and his mother. Nothing else. I can't go on losing my family, burying the people that I love, I can't bear to think that I might have another grandson I might never know. Don't you understand?"

Mateo Fernández was looking at his wife rather differently now; she noticed this and went on, her tone gentler.

"This is madness, I'm not saying it isn't, we're living in a foreign country, we have no money, there's a war on, I know all that. But it's also an opportunity, Mateo. Think about it. It's a new beginning."

As he considered what he might say, Mateo took the last of the French francs he had brought with him to Toulouse from the back of a drawer, and he gave the money to his wife. During dinner, he gazed at the girl who was to be the mother of his grandchild and smiled.

"Do something for me, Anita, give us a little boy," he said, "There are too many women in this house already."

"I'd rather have a girl," she said, "on account of the balance of probabilities..."

"Don't be silly, woman," Paloma laughed, and the family realised that they had not seen her laugh for a long time, " Probability has nothing to do with it."

It was a boy and he was born in January 1943, two weeks before his father managed to escape for the second time, the last time, from the tyre factory where, every night while Anita was pregnant, he dreamed that she was by his side. As his son began to distend the soft, pale adolescent belly that he could still see when he closed his eyes, Ignacio Fernández Muñoz discovered a new channel for his daring: all the energy he had previously put into escapes, he now devoted to sabotage. The Nazi occupation of Vichy France heralded a change, something which affected even the commandant in charge of the factory, who was relieved of his duties when he proved incapable of putting a stop to the constant disruptions to production at a difficult time for the German army. This was not his fault, though it was true that screwdrivers began to slip mysteriously from the hands of the foreign workers and an equally mysterious hearing problem began to afflict the men.

"I've dropped my screwdriver," Ignacio would hear someone shout in Spanish, the time prearranged in advance.

"What?" Ignacio would bring his hand up to his ear.

"I've dropped my screwdriver," the man would say, not raising his voice while the others chuckled silently.

"Turn the machine off before it fucks up!"

"What?" the man would point to his ears "I can't hear you…"

The machine would seize up, the commandant would be livid, whoever was responsible would be sent to the cells, Ignacio and Amadeo with them, even if they had not been directly involved, and the supply of tyres for the German army would dry up again. They did not care about the punishment. They all remembered the story of the German bomb that fell behind Republican lines in Guadalajara and failed to explode. The terrified artillery man sent to deactivate it found a message in rudimentary but intelligible Spanish inside: "Comrades, my bombs they do not explode." Some unknown German workman had felt that the civil war was also his war, just as this war was also theirs. They did not care about the punishment, until the new commandant arrived. He increased the severity of the punishments, put supervisors on the factory floor, and when he realized that even this was not enough, he declared that any saboteur would immediately be turned over to the occupying forces. The threat did not make them stop, but they had to be more careful. Luckily, a comrade from the Pas Valley was about to discover a foolproof way to disable the factory permanently.

"All we have to do," he proudly told them, "is gradually, very gradually, loosen two of the screws on the machine over a period of a week or so. That way the friction will grind away the axle. A few days later, when the axle snaps, a couple of us can quickly retighten the screws and that's that."

Ignacio and Amadeo looked at each other, astounded.

"Don't you get it?" said the man, a mechanic whom two wars had converted into an expert saboteur. "You said we have to be careful not to get caught, OK? This way, they'll never work out why the machine broke and the factory won't be able to operate."

As predicted, the axle snapped and production came to a standstill, but the mechanic could not retighten both screws at the same time and when the commandant started shouting, the lad he had told to tighten the other one froze, ashen-faced. It was now Amadeo's turn to come up with a brilliant plan.

"We're getting out of here tonight," he said to Ignacio, as they stood around the factory waiting for the repair detail to arrive, "Tonight or the first chance we get, you me and the guy from Pas, because that little fool is going to talk or my mother's name is not Eusebia…"

Years later they discovered that, while Amadeo's mother was indeed called Eusebia, the boy had not informed. Instead, he had spent a year and a half in a German concentration camp. That day, when Amadeo pronounced his prophecy, Ignacio did not knot that Eusebia's son had already found a blind spot – a fifty centimetre stretch of the fence hidden from view – and that for the past two months he had been planning his escape. When the engineer decided that the wear on the axle indicated that the part was defective, the men were sent to their barracks while the management decided what to do with them. But Ignacio and his co-workers had no intention of waiting for their decision. At 4am, following Amadeo, they crawled through the hole he had cut in the fence with a pair of wire cutters he had slipped into his boot that afternoon "just in case".

The Party said that two of them could to go to Foix using false papers that stated they were employed by a party member there and he would put them on a truck to join the resistance in the mountains; the other man would have to stay behind in Toulouse and wait for the party to devise some mission for him. Ignacio was about to say that he would stay, but the man from Pas got in before him: he was over forty and too old to be tramping through the woods with a rifle, besides he was of no use to the resistance, his speciality was sabotage "…and they don't have any power stations in the mountains." Ignacio could think of nothing to say. Nor, as they were leaving two nights later, could he bring himself to ask the truck driver to go through the city so he could say goodbye to his parents. Had he done so, he might have seen a light on in his sisters' room, as Anita got up to feed his son.

When she saw the child suckling at his mother's breast, a wave of peace surged through María Muñoz. "Please let him be healthy," all day the same thought lingered in her mind, "Please let him be healthy." She looked at Anita, at the girl's slight, willowy body, and she regretted the deceitful God, the ruthless supporter of their enemies, whose name she called on so often, but to whom she no longer prayed. "Let him take to the breast, because if he doesn't…" Hospitals, doctors, nurses, nannies, bottles, all these things had vanished with the world she had left behind. All she could do now was trust to her grandson, believe in him. The weight he gained every day, the speed with which he outgrew his clothes had been enough to keep María Muñoz going when she found the curious envelope from the Service for Spanish Refugees in the letterbox that morning. What could they want now? she wondered, before opening it to find a letter from Ignacio telling them that he was well, that he was living in the countryside, working in the open air and was enjoying his new job - a job just like the one he got in Madrid seven years ago, the year the autumn was so cold.

Inside the envelope was a smaller one containing a letter for Anita. She smiled when she read the greeting, the ordinary, prosaic greeting of someone who has every intention of staying alive: "Dear Anita…" Ignacio was not as good a letter writer as his brother-in-law had been, but he could tell Anita that he loved her, that he missed her terribly, that he could not bear the thought of her looking at another man, that he loved her more than he had ever loved anyone, that he needed her to trust him, to wait for him and he would come for her as soon as he could.

"What are you up to, Big Mouth?" They were in Ariège now, but Ignacio still called Perea by his *nom de guerre*. One evening he found Perea sitting on the ground, leaning on his backpack, writing a letter.

"What do you think? I'm writing…" Perea looked up at him.

"But how…?"

"It's like this…" Aurelio held up his pencil in one hand and the sheet of paper in the other. "You take a pencil and a piece of paper, then you put the pencil on the paper and…"

"Not that…" Ignacio accepted his sarcasm with a smile, "I mean, how do you get the letters to your family? How do you post them?"

"It's hard work," Aurelio continued to mock him, "I give them the letter and they put it in an envelope, they stick a stamp on it, they give it to someone who's going to Marseille or to Paris, and that person puts the letter in a box. I know it sounds complicated, but you're an educated man, I'm sure you'd get the hang of it…"

"What about the return address?"

"It depends, some people make up a Spanish name or a French name… I pretend mine are from the Spanish Service for Refugees, it looks less suspicious, and I make up an address - rue du Pont, rue Dumas, rue de l'Opéra – whatever I can think of. We can't write too often as the postman would get suspicious, but I write to my wife every six months or so, so that at least she knows I'm alive."

Between February 1943 and September 1944, Ignacio Fernández

Muñoz wrote to his parents three times, each time with two envelopes, one for his family, one for Anita. The first letter became shorter and shorter because, given that he could tell them nothing about what he was really doing, he only had recourse to little white lies. The second letter grew longer and longer as time passed and he was tormented by the very real possibility that Anita might meet another man, the sort of man who comes home every night. He could no longer imagine life without Anita, and tried to tell her this, but he could never find the precise words to tell her what she meant to him.

"I think about you all the time," he wrote, "you are with me when I go to sleep every night, every morning when I wake, I think about you every minute of every day." And it was true. So true that he did not stop thinking about her for a single second, even on the blessed morning when he put a bullet into the head of an SS Commandant – a commandant like that bastard Albatera. The dark, violent emotion he felt as he watched the man fall was Carlos, was Mateo. Yet a split-second later he realised that he might have been shot that night and Anita would never know. It was then that he realised that it did matter to him whether he lived or died, and he was happy that he had survived.

They had gone out to retrieve a consignment of weapons parachuted in by Allied forces, but before they got there, they had stumbled on a German patrol – who might have been bringing up the rear of a convoy, or simply have lost their way – when their truck got a puncture.

"Maybe it's one of our tyres," Amadeo whispered but Ignacio, still unable to believe his eyes, said nothing.

"They're having dinner," said Moreno, the leader, who was from Madrid like Ignacio.

"Jesus, you're right," Ignacio said, "I can't believe we've been so lucky."

His compatriot shot him a look of surprise. "We do nothing!" Moreno said unequivocally. "The orders were clear – if conditions aren't right, there's no drop, so we go back."

"Like fuck we're going back."

They argued in whispers, hidden by the rocks, close to the spot where the Germans had built a fire and were sitting around it. Ignacio felt the finger on the trigger of his rifle burning.

"We're going to take them." He said simply.

"No," said Moreno.

"Yes."

"Do I have to remind you I'm in charge?"

"You're in charge?" Ignacio Fernández Muñoz shot Moreno such a withering look that no one dared to break the electric silence that followed. "I'm in charge, because I'm a Captain and you, you're a puny little sergeant who still pisses his pants."

Then, without waiting for a response, he turned to 'his men': Aurelio, Amadeo, Nicolás 'the Confectioner' from Reus, and Salvador - 'the Kid' – who came from somewhere near Orihuela.

"We're going to take them because even though we're outnumbered, we've got cover and they're in the open, got it? He waited until they nodded. "It's going to be like shooting ducks in a fairground, but we have to take it slowly, line up the shots, divvy up the targets, and no one is to fire until I give the order..."

"What did you say you did?"

When they got to the farm where the local leaders of the Maquis were waiting, they were met by a line of resolutely bewildered faces rather than with the praise they were expecting.

"Eleven dead, two prisoners," Ignacio repeated, slowly, in French, "and we took the truck with the weapons and ammunition, two motorcycles and a tank. There was a jeep too, but we had to leave it behind because there were only six of us, so there was no one to drive it."

"A tank?" one of the Frenchmen repeated and Perea, who saw where this was heading, became nervous, "And how did you get it here?"

"We took the road." Ignacio was growing tired of what seemed like pointless questions.

The Maquis explained that this was not how things were done here, they did not take prisoners, that a tank was useless to them and they would have to destroy it. Ignacio had been expecting this, but Amadeo had been so excited when he set eyes on the tank – "Look, Big Mouth, there's a donkey for you to ride back to your village!" – that Ignacio had quickly given in to him. "Aw, Lawyer, do we have to blow it up? It's so pretty," Amadeo had said, stroking the tank, "And it's brand new, look, it's like it's been waiting for me. Let's take it, it's three o'clock in the morning and it's only a couple of kilometres from here to the track. Who's going to see us?"

"It was reckless, I admit that," Ignacio said, "But you don't win a war without being reckless."

Ignacio's brashness did little to convince the French, but Big Mouth's outburst, hurling himself at one of them when he realised they intended to take away his donkey, proved more effective: "What do you mean destroy it? You're not destroying my tank, got that?", he lifted the man off the ground, and went on screaming, oblivious to the fact that his victim did not understood a word he was saying "I'm crossing the border in this tank, got that?"

That morning, Auelio Perea drove the tank down the track, back to the camp where their waiting comrades gave them the welcome which would be immortalised the following day with a photograph. Moreno, deeply offended, refused to pose for the photo but they quickly lost sight of him on the afternoon they were summoned back to the farm where they were met by a man dressed as a farm labourer, a senior French officer they had never met before. "Are you the tank guys?" he asked, addressing them in Spanish. When they told him they were, he smiled and suggested that they join the French troops. "I get the impression your talents are underused here." "About time," Aurelio exclaimed, who was as bored as the others of being a messenger boy. Ignacio laughed, delighted at this sudden reversal of fortune, but as he laughed he thought about the risk he would be taking, about Anita.

On a morning in September 1944, as Ignacio looked up and down the station platform and did not see her, he wondered why he had left behind the carousing and the marches, the celebrations of the Liberation to come back to Toulouse. He had sent her a telegram, so that she would know he was coming home for her, so that she would not feel like an outsider, coming to meet him at the station with his family. The telegram had obviously arrived because his family were there – his father, his mother and María, pregnant with a man on her arm. Everyone except Paloma, who was probably working, he thought. Everyone except Anita.

"Ignacio!" his father called to him, waving his hat. But Ignacio did not budge: Papá, Mamá, María, María's boyfriend, no Anita. No Anita.

"*Hijo mío!*" his mother rushed over and threw her arms around him, but all she got was a perfunctory hug, a cold stare and a barrage of questions.

"What about Anita? Where is she? Has something happened?"

"No, she's fine, she's at home," María Muñoz smiled.

"Why? Why didn't she come to meet me?" he persisted.

"There have been a few changes, *hijo*, you'll see…"

"Is she married?" his sister threw her arms around him, and tried to introduce the man with her. "Tell me, Mamá! Did she marry someone else?"

"Of course not, what are you talking about? She's waiting for you at home…"

"I'm the one who got married," his sister interrupted, "This is my husband. Francisco, this is my brother Ignacio. Francisco is from Sonseca, near Toledo, you know, the village where they make the marzipan."

"Really?" Ignacio shook the man's hand, so confused that it took him a moment to remember what marzipan was. "Pleased to meet you."

The newlyweds said goodbye as they left the station, leaving Ignacio with his parents: "What did you think of Francisco? María worships him, we've know him for about a year and a half. He was besotted with Paloma, but then he fell in love with María. He's a nice lad, well brought-up, a good worker. She got pregnant straight away, she's five months gone. We're hoping for a little girl." They bombarded him with facts and questions, but they were nearing home now, and a few minutes later the taxi dropped them outside the door.

"Listen, Ignacio, before we go in..." María Muñoz took her son's hands in hers and looked into his eyes as her husband fumbled with his keys. "Only one good thing has happened to us since we left Spain, try to remember that, one good thing..."

"María!" from the hall, Mateo Fernández shot his wife an outraged look.

"What?" she protested, "I'm not allowed to talk to my son?"

"No, you're not. Because your son is a grown man, and more than capable of making his own decisions. He doesn't need your advice, let alone your blackmail."

"Mamá, what the hell is going on?" the grown man exploded, "For fuck sake, will someone tell me what this is about?"

"Ignacio, I won't have you talk like that!"

Arriving on the landing Ignacio noticed that the door was open. Paloma who had heard the raised voices was standing in the doorway, smiling, and in her arms she cradled a baby, almost a toddler, with dark hair and protruding ears, and huge, dark mournful eyes, just like Anita's, he thought still not putting two and two together.

"This is your son, Ignacio," Mateo pronounced, his tone neutral.

"He looks just like you, don't you think?" the baby's grandmother reached out and her grandson clambered into her arms, gurgling and laughing, revealing a gap between his front teeth just like the one Ignacio Fernández Muñoz saw every time he looked in the mirror. "His hair is dark like his mother's, but otherwise he's the spitting image of you..."

Ignacio said nothing, he looked from the child to his mother, then to his father, to his sister Paloma and then back to the baby. But we were careful, we were always careful... except maybe once or twice at the end, he thought.

"Here!" Ignacio's mother handed him his son, but the boy struggled out of her arms and ran to Paloma.

"But this is Papá!" Paloma explained, "You know. You can even say

Papá, can't you? Go on, let him hear you say it: Papá... pa-pá" The child had no intention of saying anything and his aunt laughed. "He's completely spoiled, of course..."

It took some time for Ignacio to react, and in that hiatus, his son's curiosity overcame his surprise; he struggled until Paloma set him down, warily came closer, and clung to Ignacio's trousers.

"Soldier," he said. This was the first word Ignacio Fernández Muñoz heard his son say.

'Where's Mamá?" Ignacio asked the boy.

"Mamá," the child repeated confidently. He dashed off down the hall and his father went after him, only to come back when he realized he was missing a vital piece of information.

"What's his name?"

"Ignacio!" they chorused. And his mother added "After you."

As he followed his son down the short hallway to the kitchen, all the emotions he had been suppressing since he stepped into the apartment suddenly thrilled through him. In his astonishment, he felt Anita's shock, the distress and worry she must have felt at discovering she was pregnant, also her fear, her determination and her strength. He almost laughed to think of all the nights he had spent reimagining her slender figure, she probably looked nothing like that now. And yet, as he stepped into the kitchen the woman waiting for him seemed to have been frozen in time; she sat calmly with her back to the stove as though waiting for her son to tug at her skirt before moving. In a clear voice, the child announced: "Papá" Only then did Anita Salgado Pérez pick up a dishcloth and take the casserole from the oven, she wiped her hands, then turned and looked at him. He saw that she was much more beautiful, more real, more desirable, than he remembered. And He felt at once utterly naked and utterly safe, felt that he was finally home.

There was a pile of well-thumbed exercise books on the table, the covers worn and creased.

"I did my homework," she said and seeing him smile, she smiled too.

"So I see."

She put the child down, took Ignacio in her arms and kissed him, her kisses kept coming, her feet lifted off the ground long before he wrapped his hands around her waist and sat her on the table, still kissing her, finally accepting the reality of her flesh. He felt so overcome that he did not recognize the cause of the sharp pain in his calf until they finally broke their embrace and, glancing down, he saw the son whose very existence he had forgotten.

"He's biting me..." Ignacio said, laughing, as he removed the hairpins that imprisoned her lush confusion of curls in a severe chignon.

"I know," she said, helping him "He's very attached to his mother."

After lunch, the rest of the family went for a walk, taking the boy with them, and they found themselves alone in a bed different from the one Ignacio remembered, in a large, comfortable room that looked out onto the street. At that moment, Ignacio Fernández Muñoz said what he felt he had to say, but it felt not like a duty but a privilege. She did not agree to his request so easily.

"Listen, Ignacio, I've thought about this a lot, and it's not as simple as that." Anita leaned back against the pillow and became serious. "Everything is about to change, it's obvious, your father goes on about it all the time: 'it might not be our war, but at least we've won this one'. And when the Nazis surrender, or maybe even before then, the Allies will deal with Franco, they'll have no choice, I mean Franco sided with the Germans and the Italians from the very beginning, he even sent troops to Russia... So some day soon the Allies are going to invade Spain, you'll go back to war, you'll kick the bastard out, everything will be fine and then what? Because everything's different here in France – here everything is a mess, all of us are penniless. Back home, things will go back to being the way they were, with everyone back in their rightful place. And it doesn't matter how communist you are, Ignacio, you'll always be rich, a gentleman, and you might say it doesn't matter, but it does. And me... there's no point lying about it, in Madrid before the war, the best I could have hoped for was to be your mother's maid."

Anita had carefully prepared this speech, and rattled it off without pausing for breath, like a schoolgirl reciting a lesson. Then she looked at him and he was smiling.

"Well, well," he was laughing now, "Honestly, you're as stubborn as a mule... I've never seen the like of it..."

"What? I'm right, aren't I?" she protested.

He did not want to answer her. He gazed at her, pushed a lock of hair from her face and tucked it behind her ear.

"Marry me, Anita."

"Why?"

"Why not?"

Though his answer made her smile, still she held out. "Are you sure you're not just asking me out of pity?"

"Yes. I'm sure."

Ignacio Fernández Muñoz and Anita Salgado Pérez were married in Toulouse in late January 1945. The man who officiated at the ceremony was a former councilor in the Popular Front who had fought with the

Lawyer in the final months of the war before taking up his post again. His wedding gift was highly unusual: he waived the need for Anita's birth certificate. She had tried half a dozen times to get a copy, writing first to the mayor then to the parish priest in her village, but she received no answer. Shortly afterwards, the newlyweds moved to Paris. For Ignacio, it was here that the reunions began, those they had spoken of during those long years of goodbyes.

Paris was fizzing with hope, with news, with great plans whispered about or broadcast loudly in Spanish. It was in Paris that Captain Ignacio Fernández Muñoz met Amadeo's fiancée, Aurelio's wife and the wife of the lad from Zamora who had spent sleepless nights worrying about his fate. Here, he met up again with friends he had known though hard times long ago and more recently. When he asked if there was any news of Roque, he found out the man from Pas had been killed by gendarmes, shot dashing through the fields after sabotaging one of the electricity pylons he loved so much. The lad from Alicante, the one they called 'the Kid' was dead too, killed by a Vichy sniper holed up in a barn who had to go down fighting even as the liberators marched through the village. What had happened to Nicolás was worse. Nicolás had been the only one of the tank squad who stayed behind with the *maquis* because his wife lived nearby and from time to time he took the risk of visiting her. On one of these visits, the Germans dragged him out of bed at dawn, and the Confectioner realised that someone had turned him in – and the only other person who knew the address was also in the *maquis* and usually came to the village with him. He screamed the man's name over and over as the Nazis were dragging him away. He was sent to Mauthausen and never came back, but his wife would forever remember those screams. When Ignacio, Aurelio and Amadeo found out what had happened, they decided to track down the traitor and kill him, but they never found him.

On the other hand, one night, in a café they often went to, 'the Lawyer' spotted a smiling, confident young man he recognized as Julio Carrión González, the eldest child of a charming woman named Teresa, a socialist schoolteacher from Torrelodones.

Raquel put the chaos pendulum on the bedside table next to the photo of her grandparents. She loved looking at it, and I loved looking at her because her lips moved constantly, her smile wavering and broadening with each impulsive twitch of the black ball.

"It's like they're chasing each other, isn't it?" she said to me once. "Of course they can't be because they're both attached to the same axis, but when they change direction and start spinning really fast it looks like one of them's trying to catch the other one..."

"Do you like it?"

"I love it."

"If I'd known, I'd never have got it for you."

"Why not?"

"Because you don't listen to me any more..."

"Oh..." she opened her eyes wide as though shocked and took me in her arms.

From my side of the bed, the pendulum blocked my view of the photo behind. The outer pendulum alternately hid the photo of the tank and revealed it at fixed, regular intervals, seemingly unrelated to the wild gyrations of the other. Sometimes when I looked at the pendulum, I thought that this ingenious, innocent contraption was an image of me: a good boy, a good son, a good citizen, an ordinary, almost boring man to whom nothing ever happened that had not been minutely planned, and the glorious, painful chaos, bitter yet pleasurable that whirled inside me.

"I don't want to talk about your father," Raquel had warned me just before the subtle, silent explosion which shifted the planet's orbit. "Neither do I," I told her. And it was true. This simple, unconditional pact laid to rest the ghost of Julio Carrión González and his last mistress dispatched him from a reality of which he would never again be a part. This was one place he had never been; here in this bed. In telling me this, Raquel gave me something more than a gift, she gave me a guarantee, that whatever we had would never be a continuation of what had gone on between her and my father in the apartment on the Calle Jorge Juan.

I had a similar experience with Encarnita's revelation. "It always was a mysterious business," she told me, and I was satisfied that what she had said was more or less consistent with the official version of events. As a girl, my mother had always spent the summer holidays in Torrelodones; this was where my father first met her, then, many years later, he had given her work to get her out from under the thumb of her tyrannical grandmother who would have kept her shut up in the house all day long. They fell in love, got married and had five children. I was number four. The idea that Mariana had gone to the Civil Guard and said Papá had robbed her, not of the little house near the train station, but of one of the most elegant villas in Torrelodones, had to be a misunderstanding. In any case, it was of no importance since the wronged woman had been a witness at the marriage of her daughter to the man who had supposedly ruined her. The mystery Encarnita had mentioned was clearly nothing more than a family squabble, the sort of quarrel that seems hugely important to those concerned, but trivial to outsiders. And by this point, I no longer wanted to think about it.

All I could think about was Raquel. Raquel was Time itself, the days, the hours, the minutes. My life was divided into the moments when I was with her and those wasted hours I spent without her in a world in which everything reminded me of her. I was falling so fast I did not even realise my own speed and before I knew what was happening, my life had become nothing more than an excuse, a façade which made it possible for me to live a life greater than my own, a life which was called Raquel.

She did nothing to stop me, imposed no limits. That spring blessed each of our encounters with the gift of simplicity, protected us, cradled us between the four corners of this bed in which nothing existed but sex and laughter, the thoughtless complicity of teenagers in love and something else, something more solemn, more vital – the Earth rotating on its axis, rotating around the Sun as we lay together, naked and entwined. Out there, was everything else. Out there was winter, ice, the slippery expanse of snow trampled into slush by passersby – guilty and innocent, faithful and unfaithful, aware or unaware of the wounds their every footstep would make on their children's future; a guilty, ravaged landscape very different from the pristine country wrapped in brightly coloured paper which they believed they would inherit. Out there was winter, but I could not feel it, and so I let the time slide by.

Raquel knew everything. She had always known everything. She knew this world we held in our hands would one day burst like a child's bubble. I knew only that I didn't want to know, not yet, and all the while my life was an excuse, a façade that concealed the only true life, which began every time I pressed the button on the entry phone.

"Hi, it's me…"

"Come on up."

She always said the same thing: "Come on up," an order, an entreaty, or a secret code. "Come on up," and up I would go. Sometimes I rang before I came, sometimes I didn't, but every time I pressed the button on the entry phone, she was there. The weather was mild, spring was in no hurry to stumble into summer and for me it was still enough just to need Raquel. This need was still a blessing. I had to control my anxiety at her absence, hoard my desire for her like a miser shutting himself away to count his money.

"Come on up," and there she was: Raquel Fernández Perea, an intelligent girl with a secret, enigmatic beauty, a woman so beautiful you had to look at her twice to see it, to truly appreciate the problem of her hips which seemed slightly disproportionate given the narrowness of her waist but which merely trumpeted the perfection of her body, her skin, velvety as a rare peach. This was the only problem I wanted to solve, the only challenge that interested me. When I placed my hands on Raquel's hips, I touched a whole infinitely greater than the sum of its parts.

But when I took her in my arms, for an instant, though I had sworn I would not do it, though I had forbidden myself to do it, I remembered everything. I remembered my charming, charismatic father, magician, wizard, snake-charmer – a poor bastard addicted to harmless but possibly fatal pharmaceuticals, grandson to a grandmother I never knew, husband to my mother, lover to this woman who broke the perfect circle of her mouth in a slow smile. I remembered all these things and they seemed so incompatible with the reality before me, that I began to babble about anything at all, simply to silence the deafening clamour in my head. The sound of my voice comforted Raquel, reassured her. At that moment, I realised that today, as every day, she had been waiting for me to make my mind up whether I would ask her about my father and, realising that I had decided not to, she responded with one of her intense, radiant smiles.

"The other day, I was thinking..." I looked at her but she looked away, shrugged almost imperceptibly as I began to babble about the first thing that came into my head. "Your husband, what was he?"

"A moron."

"Yes, but apart from that... I mean what did he do for a living?"

"He worked for IBM – still does as far as I know. But just to make you happy I'll tell you that he was an economist like me, we met at university. Apart from that..."

I smiled, "If we were at a dinner full of couples, I'd stand out!"

"As I was about to say..." she went on, "Apart from that, he had Harley that he thought was prettier than me, an Afghan hound he loved more than me, a coke habit he found more stimulating than me, and a whole group of friends with Harleys and pedigree dogs that he got on better with than me."

"Then why did you marry him?"

"Well…" She paused for a moment, "To be honest I don't know any more. We started going out in second year at college, we were together for two years, then we split up. I went off to study drama, I had this thing with an actor – I told you about him – and when he dumped me my ex found out and pestered me to get back with him. I found him a lot more interesting than before – I suppose because he had a Harley and an Afghan hound, and he earned a lot more than I did. He took me on exotic holidays and he was very handsome. I was young and a bit of a moron myself. But I've got better, haven't I?"

"He was very handsome?" I asked, frowning.

"Hang on, I'll show you…"

As she slipped out of bed, night was beginning to fall and the fading sunlight traced luminous planes on the air, swathing Raquel in an unreal, almost theatrical golden glow. As she moved towards the antique desk I loved so much, she seemed to take this shifting, defiant glimmer with her and I felt the whole world plunge into darkness, that nothing could exist beyond the compass of this body so loved by the sun.

"Look," she said. She had a pile of photos. "That's him, there."

I don't remember the date, and I don't know if it was precisely at that moment that I realised I was in love with Raquel, utterly, irrevocably and there was no way out. I can't reconstruct it because I'd never felt anything like it before, and because I had a deep-rooted tendency to smile indulgently at the sweeping, metaphysical pronouncements of my brother Julio, my friends, and my wife's friends. I just thought they were exaggerating and even the idea that I might be missing something was not enough to stop the imaginary red pencil with which I mentally divided the suffering, the loneliness, the tears and the anger from the pleasure and happiness of other people's lives. Back then, I used to remind myself that I loved my wife, my work, my life, that I did not regret anything. But that was when I believed that my life belonged to me, when I believed it *was* a life.

I don't remember the date, all I know is that it was late May, maybe June, because by now I was spending every afternoon at Raquel's apartment and the sunlight was urging us into summer. And I remember I had difficulty focusing on this tall, muscular young man with blond curly hair, a round, childlike face, and a weak chin who looked a little like a tanned teenager in some American soap opera. I know I had trouble focusing on him because, standing next to him in almost every photo was Raquel at twenty, delicate and tender as a peach still ripening on the branch. It pained me to think of all the years she had lived without me, of the hands that had touched her, the arms that had held her, the lips that had kissed her; it saddened me that I had not known her earlier and I realised I could never allow myself to be parted from this woman, that all I wanted was to grow old by her side.

"Well, come on… say something," she said. She looked scared.

"You were pretty," I kissed her breast near the nipple and managed to recover some semblance of composure. "Not as pretty as you are now."

"Álvaro, flattery will get you nowhere," she laughed.

"I'm serious. As for him… What do you want me to say?" I looked up at her. "I prefer the men on the tank."

"Me too, but we're not talking about them."

"No, that's true, I just mean I think they're more handsome. Your husband is… well… He's handsome too, mostly because he's blonde, but he looks a bit effeminate, don't you think?" She was rolling with laughter now, "I'm just saying, the curly hair is weird, even for an economist, and he's clearly put a lot of hours in at the gym, and that fake tan, I don't know."

"Well, I can tell you there was nothing effeminate about him. He was constantly cheating on me…"

"What about you?"

"I cheated on him too in the end, but…" She raised a finger. "He started it!"

Well, don't even think about cheating on me, I was about to say, but I said nothing, not because I was married – a fact I barely remembered at that moment – but because such a ridiculous cliché seemed to go beyond the neutral territory, overstep the boundaries we had set ourselves. In the distance, among the numberless men who had shared her bed before and after her divorce, stood the figure of my father, and I had no desire to know the times, the places, the names of the hotels, the restaurants, I didn't want to know the details. We could do anything, tell each other anything, talk about anything except the man who had brought us together, the man who had once been her lover and would always be my father.

What happened that afternoon had happened before, it would happen again so then, as I had done before I kissed Raquel as though I had never kissed another woman, I held her with such infinite care it was as though I held her life in my hands and she looked at me with such complete surrender as if to say that I did. Then I went home. On the scale of unreality that marked the profusion of that spring, going home far outranked the silences imposed by my father's ghost.

"Álvaro!" Mai was always happy to see me. "I'm glad you're home, here, let me show you something, I've been looking into the new kitchen.

My sister-in-law took me to this factory out in Fuenlabrada, they make units for all the top brands but you can buy them at cost, and it only takes six weeks, which is lucky, because that's exactly when the Polish builders finish at Isa's place..."

She led me into the living room, sat me down at the dining table and unfolded brochures and more brochures, floor plans and more floor plans. "I really like the layouts where you have a central island, but obviously that pushes up the price..." April went by like this, May began: "Look at this one, it looks like a kitchen out of the 1940s, doesn't it?" May sidled into June and now Raquel's face stared out at me from every extractor hood, every vegetable basket, every built in wine-rack. "What about this one? Mix and match solid wood and glass doors, I know everyone does it," as Raquel's pussy stayed on my fingers, my hands, imprinted on the skin of memory, began to appear on my face. But Mai didn't see it as I agreed with everything she said, except when she wanted me to disagree: "No, no, definitely not that one."

"OK, well that's all of them. So what do you think?"

"Whichever one you like best."

"Well I like this one best, obviously," she gestured to a group of photographs as incomprehensible, as irrelevant, as all the others. "But it's the most expensive."

"That doesn't matter. All that matters is that you like it." And I looked at her, smiled at her.

And she came over and stood behind my chair, put her arms round my neck and kissed me over and over, and I felt less and less guilty.

"I'm going to call Isa right now and tell her! I have to say it feels good to be rich all of a sudden." Just as she was about to leave the room, she remembered something and turned. "What about your book? How's it going?"

"Good, good... But I'm taking it slowly, I've only just started really..."

In mid-May I'd told my wife I was going to write a book on the educational value of interactive science museums. I had already published a few things: my masters and my doctoral theses, a collection of articles in various magazines, a four hundred page essay on the theoretical repercussions of the discovery of quarks for which I won a very prestigious but financially worthless prize, and a lot of other material I was supposed to be co-writing with Professor Cisernos but wound up writing by myself for a *History of Spanish Physics* to be edited by José Ignacio Carmona. He was the one who had given me the idea, one night when we were out together.

"That professorship is waiting for you, Álvaro, you need to shut yourself away and do some writing," he had announced suddenly, without warning.

At first I thought it was just a coincidence, but looking at my mentor, I wondered if it might be something more, a sign of complicity, or solidarity. In the end, as José Ignacio started insisting on impossible deadlines and Fernando started pretending to panic - "November, Jesus fuck, November, you poor bastard," I laughed, realising that they were winding me up, offering me the prospect of a professorship at the one point in my life when I could do nothing about it. But I didn't care, I knew that my professorship would still be waiting for me in two years time; I had some proofs to correct for a book of articles due to be published at Christmas, and two months would be more than enough time to write the passionate defence of the Educational Value of Interactive Scientific Museums that José Ignacio had asked me to publish for the good of our heroic and much maligned discipline. That night, when I came home, I simply reported the conversation to Mai.

"Did you hear what I said? I'll have to do some writing…"

"Of course," she nodded. We had spent all evening discussing her plans for redecorating the kitchen.

"I'll have to shut myself up in the University library every bloody afternoon," I said trying to sound frustrated, "and I'll have to go to the Consejo library too. I might even have to work through the summer. I don't know if I'll be able to go on holiday."

"That's terrible. It's all getting a bit much. Poor Álvaro! First your Papá dies, then all this work on the house, and now this thing with the professorship…"

"Yes," I nodded, quite genuinely, "It's all getting a bit too much."

The following day, before my first lecture, I went to see José Ignacio – to whom I had said nothing, although I was sure Fernando had told him everything – and thanked him "You dog!" was all he said when I told him why I was grateful. His informant was much more forthcoming.

"Jesus, Álvaro, what are you like?"

"To quote you: Not only am I obsessed with 'this girl's cunt', I'm also a 'prick'."

"Yeah, how right I was."

I laughed, but I realised that he was right. Not only was I obsessed, I was fixated, stunned, stupefied, the way little kids can fixate when they're playing, just staring at the leaves on a tree, or their fingertips, or the moon. I was a prick, something I had never been. I understood my predicament better than anyone, this precarious, increasingly dangerous situation, and I understood my innocence, a term I wrapped around my usual virtue, shielding me, as all unfaithful husbands shield themselves with repeated lies and excuses. I had never been a cheating husband, I had been the Midas of the curriculum, the queen bee of the research programme, a conscientious theoretician. Mai was not a factor in the problem, at least it did not seem so, not yet, and yet there was a problem that concerned her. One day the problem would have to be refomulated and on that day, I would have the solution. Or not. Just thinking about it made me fell sick and I could see the precise colour of fear, feel it in the pit of my stomach. It was easier not to think about it. I was obsessed, I was a prick, and I knew that the worst mistake I could make would be to give up Raquel Fernández Perea. This conviction persuaded me not to do anything other than laugh at Fernando's off-colour remarks. Until one day, he said something different:

"So, I think the least you could do is introduce me."

"Introduce you to who?" I was only half-listening.

"The empress of China. Who do you think? Term's over, I've already marked half my exam papers, at this rate I'll be off to Comillas without meeting her..."

I looked at him, speechless – firstly because it had never occurred to me to introduce him to Raquel, secondly because I didn't want to. It was 1 July, and three months had slipped by since my life began to be ruled by the chaos pendulum and yet nothing happened outside of Raquel's bedroom, the measureless, cosmic bed, the link to the molten core of the planet. This, I realised, was why we had barely set foot outside her bedroom.

Now that José Ignacio's request meant that science was giving back to me all the time I had selflessly invested in it, I could go to meet Raquel at the bank and we would have a quick lunch – *tapas*, sitting at the bar. It was summer now and the mild spring, felt so remote it was as if it had happened in another lifetime, as though I had been a different man: conscious of his limitations, a man who had mastered the art of deferring to a new and indescribable pleasure. That man was gone now, he had disappeared, together with his dubious array of high and low concepts, with useless virtues like discretion, caution, with the mathematical precision which he had trusted all his life.

I'd go to meet Raquel at the bank, I'd see her coming through the glass doors, I'd kiss her like teenagers kiss outside the school gates, and I could never get enough. I wasn't hungry any more, but she always insisted we go for something to eat, she always decided where, ordered the wine, ate quickly, ate my portion. And I would watch her eat and drink and I couldn't control the saliva that flooded my mouth as I ground my teeth. We could have walked back to hers: Opéra, Santo Domingo, San Bernardo, it was almost a straight line, but we always took a taxi because I could never get enough.

Afterwards was another concept that had ceased to exist. Afterwards, we could go out for a beer, we'd say, but we never did go out. "Everyone says it's a great movie, I'd love to see it." "Me too" But we never did go to the cinema. We talked about our friends "You'll like him, he's hilarious". "She's so funny", "he's so clever", "we should all get together one of these days", but we never did. We never saw anyone, never went anywhere, never got out of her bed, because I could never get enough.

Three months had not passed since Raquel offered me sanity and I had refused her. I was no longer a sane person, I no longer knew the meaning of the word 'afterwards', and maybe that's why that morning, when Fernando Cisneros asked if he could meet her, I said yes.

"OK, but it'll have to be after the 4th."

'Why?" He looked at me, eyebrows raised in astonishment, "Have we started celebrating the 4th of July?"

"No," I smiled, "It's because that's the day the builders arrive to take out the old kitchen and fit the new one. Mai is taking Miguelito to her mothers at La Moraleja, because it's impossible to do any work on the house with him there... She'll come into town with my sister Angélica every day and they'll go home together – they both work 8am to 3pm, with no lunch break. They'll take turns driving..." Fernando laughed, he could see where I was going, "I'm not going there this year. I'll go for Sunday lunch, maybe spend Saturday night there sometimes. I said I'd oversee the builders because..." I paused for effect. "Since the my tenure is coming up, I have to get a load of papers published, I can't afford the time, much less the time I'd spend stuck in tailbacks on the carretera de Burgos... I'm not even sure I can take time out to go to the beach in August..."

"You've turned into a sly fucker, Álvarito! I might have to take lessons from you..." He patted me on the back.

But after the 4th of July – on the 6th to be precise – I realised that I wasn't the sly fucker I thought I was.

"Dear heart," I said to Raquel in the deep theatrical voice she had taught me. It was the morning of 5 July and I had just woken up in her bed. "I'm awfully afraid we may have to devote some of our time to cultivating our social circle."

She propped herself up on one elbow.

"You brother Julio?"

"No," I said, though she was near the mark – he would be next, as soon as he found out about her. "But I thought we might schedule a rendezvous with my old chum Fernando, the one I took to the theatre to watch the musical comedy inspired by the works of Hans Christian Andersen, do you remember?" she nodded, laughing, "I'm afraid he's something of a muckraker and can't bear to wait any longer."

"Of course," she said, then looked at her watch and gave a little cry, "Shit, I'm going to be late for work…"

She washed and dressed and had a slice of toast before heading out. When I called her mid-morning to tell her that Fernando had rejected my initial invitation for a quick drink and countered by inviting us to dinner that evening, she did not change her mind.

"What should I wear?" she asked. I found her nervousness touching. When I hung up, having suggested she wear the same dress and high heels she'd worn when we went to the Japanese restaurant, I began to wonder whether "prick" accurately described me, although maybe I needed something stronger.

"How do I look?" she asked when I came to pick her up.

"So beautiful I think we should skip dinner," I said.

"But we're not going to skip dinner, because I'm a bit of a muckraker myself…"

Seeing her step through the door of the restaurant in front of me, Fernando made a silent gesture that spoke volumes. He had chosen an Asturian place where the food was incredibly good and the volume incredibly noisy – the small tables with checked tablecloths were wedged so close together you could barely hear yourself think. It was the last place I would have chosen, but Raquel liked it and strode confidently across the room, though her daring dress was too sophisticated, too elegant, for a *taberna* where the customers did not bother to dress up. She did not mind; she knew why people were staring at her.

I had agreed to the dinner on one condition. "Don't you go telling her the story of your grandfather Máximo, because if you do, I'll get up and walk out," I warned Fernando.

He laughed. "Fuck, I never realised I scared you so much, Álvarito!"

"It's not that," I said, which was only half-true, because I was scared of anything that might drive a wedge between Raquel and me. "It's because her grandparents are even bigger heroes than yours and I don't want you to make a fool of yourself."

"We'll see – how many years did they spend in prison?" he said.

"None," I answered, "but they emigrated to France and fought in the Second World…"

"Aw," he cut me short, "her poor grandparents had to emigrate…"

"Look, she's my girlfriend and they're my rules, either you agree to them, or dinner's off."

He agreed to my conditions, he didn't even regale us with one of the long conspiracy theories about academic politics he loved so much. I steered the conversation and as we both wheeled out tried and tested stories to make Raquel laugh, I noticed that she was drinking more she usually did.

That night, Raquel got drunk. Having delicately suggested who should pay: "This is on you, isn't it, you old bastard?" Fernando suggested we have a drink on the terrace of the first bar we found and she agreed with an enthusiasm that marked everything she did that evening: knocking back her first whisky, slowly sipping the second, complaining to Fernando about women who hoovered during IQ tests; recounting her frustrating experiences in the theatre, kissing me, holding my hand, suggesting she manage our finances and make both of us millionaires, explaining the details of a fabulous scam she'd planned with a colleague called Paco Molinero who was her best friend and my worst fear, ordering another whiskey, realising she'd had too much to drink, telling Fernando that it was all his fault because seeing us give each other sidelong glances made her nervous, insisting on paying and agreeing when professor Cisneros refused to let her. "It's the least I can do, given that it's my fault you're in this state." he explained. "I think you should take me home," she said to me finally.

"Don't leave me… the room is moving." Lying on her bed back at her apartment, she flung her arm out vaguely in my direction.

"I'll be right back…" I promised, "Have you got any Alka-seltzer?"

"Yeah, I think so, in the kitchen or maybe… I don't know."

I found it straight away, dissolved two tablets in a large glass of water and made her drink it.

"Would you like to take my clothes off" she asked when the glass was empty.

"I'd like that very much."

"Can you pull the duvet over me and come to bed, is that OK?"

"That's very okay."

"I won't be able to fuck," she said when she'd finally found a comfortable position, her head in the crook of my neck, her right arm and leg flung across me, clinging like a castaway to the only timber floating on the ocean. "I don't feel very well."

"Really? I hadn't noticed…"

"Yes…" she managed to laugh. "I did think about it… fucking I mean, but I can't move, I'm sorry."

"Nothing to be sorry for."

"But you've got a hard-on."

"Yes."

"And you don't mind?"

"No, go to sleep."

"I love you, Álvaro."

She'd never told me that she loved me before. I could feel the heavy rhythm of her breathing against my chest, my fingers rested lightly on her waist, her arm and her leg anchored me to the bed. A feeling of deep peace compelled me to stay awake so I could appreciate the experience, capture every second of this disconcerting gentleness. Eventually I did fall asleep and, four hours later, when the alarm went off, I could still feel that low-grade fever. "I love you, Álvaro." Raquel opened her eyes, and the words she said were different, different and yet somehow the same.

"You know what? Despite everything I had to drink last night, I feel great. No hangover, just a bit tired. I think getting drunk with you is good for me, Álvaro."

She took a shower, dressed and had breakfast then came back into the bedroom in executive mode: white trouser suit, flat, sensible shoes, leather briefcase.

"I've made some coffee," she sat on the edge of the bed and kissed me on the lips. "If you're not having lunch with that muckraker Fernando, we could meet up back here for a siesta."

"All right," I said, slipping my arms around her waist and pulling her – still clutching her briefcase – onto the bed. "I'll tell Fernando we'll meet for a drink later."

She let me hug her, not complaining that I was creasing her suit. I dressed and got back to my house just as the Polish builders were arriving. Fernando called at 10am and refused to meet me any later than 1pm on the dot. When I met him at the Argüelles, he wasn't sitting at his usual place by the bar, but at a table: clearly there was a lot he wanted to say.

"So?" I asked, taking a seat opposite him.

"Astonishing!" he said and began to tell me how much he liked Raquel.

His reaction didn't surprise me, I'd been expecting it, but 'Astonishing' was a curious word to begin with and it hovered over everything else he said, watching, lying in wait for the next phrase.

"All in all," he said, "I think she's the best thing you've pulled in your life."

"But…?"

"…but it's weird…" Seeing me frown he shook his head and quickly rephrased. "Not that she's weird, like I said, she's great. *That's* what's weird." He shook his head again. "No, that's not it either, it's like there's something weird about her."

"What's weird is that she's not weird?" I suggested jokingly and he didn't seem offended.

"That's it!" he said, "That's exactly what it is. The weird thing is she seems completely normal, by normal I mean like you and me."

"What is this, a riddle?"

"No," he looked serious, almost solemn, now. "Think about her and think about you, Álvaro."

"She's not right for me?" I guessed.

"No, she is right for you, you make a great couple, I realised that watching the two of you together last night.

"So?"

"Well, that's what's weird…" My best friend looked at me, closed his eyes, and said something it seemed he had hoped he would never have to say: "She is right for you, Álvaro, you're right for each other. But you're nothing like your father. The person she's wrong for – I mean *absolutely* wrong for – is him." He paused and looked up at me. "Don't tell me it hadn't occurred to you."

It hadn't occurred to me.

"I don't want to talk about your father," she'd said. I didn't want to talk about him either, so that had been that. The last thing I had thought with my old head, the head I lost the moment I laid it on the pillow in that bed where he had never been, was that I wasn't going to think about him. I had followed my own orders to such an extent that I had not been tempted to link the figure of my mother with the flimsy cable given to me by a frail old woman. I was in bed with Raquel and that was all that mattered. Since then, I had not spent any time alone with my mother, I hadn't wanted to, and I was not about to let some mystery about my father's life ruin my own.

Conscious of the long, horrified silence with which I greeted his words, Fernando Cisneros told me to take no notice of what he'd said. "What do I know?" he muttered, but it was already too late. I knew what he meant.

That was the worst of it. I completely understood his surprise, the radical disparity between what he knew and what he had imagined.

Raquel turned up and everything about her was completely normal, the way she looked, the way she talked, the way she moved, she was an ordinary girl. That was why I'd fallen in love with her, why it had been easy for me to evict my father's ghost from her bed. The worst thing was that I understood Fernando, I could easily imagine what he had been thinking, visualise the woman he had been expecting to meet; there was no vampire sucking my blood at night, no big-breasted floozy trying to make me forget she was an airhead, no cold, calculating bitch trying to lure me into her web, no brazen schemer after me for my money. Raquel Fernández Perea was none of these things, I had known that from the beginning, just as I'd known that I was not attracted to her because she had been Julio Carrión González's lover, quite the reverse.

As we ordered two more beers and went back to talking about trivial things, I began to feel again the happiness I had felt the first time I had seen Raquel's room, and this feeling became a problem that I should have considered before now. It was a beautiful room, agreeable, furnished with a few well-chosen pieces: an antique, hand-painted lamp, a richly coloured Turkish or Moroccan kilim. The stark contrast between this room and the vaulted bedroom with its stucco walls and plaster niches and the vast plasma TV positioned so that it could be watched from the bed underscored what Fernando had said with a thick red line. The first time I had thought about both rooms, I had thought only about my privileged position, that I had exclusive access to a place in Raquel's life, I didn't stop to wonder what a girl like her with a beautiful apartment in an old but well-maintained building in a historic area of Madrid had been doing in the type of slick bachelor pad where married millionaires took their mistresses – usually married women of the same social class, or younger women of modest means determined to improve their lot. Raquel did not fit into either category, but seeing the alarm clock on the nightstand, I reminded myself that she wasn't some lost little girl and I couldn't dismiss the possibility that she had had other motives – ambition, maybe, or greed.

The man who had shared Raquel Fernández Perea's bed before me had left no trace in her life. The chaos pendulum in his lover's apartment hid a photo of an old German tank, there were no photos of him, nothing that belonged to him. I'd given Raquel other cheap presents: Physics for Dummies, a set of magnets I'd bought long ago in the Natural History Museum in New York, a wooden box she'd admired on a stall one afternoon and the photo of me receiving a prize for arithmetic at school in which I stood, hair neatly combed, in front of a statue depicting the Virgin Mary hovering above a plaster cloud; I was dressed in a blue blazer, white shirt, striped tie, and grey trousers, and was holding the trophy in one hand and a certificate tied with a red ribbon in the other.

"Go on, give it to me, please," Raquel had asked when I showed it to her, "I love it. What year was it taken?"

"I don't know. I know it sounds conceited, but I won the prize every year. How old do I look? Ten, maybe eleven?"

"Something like that... Go, on, let me have it..."

"OK, I'll have a copy made for you."

"No! That's not the same at all! I don't want a copy, anyone could have a copy..."

I'd always had the photo in my wallet, but she asked for it and I gave it to her. She put it on a shelf in her bedroom next to a photo of her with her friend Berta – unrecognisable, both of them, with white faces, red plastic noses and black baggy trousers. Sitting next to each other on the shelf, my photo and hers, the swot and the clown, made the perfect comic coupling; a photo of my father would have ruined the effect. After less than three months, even a bungling detective would have noticed clues that a physicist who won prizes for mental arithmetic as a boy had been here. Souvenirs of the physicist coexisted with those of her heroic grandparents, her moronic ex-husband – "I got that rug in Tangiers with Josechu... Why are you laughing? I don't see what's so funny about his name...", her actor ex-boyfriend, "he designed the poster too", and actress friend, "Berta lent me that wig and liked it so much I hung onto it", a close friend – too close for my liking – "the software is Paco's, he came to help me buy the computer, and the manual belongs to him too. I told you we slept together, didn't I? But it's no big deal, we're just friends. I know you don't go round sleeping with all your friends but this was different, I'd just got divorced...", and a number of other men, "the mirror was a present from an old boyfriend, Felipe, he brought it back from Peru, that's from Manolito, my next door neighbour, he gave it to me the day I said I'd go steady with him...", but nowhere was there any gifts from an elderly, rich businessman.

In Raquel's bathroom there was only one perfume bottle, the only perfume she ever wore, expensive, but in keeping with her income, nor was her apartment crammed with antiques, all the pieces of furniture, books, albums, figurines, ornaments and oriental vases that exiles leave behind whenever they leave home. It was the same with her jewellery, she kept only what she wore, pieces that she liked, whether antique or modern, but none of the opulent pieces a filthy-rich sugar-daddy might have chosen. There was one exception, a bracelet, but it was too precious to have come from him. She had worn it the night we had dinner at the

Japanese restaurant. The night when all the laws of physics were suspended, it lay on the bedside table as though Raquel had intended to wear it but had changed her mind at the last minute. The afternoon after the storm, I noticed it again and asked:

"Does it mean a lot to you?" she looked at me, mystified, "...the bracelet?"

"Of course it does!" she picked it up and handed it to me. It was very old, a simple band encrusted with a spectacular constellation of precious stones, waves of diamonds, sapphires and more diamonds, with a single, enormous pearl in the centre. "It was an engagement present to my great-grandmother María, the mother of my grandfather Ignacio."

"The one who lived on the Glorieta de Bilbao?"

"That's her. It's all that's left of the family fortune, the only thing that survived the shipwreck."

The previous evening, when I had got dressed to go home, Raquel had asked me to wait. "I'll go with you," she said, "I'm meeting someone at the Café Commercial." "Who are you meeting?" I asked, spinelessly, thinking of Paco, and she answered with a question "What the fuck do you care?", then she laughed and told me she was having dinner with Berta.

As we arrived at the café, we saw Berta inside, waiting at the bar. She waved at us. "Do you want to come in for a drink?" I followed her inside and immediately ran into one of my fifth-year students, a dull boy I barely recognised, who had come to my office a couple of weeks earlier to ask if I would supervise his thesis. He said hello and I stopped to talk to him for a minute, but Raquel didn't wait. When I went to join her, she apologised. "What for?" I asked, kissing Berta. "I'm sorry you were seen with me," she said. She was so obviously joking, half-flirting with me, that I laughed, took her in my arms and gave her a long, hard kiss, long enough for everyone at the bar to turn and stare, including the tedious physics student who had never met Mai and probably didn't even know that I was married.

I had learned two things from this encounter. The first was that had the person who had seen us together in the café been potentially compromising, I would have done exactly the same thing, and knowing this absolved me of the sleazy calculatedness of the inveterate womaniser. The second was that Raquel had been thrilled by my performance, all the more so because Berta had been there to witness it. This may have been the reason why she chose that evening to tell me something she could have told me earlier as we crossed the same square. When we finished our beers, I announced that I would pay. Berta went to the toilet and Raquel took my hand and led me out of the café. We stood on the pavement, between the newspaper kiosk and the entrance to the metro, and she pointed to something.

"You see that house?" I nodded, not really looking at the building which I had seen a thousand times before, "That's where my grandfather Ignacio was born."

"Really?" I said, genuinely surprised. It wasn't a palace, but it was a mansion.

"Really. They lived on the second floor, in a huge corner apartment, with two balconies looking out over the Glorieta and the Calle Carranza..." She pointed confidently to the apartment in question. "That one there, see?"

"I didn't think anyone lived there, I thought the whole building belonged to an insurance company," I murmured.

"Now maybe, but not back then."

"What happened? I mean if he owned that apartment, it doesn't make sense that your grandfather would live where you live now. Did they sell this place?"

"No. They lost everything they had in the war, this apartment, their place in the mountains, my great-grandmother's land..." she stared straight ahead. "To be more precise, they were robbed of everything they had."

At that moment, Berta had emerged from the cafe and said something to Raquel that I didn't quite catch, because Raquel looked at me with the same smile she had hidden behind the first time she had talked to me about her grandfather Ignacio. There was something compelling about that smile, a desolate, hopeless tenderness; I could not resist that smile and at that moment I would have given anything to comfort Raquel, to save her from her own expression, snatch that pained rictus from her face and make her laugh out loud.

"If I wanted to join you for dinner..." I said apprehensively. "Would that ruin things ...?"

"I don't know." Berta looked at Raquel with the same brazenness she had displayed the first time we met. "... the thing is, you were the first item for discussion on the agenda."

"It would ruin everything," Raquel said, pressing herself against me. "But I'm sure we can find something else to talk about...".

We had already ordered when I got up to phone Mai. I told her I had run into an old friend at the library, someone she knew, who at that moment was probably sitting quietly in his office in Columbus, Ohio. Before I could even say that I was calling not to suggest she come and

388

join us, but to let her know I wouldn't be home for dinner, she had yawned and told me there was no point expecting her to come, that she was tired and was on her way to bed. When I went back and sat down, Raquel laid her head on my shoulder and let it rest there a moment. I realised that she knew precisely what I had been doing when I said I had to go to the toilet, and for the first time, despite the trivial nature of my offence, I felt I owed her more than I owed Mai. The feeling was a first step on the slippery slope, the plateau from which I began my descent, but that evening all I could think about was Raquel. The star of the evening, however, was my grandmother Teresa.

"OK, I propose we move straight to the second item on the agenda," I said, breaking the somewhat awkward silence that followed.

"There is no second item," said Raquel.

"Really? I didn't realise that I was such a complex subject..."

They both laughed, but neither of them said anything, so it was left to me to speak. I could have waited for a more propitious moment, for a quieter, more private place, but I had been holding my silence for a long time. Too long.

"In that case, I'd like to suggest a topic. Earlier on, when you showed me the house where your grandfather was born, it reminded me... Actually, I didn't need to be reminded because it's something I've been thinking about ever since I found out... Strange things have been happening to me recently and I had always thought my grandmother, my father's mother, died in 1937 during the civil war. Then two months ago, while I was going through my father's papers, I found out it wasn't true..."

That evening I was the one who spoke, who brought Teresa González Puerto back from the grave in which her son had buried her, and I told them everything, what I had thought I knew, and what I now knew, what I had been told, and what I had discovered. It was something I knew I would have to do sooner or later because the secret about my grandmother was suffocating me, because my jealous, loving silence made my complicit with my father's unjust, unjustifiable silence, and because I could not stay silent any longer. I had to talk about it so that my grandmother could live again, if only through my words, so that her true life could be restored to her, the path she had chosen which had cost her her life. And the more I talked the better I felt, I felt like a better, a braver person, more like the son she would have wanted, this gentle, moving presence that hovered over us like an ancient blessing, outlasting the horrors of the war, the deathly silence of cemeteries, the still smiles of photographs.

This was what I felt, and I felt her, my grandmother Teresa, not the meek wife of a brutal husband but the adulterous girlfriend of a magician, the incorrigible young girl who, at the age of thirty, had decided to let down her hair and spend her days shouting in the streets, the woman who had dared to write that perhaps she was wrong, but she was doing what she felt she had to do, and she was doing it out of love. That Teresa was a part of me, she was with me as I told her story; she had been brought back from the dead by my love, my pride, and she would go on living through the love, the pride of my children and my grandchildren. Because the end of the chapter is not necessarily the end of the story and the life of a brave woman does not end with her death. I felt all this, talked about it, her voice through mine, so that my grandmother might return and win her war that night. And Teresa González Puerto did win, and in winning, reason won through and the light for which she had so long fought glinted in the startled actress's eyes while the woman her grandson loved listened in silence, burying her face in her hands.

"It's amazing," Berta was the first to speak, "You must have been… it must have been awful for you, I know because I come from a pretty fascist family myself, and if I found out something like that, well… On one hand I'd feel terrible, but on the other hand I think I'd feel proud … it's like you said, but it must be tough, thinking about your father in retrospect?" I nodded and glanced at Raquel but she hadn't moved and her hands were still pressed to her face. "Could you make a photocopy of her letter for me? I've got loads of letters like that, from people who were in prison, who were executed, from soldiers. I've often thought of putting on a play about them, I'm not sure exactly what. It's not easy, because you can't read a lot of the letters straight through. They're full of mistakes, clichés, they can be muddled and repetitive. They're letters written by people who didn't read, who weren't used to writing. But that's not the thing I find most surprising. What I find surprising is that anyone reading those letters should be able to tell that this country has gone to the dogs."

"Yes," I said, smiling, "That's what I thought."

"I mean, I know your grandmother's letter is well written, you can tell she was a teacher. It's nearly as good as the letter Raquel's uncle wrote to his wife when he was sentenced to death. You'd like that one…"

"I don't feel well…"

Raquel stared at us, shoulders hunched, face ashen.

"What's the matter?"

"Raquel, you're white as a sheet…"

"It's really hot in here. I just felt faint for a minute, I don't know... I'd like to go home."

"Of course," Berta and I answered together, but Raquel looked only at me.

"Could you walk me back? I think some fresh air would do me good."

"Of course," I said again and asked for the bill.

We split the bill before going our separate ways; Berta grabbed a taxi outside the café and we waited until it had driven away before setting off on foot.

"We can take a taxi if you want..." I suggested, but she shook her head.

"No, I feel like walking. I'm a lot better, and it's a beautiful night... especially given how hot it was in the restaurant..."

I respected her wishes and made no comment. We headed towards the Glorieta de Bilbao, past her grandfather's house, turned up the Calle Carranza, and I found myself thinking aloud.

"It's weird how things change, isn't it? There's your family, who lived in Madrid, owned that big apartment and then lost everything. And then there's my father, the son of a shepherd and a penniless schoolteacher who grew up in some village in the mountains and never even went to university. He wound up so rich he could buy that building, and others, all within the space of a couple of generations, and now here we are, you and me..."

She didn't say anything. I hadn't expected her to, nor had I expected her to start crying, which is what she did, crying like a little girl, giving in to great heaving sobs that needed no words. Her tears left me defenceless, lost, almost naked there in the street.

"What's wrong, Raquel?" I pushed back her hair, dried her tears, took her face in my hands and I felt a twinge of panic when I realised I couldn't bear to see her like this, "Don't cry, Raquel, please don't cry..."

I held her tight and she buried her face in my neck. All I could do was wait, and I waited. I waited and watched as she gradually calmed herself, stopped trembling, then drew back and said to me in that thick, guttural voice that follows tears.

"What must you think of me?" Her words, the frailty of her voice, the deathly pallor of her face terrified me.

"I think the world of you, you know that." I said, stroking her face again.

"No!" she shook her head, her gesture emphatic, almost childlike. "You can't possibly think I'm wonderful. At least not tonight. Earlier on, when I was listening to you talk about your grandmother, I was

391

wondering what you could possibly think of someone like me, of me being with your father, and the only answers I could come up with were horrible…"

"No, Raquel…" I hugged her again, kissed her forehead, "I never think of you being with my father. The only person I can think of you with is me. I don't care about anything else."

She wrapped herself around my neck and kissed me for a long time, and when she finished, she looked up at me with a look of such complete surrender that it seemed to say her life was in my hands. I kissed her again, and then we walked on, clinging to each other as we walked.

"I'm sorry, Álvaro, please forgive me. I shouldn't have made a scene… It's just that… sometimes I can't cope with things."

"Am I so very difficult?" I suggested, because although I had heard her, I didn't want to talk about my father.

"No," she smiled, "It's not you, you're easy to cope with…"

I didn't say anything else, I didn't need to. Sometimes the love I felt for this woman confused and overwhelmed me, and sometimes, as this time, she realised it.

"Can I ask you something?" we were almost at her place and she didn't wait for me to answer, "What did you say to your wife? When you called her earlier…"

"I said that I'd run into a friend from Bilbao I'd met when I was living in Boston, that I was having dinner with him."

"Has it been a long time since you've seen him?"

"Nearly three years." I didn't need to lie, not then and not later. She laughed as though I'd invented the whole thing to cheer her up. "He used to come over every summer, he married an aerobics instructor called Ingrid, she's black and has a body to die for. He brought her over once to show her off and he hasn't been back since. He's working in Columbus Ohio these days. He emailed me some photos of his son, he's really cute…"

"So if you were really having dinner with him, you'd have a lot of catching up to do."

"A whole lot…"

"And after that, you'd go for a drink…"

"Not one, at least two or three…"

"Do you want to come up?"

"Yes."

Before, I had told her that I could only imagine her being with me, that what had happened before we met didn't interest me. I had said it without thinking, as though no one before me had ever trotted out these hackneyed words rendered all but meaningless by millions of men and women who had felt just as I did and who said the same words, in different languages, in different epochs, in every country in the world.

After, having gone back with her to this place where the past did not exist, where everything was now, I felt at one with this woman; felt as though we were one, that we made up something whole, some perfect number, something precisely equal to the sum of its parts. Loving Raquel was as easy, as ineluctable as breathing. It was enough for me to gently stroke her perfect skin, to be reborn again and again, for every word I knew to be born again, so that "before" no longer existed and "after" would never exist.

"About your father, Álvaro…"

"I'm not interested."

"You might not be, but I am." I didn't want to let her go on, but she pulled away, stretched out on the bed and stared up at the ceiling. "My affair with your father was the stupidest thing I ever did, Álvaro, the biggest mistake of my life." She looked at me then and I was afraid she would start to cry. "Please, listen… It's not that I don't want to talk about it, I can't talk about it, I can't even remember it. I can't bear it and now, I can't even understand how it happened… There are times in life when everything is weird, when you forget everything you ever knew… It's difficult to explain, but I just want you to know that it wasn't *me*. Honestly, it wasn't me. You know me, Álvaro, I'm not like that. The woman you know, that's me."

At that moment, I didn't realise the full significance of the words I had just heard. I was so moved, so much in love, that all I could do was kiss her, hold her. It was the only thing that mattered, the only thing that could banish 'before' and 'after'. But two weeks later, as I was sitting at a table pretending to listen to Fernando Cisneros at the Argüelles bar and once again doubting my celebrated intelligence, that obscure, episodic conversation peppered with allusions took on a greater significance.

Raquel's curious, partial confession, "this is who I am, that wasn't me", not only meant that Fernando was right, it placed the figure of my father on a different plane. Having said that she had never loved him Raquel Fernández Perea had not mentioned Julio Carrión González again, leaving in the air only an agreeable, rose-tinted trace, his charm, the innate gift for seduction that had made my father popular. At the end of the long, exhausting night we spent together with our ghosts, Raquel had spoken of him as an enemy, or worse, as someone capable of making her an enemy of herself, making her forget everything she knew. And I, unable to understand what I was hearing, accepted it unquestioningly, in fact I was foolish enough to think myself lucky to have heard it.

When Raquel told me who she was and who she wasn't, all that mattered to me was that her words confirmed the intuition that had led me across the threshold of madness, the certainty that this woman was mine; mine and not my father's. It was not merely an illusion, it was stupid; I had been single-minded and, more than that, I had been a fool; for the one thing I knew, I had known from the first, was that my father was lying in wait, watching this ridiculous, absurd infatuation. His immense, daunting shadow turned it into a necessity, a rite of passage, though I had never aspired to be like him. I had had no problem isolating Raquel from the other upheavals associated with his death, but I could not rid myself of him completely. I could not bring myself to do it, until Raquel did it for me, obliterating him with a few words; this was what I had thought when I heard them, that my father was gone, that he would never again come between me and this woman

As I glanced at my watch as though I needed to be elsewhere, and said goodbye to Fernando Cisneros as though nothing had happened, and started down Cea Bermúdez as though heading somewhere, and turned into the first side street without knowing why, and turned again at the next intersection, wandering aimlessly, I tried to fit the pieces together. Raquel had never seemed worried about what I might think of her until my grandmother Teresa had sat down with us in that restaurant, but my father's role in that story seemed too insignificant to have triggered such a response, even if it heightened her feeling that her relationship with my father was a betrayal of her grandfather, a distant, dead man whose very name lit up her face with an expression that was like no other. Raquel had exploded that night, and she had said things that took on new meaning in the light of the unease Fernando Cisneros' words had left in my mind.

"Sometimes I just can't cope with things," she had said, and then stopped. I had assumed she was talking about my father and me, about the fact that we had both been her lovers – it seemed logical in such a situation you might feel overwhelmed, the way I felt overwhelmed, though I refused to think about it. What did surprise me was that I had never noticed even the slightest sign of awkwardness or tension in her. On the contrary, it seemed she didn't find it difficult not to think about my father, didn't have to *make* herself forget. Between Raquel and me everything was now, and everything was easy, as though we had both been born the moment we met. But she had a past, I had a past. "Don't say anything to Berta, she doesn't know anything about it," she'd said when she told me what sort of woman she really was. "She doesn't know about my father?" I asked, astonished, because they told each other everything. She hesitated a moment then said: "She knows about him, she just doesn't know he was your father." "Then who am I?" I asked. "You're the son of some client or other, you showed up at the bank one day and started flirting with me." Then she smiled, "That's more or less the truth, isn't it?"

She had a past, I had a past, though I didn't know what to do with it. I still had no solution when I looked at my watch again and realised that I had completely lost my skills in mental arithmetic.

"You're late," she was leaning against the wall and didn't move.

"It's not even five minutes. In Spain that's not considered late," I argued. "How are you?"

"Pff!…" she stepped away from the wall with a weary, almost pained expression, "I'm exhausted. I don't even feel like eating, that says something…"

Stepping into her apartment, she didn't even hang her bag on the coat hook by the door as usual, but carried it over her shoulder into the bedroom, where she let it fall to the floor before collapsing on the bed. I went over and took off her shoes.

"Do you want me to take off your clothes?"

"Yes." She opened her eyes and looked at me. "Please."

"It's like I said to Fernando, she has only one fault," I talked as I undressed her, "Don't get me wrong, she's a wonderful girl, but she has one failing, she drinks, but what can you do? She likes a drink, and when she drinks, well…"

I lay down next to her but she was already asleep. I fell asleep shortly afterwards, and still everything seemed OK. It was only later that the screw came loose, that cracks began to appear, that the well-oiled machine we had been until then began to creak. I was awake and Raquel slept on; I liked to watch her sleep, Raquel slept naked, abandoned to her nakedness, so accessible, and vulnerable, so confident and desirable that it was almost painful to look at her. And my eyes yielded to the dictates of this painful desire, wounded by this hostile, alien image, this other image, something I had never seen when looking at Raquel, this extraordinary woman who was so ordinary if ordinary was defined by me.

That afternoon, as I watched Raquel, I imagined her, conjured her in gestures, positions and situations which, to someone other than me, would have seemed perverse and obscene, a young woman slipping into a jacuzzi surrounded by candles where a man old enough to be her grandfather was waiting. To someone other than me, because I had appropriated these images, my gaze had incorporated them as useful elements in the creation of a intimacy which had its rules, its own language, its own grammar, its own syntax. Raquel and I didn't talk about sex, we didn't need to, but she liked to describe her pleasure, to define it with an expression of almost childlike joy: wow, that's great, that's... We didn't talk about sex, we had sex, spontaneously, impulsively, wordlessly, to the point of exhaustion. I had never known such pleasure, or given such pleasure to any woman. This had been the nucleus of the endless ties that bound us. Every day, I learned new things about Raquel, and nothing had induced me to change even the smallest detail of the rules of our shared intimacy.

Nor did it happen that afternoon, by which time I knew of the woman sleeping next to me the way a talented musician knows his instrument. It wasn't that, nor was it the fault of some *thing* – the jacuzzi, the candles, the purple rubber dildo. No, it was something else, something vague and difficult to pin down, something about the precise point where three identities intersected: mine, Raquel's and my father's, but where there were only two attitudes, two ways of seeing the world, of thinking about things including sex. It was a question of identity, of attitude. If Raquel Fernández Perea was truly the woman I knew, the body with which my own body intertwined, which opened to my least touch, then she could not be this other woman, the woman I imagined alone in the apartment on the Calle Jorge Juan, the stranger lighting the last candle before slipping naked into the water, resting her head against a pile of pillows, her legs spread wide and a broad smile that showed the gap between her teeth.

At that moment, Raquel woke, she smiled without opening her eyes and pulled me to her, reached out her hand until it grazed my penis, stroked it with a finger, then two, caressed it with her palm before closing her hand around it and only then did she meet my gaze, her eyes wide, her lips an almost perfect circle, she breathed a sigh and began to purr as she often did. I recognised the signs, what I did not recognise was myself, the unfamiliar, borrowed gestures with which I tried to put her to the test and succeeded only in proving my own weakness.

"Stop, Álvaro," she opened her eyes and drew her legs together.

Raquel Fernández Perea had never done anything to stop me, had never imposed limits, but this was not me, and she realised that.

"Why?"

"Because you're looking at me the way your father did." She covered herself with the sheet, turned her back and stared at the wall, "It was bound to happen sooner of later. And the worst thing is, it's only what I deserve."

I loved this woman. I loved her so much that sometimes it confused and overwhelmed me. Suddenly I was myself again, and I went to her, slipped under the sheet, put my arms around her and kissed her over and over, begged her to forgive me, told her I loved her. "Say it again," she said, and I said it over and over until I was hoarse.

At that moment I understood the full meaning of what I had said, something I would have to learn to live with, to love her in spite of Fernando's disbelief, just as I had learned to love her in the shadow of my father's ghost. And as the world resumed it course, running gently like water, I realised that the best thing for both of us would be if I never found out the true nature of Raquel Fernández Perea's relationship with Julio Carrión González, I realised that the solution to the problem we were both thinking about at that moment had nothing to do with me.

And so I discovered the precise colour of fear, felt in the pit of my stomach the exact volume of nothingness it takes to fill the void.

On 12 September 1949, the sky clouded over suddenly in mid-afternoon. When the first clap of thunder came, Julio Carrión González was leaning against the granite columns of the porch of the Casa Rosa, the most beautiful house in the village, watching the taxi-driver struggle to secure the boxes and trunks on the roof of the car. The second thunderclap boomed a few seconds before the rain came and the taxi driver gave up.

"I'm sorry, *señora*, but you're going to have to take this one with you."

Mariana Fernández Viu did not reply. She took no notice of the suitcase he set down at her feet. Taut, like a dead woman, she stared at her enemy and clutched her bag as though it contained her last hope, the one thing that might save her from tumbling into the abyss. But there was nothing in her bag that could save her. Julio knew that, and so he could stand, patient, smiling, and stare into those eyes that burned with hate. He had seen much greater hatred in eyes more beautiful than these. "Ruin her, destroy her, and when you're done, tell her I sent you. This is what you wanted, isn't it, Paloma?" he thought as he lit a cigarette. "Never let it be said that I don't keep my promises..."

"*Señora*, please! Get a move on, we'll get drenched!"

The taxi driver ventured to put a hand on her shoulder as the rain began to fall. Finally, Mariana lowered her head and climbed into the car. When, a moment later, the engine roared into life, the man smoking on the porch thrilled at the sound. That man had come to the end of his journey, a journey that had been long and tortuous but none of that mattered now. He had finally made it: Julio Carrión González, the son of an alcoholic shepherd and a political prisoner who had died in jail, was rich, he was a gentleman.

"It's theft, Julio" Eugenio had said, in his eyes the fierce glint of integrity he knew of old, "Even if it's legal, even if everyone is doing it, it's still theft and I'll have nothing to do with it."

Eugenio Sánchez Delgado was the first person Julio sought out when he returned to Madrid in April 1947. Before that, he had gone to see his father, or what was left of his father, a gaunt, bewildered thing, just one more useless stick of furniture in a house that was filthy, filled with broken fragments salvaged from a previous life that were carefully arranged on the same tables and shelves as before.

"Father..."

The first thing Julio recognised was a cracked glass vase, then the yellowed tablecloth, an old coffee grinder with the handle missing. Everything was dark with layers of dust, slick with rancid grease. The air stank of mildew and misery.

"Father…"

Julio crossed the room and noticed that Benigno smelled even worse than his surroundings. The old man did not look up, did not move when a gust of wind whipped away the old newspapers, sending terrified cockroaches scattering for safety. Julio had to shake his father, but Benigno was so drunk he didn't recognise him.

"How did you get in here? Who are you?" It was painful to make out what he was saying, more difficult still to see the blackened teeth, smell the stale breath.

"It's Julio, father, your son." Benigno studied him more carefully, "How can you live like this, father?" In answer, he got only a weak, befuddled look. "You didn't spend my money, did you father?" neither of them moved, fused in a moment of permanent sadness. Then Benigno lowered his head to sip from a glass of clear iridescent liquid. Julio ripped it from his hands, dipped his fingers into it and smelled them. At least it was cheap, the dregs.

"All right, father, I've had enough of this." Benigno did not even try to move his head, "Come on, get up!"

Julio lifted him by his armpits and hauled his father to his feet. It was 11 a.m., but Julio couldn't tell whether his father had been to bed, or had got up early and started drinking, or had been so drunk the night before he hadn't made it to bed. It didn't matter. There was a mattress with a filthy blanket on the floor by the kitchen door. Julio was so heartsick, he laid his father there and went out into the yard. There were no chickens now, just rows of empty cages, most of the doors hanging open. But the bags were where they had always been. He filled one with out-of-date newspapers and all the broken ornaments he had seen when he first arrived, then headed upstairs. His old bedroom was as dusty as the rest of the house, but no one had touched it. His bed was made, his old school books and few toys were untouched, and a handful of photos of naked women remained at the back of the drawer where he had hidden them. This did not console him – quite the opposite. He suddenly felt faint, and opened a window, splashed water on his face, then went out into the street where he could breathe.

"She doesn't live there any more." A woman he did not recognise peered at him suspiciously from the doorway of Evangelina's, the grocers.

"Did she leave the village?"

"No, but she lives up by the train station, on the left, one of those big concrete houses."

Julio nodded and thanked her. He knew the houses she meant, they were really storehouses that belonged to the railway that had been disused even before he left for Madrid. It did not surprise him. Evangelina had just married a friend of his mother's when the war broke out and had been widowed long before the war was over. Her husband had died defending Bilbao, but her grief had not stopped her work, she had been second in command to Teresa González on every committee they set up. This was why he had thought of her. Because if she was not in prison, she would be in need of money.

"There'll be a lot of work involved..."

At thirty-four, Evangelina sometimes missed prison life. In prison she had not had to worry, had not had to look after anyone but herself. During her visits, her mother always told her that her little girl was fine, that the family was fine, that there was nothing for her to worry about. Everything was different when she was released. She came out of prison to a new war, a sordid, petty war, the daily battle against unemployment, paltry wages and astronomical prices, the constant harassment of the Civil Guard, the doors slammed in her face, the neighbours who refused to give her the time of day, the struggle of seeing her own daughter treated like a leper, and the hours waiting at the gates of another prison with a parcel of fruit to visit her little brother, to whom she would lie: "Everything's fine, we're all fine, there's nothing for you to worry about." He had headed into the mountains in 1939 and had held out until one of his comrades decided to surrender and turn him and a number of others in early in 1943. Evangelina sometimes missed prison life

"I haven't been to your house for a long time," she said, trying to hide her excitement, the nervous flicker of greed as she looked at Julio, her eyes so sunken that it would have been impossible for anyone to guess her age. "But with things the way they are..."

"I'll do it," a young girl of about twelve who had been standing listening to the conversation from the doorway of the old storehouse, which had been divided into small rooms, by hanging matting from two cables to create a makeshift corridor, came, forward, smiling. "I don't mind if it's a lot of work, I can do it..."

"Juana!" Evangelina interrupted the girl with an expression of mingled embarrassment and fury. "He came to see me. And I never said I didn't want to do it."

"I'm sorry, I thought..." The young girl gave her an imploring look.

Julio watched them as they eyed each other: outside was a muddy track, there were no pavements, no electricity, no water, no cars. There were no young men here, only old men and women of all ages, single women with children, young girls more than happy to take on an adult's job, who would work harder for less money and never argue.

"I know there's a lot of work involved," said Julio reassuringly, "But I'll pay well."

"Well, then why don't we both do it, that way it'll be faster. When do you want us to start?" Evangelina yielded to the embrace of her forceful little friend with a weak smile.

"Straight away."

On the way back to his father's house, Julio enquired about Benigno's land, his sheep. Evangelina told him the land was all leased, confirming Julio's suspicions. He left them to their work and set off to find the bastard, who greeted him with a salute: *"Arriba España!"*; Julio did not respond with the habitual *"arriba siempre"* but simply said, "I'll waive the outstanding money." The bastard swore that he had kept no receipts of the fair, scrupulously exact payments he had made to Julio's father."

"Well, from now on, I want everything in writing," Julio said, "and I want you to play the leasehold money into the bank immediately because I'm betting you haven't paid it yet this month, have you?" Before leaving, Julio turned, happy, but surprised that his threats had been so effective, "And don't let me have to tell you again."

In the village bar, it was the same. The villagers clearly remembered the morning when he had strolled through the streets with a uniformed Falangist, and they remembered his previous visit, too, when he had been wearing a blue shirt and a red beret, ready to ship out to Russia. It had been three years since the only other inhabitant from Torrelodones to have survived had come back, but he told them that Julio had stayed behind, that he had enlisted in the rear-guard, that he was friends with the senior officers and that's why he had stayed. Now, here he was, well turned out, with money in his pockets, looking like a man of the world and although it was already April 1947, still nobody asked, it was better not to ask questions, better to be nothing, to be no one. So everyone was happy to see him, they clapped him on the back, smiled in the street, and they didn't ask questions.

Had Ignacio not been mistaken for a third time, had he gauged the situation correctly, his expectations, being for the first time in sympathy with those of Spaniards on either side of the French border, everything would have been easy. Nobody imagined that the Allies would leave Franco in power. Not even Franco. The exiles in Paris knew that. "They're running scared, they won't be there for long now," they chanted outside the Spanish embassy.

Tens of thousands of Spanish resistance fighters, the same Republican soldiers Daladier's government had treated like dirt in 1939, had since fought with the Allied Forces and defeated the Germans. They had made an important contribution in several key battles, had been crucial in the South where they had single-handedly liberated towns, villages and whole districts. But they were not fighting for France, they were fighting for Spain, so that they could come back and fight for Spain, and the Allies knew it. Your turn today, our turn tomorrow, they thought. But no. Today it was the Allies turn, tomorrow it was Franco's. True, Spain was not accepted as a member of the United Nations, but the snub mattered little to Franco. True, the advocates of world democracy had a few words to say to him, a little gentle scolding of the sort an affectionate grandmother might give her mischievous grandson. "If you don't behave yourself, then one of these days you'll end up with no dessert." That was all. Not a word more.

"Betrayal is the one constant in my life," Ignacio Fernández had said to him. "I live to be betrayed. I get up and I go to bed, I eat, I breathe, I struggle, I risk my life only to find myself betrayed, by my friends and my enemies, in my own country and abroad, because betrayal is the rule, the one constant..."

It was December 1946; ten years had passed since the first time they had been betrayed, and in the intervening years nothing had changed. When the radio announced that the United Nations would take no further action, the waiter in the bar where they were drinking started to cry like a child. Tomás, from La Rioja, who was tall and heavy set; Tomás who had marched into Paris with the 9th Company deaf in his right ear and with three toes missing on his left foot, started to bawl.

Had Ignacio not been mistaken, everything would have been easy. If the world had not betrayed these men, had not abandoned them, they would have strode home to Spain. When Juan Manuel, a taxi driver from Madrid who now worked in Orleans as a metal worker, asked him how he'd got there, Julio lied a little, but just enough.

"I enlisted with the Blue Division for the money, and so I could get across the border, but as soon as I tried, they caught me." And so, in the first person, he recounted Pancho Serrano's story, though he made up the last chapter himself. "They had no evidence against me, they'd already shot three of us that week, and I denied that I'd been trying to desert. I told them I'd got lost out there, what will all the snow, because it all looked the same, and the fascists didn't like admitting to deserters..." he paused and gauged his audience, but saw no suspicion in the three pairs of eyes gazing back at him. "The Nazis were sick to death of Spanish deserters, there were ten times as many Spaniards as Germans deserting, so they had me up for insubordination. They put me in a prison detail, we weren't armed, and they gave us all the shitty jobs, digging trenches, making timber pathways, that kind of thing. I was still there when the Blue Division was recalled, so they put me on a train to Spain and told me I'd be free when I got there, that I wouldn't be court-martialled, but I jumped the train at Marseilles. I've been wandering around for five or six months now, hiding from the French police, working whenever I get the chance...'

Neither Juan Manuel nor his two friends asked Julio anything else, because he was not in Spain, but in France, and the exiles of 1939 were accustomed to hearing stories like his. Martín had been a shepherd in Biscay but now worked in the same factory as the taxi driver. If he didn't have as many children as Pablo, he still shared a small apartment with his sister, his brother-in-law and his two nephews. Pablo's children were not in France. The eldest was in jail back in Spain, and the two youngest, a boy and a girl, were in the Soviet Union. "At least we think so, that's where they were sent, but it's been ages since we've had any news..." he said as they walked back to his place. His wife Maruja, who, like him, was from Murcia, was happy to have a young man in the house once more.

Some days later, the man who had been the most elegant and mysterious Spaniard in Riga was working for a Frenchman who helped his workers by supplying them with false papers in return for half their salaries. Julio did not care, it was exactly what he wanted. While he broke his back lifting boxes and lugging them from one place to another, he imagined Romualdo Sánchez Delgado back in Madrid, well dressed, with money in his pocket, prattling about the invisible tanks the Germans were still secretly working on. There are no invisible tanks, Romualdo, but there are prisons. And that's where you'll be when I'm rich and sitting on a terrace on the Calle Alcalá, Julio thought whenever he felt exhausted, or depressed.

This was what would happen, it was logical. Julio did not doubt it, nor did Juan Manuel or Pablo or Martín, still less the young people he met the following year when he decided to try his luck in Paris. Tomás, Aurelio, Amadeo, Ignacio, their fingers still stained with the gunpowder of victory, their ears still ringing with the Spanish Republican anthem, *el Himno de Riego*, played after *La Marseillaise* in every village and town during the parades that followed the Liberation. Their weapons were different. He had two decks of cards, identity papers that seemed completely genuine, and something even more uncommon and more valuable. Some are born handsome, are born rich, are born princes. Julio Carrión González was born charming and he knew it, he knew that people liked him, that men instinctively trusted him, that women desired him, and he also knew that the most intelligent people could be fools when confronted with someone more intelligent than they are.

"*Buenos días*, I'd like to speak to don Ernesto Huertas," he said with his habitual smile. On that morning in February 1947, at the desk of the Spanish embassy in Paris, it was not a woman who greeted him, but a brusque, dark-skinned civil servant.

"I'm afraid that isn't possible," the man looked him up and down, making clear his distaste. "There is no one by that name working here."

"Oh, well, if he does come in some day, or if you suddenly remember someone by that name, would you be so good as to give him this envelope?"

The receptionist looked at him again before stretching out his hand and Julio took his leave with great ceremony.

Ernesto Huertas kept him waiting for three days, but on the fourth, he came to meet him at the newsstand where Julio, in his note, had said he would be waiting every afternoon at 6pm.

"Your name is not Eugenio Sánchez Delgado," he said as soon as he saw him, "Your name is Julio Carrión and you're one hell of a turncoat."

Julio accepted the insult with a smile. "Maybe, but I didn't arrange to meet you so we could talk about my faults."

Huertas, who was head of Spanish military intelligence and responsible for keeping an eye on Republican expatriates, knew everything. For his part, Julio knew quite a lot about Huertas, and he was counting on that fact, for he had no intention of going back and tending sheep with his father.

"So why did you bring me here?"

"I'd rather we talked in private."

Huertas nodded, then followed Julio to a café with a small private space at the back, a few tables behind a partition out of sight of prying eyes. Carrión ordered two coffees, then leaned across the table and said in a whisper:

"I want to go back to Spain." Huertas smiled. "To Madrid."

"I think that sounds wonderful. That's what the consulate is there for, it's open every day from 9am until noon."

"I know," Julio took a deep breath and crossed his fingers under the table, "and after that, there'll be a trial, to... apportion blame. Isn't that how you put it?"

404

"Precisely," Huertas gave a mocking grin.

"Of course. But I want to be exonerated, I want to go back a free man."

"And what were you planning to go back with?" Huertas took out a small, well-thumbed notebook and leafed through it for a moment before continuing. "Your membership card as a Falangist, or the one from the JSU, or maybe your military service record from the Blue Division or the file I have in my desk back at the office?" He looked up and smiled sardonically at Julio, "What would you like to go back *as*, Carrión? Tell me, I'm genuinely interested."

"I want to do a deal," Julio, who had meticulously anticipated every possible turn of this conversation.

"Oh, really?" Huertas raised an eyebrow, took his time, "And what exactly can you offer me?"

Julio answered the man's question with another: "What do you want to know?"

It was his plan, one that he had conceived and carefully worked out on his own, even if Ignacio Fernández Muñoz had thought that it was his, and would go on thinking so for the rest of his life. Two months earlier, on the afternoon when Tomás turned off the radio and cried like a child, Aurelio had looked at him and asked: "What are we going to do now?" The Lawyer had kept his mouth shut. "What are we going to do, Ignacio?" el Boquerón said again. His friend drained his glass, "What do you think we're going to do?", he said finally, "We're going to go on hoping, go on living... What else can we do?"

But, as they left the bar, another idea occurred to him. "I'll talk to my father," he said "because the way things are going it makes no sense to stay here, living on top of each other, with him and Mamá working themselves to death when he still owns property in Spain..." Mateo Fernández Gómez de la Riva had sold nothing, not the house in Madrid nor the house in Torrelodones, not the apartment he had bought his daughter on the Calle de Hartzenbusch nor the land his wife owned, nothing. "I've a feeling I'll never set foot in that shitty country again," he had said, but it was not true. He did not believe it. He had believed he would go back, that his wife, his children, his friends, everyone would go back. But what should logically have happened, did not happen, and never would. Julio realised this before anyone, because the only thing that mattered to him was his own future. He knew that the Fernández family was rich; he had never imagined quite how rich until Ignacio reeled off a list of the property they owned. The rest was easy, even if Julio, an ordinary soldier with no contacts in the new regime, was in no position to sell his treachery cheaply.

"What you've told me isn't worth shit." The commander closed his notebook and slipped it into his pocket. Julio held his gaze and said nothing, though he had seen Huertas make notes several times during the conversation.

"I know," he said simply, "but I'm not who I seem to be."

Huertas, an old hand at these things, looked at Julio curiously as though the truth was only now beginning to dawn on him: the lad played the innocent, but he had clearly known from the start that the information he had to offer was not worth the favour he was requesting. Julio had brought him here to tell him something else.

"I was colonel Arenas's right had man in Riga, but I was working under cover. As far as anyone was concerned, I didn't exist, and coming back here wasn't easy. But I never intended to stay in Paris, I always intended to move on. I should have gone back to Spain two years ago, but I fell in love with a woman who drove me mad."

"Aw!" Huertas laughed, "How romantic!"

"Yes, actually" Julio smiled with him, "...it was romantic. Paloma Fernández Muñoz, I believe you know her?"

"The beautiful Paloma..." the commander nodded slowly, "Of course I know her, who doesn't? Tell me, Carrión, just out of curiosity, have you fucked her?"

"No, I haven't." Julio shook his head, looking pathetic, and Huertas laughed harder.

"Well, I'm sorry son, because I have to say that would really bring you up in my estimation... Even my men who've infiltrated her group have tried their luck, but nothing. The Red Widow, that's what they call her. I'd like to go and proposition her myself some day, because I must be the only Spaniard in Paris she's hasn't turned down."

"Yes..." Julio paused and took a deep breath "Your accent... you're from Andalucía, Commander?"

"Yes."

"From where exactly, if you don't mind me asking..."

"No, I don't mind. I'm from Córdoba."

"From Córdoba...?" Julio frowned, twisting his mouth in an expression of annoyance, "Pity..." Then he said, as though to himself. "I was just thinking... Paloma's mother is Andalusian too, she owns a lot of land, acres and acres of olive groves, worth a fortune. And she hasn't lost a single tree, because one of her nieces has contacts high up in the administration, and she's been watching over it. But in Spain property is everything, obviously, and she wouldn't want anything happening to it.

That's why, when she heard I wanted to go back, don Mateo gave me power of attorney so I could oversee the sale – on his behalf obviously..." Julio looked up and was dazzled by the greed he saw in the man's eyes "Since you're from Córdoba, and Paloma's mother's lands are in Jaén, but then it looks like I won't be going back..."

A week later, after Ernesto Huertas had checked to make sure that Julio Carrión was not simply selling smoke and mirrors, Julio was told that he could apply for a passport. Two days later, Huertas himself appended a flattering report concerning the Falangist, a member of the Blue Division with an irreproachable record who had been living in Paris for personal reasons, he added parenthetically with no further explanation, but who had always made himself available to the embassy. The passport arrived a month later and Huertas personally gave it to Julio together with two pieces of advice. It was the last contact between the two men, but on the morning he left, Julio Carrión sent Huertas a letter: "Paris, 3 April 1947. I screwed her, you son of a bitch, I screwed her." He signed it, reread what he had written, then laughed and tore it up. He would have liked to have sent it, but he didn't dare.

"Ruin her, destroy her, and when you're done, tell her I sent you." Paloma Fernández Muñoz had looked at him and Julio had shuddered at the ferocity he saw in her eyes, dark with rage.

"Promise me."

"I promise."

"At first I thought of asking you to kill her, but I'd rather she lived. I wanted her to remember me, I want her to see my face when she gets up and when she goes to bed every fucking day of her fucking life. Do this for me, Julio, then come back for the rest, because there is nothing in the world, and I mean nothing, that I would not do to repay you."

What a pity, Paloma, Julio thought, what a pity, as he dressed, feasting his eyes on the woman who was getting out of the other side of the bed. As he left the house, as they walked along the street, as he kissed her for the last time, a fierce, desperate, hopeful kiss, "What a pity, Paloma." This was his plan, one that he had conceived and carefully worked out on his own, although he had allowed Ignacio Fernández Muñoz to think that it was all his idea, not expecting this gift, this dazzling night when he had discovered what a woman was capable of. He suddenly felt blessed, and for the first and last time on his path to glory he felt guilty, a traitor.

"Hello." A tall blond man, a distant acquaintance, had greeted him with the frank, honest smile Spanish exiles accorded their own in the short, deceptive spring that followed the Allied victory. "You're Teresa's son, aren't you, the schoolteacher from Torrelodones?"

Since the Lawyer had recognised him in a café heaving with other expatriates, Julio Carrión had been dropping in so regularly on the Fernández family it was as though he was one of them. He had known about them before that, had seen their large, comfortable villa with its vast garden, the pine trees so tall they could be seen from the road. And yet he had almost no memories of them, for he had been a child when they stopped coming on holiday to Torrelodones. Ignacio was the only one he had seen since, when the front line on the road between La Coruña and Torrelodones had become a loyalist stronghold. At first, he thought this was the only reason that the lawyer had heard of his mother, but he quickly discovered that the summer before, Ignacio had gone with his brother Mateo to the meetings at the Casa del Pueblo and that, sometimes, Carlos – Paloma's future husband - went with them. In Paris, in 1945, a Spanish expatriate needed no other qualifications to find himself welcomed with open arms. "We're all in the same boat," María Muñoz would say, "We help you out, maybe tomorrow you'll be helping us out." "And besides, he's charming, he's funny," said Paloma. Anita liked him too, he did magic tricks, and played with the children… They adored Julio, who would make sweets appear magically from their ears, make a whole host of things disappear under a napkin.

He allowed himself to be loved, he did not have to work at it, and he became quite fond of the children, he even stayed over sometimes on Saturdays to look after them when Ignacio's parents went out. But everyone knew he was not there for them; he was there for Paloma. She had found a job at a newspaper and came home late.

"Go on, Julio, go out and enjoy yourself," she would say when she opened the door and found him standing, waiting for her, in the hallway. "I'll look after the kids…"

She knew that he didn't want to go, and would allow him to stay, to sit opposite her at the kitchen table while she ate her dinner, then sit next to her on the sofa, worshipping her like a goddess. This was the one true thing that Julio would tell Commander Huertas, even if it was only a half-truth. He had been head over heels in love with Paloma but she had never driven him mad. No woman would ever drive Julio Carrión González mad, he was too attached to his own idea of sanity. And yet in his own way he did love Paloma Fernández Muñoz. To him, Paloma was both the quintessence of harmony, grace and beauty and a torture willingly borne, a pleasurable, inexorable suffering, but one that caused him no pain, since Paloma belonged to everyone and yet no one, she was loved by armies of living, breathing, men but was a faithful wife to her dead husband.

"Live on without me Paloma, find a companion worthy of you, I only pray that he loves you even one-tenth as much as I have loved you, my darling…" This was the favour Carlos Rodríguez Arce had asked of his wife before he died, but it was one that she still was not willing to grant him. It was a decision that did not please her parents or her brother, still less her sister, but no argument could sway her.

Until the penultimate night of 1946, when Julio Carrión González stood in her living room and announced that he was going back, that he had no choice. Before he'd even had time to explain that his sister had written to say she was marrying an older man who was disinclined to spend his life looking after his new father-in-law, and that unless Julio came back to take care of him, they intended to commit the old man to an asylum, he saw Paloma's eyes shine. "I have no illusions, obviously, I don't want to go, but my father is very ill. My sister's turned into a harpy but she says my future brother-in-law is prepared to stand guarantor for me." At that moment, nothing more was said. Then, the Lawyer thought he had an idea. "Listen, Julio, can you do something for me…?" "Of course, whatever you need me to do, you know that. I'll go and see your cousin as soon as I can. I'll find out what the situation is and write to you." Julio said no more, thereby ensuring that Ignacio would go on brooding about the problem.

"I want to give you power of attorney, Julio," Ignacio's father said the following day, "Ignacio and I have been talking about it and he doesn't think you'll be able to do anything unless you have documentary proof that you're acting on my behalf." "Do you really think that's necessary?" Julio ventured. "Of course it is," said Don Mateo, "Otherwise, anyone could have taken the property away from us already." "True," Julio conceded, and as he did, he saw that something had changed in the way that Paloma looked at him, she was staring at him almost in awe. The afternoon before his departure he went to the house for the last time to say goodbye.

"Do you have any plans for this evening, Julio?"

Paloma came out to meet him at the door, and her arrival suspended reality.

"It's just that it's been a long time since I've gone out, but…'

Carlos Rodríguez Arce's widow was wearing a tight, low-cut black dress in a soft fabric that clung to her body with terrifying obedience. The dress left bare the beautiful arms, the beautiful legs which until now Julio had had to be content to divine beneath the modest, almost monastic clothes that concealed her body. Now, however, she had put herself on display for him. Her hair had been curled and she was wearing dark red lipstick.

"So...?" she said and came up to him, "What do you say? Will you take me out?"

"Of course..." Julio was choked with excitement. "Of course I will..."

Paloma took his arm and, in the doorway, turned to look at her family all of whom seemed bewildered except her mother, who had brought her hands to her face and was silently shaking her head, her eyes wet with tears.

"What's the matter, Mamá?" Paloma's voice was dispassionate, but her expression seemed to dissolve as she looked at her mother's face, "Aren't you the one who's always telling me I should go out more?"

At that moment, Julio, afraid that their evening together might never begin, took her elbow and gently led her outside. Paloma allowed herself to be led, closed the door behind her, and there in the hallway, she showed him that he had nothing to fear.

"We're going to have fun tonight, you and me," she said, after she had kissed him passionately with a hunger that was not calculated, "You'll see..."

Julio realized Paloma's intentions at the same time her mother did, but he was surprised by the passion, by the recklessness of this woman who was prepared to stake everything she had to ensure her revenge, prepared to give herself completely to a man who was not her tool, but her knight, the champion who would conquer in her name.

This was what Julio Carrión felt, was what made him hesitate, as the most coveted Spanish woman in all of Paris, the woman who always said no, walked arm in arm with him, this extraordinary, magnificent, impossibly beautiful woman who could stop traffic, hush conversations, was stepping out with him. Julio Carrión felt the nudges, heard the whispered comments, saw the astonished stares, *la bella Paloma* stepping out with a man, laughing with him, kissing him, the Red Widow, in a low-cut dress, her arms, her legs, exposed, resting her head against the chest of this boy as a passing photographer took a snap. Julio had understood Paloma's intentions, but he had not expected this abandon, the genuine, boundless passion of a lady choosing her knight.

"Well what do you know, I'll even get to fuck you for free, my little Paloma." Julio had expected a clean, uncomplicated negotiation. "You toss my bitch of a cousin out on the street and I'll pay you in advance." "Fine," he'd said to himself, "but pay me now and afterwards, we'll see..." But it had not just been a fuck, and it had not been free. Paloma

Fernández Muñoz would never know it, but Julio Carrión González would spend the rest of his life trying to obliterate that night from his memory. For the rest of his life, he would compare every woman to Paloma, and where other men have a heart, Julio would have a hard, dry scar that could still soften, still throb on long wet afternoons. But even the most intelligent people can be fools when confronted with someone more intelligent than they are. And Paloma was more intelligent than he was.

"You can't imagine how much I loved him," and what sounded like an end, was the beginning of something new.

She was naked, exhausted, sprawled across his bed, and the dim light of his tiny room in his cheap boarding house shimmered, gilding her body with the light of a hundred candles. She gazed up at him, her face still flushed, pushing away the sheets, shameless and conscious of her. He could not resist the power in her eyes, could do nothing but gaze at her, listen to her, inhale the perfume of her sex that pervaded the whole room, and begin to commit her to memory. And just as he thought that she had no more to give him, his skin weary of responding to the limitless offer of a woman prepared to show him everything she was capable of, Paloma said: "You can't imagine how much I loved him," and it all began again.

"Carlos loved me so much, gave me so much..." her eyes glittered, but her voice was calm, gentle, sweet, "He was so much in love with me that no one noticed how much I loved him. Now they do, now they finally understand. He was a better person than me. He would not have nursed a grudge, or constantly waited for revenge. But he's dead, and I'm alive. I'm dead but I'm alive, every day for seven years I have been a living corpse, until tonight." She shifted slightly, pressed her body against Julio. "I am not as good a person as Carlos was, but I survived, and the only thing that gets me through the day is the love I have for him and the hatred for those who took him away from me. I am not as good as my husband was because I want revenge. I don't care that it's immoral, or pointless, I want revenge. It's the only thing that matters to me. Avenge me, Julio, and you'll never regret it. I won't lie to you. I don't think I could ever love anyone the way I loved Carlos, but if you avenge me, I can begin to forget and maybe I can start to live again."

This is what she said, then she straddled him, claimed him with unspoken words that only he could hear, words that he would never forget, that seemed to say: "This is me, Julio Carrión, and you are my champion. This is me and all this will be yours if you champion my cause, if you fight for me, because you are the only man who can bring me back to life, the only man who can make me happy."

"I won't lie to you," she had said to him, and she did not lie. Julio knew that, knew she was not putting on an act to draw him in. Paloma had treated him as she had every other man, with the same cordial detachment, until he had set himself apart, had subtly offered himself to her. Only then had the beautiful, grief-stricken widow noticed him, only then had she decided to bring him into her plans and offer herself so completely. "Do you like that? Wait, don't be so impatient, let me…"

"What a pity," he thought afterwards, "What a pity, Paloma" And yet, their last embrace moved him, bound him to her more than he could know when he left her standing in the entrance. That last, fierce, desperate, hopeful kiss did not stop him from writing to Huertas the letter he would never send: "I screwed her, you son of a bitch", but it travelled with him on the journey back as though stitched to his lips.

Afterwards, though he could hardly believe it, he did have doubts, he even went so far as to make a decision only to change his mind and change it back again. There was still time. The passport that permitted him to cross the border at Irún as though the past three years of his life had never happened had cost him little compared to what he had to gain. Paloma's father would not frown on him if he came back to Paris with Don Mateo's fortune to claim his prize, to worship his goddess, to win the heart of his fair lady. There were moments when Paloma seemed more important to him than his greed, than the thought of the sheep that had been his father's whole life and which he had vowed would not be his. But he had plotted his future, he had promised himself that never again would Julio Carrión González be on the losing side, and that promise freed him from all other considerations. He wasted no time wondering who was worse and who was better, who was right and who was wrong, he cared only about winning, and yet, afterwards, though he could hardly believe it, there were moments during his long journey back when winning meant Paloma Fernández Muñoz, when his prize would mean a different life.

Until he arrived in Madrid. On 4 April 1947, Julio Carrión González stepped off a train in the Estación del Norte to a warm, bright spring day. He glanced around him, gave thanks for the sun's warmth, breathed in a familiar scent and reminded himself that the world was full of women; other women. There were several of them right here on the station platform and one of them, in a red dress, was walking slowly, swaying on her heels. As he watched her, he could feel Paloma stinging his eyes, a parched dryness in his throat, pins and needles in his sides. He decided to ignore it, and remembered that one night in Paris he had participated in a frivolous but entertaining discussion between those who defended Freud's theory that sex makes the world go round and the Marxists who maintained that money makes the world go round. He smiled. Maybe, he thought, I'm a Marxist after all.

He chose a good hotel on the Gran Vía, he appreciated the burnished furniture, the roses in a cut-glass vase, the vast, soft, bed. This is the life for me, he thought. At that moment, the pain faded away, but when he brought his hands up to his face, still, above the scent of soap and water, he could smell Paloma. To shake her off, he went out for a walk, strolled along the boulevards, glanced into the shop windows, went into a tailors and bought a new suit, sat on a café terrace and watched the world pass by, listening to fragments of conversation; he realised that what the Spanish expatriates in Paris had said was true: Madrid was utterly different and yet completely the same.

Whereas in 1941, there had been rage and hostility in the voices now there was only fear. Where in 1941, there had been fear, there was now something else. The people of Madrid might not notice it, but he had been away for six years and he had returned to a city that had been beaten into submission, a city inhabited by stiff bodies and silence, where a wide corridor opened up before any uniform even on the most crowded pavements, because the moment they saw a policeman or a soldier, civilians – of whom there were more women than men – stepped back as though they had received an electric shock. Here in the centre of the city, he could see no sign of poverty, but, like the fear, he could smell it in the distance. This was his country, and yet it reminded him of a different, far-off country. Here, mingled with the smells of his childhood and his heady, passionate youth, Julio Carrión González could smell Riga, and he realised that his country was not calm, it was caged, it was an occupied territory where there were no victors, only masters. Others might have pondered this, but Julio did not need to – he realised that he found himself in a paradise for imposters, usurers and opportunists. A place where he might thrive.

Jesus, Madrid is expensive, he thought as he paid for his coffee. He did not have much money left, the trip to the tailors had eaten up almost half his final pay packet, but it did not matter. Tomorrow, he would go to Torrelodones and he to see wanted everyone to notice him to see that he was back. He felt a sudden urge to head for the Calle de la Montera and say hello to Señor Turégano, but he resisted.

At dinnertime, he headed back to the hotel, went into the bar on the ground floor, and ordered a Martini. Almost immediately, a woman with bleach-blonde hair and too much make-up came over and asked him for a light, but Julio was not interested in her. She sat next to him, smoking, but realising that he had no desire to talk to her, she stubbed out the half-finished cigarette and slipped it back into her packet. Her place was quickly filled by a skinny young girl who also realised he was not interested and did not even bother asking him for a light. As she got up, Julio noticed another woman, about thirty – the age he preferred – with dark hair pulled up into a chignon, large eyes and a pretty mouth; she looked completely ordinary, married probably, but in a fix. At that moment, he saw Paloma Fernández Muñoz at the bottom of his glass, perched on the empty stool beside him, and he signalled to her.

"Hi," he said, "Can I get you a drink?"

"Yes," the woman's conversational skills were no better than his own, "A chocolate milkshake, please."

"What's your name?" he asked, after he had recovered from his astonishment at her, nutritious request.

"Julia," she said, smiling.

"Really? Mine's Julio!"

"Call me María if you like," she said, drinking down half the milkshake in a single gulp. "I don't mind."

When he suggested that they might spend a little time together, she indicated a price, pressing the fingers of her right hand against the palm of her left and he quickly asked for the bill. "Jesus, Madrid is cheap," he muttered to himself as he signed the bill. The woman turned to him: "What did you say?"

"Nothing, it was nothing…"

Stepping into his room, she took off her old, moth-eaten gloves and put them in her handbag, then laid out the ground rules:

"I don't kiss. I'll do anything else, but not that."

"Even if I pay extra?" Julio asked, out of curiosity.

"Even if you pay extra." She picked up her bag, took out her gloves. She's probably thinking at least she got something to eat, thought Julio.

"No, it's OK. We don't have to kiss, I don't mind." Watching her as she undressed in a diffident, emotionless manner that indicated she was no professional, Julio asked: "Are you married?"

"None of your business."

"She's married, or she's a widow, no, she's married but on her own," he thought, "she's young, pretty, she has a good body, her husband must be off somewhere, in France maybe, I might even have met him. Maybe he's in prison here, or in a labour camp, working off his sentence, thinking about his wife, waiting for her letters so he can write back by return post. So what? When he gets out, she'll give up all this, and go

414

back to being a polite housewife…"

After they had finished, the woman got up without saying anything, dressed quickly, and was gone. Then, Julio Carrión González, who two nights previously had been the chosen one, the most powerful man in Paris, found himself alone with his poverty, and he realised in spite of himself the true price of a kiss. "Fine," he thought, "better now than later." But he could think of nothing else, and suddenly the memory of Paloma's kisses stung his eyes, parched his throat, sent pins and needles stabbing through his sides. "It's alright, Paloma, I'm done with tears," he said aloud as though she were lying next to him. And it was true. Julio Carrión González had a long life ahead of him, but never again would he succumb to the urge to weep.

No tears troubled him when he came face to face with the ruin that was his father, the shambles that had been his home, in fact he felt a profound sense of relief, after having ordered the most expensive meal possible in the bar on the village square and bought a cognac – the good stuff – for those acquaintances who stopped by his table to say hello. Evangelina, who did not have the looks to tout herself around the hotels on the Gran Vía, had worked quickly and well. The room that took up most of the ground floor, what they had always called the dining room, was as immaculate as if Teresa González had never left. At one end, sitting at the table, his hair combed, wearing a jacket over the shirt he had always worn, Benigno stared vacantly in front of him.

"Julio," Evangelina clattered down the stairs when she heard the sound of the door. "I've finished downstairs, though I only gave the kitchen a quick once-over. You can't imagine the state it was in."

"Oh, I can imagine, Evangelina."

"I made your father a couple of fried eggs, there was nothing else in the cupboards. The bread was a bit stale, but he ate it anyway. There's still a lot to do, so we're going to need more time – two or three days if we're going to launder everything, all his clothes and so on…"

"That's fine. Don't worry about it…" He looked at the woman and smiled again, "Take all the time you need. All I want is for the place to be clean. And I'd like you to come in regularly – to clean, do the laundry, the shopping and the cooking, because I can't stay, I have to get back to Madrid. We'll talk about it before I leave, all right?"

"Of course." Julio was far from sure that a woman like Evangelina would want to take care of a man like his father, but she looked at him as though he had saved her life which, he realised, was probably the case. He had not wanted to agree a price with her because he was not yet sure how much money he had. This was the detail he had not thought about in

Paris. Now, the state of his father cast a shadow over his carefully laid plans, so he forced himself to behave like a repentant prodigal son.

"Father!" He hugged Benigno, and sat down next to him.

"Julio… So it is you… you've come back," his father said, staring at him as though he could not believe his eyes.

"Yes, I'm here now."

"Your mother died in prison, the penitentiary in Ocaña, the little whore." His eyes flared, suddenly alive. "Did you know that?"

"Yes, father. You wrote and told me."

"She's to blame for everything, it's all your mother's fault."

The old man made no attempt to explain himself. Julio closed his eyes because he did not want to remember, because he had promised himself he would never cry again He refused to remember that odious letter he had ripped to shreds before he had finished reading it, his father's words "I'm not sorry for her, she had it coming. I don't know where your sister is and I don't want to know…" Julio remembered the terrible loneliness that had kept him awake that night in Grafenwöhr, the feeling that he was an orphan. But that was in the past, he quickly reminded himself.

"Where is my money, father?"

"What about my things?" Benigno looked at him again, his eyes vacant, "Where are all my things? Can't you see, they've stolen everything I had."

"There was nothing here, father, only rubbish. I threw out everything that was broken. I'll replace it all for you, but to do that, I'll need my money. Where is it?" Benigno frowned and grinned. "The money father. The money that was sent to you, my salary for the time I was in Russia – both salaries, the Spanish and the German. Where is the money, father?"

"What did you think?" Benigno reacted at last, shooting Julio a lopsided smile and pointing to the chest of drawers, "You think I spent it?"

That night, back in Madrid, the city seemed more beautiful to Julio, the lights brighter, the women more beautiful.

He was rich. Only a fraction as rich as he planned to be, but he was rich. He had more than enough to live the life of a gentleman for several months, which was more than enough time for him to make contacts, finalise his plan and set to work. The money soothed him, it was enough to draw a line through time, rub out the past, rub out the fear and the fatigue of the garage on the Calle de la Montera, erase the cold and the mud and the lice in Russia, the grey routine of an expatriate labourer first in Toulouse, then in Paris, erase his mother and Paloma. In the morning, he took the train to Torrelodones, but for the return journey, he hired the only taxi in the village. "I just want to say, Julio…" Evangelina had been staring at him since he had accepted her conditions without argument, "I was very sorry to hear about your mother's death, it broke my heart, really it did. Everyone loved her. She was a wonderful woman, intelligent, generous, brave, she was the best person I have ever known…" Even this, he forgot as soon as he stepped into the taxi to Madrid, that took him back to his fine hotel on the Gran Vía, with its vases filled with fresh roses and the burnished wood.

His body was eager for pleasure, and for a day and a half, he yielded to its demands. In this, at least, Madrid was unchanged, even if Franco, like his father, was holier-than-thou. The oldest bar in the city, La Villa Rosa, was still open for business, and lurking at the bottom of the narrow stairwell next to the kitchen of Los Gabrieles on the Calle Echegaray was the city's finest brothel. It was a meticulous reproduction of a place where young bulls were tested out *Plaza de tientas*, a place where young bulls were tested out, where once Primo de Rivera, the old dictator, had once liked to play the bullfighter with his favourite whores. Romualdo, who liked to boast that he had been there many times, had told Julio about the place when they were in Russia and Julio had been impressed by his tales.

He needed little time to recuperate and so, after forty-eight hours of dissipation and twelve hours of sleep, he got up two days later, showered, shaved, dressed and went down to the dining room for breakfast. He picked up a newspaper and, leafing through it, asked for a telephone directory, hoping to find Eugenio's number. He assumed that his old friend would be delighted to hear from him, and when he called, the two men arranged to meet at 2.30pm.

Eugenio Sánchez Delgado lived at the Retiro end of the Calle Castelló, in a nice, bright apartment with his wife Blanca who was four months pregnant though they had been married barely six months. As he made his way there, Julio's senses, still fogged from an excess of subterranean pleasures, were met by a wholesomeness, a crispness, like the scent of freshly laundered sheets in this neighbourhood filled with the comfortable well-heeled middle class. He felt the same sensation as he stepped into Eugenio's apartment, and as he kissed Eugenio's wife. She smelled of eau de cologne and she was plain: an ordinary girl, too broad-hipped for her age, she had a homely face, and her lips bore a permanent expression of calm.

"You're in fine form, Eugenio!" Julio said honestly, hugging his friend. Eugenio slipped an arm around his wife's shoulders before responding. "It's true, I've never been better, but Blanca deserves all the credit."

"Oh," So that's how it is, thought Julio, giving his hostess a smile so charming that it made her nervous. "Matrimonial bliss..." It was true that Eugenio looked well, he seemed more confident, more mature, no longer a gangling youth, but a slender, well-built man. Yet, when his wife went back to the kitchen and left them alone together, Julio thought he detected an flicker of sadness in Eugenio's eyes.

"So, how are things?" Eugenio took him by the arm and led him into the living room. "Tell me... where've you been all this time?"

"Well, it's a long story... "I stayed in Riga, you remember Colonel Arenas asked me to?" His friend nodded.

"Romualdo said something..."

"Well, that's where I've been... Arenas asked me to act as a liaison of sorts between the Blue Legion, the Wehrmacht and his head office back in Madrid, so `I stayed on until the end. When the Germans had to retreat, I settled in Berlin. I had no official standing with the embassy, but in theory I had the support of the Spanish army, although as you can imagine, given the way the war was going by then, that wasn't worth much. I should have come back, but I ended up getting involved with a woman – Gertrude her name was, she was blonde and as tall as I am, with green eyes..."

"Well at least you got to learn German!"

"You'd think. I learned about three words. She and I spoke French to each other, but I didn't care because... what can I tell you, I fell for her. The night I met her, she looked right through me, I felt like a fool, you can't imagine, by the next morning, I barely knew my own name." Eugenio laughed, "I was head over heels and, well, by the time the Allies turned up, I couldn't come back. Apart from the fact that most of them had already done a runner, it would have been more dangerous to go looking for a Spanish diplomat in Berlin than to sit tight, so I hid out with Gertrude, until eventually she went back to her village and starvation forced me out, and the American troops arrested me."

"Just as well," Eugenio was not laughing now, "Because if the Russians had got you..."

"I know... it took me more than a year to convince the Americans that I hadn't done anything... In the end, they let me go with only the clothes I stood up in. I had no money and no way of making any. Things were tough for a while, I lived in a bombed out hovel and depended on handouts for food, on the Red Cross, until they offered me a place on a refugee train to Paris. I got there last June. Things were easier in Paris because the place is full of Spaniards – Republicans – they all help each other out. Of course I had to pretend I was one of them, that way I could earn enough money to get by..."

"What about the embassy?" Eugenio looked at him, surprised, "They should have helped you, I mean..."

Julio cut him off. "They don't trust anyone at the embassy, nobody. I went and talked to them, I went again and again, I told them to call Madrid, to call Arenas. But it did me no good, it turned out he was dead, they said my safe-conduct was a forgery, and there was no one else I could turn to – in Riga, I'd been undercover, in Berlin too. I suppose they didn't want to take the risk... I was terrified that the French would just deport me, so I disappeared for a while... Shit, back then I was furious, but now I understand..." Eugenio nodded, though Julio could not read the expression on his face. "Anyway, I don't know what happened after that, but about a month ago they gave me a passport. I didn't ask questions, I just went straight to Torrelodones so I could see my father, so I could eat well for once... And here I am."

It all came out in a single breath, his tone cheery, casual, just someone recounting an adventure that was over, a pirouette with no more grace than its inevitable whirling, and yet not one word of what he had said had been left to chance, not one was spontaneous.

"Wouldn't it be funny," he had said to Huertas when the man had met him to give him his passport "If, now that the hard part is done, everything went wrong and the deal fell through?"

"Why should it go wrong? You said had contacts, didn't you? I've told you where you can find Sánchez Delgado, I've done my part. "

"Yes," Julio said, "And I'm grateful. But suppose I see Colonel Arenas strolling down the street. What do I do? He's a soldier of the old school, an honourable man..."

"Yes, yes..." Huertas interrupted, "Maybe Colonel Arenas was all those things, but he's not anymore; he's dead. Died of a heart attack eighteen months ago. You think I'm a fool, Carrión? Arenas was a good friend of my father's, you think if he was still alive I would have anything to do with this scheme of yours? And in Madrid these days, the sort of people we're interested in aren't going to go asking a guy like you any questions. Take my word for it."

At that moment, Julio Carrión dared to meet Ernesto Huertas' gaze, man to man, and the Commander did not blink. This man who, for two years, had known everything there was to know about the Spanish communists living in exile in Paris must have known that Julio moved in the circles Huertas was investigating When he went to meet him, Julio knew Huertas was from Córdoba, knew he came from a military family, and was married to a woman with a lineage as notable as it was decadent. Though she too was from Córdoba, she had not gone with him to Paris, preferring to stay in Madrid with the five children they had had in the space of seven years. Julio knew all this; he knew, too, that in spite of his unfailing allegiance to the Cause, Huertas had a French mistress and considerable expenses. It was rumoured that he trafficked in passports, Julio held proof of that fact in his hands, and that he would intervene in judicial proceedings to have a prisoner released, a sentence quashed, even have the death penalty commuted. In Paris, Julio sensed, he was much too shrewd to take such risks, in Madrid he was not so sure, but as he looked Huertas in the eye, he was in no doubt as to the man's greed.

"I'm going to tell you a story Commander, let's see how believable you think it is..." Huertas listened attentively, offered suggestions, genuine details, it was he who suggested the bombed out building, suggested Julio mention the Red Cross. It was Huertas who told Julio to say he had arrived in Paris on a refugee train. "Don't be a fool Carrión, how could you possibly have made it from Germany on foot?" Julio had accepted Huertas amendments, committed every detail to memory, but the person on whom he had chosen to try out his story for the first time, demanded no details.

"Poor Julio," he said simply, looking at him with genuine compassion "What rotten luck."

His guest lit a cigarette: "I suppose, but all's well that ends well. Some people have had it worse."

"Of course. Pablo, for one... You know Stalin sent him to a labour camp, the same camp where the prisoners from the Blue Division are being held."

"Really?" Julio's eyes widened.

"Boys!" Blanca popped her head round the door, "Lunch is served."

"I'll tell you about it later." Eugenio murmured as they got to their feet, "My wife doesn't know anything about it."

Señora Sánchez Delgado was a fine cook and an attentive and generous hostess. She doted on Eugenio, always made his favourite meals, was proud to watch him put on weight. "My mother-in-law doesn't approve," she said to Julio with a smile, "she thinks I spoil him..."

"It's true," Eugenio said, "But I'm happy for you to spoil me..." They held hands across the dinner table, were always kissing, had pet names for each other. Julio felt awkward, and Eugenio noticed.

"What's the matter?" he asked, his tone cheerful.

"Nothing..." he said, "It's just that, I can still picture you back in the trench, with your rifle and your uniform and suddenly seeing you here, in your own home with a wife and a baby on the way... I can't take it in."

"I know."

Eugenio and Blanca smiled at him, then she glanced at the clock and leapt to her feet.

"It's a quarter past four, I'll just change then I have to go."

She excused herself, explaining to Julio that every afternoon she went to visit her parents who lived nearby, "I'm an only child, and they miss having me around. Of course, I won't be able to go after the baby's born..." Julio realised that Eugenio thought this entirely reasonable. That's how he is, Julio thought, if he's decided to be happy, he'll be the happiest man alive. And yet, he noticed, without Blanca nearby to put a twinkle in them, his friend's eyes no longer blazed as they used to do, as he followed Eugenio back into the living room, warming a glass of cognac between his hands, he wondered what had happened.

"I don't want to hold you up, Eugenio, but... I don't know, I have so many questions..."

"Ask away..." Eugenio said, sinking into an armchair. "I've been looking forward to seeing you, and these days I only work mornings."

"Jesus, you civil servants have it easy!"

"I'm not a civil servant, Julio."

"No?" Julio raised an eyebrow in surprise, this was the first point on which Huertas has been mistaken. "I thought you had some job at the ministry?"

"I was in the Department of Public Works, but I left just before Christmas. Nowadays, I work for a private construction company from 8 to 2 and I spend the afternoons studying. I want to finish university."

"University?" Julio did not know what to think, "But when we left for Russia, they said... Weren't they supposed to take your service into account as part of your degree?"

"I know what they said," Eugenio cut him off, smiling, "And they did. I studied shit and they gave me a degree in shit. In theory I'm a qualified engineer, but in practice I know what I am and what I'm not. That's why I want to finish my studies, proper studies, like everyone else." He sipped his cognac, "Are you surprised?"

"Yes," Julio said truthfully.

"Things aren't going well here, Julio. They could be, but they're not. It was different when I came back, because the Germans were fighting a rearguard action, whereas here, at least on the surface, nothing was happening, nobody was doing anything, just in case... Of course, Franco betrayed the Germans just in time, and the British paid him well for it. I know it sounds harsh, but it's the truth. It was the British who put Franco in power, and it's the British who kept him there. And I'll tell you something else. I don't know what would have happened if Roosevelt hadn't died so soon, but I do know that if Hitler had won the war, Muñoz-Grandes would be sitting in El Pardo today: he was their man, he was the one they trusted. But Hitler lost and Franco won again. Oh not honourably, he was a turncoat, but he won and that's all that matters. So a year and a half ago… I don't know… I was completely disgusted by the whole thing…"

Eugenio Sánchez Delgado had aged, not just in the way he moved or the way he talked, but in his mind. And yet the faith he had once had was so important to him that he had been prepared to sacrifice everything: power, status, money, even his own happiness to keep alive a flame that would never again burn with the ardent, youthful passion in which it had been born. Julio knew from the first moment that he had never met anyone like this man who could be so innocent, so open, occasionally shrewd but more often foolish. But not until that afternoon when he heard the tremor of indignation in his voice, did Julio realise what it meant. Eugenio had abandoned his innocence, had given up on his theory about the little mistakes made necessary by great causes so he would not have to give up on his own principles. But Julio no longer surprised by him, no longer admired him in spite of himself, no longer considered Eugenio a better man than he. He could not even admire his courage for Julio Carrión González had also aged. And even though he still liked Eugenio, still thought of him as his only friend, the only thing this conversation inspired in him was weariness.

"People are still dying of starvation, and that's not a figure if speech. I know you've only just got back, but you must have seen it?" Julio acknowledged the fact with a shudder. "I know there's been the war, and the drought, and the economic sanctions… In the beginning, maybe, it was understandable, but not now."

Eugenio fell silent, he took off his glasses and wiped them with a corner of his shirttail.

"Let me give you an example. You remember Ricardo, my brother-in-law?" Julio nodded though he had only met the man twice. "When my sister Pilar married him, he was only a second lieutenant but today he's one of the richest men in Madrid. You're thinking maybe he's a government minister, or a banker, maybe his father is a millionaire? But no…" Eugenio paused as though waiting for Julio to say something.

"What is he then?"

"He's a clerk in the municipal Department of Supplies." He

underscored the remark with a bitter smile. "Nothing more, nothing less. In any civilised country, he'd be in prison, but Spain isn't a civilised country any more, Julio. Everything, anything is permitted. The people who had nothing are starving, those who have lost everything are starving too... Last summer, I took my brother Arturo out to a reception at General Camilo Alonso Vega's villa in El Viso, a big modern house with a nice garden. Ever wonder why El Viso didn't get bombed during the war?"

"No," Julio did not see what Eugenio was getting at.

"I did... I thought it was strange, because Salamanca was on our side, there were no communists there, but El Viso? The Socialist Besteiro was living there and half of the members of the Institución Libre de Enseñanza, socialists and Republicans, I mean they were the ones who founded it, weren't they? Anyway, that afternoon, at the General's reception, I realised why. 'You have a lovely house,' I said to his wife. 'Yes,' she said to me, 'it's a beautiful setting, isn't it?' Then, without trying to justify herself, as if it was the most normal thing in the world, she told me that the house used to belong to some man called Ganvinet - a communist living in exile in London – and his wife, who had committed suicide in prison. I wanted to ask her 'But didn't these people have children, family, or even friends, surely they must have had someone with a better claim to this house than you, Señora?"

Stop busting my balls, Eugenio, thought Julio for the first time, but he did not say it aloud, did not try to fill the silence that now separated him from this stranger who had once been his oldest friend.

"I nearly asked her, but of course I didn't. In Spain, no one asks any questions, that's how people get a job in Supplies, in Public Transport, in Public Works. 'But they were communists.' You don't need any other excuse, it's like saying 'Open, Sesame!' It's 1947 but we're still behaving like it's 1939. All you have to say is 'They were communists,' and you can get away with anything."

"It's not like that, is it?" said Julio Carrión. He frowned, adopting a concerned tone while he tried to contain his excitement. "I mean it's legal, there are laws..."

"It's theft, Julio." Eugenio stared at him, his eyes shining with something of their former passion. "Even if it's legal, and everyone does it, it's still theft, and I'll have nothing to do with it."

"So that's why you left the Department?"

"Yes. That, and because they put me in charge of the expropriations..."

"What about Romualdo?"

"Him? Oh he's doing fine, you know him. As far as he's concerned, things have never been better. He's one of the gang."

"And you never talk to him about it?"

Eugenio refilled Julio's glass and his own, then sat down, " I haven't spoken to him in months."

Or longer, for almost a year and a half; ever since Eugenio Sánchez Delgado had become interested in what had become of the members of the Blue Division who had been captured in Russia. He had not stopped being a Falangist. Quite the contrary. The shame and disappointment he felt had left him no other possibility than to redouble his efforts, to become more deeply involved in what he still thought of as his party, the secular, Republican fascist party whose emblem appeared on every public building, every train station, every street, on every letterhead, every uniform, a party which, first and foremost, was clerical and reactionary, which over time appeared as a humiliating, endlessly deferred, exercise in restoring the monarchy.

From this moment on, until the day when a policeman would blow a hole in his daughter's spleen − the daughter who had been born five months after this reunion with Julio Carrión − Eugenio Sánchez Delgado attempted to be true to himself. In order to do so, his only course was to undermine the regime from within, without ever admitting the contradictions in this fundamentally fruitless task which was doomed before it even began.

Eugenio Sánchez Delgado maintained this dual aspect of his character until the age of forty-three, until he had no choice. But on the afternoon Julio saw him in his apartment on the Calle Castelló, he still had passion, still had hope.

"I told you that Pancho is in a labour camp in Russia? I found out by accident, because obviously I was expecting any name but his… I work with an organisation that looks after the interests of members of the Blue Division who were captured. We work through the Red Cross and the Swedish embassy. We can't do much, obviously, because it's not official, and we can't risk provoking the English and the Americans now that we're all friends again. That's why we only recently managed to get a list of prisoners and there it was, Luis Serrano Romero. I could believe my eyes. I thought it had to be a mistake, so I wrote to the Swedes and explained and they wrote back and said there was no mistake, that Stalin had incarcerated the deserters in the same camps as the men from the Blue Division… I was speechless."

"It is odd," said Julio, making light of the news, little expecting that the shock would transport him back to a German train, an autumn day, en route to Nuremberg.

"Odd?" Eugenio raised his voice, "You think it's odd? Jesus Christ, it's grotesque! It's appalling... Pancho Serrano was a hero, he may have been a communist but he was a fucking hero! He was willing to march across Europe with a ID card hidden his boots and he had enough balls to fight for *them* and they've gone and put him in a prison camp!" His face softened and took on the dazed expression of a lost child. "I just don't understand. I mean it would never have happened here in Spain. In our war, Pancho would have got a medal, a promotion, from either side... wouldn't he? I mean that would be fair. Oh, I don't know..."

"He was looking for trouble," Julio said, hoping they could get back to the subject that really interested him.

"*No!*" Eugenio said, his eyes flashing, his cheeks flushed with righteous anger. "He was *not* looking for trouble! He was looking for something different, and you know it, you were the one who explained it to me, Julio, and they have no right..." He paused and struggled to regain his composure. "Poor Pancho, I often think about him, I wonder how he feels, to have been betrayed by his own kind, by everything that mattered to him. It's awful. Apparently the Russians trust them, give them power over the other prisoners, they don't make them work so hard. But he wouldn't do it. And I can understand. He had the balls to refuse. Poor bastard, I think about him a lot, about that night - '*tovarich, spanski tovarich! Don't shoot, I'm coming over!*' – you remember? And I think, what would we have done, what would the Spanish have done?"

'We are the wretched of the earth', thought Julio Carrión, who could see in Eugenio's eyes the trembling lips of Ignacio Fernández. He dared not say the words aloud. War and peace had come and gone and they had both grown older, Julio no longer knew what to say, how to act, what to do to ease Eugenio's suffering, this pain that was not simply inconvenient but possibly dangerous.

"I went to see the real Pancho, you know? His little brother, the one who was actually called Francisco Serrano Romero. I had to go and see him, it was the only way I could get to talk to him. 'Those people don't have a phone,' someone told me when I called the town hall, 'and nobody round here lets them use theirs.' I said 'Couldn't you go and get him, that way I could talk to him on this phone?" But he said no, said he wasn't about to get up from his desk for anyone, and certainly not for Pancho. 'Thanks for your help', I said and hung up... So in the end I went there."

"Why?" Julio could no longer hide his astonishment. "I'm sorry, Eugenio, but I don't get it."

Eugenio did not bother to answer, he just smiled and went on:

"So, anyway, he lives in a kind of farm, an old ruin he fixed up himself, on the outskirts of town. He's the only man left in the family. His older brother was killed on the Ebro, his father is part of a prison work detail building a dam in Cuenca, and Pancho – or rather Luis – is in Russia. He and his wife, his mother, his brothers' wives, and his older sister – she's not long out of prison in Alcalá, she's a widow too - they all live in the same house, with a whole crowd of kids. The younger sister has married and moved to Badajoz and she wants nothing to do with them.

"What were you expecting?" Julio filled his glass to the brim. "They lost the war, didn't they?"

"Yes. They lost the war. And now here I was telling him that Stalin had his brother banged up in a prison camp. When the real Pancho heard, he went white as a sheet. 'What did he do?' he asked me. 'Nothing', I told him, 'He didn't do anything, he went over to the Russian side.' When I said that he went quiet, then he grabbed me and started screaming 'You fucker, you bastard, I'm going to kill you.'"

"He didn't believe you."

"He didn't want to believe me, but it was the truth, and in the end he accepted it. He backed away and sat down on a stone bench next to the door. Then he said 'I am Pancho.' And I'll never forget it, the tone of his voice, the expression on his face. He looked like a corpse, Julio, like a dead man, it was terrible. I was sorry I'd come. You'd think he had been through enough, then I show up and fuck up his life a little more... But there I was, and I had to tell him. He reeled off two or three names and a stream of kids appeared from the house. He said to the oldest lad 'Go and ask your Aunt Lupe to come here'. 'She's Luis's wife,' he said to me and he didn't say another word until his sister-in-law arrived. She was a tall woman, young and slim, dressed in black. She stood there, leaning in the doorway, and she listened to me, saying nothing, though by the end she had her face in her hands. She was crying, but she wouldn't let me see her cry. When she calmed down, she looked at me, and she said something, I'll never forget, she said, 'You know, I thought he'd gone off with another woman, I think I would have preferred that.'"

"I don't understand," Julio stared enquiringly at Eugenio.

"I do...' Eugenio said, "And I understand what Pancho said when I was leaving. He said 'It must be some mistake, it can't be true. I'm not saying you're a liar, it's just that I don't believe it. But if there's anything you can do for my brother...' I realised that maybe he and I were not so different, both of us believe what we need to believe in order to keep going in this fucked up world. And I did try to do something for them, not just for Pancho, but for his family. I talked to Romualdo, who's lining his pockets in the Ministry of Agriculture, I told him the whole story and asked him to do whatever he could to help, to give the family a grant or a subsidy, an advance against the harvest. He'd barely have had to lift a finger. 'I'm not asking you to do it for them,' I said, 'Do it as a favour for me.' But he wouldn't. You know what he said? 'They can go fuck themselves.' I haven't spoken to him since."

When he left Eugenio's apartment, Julio Carrión no longer felt that freshness, no longer smelled the clean smell like freshly laundered sheets, that had welcomed him when he arrived. He was annoyed, though he had no reason to be, since what Eugenio had told him confirmed his hopes, but he could not rid himself of a bitter taste, like a scrap of food rotting between his teeth.

Julio could not understand why he missed the old Eugenio, the happy, enthusiastic, passionate Eugenio only now that he was gone for good. Madrid seemed depressing, cruel, complicated. Against his better judgement, through his friend's eyes, he could see the other side: the hardship, the worry, the subdued fury of the desperate. But he stifled this surge of nostalgia, intent on playing his hand as quickly as possible. At the end of the day, Eugenio Sánchez Delgado had always been a queer fish, thought Julio, and most people out there probably didn't think the way he did. Two days later, he discovered how right he had been.

"Julito! Jesus Christ!" Romualdo gave him a broad smile. "You don't know how happy I am to see you. Shit! You know every morning I wake and see these legs of mine and I remember you! Come here, give me a hug!"

This long, tender embrace, which drew raised eyebrows from one or two of the customers having an early evening cocktail in the expensive bar on the Gran Vía, was the dawning of a new life for Julio Carrión, a life of drinking and whoring and private rooms, of calculations, percentages, profits, of dinners that went on into the early hours, more drinks, more whores, more private rooms, clandestine meetings with men who, though charming, where not as charming as he was, in formal rooms and private offices, in bars and cafés, alone and with Romualdo, more dinners that went on into the early hours, or early dinners in family dining rooms, presided over by a reproduction of the Last Supper and a plump, charmless hostess who would inevitably ask if he preferred prawns or clams before she served him fish soup with a silver ladle.

Romualdo inevitably declined these high Catholic invitations, and Julio would accept in his place. From the beginning, Julio took the

427

calculated risk of telling Romualdo everything, and it proved to be the right decision. 'If it weren't for you they'd have amputated my legs,' Romualdo said when they met again. Romualdo introduced him to half a dozen well-placed men and advised Julio how much of the truth he should tell each one. Julio was in no hurry, and his patience was to his advantage. So it was almost a month before he knew where to begin, how to proceed, a month before he rang the doorbell of an apartment on the second floor of a majestic old apartment block overlooking the Calle Manuela Malasaña and the Calle Carranza.

"Hello," a young girl, tall as a grown woman, with hair so blonde it looked unnatural gazed at him curiously.

"Is your mother home?"

"No. Who are you?"

"Angelica!" A second girl, shorter than the first though older, rushed into the hallway and grabbed the first by the arm, whispering fiercely "How many times have I told you, you're not supposed to answer the door? That's my job. Your mother will tell me off."

La Señora was not at home, she had gone out but would be back shortly, of course he could wait, would he care for something to drink? The maid implemented the protocol for unexpected guests and showed Julio into a study lined with books. He had the impression that everything – the furniture, the paintings, the décor, even the marks of the silverware that had once stood on the now bare sideboard – belonged to the previous owners of this house, and still reflected their taste, their past, their way of life as though some gossamer thread linked everything he could see to that small, sparsely furnished apartment in a cheerless Paris suburb. He was attempting to imagine them - Ignacio, María and Paloma – here in these rooms, sitting on the sofas, leaning over the balconies, when the little girl who had opened the door to him tiptoed soundlessly into the room.

"Don't take any notice of Matilde, she's a pest," she announced taking a seat facing him. "What's your name?"

"Julio Carrión."

"My name's Angélica. But you already know that..." Her eyes were deep blue and disconcertingly attractive; she was physically mature yet obviously still a child, her face was round and chubby, her legs were scabbed and scratched, and she had an abruptness more in keeping with her age than her body.. "I'm twelve... at least I will be soon. How old are you?"

"Twenty-five."

"That means, when I'm twenty you'll be..."

428

"Thirty-three…"

"Twenty and thirty-three," she thought about this, "That means that in eight years, we could get engaged…"

"Really?" Julio laughed.

"Of course," she said solemnly, "My father was eleven years older than my mother."

"What are you doing here, Angélica?"

They both turned and, standing in the doorway was a woman Julio did not know, but who surprised him as much as this little girl had.

Julio had not dared to hope that Mariana Fernández Viu would look like her cousin Paloma, but the difference between them was even, more profound than he'd expected, making it difficult to believe that this timorous woman, with her blouse buttoned up tight, her low-heeled shoes and a black hat pushed down over her forehead could possibly belong to the same family. Had he not known that Mariana was thirty-five, Julio would never have guessed her age, blurred as it was by the primness particular to Spanish matrons intent on defending their virtue. She was neither pretty nor ugly, she was simply abrasive.

This abrasive outer shell surprised Julio, as it was so completely at odds with her daughter's grace. Angélica might have inherited her piercing blue eyes from her mother, but not her sensuality, her boldness, that precocity that had made him listen to her plans for their engagement. Mariana, too, was tall and stout, though not overweight, a heaviness that distinguished her from her cousins.

Looking at her, Julio was reminded of Ignacio's little sister María, who had the same thick ankles, the same dark hair, though María's hair was invariably a tousled mess as she dashed down the street, rushed about the house, fussed over the children, always in a hurry, something that you could hear in the way she spoke, the way she laughed, it was a trait that to some extent she shared with her brothers and sisters, and with her sister-in-law. "That's what it is," thought Julio, getting to his feet as he saw Mariana come toward him with a slow, indolent, gait.

"Hello, my name is Julio Carrión," he offered his hand and she shook it limply, which reminded him of the nickname her cousins in Paris had given her. "I've just arrived from Paris. I'm a friend of your cousin, Ignacio Fernández Muñoz…"

"Ignacio, oh yes, of course…"

By the time she had said these words, everything had changed.

"Angélica, go to your room."

"But, Mamá…"

"I said go to your room."

429

By the time they were alone, she had been careful to soften her dour expression as soon as the blood which had drained from her face returned. Julio witnessed the sudden metamorphosis. As Angélica slowly got up, dragging her feet in a mute, childish protest entirely appropriate for her age, he watched the frantic play of light and shadow on Mariana's face. Mariana Fernández Viu was worried, and beneath her nervousness, Julio Carrión could also sense fear, contempt, and rage as the woman vacillated between the urge to challenge the newcomer and the urge to win his trust.

"Don't be afraid. I'm not going to hurt you," Julio flashed her his most charming smile.

"At first, I thought of asking you to kill her," Julio remembered Paloma's words and realised that this woman was terrified of just such a threat. You have every reason to fear me, he thought, but he smiled again and sat down. With the effortless grace of the master of the house, he gestured to the armchair where Angélica had been sitting.

"Please, sit down." She obeyed, as though she had finally realised who was now in charge.

"How is everyone?" Julio's silence compelled her to be more precise, "My cousins, my uncle and aunt... Are they well?"

"They're in good health, yes. Those who survived, obviously. Mateo was shot. Ignacio married a pretty girl from Aragon, they have two children. María is married too. A boy from Toledo. They have a daughter and she's expecting another child. Paloma... Paloma didn't have any children. Her husband was shot, too. But you know all this, don't you?"

Mariana did not reply. Her whole body tensed, she closed her eyes and made the sign of the cross. Julio was in no hurry to reassure her.

"I'm not carrying a gun," he said after a moment, but still she would not look at him. "I'm not a killer, or a communist, so you needn't be afraid. As I said before, I won't hurt you, but if you don't calm down, I don't see how we can talk business."

"I don't suppose anyone gave you any trouble back in 1939, did they?" he continued "I mean, you'd helped them arrest your cousin's husband... He was quite a catch, a high-profile Red, and that sort of thing mattered back then. But it's not 1939 any more, and this is a serious country, so although your friend Dorita and the nuns of the Convent of the Divine Shepherd may speak highly of you, and I have no reason to doubt their word, you must admit that the situation with this house and the other properties belonging to your uncle and aunt is highly irregular. I'm sure we can work out something to keep everyone happy."

He did not say another word. Two days later, Mariana invited him to

430

lunch so they could talk things over. That afternoon, she herself answered the door. She was wearing a close-fitting dress of maroon velvet with a deep décolletage above which swelled her pale, flabby breasts stippled with a large number of spots. To minimize her remoteness, she had applied red lipstick similar to the shade Paloma had chosen to wear on the night they had gone out – a night that now seemed as if it had happened at the beginning of time. Seeing Julio, Mariana smiled broadly displaying a crimson stained tooth and a brazenness so clumsy she would have been better taking lessons from her daughter. Julio returned her smile, thinking 'I've got you now..."

When Mariana signed the document by which she relinquished all rights and monies in the sale of her Aunt María's olive groves, she did not know that the money Julio would receive, after charges and commissions were paid, would never reach her uncle Matéo. Nor did she imagine that this document would be torn to shreds and tossed into the first rubbish bin her guest happened on as he left the Glorieta de Bilbao.

The disclaimer she had signed was designed merely to reassure her and to give a spurious appearance of legality to the scheme, just as the power of attorney Julio had brought with him from Paris was simply a safeguard. His new friends recommended a course of action more convoluted than the simple sale and purchase of properties which, though it had the drawback of increasing the number of intermediaries, had the advantage of protecting him from any present or future claims. Because not one of the Fernández Muñoz properties still belonged to them by the time there was a series of supposedly public auctions, in a sealed office at 6.30am, each lasting barely two minutes, in which ownership was granted, for a peppercorn sum, to the sole bidder – one Don Julio Carrión González. The resulting deeds detailed many names, but nowhere on them were the names Mateo Fernández Gómez de la Riva, nor that of his wife nor any of the children. By that time, they no longer had any legal claim on lands or dwellings which had been legally expropriated in accordance with a law that had been repealed two years earlier, but which postdated the mysterious dates that appeared on the documentation.

On the day the first document Mariana Fernández Viu signed was tossed into the bin where every subsequent document would end up, Julio Carrión González sold one third of the lands formerly belonging to María Muñoz. The transaction was so favourable that not only was he in a position to settle his debts with Ernesto Huertas, he also decided to settle his account with Freud.

"How are you?" He apporached her under the arches of the Plaza

431

Mayor and she stared at him, open-mouthed, as though she was looking at a ghost.

He had already been here, had been tracking her for weeks, with the patience of a hunter, waiting for the perfect moment. Madrid had changed so much and had not changed at all, and Doña Pilar, his former landlady, was still in residence at her boarding house on the Calle de la Sal, her tongue as loose as it had ever been. In order to know what was going on, however, he had to risk news of his return filtering back, but when he saw her, and saw the way she looked at him, he realised that would not be a problem.

"Where did you spring from, you bastard?"

"Well that's a fine welcome, Mari Carmen!" Julio laughed, and saw the woman who had refused to be the love of his life smile in spite of herself.

Peluca's daughter, who had been such a beautiful girl, had grown up to be an astonishing woman. Mari Carmen Ortega was not as beautiful as Paloma Fernández Muñoz, but she still had the prettiest legs in all of Madrid and a face so passionate it made virtues of her flaws. Before she was twenty, she had had a spectacular body, now, to say she had curves in all the right places would be a shameful understatement.

"It's not that..." she looked him up and down, then with the habitual air of superiority which had once annoyed and now excited him, she said, "It's just that all the marching bands were booked up."

Considering the encounter to be over, Mari Carmen walked on, pretending not to notice that he was walking next to her.

"And where are you going, if you don't mind me asking?" She stopped and stared at him. "I mean, I haven't seen you in a long time and we used to be friends, didn't we? Comrades..."

"Be careful, Julio," Mari Carmen thrust out her chest, stuck out her chin, "Be very careful, don't make me call you a son of a bitch!"

"Jesus, Mari Carmen, you've got some tongue in your mouth!" he laughed again, as though her insults amused him. "My mother was not a bitch, I'll have you know, she was a schoolteacher, a good Republican and a communist, she died of pneumonia in 1941 in a detention centre in Ocaña."

"That's true," she nodded, "And I apologise. To your mother, that is, not to you..."

"That's OK, I accept your apology," he took her by the arm and for a moment she was so surprised she let him, "Now, let's go and have a drink. I'm buying."

"What?" she tried to resist, but he held her arm "You and me go for a

432

drink? Are you joking?" Julio looked at her, nodded and walked on.

By the time he opened the door of the bar on the Calle Mayor, Peluca's daughter had stopped protesting.

"What would you like?"

She didn't answer immediately. Standing at the bar in her simple white blouse and an off-white skirt which was clearly out of fashion, Mari Carmen Ortega felt awkward in this place which Julio had thought was neither too expensive nor too classy. He saw her glance around at the women with their jewellery, taking tea and gossiping.

"I don't know," she said after a moment, "what are you drinking?"

"Brandy," said Julio, " I need to get over the shock of seeing you again."

"No, nothing alcoholic," she ignored the compliment. "I'll have a white coffee and some toast."

"Aren't you conventional!" murmured Julio, signaling to the waiter.

"Or maybe... hang on... I'll have one of those new grilled sandwiches. I'm sure they must have them here, you know, with ham and cheese?"

"I know."

And he knew that he had won, knew it even before he saw her look at her cup, at the waiter, then say in a tone that came from a different age, "Would you be so kind as to bring me another sachet of sugar, please?"

When the waiter brought it, she put it with the other sachet in her handbag.

"You're not going to put any in your coffee?"

"I don't mind either way," she said with a smile, "I don't usually have sugar in coffee. Anyway, that way you can really taste the coffee, and the children like sugar."

Julio ordered another coffee with two sachets of sugar which he gave to her. She smiled and thanked him before stuffing them into her bag.

Then, eating slowly, as though savouring every bite, he asked her a few questions to which he already knew the answers, careful not to reveal his intentions.

"Me? I've only got one, but I'm looking after my sister's daughter, my sister's disappeared and no one knows where she is."

"It's hard work."

"Yes, I have to admit that. I mean, I sort of know how she felt, I can understand why she might have had enough. We've never had things easy, it's hard to find work and a day's pay doesn't go very far. And there's no salary where I work, there's just the three of us, making dresses... Pura was seeing some guy, I know that. She always denied it, because obviously she's still married, and she thought it was seedy, having an affair, even if her husband hasn't written to her in two years..."

"Where is he?"

"France," she shrugged, and made a face, "I mean, I think he's in France. He's probably got someone else, he might be dead for all I know, we haven't heard a thing. That's why I said I know how she must have felt, but walking out like that and leaving her daughter behind... It's not fair on the girl and it's not fair on us."

"What about your husband. Is he in France?"

"No," she laughed, "Antonio's a lot closer to home. He's in prison, in Yeserías, just down the road."

"Still?"

"He got out in 1944, got a job, got me pregnant but before the baby was even weaned, they arrested him again."

"You say it like it's funny."

"No, it's not funny, but what can you do?" Her face was serious, though her tone was still light. "That's life."

"For the good guys."

"Yes," her eyes glinted, "For the good guys."

Mari Carmen Ortega did not know and did not want to know what kind of city, what country, what reality she was living in and Julio Carrión, an expert in cocktails, whores and private rooms, did not waste time attempting to explain it to her.

"What about you, Mari Carmen? Wouldn't you like to change your life?"

He took a wad of banknotes from his wallet, and put a hundred-peseta bill on the bar, and another, then another. He had expected her to be angry, and she was angry. What he had not expected was that she would misunderstand the nature of his offer.

"What do you take me for?"

Her tone was shocked, but she was not shouting. Then she got up, her back straight, her chest out, her head high, and began to scream at him:

"You think I'd inform? I'm not some grass, some traitor like you, Julio. I'd rather starve, I'd rather beg in the streets, I'd rather die than betray my own, you'll get nothing out of me, understand? I won't be bought..."

"That's not what I meant, Mari Carmen..." Julio took her arm, and pulled her to him. "What do you take me for? I'm not with the police, I've nothing to do with the police, I don't care what you know and what you don't... I was talking about something completely different. And, forgive me for saying this, but you look like a complete fool."

Mari Carmen took a moment to react. Slowly, she sat back down on the barstool, sipped her coffee, and smiled to herself.

"Oh, so it's the other…" she said shaking her head as though she could hardly believe it, "You want to sleep with me, is that it?"

"Yes," he said, thinking that he had nothing to lose.

"Jesus Christ," she laughed, "After everything that's happened you still want to sleep with me."

"What do you expect? I'm a one-woman man."

"Really…?" Mari Carmen laughed again, she was nervous and she was flattered by the fact he still wanted her, but neither her nervousness nor her vanity stopped her from picking up the money on the bar so quickly he was taken aback. "Well, I'll take this for the moment, and I'll think about it."

"Take my phone number, that way you can call me." He scribbled his number on a business card, "I usually go home for a siesta and I never go out before 7pm."

"All right. But I don't think it's likely," she took the card and put it in her purse.

And then, the prettiest pair of legs in Madrid walked away, taking her astonishing body with them. As he watched her go, Julio replayed the scene as though it had happened to someone else and found himself with a quaint moral dilemma. Though the integrity that had prompted Mari Carmen's fury was strange, Julio Carrión knew that it was not feigned: she would genuinely prefer to starve than to betray one of her own. But her integrity had not stopped her from taking three hundred pesetas from under his nose as an advance against possible favours she might just as easily have granted him for considerably less. But even if she did, Mari Carmen, had never been fickle. Julio had seen her with more than one man, but he knew that she had been faithful to each of them until she slept with the next. And since her marriage there had been no one else as far as Doña Pilar knew, and in such matters she was as all-knowing as the Almighty. Strange woman, thought Julio, and then he thought of Eugenio and laughed. It would not have occurred to him to introduce Mari Carmen Ortega to his old friend, but he realised that were he to do so, Eugenio would probably think her decent, even admirable, a real hero. It was a foolish idea, obviously, but he might introduce her to Romualdo…

Mari Carmen Ortega had told him she would not call him, and she did not call, but ten days later she showed up at his place at 6pm.

"No kissing," she said, standing in the doorway.

"Like the whores?"

"Exactly." She stepped inside, put her bag on the sofa and looked at him. "That's what I am, isn't it? A whore. But I'm a better person than you and I don't want either of us to forget it."

"You are…" Julio caught her around the waist, then ran his hand slowly over her breasts, her shoulders, her arms, "You are the better person, Mari Carmen, but you're totally screwed."

That afternoon, Julio Carrión González settled his scores and put the finishing touches to his plan.

The remaining stages of the plan proceeded slowly and without incident until the last storm of the summer of 1949, when Mariana Fernández Viu reluctantly climbed into the taxi, along with her daughter. Angélica, who was only fourteen, was the only character able to play a role other than the one Julio Carrión had assigned to her.

"Where are you going?" her mother called, as her daughter clambered out of the moving taxi, the rain dashing against the windscreen. "Angélica! Come back here!"

"I forgot something, Mamá," the girl did not turn, "I won't be a minute."

Still leaning against one of the stone columns, smoking, Julio Carrión watched her rush back, but he thought nothing of it. Angélica was an only child, she had always been spoiled, impulsive, disobedient, she always did as she pleased. She knew nothing of Julio's last conversation with Mariana, had not heard her mother's vicious insults and Julio's cold indifference. And yet, this young girl knew something that he could not have guessed.

"Angélica!" Mariana opened the car door, stuck out her leg, but did not dare get out. "I said come back here at once!" But her daughter had already reached the top of the steps.

"Come with me," she grabbed Julio's hand and dragged him inside, "I forgot something."

In the hallway, she pushed him against the wall. What happened next did not seem like much, and it was over very quickly, but before her mother had time to call to her again, Angélica closed her eyes, kissed Julio hard on the lips and ran out.

In mid-July the countdown began.

"What's the matter?" I'd ask Raquel from time to time.

"Nothing," she'd say, and I didn't believe her, but I hugged her and saw her smile.

Her smiles were not different from those I had seen before, but now there was something new, a kind of insistence that made them linger just a second longer than necessary. The same was true of her kisses and of the sudden urge that compelled her to hug me as we were walking down the street. I know it should have worried me, but at the time I barely noticed, because aside from these subtle changes, Raquel expressed no doubts, showed no sign of tiring of me. On the contrary, what I most noticed about her was an absorption, an intensity in her most serious and her most frivolous gestures, the way she stroked my face as though attempting to leave some indelible trace, the sentences left unfinished, her wide eyes studying me as though trying to memorise ever line, every detail, every wrinkle of my face.

I noticed and interpreted these clues, but I was wrong about every one. I would probably never have guessed their real significance, but other factors conspired to mislead me. The most important was my particular interpretation of the relative speed of time. If the Whole had been merciless to me, Time was more cruel still, stripping me of everything I had once known, of every scrap of knowledge, all my suspicions, my intuitions, my certainties. The calendar was no use. I knew how to read it, I knew that if sex counts as the beginning, then my affair with Raquel began on 22 April, but even the date – '22 April' – was just words, meaningless words in some altered reality.

"What's wrong, Raquel?"

"Nothing." she looked at me and smiled, "Honestly, there's nothing wrong."

I matched her smile, her silence, with my own, never saying what I never found the right moment to say – 'Of course there's something wrong, and I know what it is'. Looking at the pages of a calendar, not only did our situation not seem tragic, it looked as though it might still aspire to the breezy foolishness that is the first flush of love. But our lives were not lived in the pages of a calendar but on a tightrope which every day grew more taut, which had begun to flay our feet. This is what I felt, what Raquel must have felt: we had exhausted our resources, cut every corner, and time was running out.

On one of the many surreal mornings when I arrived back at my own house, feeling strangely as though overseeing the team of builders was my sole occupation, I discovered a package from the Registry Office in Madrid in the letterbox, containing the death certificate of my grandmother, Teresa González Puerto, deceased on 14 June 1941, in the famous Ocaña penitentiary just as Encarnita had said. The certificate specified the immediate cause of death – cardiac arrest – and the secondary cause – pneumonia, the result of tuberculosis. It also indicated her date of birth, her marital status, the fact that she was a prisoner, and her age – she was forty. She would have been forty-one on 3 August, but she did not live to see it.

Two days later, in the same letterbox, I found a class photograph, some fifty pupils posing with their teachers, and two good quality enlargements; one of Teresita Carrión González, with her hair in pigtails wearing a spotless school smock, and a second one of my grandmother, her hair loose, standing next to Manuel Castro. Inside the envelope was a short, affectionate note from Encarnita's daughter in which she apologised for the delay, explaining that it was because her mother had been upset after my visit. "It was two weeks before I could get the photo away from her."

For my part, I had not stopped thinking about my grandmother. Every time I was surprised by the peculiar lack of feeling, the guilt of the cheating husband that should have kept me from sleeping at night, I wondered if she had felt something similar, whether, when she looked at her husband, my grandfather, she felt the slight uneasiness, almost annoyance together with a vague feeling of pity that I felt when I looked at my wife. It was possible that, when this photograph was taken, this freedom fighter was no longer free. Maybe she had already sacrificed her freedom to this man who stood gazing at her as though she was the only woman in the world. Going into the house, I placed the photo Encarnita had sent me next to the bland portrait which stared back at me from its silver frame.

That morning, Mai arrived to see how the work was going. She came during her lunch break every two or three days, and never stayed longer than ten minutes or so.

"It's like a madhouse!" She hugged me and laughed. "I don't know how you get any work done."

"This is nothing! The jackhammer in the early stages was much worse!"

The Poles were conscientious and hardworking, and I had no problems with them. Mai was thrilled with the results, and talked about

438

them on the way back to her office. Sometimes we had lunch together, sometimes with Angélica, sometimes just the two of us, and recently for reasons she never quite explained, Mai sometimes had a little extra free time. On one of these afternoons, she skipped dessert, ordered coffee with an ice cube so she could drink it immediately, smiled at me and wondered aloud whether I might not reschedule by half an hour, since the library was hardly likely to be invaded by hordes of knowledge-hungry physicists mercilessly commandeering every book I needed.

At which point, my body suffered something akin to frostbite. It was the middle of summer, the weather was warm, but I felt my blood drain away and my veins fill up with some icy, metallic gas. But I would smile, and everything would be fine. It had to be fine, since Mai was still looking at me with the same expectant smile she had when giving Miguelito a surprise present. "I thought you might enjoy a less – um – cerebral *siesta*" I realised that that was precisely what she was doing: giving me a surprise present. And I tried to behave like a well-mannered child, I was effusive in my thanks, displaying a gallantry that at the time she did not find suspect.

These impromptu quickies had the virtue of being so infrequent that it was as though my wife and my mistress had swapped roles, and were also impeded by the collusion of the Polish builders, hammering, pounding and drilling, and chattering in a foreign language on the other side of the bedroom door.

"I suppose it is difficult to concentrate here these days," Mai admitted.

I nodded enthusiastically and continued applying myself to this bizarre exercise in concentration until I had delivered satisfactory results, although it was beginning to require more and more effort on my part.

Mai didn't seem to notice that anything was wrong. At first, the state of frenzied excitement aroused in me by the mere existence of Raquel meant that conjugal duties were no problem. Later, my cock became a little more demanding, but by then the pressure of this professorship I was working towards came to my rescue. In the end, even during the act itself, I would feel the terrible void of the holidays looming and start to tremble but even then Mai seemed to see nothing worrying about my sudden lack of muscle tone. Raquel, on the other hand, recognised the symptoms.

"You've been fucking your wife."

She would guess even before I stepped inside, as she stood in the doorway.

"No," I'd lie brazenly. After all, how could she know?

"Yes…" She would step aside to let me in, close the door, put her arms around me and gaze deeply into my eyes. "Yes you fucking have."

"How can you tell?"

"Because… I can tell. I can smell it, Álvaro."

"I've just had a shower."

"You see? That's how I can tell."

"I took a shower because it's five o'clock, its sweltering outside, and I knew I had to walk here," I explained, adopting my most scholarly tone.

"OK. And because you've just been fucking your wife."

"No."

"Yes." Her certainty rattled me, I was so angry that she was right, that I responded with the abrupt and insolent logic of a child.

"If you're going to be like that, I'm going home." But she just laughed harder.

"You don't have to go. I've got TV. And I've got microwave popcorn…"

Bt we didn't turn on the TV, we didn't microwave the popcorn, we went to bed, and we fucked, and we fucked because the Earth turned in her bed, because Time, molten and shifting, suspended the laws of physics in this bed where we made love, and because I loved this woman, loved her so much that afterwards, when she lay serene and silent next to me, I could calculate with blinding, almost painful accuracy, the precise nature of fate.

Happiness is priceless. There is no task, no effort, no blame, no problem, that cannot be overcome when the goal is happiness. I knew this because I had been intimately familiar with greyness during my years of poverty, those years of believing my life was a life and that it was mine. So, when Raquel sat up and looked at me, and when I saw in her eyes a light that was the same and yet different, I realised that this sudden insistence had initiated the countdown, and I knew what I had to do, what I would do.

And yet there was something else. There was something more, something unrelated to Raquel, something beyond the scope of those looks that terrified me, insisting that I never again look at another woman. There was something more, but it was far beyond Madrid, outside this city, away from this refuge which gradually faded as my car carried me closer to Castellana, away from her, to a place that seemed increasing alien and strange, a place that made me ache me even before my son came running down the gravel driveway towards me like a bull out of a pen.

"Papá!" he yelled. I crouched down beside the garage and flung my arms wide.

"Miguelito!" He leapt frantically into my arms, trying to knock me down.

I had begun to understand my brother Julio a little better, his embarrassing, almost maternal love for his children, his constant, systematic self-denial designed to reassure them that he would always be their father, that they could always count on him, even when their respective mothers were no more than faint notches on his gun belt. It made my brother seem simultaneously more noble and more grudging although it was good for his kids, obviously - and maybe that was the only thing that was important. Because one Sunday that summer, I no longer knew what to think of him, or me, or anything.

I had arrived at La Moraleja before lunch with a plan that I implemented as soon as I arrived. I put on my swimming trunks and went to find Mai at the pool. She was lying with her eyes closed, tanning herself, and she smiled when she felt my finger slowly travel down her body from her collarbone to her belly button. She sat up and said my name, and everything went according to plan. I hadn't reckoned on Julio being there, so I didn't pay him any attention when we sat down to lunch, Mai smiling and still flushed, me as happy as I was when I was a kid, after I'd done my homework and knew I could spend all day Sunday playing. I casually told Mai that I had to go back to Madrid that night, then she went for a siesta with Miguelito. While I was settling myself on the porch to read the paper, my brother stopped me.

"What's her name?" he asked out of the blue.

"Who?"

"The girl who's got you so worked up."

"Julio!"

I sat up with a jolt, looked around but saw we were alone.

"Don't worry, everyone else is taking a nap." He laughed, and proffered one of the cuba libres he was holding. "Let's try again: what's her name?"

"How did you know?"

"Álvaro, please! I'm the expert in this family."

"Her name is Raquel, but tell me how you knew."

"You're fairly good at hiding it, if that's what you're worried about." We heard a door close somewhere inside the house, and Julio dropped his voice to a whisper. "I wasn't completely sure, to be honest. I've thought you were behaving oddly, but what with the professorship and the fact that you always were a bit odd... But this morning... it was glaringly obvious, Álvaro..."

"What was?" I knew exactly what he was saying, but I wasn't sure how he had spotted it.

"The defensive fuck." It was so funny, I laughed in spite of myself.

"Attack is the best form of defence," I said, and he nodded.

"Absolutely, no doubt about it. Do you know how often I've pulled that one? The spur-of-the-moment fuck to make sure I had the evening free, or the morning after fuck so I'd be forgiven before anyone started asking awkward questions? Best thing you can do – a quick, hot-blooded fuck. Works every time. When I saw you down at the pool, I thought, *ah-ha!* And the best thing is, we're only too happy to fuck them."

"Who?" I was still laughing.

"Our wives, who do you think?"

"I'm not." Suddenly I was serious, and I saw the worry in his eyes. "I mean, maybe it's because I'm odd, but more and more I'm finding I don't want to."

"That's worse, Álvaro," He came over and squeezed my shoulder, "Or better, depending how you look at it…"

The conversation left a bad taste in my mouth. I had never wanted to be like my father, nor did I want to be like my brother Julio, and yet I was starting to understand him, I thought about him when I was with Miguelito, I found I was more attentive to my son, and enjoyed my time with him more. Miguelito hadn't yet turned five, and, by the time he grew up, he would have only the vaguest memory of this summer, but I did my best to make sure my unconditional love was a part of that memory because sometimes, when I looked at him, I would unintentionally imagine myself with other children, mine and Raquel's, and suddenly I felt a surge of pain and guilt, all the feelings Mai could not stir in me. This was why, when I arrived at La Moraleja, the first thing I did was crouch down, arms wide, and wait for him to throw himself at me.

There we stood on the porch, my whole family – or what I thought of as my whole family – my mother, my brothers, my sisters and their wives, their husbands, all happy to see me. And then I suddenly remembered what I knew and what I did not want to know, what I had wanted to forget and should not have forgotten, what Fernando Cisneros had noticed and what I had suspected. Raquel's voice when she said I looked at her the way my father did. And I realised that the best thing, perhaps the only thing, would be if I never found out what had brought together my father and the woman I loved.

Then my mother kissed me, my wife kissed me, my brothers kissed me and we missed him, we would always miss him, our grief was a part

442

of us, as I settled into telling them how well my life was going. "You must be thrilled, Mamá, having a son who might be a professor..." Clara said. My mother looked at me and nodded, but I knew it did not matter to her. What was surprising was that it no longer mattered to me, because Raquel Fernández Perea had come into my life, as fate or death might come into your life.

And yet I sensed my father's ghost more strongly in his house than anywhere else, a place I could be sure Raquel had never been, where she was his mistress, not mine. My grandparents wedding photo still hung in the same place, Teresa, young and confident, smiling broadly for the camera; the photo of my grandmother Mariana, who had not a whit of mystery about her, hugging my older brothers and sisters. I had never really looked at it before. I studied their faces, looked carefully at Mai and at my mother, and suddenly I saw Raquel, young, naked, slipping into the arms of an old man in a jacuzzi surrounded by candles, and the image was so shocking, so unbearable, that I could not reconcile it with my memories. I started to choke, I felt as though I was suffocating so I went to find Miguelito, to take him to buy sweets, to play football at the bottom of the garden, anything to get as far away as possible from this porch.

I thought that was enough but one afternoon, Lisette came down to the pool to talk to me. She was wearing one of those Brazilian bikinis that all but gave Julio a heart attack, and she was carrying Clara's baby. She did not say anything until Miguelito was in the water, out of earshot.

"Álvaro, baby, what's the matter? I can tell something's up." Her smile was mischievous, almost malicious.

"I don't know," I said, "What kind of thing?"

"You don't look at me any more."

"I'm looking at your right now, Lisette."

"I know, but you don't look at me the way you used to."

"Oh, I see..." I smiled back at her, "Well, I'll try and do better in future..."

It was a Wednesday, one of my nephews birthdays, which was why I had come down to La Moraleja. I had been thinking of staying the night – so I would not have to stay on Saturday night, but Lisette's comments had unsettled me and I couldn't find the energy to make love to Mai before I left.

"Jesus, this is a complete bitch." Staring at my mobile, I wandered over to Mai just as the strains of 'Happy Birthday' died away, "This is going to sound stupid, but I have to get back to Madrid tonight. I've just remembered that I've got a meeting with the director of the museum at half eight tomorrow morning."

"In July?" My wife's expression was less surprised than sardonic.

"It's a planning meeting for next term's courses," I came back coolly.

"But surely you can go straight from here," she said, "I mean, it's not much farther than it is from our place."

"I know, but the meeting is at the headquarters of the bank," I could see that she wasn't convinced. "José Ignacio just sent me a text to remind me."

Mai did not say anything, but she gave me a cold look, the first, and I thought this was bound to happen sooner or later. This was why I hadn't blamed my quick getaway on the pressures of work or my nervousness at my fictitious but hugely useful application for professorship. I never forgot important meetings, as my wife knew only too well having lived with me for almost ten years. I didn't want to say any more, but I grabbed a phone and a sandwich and went into the bathroom to call José Ignacio before I left, because I knew that Mai would call him as soon as I was out of sight.

"Put a sock in it, Álvaro," he said before I'd even had time to explain.

"Please, José Ignacio, just this once. I've never asked you to do anything like this before."

"I don't like the idea."

"I know, but I'm not asking you to lie, or to make something up… all you have to do is say yes. A simple answer to a simple question, that's all. I'm not even sure that Mai will phone you."

He agreed, half-heartedly, and I felt a surge of joy entirely disproportionate to the favour he was doing for me, an intense feeling of euphoria so powerful that when I turned to leave the toilet and caught my reflection in the mirror, the man staring back was younger, brighter, and more handsome than I was. I did not try to understand the phenomenon, nor the unexpected transcendence I felt at the prospect of an encounter which, if I had postponed it by less than twenty-four hours, would have spared me asking any favours and arousing my wife's suspicion. But need cannot be explained, and I needed to see Raquel, although I had had lunch with her that day, although we had gone to bed together afterwards, although it had been barely three hours and forty-five minutes since I had left her.

Coming out of the toilet, I grabbed another sandwich, said a general goodbye to everyone, and kissed Mai on the cheek since she would not turn her face towards me.

Lisette walked me to the door, and her smile reminded me what had triggered this pointless, extraordinary panic. So although I took no pleasure in doing so, I gazed at Lisette for a long minute, and then asked: "Better?"

"No," she laughed.

She was still shaking her head as I climbed into the car. I thought about phoning Raquel before I hit the motorway to tell her about my change of plans, but José Ignacio phoned before I could.

"How long since you left the house?" I couldn't tell him precisely, only that I was still stuck in traffic outside La Moraleja.

"I don't know, four minutes, maybe five, I'm not sure...'

"OK, well I've just got off the phone with Mai..."

"Really?" I was shocked, "So, how are things..."

"What do you mean how are things?" José Ignacio was whispering so that his own wife wouldn't hear, but I could tell he was angry. "They're shit, Álvaro, completely shit OK? Because I lied to her, I lied because you asked me to, but I'm happy about it... Apart from anything else, I'm a terrible liar. So listen to me, this was a one-off. Next time..."

"Don't worry, José Ignacio," I cut him off, "There won't be a next time."

In the silence that followed I realised that not only had he heard what I had said, he had understood.

"You're moving out?" he asked, his tone neutral.

"No, not yet," I reassured him before casually blurting out a decision I was not sure I had yet made, "But I don't think I'll last the summer."

"For God's sake, Álvaro."

He asked me to promise not to do anything stupid and I promised, I didn't bother to remind him that he had been married three times, that his first wife had left him for another man, and that he had left his second wife to live with his third; I just thanked him and hung up.

"I've just come from my mother's house, and I haven't fucked anyone. Smell me if you like..." Raquel was waiting for me at the door.

"No," she smiled, "I don't need to. The thing about the smell is just a metaphor, Álvaro."

When I arrived, she was eating caramel ice cream and drinking whiskey on the rocks. "It's a great combination," she said, offering me some. I accepted and told her about Lisette, I told her what Julio had said the first time he saw her and how right he had been, I described how Lisette greeted me when my mother or my wife was around and how different she was when it was just the two of us. I told her about that summer day two years earlier when something would have happened between us if Clara hadn't wandered into the kitchen just as Lisette was showing me how to make mayonnaise, our right hands on the whisk as she held my other hand to show me how to drizzle the oil.

"And did you learn?" Raquel laughed.

"No, she's not a very good teacher. She was too interested in what was going on behind her back."

"What about you?"

"I was happy to let it drop. Anyway, this afternoon, Lisette complained to me that I don't look at her the same way any more."

"Really?" Raquel sounded surprised.

"Yes. I thought it was some sort of bluff so when she walked me to the door, I stared at her, but she just said no, it wasn't the same."

She didn't say anything, but she came back to the sofa, took my head in her hands, pressed it back against the cushion and kissed me slowly, languidly with such attentiveness that it was as if time rolled backwards and she was twenty again, a fresh and tender peach, still ripening on the bough. And that's when it happened. That's when I remembered that I could never leave this woman, nor could I ever imagine allowing some other imbecile into her life. All I wanted was to grow old with her, to see her face every morning when I woke up and every night before I fell asleep. These were not just words to me anymore, clichés drained of meaning through centuries of use by other men and women. But I could no longer think this because thought is the enemy of action, and I couldn't think any more.

"Maybe we should do something?" I said, as she drew back. "We can't go on like this forever, Raquel."

"Are you asking me to run away with you?"

"Well..." I said, smiling, "I don't know about running away... I like Madrid."

"So do I."

"But I'd like it even more if we were living together."

That's it, I've done it I thought, as she kissed me again and I responded to her kisses. I've done it! I surrendered to her tender kisses, her eyes shone with a gleam akin to tears to an emotion that stung my eyes and I kept thinking I've done it!

I had done it. I didn't care about anything else. I didn't care that my decision had been triggered by a trivial event, or that it would turn my life upside down, the only thing that mattered was the explosion, the cataclysm, I needed to smell the gunpowder that would explode my world. I needed to feel in my flesh the teeth marks of that joy that pronounced it dead. Nothing else mattered, as long as I could feel Raquel's lips on mine, feel her fingers caress me, her arms hold me as though fusing her body with mine. This was what I felt, and it seemed so reasonable, so fair, as to quash the doubts, and fears, the callous self-justifications of men who were not like me. Because at that moment I dared everything, I knew everything, I was master of everything.

I was master of everything until Raquel drew back so she could look at me, and I realised that what I had seen in her eyes was not the glow of unconditional joy I had imagined, but of real tears.

"Say something," I begged her, though I already knew that it was bad.

"What do you want me to say?"

"Say yes."

"You want me to tell you that I love you, Álvaro?" she smiled, "That I want to live with you, that I'm in love with you, that I can't bear the thought of you being with another woman? Is that what you want me to say?"

"For example..." I stroked her face with my fingertips.

"Well then I've said it. Because it's true, Álvaro, everything I've said is true."

"Well, then, that's it."

"What?"

"Let's go away together, Raquel, let's leave now, as soon as you can get time off, we'll go wherever you want to go. I'm rich, remember?"

"Yes, but..."

"But what?"

"It's not that simple." She fell silent. "I'm just surprised, because... We've never talked about it. We were together here this afternoon, you were right here, and you never said anything and now suddenly, you come out with all this..."

"I know, but it makes sense, doesn't it?" I realised that it was not in my interest to lose my cool. "We've never talked about it, but we both knew it was coming, Raquel, we knew it was bound to happen some day."

"Yes, but not so quickly... we've only been seeing each other for three months, and I thought... I thought we'd carry on like this, the way things are now, for much longer."

"What do you mean, the way things are now?" and I was surprised to hear my voice had grown hard, "Sleeping together every night, like we do now or meeting up in the afternoons like we did a month ago, or seeing each other occasionally the way we did at the beginning? How exactly did you think we would carry on?" She did not look at me as I spoke and this made me angry. "Or do you want something else, Raquel? You want me to set you up in an apartment so I can come round after lunch on Wednesdays to fuck you? Is that what..."

447

"No!" she screamed, throwing herself at me, her voice almost a howl. "That's not what I want, I want to live with you, Álvaro, I love you, but I can't... not right now... I need time, I need a bit more time."

"Time for what?" I put my hands on her shoulders and looked into her face. "I'm the one who's got something to lose, Raquel. I'm the one who's married, who has to deal with the fights, the arguments, the lawyers... Me, not you." She felt weak and limp in my arms. "I don't understand you... I always thought that women were supposed to be brave."

"Really? What gave you that idea?" she had slipped her arms around me again, pressed her face against mine.

"I don't know," I said, smiling. Suddenly, the whole thing felt ridiculous. "Magazines, television, women writers..."

"The sort of writers who claim married men never leave their wives."

"Exactly."

"Well, they're wrong." Her kisses had a poisonous tenderness. "They're wrong about you."

"No, I'm the one who's wrong. I was wrong about you."

"That's not true, Álvaro. I swear it's not true," she said, pouting like a little girl.

"Really? Then let's go away!" I don't know where I found this last gasp of hope, "Let's go away and never come back, Raquel. Why not? I don't understand. Things are easy for you, but I can't go on like this – you don't have to lie, you don't have to go away on holiday with someone you don't love anymore, you don't have to explain yourself to anybody."

"I had to explain myself to you."

Slowly, she got up, but though my legs were numb, I could still feel the weight of her body against them like an premonition. I watched her wander across the bedroom, heard the sound of ice clinking and watched her come back, a pale shadow of herself, weak, ashen.

"I'm still waiting..." I said, as she sat in an armchair facing me.

"For what?" she said, after draining half the glass in a single mouthful.

"For your reasons"

She began to cry softly, silently, like the tears I had seen her cry one night as we walked along the Calle Carranza together.

"I love you, Álvaro. It's true. It's one of the few things I know for certain, I love you so much that I couldn't bear the thought of you... hating me, or despising me, I couldn't bear for you to feel miserable or humiliated because of me. That's why I need time to make sense of things, of …" she didn't finish the sentence, but looked at me almost fearfully, as though she sensed the cataclysm that would be triggered by her words, the very words that she had refused to utter since we first discovered that the Earth turned beneath our feet. "I was your father's lover, Álvaro."

"Leave my father out of this, Raquel!" I was so angry that I jumped up. "My father is dead. Dead and buried. He's dead, and I'm alive. I don't give a fuck about my father, got that? I don't give a fuck what you and he you got up to with that dildo I found while you were watching your carefully catalogued porn films…"

She did not react, she did not speak, and I felt so alone, so abandoned, that I barely knew who I was any more. I knew the best thing to do would be to shut up. I knew it, but it didn't matter because she wouldn't even look at me. Don't do that Raquel, don't, please. I had offered her everything and she had rejected it, so I succumbed to self-pity. I wanted to ask her why she had dragged me away from the humble, passionless patch of garden that was my life, why she had taken me to such heights only to drop me. I longed to ask her, but I couldn't bring myself to, so I said things I should never have said, things that I had tried to blot from my mind.

"You want to know the truth? You want me to play truth or dare with you? OK, well, let me tell you something, Raquel, the fact that you slept with my father does bother me, it fucking kills me. It kills me to think you could fuck that geriatric millionaire in that bath surrounded by little candles. I feel disgusted and ashamed just thinking about that tasteless apartment, I feel disgusted just thinking about you and my father and that fucking dildo, it's pathetic, Raquel, it's completely repulsive. Do you take me for a idiot? Well I am an idiot, because I fell in love with you, and I just decided to accept it…"

Only when I had stopped shouting was I able to think again. That's it, was what I thought, it's over. I've had my whiff of gunpowder, I've seen everything explode, and I couldn't even blame her.

Raquel had curled into a ball, slowly folding in on herself as I screamed at her, like the maniac. I was trembling with rage, with pain, with shame, with helplessness, and with love.

"I'm so sorry, Raquel." I waited for a moment for a reply that ever came. "Honestly, I'm truly sorry. I should never have said those things, I'm not like that, I… I don't know what came over me, but I'm truly sorry, I swear… Please forgive me."

As I walked towards the door, I was convinced that it was all over, but suddenly she got to her feet, and threw herself in front of it, as though crucified there.

"Don't leave, Álvaro, please..." Finally, she looked up at me. She seemed desperate, baffled by her own pain "I'm begging you, don't go..." she launched herself at me and gripped me with such force that it would have hurt, if I had still been capable of feeling pain. "Don't go, Álvaro, please, don't leave like this. Forgive me, I need you to forgive me..." Gradually she released her hold, still murmuring this soft, frenetic litany in which she seemed to find some small consolation.

I was stunned, dazed, shaken, but I had come alive again and Raquel did not realise it. She grabbed my sleeves, gently this time, almost fearfully, and slumped down until she was sitting on the floor. I looked down at her for a moment, then helped her to her feet, hugged her with every ounce of strength I possessed and told her that I loved her, I loved her, I loved her.

'The number you have dialled does not exist.'

"Come on, señorita..." The first time I heard the message, I thought of Fernando Cisneros, remembered his most surprising, furious, fit of stubbornness. "No, I know it's not your voice, of course I know you didn't say it, I know it's a recorded message..." We were at the university bar, he had misdialled a number, but he deliberately misdialled again. "I can't believe it!" he said, "This is unacceptable," then, determined to speak to someone, anyone, he dialled directory enquiries, and kept dialling until he happened on some poor girl who had clearly never had to deal with anyone like him before. "Of course it's important, it's extremely important, because I can assure that the number in question *does* exist, it has existed since the dawn of time, from the moment man first crawled from the primeval ooze..." José Ignacio looked over at me and brought his finger to his temple. "Let it go, Fernando," I said but he wasn't listening. "What do you mean 'just a turn of phrase'? No I'm afraid I can't possibly accept that as an excuse. There's no point telling me you don't know what I mean. It's very simple. The first digit, 9, is the number of units and 9 exists, the 1 is the tens, and that exists, the 6 is the hundreds and 6 exists, 7 is the number of thousands and that exists..." He stopped suddenly, held the received away from his face and gave a look of comic distress. "She hung up on me," he muttered. "I'm not surprised, said José Ignacio. "What do you mean, you're not surprised?" He pointed at us, drawing an imaginary circle around us. "Come on, you're not going to tell me that this sort of thing doesn't matter to you? What's going on, am I the only champion of popular science left round here?"

*'The number you have dialled does not exist.'*

The first time I heard the message, I thought I had dialled a wrong number, but I didn't blindly persist as Fernando had done. I looked up Raquel's number in my contacts list, made sure it was highlighted and pressed the green 'dial' button. Usually I didn't do this, because I enjoyed pressing the digits of her phone number, but I didn't want to risk hearing that the number did not exist a second time. And yet that is what I heard, once, twice, three times.

The weather that day was more than cloudy, it was vile, and by noon it had started to drizzle. Miguelito was irritable at the thought of another day at the beach ruined in this tiny village on the Cantabrian coast where he had spent every summer. Mai liked spending summers at Comillas, where her mother's family was from and she uncomplainingly accepted, almost prized the panoply of greys that marked the Cantabrian sky. Personally, I had never seen the appeal of the place which was why, much as I enjoyed Fernando Cisneros's company (he was much less negative about the traditional summer haunts of our collective in-laws), I hadn't yet decided to invest our savings in any of the series of houses Mai spent every August finding. Instead, we went on renting an apartment – not very big, but big enough – on the second floor of a building that belonged to Mai's parents.

Comillas had been the one major problem in our relationship back when I had no problem with our marriage. However, the sudden elimination of the second proposition quietly solved the first, and Mai made no mention of looking at properties as we left Madrid. We drove in silence, Miguelito sleeping, Mai saying nothing, simply feeding disc after disc into the CD player. I was distant, absorbed in contemplating the depth and number of my wounds and the nebulous state brought on by the sudden, terrifying remoteness of Raquel. However even the considerable energy needed to feed my misery was not enough to hide the glaringly obvious, and to Mai, who had been a stranger through the upheavals in my life these past months, it had become glaringly obvious.

Everything's gone wrong, I thought as we headed north. It had all gone wrong. And I thought that maybe I should have stayed in Madrid. I had almost stayed behind, but at the last minute, I had thought of my son.

I was no longer certain of anything, all I knew was that my life would never be the same again, and that Miguel was the only constant that would survive in the new landscape after the destruction of the old. I'd often imagined scenes, desks, notes, dossiers, strangers coming and going in a corridor, like shadows stripped of their owners. I had imagined these things, moreover I had prepared myself for them, steeled myself for what was to come, because at the end of the tunnel, beyond the cacophony of shock and resentment, Raquel was waiting, the love of my life. I was a good boy, a good son, a good husband, a good citizen, yet now I was prepared be stripped of these medals, to become a topic for gossips and scandalmongers, to be labelled a scumbag, to ruin myself financially and do it willingly because I had was in love with a woman who loved me and that made me brave, decent, good, innocent. It was precisely because I had already decided how the rest of my life would pan out, that Raquel's distance crushed me. Her confusion and ambivalence which had seemed impulsive at the time now seemed to have a certain lucidity, a compelling logic that hurt me more than I could have imagined.

All the same, when confronted with the dilemma of the holidays, I had a choice, and I chose Miguelito. If I was going to walk out on my marriage, I wasn't going to do it until the time was right, I wasn't about to give opposing counsel ammunition. I remember thinking that, I remember that very expression 'opposing counsel', and a second later I felt sick, I felt vile, cynical, a traitor. A traitor going on holiday behind enemy lines, prepared to do anything if it would further the cause of my treachery.

"It's not that I don't understand that it's harder for you than it is for me," Raquel stirred up her doubts and my certainties after a night that was terrible and magnificent. "I understand, Álvaro, honestly I do. And the worst thing is, you're absolutely right, but this is the way I am and there's nothing I can do about it... I know I'm not being very clear, but I need time. I told you before, sometimes I can't handle things, you remember?" I nodded, I remembered. "It's just... everything is so fucked up. Because if I've fucked up, it was with your father. If there's one thing in my life I regret, it's that. But if I hadn't done it, I'd never have met you, Álvaro, I'd never have fallen in love with you."

"And what am I supposed to do?" I looked at her and realised, stripped of the rage that had fuelled it, all the resolve of the previous night had abandoned me. A few hours earlier, I had wanted an unconditional surrender, now I was so weak I was prepared to settle for anything as long as I did not lose her. "What do you want me to do?"

"Wait," she closed her eyes, "Wait until I find... There must be a way to get through this, and I need to think...'

"What?" I took her hands and squeezed them, "to get through what?"

"You said it yourself last night. You said that the thought of me being with your father disgusted you, and I knew it. Remember, I said it myself, that night when you told me about your grandmother. I asked what you must think of me and you said 'I think the world of you'. But that's not what you thought last night, Álvaro..."

"Okay..." I laid her hands on the table. "You want me to wait, so I'll wait. I don't want to talk about it any more, I'm not exactly proud of ..."

"...of telling the truth?" A flash of irony suddenly lit up her dark, trembling face.

"It's not the truth, Raquel."

"It is."

"No, it's true, but it's not the truth. The truth is that I love you, that's the only truth that matters, and you come with baggage, your past, your successes, your mistakes. I'm not a better person than you, there are lots of things I'm ashamed of, including what I said last night."

Excellent, Álvaro, you've behaved like a gentleman, I thought, as Raquel took both my hands and kissed them.

I had behaved like a gentleman, and I knew it, but this irony was bitter, corrosive and powerful. I loved a woman who loved me, and that made me decent, pure, good, innocent. I loved a woman who loved me and who may not have been lying to me, but she was not telling me the whole truth and that was worse. And the worst thing was, I didn't dare ask her.

These thoughts hung in the air after that serene and sunny conversation. I behaved like a gentleman and she like a lady and both of us were keenly aware of the kid gloves. Nine days later, we said goodbye, having fixed no firm date when we would see each other again. Raquel went to Málaga to spend two weeks at the beach with her two grandmothers. "They've been friends since they were little girls, and now that they're both widows, my grandmother from Madrid spends the summer with my grandmother in Málaga. I go every year, I love spending time with them, because they spoil me. I take them out, drive them around, take them to a Chinese restaurant. I don't think either of my grandfathers ever set foot inside the place, but my grandmothers love Chinese food..."

I listened to her talk, heard her describe this heart-warming film, adult themes, but suitable for all audiences. She looks so cute, so young, so innocent, I thought, and so I smiled and didn't tell her what I planned to do for the holidays, a film rather different from her romantic chick-flick, a bleak drama set in a gray building overlooking a blustery stretch of beach, an overcast sky, the little boy playing with his Spiderman in the shadows, the distraught, heart-broken wife who did not deserve what was happening to her and a psychopath trapped in the depths of his own silence. This was what awaited me, this was the part I would be playing;

all I had to do was smile like an idiot and behave like a gentleman, because that was the best way of ensuring nothing happened.

Nothing that was happening to me made any sense. Raquel's absurd reaction, this studied nonchalance that alternated with tears made no sense and yet, the moment we were apart. Nothing that was happening made sense. Raquel's absurd reaction, this studied nonchalance that laternates with tears made no sense, yet the moment we were apart I began to see a certain compelling logic to her attitude.

"There's someone else, isn't there, Álvaro?" Mai asked on our first night in Comillas.

I spent a lot of time trying to catch this ephemeral thread that slipped through my fingers, and yet I could still see it, bringing with it the information I needed to solve a problem of misleading significance.

"If you're seeing another woman, tell me, Álvaro, I need to know." Mai asked again two nights later. And I said yes, I said I hadn't deliberately gone behind her back, that I hadn't wanted it, but yes, there was someone else. I can't pretend that the confession did not affect me, that I didn't feel terrible immediately before and after I told her, but then I didn't spend much more time thinking about it. I needed all the time I had to analyse the words Raquel had said, the silences that punctuated a series of disconnected phrases filled with implications that seemed to be beyond my understanding.

Mai let another couple of days pass before asking: "Is it serious? Tell me, Álvaro, is this just a fling or…"

"It's serious, at least for me. I don't know about her."

I didn't take me long to work out that Mai had not much liked my last response: "So, you're just planning to stick around until she makes up her mind, is that it?"

"No, Mai, it's not like that." I held her gaze, did not raise my voice. "But if you want me to leave…"

She asked me to stay and I stayed, and when I was alone I went on thinking about Raquel, while Mai spent her time talking about me to her sisters, her cousins, her girlfriends and a whole army of women and their various partners who began to give me black looks over the dinner table.

"You shouldn't have come, Álvarito." Fernando Cisneros said, although he was happy to see me there, "They'll rip you to shreds."

"I've already been ripped me to shreds," I said, and told him what had happened.

"I don't understand," he said, "it doesn't make sense. I mean, we belong to a structured society governed by norms based on the recurrence of specific events…"

"OK, Fernando!" I held up my hand, hoping for a truce. "I know the theory."

"But it's not just a theory. Come on, Álvaro, look around you, and think about it… A divorced woman with a good job, no kids, no ties, has an affair with a married man whose only problem is the fact that he's married. He tells her he's prepared to drop everything to be with her… she should be biting your hand off."

"I know." I said. "She should, but she's not."

I spent a lot of time talking to Fernando, but instead of helping, his contributions only depressed me. I found it easier to think on my own, but although every bleak afternoon in the worst month of my life brought me closer to an explanation, by the time I finally understood, it was too late.

*Goodbye, Álvaro, I love you. I LOVE YOU, Raquel.*

On 19 August, I turned on my mobile phone and heard the tinkle of a message alert. It wasn't her first text message, she'd sent others – not many 'Hi,' 'Goodnight', 'I love you.' 'I'm at the beach and I'm thinking of you.' 'I'm eating chop suey and thinking about you' 'Is it raining up there?' When I received this one, the last one, it had been two weeks since I had spoken to Raquel. Her phone was always switched off and I was sure she only turned it on long enough to send these few words which fell like cool raindrops on the tongue of a man lost in the desert. Until I received this one.

*Goodbye, Álvaro, I love you. I LOVE YOU, Raquel.*

The first time I read it, I allowed myself to be taken in by those capital letters, by my own fear, by a panic that had the form of her face, the colour of her eyes, the shape of her lips. The first time I read it, I didn't understand it any more than I understood anything that had happened to me since Raquel Fernández Perea had come into my life. My own telephone finally helped me understand the message. 'The number you have dialled does not exist.' Once, twice, three times.

*Goodbye, Álvaro, I love you. I LOVE YOU, Raquel.*

The weather the following day was vile, and by noon it had started to drizzle. *The telephone you are calling has been switched off or is out of range.* Miguelito was irritable at the thought of another day at the beach ruined in this tiny village on the Cantabrian coast where he had spent every summer and so, because I could think of nothing else to do, I suggested to we go down to the harbour and feed the fish. Mai was out. She had gone out earlier without saying where she was going. This was not an oversight, it had become routine.

"Come on, I don't want you getting cold," Miguelito was bizarrely compliant, he didn't complain as I put on his yellow fisherman's raincoat and buttoned it all the way up. "Maybe it'll be fine tomorrow…"

He stood silently for a moment, staring at me with an almost adult intentness, then he asked me the last question I wanted to answer that morning.

"Why is Mamá crying?"

"Mamá's not crying," I put on his hat, not thinking what I was saying.

"She is too, I've seen her," he insisted, "Why is she crying, Papá?"

"I don't know," I crouched down beside him. "She's probably sad. People get sad sometimes…"

"I know," he frowned and looked at me. "Are you going to cry too?"

"No, I'm not going to cry…"

Two minutes later, he was laughing like a lunatic, running ahead of me in a race that, as always, he was going to win. At the harbour, we fed the fish stale bread we'd brought from the house, and some more we scrounged from nearby restaurants who knew us, and I thought maybe this is my life, and it was good, peaceful, happy, as my son giggled, watching the fish stuff themselves, following him along the harbour. Then I thought about Mai, I pictured her the way she had looked when we had first met, before I had ever seen her cry, when I loved her the way I might have gone on loving her my whole life if my father hadn't died, if Raquel hadn't gone to his funeral, if my mother hadn't insisted that I should be the one to meet with the investment manager. But all these things had happened, and now everything was lost. Then, as though I thought there was still one more step to go, one false move I had to make before I tumbled into the void, I turned on my phone and called Raquel.

I expected the message 'The telephone you are calling has been switched off', but I dialled the wrong number. So I did not redial the number, I looked for her name in my contacts list, made sure that her name was highlighted, pressed the green 'dial' button, and for the second, third, fourth time I heard the message:

'The number you have dialled does not exist.'

I dialled other numbers, the landline at home, but the answering machine was turned off, my number at the office, but nobody answered, the bank where she worked where, after half a dozen attempts, I was informed that it was not company policy to give information about the status of employees to strangers.

Directory enquiries was worse. Yes, the subscriber had closed that account, no, they could not tell me if she had opened another account, yes, the information was confidential, no, the operator didn't care who I was, yes, she understood that I was desperate to get in touch with this

456

woman but if I continued to pester her she would have no option but to contact the police. "Believe me, I've come across husbands like you before," she concluded. "Go fuck yourself," I concluded and she hung up on me.

"You told me you weren't going to cry…"

Miguelito was looking up at me, his mouth quivering.

"And I'm not going to cry. I hardly ever cry, you know that."

"But you're crying now, Papá."

"No," I said, smiling to prove he was wrong. "It's just the wind making my eyes smart. Are you out of bread?"

"Yes. And I'm cold."

"Let's go."

As we headed back to the apartment, I listened to the message again. 'The number you have dialled does not exist.' I promised myself this would be the last time, although I didn't know if I would keep my promise.

Raquel needed time to escape, to run away. She wanted to disappear, and all that was left on the other side of her pauses was a man abandoned.

I felt physically ill, a flash of hot and cold, a deep stabbing pain like fever. The future had ripped itself in two; all that was left on this side was me and my son, the four-year-old boy walking beside me, holding my hand, trying to avoid the cracks in the pavement. At first, that was all I could think. Then I realised that there was only one possible solution for a ruined, lovesick, abandoned man; his only possible salvation was to rip off all these adjectives in a single blow.

Beyond the sea of loneliness, I could see contempt looming like a familiar horizon. When I knew I had this, I realised it would not be difficult. All I needed to do was hang on to the repulsive images: a jacuzzi as big as a swimming pool, a vaulted bedroom, two dozen candles and as many films carefully arranged on a metal stand and that purple rubber dildo I'd found in a drawer. The solution consisted of replaying over and over in my mind the very images that for months I had forced myself to forget. These were the elements of the equation, it was simple: I merely needed to subtract where previously I had added, divide by the same amount I had multiplied. It was a costly solution, but it was worth it, because if I could feel contempt for Raquel, perhaps I might come to hate her, perhaps even hate her as much as I had loved her. It would not give me back my life, but it would give me peace.

I was convinced that the only thing that could save me was to throw my passion into reverse, and so I tried. I used every ounce of energy I still possessed, I abjured my body, cursed happiness, renounced madness. I tried to despise Raquel Fernández Perea with everything that I had left, with the little she had not taken with her, but I did not succeed. Don't do this to me, Raquel, why are you doing this to me? I was convinced that I had to despise her so that I could come to hate her, but her eyes had never shone as they did now, her skin was never so soft, so flawless, her body so large and I so small, a tiny insignificant man, with no map, no compass lost in the vastness of a world that had suddenly stopped and would never turn again.

When Ignacio Fernández Muñoz realised that Julio Carrión González had robbed his parents of everything they possessed, he broke down. It was not the first time he had experienced defeat, but it was the cruellest, for in none of the defeats he had known had he been responsible. He could not have fought more than he had fought, could not have been more committed that he was; and he would do it again, he would give his all for a second chance that would never come. Others might have been able to do more, or to do it better, but not he, he had done his best and it was this knowledge that kept him going, that kindled his sense of pride. This – the conviction that he had no regrets – was what Julio Carrión González stole from Ignacio when he robbed his parents of everything they owned.

By the spring of 1964, when his youngest child would be the first person in the family to go back to Spain since 1939, this wound had not completely healed. It would never completely heal. This was why, when his son Ignacio, who could not know the impact of his words, casually mentioned over the dinner table that Spain had beaten Greece as the choice for his school trip, it plunged Ignacio senior into a silence that even he did not understand.

"You don't like the idea, do you?" Anita asked him that night when they were in bed.

"I don't know…" he replied truthfully, "Why do you ask?"

"It's just…" His wife pressed closer to him, nestled her face in his neck. "I don't know either, but I don't like it one bit."

That night, Ignacio Fernández Muñoz did not sleep. As he tossed and turned, his whole life flashed through his mind – the images, the colours, the sounds and smells, precise or intangible sensations shot through with shafts of light and pools of shadow. Ignacio Fernández Muñoz envied his son and feared for him in equal measure.

That night, as he tossed and turned, he would have given anything to slip beneath his son's skin on the day he set off, so that, without sacrificing his own memories, he might see with his son's eyes, hear with his ears, experience this land, this country that he longed to go back to with the same passion that prevented him from going back. He could not go back, perhaps he would never go back, but no one could stop him from returning to Spain in his mind, through the sensations of a young man setting foot there for the first time. It was exhilarating and sad, bitter and joyful, but most of all it was strange. And so when he told his wife that he envied and feared for his son, he was telling the truth.

It was not merely a physical fear, though he could not completely rid himself of that. His son had been born in France and would cross the border with a French passport, a genuine passport, not like the meticulously crafted forgeries he had so often marvelled at when bidding farewell to comrades. But the validity of the passport would not change the fact that the border guards would see the name: Ignacio Fernández Salgado, son of Ignacio and Anita, born, 17, January 1943 in Toulouse, and draw their own conclusions.

In 1964, France was teeming with Spanish exiles who had children the same age as his. Ignacio Fernández Muñoz knew that the passport was sacrosanct, that Franco's police would not touch the person carrying it, but that would not stop the harassment, the comments, the needling questions, 'son of a communist, are we?' I should tell him to say nothing, keep your mouth shut, don't give them the satisfaction, thought Ignacio as he watched his life flash through his mind. I should tell him to stay calm, but I won't need to, his mother will take care of that. This thought reassured him, freed him from the responsibility of offering what might have sounded like simple fatherly advice but which, to him, represented something more – for to say these things would be another defeat, belated perhaps, but an unconditional defeat all the same.

Ignacio Fernández Muñoz tossed and turned in his bed, attempting to choose between the lesser of two evils. Maybe his son would not like Spain, that would be bad. Maybe he would like it too much, that would be worse. He might come back thinking that the butchers who had laid waste to his country, his family, his future, were good people, well-meaning, that the Spanish people were happy with their lot, content to live and prosper beneath the fascist boot. Ignacio knew this was not true, not everywhere. The communists in Paris had close ties with people back in Spain, they had many contacts there, and information was passed back and forth. Until very recently, the *guerrilla* could count on vast, efficient support networks in certain areas, even during the worst of the crackdowns; there were the miners who were constantly waging their own war, the students who had brought Madrid to its knees in 1956, and the tram drivers striking in Barcelona. Eight years later, with the official unions infiltrated at every level, the major universities had become strongholds of the underground movement, but such progress, which looked so attractive from Paris, might not have been as popular on the ground. Ignacio Fernández Muñoz tossed and turned, he could not sleep wondering how he would react if his son came back from Spain and said the unthinkable: 'It was great, really beautiful, the monuments, the wine and the flamenco, I loved it, and the people are really nice, they're so happy, the standard of living is pretty much the same as here, it's obvious that the economic development is really working, they have a good life, and they don't seem to be missing out on anything..."

Ignacio looked at the alarm clock and saw it was 4.20 am. He got up, went into the living room and sat in an armchair. *Cuanto peor, mejor* – "The worse, the better!" A phrase attributed to Nikolai Chernyshevsky indicating that the worse social conditions become for the poor, the more inclined they are to launch a Revolution. He had repeated this phrase so often, heard it said so often, but he had never really thought about what it meant. What an unfair unjust fate, he thought, it's absurd. But this was his fate, the life he had chosen; he had fought and lost, and had rebuilt his life from the ground up to fight again for the very people on whom he now wished not simply poverty but misery, the bitter, profound misery capable of stirring them to revolution.

It's appalling. Ignacio Fernández Muñoz felt terribly alone. Exile was a terrible fate, one that took its toll not only on the surface, but deep within, distorting love, swelling hatred until good and evil became a single thing. The horror of this stagnant life, this river flowing nowhere, with no sea, no lake to meet it. And at this, the darkest moment of the night, Ignacio saw Julio Carrión exactly as he was that last evening, standing in the hallway of their family apartment in Paris, the evening when Paloma had stopped him with a question.

She had suffered the most, she who had already suffered so much. In 1949, when the inevitable came to pass, like a slick of black oil fouling a crystal sea, his parents had put on a brave face, Anita was more worried about comforting him than she was about having lost a fortune she had never had, but Paloma tried to commit suicide in the bathroom of that same apartment, a home he had since left to live with his wife and children.

Ignacio would never forget Anita's cries, his mother sobbing on the telephone, the fear he could feel in his legs as he ran to the apartment, his sister, sitting on the edge of the bath, her eyes vacant, her wrists wrapped in white bandages, stained with blood. "The ambulance is on its way," he said to his mother, "The ambulance is on its way," he whispered again, this time to Paloma. He crouched down next to her, but she did not speak. "Forgive me, Paloma, forgive me," he begged her, "This is all my fault." She shook her head slowly. "But it is, it's my fault, the whole thing was my idea, that's why I need you to forgive me, Paloma, please...'

"It wasn't your fault, Ignacio." This was the first thing Paloma said

461

when she came home from the hospital, then she said that she was very tired and wanted to be left alone. She did not attempt suicide again, but followed an insensate pattern of eating, drinking, sleeping, getting up in the morning, kissing her parents, hugging her nephews. "Leave me in peace, please, just leave me in peace," she would say. They watched her closely, on the alert, but Ignacio did not simply watch her, he saw her, saw in her dry emaciated body a woman who had lost the capacity to desire, watched as despair turned the beautiful Paloma into an ugly, disagreeable woman.

Carrión had been clever, so clever that, by the time Ignacio began to realise something was wrong, it was too late. Initially, until the end of 1947, Julio wrote more often than necessary, talking about how slow the process was, the bureaucratic difficulties they could not have foreseen. The letters became more infrequent in 1948, but Ignacio remembered his own wedding, remembered Anita's panic when the parish priest and the mayor of her village refused to respond, the simple birth certificate which even now had not arrived. Besides, in the spring, Julio had sent some money, a paltry sum in itself, but important because it was the proceeds of the sale of the first of the olive groves. But they received no more money, and by the beginning of 1949 Julio had stopped writing altogether.

Ignacio had waited for two months, it was two months before he began to worry, and it took him some time to find a lawyer in Madrid he could trust; after that everything happened quickly. By the time his new agent had made enquiries, not one of the properties still belonged to the Fernández Muñoz family. Paloma was the one who suffered most, but her brother would have suffered as badly had his father not intervened.

"Listen to me, Ignacio," It was a Sunday morning, the women were cooking lunch and the two men walked to a nearby café where Ignacio's father chose a small table by the window in the sun. "Nothing has changed, understand? We had nothing before, and we have nothing now. It's no different than if they'd commandeered everything ten years ago, or if your cousin had robbed us of everything rather than this bastard. It's not your fault. "

"But it is, Papá." Ignacio would never be in any doubt about this fact.

"No," his father raised his voice. "No. It doesn't matter that you met him and brought him home, it doesn't matter that it was your idea to sell the property. It was a good idea, it might have occurred to any of us. Yes, he swindled us, but what could we do about it? We were all taken in by him, not because we're stupid, but because it's easy to deceive honest people. That's all there is to it." Mateo Fernández Gómez de la Riva

462

paused, looked at his son with all the wisdom of his sixty-two years, and a flash of his former authority. "I need you, Ignacio, and in the state you're in now, you're no use to me. I need you to be strong, to look after the others. You're the head of this family now, understand? You, not me, especially now that María has decided to stay in Toulouse. She's a strong woman, but she's not here, and I'm an old man, Ignacio. I'm old and I'm tired, and I can't take much more. So let that be an end to it, I don't want to hear the name Julio Carrión ever again, understood?"

"Yes, Papá."

"Promise me."

"I promise, Papá."

You saved my life too, Ignacio thought that night, so many people saved my life so many times that I should have done something remarkable with it, something other than simply survive and finish my studies, fall in love, get married and have children. 'But you've helped so many people,' Anita would say to him when she found him in this mood, and perhaps it was true, but it was not remarkable or important, it was not enough to justify the effort that so many people had invested in him. And now, when the benevolence or the cruelty of the times made it possible for him to leave work at the same time as his colleagues, when there was not always one more confused old man sitting in his waiting room, no woman gazing vacantly at her brown dress, her hands clutching the hands of two children, now that he had all but forgotten their gestures, their problems, the words with which they told their very different stories, especially now, he wished them the worst, the cousins, brothers, parents of the Spanish exiles he had counselled, helped and defended for free. And all this because his son had decided to go back to Spain on a school trip.

"Well, then, don't let him go."

When the alarm clock rang a few hours after his mind finally allowed him to sleep, he found Anita sitting up in bed, her arms folded. This was how she was, quarrels made her tired, but she always woke to them again.

"What?" he muttered.

"He doesn't have to go back. We can exchange it for something else, he can go to Greece with a friend."

"No," he looked up at Anita, her expression was more worried than confused. "We can't do that."

"Why not?"

"Well, I don't know…"

"Thanks…" Anita got up and stood staring at him for a moment before storming off to the bathroom, "A lot of good you are to me, Ignacio, 'I don't know, I don't know, I don't know'. Sometimes I think you don't know how to say anything else."

Neither of them could have imagined that their son also did not like the idea of the trip. Ignacio Fernández Salgado would have preferred to go to Greece, or Italy, or Holland, to any of the places they had voted on until there was only one option left.

To him, Spain was not a country, it was an accident, an anomaly that mutated according to time and circumstance like a hereditary illness, capable of erupting and disappearing by itself. Ignacio Fernández Salgado, who had never been to Spain, was sick to death of *tortilla de patatas* and dancing *sevillanas*, of Spanish Christmas carols [ii] and Spanish proverbs, of Cervantes and Lorca, of Spanish shawls and guitars, of the siege of Madrid and the Fifth Regiment, of eating 'The Twelve Grapes' as midnight struck on 31 December and raising a glass of champagne only to hear the same words every year *'next year, we'll be home'*.

It had nothing to do with the fact that his parents were foreign. Paris was full of foreigners, that was bearable. What was unbearable was to be the son of Spanish exiles, to have been born, grown up, to have become a man in this dense, impenetrable exile constantly tormented by a border which was so close and yet unreachable, like a plate of sweets a centimetre beyond the reach of a starving child. Exile was a terrible thing, this curious exile he had been forced to live out as his own, because he had been born, not into a country, but into a tribe, a clan, that fed on its own misery, a society of ingrates unable to appreciate what they had, for there was always something they did not have, who lived half-heartedly, constantly miserable, constantly shut away inside their portable country, a ghostly, posthumous presence they called Spain which did not exist, it did not exist.

It was probably different for those who had gone to South America, since they were separated from home by a vast ocean, by thousands of miles, different accents, the same language. Ignacio Fernández Salgado would have been happier had his parents met over there, in one of those hot countries, a country where Christmas came in summer. Over there, the refrain 'Next year, we'll be home.' would be an idle boast, made with a smile, shorn of the solemnity which hovered above the dining room table each year. You're such fools, thought Ignacio, what home do you have but this one? Then he would look at his mother, his father, his grandparents, the insubstantial phantom of his aunt Paloma, and regret having thought it, but he knew that a year later, he would think the same

464

thing again.

Though his parents did not realise it, Ignacio Fernández Salgado was acutely conscious that he was not going back to Spain. He could not go back because he had never been there. And so he did not understand their frowns, the brooding air, the weariness that came over them at Christmas and New Year, an expression that greeted him again that morning over the breakfast table.

"Tell me, *hijo*, do you really want to go?" his mother took the initiative.

"Go where?"

"To Spain, where do you think?"

"I'd rather go to Greece, but I'm happy to go because all my friends are going and I suppose it'll be fun. It's just that..." He paused, careful not to choose words that might offend or upset them. "I'd prefer to have gone somewhere else, because it's like I already know Spain, even though I've never been."

"But you don't know it," he father's tone was unfathomable. "You have no idea what it's really like, deep down."

"You don't have to go if you don't want to. You can go somewhere else instead, we'll pay," Anita added.

"But..." Ignacio could not believe what he was hearing. "I don't understand. You spend your whole life talking about Spain, comparing everything here to what it was like back there – like that thing about the aubergines, Mamá. Spain is like an illness with you two and now... You don't want me to go? Why not?" They looked at him, but neither wanted to answer. "You don't even let us speak French at home. We have to stop as soon as we're inside the door... I don't get, I just don't get it..."

"It's not that I don't want you to go," his father said, "But it's true I don't like the idea. It's complicated."

"It's dangerous." His mother was more honest, and dealt calmly with the mounting astonishment in her son's eyes. "Don't look at me like that. It is dangerous. Not for your friends, but for you. I'm not saying something would happen, but your father is right. You don't understand, *hijo*, you were brought up in a democratic country, a country where the police are officials who represent the government, where there are laws and people respect those laws, but Spain is not like that, not any more..."

"Do me a favour, Mamá..." Olga, who was four years younger than her brother, and had been quietly dunking biscuits in her coffee, heaved a sigh: "Don't start, please..."

"Oh, I will," Anita got to her feet, raising her voice, "I will start, because I know what I'm talking about and you don't have the first idea,

465

either of you."

"I won't go looking for trouble, Mamá, I promise. Nothing's going to happen to me, I haven't done anything, and I'm not *going* to do anything."

"That's what my father said when they came and arrested him."

"Come off it, Mamá," her son exploded, getting to his feet and heading for the door. "It's always the same old story…"

"Of course it's the same old story…" she shouted after him "Because that is what my father said, I can still hear him, 'nothing's going to happen to me, I haven't done anything'. And they shot him, understand? He was thirty-six, he had four children, and…" Her whole body was trembling, "And I'm the only one left, the only one of my family who survived…"

Ignacio Fernández Muñoz went to his wife, took her in his arms and whispered her name: "Anita."

"What?" she did not look at him.

"Let it go…" she struggled and glared at him, but he calmed her. "Let it go, please… Think about it. He's not going to war, he's just a tourist…"

That night, when she came home from work, Anita Salgado apologised to her son who was sitting in the living room waiting to apologise to her. It was not easy for either of them. She felt the same cold chill she had felt when her father pressed the freshly washed apricot he was about to eat into her hand and said, "Don't cry, silly, nothing's going to happen to me, I haven't done anything." He had leaned down to kiss her, but before he could the Civil Guard gripping his right arm had dragged him out of the house.

It had been twenty-eight years since Anita Salgado ate that apricot, but she still hadn't digested it. She did not eat apricots any more, but she could remember the taste. She wished she had kept the pit, which she had bitten and sucked until the last thread of pulp was gone so that she could slip it into the pocket of her apron without knowing why she was doing it. She did not need it to remember her father, and so that she could still be with him, she had slipped it into the pocket of his shirt when she next saw him, stiff, blood-stained, his eyes closed, on the day they buried him. Then, as though she were an adult rather than a girl of twelve, she had gone to a fountain, soaked her handkerchief, and cleaned the bloody face and neck of the corpse. After that, she passed out. A neighbour took her home, sat her in an armchair, gave her a glass of water, and talked and talked, desperate to distract her from the funeral. She was sorry not to have been at that brief, pitiful ceremony, but she was sorrier still that she had not kept the apricot pit so that she might slip it now into the pocket of her son.

He knew the story of the apricot pit by heart, but he also knew that almost thirty years had passed since then. Almost thirty years according to the clocks, according to historians, but not according to his mother. That was what was so unbearable, agonizing and grotesque about his situation. And now he was going to Spain with friends who would expect him to play a role he would have given anything to avoid: that of translator, interpreter, expert in this absurd country which even the Spanish did not understand.

Laurent had already spent the summer in Spain twice, once in Majorca and once in Torremolinos, and what he had told Ignacio on his return bore no relation to the descriptions he had heard at home. To Laurent, who was one of his best friends, Spain was a charming, inexpensive country, the people were friendly, a little strange, but welcoming. True, there were a lot of police in the streets, the women in the villages always wore black, everyone went to mass on Sunday, and it was very difficult to pick up girls, not because the girls didn't like the idea, but because they were constantly being watched. Normal girls were not allowed out at night, nor were they allowed to talk to strangers. At the beach, during the daytime, things were different, but the girls always insisted on immediately introducing any boy they met to their mothers. So, in spite of the killjoys constantly dressed in mourning and the heavily guarded girls, Laurent thought Spain was great, he liked the music, the cooking, the bars and the insatiable Spanish compulsion to have a good time. His sister thought so too, in fact, she had signed up to go with them.

"Book another place," his father asked him early in March when he finally seemed to have come to terms with the idea.

"Why?" Ignacio looked at Olga, who was sitting next to him on the sofa watching television. "Are you coming?"

"Are you out of your mind?" Olga rolled her eyes and used one of her mother's favourite expressions. "Not if I was drunk as a skunk."

"Who then?"

"It's for Raquel, isn't it?" Anita smiled and her husband nodded before turning to his son. "You know Raquel, Aurelio and Rafaela's daughter…"

"What?" as he glared at his parents, Ignacio Fernández Salgado kicked himself for being so stupid, he should have known that something like this was coming. "There's no way I'm looking after some kid."

"What kid?" his mother cut him off, "she's older than your sister, she must be… nineteen, I think." She glanced at her husband again, but this time he did not come to her rescue. "Let me think… I met Rafaela when she was pregnant and that must have been just after we arrived in Paris, at the beginning of 1945, so…'

"I don't care, Mamá! I don't care whether she's nineteen or twenty, I'm not looking after her!"

"Of course you're not looking after her, Ignacio," his father said in the calm tone he employed when his authority was not to be questioned. "She's a big girl, she can look after herself."

"No, Papá, don't do this to me! It's always the same, why can't I be like other kids?"

"Laurent's sister is going with you," Anita reminded her son.

"But she's his sister! Don't you get it? She's his sister, so it's different! He can hardly say no, and anyway…" He knew he was lost, but he tried once more. "I don't even know this girl."

"Of course you do," his mother laughed, "You remember, you used to see her at the party the newspaper *L'Humanité* used to give when you were both little. She always wore a flamenco dress with a flower in her hair, I think she still dances…"

"*L'Humanité*, Jesus. I remember… 'a galopar, a galopar' From the poem Galope by Rafael Alberti that became a popular anti-Franco refrain. "Please, Mamá, do you have to remind me?"

"You used to love to going to those parties…"

"I loved going?" It had to come to this, he thought. " I did *not* love going, you know very well I never liked going. You made me go, it's not the same thing…"

"I don't want to hear any more about it," his father brought the discussion to a close. "Either Raquel goes to Spain with you or neither of you is going. It's as simple as that. I'm paying for this trip, so what I say, goes."

"You see? Marxism in action," Anita looked at her son and smiled.

"Anita, please…" her husband looked shocked. He turned to look at his son. "She may not be your sister, but that girl is part of this family. Her father has been like a brother to me for years."

"No, Papá…" Ignacio Fernández Salgado shook his head, "That girl is *not* part of this family, because we're not a family, we're a tribe!"

"OK, then…" Ignacio Fernández Muñoz smiled at the inventive turn of his son's anger, "maybe we are a tribe, but we're your tribe. You're just one more savage, I'm afraid, but that's the way it is. One more thing, I want you to go and visit your aunt Casilda, and that's even less up for discussion. How much free time do you have in Madrid?"

The day in 1964 that Anita referred to as the Friday of Sorrows,

Ignacio Fernández Salgado took a taxi to the airport. His parents had offered to drive him, but he had refused their offers, pointing out that they would at work. Thankfully he would not have to face the embarrassing goodbyes, more scenes, more tears, 'a galopar, a galopar', so he headed off alone, and found his friends happy and excited at the prospect of the trip and this new girl.

"Don't get your hopes up." He had not wanted to say more. It would not have made any difference, since when they were young, none of his friends had been forced by their parents to go to the party given by *L'Humanité*. That last argument had brought it all back: the taste of *churros*, the lyrics of the fandangos, the sound of cider trickling into a glass, and the disturbing, almost terrifyingly sight of the huge, lumpy *empanadas* they called 'pregnant buns'. The same greasy *paellas*, the same women wearing mourning dress, the same men wearing berets, and the shame of having to walk through the streets dressed in an Aragonese peasant outfit, with the same checked scarf his mother forced him to wear every year tied round his head, especially after Olga opted to wear the regional costume of her father's province.

"You're a cheat, Ignacio!" Anita said to her husband when he first showed up with the tasselled black shawl embroidered with flowers that Casilda, his sister-in-law, had sent him from Madrid.

Even without the shawl, his sister much preferred the long close-fitting white dress with red polka-dots, with which she was allowed – like Andalusian women – to wear high heels. Once Olga saw the shawl, there was no going back, and Anita, having painstakingly cut and sewn a skirt, a corsage and a fichu, exacted her revenge on her son.

"Ah, look at him! Doesn't he look cute in his scarf?"

It was awful, all the more so because the scarf was called a *cachirulo*, it was completely awful. It was beyond awful.

At first, Olga enjoyed it because Mamá would put her hair up, paint her eyes with eyeliner, put carnations in her hair. She looked pretty in her little dress, but him... every year it was the same, a piece of fabric wrapped several times around his waist and his *cachirulo* perched just above his jug ears making them even more noticeable. And every year, Olga would step out into the street, smiling, hands on hips and Ignacio would follow, staring at the ground, trying to hide behind his father or his mother so as not to be noticed. But someone always spotted him, some neighbour would always ask 'Hey you, what are you dressed as?', and there'd be a skinny girl with braces on her teeth waiting for any occasion to stamp her feet, ¡olé! ¡olé! lifting her skirt and twisting her lips as though in pain. He could still remember that she had a forest of hair on her legs, could remember that final pose, one leg forward, the other hidden, one arm raised, the fingers stiff as though she were suddenly paralysed down one side, a broad smile, her hair plastered to her forehead with sweat.

"Are you Ignacio?"

This was why he had said to Laurent and Philippe, who was the sex maniac in the group, not to get their hopes up. This was why he was unable to make sense of the question asked by this pretty French girl, defiantly modern, wearing a white dress, her hips accentuated by a belt in the same fabric, and barely a few inches below, her long, smooth, beautiful legs.

"Is your name Ignacio Fernández?" her French would have been perfect but for the fact that two rival accents, French and Andalusian, clashed with every word.

"That's me."

"Hi," she held out her hand. "I'm Raquel Perea. I think you've got my ticket?"

"Yes." He was dumbstruck.

"Well, could you take my suitcase as well and go and check the bags in…" the vicereine of India addressing a servant could not have mustered greater condescension, "I'll be right back, I just have to say goodbye."

"Oh…" He picked up the suitcase and immediately put it down again when he realised it was twice as heavy as his own. "Wait, I'll go with you. I'd like to say hello to your parents."

She turned and looked at him, puzzled, "My parents?" then continued walking until she came to a tall, stocky boy with the loathsome look of someone who had been champion of something or other at school.

Clearly - ¡olé! ¡olé! - Raquel Perea now had a boyfriend. Ignacio Fernández Salgado noticed as much in the twenty minutes that followed, his friend Laurent noticed, Philippe noticed, as did a number of other passengers who passed the two-headed monster embroiled in a steamy kiss.

"So who was that," he ventured when she condescended to recover her belongings.

"He's my boyfriend, who did you think he was?" He's leaving for the Dordogne tomorrow, going to his grandmother's to eat *foie gras*. I thought about going with him, but my father was determined to pack me off to Spain with you," she paused, jerking her chin upwards, almost defiantly, "to eat garlic."

Her jibe stung him like a mosquito. "Look, I didn't ask you to come."

"Just as well. I recognised you by your ears, though they're not as

470

obvious with your long hair."

Nice, thought Ignacio, and he almost shot back that he didn't recognise her without the forest of hair on her legs, but he didn't because he realised that she would probably take it as a compliment. He couldn't think of anything else to say, and they did not exchange another word until he found her sitting next to him on the plane.

"We're not even going to Málaga," she sounded less like a fractious empress than a disappointed child.

"I know, but we're going to Seville," he said, without asknig himself why he was trying to cheer her up, "And to Córdoba and Grenada... It's still Andalucía, isn't it?"

"Yes, but it's not the same. Listen I'm sorry for that crack about your ears earlier. It was rude, it's just... I didn't want to come, but my father wouldn't let me go on holiday with my boyfriend, you know what it's like, they're old and they're square. I said: 'I don't understand, Papá, you won't let me go on holiday with Jean-Pierre, who you know well, but you're determined to make me go away with some boy you don't know from Adam because you haven't seen him in years.' You know what he said? He said it wasn't the same thing, because you're your father's son and you're Spanish. Have you ever heard anything more ridiculous? They're insufferable, honestly, there's no talking to them!"

"You think that's bad?" Ignacio smiled, "My mother told me she didn't want me to go because it was dangerous, and when I said nothing was going to happen to me she told me that's what her father said just before they took him out and shot him."

"Really?" she looked at him, wide-eyed, "It's unbelievable they're still going on about that stuff even now. It's like they get off on it."

Only when the air hostess announced that they were beginning their descent did they finally stop criticizing their fathers, their mothers and the rest of their tribe. As they landed, Ignacio looked out at the runway of grey tarmac and white paint identical to the one in Paris. There was nothing special about the runway and yet, looking at it, contrary to what he had expected, Ignacio Fernández Salgado felt a hole in the pit of his stomach, a lump in his throat. He also felt pressure on his arm, but was so absorbed by this unforeseen mutiny of his own body that it was a moment before he wondered what the pressure was. When he did, he found Raquel Perea leaning over him, looking at the same unremarkable stretch of Seville airport runway.

"Spanish soil," she murmured in a humble, nervous, almost gentle tone.

"Yes," he discovered he too was whispering.

471

"I'm not sure I'm going to like it."

"Me neither, but I had to come sooner or later."

"I suppose. So you've never been before either?"

"No."

"Well," she smiled at him, "at least this way we'll get through it together…"

"Like chickenpox." Ignacio smiled back and Raquel laughed.

And then Raquel stepped out of the plane with him and did not leave his side until they had collected their bags. They moved at the same pace, serious and silent, not looking at each other, as if they had nothing to do with each other, and nothing to do with the gaggle of noisy French students laughing and chasing each other down the corridors. At first, Ignacio's only thought was that he could distinctly taste apricots. Then a woman's voice came over the loudspeakers.

"Hey!" Raquel grabbed his arm and squeezed. "Listen to the way she talks…"

"She has a nice voice," he said after a moment.

"No, I mean her accent, she talks just like my mother does in Spanish."

She didn't let go of his arm, but squeezed it harder as they queued at passport control.

"The Civil Guard…"

"Yes," said, Ignacio, who had just read the sign.

Ignacio Fernández Salgado suddenly felt grateful for his father's dictatorial contrariness, he was even grateful for the 'punishment' that had meant bringing Raquel Perea with him on this trip, because until this moment, Ignacio had simply felt nervous, excited, perhaps a little shaken. Now, as he moved towards that little window, he could taste every apricot he had ever eaten grow rancid in his mouth. With each step, Ignacio Fernández Salgado could feel his palms sweat, chills running up and down his spine, his legs giving way. But with each step, he could hear Raquel's ragged breathing, could feel her nails digging into his arm, and he knew that she was trembling, he knew it, and that was enough to keep him going. If he was calm and composed, she would be calm and composed. When his turn came, they both stepped up to the window. He pushed his passport over the counter, looked at the man in the green uniform who returned his stare, and greeted him in Spanish.

"*Buenos días.*"

"*Buenas…*" the guard opened the passport, glanced at the photograph, then at Ignacio, then wrote on a piece of paper. "Fernández Salgado. So you're Spanish?"

"No," he reeled off the answer his father had suggested. "French. My parents are Spanish."

"I see…" the guard flicked through the passport, studying the stamps. "This is your first time here?"

"Yes."

"Very well," the man pushed the passport back to him with a smile, "Welcome."

'God I'm so stupid', thought Ignacio as he watched the same scene played out again by Raquel: "Perea Millán?" "Yes. I'm French, like him. My parents are Spanish."

"Could you be any more stupid?" Ignacio thought of his father's preferred put down, and he felt obliged to answer "No" with the same rage, the same pig-headedness he felt every year as he watched his grandparents, his parents, his aunts and uncles raise a toast on New Years eve. "Very well, welcome." That was all there was too it, it had been so simple, so straightforward, that once they were on the other side, Raquel seemed ashamed that she had been trembling.

"Well, I suppose that's it," she looked at him sceptically, "It wasn't so bad after all…"

Ignacio shrugged. It was true, it hadn't been so bad, in fact it had been nothing. During their first days there, everything seemed to be like that. True, Seville was astonishing beautiful, as was Córdoba then Grenada, as ravishing as a bride, her veil of white houses spread below the snow-capped mountains. That was his favourite photograph, although he had taken some good shots of the Santa Cruz district and a portrait of Raquel at night, dazzling and half-drunk, in front of the statue of Cristo de los Faroles.

He loved Andalucía, because, his father being from Madrid and his mother from Aragón, he had not known what to expect. He genuinely liked it because, what he had been expecting – the stiff gentleman accompanied a dark-haired dancer in a flamenco dress of flounces and ruffles, was poorer than what he found: the unhurried pace of these cities, slaves to their own beauty, to the ancient rhythm of water constantly gurgling through the chalk, the flowers, the narrow labyrinthine streets. It was beautiful, extraordinarily beautiful, and it filled him with a curious stillness, but a sadness too, for this place, with its chalk-white houses, their stone terraces groaning under the weight of potted plants as tall as trees, was surely a wonderful place to live, but it was not his home. He would have liked to live here, but it was impossible. He would never lean over one of these balconies, with their black railings, their red geraniums, where his mother, who for decades had struggled in vain against the

473

winter frost of Paris, would have been so happy.

The weather – warm but temperate, neither too joyful nor too sad – reflected how he felt on his first days in his parents' country, for it was not his country. He was finally in Spain, and it turned out that Spain really did exist, that it really did occupy a specific part of the planet. But because it was nothing like the ghostly, posthumous country in which his tribe had pitched camp, the real Spain seemed to him a strange and unfamiliar place.

"Are you still in Seville?" his mother's voice at the other end of the line was tremulous.

"Yes, still here. We leave tomorrow."

"So what is it like?" Anita Salgado had never been south of Teruel.

"It's beautiful, Mamá, you'd love it here." In the silence, he could hear her anxiety, "You have to come and see it some day."

"Of course, *hijo*. I'm so happy just knowing you're there, Ignacio…"

"Let me talk to him Anita! We might get cut off like we did yesterday." Ignacio heard his father's voice. "You should call your grandmother, she's from Andalucía… she'd be so happy to hear from you."

As he hung up, Ignacio felt puzzled and guilty. These feelings were all too familiar to him, but in Seville, in Córdoba, in Granada, the guilt seemed to outweigh the confusion. It had been obvious that his mother would have preferred him to go anywhere but here, and yet every time he spoke to her on the phone she seemed to be close to tears. Nor could he understand his own feelings in this unfamiliar country where everything – the language, the food, the customs – was so familiar, where certain people, certain scenes left him reeling with the unsettling sensation of déjà vu, the impossible conviction that he had lived these moments before.

In Andalucía, Ignacio Fernández Salgado belatedly realised that his parents had been right, that he had 'gone back' even though he had never set foot on Spanish soil. But it was they who should have been here, they who should have 'gone back' since they would recognise themselves in this world he did not feel able to decipher. This was what he thought, what he believed, as he embarked on his last night in Andalucía.

They had been told it was a cave, but it did not look like a cave. The walls of the vaulted room, which was long and narrow as a tunnel, were rough-hewn and whitewashed but the copper pots and pans, the ornate glazed earthenware plates that covered every inch of wall, gave the place a vibrant, baroque feeling entirely at odds with its subterranean location. And yet it was a real cave, one more peculiarity in this savage land of garlic-eaters.

"Flamenco, oh great!" He had said that morning when they found out that they were to spend their last night in Andalucía at a flamenco show in a cave in Sacromonte, "That's all we need..."

"Don't be like that..." Raquel spoke to him in Spanish, before reverting to French, which they spoke when the others were present, "You'll love it, it's unique, it's moving, it's like no other music on earth."

"I loathe flamenco," said Ignacio slipping back into Spanish.

"Well, then you're an idiot." she said, and turned to the others.

As she did, Ignacio thought again how much better she was handling this than he was. Maybe it was because her parents were from Andalucía, but her French accent was starting to fade. Ignacio witnessed this evolution in her pronunciation which culminated in a shop on the Calle Zacatín, when the shopkeeper closed the display case too quickly.

"*AY, mi deo!*" yelped Raquel, sucking her injured finger.

"What do you mean *mi deo?*" said Ignacio when the assistant had finally finished apologising, "Don't you mean *mi **dedo**?*"

Raquel stared at him for a minute, confused, and when she did reply, it was clear she had not understood.

"Yes, my finger... I pinched it in the case..." she pronounced it *pillao* rather than *pillado.* So, I suppose now you've got *diez deos* on your hands and *diez deos* on your feet, he thought, not bothering to explain that he was sure that back in Paris he had heard her say *dedo* without the Andalusian accent. And it was not just that. If she ever gave a thought to the Dordogne and the indigestion her boyfriend must be suffering from an excess of *foie gras*, it did not show. Raquel was enjoying Spain more than Ignacio thought was reasonable or indeed healthy. He too liked the fried fish, he loved the *pata negra* ham, the tomato salad flavoured with garlic, the taste of extra-virgin olive oil, he loved the sweet dessert they called *tocino del cielo*, even pale dry *manzanilla* sherry, he liked all these things but... the religious processions? She didn't miss a single one. She would send Philippe on in front like a guide dog to clear a path all the way to the railing, and there she would stand until the last pilgrim passed holding his lighted candle. This was too much for Ignacio, who would go and sit in a crowded bar and drink, little realising that the tradition of heading for a bar to avoid a religious procession was as Spanish as the procession itself. But there was more to it than that, too.

Ignacio looked at Raquel and saw her eyes grow wide, lips parted, and he realised that he liked to look at her, needed to look at her, as though he might feed on her enthusiasm, her happiness, this warmth that tempered his spirit which was frozen with confusion and guilt. On the sixth night of their trip, the last night they would spend together in Andalucía for a long time, not only did Raquel no longer speak disparagingly about Spain, she would not tolerate anyone else to criticise or complain, not even him. Two nights earlier, in Córdoba, just after posing for the photo, she had confessed to him that she had never imagined she would love her parents country as much as she did.

"Don't you feel that?" Ignacio shook his head. "Well, I do. Isn't that weird? To be honest I was sick to death of Spain and Spanish proverbs and Spanish battles, I was sick of hearing that Spain was better at this and that but... I don't know, now I feel like this is my home. I know it's not, it's just an illusion that will probably vanish the minute I get back to Paris, but right now, that's how I feel."

"You must have Moorish blood," Ignacio joked.

"That must be it," she smiled, "But that's not so bad, is it? Just look around..."

She was right, and Ignacio was happy to admit it, to watch the mysterious alchemy of exile at work in her, even if it produced no results in him. This was why, despite Raquel's infectious happiness and enthusiasm, despite the thousand reasons that went through his mind, he still hated flamenco when he stepped into that cave in Sacromonte.

"I don't know how you can listen to that, Papá." He had dared to say one day after three-quarters of an hour of aural agony. "I don't like it, but I like listening to it," his father had said. They were working together, building a wooden boat, out on the porch of the house in Collioure that his parents rented every summer when he and Olga were young. Ignacio loved working with his father because he was patient and skilful. Ignacio Fernández Muñoz would always say that he had been useless with his hands when he arrived in France, but that he had an excess of time in the concentration camp and was so bored that he decided to learn some trades. He was an able carpenter, which was the only trade he practised after his release. When they began working on the boat, Ignacio remembered the torment he had endured while they were building the four-storey doll's house for his sister, and to spare himself more pain, he said: "That's impossible, Papá, you can't like listening to something you don't like." His father smiled. "Of course it's possible, but, if you prefer, let's just say I like flamenco.

"Well I don't, I don't like it at all." This is what he had said to his father, and this is what he said as he settled himself on one of the hard wooden benches that lined the walls of the cave, having tried and failed to wangle a place next to Raquel.

But he liked the wine, and at first he thought it was because of the wine, because he had had quite a lot to drink. The company – a pretty, plump gypsy woman and another, slimmer but considerably less attractive, both middle-aged, a number of young dancers with dark hair and heavy eye makeup, two guitarists dressed in black and three young men all sat together around a stage at the far end of the room. There were a few words of welcome, a few off-colour jokes and then the guitars began.

"Tonight, I'm going to start with some *bulerías*," announced the plump gypsy, and began to sing.

Ignacio heard, though he was not listening. He was not watching the performance so much as watching Raquel who sat grave and intense, her eyes fixed on the singer. Then the gypsy fell silent, there was applause and the guitars started up again, and one of the young men sitting next to the guitarists, a skinny, nervous boy with a narrow waist, began to beat out the rhythm with his hands, at first soundlessly, his hands barely touching, as though keeping time merely for himself.

"I'm going to sing *granaínas*," he announced.

"*Desea el hombre una cosa, parece un mundo, luego que la consigue, tan sólo es humo, tan sólo es humo, prima, tan sólo es humo. Desea el hombre una cosa, parece un mundo...*"

The boy's voice was diaphanous, pure as crystal yet cracked, rich and deep, intimate yet strange. All these things Ignacio could hear in this voice as he listened, and he had not even been aware that he was of listening, but the words had come to him, and he welcomed them, embraced them and allowed them to enter his ear, his body, his memory.

"*A man may yearn for something, it seems like all the world, but once he possesses it he finds, it's nothing more than smoke, it's nothing more than smoke...*" The singer was young, barely older than Ignacio himself, and he closed his eyes as he sang these words. And Ignacio liked the wine, not the flamenco, he was enjoying the wine. That had to be what it was, because he suddenly realised that he was excited, that he had been moved by these words, this song, *it's nothing more than smoke, it's nothing more than smoke*, the young man's voice took him to places he did not recognise, places that set his heart racing, though he had never heard the song before. And he thought that perhaps this song, just this song, this encapsulation of the human condition, might be Spain for him. *A man may yearn for something, it seems like all the world, but once he possesses it he finds it's nothing more than smoke.* Words so simple yet so complex, so precise yet so universal sung in this high, hoarse and faltering voice, as fine as crystal, as a needle, an invisible weapon.

Emotion is strange, and this one was stranger than any, though the wine was probably to blame, he thought. He knew the words to this song though he had never heard it before, maybe his grandmother María who was from Jaén and a fine singer had sung him to sleep with it.

Then everything suddenly changed. The singer finished and he applauded enthusiastically, Raquel shot him a surprised look, and the dancers began to flick the ruffles of their skirts to the rhythm of the guitars and the clapping of the others. Ignacio realised that this was the highlight of the show, the one the tourists had come for, but while his friends tensed, leaning back in their seats or craning forward the better to admire the furious *taconeo,* heels cracking against the boards as though the dancers were wielding bullwhips, Ignacio found himself missing the unexpected surge of emotion, the crack and caress of that voice which, with humble words, said such extraordinary things.

He could still hear them, could still feel their caress when Raquel began to move in her seat, her feet, her shoulders, her whole body swaying to the rhythm of her hands which made a powerful, hollow sound, something like applause yet not, because the air in the slight space between the curved palms makes of them a percussion instrument. She's about to stand up, he thought, and as he did so, one of the gypsies, a tall, dark-skinned man with a hooked nose, reached out his hand and led her onto the stage. A moment later Raquel Perea Millán, daughter of Aurelio and Rafaela, the skinny little brat, who used to go the *l'Humanité* parties dressed in flamenco frills and clamber up on to a table to show off, was dancing in a cave in Sacromonte in her yellow and white miniskirt, with no ruffles, no combs, no brightly beaded necklace, but a great deal of talent.

The performers said as much – *¡olé! ¡olé! you have a gift, hija!* She twirled, moving her feet and her arms to the rhythm of the music, leaned down to flick the ruffled pleats of her imaginary skirt, then straightened quickly, and strode across the stage in quick graceful steps, as though about to step down, but she did not, she started all over again *¡olé! ¡olé!* they said, *just look at the girl dance.* Raquel was dancing, and dancing extremely well, so well that it was as though she had only ever danced here, now, with the tall, dark-skinned gypsy, who moved with unerring instinct, matching his movements to her body. They came together and parted with the tense languor of an animal in heat, as his arms encircled her, never touching her, to envelop her in the grace that enveloped him. The singer clapped his hands, gazing at the couple, everyone was staring at them, they seemed aware of nothing and no one else, they did not need to look at anyone else only at each other, lips parted, in an expression of

478

fierce, almost savage recognition that excluded all those who were not part of the reality they shared, of the only thing that existed for them in that moment.

"So, where are you from?" the gypsy asked her, after the show was over and the performers mingled with the audience. "Dancing the way you did is something you can't learn."

"I'm from Málaga," said Raquel, her back to Ignacio, oblivious to the look of astonishment he gave her, "I live in France but I'm *malagueña.*"

"Of course," the gypsy smiled, revealing perfect white teeth. "It shows."

*Me cago en tu padre, cabrón!* I shit on your father, you bastard! As he half-turned to evaluate the situation, Ignacio realised he was no longer even swearing in French. Nor was he cheered by what he saw. He couldn't count on Philippe, whose unconditional devotion to Raquel had proved in vain. He was completely drunk – Laurent was trying to hold him up and calling to Ignacio for help. Nor was he the only casualty. One of the girls had had to be taken out just before she threw up, and all the others had their jackets on. In the meantime, the gypsy had made some progress, as could be seen in the flushed cheeks of his prey. Ignacio took a deep breath and walked over to them.

"Raquel," he said, barely touching her elbow and addressing her in Spanish, "We're going."

She looked from him to the gypsy and back again. She was hesitating, as both men realised, they both had the same desire in their eyes, each aware of her power and her frailty, the symbols of their respective tribes, at once exotic and distinct.

"Are you leaving with the Frenchie?" the gypsy was the first to crack.

"He's not French," she said at length, "He's Spanish..." she looked at the dancer and smiled. "Yes, I'm going to go too, we're setting off for Madrid early tomorrow, and we've had a lot of late nights."

He accepted the decision with good grace, Ignacio was forced to admit as he watched the man take Raquel's hand in his, slowly kiss it, and say a simple *adiós* before turning away and leaving the two of them alone. Then, because he needed to do something, Ignacio placed his hand on Raquel's arm again and led her very gently towards the door. When they got outside and found themselves flayed by the dry, icy wind of the *sierra*, which in the early hours belies the benevolent constancy of the noonday sun in Granada, he turned to her but had not expected her teasing smile, which made him think that, perhaps, she had realised her great conquest on this trip would not be Philippe, but himself.

"I thought you were from Nimes," he said after a moment, returning her smile.

"And I thought you hated flamenco," they both laughed.

"Now I like it," he confessed, "Thanks to you."

"I'm glad, because... I have to say that when we were little, I didn't like you very much, Ignacio. I can still remember at the *L'Humanité* parties, every time I saw you I felt ill. You were the only person who never clapped. I'd dance, because I loved dancing, and in France I didn't have much opportunity, so I'd spend the whole year waiting for those parties, practising in my bedroom on my own. And then, bam! There you'd be, in your red and black scarf with your jug ears, and suddenly I'd get nervous, because I knew what was coming next. What I never understood was why you always gave me that look of contempt. When I finished your mother would come over and kiss me, and every year she'd tell me I was getting better, and there you were, standing next to her with your *cachirulo* and that pained expression like you'd been tortured..."

They were walking down the Cuesta del Chapiz, towards the Paseo de los Tristes when she stopped and turned to him.

"Why did you hate me so much, Ignacio? And why did you always watch if you didn't like my dancing?"

He did not know, but he knew what he had to do, knew what she was expecting.

The kiss did not last as long as the one Raquel and her boyfriend had shared at the airport in Paris, but it was sweet and crisp as the first bite of a piece of fruit, and its intensity surprised them both. They were coming to the hotel; neither of them spoke, they could think of nothing to say. Ignacio was wondering what had happened, what might happen next. Raquel, walking a pace in front, was simply wondering when, how and where it would happen. It would not be in Granada, but neither would it be in circumstances she could have imagined.

"I'm not crying because I'm sad," Ignacio looked at her as they stood at a traffic light in Madrid. "It's not because I'm sad."

And at that moment, Raquel Perea Millán, who had a tall, stocky boyfriend waiting for her back in France, gorging himself on *foie gras*, realised that her life was about to change.

"Where are we going?" she had asked Ignacio that afternoon, after the others had gone off to spend their free time shopping.

"To tell you the truth, I don't really know," He smiled, still dazed by how lucky he was. "My aunt told my father she lives at the end of the Moratalaz, but he couldn't remember where that is... The best thing would be to take a taxi."

"I have to go and visit someone this afternoon," Ignacio had told her over breakfast on their first day in Madrid. "Who are you going to see?" she asked him later, as they were walking down the Paseo del Prado. "My uncle's wife," he said, and told her the story of this woman he had never met, whom no one in the Fernández family had seen since 19 February 1939, but whom he had grown up calling aunt Casilda. "Well, maybe I could go with you..." she said, as though it had just occurred to her, "I mean, we've been here a whole week, and we haven't really seen how people live... if you don't mind," she added quickly, because they had not kissed again since that strange night, and were not close enough to dispense with formalities. "No, of course not," Ignacio said quickly, "I'd love you to come."

"Where did you say you wanted to go?" the taxi driver turned to him, astonished, and he slowly repeated the address, "Well, I have no idea where that is."

"It's at the other end of Moratalaz," said Ignacio, "At least that's what I was told."

"OK," he started the car, "Well, let's head for Moratalaz, and after that, we'll see..."

They headed down Gran Vía and turned onto an even wider boulevard with La Cibeles in the distance, passed the Puerta de Alcalá and drove for a while alongside the Retiro; this was Madrid, Ignacio knew that, had seen it a thousand times in photographs and films, and heard about it even more. Perhaps this was why he felt more at home here than Andalucía because here, finally, in the buildings and the street names, in the trees, the *palacios*, the boulevards and the statues, his two countries finally came together.

Arriving in Madrid he found it exactly as he had expected it to be, a sprawling city with too many houses, too many shops, too much passion to be disrupted by this new thing called of tourism, and he liked that. He liked Madrid, and so did Raquel, though her approval barely counted since she had even claimed to love the monotonous scenery of La Mancha they had seen from the bus. And yet, beyond the Retiro and the Calle O'Donnell, Madrid began to blur and fade. Ignacio had the impression that he was no longer in his father's city, and yet this was still a city, new areas of cheap, ugly houses, tower blocks, it could have been any city in the world, but it was Madrid. The taxi driver was still driving fast, he knew his way here, but he did not linger when he stopped and rolled down his window to ask for directions. If what they had been driving through was Moratalaz, they had clearly arrived at the far end of it, because before them were fields, an arid wasteland of building sites with a train track in the distance. "I think we might have passed it," said

481

the taxi driver, and turned the car around, drove a little way, stopped and asked for directions, announced they had taken the wrong turning again, and this sequence of events was repeated twice more before they came to the house they had been looking for.

"Well, here we are at the end of the world."

It was an ugly, three-storey building running the whole length of the block with several narrow aluminium doorways. The walls were of whitish brick, and on the terraces and the balconies there was laundry, bits of junk, ladders, and here and there a withered plant, utterly unlike Granada with its geraniums. This was not a pleasant place to live, thought Ignacio as he pushed open the door and found himself in a narrow hall lit by two bare bulbs. On the right hand wall was a row of postboxes, two of the doors were hanging off and others were missing, one of the latter had once been his aunt's mailbox, but Ignacio already had her full address: staircase C, second floor, left hand door.

"Are you nervous?" Raquel asked as he rang the doorbell.

"Yes."

She took his hand and squeezed it as they heard the sound of a bolt being shot back.

"Hello, You must be Ignacio..."

In the doorway was a rather tall young man with the Fernández family nose which Ignacio had been lucky enough not to inherit, and the misty eyes which, unfortunately he had not inherited either.

"Yes, I'm Ignacio. You must be Mateo."

"Yeah..." the young man smiled then stood aside to let them pass, "Who's the girl?"

"This is Raquel. Her parents are Spanish too, they're good friends of my parents. I asked her to come. I hope you don't mind."

"No, course not... anyway, don't stand there, come in."

The pressure of Raquel's fingers relaxed, but he shot her a glance, pleading for her not to let him go. She nodded as they stepped into the hall. On the right, a door with a wooden architrave led to a narrow living room where there was barely space to move between the furniture: a three-piece suite, a low table with four chairs at the end next to the door to the terrace, and a sideboard opposite the sofa. Hanging on the wall above the sideboard there was a rug. Ignacio was so taken aback he had to look twice – a wool rug with a picture of two stags woven in darker wool, with long white tassels: a carpet on the wall, and a hideous one at that. He was standing, dazed by the sheer awfulness of the décor, when he heard a shout and turned and saw a woman who could not be much older than his mother, but who seemed much older. Short and stocky with dark curly hair, she came into the living room wiping her hands on a dishrag which she dropped onto one of the chairs so that she could hug Ignacio with such force it was as though they had been through some disaster together.

"Ignacio! Oh, my God! Ignacio," she took a step back to to look at him and he could see tears in her eyes. "I can't believe it, let me look at you, *hijo*. You look just like your father. How old are you now?"

"Twenty-one."

"That's how old he was the last time I saw him, I still remember, every day...*ay!*" Her eyes no longer held back the welling tears. "You're just the same, your eyes, that forehead, your ears ... It's like looking at your father!" Then finally she turned and saw Raquel. "Who's this girl? She can't be your sister?"

"No, no..." Ignacio cut in, "She's the daughter of some Spanish friends of my parents, her name's Raquel."

"Oh! It doesn't matter, *hija*, my home is your home." She kissed Raquel on both cheeks, then picked up the dishrag and gestured to the sofa. "Well, don't just stand there, take a seat... What would you like to drink? I've just made a sponge cake. Maybe you'd prefer beer?"

Just then a thin man of about fifty, prematurely old with sparse grey hair and a sad, drooping moustache came in and crossed the living room without a word. His rubber-soled slippers glided soundlessly over the tiles as though he were floating.

"That's Andrés," Casilda looked at him coolly, "My husband. Andrés, this lad is..."

"Yeah, yeah, I know..." He looked from his wife to the new arrivals. "Hello." He slumped into an armchair.

"Good afternoon," said Ignacio then everyone fell silent.

"Well, I'll just pop into the kitchen..."

Casilda disappeared and the silence remained unbroken until her son asked: "So, what have you been doing? Do you like Spain?"

"Oh yes," Raquel smiled, "Very much."

"You know what I think?" Mateo focused his attention on the girl, ignoring his cousin. "Nowhere in the world can you live the way we do here. Just look at all the building working in Alicante, you wouldn't believe how many tourists come in the summer. And that's just the beginning... We live like kings here, honestly, the weather is perfect, the sun shines all the time, it's not like those northern cities where you get up to grey skies and rain ... And the food? What did you think of the food? I've got a friend who's just moved to Cologne and he's already sick to death of eating pork and sausages and potatoes, it's just not the same. I mean, obviously, he earns a lot more money there, but I don't think he'll stick it out… It's just we have everything here, just look at the fruit … And then there's the ham, I don't know how anyone could live in a country where there's no *jamón Serrano*. And it's so peaceful too, you can walk the streets any time of the day or night …"

As Mateo prattled on, and Raquel listened with an inscrutable smile, Ignacio compared the boy's words to the things on the sideboard facing him: six glasses, each a different colour, a school sports trophy, a small teddy bear, two small earthenware jugs painted yellow, a white china pot embossed with flowers, a perfume bottle and a box made of painted sea shells. Nothing more. And not a single book.

The poverty of the furnishings shocked him more than the rug hanging above his head. Ever since they had stopped thinking of him as a child – some six or seven years ago – his parents had stopped forcing him to accompany them to dinner with their Spanish friends, but he still remembered their houses, and his uncle's house in Toulouse, his grandparents' house, his own home. He had been born and raised in a home of exiles who had arrived in France with nothing but the clothes on their backs, who for years had worked like dogs so as to be able to live in a foreign country as they might have done in their own, or at least that was what he had believed. Until this afternoon, when he discovered the unexpected, grotesque reality, this ugly, ramshackle sofa, this house where even a perfume bottle might be considered an ornament. This was how they lived, those who had stayed behind, those whom the exiles envied, the men who had never had to sleep on a beach, the women who had never had to steal a petticoat from a dying woman. And still they wanted to go back, he thought, still they raised a glass every New Year's Eve to toast the possibility that they might go back to this country. Before he had time to come to any conclusion, the lady of the house reappeared with some green cups and a sponge cake.

"…and the women? Spanish women are stunning, of course, you'd know that being Spanish yourself. You should come back, honestly, there's no place in the world where you can live like you can…"

"Don't talk rubbish, Mateo."

Casilda did not look at her son as she poured the coffee.

"It's not rubbish, Mamá, it's the truth. And…"

"No," his mother interrupted, looked at her nephew and the girl who had come with him, "It's not the truth. We're not happy here. You can see that for yourselves."

"You might not be happy, Mamá," Mateo raised his voice, "You're never happy with anything!"

"Maybe that's it..." she conceded, her voice calm. "I'm not happy here. Andrés, would you like some coffee?"

"I'd like you all to shut up."

"...and some coffee?" his wife asked sardonically.

Her husband merely nodded as a girl of uncertain age commented from the doorway: "Mamá's right," then crossed the room towards the guests.

"Shut up you brat," from his suddenly harsh, authoritative tone, Ignacio and Raquel realised that the man was clearly her father.

"I'm not a brat," she, however, took after her mother, "I'm sixteen." Then with a sincerity her older brother lacked, she went over to Ignacio and kissed him on both cheeks. "Hi, I'm Conchita."

"There's still one missing," Casilda smiled, "Andrésito, my youngest, he's twelve, but he went out with his football a while ago and god knows where he is now..."

The football fan did not appear, and coffee and cakes proceeded without further interruptions, the women asking questions, the little girl eager to know everything about the guests - what they were studying, where they lived, what their parents did, what the French thought about Spain. Ignacio and Raquel answered her questions, choosing their words carefully, because they guessed that this was not the first time the family had had this argument, and they did not want to make things worse, but from time to time, Ignacio glanced at his cousin, who greeted his mother's words - "so you're studying engineering? That's good. You're just like your grandfather," with a contemptuous toss of his head, and he did not understand him, did not understand how Mateo could be so happy at the success of his father's murderers.

Again Ignacio thought that Spain was an impossible place, but he did not have time to think any further, because Raquel glanced at her watch and nudged him gently.

"It's already eight o'clock, we should be going," she said.

"We only have half an hour to get back to the city for dinner," he added.

Mateo looked at them wide-eyed. "You're have dinner at half eight?"

"No, well, at home, we have dinner at half nine, sometimes as late as ten," Raquel said.

"OK, but just wait a minute," Casilda said, "I've got something I want to give you. I'll see you out."

As she went to fetch it, Mateo said his goodbyes to Ignacio and Raquel. He gave his mother a withering look when she reappeared with a plastic bag.

"Don't mind them inside," she said as she walked down the steps with them, "It's the fear talking. They terrified, and they don't know what to say." She stopped and turned to look at them. "We've had a hard time, and there's more to come. That's why people don't want to know, they don't want to acknowledge the problems. They end up believing what they've heard and forgetting what they've gone through."

"But not you," Ignacio ventured.

"No, not me..." Casilda smiled and carried on down the steps. "But they don't understand. That's why I wanted to walk you out ... and besides, Andrés has always been jealous of my first husband, Mateo. In the beginning, I could understand it, because, before he asked me to marry him, he asked me straight out and I told him the truth, I told him I didn't love him as much as I loved Mateo. And he said 'it's because he was executed, isn't it?' and I said no, I didn't think that was the reason, but he's always said it was... He took it very badly, but he still insisted on marrying me."

She looked at them again, Ignacio looked at Raquel and saw that she was looking at him. Neither Ignacio or Raquel knew what to say, and they carried on down the stairs in silence, concentrating on her words, because Casilda, for her part, had a lot to say: "He'd only just got out of prison. He spent five years inside. After he got out, he gave up on politics. He was all alone, he didn't have any family, and he was living in a boarding house. Things were even harder for me. I used to work as a cleaner and I didn't even make enough money to pay the rent. I'd had to give up my parents' apartment, and all I could afford was an attic room with a leaky roof on the Calle Venture del Vega... It was no kind of life for me or for my son, that's why I married Andrés. I'm not sure I did the right thing, that's the honest truth, , because although we got married, and had two children, he still hasn't forgotten. He's alive and Mateo is dead, he's been dead for more than twenty years, the 'twenty years of peace' those bastards are celebrating...I've been a good wife to him, but it's not enough, and I can't do any more. Things are going from bad to worse because he's still jealous of a dead man, he gets furious if I so much as mention his name, and my son... Well, Andrés is the only father he's ever known and that's why he hates it when I talk about my first husband, that's what he calls him 'my first husband'. It makes me angry, but what can I do?"

They had arrived at the front door of the building, but she did not go outside, she leaned against the wall, as though afraid someone might see her, and slipped her hand into the plastic bag. She glanced back up the stairs to make sure they were alone, and only then did she open her hand:

laid across her pale palm was a gold bracelet encrusted with diamonds and sapphires and an enormous pearl in the centre.

She took Ignacio's hand and placed the bracelet in it. "Here. Look after it, don't lose it, it's worth a lot of money. That bracelet was your grandmother's dowry, she gave it to me the last time I saw her, when she found out I was pregnant. I was very fond of her, she was always good to me. That's why I want you to give it back to her."

"But why?" If she gave it to you, then it's yours."

"I know, but I want her to have it, or one of your aunts, or your mother ... 'Take it', she said to me, 'if things get worse you can always sell it, you might need the money.' And she was right, the money would have come in useful, but I never could bring myself to sell it. In any case, it would never have worked, they'd probably have locked me up for theft."

"Why would they?" said Raquel, "I mean, you're her daughter-in-law..."

"Not to them. They said my marriage – all marriages performed during the Republic - were invalid. I was a communist, and a communist couldn't possibly have a bracelet like this unless she'd stolen it," she smiled, "No one would have dared buy it from me, they'd have called the police... For people like me, everything was dangerous..."

"What about now?" Raquel said, "Surely now you could...?"

"...sell it? Of course I could sell it now, but I don't want to any more. If Mateo had been a girl, then maybe, I might have kept it until he was a bit older, in case he came to his senses and I could have given it to him, but...," she turned to her nephew. "I'd rather you took it back to your grandmother, tell her how much I love her, and thank her for me. And, oh, there's something else I want you to have..." Her lips suddenly began to tremble as her hand slipped once more into the plastic bag and took out a photograph with a scalloped border, the whites yellowed and the blacks mottled with grey. "I'm sure you've never seen this, have you? Take it. I have another one taken on the same day."

"It's very beautiful," said Ignacio, who had never seen the portrait, but he immediately recognised the smiling solider as his uncle Mateo, his arm around a slim, graceful girl.

"Yes," Casilda smiled, "Mateo is very handsome in that photo, and I look pretty too, I was pretty back then. That's why I want you to take it to your grandparents and tell them... Tell them I think about Mateo every day, every day without fail..." for a moment, her face contorted in a paroxysm of grief and she could not go on, but then she composed herself. "Fifty-six days of my life we spent together. Fifty-six days, not even two months, over a period of two years, and often I didn't even get to spend the whole day with him, a couple of hours, maybe three ... But still... I remember that first night he showed up at my house in the early hours, dripping wet, I remember him leaving in a hurry because his commander had said that if he was late back, he would be court-martialled and shot for desertion." Though there were still tears in her eyes, she laughed, "Every morning, I think about that night, I remember every detail so as not to forget, and I can still see him, still hear his voice, I still remember the things he said to me right up to the fifty-sixth time, the morning when he picked me up and took me to the truck that was taking me to Cartagena. I was inconsolable and there he was smiling and waving, and even after the trucked pulled away I heard him shout 'See you soon, gorgeous!" That was the last thing he said, 'gorgeous', and I never saw him again..."

She wrapped her arms around herself and began to cry, to sob with such grief that it was as though it had been yesterday, as though twenty-four years had not passed. She had been a widow for almost twenty-five years according to the clocks, the calendars, but not to her. Not to her.

Ignacio Fernández Salgado knew how badly Mateo's death had affected his father, his grandparents. They had often spoken about it, too often for his liking, and yet he felt an instinctive shudder of pain run through him, because he could not doubt the grief this woman still felt, this woman who had a second husband, three children, and a life that did not matter to her. If someone had described this scene to him, he would have found it laughable, just one more pitiful example of Spanish foolishness, but he was here, he could see it and hear it, there was a taste of apricots in his mouth, and he felt an overwhelming need to hug this woman, to hide himself within her so that he could weep for all the dead, all those people for whom, until now, he had not shed a single tear.

"I remember it every morning." Casilda's voice was firm now. "I wake up every morning before the alarm clock goes off, and I remember those fifty-six days, because no one can forbid me, no one can stop me, not my husband, not Franco, not his fucking mother... Tell your grandmother that, and tell her..." she closed her eyes, gritted her teeth and carried on. "Tell her that on the 29th of every month, I buy a bunch of flowers, I put on a black dress and I go and stand by the cemetery gates because I don't know where he's buried... They won't tell me where he's buried ..."

She fell silent, as though she could not bear to go on, and Ignacio took her hand and squeezed it.

"I wasn't allowed to wear mourning when I went back to Madrid.

Everyone in my area knew me… I was a coward, I didn't dare. The second day I went out wearing black, a policeman who lived next door took me to the station and they asked me how I could possibly know who I was mourning for, they said I was a whore, that I slept with anyone and everyone. That was just the start …" she paused, looked at Ignacio and Raquel, then gestured with her hand as though waving away temptation. "Pff, why would I bother tell you what they said all those years ago…? The fact is I couldn't mourn, and I was a coward, I didn't dare…"

"It doesn't matter, Casilda," Raquel spoke the words Ignacio had been thinking. "Wearing mourning doesn't mean a thing, it's just clothes, it's just a colour."

"It does matter," Casilda was insistent, "It mattered to me. But I was scared, and I had a baby … That's why I wear mourning now – in secret, obviously – but only so that I don't have to fight with my husband. I take the clothes to work, and I change again before I come home. My son knows, he says I'm crazy, but I don't care. On the 29th of every month I buy the biggest bunch of flowers I can afford, and at lunchtime I go to the cemetery and I leave the flowers by the wall and I stay there for a while, until they throw me out, because sooner or later a guard always shows up and moves me on… I know the flowers don't last. I know the guards give them to their wives or their girlfriends, but I don't care. I go on buying flowers just to piss them off, I leave them by the wall where they shot him just to piss them off …" For a second, her eyes flared with the fire of the young girl in the photograph. "One day, about ten years ago, I saw a name written on the wall in chalk: Victoriano López Aguilera. I don't know who he was, but I'll never forget his name. I asked around – because I go to the cemetery so often, I've got to know the other women who go – but nobody knew who had written it. One of them said 'It must have been written on one of the other days, I come on the 29th.'" Since then, every month I write his name on that wall: Mateo Fernández Muñoz, and I write 1915 – 1939. I know they rub it out as soon as I'm gone, but before they can erase it they have to read it. Fuck the lot of them! Because what they want is for Mateo never to have existed. Do you understand Ignacio?"

She looked at her nephew and he nodded without quite knowing why, because he did not yet understand, but she sighed as though she had finally reached a place where she might rest.

"It's not enough for them that he's dead, they want him never to have been born, that's why they claim he was never married to me, that his son has no right to take his name, that's why there's no tombstone. But Mateo did live, and I lived with him, and that's the only reason I go on…

'How can you go on like this, Mamá? What good do you think all this hatred, this bitterness will do?' That's what my son asks me." She closed her eyes then and smiled a bitter smile. "He doesn't understand that it's the only thing that keeps me going in this fucking awful country, until all this is over, until your father comes back, until your grandparents come back, the people he knew, the people he loved. For the moment, he only has me, but I'll go on wearing mourning, I'll go on buying flowers, I'll go on writing his name in chalk on the wall where they shot him until the day I die. Tell that to your grandparents, Ignacio, and tell Paloma that whenever I have time – because sometimes the guards move me on straight away – I write her husband's name, I don't remember the year he was born, but I write 1910, because he was older than Mateo."

"He was born in 1911," Ignacio would never know where the voice came from that uttered these words, but he knew that he could not leave without saying them. "It had to be 1911, because he was twenty-eight when they shot him."

"From now on, I'll write 1911," she brought her hands to her face again as though to wipe away her tears, her anger, as though to put things in place. "I'm so happy to have met you, Ignacio." In 1971, when their first son was born, Ignacio Fernández Salgado and Raquel Perea Millán would decide to name him Mateo. No one asked them why, but everyone assumed that it was to close the gap that had opened in September 1944 when Ignacio Fernández Muñoz said to Anita Salgado Pérez that he would have preferred his first born son to have taken his older brother's name rather than his own.

No one saw them on that April evening in 1964, as they walked together along the deserted pavements, in this deserted district of a city they did not know. She was watching out for taxis but there were none, he was wondering whether he was going mad or whether he had miraculously recovered his sanity.

"Tell your father I think about him all the time," this was the last thing Casilda had asked, hugging him fiercely, "No one would think it to see us now, but once upon a time we did something great here, something truly magnificent. They were the best years of our lives, despite the war, the bombings, the starvation, because we were doing something important and we believed that what we were doing was worthy of the sacrifice..."

Casilda's words resonated in Ignacio's head and brought back other words he had often heard but did not understand until that afternoon. *No, Gloria, not with the rabble. With the people of Madrid – The first man to run, I'll shoot him – We're not like them, Mamá, they were the ones who*

490

*started it – Don't cry, silly, nothing's going to happen to me, I haven't done anything. – We are what we are María, and our place is here with our own people – The fascists won't set foot here, not even over my dead body, because even if they kill me, I'll come back from the grave – and the salchichón... 'why don't you hang it up in the pantry and we can worship it for a few days before we eat it?' – 'I've thought about you so much, Papá... After I was arrested in Madrid, I thought about you all the time, I was so happy that you weren't there to see it, to see how we were betrayed' – I have loved you with all my strength, Paloma – Mateo was killed not just for being who he was, but for being Papá's son, Mamá's son, for being your brother, Ignacio, for being Carlos' brother-in-law – We have nothing to be sorry for, Ignacio...* That afternoon, his grandfather's voice seemed to be speaking not to his father, but to him, *I don't regret anything, hijo.*

Ignacio Fernández Salgado - who was not Spanish, who was not French, who did not know where he was from and who had been born into a fucking tribe – finally realised that his mother was right, that this trip had been dangerous for him, because he could not go back to being the person he was before. Suddenly face to face with the maelstrom of contradictions that he had spent a lifetime avoiding, when Ignacio finally accepted his destiny, he found he was at peace with himself and, though he hardly realised it, he was crying.

They were standing at a traffic light.

"I'm not crying because I'm sad," he said, "It's not because I'm sad." And Raquel kissed him.

After that, everything happened quickly, easily, even the taxi ride was merely a formality between two halves of a single kiss.

They did not get back to the city centre until 9.15 pm and neither of them wasted time asking the other if they wanted to go for dinner. From that night, Laurent shared a room with his sister and they slept together, firstly in Madrid, then in Barcelona. When they got back to Paris, Raquel dumped her boyfriend, and her parents were as delighted as Ignacio's were the first time their son brought her home to lunch. They were married two years later and in the spring on 1969, their first child, a girl, was born.

When Ignacio Fernández Muñoz took the baby in his arms for the first time, he felt proud and emotional at being a grandfather for the first time. It was a feeling he would relive with the birth of each of his grandchildren, but he would never love any of them as much as he loved his first granddaughter, whom they named Raquel Fernández Perea.

"Excuse me...?" It wasn't her voice.

"Raquel?"

"No, Raquel's not here..." It wasn't her voice, it wasn't her voice.

"I'm sorry." It was a young woman who spoke with a French accent. "Bye."

When I saw the light shining out across the balcony, I felt so nervous that I didn't know what to do and I walked around the block three times, the first time quickly, then more and more slowly, my heart in my mouth. Then I went into a bar, ordered a drink and downed it quickly, never taking my eyes off the door to the building. I had been watching the apartment for almost a fortnight but until that night, nothing had happened.

I was looking for Raquel. I was searching for her because she wanted me to search for her. This was the one thing I felt sure of when I got back to Madrid on 26 August, exactly a week after receiving her last text message: *Goodbye, Álvaro, I love you, I LOVE YOU, Raquel.* I hadn't erased the message, and sometimes I would pick up my mobile just to make sure it was still there, to be sure she had definitely sent it. Definitely. I no longer knew anything for definite, no longer knew what was true and what was a lie, but every time I pressed the message button, those seven words appeared, and they comforted me. Raquel had written this message and she had sent it to me, just as suicides who don't really want to die pick up the phone immediately after swallowing the bottle of sleeping pills. The message was not a message, it was a cry for help. Raquel had left, she had disconnected the answering machine on her landline, had changed her mobile phone number, changed offices and moved away, but before she did all these things, on 19 August 2005 at 11.39 am, she sent me that message.

"I'm afraid Señora Fernández Perea no longer works here."

On the first of September at five past nine, I stepped out of the lift into the foyer, but this time the receptionist at the Department of Asset Management at the Administrative Society of Cooperative Investment Institutions S.A. did not direct me to Raquel's office.

"She applied for a transfer to another office," Mariví, as over made up as she had been in April and considerably fatter, anticipated my first question.

"Could you tell me where she's working now?" Mariví looked at me, shook her head, and I was surprised to see a glimmer of compassion in her eyes. "Please…"

"No, I'm sorry," she looked away, "I'm only a secretary, I can't…"

"I wouldn't tell her you told me …"

"Let me finish," she smiled and I knew then that I was lost, "I can't tell you because I don't know. Nobody told me and I didn't ask. It's a big company, and people get transferred all the time. I'm really sorry, but I can't help you."

She wasn't telling me the whole truth. Shocked as I was, I realised that Mariví was lying, but I also saw there was sympathy in her gaze.

"However…" she lowered her voice and leaned across the desk as though to indicate that she was on my side, "When you first came, it was something to do with settling an estate, wasn't it?" I nodded, "Well, you know, sometimes these things can drag on forever."

When she was twenty years old, thirty kilos lighter and only smoked after meals, her childhood sweetheart had left her for another guy while her wedding dress was still hanging in the dining room of her parents home. Raquel had told me the story once, and Mariví told me it again that morning. Heading back to the lift, after I had thanked her, I felt exhausted.

I walked back to my place, shambling along dragging my twin temptations with me – the urge to give up hope and the need to salvage the slender thread of hope I still held between my fingers. I wanted to go on believing. *'To believe'* is more ambiguous and more precise than any other verb, even condemned men walking to the gallows prick up their ears and die waiting for a last-minute pardon. When I resigned myself to the incomprehensible, that Raquel had wanted to disappear, I could still see a light at the end of the well shaft into which I was tumbling. They were black, terrible days, heavy and slow, made up of heavy, interminable grains of damp sand, one last grain then another last grain and another falling on my head.

"What's the matter, Papá?" Miguelito asked. "Are you not feeling well?"

"No, I'm not feeling well," I said and he went off to the beach with his mother.

The weather had improved and everyone was happy, everyone except me. So I went back to bed before they came back for lunch and when they went out again, I got up and sat on the sofa. I spent one day like this, two days, three days, and when I woke at dawn on the fourth day, convinced that anything was better than this uncertainty, I realised the significance of that light in the distance. *'To believe'* is more ambiguous and more precise than any other verb, more compassionate and treacherous. Anything would have been better that this uncertainty, I thought, it would have been better if she'd told me she was seeing someone else, if she'd told me she didn't love me, if she'd dumped me. I would have preferred it if she'd dumped me, but that was something she hadn't been prepared to do... I thought about this.

Raquel had disappeared, but she hadn't dumped me. At first this sounded like a ludicrous theory, a fool's comfort, but thinking about it carefully the logic made a certain sense: it was shaky, but it held up better than anything else I could think of. If Raquel had wanted to dump me, she would have done so. It would have been easy. It would have been as simple as not asking me to stay on that last stormy night when she stood crucified in the doorway of her flat begging me not to leave. All she had to do was let me leave, but she had begged me to stay.

Why? I wondered as I got up from the sofa, washed my face, brushed my teeth, put on my clothes, and went out. Why? Raquel had disappeared but she hadn't left me. She had disappeared, but before doing so she'd taken the precaution of saying goodbye, of telling me she loved me. If you said it over and over, it was almost like music, like a dreamy old melody. *Goodbye, I love you.* It was warm and sunny out and as I wandered slowly along seafront, I soaked up the sunlight, the sight of people bathing, like a convalescent.

Raquel wasn't dying, she wasn't married, she didn't have a boyfriend who'd just come back from the far side of the world, she wasn't pregnant, she didn't have an incurable illness, wasn't about to be sent to prison, she wasn't a drug addict or an alcoholic, she didn't have a secret love child, she wasn't a member of some religious cult or a terrorist cell. I examined and rejected each of these possibilities in turn. "For a physicist, you have a vivid imagination..." And maybe I had, but I harried my imagination, I twisted it, wringing out every possibility, and I came up with nothing. I couldn't rule out the possibility that she had a secret lover, some dark shady connection that made it impossible for her to share her life with me or any other man, but if such a man had existed she would have told me. Raquel Fernández Perea was a normal woman, if by normal you meant like me. She had been working for the same company for years, been living in the same apartment, everyone in her district knew her, she was on first-name terms with her local shopkeepers. There was nothing strange about her, and yet her disappearance confirmed Fernando Cisneros pronouncement, a verdict that sounded like a riddle: the strange thing about her was that there was nothing strange about her; that she did such strange things without being strange. If Raquel had really wanted to disappear, she wouldn't have picked up the phone like a half-hearted suicide. If she hadn't wanted me to look for her, she wouldn't have said goodbye.

This conclusion gave me back the decisiveness that I'd lost during the sterile period of exhaustion. If Raquel wanted me to look for her, I would look for her. Uncertainty is a cold, unwelcoming house full of invisible terrors. Better to suffer, better humiliation, anger or ice, better the taste of blood in my mouth, any of these was better than this limbo of stale air. I wanted to know and I was prepared to pay the price for that knowledge. At times, Raquel had looked at me as though I held her life in my hands and I had felt that was true. Now, I held my life and hers in my own hands, and the archived message on my mobile phone was a white kerchief, the ensign of a knight urged on by a fair maiden to slay the dragon. I was prepared to slay that dragon, but before I could, I had to find it, to know who or what it was. That night, I went out to dinner with my wife and son, I sat on a terrace and stared at the sea, added my voice to the voices ripping me to pieces, and on the way back, I announced that I was going back to Madrid. "OK," Mai did not even look at me, "But I'm keeping the car."

I took the train back to Madrid on 26 August, caught a taxi outside the station and asked the driver to take me to the Plaza de los Guardias de Corps. There was no one at Raquel's apartment, or at least, no one answered the door. The signs of the holidays were evident – all the shops were closed and there were parking spaces on the Calle de Conde-Duque. I sat on the terrace of the only bar I could find and waited for nightfall. No light appeared beyond the twin balconies of her apartment, but I carried on waiting, then finally I went back to my house, which welcomed me with the strange indifference of new smells, paint and plastic and silicone. This shiny new space was not home, and it sent me out again in search of the colours, the smells and warmth of the home I had lost.

I had come back to Madrid to look for Raquel, and I looked for her everywhere, but it was useless. Two days after I got back, the doorman of her apartment building told me he thought she'd probably be back in a day or two. On the 31st when I saw him again, he looked at me suspiciously, almost alarmed by my persistence. He hadn't heard anything, but it didn't matter because I was convinced I would find Raquel at her office. When Mariví explained the lengths to which Raquel had gone to disappear, I almost broke down. But I had decided to hold out until the end, and before heading home, I sat on a bench and phoned my brother Rafa.

"No, no, everything went fine. I told her we wanted to sell up, and she didn't have any objections," he told me. "I was surprised, I expected her to try and talk me out of it, but when I got there, she had the papers ready for me to sign, we both signed and I left. I can't have been in her office more than ten minutes, that's why I don't really remember much about her... A brunette, polite, friendly... but why do you need to get in touch with her?"

I'd already prepared an answer: "When I met her, she gave me the address of a bookshop... It's not important, but we talked for a bit. I told her I taught physics and she told me she knew a secondhand bookshop that often had monographs and old manuals. I jotted down the address on a bit of paper and now I've lost it... I only thought of it because next week it's a friend's birthday ..."

My brother, ever conscious of his status as a rich, powerful man, wasn't interested in sentimental details: "Well, then call her... The thing is, I can't actually remember her name, but I can look it up if you like..."

"No, that's OK, I've found the letter she sent to Mamá."

I had hoped he'd give me a clue, something specific that might help me track her down. I thought about calling Julio and asking him what kind of financial hassle might crop up with a legacy, but I guessed that a vague reference would be enough. I was right, but when I spoke to the girl at the bank, she didn't transfer me to Raquel.

"I'm sorry... I've looked but I can't find an extension number for her. I think maybe she doesn't work here anymore."

"That's impossible," I said, as much to myself as to her.

"What I mean is, she no longer works for any of the departments in this building," the girl sound young, dynamic and she was patient, "It's a big bank, there are hundreds of departments, there are any number of places she might have transferred to... But she's not my list."

"In that case I'm not really sure what I should do..."

"Don't worry, I'll take your details and send them to the right department. Even if the assets have been liquidated, someone will still be dealing with your file. If you give me your phone number, I'll make sure whoever has taken over gets in touch."

I made a big deal of thanking her. I didn't hold out much hope, but three days later a man named Francisco José Reguiero called and told me he was at my disposal if I needed anything. He had qualified a few months earlier and had only started working at the bank on 1 September. He still had no idea how things worked, so they'd put him in charge of unresolved files "to get used to asset management." He was as chatty, as friendly, and as useless as everyone I had spoken to over the past few days. Obviously he didn't know Raquel, didn't know where she might have gone, he didn't know anyone who might know except maybe her secretary, Mariví, who knew everything. "What about Paco?" I ventured.

"Paco?"

"Yes," I was mortally embarrassed now, yet I ploughed on regardless, "Raquel mentioned a colleague named Paco, maybe he might…"

"What's his surname?" Suddenly, Reguiero seemed considerably less forthcoming. "There are lot of people called Paco in the department."

"I realise that, but I don't remember his surname…" In fact, I'd never know it, any more than I knew Berta's. "It doesn't matter… Thanks for your help."

I called directory enquiries, once, twice, three times, until I finally happened on an operator more sympathetic than her colleagues, she gave me the same number I had been vainly calling at all hours since 19 August.

Don't do this to me, Raquel, why are you doing this to me? I felt as though I was trapped inside an impenetrable maze whose walls closed behind me, forcing me to take two steps back every time I thought I was getting somewhere. And yet somewhere in this city a dragon awaited. I tracked it with a single-mindedness that could no longer be called determination, it was more like an illness, a morbid obsession that could only be described as temporary madness.

That must be what other people thought, all those people I pestered relentlessly in those first days of September: Raquel's doorman, the caretaker at the building on the Calle Jorge Juan. Mariví, whom I went back to see at least twice more, Reguiero, not to mention the host of secondary figures who had had some loose connection to her. I asked anyone if they had seen her: the woman at the florists who had sold her an automatic sprinkler system in late July, in the bakery where she usually bought her bread, the man at the newsstand outside her building, waiters in the two or three bars we'd gone to over the summer. All of them remembered Raquel, some of them even remembered me, but they all shook their heads. Little by little any sympathy they had turned to irritation as I insisted on explaining how important it was for me to find this woman. Raquel had just been part of the scenery to them, one of the hundreds of women they saw every day. "Why don't you hire a private detective?" the man at the newsstand asked when I gave him my card and asked him to call me if he saw Raquel. One of the waiters said it was a pity the TV series that traced missing persons wasn't on any more. "Of course, they've got a list people can sign up to, to say they don't want to be found," he added, "so maybe your girlfriend…" He didn't bother to finish the sentence.

Yet if she hadn't wanted me to find her, she wouldn't have said goodbye. I didn't mention this belief to anyone, but now and again I'd switch on my mobile phone and read her message. I wasted the last few days of my holidays prowling her district, hanging around the stalls selling curios where she had liked to browse, wandering aimlessly around Canillejas. Meanwhile, September rolled on with the languor of a transitional month, halfway between summer and autumn, between the last warm days and the first cold snap, and I adapted to its rhythm.

I didn't dare talk to anyone anymore, not the doorman or the man on the newsstand, but I saw them and they saw me. "There goes the head case again", they probably thought as they turned away. I usually strolled through the Plaza de los Guardias de Corps at sunset, and every day the same thing happened: nothing. I'd get to the door of her building, press the button and remember her voice. "Yes?" But no one answered. I could remember my own voice: "Hi, it's me." and Raquel saying "Come on up," but the silence dulled the memory of her voice and mine so much that, for a moment, it made me doubt everything.

*'To believe'* is more ambiguous and more precise than any other verb, and every night this vagueness gripped me, covered me in the ashes of a joy I had lost, one that, in truth, maybe I had never possessed. I felt worn out, depressed, worn out with being depressed and depressed by how worn out I felt. Maybe this is how it ends, I thought, maybe this is it. Term starts again soon and some day I won't make it to my daily appointment with this intercom, some day I'll start to forget Raquel, I'll be myself again.

These days, Mai was the one always waiting for me at home. We barely spoke to each other, but she knew that something had happened. It wasn't hard to guess since I was spending more and more time at home. I didn't feel like going out any more, I didn't feel like working, I did nothing except walk every afternoon to an empty flat and sit for an hour or two on a café terrace watching the building. Mai wasn't crying any more, she wasn't attacking me, and every night she made dinner for me. Sometimes, in the middle of the night, she'd slip her arms around me; she wasn't to blame for any of this, she didn't deserve this. I didn't want to go back to the way my life had been before, and yet this was the landscape that was beginning to appear on the horizon. Maybe this was how it would end, in September, maybe October, November, the Earth would go back to its usual prosaic orbit and I wouldn't even know what had been true and what was a lie.

"But surely it's better this way?" Fernando Cisneros said with a smile on our first day back on Campus.

"No it's not," I said, determined to hold out to the end. It's the worst thing that's ever happened to me.

He looked at me pityingly and said nothing.

"What about your friend?" I asked.

"What friend?"

"The girl who was looking into that thing about the theatre...

"Oh her... She never called me back. I told you it was difficult."

When he'd got back from Comillas two days before my wife, he had adopted a different tactic for reassuring me.

"You look like shit, Álvaro," he said. I told him about my conversation with Mariví. "Look, Raquel can't just disappear, it's impossible – there's bound to be some trace. She could go and live on the other side of the world I suppose, but some day or other you're bound to run into someone who knows where she is," he reassured me. I said I wasn't so sure but he was obviously thinking about Elena Galván, about the time I was Christmas shopping and had run into her on the Plaza de Callao. Then I remembered Berta, remembered the play she'd been rehearsing – actually it's a trilogy that runs to six hours.

"There you go then," Fernando said.

"But I don't remember the name of the play or the writer, though I do know he's Spanish and well known. I recognised his name when Raquel mentioned it, and the name of the play, but I can't remember it now..."

"That doesn't matter, I have a friend, Pilar, she's professor of literature and she knows all that stuff ..."

It had all seemed so easy to him that afternoon, but now, two weeks later, he had forgotten what he'd said. This might take a long time, I thought, that evening, as I stared at the door of the building, at the dark window beyond the balcony, but some day, somewhere, I'd run into Raquel again, although by then it could be too late.

Everything about the Plaza de los Guardias de Corps depressed me, the name, the place, the stubbornly closed door. You can't slay a dragon if it hides from you, and I was worn-out, I was completely worn-out.

"Maybe it's for the best, don't you think?" Fernando Cisneros said that morning, but the following morning, Saturday 17 September, I finally spotted a thriving plantation of geraniums on the balcony.

When I saw the light was on in the room beyond the balcony, I felt so nervous that I walked round the square half a dozen times like an ox tethered to a waterwheel. And while my legendary intelligence stalled at the prospect of this impossible conversation, my feeble body showed me that it was capable of coming back to life. I felt the sweat, the frenzied pulse of my blood, the sudden state of alertness that sent pins and needles shooting through my fingers.

If ever I believed in fate, it was that evening, and if ever I needed a drink, it was at that moment. The mixture of belief and alcohol was so effective that not for a moment did I doubt that Raquel would be there. "Yes?" I imagined. "Hi, it's me." "Come on up!" I savoured the sound of these words as I pressed the button on the intercom, I could taste them, feel their warmth in my belly.

"Yes?"

"Hi, it's me."

"I'm sorry?"

When the unfamiliar French accent slashed through the sails of my hope, the shock all but paralysed me, but fate intervened in the person of the charming, elderly woman from the second floor who appeared at that moment and made my decision for me.

"Hello," she said handing me a rectangular package tied with string. "Could you hold these cakes for me?"

"Of course," I said, taking the box without really knowing what I was doing.

"Thank you," she said, rummaging in her bag, "Cream éclairs, they melt if you so much as look at them..."

She found her keys and went inside, not even looking to see if I'd followed her. When we stepped into the lift, she took back the box of cakes, pressed the button for the second floor and said: "You're going to the fourth?"

"Yes," I gave her a smile.

She knows. At least she knows. That was what my smile meant. This woman I didn't know had recognised me, had acknowledged me, borne witness to a story that was true. She knew who I was, she knew my place in the world, she did not doubt my sanity or my intentions. She's going to disappear now, I thought, she's going to vanish in a puff of smoke. But she stepped out of the lift with her cream cakes and said goodbye; she was real, she was flesh and blood. When I got to the fourth floor, the shadow of her presence gave me courage as I stepped up to the door, and without a flicker of hesitation, pressed the buzzer.

"Hi..."

That was all I could say before I froze, speechless as I stared at the space, the table, the coat rack, the paintings, the light still hanging in the same place, still with one burned-out bulb, exactly as it had always been.

"Hi..." a young woman said. She was about the same age as Raquel, about the same height, she was pregnant, and she had glasses and a ponytail.

I studied her carefully and saw that her skin was unremarkable, her eyes were blue, she had a square jaw with a protruding chin, utterly unlike the graceful curve of Raquel's neck, her face, but I also noticed that in some small way she looked like Raquel; it might have been the proportions of her features, it might simply have been the vague similarities common to even distant members of the same family.

"I rang the intercom a minute ago," I said, after a protracted pause which the girl accepted without any sign of impatience, though her neighbour, coming back from a walk with his dog, noticed. "My name is Álvaro, Álvaro Carrión, I'm looking for Raquel Fernández Perea, she owns the apartment..."

The girl nodded: "I know, but as I told you, she's not here..."

"No, of course..."

The neighbour was pretending to search for his keys, or maybe he had really lost them, but his presence made me even more nervous. The girl looked at him, and I realised that she too thought he was pretending so that he could eavesdrop on our conversation.

"Can I come in?"

She opened the door and stepped aside, then closed it behind me with the exaggerated grace, the excessive warmth one might offer a stranger.

"You've been expecting me, haven't you?" I ventured.

"Well..." she spoke with a strong French accent, pausing from time to time to choose her words. "My mother told me that Raquel... she have a... relationship?" She looked at me and I nodded. "With a man, but this is over ..."

"But it's not over!" I protested. Her eyes flew open and I knew at once that I needed to temper what I said. "What I mean is, that's not the way I saw it. She just disappeared without telling me why, but before she did, she sent me a message..."

"Listen..." the girl interrupted me, "I know nothing. I do not see my *cousine*. Tomorrow, I go back to Paris, the holidays they are over."

"I see... So you're not here for long.?" She nodded. And you're Raquel's cousin?"

"Yes, my mother is a sister of her father. My name is Annette."

"Like your grandmother?" I smiled.

"*Oui*... like my grandmother," then, for the first time, she smiled too and I realised that she had understood what I meant, had realised that this casual remark was proof of how close I was to Raquel, an assurance that I was telling the truth.

"You know, you look a lot like Raquel when you smile."

Just then, a man about my age carrying a little girl who was wearing a bib spattered with baby food popped his head round the door and glanced at the Annette questioningly.

"*C'est un ami de ma cousine,*" she reassured him, then turned back to me, "That's Claude, my husband, he doesn't speak Spanish."

Her remark was intended to bring my visit to an end, but we were all so well brought up that he and I shook hands and he led me into the living room.

"Listen, Annette, I..." I was about to say 'I'm desperate', but the word was too theatrical to be true. "Could you do me a favour? Even if you're not going to see Raquel, I assume you have to leave the keys for her somewhere?"

"At my mother's house... well, it's my grandmother's house too," she smiled again and her smile was so like that of her cousin that it hurt my eyes, "At my grandmother Anita's house."

"Would you mind leaving Raquel a note? It'll only take me two minutes to write, I don't want to disturb you, it's just... I'm in a bad way. I need to..."

"But..." she looked down, twisting her hands as though trying to dissuade me, "I don't have any paper. I don't know where there is any."

"I do," I was counting on my self-assurance to dispel her doubts.

"*Alors...*" I headed down the corridor and she followed me, her daughter was whimpering now and her husband was trying to comfort her, making soft rhythmic sounds like a train. This strange music followed me all the way to Raquel's room, this bedroom where the most astounding moments of my life had been played out. And yet, when I opened the door, all I saw was a suitcase open on the bed, unfamiliar clothes strewn over the duvet, pots of cream and cologne bottles on what had been my bedside table. I noticed that Raquel's was empty, there was a space where the photo of me being awarded my prize for mental arithmetic had been. If she'd left the frame, I would have assumed she'd torn up the picture and thrown it away, but the photo of her grandparents was gone too, and the chaos pendulum. She's taken them with her, I thought, she's taken the photo of me and the one of her grandparents. I could almost see her. But her cousin was staring at me anxiously, as though suddenly wary of this strange man standing stock still in the middle of the bedroom. I opened the desk drawer and took out the notepad.

I sat down in the leather armchair, took out my pen and wrote:

> "Call me, Raquel. Please, call me, tell me what's happened. It doesn't matter what it is, I'm not afraid of anything. I love you Raquel, I love you, and nothing else

matters. Call me. Don't leave me like this, I'm begging you. I love you so much, you can't imagine, I love you so much I think I'm going mad, I love you more than anything, more than anyone in the whole world, I love you. Álvaro."

When I'd finished, I reread what I'd written and thought it was terrible. It was clumsy and stupid. It was full of repetitions and clichés, I could do better than this, I could have written something better if I'd taken the time, chosen my words carefully, but I ripped the page from the notepad, folded it and gave it to Annette, without even bothering to put it into one of the envelopes I'd seen in the drawer. It was best to leave it as it was, awkward, clumsy, and full of clichés. It was best if her cousin, her aunt, her grandmother read it before she did. It was best to have them on my side. There was only one good thing about the note: the touching sincerity of despair. And yet, when I thought about it, I realised that I was no longer a desperate man.

Maybe it was a premonition. Maybe it was just that I was so devastated that the simple news that Raquel was still alive, the possibility, the probability that sooner or later she would read this note was enough to shake me out of the stupor and the self-pity I'd been wallowing in. I didn't know where Raquel was, yet I could see her reading this note, I could imagine her astonishment, the shudder that she would feel when she got it.

Maybe it was because I had been so devastated that the smallest of things could comfort me, for a couple of days later, as I watched my students take their resits – the same innocent fools who in their first term had heard me say that the whole is only the sum of its parts when those parts do not interact – I told Fernando Cisneros that I was feeling much better.

"In that case, I'm not sure I should give you this," he said, handing me a web page listing times and ticket prices for a theatre in Salamanca.

It was 11.10pm and I was already in my pyjamas. It was Wednesday 28 September  and one of the TV stations was showing a repeat of "Walking with Dinosaurs", a programme I never tired of watching.

I was sitting on the sofa waiting for the wicked tyrannosaurus to savagely attack the poor, gentle triceratops when I heard my mobile phone bleep to say I had a new text message. The phone was on the coffee table next to me. I picked it up, still watching the TV, and didn't look at the message until the prehistoric homicide had been committed. At that moment, everything stopped: time, history, the pitiless chronicle of extinct cruelty. It only took me a second to read the message, from an unknown number, only six words. *Am at Calle Jorge Juan. Come.* Six words, only twenty two letters, twenty-nine including punctuation and spaces. *Am at Calle Jorge Juan. Come.* No greeting, no sign off, nothing to mark the dividing line between good and bad, between peace and dread. *I'm on my way,* I replied, *Wait for me.* When I got to my feet, I was surprised my legs could hold me.

Mai was in bed watching a film. "More dinosaurs?" she'd asked after Miguelito had gone to bed, and I'd nodded. "Are these new episodes or repeats?" I'd smiled "I'm afraid they're repeats, but don't worry I'll go and watch them in the bedroom." "No, no..." she'd insisted with the same gentle consideration she had treated me with since she'd discovered that something to her advantage had happened, "I'll go into the bedroom, although I love films, I always end up falling asleep..." This was true. When I stepped into the bedroom, she was already half-asleep. I walked past the bed, took a clean shirt from the wardrobe and when I turned round she was suddenly wide awake, sitting up in bed.

"Are you going out?"

"Yes."

I went into the bathroom to get dressed and when I looked at myself in the mirror I realised that she would have seen the alarm signals even if I hadn't changed before going out. I was ashen, my eyes were wide and red-ringed. This strange face fascinated me as though it belonged to someone else, to a very different man to the one I felt inside. The worst is over, I thought, I'm not hurting any more, but my face refused to listen. There was an obscure, almost tragic wisdom in the face I saw in the mirror. Something I couldn't decipher.

"Álvaro, Álvaro..." Mai was hammering on the bathroom door.

I quickly buttoned my shirt and unlocked the door.

She stood there, wrapped in the velvet shawl I had once brought her from La Coruña, her arms folded, shoulders tense, in her eyes a look of anger and pain.

"If you go, don't bother coming back."

I was about to say 'Fine', but the answer sounded so flippant, so cruel in its terseness, yet this was the only sentence I could formulate. "Fine, in that case, I'm going out and I won't be back." Mai glared at me, then turned on her heel. I finished getting dressed. I didn't want to think about her ultimatum. Raquel is back, she's waiting for me, I said to myself over and over as I slipped on my shoes and my jacket and checked my pockets.

I was leaving my wife, I was finally leaving, not really knowing where

I was going or what I might find there. I left with no guarantees, nothing but an address, a meeting, six words, but I didn't want to think about that, I didn't want to admit that the best thing, the thing any sane man would have done, would have been to ring this unknown number, talk to her, postpone the meeting by a few hours, burn no bridges. But I didn't have any bridge to burn because Raquel was back, she'd sent me a message, she was waiting for me, and that was all that mattered. That was why I was leaving, not really knowing where I was going or what I might find there. I wanted this to be over quickly, I didn't care how it happened as long as it happened quickly. I knew that what Mai had said was just words, that she did not really mean what she said, that I could come back once, twice, ten times if I wanted to, but I also knew that I wouldn't want to, that I wouldn't do that to her. I knew that even if Mai had held a gun to my head I would have left just the same, because Raquel was waiting for me and nothing would stop me from going to her.

"Did you hear what I said, Álvaro?" Mai was standing in the hall by the front door.

"Yes."

"You know I mean it."

"Yes."

"But you're going anyway?"

"Yes."

Outside, I waited for a surge of happiness, I tried to feel it, but I felt nothing. But my joy was there somewhere, it had to be, I knew this with the certainty that I knew the dragon would cower meekly at my feet, surrender rather than face my sword. I knew it because I had heard it, though in words that were more circumspect.

"Raquel will come back, she'll show up when you least expect it," Berta had told me the previous Saturday, "She'll come back because it's the last thing she should do and in the state she's in people never do what they ought to."

When I tried to ask her what she meant, she raised her hand. "Don't ask me any questions, Álvaro, I've said too much already..."

"Why are you a woman, Pichona?"

The actor playing Silver Face had already slipped his hand down the front of Berta's dress. She threw her shoulders back to assist this provincial Lothario in his machinations, all the while staring into his eyes, her head held high, her face a mask of satisfaction in spite of her protestations.

"Please don't..." but her arms hung limply by her side and she did nothing to stop his greedy hand from capturing her breast.

"They are firm."

"Do not touch them."

"Why are you a woman?"

"You should know."

"But I don't know."

"I am a woman, I need to be a woman so that you will come to see me for a day, for a year if it should last so long. To squander an ounce with you, if I should have it. But I cannot admit that you should flaunt it publicly."

Convinced that she will have Silver Face in her bed that very night. Pichona dares to shift from the formal *usted* to *tu* without warning. "You don't mind if I address you as *tu*, do you?"

By the time Fernando Cisneros took his leave, there were only three students left in the exam hall. One departed before the end, but the other two took advantage of the extra half-hour I had added to the two hours of official time for the exam. The last student to leave, a tall, leggy blonde with large breasts and a tiny waist flashed me a sly smile and murmured that she hoped she would pass. She paused for a moment, in case I had something interesting to say, but I simply told her that she'd have the results in ten days.

Then I locked myself in my office and typed in the URL for the website Fernando had shown me, a theatre putting on Valle-Inclán's *Barbaric Comedies*. And there was a picture of Berta with long dark hair tumbling over bare shoulders in the poster for *Silver Face* and *Emblematic Eagle*. She didn't appear in the last play, *A Romance of Wolves*.

"They've obviously decided to perform all three as a single piece," Fernando had said, but they were performing them in chronological order over several days. They had spent the summer touring the production around Spain, but had taken a break in September, which was why Fernando's friend had taken so long to track them down.

That morning, I bought a ticket in the fifth row of the stalls for the first performance of *Silver Face*, then I went to the library in the Department of Philology, took out a critical edition of the three plays and spent the next few days reading them from start to finish. Mai did not comment on my sudden interest in the plays of Ramón del Valle-Inclán, didn't bat an eyelid when I told her I had to go to Salamanca on Saturday on some university junket, though I was vague about the details. In the end, the play which, when I bought the ticket, I'd no intention of seeing, now fascinated me.

"Open the door, Pichona!"

"I am naked in my bed."

"That should save me some little time!"

"Oh, Moorish king! Tell me who you are?"

"You know all too well."

"I tell you I do not know you."

"Open the door!"

"Let me put on a petticoat. Do not break down the door, my darling." But Berta, who was indeed naked in her bed, simply slipped her arms into a white lace bed-jacket, which she did not even button as she crossed the stage to open the door. I remembered Raquel telling me "Directors are always getting her to take her clothes off, she's stunning when she's naked." She had been right on both counts.

Raquel had also said that Berta was a fine actress, and she was, so much so that as she crossed the stage, it seemed that she was fully clothed by the talent of the playwright whose lines she spoke with such artlessness, such conviction. Her nakedness was less arousing than it was poignant, and her performance overshadowed the other actor.

I felt that this guy didn't really understand the shadows of the passions that motivated his character, the impotence of a younger son challenging his father for a woman they both desired, the malevolence that pushed him towards la Pichona, his casual betrayal of his beloved Sabelita, a girl more faint-hearted than feeble whom his father Don Montenegro would seduce then cast aside in a heartless show of arrogance that broke every law, human and divine. Silver Face was handsome, strong, young, ambitious, capable of inspiring in Sabelita that same love that he felt for her, a love he was prepared to swear before God, to commit to for life, but his father was more powerful and wanted the girl for himself. His desire marked the alpha and omega of all things. When I bought my ticket, I wasn't sure I wanted to see the play before I'd had a chance to speak to Berta. But I'd finished correcting my exam papers and needed to find some other way of killing time, and so I read this brutal, brilliant, savage play. I remembered Raquel saying "Spanish stories ruin everything." This particular Spanish story seemed to have been written in a frame of mind that precisely anticipated my own mood when I arrived to see it.

"Álvaro!" Berta emerged, dressed now, with no make-up, from the stage door where I had been waiting for about a quarter of an hour. "How are you?"

She looked exhausted but elated. She had been a great success, if an actor's success can be judged by the bravos and the applause at the last curtain call. I'd watched her smiling, looking down into the stalls, then her eyes happened on me and her face suddenly became serious. That was what I thought I had seen, but when she appeared she kissed me so spontaneously that I gave a truthful answer to her question.

"Not good. Not good at all, that's why I'm here."

"I'm not surprised…" she started walking and I followed her, "Let's go for something to eat, I'm starving. Did you see the play," I nodded. "Did you like it?"

"I liked it a lot," I wasn't lying, and she thanked me with a smile, "Given my situation, it's pretty close to the bone."

"Really?" I realised she hadn't understood but then the penny dropped. "Oh, you mean because of the relationship between the father…"

"And the son," I finished the sentence, "except I'm not planning to head off to war."

"I see you've read the plays." She sounded surprised

"Yes. I started reading "Silver Face" to see what the story was about but then I had to find out how it ends."

"It's not exactly a happy ending."

"It's a very unhappy ending, but at least your character is one of the good guys."

"That's true." She slipped her arm through mine and led me to a bustling café. "Poor little Pichona, living on the streets, hardly better than a whore, but she's big-hearted and she's the only one in the play who's really capable of love. That's the genius of Valle Inclán. There's always a whore, or a tramp, or a child or a lunatic that he treats with such tenderness it compensates for his cruelty to everyone else. Anyway, Álvaro… you shouldn't be so quick to judge. Silver Face is good in his own way, he's a better man than his father and he's a saint compared to his brothers. That's why Valle-Inclán has him go off to war, to redeem him, so he plays no part in pillaging his mother's inheritance, so that Montenegro doesn't get to curse him the way he does his other sons. But Silver Face is nothing like you, whatever you might think. Shall we take this table?"

The café looked jammed, but Berta found a table at the back, and ordered a club sandwich and a beer.

"Berta, where's Raquel?" I asked as soon as the waiter left.

"Um…" she thought for a moment, "She's in Madrid."

"Where in Madrid?"

"You know I can't tell you that. Raquel's my friend and you don't betray a friend."

"But…"

"Don't push it, Álvaro... If you keep asking me questions, I might just start telling you any old shit. I'm good at that, I'm an actress, remember? The whole thing was madness... All I can say is I didn't know anything about it until that dinner when you showed up at the pizzeria with her and she had a funny turn, remember?" I remembered, and I believed her, I could sense that she was telling the truth. "When I found out, I was thunderstruck. Until then, I'd had no idea and the whole thing seemed incredible. If I'd known I'd never have let her..." she let the sentence trail off, "Raquel's always been the sensible one in our group. I was always the one who fucked up, got involved with unsuitable men, married with sick children and wives, all that baggage..."

"But I'm willing to get divorced, I want to marry her if she'll have me, and Raquel knows that ..."

"Álvaro... Oh, Jesus... Álvaro!" she said my name as though it pained her, then stretched out her arms and took my face in her hands as though to shut me up and console me.

"Then that's not the problem?"

"No, that's not the problem." She let go of my face, but in her eyes I could see a guilty compassion.

Our order arrived, forcing us to stop for a moment. Berta was frowning, she didn't like the way this conversation was going.

"What happened Berta?"

She took her sandwich in both hands, then closed her eyes and bit off as much as she could.

"I can't tell you, Álvaro, really I can't..." She began the sentence with her mouth full, then waved her hand signalling me to wait until she was finished. "...it's not my place to say, you wouldn't want to hear it from me. This is something Raquel has to do. What I can tell you is..." She took another bite and I realised she was not starving so much as giving herself time to choose her words. "Raquel's in a bad way, Álvaro. As bad as you, maybe worse, because this is all her fault. She left because she doesn't want to hurt, but, I don't know... Sometimes I think the cure is worse than the disease, because, in the beginning it did seem that leaving was the best thing she could do, even I thought that, but now... How was I to know how things would turn out? The guys I fall for never chase after me, not to this extent. How could I have known you'd be so persistent? I stayed with her a couple of nights ago and she showed me your note ... She was devastated, she wanted to call you and I... Maybe you'll hit me for this, but I was the one who persuaded her not to, because she has to think things through, she can't just call you without knowing what she's going to say ... Don't angry with me, Álvaro, please... I just want things to work out, and I can't always be there for her, because I'm touring ... Anyway, what I'm trying to say is Raquel will come back, she'll show up when you least expect it. She'll come back because it's the last thing she should do, and in the state she's in people never do what they ought to."

"What do you mean...?"

"Don't ask me any more, Álvaro," she raised her hand. "I've said too much already..." But before she left, she told me one more thing, after she'd insisted on paying, after I'd told her yet again that honestly, no honestly, I wasn't angry with her. I hadn't left. I watched her from the doorway of the café, silently betting that she'd take out her mobile phone and call Raquel before she got to the middle of the square, but suddenly she came back.

"One more thing, Álvaro... There isn't another man, not now, not before the summer, there's never been anybody else. I'm just telling you because...Well, I know we're all grown-ups but I'm telling you because if I were you, it would be something I'd be happy to know."

"Thanks, Berta," It was something I was happy to know.

We kissed goodbye again and she left, and before she'd even reached the place where she had been, she took something out of her bag. A second later I could see she had her phone pressed to her ear. For a second I thought of running after her, ripping the phone out of her hands and talking to Raquel. But we both knew I wouldn't do that. So I just watched her go until she disappeared beneath one of the arcades on the square, then I went to my car and headed back to Madrid.

As I drove, I tried to make sense of what she'd told me. It seemed very little and yet it was more than I had been able to find out in a month. Berta's silences, the irregular sequence of hesitations, the dot-dot-dots of sentences that trailed out into silence had seemed more revealing than her words, and what she did say seemed to me more darkness than light, except for her last comment. It might not have seemed important to her, but it meant a lot to me, not so much to my sense of pride, but because it refuted a hypothesis which had begun to form in my imagination. The vague language with which Berta had predicted that Raquel would come back, her discreet convoluted way of letting me know that Raquel loved only me was useful too, especially the bit about the phone call she had persuaded Raquel not to make, proof that my most awkward words had also been the most effective. And yet none of this new data took me to any place other than where I had been the moment I found out that Raquel had disappeared. I had to wait, that was my only conclusion, the only thing I learned. I couldn't have imagined that I would not have long to wait.

In the taxi that took me back to the place where everything had begun, the opulent apartment on the Calle Jorge Juan, the last place I would have expected to see her, I felt a strange sense of nostalgia for that wait, an incomprehensible desire to postpone the moment for a few more hours. *I'm not afraid of anything*, I'd said in my awkward, clumsy note to Raquel, *I'm not afraid of anything*, but it wasn't true. The taxi driver, however, took less than ten minutes to get to the building, pulling up in front of the cold marble doorway. The door was closed, but I took the precaution of pushing it before gently touching the doorbell for Apartment E with a trembling finger. I felt a sense of unreality that was intensely physical yet light, a frothy whitish mist, like the nebulous light of dreams.

This isn't real, I thought. But I pressed the button and someone upstairs released the catch. My shoes made a soft squeaking sound on the freshly polished marble, and the lift screeched as it came to a halt on the ground floor. As it climbed towards the seventh floor, I looked at myself in the mirror and felt a surge of pity for this face which I understood better than before. It was the face of a man who was terrified, hysterical, alone exhausted. But when I got to the seventh floor, I found myself standing before an open door and, on the other side, Raquel, dressed exactly as she had been the first time I met her: a black t-shirt with a white pattern and a pair of black jeans that did little justice to the shimmering asymmetry of her hips. She seemed thinner, paler, her eyes were puffy and the skin around them was as translucent as parchment. Looking at her, I saw a woman who was terrified, hysterical, alone, exhausted, a face so like my own yet so different. But I also saw Raquel, a clever girl, so beautiful you had to look twice. I saw the love of my life.

"Álvaro." She took a few steps towards me, so slowly my whole body ached. I couldn't move, I couldn't speak, I could do nothing but stare at her. "Álvaro, there's something I need to tell you…"

"Don't ever do that to me again, Raquel."

My arms took the initiative, wrapping themselves around her and hugging her hard, my hands moved over her back, slowly recognizing her, recognizing myself, I could now become myself again as I breathed her in, as I touched her, I was intensely aware that I was about to kiss her, and when I kissed her everything was calm once more, flowing gently like water.

"Don't ever do that to me again…"

Clinging to my neck like a castaway she hugged me, kissed me, gazed at me as though I held her life in my hands.

"If I could, I'd eat you right now, I'd swallow you up so that you'd always be inside me, so I'd always know where you were, because I was dead, Raquel, it was like I died, and I can't bear it, I couldn't bear it if… Don't ever do that to me again, ever, for the love of God."

Then, without letting go, she looked into my eyes and said the only thing I needed to hear.

"The only thing I love is you, Álvaro."

"And I love you," I felt a rush of tenderness, a sharp pain like a knife wound, "I love you so much…"

"There's something I need to tell you."

"Not now." I hugged her again, kissed her, "Please, not now, I don't need to know now, I don't care Raquel…"

When I'd arrived, I knew I was going to kiss her and the mere knowledge had moved me. Later as we lay together naked in that unfamiliar bed, I was more conscious than ever of beauty, of pleasure, of joy, of the existence of all living things, for the whole world was suspended on Raquel's lips.

I was risking everything on those lips.

I was aware of it again when she moved away from me.

"I never slept with your father, Álvaro."

This is what she said.

She told me that she had never slept with my father and suddenly I felt a terrible urge to laugh and cry at the same time.

On Saturday 5 May, 1956, Don Julio Carrión González, thirty-four, was joined in holy matrimony to Señorita Angélica Otero Fernández, twenty-one, at the church of Santa Bárbara in Madrid. The bride, the great-granddaughter of the Conde de la Riva, wore a white silk dress designed by Cristóbal Balenciaga and a veil of Mechlin lace, a family heirloom. The witnesses to the marriage were the father of the groom, Don Benigno Carrión Moreno and the mother of the bride, Doña Mariana Fernández Viu. After the ceremony, the newlyweds celebrated with a dinner for two hundred guests in the state rooms of the Palace Hotel.

"Listen, Julio, you may be rich, but you're not respectable," Angélica turned on him those liquid, piercingly blue eyes that both captivated and unsettled him. "Until now, that didn't really matter. In Spain we've always believed it's good for young men to sow their wild oats, but you're over thirty and no respectable man is still single at that age. Not in this country. How much longer do you think you can get away with being single, showing up with dark circles under your eyes to receptions full of bishops and generals' wives? It can't last, Julio, and you know it, unless you settle down quickly with a pretty little virgin from a good family and give her two or three children. That's what you need, but it's not an easy thing to come by, no matter how rich you are. There's only one woman in the world who would make a suitable match for you, and that's me. Firstly, because my surname is Fernández, and that might be useful later, in certain situations. Franco can't live forever. But mostly because I know who you are and what you are, Julio... You're a thief, an impostor, a liar and a scoundrel with a taste for whores. I know all that, but I still love you. I've loved you from the first moment I saw you." Her voice as she spoke was so calm, so cold that it was clearly a speech she had rehearsed many times. "Think about it, Julio."

He smiled almost shyly and said nothing. They were sitting on the Rosales terrace, enjoying a warm September evening; the autumn sun was fading but was still bright enough to dupe the trees which had not yet shed their first leaves. It was not cold, but when Angélica, feeling the silence drag on, picked up a cigarette and tried to light it, she found that her fingers were trembling. Julio smiled more broadly and felt a vague, diffuse warmth course through him fuelled by his vanity and his utter admiration for this woman.

"You're nervous," he ventured.

"Yes," once again Angélica proved to him that there were different ways of being brave, "I'm very nervous."

Julio Carrión González had always been attracted to Angélica Otero Fernández. From the very beginning, in spite of her insolence, the almost suicidal arrogance that erupted into daily tantrums, making her his most troublesome employee. When she stared him down, chin held a little too high, nostrils flared, he found Angélica unbearable, irritating, stupid, but even then he found himself attracted to her. He had played with her often when she was a young girl, and he sometimes felt that this was why she had come back from Galicia, so they could go on playing.

"Do that Russian trick for me, Julio…"

Even as a child, when she spoke to him, there was a tremor in her voice that troubled him, a wisp of precocious, ambiguous promise that cloaked those innocent words, for they had to be innocent even if at times there seemed to be an unconscious sexual undercurrent. Maybe even conscious, he had sometimes thought, even if it's tentative and vague. This was why he had enjoyed flirting with her when she was twelve, thirteen, fourteen, looking at her body that was mature beyond her years, as she posed like a vamp, showing the scabs on her knees, the smooth pink of her girlish cheeks. She would make faces at him and toss her head.

"Do it, Julio…," she would say in an affectionate little voice, pretending to be coy. "Go on, do it for me.

He could not suppress a smile as he remembered how many other women had asked him that same question, in the same tone of voice.

"OK, you wait here, I'll just go to the kitchen to get a cup and a glass."

Back then – from the summer of 1947 to the summer of 1949 – it had been one of his favourite tricks. It was such a hit, particularly with women, that he always kept a piece of sponge in his pocket. When he got to the kitchen, he pressed the sponge into the bottom of a opaque glass, took a pick and, from one of the blocks of ice they used to keep meat and fish cool, chipped off a sliver and placed it on top of the sponge. Then he went back into the living room with the cup in one hand and a small glass of water in the other.

"I had a girlfriend in Russia," he would say looking at Angélica, who clapped and smiled, craning forward. "Her name was Nadia, and I loved her very, very much. I loved her so much that when I had to leave I cried. I kept my tears in this glass and sent them to her in the post." With a theatrical flourish he had learned from Manuel Castro, he tipped the glass into the cup where the sponge immediately absorbed the water. "And she sent me her tears, but it was so cold in Russia that they froze before I got them." He tipped up the cup and, instead of water, a sliver of ice dropped into his palm. He handed it to Angélica and while she was staring at it, open-mouthed, he used his thumb to retrieve the sponge from the cup, wringing out the water onto the carpet, and placed the cup down next to the glass.

"That's amazing! How did you do it?"

"I can't tell you that. A magician never reveals his secrets."

But, although he was convinced that she would do so some day, Angélica never asked to be his apprentice. She did not want to be like him; she wanted to be with him.

"I'd never make you cry like that Russian girl," she would say whenever her mother was out of earshot.

"Go to your room, Angélica." Because whenever Mariana appeared, the magic between them was over.

Julio often thought that he would not have found the girl so amusing were it not for the fact that she was so unlike her mother. The only thing they had in common was that both looked older than their age. Mariana was only two years older then her cousin Paloma, who was almost six years older than Julio, but everything about Mariana belied those years. When they first met, Angélica's mother had just turned thirty-three, only a little older than Julio liked his women. Even so, she tried to seduce him.

In the beginning, when she knew nothing about the true intentions of this charming young man, Mariana had thought that the best possible solution to the problems his sudden appearance might create was to marry him. Julio would call her twice a month to tell her that he would like to come to lunch or to dinner, and he was so skilful that when she hung up she was never quite sure whether she had invited him or he had invited himself. At first she did not mind his visits, in fact she enjoyed them. He was invariably punctual and never came empty handed. He would send flowers, or bring dessert, cakes or chocolate, and when the previous bottle was almost empty, he would bring a bottle of Pedro Ximénez because, though she was fond of food, his hostess was even more fond of dessert wine.

"Oh, Julio, you shouldn't have," Mariana always accepted his gifts with evident pleasure and the same polite protest. "It's no trouble at all." Julio would reply with his most charming smile. "You're always so generous, and I..." she would turn her head in a coy gesture that was wasted on her guest. "...I have nothing to repay your kindness, I'm only a poor woman..."

...and fat, he added to himself as he stared at the folds of flesh that spilled out over a corset as stiff as armour plating. *...and clumsy,* he thought noting that she couldn't put on lipstick without getting it on her teeth *...and stupid,* he thought, since only a complete idiot would think she had any hope with him. *...and a whore, you're worse than a whore,* because for all the years she had spent going to mass every day, she would still have been happy to spread her legs if he'd asked. This was what Julio Carrión González really thought about Mariana Fernández Viu, but he was careful not to tell her until the right moment.

"Please, Mariana," he would say, "I'm the one who should be grateful."

"Don't be silly, you're like one of the family now. Come in."

Then, as she disappeared down the hall, pretending to blush and trying unsuccessfully to get the wrinkles out of dress, Julio turned and there, leaning against the wall or in the doorway, one hip thrust out, would be Angélica in her school uniform.

"What about me?" Angélica would feign anger with an instinctive grace, a charm that Mariana would never possess, "Didn't you bring anything for me?"

He crept towards her, slowly, sure-footedly, as noiselessly as a cat. "Let me think, ... I'm not really sure ... Although, maybe... Hey, what have you got...?" He stretched out an open hand towards her and closed it into a fist next to her ear. "What's this? Have you been growing chocolates in your ears?"

Delight transformed Angélica, turning her into the little girl she was; she was suddenly impetuous, uncoordinated, leaping up and throwing her arms around his neck. Julio let her hug him, inhaled the child's perfume she wore, thinking that it was a good thing she was so young, because if she were to proposition him the way Mariana did, he might very well succumb. Then the mistress of the house reappeared with aperitifs for two, delicately laid out on a tray filled with linen napkins and crackers, and as she poured the vermouth, ignoring her daughter's existence, she marshalled all her meagre talents as an inept seductress. These were the moments Julio genuinely enjoyed, because every time her mother leaned a little too closely to her guest or touched his arm for no apparent reason, he could see Angélica scowling, puffing out her cheeks, shaking her head or closing her eyes in horrified embarrassment. Then, all three of them would eat together, but Mariana did not speak to her daughter until Matilde appeared with the coffees.

"Go to your room, Angélica."

It was over coffee that her guest chose to deliver his blows, but he played his part with calm and cunning. He would wait until Mariana had completely recovered from their previous quarrel before persuading her to take one more step towards her downfall. Julio generally believed that the first of those to expropriate the fortunes of the Fernández Muñoz family was not a clever woman, and she had little foresight, since she seemed incapable of divining her guest's true plans. From time to time she would thank him profusely for everything he was doing for her family in exile, but now and then a flash of lucidity in her eyes would make him doubt his assessment of her. He reminded himself it did not matter: there was nothing Mariana could do, he held all the cards.

"Don't you ever feel lonely, Julio? A young man like you with no one to look after him? I don't know, there are nights when I think even I might..."

"Don't worry about me, Mariana, I've always been a loner."

This was the pattern of most of their meals together: he would arrive, give them presents, there would be a little conversation, unproductive at first, though gradually Mariana had shifted from anxiety to a point where she was all but frantic. Julio, smiling and gracious, allowed himself to be admired. He tried not to discourage Mariana too much since her present attitude seemed much better than declaring hostilities before it was time. In fact, Julio did toy with the idea of bedding her. He could have done so easily, but beneath her makeup and tight-fitting clothes, Mariana Fernández Viu was still abrasive and her executioner was in no hurry.

"My husband was a good man, hard-working and serious, but his health was always very delicate, he fell ill when he was young and never really recovered. I've never known what it was to have a real man, a man with drive and ambition ..."

"You're still a young woman, Mariana," *don't get any ideas, it's never going to happen* "You'll find a man, someone who deserves you."

1948 was Julio Carrión González's first good year since 1933 when his mother had decided to go into politics. He spent the spring selling off the last of María Muñoz's olive groves and in late summer; he sold the farm for considerably more money that he had expected. He had already begun reinvesting his money as he made it – on drinks and whores and private rooms – but also on building permits in a Madrid that had been razed to the ground by bombers and was inhabited by a dark mass of fearful souls whose single preoccupation was finding somewhere to live. Construction companies proliferated in a climate of frenzied speculation that would make fortunes for charming, intelligent, gifted men like him. He had more than enough of such qualities to know that he did not need to hurry, to draw attention to himself, to get rich too quickly and arouse the suspicions of the gilded elite to whom he would always be a parvenu.

Julio Carrión González had not forgotten that even the cleverest men can be fools when confronted with someone cleverer than they are. And so he proceeded cautiously, never flaunting his newfound wealth nor saying any more than was necessary. His frequent visits to Mariana Fernández Viu were merely parts of a perfectly regulated machine.

"I'm worried about Angélica, Julio. She's so impulsive, so capricious… She'll be the death of me one of these days. Obviously, with no father figure, what can I do? But I'm afraid to bring anyone home because… I think you're the only person she really gets along with."

"I don't think you need to worry about that. Angélica is just high-spirited. She's intelligent and strong, and more than capable of taking care of herself. And she's very pretty."

"You think so?" Mariana asked, frowning so that her guest would see how much this idea upset her. But Julio enthusiastically repeated his opinion: "Of course. You have a very pretty daughter, and she'll grow up to be a beautiful woman. It won't be long before she is taking care of you."

Mariana Fernández Viu was never able to prove that Julio Carrión González was a thief. She never saw nor heard anything to corroborate what she knew, what she suspected when it was too late, and even then he would not give her the satisfaction of a real confession. Julio called, he came to visit, he brought flowers or chocolates, and in everything he did he behaved like a gentleman. Mariana did not know exactly what he did "oh, I've got a few irons in the fire" nor how much money he had "things are going well, I can't complain," nor where he stood politically "we're living through difficult times, don't you think? The most important thing is that we're working for the future of Spain," nor what he wanted from her, "thank you for lunch, Mariana, and for your charming company …"

He deliberately mislead her, sometimes adopting a false shyness, or he charmed her by being a little carefree, a little insolent, but he always remained true to his essential character. Julio Carrión González decided he needed to be something more than an acquaintance but something less than a friend; well connected to those in the administration and yet also to the Fernández Muñoz family, which indeed he was. He never missed an opportunity to bring Mariana news of Ignacio and his parents, nor did he miss a chance to tell her stories involving the Sánchez Delgado brothers and their family. Over time, he found that the most effective approach was to bring these two worlds together.

"You know, it's strange," he began offhandedly, after Mariana had sent Angélica to her room, "The other day, I was introduced to a general

– I can't remember his, but it doesn't really matter – Romualdo Sánchez Delgado introduced me to him, I'm sure I've mentioned him to you, he's undersecretary at the Ministry of Agriculture." Mariana nodded prudently and gave a forced smile. "Anyway, it turns out this general was a great friend of your uncle Mateo before the war, he spoke very highly of him. Said he was prepared to cut through whatever bureaucratic nonsense was necessary to have him back. I wrote to Ignacio the other day and mentioned it..."

Mariana never made any comment on these snippets of information, but Julio would see her grow pale and wring her hands, and this sight reassured him. Everything seemed to terrify Mariana - the thought that her family would come back and the thought that they might stay in France; she was unsettled whether Julio was happy or when he told her that things were not going well. Over the months, Julio discovered that Mariana had no connections, no protection aside from her friendship with some parish priests and a few priggish local women, connections she had not had the wit to leverage eight or nine years earlier by attempting to legalise her claim to the Fernández Muñoz estate.

"It's warm out today, don't you think? Almost like a breath of spring ... I feel a sort of tingling all over, the feeling you get after a glass or two of champagne, when you feel like throwing caution to the wind ... What do you think? Should we open a bottle and toast to..."

"No, Mariana, no toasts..." she had already slipped off her jacket and was leaning over the table, her lips pursed in a grotesque moue which Julio could not bear a moment longer, "We need to talk. It's about the apartment on the Calle Hartzenbusch."

"The apartment on the Calle Hartzenbusch..." the last wisp of her clumsy sensuality vanished in that dot, dot, dot. "Why, is there a problem?"

"Not at all," he guest was not smiling now, "Quite the opposite. I went there a couple of days ago and spoke to your tenants, they were very gracious and showed me around. A lovely apartment, on the fourth floor overlooking the street, with a large kitchen, two reception rooms and three bedrooms, that's the one?"

Mariana nodded grudgingly and rebuttoned her jacket.

"Afterwards we... had an exchange of views. I had to explain the situation to them, obviously, let them know that you don't actually own the apartment, that you had no authority to rent it to them, that for ten years you have been receiving rent that is not yours... They weren't happy, obviously, but we came to an understanding. They've agreed to vacate the apartment by the beginning of June in return for some small compensation, though I don't expect you to pay that, don't worry... They'll move into a new apartment in a building I'm just finishing near the Plaza de Toros. Initially, they didn't like the idea, either, but eventually they grasped the situation, they know that they have to move out. And now you know too."

"Me? But why do I need to know?" By a supreme effort, Mariana had managed to keep her composure, but she could do nothing to stop herself from shaking. Julio had never seen her so distraught, but he was not surprised. Until that night in February 1949, he had divested her of assets that, though very valuable, were remote - olive groves she had never set eye on, not even before the war. The apartment Mateo Fernández Gómez de la Riva had bought for his daughter Paloma on the Calle Hartzenbusch was worth considerably less but it represented the advance of Julio Carrión into her territory, Madrid, into the closed circle which until now had remained unaffected by the other changes. Julio knew this, and he knew too that Mariana had been forced to adapt her finances, that the rent from this apartment was her only source of income aside from her pension, but from his arsenal he adopted his most reassuring tone to explain his plans.

"This apartment is vast," he gestured to the surrounding rooms, "and very valuable. And it's much too big for the two of you and poor Mathilde who can't possibly keep it clean all by herself. How many bedrooms do you have - five, six? Not counting the study, which you never use. If you think about it, the apartment on the Calle Hartzenbusch would suit you much better. It's smaller, cosier, easier to keep clean. If you wanted, you wouldn't even need to retain Mathilde and you'd have even more space. As you know, it was Paloma's apartment when she got married and I suppose she probably had a maid, more or less like you, although at the time you were living in a place on the Calle Blasco de Garay, and from the look of the building, I'm guessing it was considerably smaller and less attractive than her place. So I was thinking it would be best for you to move into the Calle Hartzenbusch at the end of the summer. Angélica wouldn't even need to change schools, her school is just down the road."

"Yes... no... I mean, you're right about the school, but..." Mariana wrung her hands, as she struggled fruitlessly to find some way of explaining what she meant.

"And I'd have no trouble finding a buyer for this place," Julio went on, "It would be ideal for a large family, or it could be used as offices."

"Maybe," said Mariana, raising a hand to interrupt her guest, "But the rent from the Calle Hartzenbusch apartment is my only income."

"Mariana!" Julio looked at her wide-eyed, as though he could not believe what he had just heard. "Mariana, please, do I really have to remind you …"

"No, No, I know," her shoulders slumped, her eyes welled with tears, but still, in a shrill, terrified voice she insisted. "All I was trying to say is … that rent is my livelihood."

"But you have your pension? I thought that your husband's friends had arranged things so you would get the maximum, the same as you would have got if he'd died fighting the Reds?"

"They did, but that pension is barely enough to survive on."

"What more do you want?" Julio's tone grew harsh. "Your aunt and uncle would have been grateful for enough to survive on when they crossed the border. Besides, you're not badly off, considering. You have an apartment rent-free, and as I said, you'll have more than enough space to rent out a room, even two if you and Angélica sleep in the same room…"

"Lodgers? You're telling me to take in lodgers?"

"I'm not telling you to do anything Mariana, I'm just giving you some advice. You can take it or leave it, but I feel I should say that there's nothing shameful about taking in lodgers. Lots of respectable widows do it and they don't seem to have any problems … That's why I thought you might consider it, but there's no hurry. You won't have to move until September. You can spend the summer in Torrelodones as you do every year. After that, we'll see…"

But there was nothing to see. Mariana would never move out, would never vet any prospective tenants because by the time the holidays arrived, the apartment on the Calle Hartzenbusch had already been sold. Julio wanted Mariana out of Madrid so there would be as little fuss as possible, her absence would just like that of her neighbours who spent the summer in the country, he wanted to curb the number of people she could call on for support. Not that he was worried by her connections, but he did not want to be the subject of gossip in certain circles, regardless of how innocuous they seemed. He was determined preserve his image as a kindly, charming man. At the beginning of July, a few days before he sold the apartment on the Glorieta de Bilbao, he had all of Mariana's personal belongings packed up and put into storage in one of his warehouses until the end of August. Over the summer, his visited Torrelodones less frequently than he had in previous years, to Mariana's mounting exasperation.

"Julio, if you wanted…"

"Put on your clothes, Mariana, please. I don't want to take advantage

521

of you."

Until 12 September. On which day, at 10am, Julio arrived through the gates of the Casa Rosada in a taxi piled high with boxes, trunks and suitcases which Mariana recognised even before the taxi driver had unloaded them.

"What is this?" Mariana cried. The blood seemed to have drained from her whole body like a routed army in retreat.

"It's your things, Mariana. I hope I didn't forget anything. I've sold the apartment on the Glorieta de Bilbao," Julio smiled.

"Already? But that means…" she fell silent, swallowed. "But you said we should move to the Calle Hartzenbusch, and I think that's a good idea … I didn't expect things to happen so quickly, I would have liked to tidy up the house, take a few pieces of furniture…"

"The furniture doesn't belong to you, Mariana. I've sold it all."

"But what about the apartment on Calle Hartzenbusch…? Of course, there's all of Paloma's furniture …"

"No," Julio's smile never wavered, "The apartment on Calle Hartzenbusch is empty. I don't think the new owners have moved in yet. I sold it last month.

"But… but…" Mariana Fernández Viu staggered, took a step back and collapsed into a chair. "You're throwing me out on the street?"

His smile finally vanished, "Which is precisely where you deserve to be."

"This is what you wanted, isn't it, Paloma." Standing on the porch of the prettiest villa in Torrelodones, Julio Carrión lit a cigarette, glanced around him and felt a throb in the hard, shrivelled scar where other men have a heart. "You can't say I don't keep my promises."

"You know why I didn't sleep with you, Mariana?" She stared down at her dress, not daring to look at him. "Because when I was in Paris I was sleeping with your cousin Paloma."

"You bastard!"

Mariana Fernández Viu suddenly got to her feet and hurled herself at Julio Carrión, punching and scratching and kicking. Julio was able to restrain her, but he could not stop her from spitting abuse with the desperate impotence of a snake crushed underfoot.

"You son of a bitch, you bastard! How dare you speak to me like that! You stupid bumpkin, I'll ruin you, do you hear me, I'll destroy you, you're nothing but a pig, a monster …"

"No, Mariana." Julio was perfectly calm, "You're not going to ruin me because you can't. You're right about one thing, I am a bumpkin, but apart from that, everything you said about me applies equally to you.

With one difference: I'm the more intelligent one, and I have everything on my side. The law, for a start."

"Who are you, Julio, what are you?" She extricated herself from his grasp. "Are you a communist like my cousin? Are you a spy, a thief? What do you really do for a living, what are you doing with all this money? Keeping it for yourself, sending it to my uncle, or giving it to the Party? If you're not a thief, how is it that your business is doing so well?" She paused then looked up at him with the immense pity that she felt for herself at that moment, "Why have you destroyed me? What have I ever done to you?"

He lit another cigarette, inhaled deeply and looked at his victim with the trace of a smile playing on his lips, the serene charm of the most charismatic man in the world. "Nothing. You've never done anything to me, Mariana, you were just in the wrong place at the wrong time. That's all. I have no score to settle with you. In fact, I want to help you. In here…" He slipped a hand into the inside pocket of his jacket and took out a white envelope, "…are two first class tickets for the Madrid to Galicia express train leaving tomorrow morning at 8.30. I've booked a double room for you at the Carlton, in case you'd rather stay in Madrid overnight instead of getting up early. And I've put in a little money to cover your expenses on the trip. This way, when you get to Pontevedra, you'll have enough to take a taxi to your parents' house. I'm sure they'll be thrilled to see you. Actually…" Julio looked his watch to signal that he was running late. "…I'm just going down to the village to see my father. He'll be back from mass by now. The two of us will have lunch in the little bistro on the village square – he loves roast lamb, poor man. I'll come back this afternoon to say goodbye …" Walking towards the steps, he turned back, "Oh, one more thing. Take your time, there's no rush, I've booked the taxi for the whole day. The driver will wait here until you're ready to leave."

"And if I refuse?"

He had already started down the steps when he heard her question, and when he turned Mariana was standing, purple with rage, clutching the envelope in both hands.

"You could do that, of course, but I wouldn't advise it. There's nothing you can do, Mariana, and I might not always feel so generous. You could stay here until I get an eviction order. I'm not the kind of man who would drag you out by the hair, and you'd gain a couple of days. But only a couple of days, because I am still the legal representative of the owner of this house, and you are an unwelcome tenant who has defaulted on the rent. It wouldn't take me long to convince a judge, and then you would have to deal with the shame of the police removing you by force. Do you really think it's worth it? Or you could go back to Madrid and stay in a boarding house, because I don't think your pension would run to anything else, but what would you gain? Everything is so expensive, you'd have a hard time paying your bills let alone buying two train tickets a lot less comfortable than the ones I'm offering. But if you accept and you go back to your parents tomorrow, with your widow's pension you'll have more than enough to take care of yourself and your daughter. I know you'd rather live in Madrid, but sometimes in life, you have to choose between what you want and what you can do, and you can't do anything else. You've already spoken to a lawyer, haven't you? A young man called Tejerina, I can't remember who told me, I know that he told you exactly the same thing I'm telling you now. You can always get a third opinion, it wouldn't take you long to find another lawyer, but they've all read the same books, studied the same laws, they'll all give you the same answer."

Mariana held his gaze for a moment, but said nothing. When he realised there was nothing more for him to say, Julio headed down the steps without looking back, he spoke to the taxi driver who was parked just outside the gates and then walked towards the village taking the route he always took. He paid Evangelina, said hello to the people he passed, reserved the best table in the *mesón* on the square, arrived back at the restaurant at 2pm precisely, smiled to see how much his father enjoyed the roast leg of lamb Julio had ordered, and bought several rounds of drinks for Benigno's friends with whom he spent a while playing dominos. Then, at about seven o'clock, he took his leave, and slipped some money into the pocket of the new jacket he had bought for his father. "Here, father, this is for you. And if you need anything else, just call me, or ask Evangelina to call me, she's got my number."

When he got back, the taxi was no longer outside the gates, but inside, near the porch, its boot open and packed with boxes. Mariana, wearing a hat, her face as impassive as a statue, was supervising the efforts of the driver and of Mathilde who was perfectly relaxed for a woman who had just been fired. The maid was careful not to tell anyone that don Julio had already asked whether, when she got back to Madrid, she would like to work for him and she had accepted, of course she had accepted, he had offered to increase her salary on condition that she said nothing to her mistress.

"I'm pleased to see that you've decided to be reasonable, Mariana."

"This is not the last of it, we'll meet again Julio," she did not dare look at him, "You mark my words."

After that, everything went according to plan. Time passed, 1949 ended and 1950 began, he sold the house in Torrelodones for a good price, was aware that no one linked his name to that of the Fernández Muñoz family, and he felt more relaxed, and began to go out in society where he proved very popular with the men and even more popular with the women. His name began to appear in the society columns alongside those of the other guests at fashionable receptions and banquets, and he became accustomed to the fact that everyone addressed him with the respectful title *Don Julio*. Until, one morning in 1954, when his secretary knocked on his office door.

"You have a visitor, Don Julio."

"At this time of the morning?" he frowned and checked the diary on his desk.

His secretary Amparo, a very beautiful girl, smiled and explained.

"It's a girl, she's very young, and she doesn't have an appointment. I don't know her, but she insisted that she was sure you'd see her, because she's almost family. Her name is Ángela... no, Angélica. Angélica Otero Fernández."

"Angélica!" Julio stared at his secretary open-mouthed.

"So, what should I do? Do I send her in or shall I tell her to come back another day?"

"No, no," he looked down at his watch to stall for a moment, wondering what this sudden visit might mean. "It's easier if you just send her in now."

A moment later, she stood before him, with that same curly, impossibly blonde hair, her chin held a little too high, her eyes the colour of a limpid ocean. She had not changed much, the woman she had grown into was merely an older version of the little girl Julio remembered, and those details that were new - the high heels, the handbag, the voluptuous swell of her breasts, the hips - did not surprise him so much. He was more taken by her clothes, a trouser suit that accentuated her body and was completely up to date, although clearly a cheap copy, since the material was inferior.

"Angélica, what a surprise!" Julio greeted her from behind his desk, then got to his feet and moved towards her.

"Yes, I'm guessing you weren't expecting me," she said with a malicious irony that was typical of her. "Aren't you going to kiss me?"

"Of course," when he got close to her he realised she was wearing the same childhood perfume. "Please, take a seat... how are you?"

"Not good, to tell you the truth." She sat stiffly, like a lady, crossing her legs then lighting a cigarette and exhaling a puff of smoke. "That's why I'm here. I don't really like life in Galicia. Santiago is a beautiful city and there's lots to do, La Coruña too, but I live in a tiny godforsaken village in Pontevedra where it's always raining, there are more cows than people, and I'm bored to death. I don't know anyone in Santiago or La Coruña, so I decided... to come to Madrid to see you."

"That's wonderful. It's lovely to see you. But I'm not sure I really understand."

"You understand me perfectly, Julio, you're an intelligent man. I want to live in Madrid so here I am. I know people here, friends from school and my old district. They miss me, and I've missed them, we've been writing to each other."

"That's nice."

"Isn't it? But if I'm going to stay here, I need a job. I'm poor – you know that better than anyone. You, on the other hand, are doing very nicely, you only have to look at this office to know that. I'm sure you could find me something. I turned nineteen last December, and the girl who came to Madrid with me can't be much older. I'm taller than she is, and intelligent, I speak French and before you ask, I have a diploma in shorthand and typing. Julio took a moment to look at her, he recognised her boldness, her wild, dangerous arrogance which, when she was a child had amused him and which now seemed much more interesting that the meek, inexperienced availability of all those girls of marriageable age whose mothers sent them to see him with "Do Not Touch" tattooed on their foreheads in invisible ink. Angélica held his gaze as though she could tell that strong women were Julio Carrión González's weakness, but Julio was thinking about something else. He foresaw that employing Angélica might cause him problems, and not hiring her presented much the same risk.

"What about your mother?" he asked, "What does she think?"

"My mother knows nothing about it, as you can imagine. She thinks I came to Madrid to ask my friend Maruchi's father for a job. It goes without saying that she despises you, still prays that you'll be ruined. But I'm not my mother. She's lived her life, now I intend to live mine."

"Working for me."

"That would be a start."

Julio Carrión looked at his watch, frowned, took a business card and handed it to her. "OK. Call me the day after tomorrow. Where are you staying? With your friend?" She nodded. "Is there anything else you need?"

"Just a job." She glanced at the card, then slipped it into her purse. "I think I'd rather call you tomorrow, if that's OK..."

Julio smiled, kissed her goodbye and the following day he took her call and invited her to lunch. He had decided to postpone his decision until dessert, but she didn't give him a chance. When he offered her a job as a receptionist at a salary slightly higher than his secretary, he saw her glow.

"What about your receptionist, what are you going to do about her?" she asked.

"I'll put her on the shop floor, she's not as pretty as you are."

This was true, and the reception desk at Carrión Construction fared much better with Angélica Otero Fernández at the helm. "Where did you find the pretty little thing?" Romualdo Sánchez Delgado asked him one day, when Julio found him flirting with Angélica. "Nowhere, as far as you're concerned," Julio said with a smile. His friend gave a little laugh and slapped him on the back "You dirty bastard." After he walked Romualdo out, Julio gestured to his receptionist to come into his office.

"I've already told you that I don't like it when you flirt with the visitors, Angélica," he said as he closed the door, "It's unprofessional."

"But I don't flirt, Julio, I swear I've never encouraged them…"

"And I've told you more than once to use the correct form of address."

"Yes, *Don* Julio."

"Without the sarcasm."

"Of course."

In the first months, things went no further. Angélica proved to be a good worker, punctual, conscientious, patient and friendly. Julio followed her progress from a distance and then lost interest. He found his receptionist attractive, but he had always found his receptionists attractive and he was not about to make the mistake of responding to her flirtation with anything other than a smile and a chaste, inoffensive kiss on the cheek. He never managed to get her to address him with respect as he would have liked, but her languid smiles more than made up for her not calling him Don.

Moving back to Madrid had been good for Angélica Otero Fernández. She had moved in with an old friend of her mother, the widow of a Commander in the Civil Guard, who rented out a couple of rooms in her beautiful house on the Calle Mejía Lequerica, the closest thing she could find to the Glorieta de Bilbao. She did not have to send any money back to Galicia, but even so, the effect of her first salary on her appearance was astonishing. Although there were certain constraints on her budget, her clothes – daring and fairly successful copies of designer outfits - and two pairs of plain court shoes - made her look very elegant. To the charm and instinctive grace she had always had, Angélica had added a singular gait, she clacked along the pavement as though trying to puncture the concrete with her heels, a walk natural to women who are never surprised to find every man's eyes on them. And she liked to please, she knew the right thing to say to everyone, smiled even at the men who did not interest her, dropped subtle, carefully worded hints to those who might, but she neither encouraged nor discouraged any of them. Julio studied her, and he was not worried, even if he sometimes felt that Angélica was toying with him the way he had once toyed with her.

"You have a visitor, Julio."

The day he realised that this was true, she knocked softly on his door, but rather than leaving it ajar, she came into the office and closed it behind her.

"It's that fat girl. I think her name's Rosi, isn't, it?" He looked up at her with amazement as she screwed up her face and held her nose, "You should tell her not to wear so much perfume, not unless you're prepared to buy her real perfume, because it stinks. And tell her to buy clothes that fit her, because those clothes are too tight."

"How dare you, Angélica!" His receptionist's tone had finally succeeded in making him angry, and he did nothing to disguise the fact. "How dare you! What did you say?"

"You have a visitor, Don Julio," she pushed her hair out of her face and smiled, but not for a moment did she look away. "Señorita Rosi. Shall I show her in?"

"Yes, please. And make sure this doesn't happen again."

Rosi was his official mistress this season, a chorus girl who had just turned twenty-eight and was stunning, just the way he liked his women – robust, perfectly proportioned and spectacular; she was pretty enough, although her face was a little too round, she allowed herself to be admired but she also knew her place. This was all Julio expected of his lovers, ever since Mari Carmen Ortega has slipped through his fingers.

"Listen, Julio…" He had immediately notice the wild, angry tone in her voice when she had called one day in June 1950. "It's over, and this time it's for good. I'm just calling to let you know. My husband gets out of prison next week. If he hears so much as a word about what's been going on between you and me, one word, he'll kill you. And if he doesn't kill you, I will, is that clear?"

When he hung up, Julio Carrión was smiling, though he was almost certain that this really was the last time that he would speak to La Peluca's daughter. It wasn't the first time that Mari Carmen had left him, but until now, he had always known she would come back.

He had been the proud proprietor of the prettiest legs in Madrid for three hectic years of tears and tantrums, quarrels and break-ups. Mari Carmen had never really liked him and whenever she forgot and allowed him to take her to the cinema, or to dinner, or to buy toys for the children, when she was so depressed or so worried that she went out with him, had fun, drank until she was almost unconscious – the only state in which she'd ever kiss him back – she would wake up the next morning hating him all the more. Then she would break up with him, but he was persistent, he would find her, give her presents, tell her jokes, make her laugh. And sooner or later she would show up, furious with herself, red-faced with shame and more desirable than ever, and she would wave her hand and say: "OK, you can shut up now. Don't say a word unless you want me to leave straight away." He would not say a word, but would slowly undress her, run his fingers over her body, cover her with kisses, careful never to come too close to her mouth. She would calm down, and become almost gentle and by their second date, she would talk to him, by the third she would smile, and by the fourth and fifth, she would allow him to bring her to orgasm, a pleasure she did not allow herself under any other circumstances *Julio, you're complete bastard* for some obscure reason that he never quite fathomed, but did bother to try and understand *Jesus, you son of a bitch* because he loved to watch her body relax completely, and the the stream of abuse she rained on him could not hide the smile of pleasure on her face *you're a bad, bad man* then he would burst out laughing and she would laugh with him, thus preparing the ground for their next break up.

Julio Carrión was attracted to strong women, and in a confused way he felt that possessing La Peluca's daughter somehow compensated for the loss of Paloma. Strictly speaking, however, being shamelessly selfish, he realised that Mari Carmen's great strength was also her great weakness.

"I don't understand why you're with me?" she would ask him on a regular basis, "There's plenty of girls in this city who'd be only to happy to spread their legs for next to nothing."

He smiled, but said nothing, because he was not sure that his mistress would appreciate the truth, that what attracted him to her was her uncertainty, the violence she did herself every time she undressed in front of him and yet, after a while, she would always end up treating him as an old friend, a traitor, certainly, and yet someone she felt sufficiently close to, that she instinctively confided in him. Headstrong, insolent and foolish as she was, Mari Carmen was also a nice girl, too nice to feel comfortable with the emotionless pleasure of the professional whore. And so, against her better judgement, she slept with him, confided her problems to him, told him about her work, her meagre salary, her terrible relationship with her mother. Julio was grateful for this because he was still half in love with Mari Carmen Ortega.

She had warned him that she would kill him if she so much as saw him crossing the street, but he knew that she would never go through with it. At least as long as he kept his mouth shut, and he had nothing to gain by opening it. He did not want to lose her forever, and he realised that Mari Carmen was right, that Madrid, Spain, the world was full of women who were prettier, younger, more generous, and less expensive, but this was something he remembered only on those afternoons when he strolled around the Plaza Mayor like a jaded tourist, hoping to see her in the warren of narrow streets. One day, he spotted her in the distance. Later, he met her by chance but did not dare speak to her because she was with two other women. She pretended not to see him, but still he would go out looking for her, until that Saturday when, just as he was about to take a table on a café terrace, he saw her sitting at the bar.

*Well, well...* When he pushed open the door he saw that she was not alone. Sergeant Antonio was not as tall as her Russian aviator, but he was twice as broad, his hair was almost white and although it was close cropped, it was noticeable, too much so for a man of thirty. Tonight Mari Carmen Ortega did see him, she was hugging her husband, hiding behind his shoulders, still powerful though slighter than they had once been. She was stunning. Her hair was washed and curled and tumbled like velvet ribbons onto her shoulders, on to the straps of a new, low-cut, figure-hugging yellow dress just like the dresses she used to wear to go out with him. Julio felt a spasm of anxiety at seeing this man again after so many years, though he could not see Antonio's face, only his profile as Mari Carmen took her husband's face in her hands and kissed him with a sudden, exaggerated passion; she stared into Julio's eyes as she shared this feverish kiss with Antonio Rodríguez Méndez, a communist who had spent time in prison and had every chance of going back there, a failure, a loser.

"Idiot!"

The waiter raised an eyebrow but realised that the insult was not directed at him – on the wall behind him was a mirror, but Julio was not looking at himself as he slipped double the price of a drink he would never drink onto the bar. Had he looked up from his shoes, he would have seen his face, crimson with rage mingled with the dark shadows of an old humiliation, unbearable for a man who could not tolerate pity, not even from himself. As he stepped out into the street, he felt as small, as hopeless, as powerless as the first time he had crossed the Plaza Mayor, weighed down with trunks, his father's birdcage dangling from his little finger.

"You little idiot! You'll be back. You'll come crawling back and beg me to forgive you. You think this is over? It's not over, Mari Carmen, it will never be over …"

Seeing passersby staring at him, Julio realised he had been talking out loud, which only made him even more angry. He turned onto the Calle Mayor, hailed a taxi and went home. He knocked back two glasses of whiskey and felt calmer, able to think. Eugenio and Blanca had invited him to dinner 'with a few friends' that night, and he knew that meant another couple as perfect as they were and a few of Blanca's dreary single girlfriends. When Blanca introduced him to them, he was as charming as ever, but losing Mari Carmen Ortega had made him think about the kind of woman he needed in his life. From that day, Julio Carrión González gave up on strong women in favour of simpler qualities. Since then, all he asked of the women he slept with was that they caused no trouble.

Rosi, the chorus girl he had started seeing shortly before Angélica reappeared was not only plump, voluptuous and stunning, she also satisfied this condition admirably. So much so that her unexpected visit that morning was simply to consult her benefactor about whether she should go on tour. She had to decide by the afternoon whether to go on tour with her current theatre company or stay in Madrid and look for something else.

"The thing is, Julio…I don't really know what to do."

He looked at her, thought for a moment and decided he was tired of her. Rosi was nice, she was obliging, she was generous, all this was true, but she had no real charm. He could easily find a dozen girls like her out there.

"It's complicated, Rosi," he said eventually, giving her his most charming smile, "I don't want to get in the way of your career. I know how important it is to you, so I don't think you should pass up the opportunity. Go on tour…Where is the opening night?"

"Zaragoza, 20 December."

"That's a good time to open, so close to Christmas, and Zaragoza isn't far away… I'll come and see you."

By the time the surprised smile lit up her face, Julio had already put a note next to the date in his diary: *Rosi, flowers.* "A nice little bouquet and everything will be fine…" He walked her out, consciously more affectionate than usual just to annoy Angélica.

As soon as Rosi was gone, she rushed into his office with a clumsy pretence of panic, "I'm really sorry, Julio, I don't mean to annoy you, it's just that... That girl isn't right for you, it's not good for you to be seen with her. She's so common, so ordinary. She can't even speak properly!"

"Angélica!" his tone was enough to cut her dead. "I don't give a fuck what you think. And if you want to go on working here, don't even think about overstepping the mark with me again. I'm in charge here, and my private life is none of your business. Is that clear?"

She didn't answer immediately, but when she did, there was no trace of the apologetic little girl who had stood in his doorway a moment before.

"You're going to fire me? I don't think you'd dare," she said arrogantly.

"Are you threatening me?" He got to his feet and slammed his fists on the desk.

"Me?" She was twittering again like a frightened bird.

She left his office without a sound and for several days, she did her best to be invisible. She was so successful that on 19 December, as he looked at his diary for the following day, Julio decided to ask her, rather than his secretary, for advice. On her first day, Angélica had asked him why there were no plants or flowers in the offices. Julio had shrugged his shoulders. "No reason, nobody thought of it." She had raised an eyebrow, because someone should have thought of it... In the months that followed, Julio noticed the stream of ideas his new employee came up with: aside from the fridge, the cold drinks, , the linen napkins, "paper napkins are so tasteless", she now bought fresh flowers once a week, and put them where the customers could see them. She was an expert, and the florist now gave her a discount, but what interested Julio was to see her face as he consulted her about today's order.

"Gladioli?" she said simply, when he had finished. "I only say that because they take up a lot of space, they're very showy, but I suppose they're cheaper than roses."

"Maybe I should get roses, then..." he said in a burst of generosity.

"A dozen?" She didn't look up from her notepad. "Two dozen?"

"Let's make it two."

"Red?" her lips curled into something resembling a smile.

"No," he smiled too, "Not red..."

"Pink, then," she said, finally looking up at him. "Yellow roses are pretty, but I don't think it looks good, a man sending yellow roses. And white roses are more appropriate for an older woman, or for a little girl, though obviously it's your decision."

"That sounds fine. Two dozen pink roses..."

"Good. I'll order them straight away..." She was turning to leave when she changed her mind. "I'm on your side, Julio, I've always been on your side. I'm amazed you've never realised that."

She left the office without waiting for a reply and, a few hours later, when she came back to tell him about the Christmas party she was planning for the staff on the 23 - "You mean you don't have a Christmas party?"

"No, we've never had one."

"Well, you should have thought about it, because it gives out the wrong signals" - neither mentioned Rosi or the flowers.

The Christmas lunch – less tasteful than it was plentiful - which she forced him to attend - would not have been such a success had she not persuaded him to give his employees the afternoon off - *"Surely you can't expect them to go back to work when they're plastered?"* – and so confirmed her popularity, this receptionist who had been working there for less than a year, but already had more influence with Julio than any employee had ever had.

"And I'll tell you something else, since I'm a bit tipsy" Angélica only spoke to him once at the party, by which time he was sick of listening to bad jokes and had retreated to a corner "If you were clever, you'd give a Christmas present to the children of everyone in this room..."

"Really?" he gave her an anxious look, "Anything else?"

"No. Just that ... I don't think you understand... Do you know how much this party cost?" She gestured to the tables still groaning with sandwiches, unopened bottles of wine and beer and half-eaten plates of crisps. He shook his head. "Less than the price of a meal for two in a decent restaurant. The toys would be even cheaper, but people would think a lot more of you, and not just the ones with the children."

"Tell me something, Angélica," he said, smiling, "What do you think of me? You think I'm a bumpkin, don't you?"

"No, you're not a bumpkin," she moved closer, brushing against him deliberately, he thought, her lips seemed uncomfortably close. "Not any more. But you still have a lot to learn."

"...before I'm a gentleman," he whispered.

"Exactly. Before you're a gentleman."

"Good," Julio turned to face her and, if they had been alone, he might have kissed her, but luckily they were not. "So who's going to buy these toys?"

"I will, if you want." Angélica took a step back, "On the 27th, when I get back from Galicia.[1] I've already thought about it: toy trucks for the boys and dolls for the girls."

On 23 December 1954, Julio Carrión González finally saw where Angélica Otero Fernández was coming from, and he liked what he saw, though he did not attach great importance to it. However things did not turn out as he expected, as he discovered that same night when he thought he could take advantage of his receptionist's inebriation.

"Don't get the wrong idea about me, Julio." She rebuffed him, still smiling, as she buttoned up her coat, "In your position, one false move could be fatal."

This was what she said, but she left so quickly that he did not have time to get angry or consider what he had just heard, a warning that would make more sense on the first night of the New Year.

When he saw her appear in the living room, he was so stunned that he did not even look at the man who came in with her. Angélica was wearing a short black sleeveless dress so simple that on most women it would have looked unremarkable, but on her it was amazing. The same was true of the velvet ribbon that held her long hair off her face, the plain stiff tulle shawl she wore over her décolletage, and the ornate jewelled brooch she wore just below her left shoulder. Standing at the top of the steps leading down to the living room, she looked like an exquisite porcelain figurine. This was what Julio thought when he saw her, before he turned back to the neophyte actress standing next to him. She was in her late twenties, her hair was platinum blonde to highlight her resemblance to Lana Turner, and she did not even expect money in return for sleeping with him. She was stunningly beautiful and he had thought he found her very attractive until Angélica appeared. At that moment, Gustavo Aguirre, whom he had not noticed, gently led Angélica down the steps, and only then did Julio realise he was her partner, which explained why his receptionist was attending Romualdo Sánchez Delgado's annual New Year's Party.

The man with Angélica was young, tall and slim, and until that evening had never seemed particularly handsome, he was a mediocre architect from a good family and it was his name rather than his talent that had prompted Carrión Construction to engage him two years earlier. As he watched the young man move around the room with unexpected poise, Julio thought to himself that Gustavo Aguirre was the reverse side of his coin, the antithesis of the clever boy with no family, no social

---

[1] In Spain, presents are exchanged on 6 January.

status to speak of, who had nonetheless succeeded in becoming what he was today. Perhaps this was why this lanky, awkward boy had seen in Angélica what he had not seen until now. It was a feeling that he did not.like.

"Good evening, Don Julio," her tone so subtly mocking that it was lost on everyone but him. "Are you enjoying yourself?"

"How are you, Julio?" Gustavo said, proffering his hand, though his eyes were on Angélica, "Nice to see you. Shall we get a drink?" Gustavo took her arm, "I'm simply parched."

*I'm simply parched*, Julio whispered to himself sarcastically as he watched them move towards the buffet table, *I'm simply parched*, it was the sort of pretentious expression he might expect to find in a cheap novel. Well, I'm not going to ask you to dance, Angélica, he promised himself, and he did not. She didn't seem to notice.

1955 was Angélica Otero Fernández's year, not so much because of her growing popularity among the men who flocked around her, as for her skill in attaining the one prize she sought, the prize she had been thinking of since that spring afternoon in 1947 when she had entertained herself working out how old Julio Carrión González would be when she turned twenty. Gustavo Aguirre, whom she did not much like, was only the first of her suitors and did not even last until March. His successor, whose name was Emilio Alvar, and who had an important position at the Ministry for Public Works, proved much more effective.

"Are you going to marry him?" Julio asked one afternoon in May.

"Why? Would it bother you?"

"No." He rearranged the papers on his desk, "I'd just like some advance notice so that I can find a replacement. But..." He looked at her and changed his tone, "You're very young, Angélica, I've know you since you were a girl, and I'm not sure that a forty-year old widower with two children is a good match for you."

"He's just turned thirty-nine," she interrupted him, "And I've always liked older men."

Julio, who was only six years younger than Alvar, fell silent, he felt a sudden urge to ask her to marry him. But he did not ask because he thought, and it was not the first time that the thought had occurred to him, that she would never accept. He was attracted to Angélica, he had always found her attractive, but she was not the sort of woman he was looking for, straightforward and unproblematic, and he was not much interested in exploring other variants of the feminine psyche.

"He wants to get married," she said as though she could read his mind, "But I'm not so sure because... I don't know, he asks too many questions."

"About what?"

"About you."

She looked at him calmly, then turned and walked out of the office leaving her boss to stew in his uncertainty for the rest of the afternoon.

"What did you mean earlier?" Julio tried to sound less curious than he felt.

Angélica looked at him with all the innocence she could muster: "Earlier? When?"

Julio balled his fists and took a deep breath.

"Don't play games with me, Angélica, it doesn't suit you."

Angélica simply laughed.

"Oh, I get it... I don't think it's anything important." They had reached the front door, Angélica looked out and waved to someone outside. "Look, there he is, that red car over there." Julio saw him and waved, forcing himself to smile. "Well, it's normal that he would want to ask me questions, isn't it? I mean he wants to marry me... He knows I've known you since I was a little girl and he's interested, that's all, about how we met and when and why, what made me think of asking you for a job..." Emilio had begun to beep his horn, "I'm sorry, Julio, I have to go... We've got tickets for the theatre. I'll see you tomorrow."

That afternoon, she didn't kiss him goodbye, she simply left, dashing across the road and slipping into the passenger seat of the red car which, a moment later, merged into the traffic, leaving Julio alone on the pavement. It took him a moment to react, but he recognised the metallic taste that filled his mouth, the hollow sensation in his limbs, the old, dazzling brightness blinding him. Suddenly, almost treacherously after so many years, Julio Carrión González was scared.

That night, he had a date with a girl but he did not even take the trouble to cancel it. He wandered the streets for a long time, trying to think. "Money, I could offer her money. No, I could fire her, I could talk to Emilio, tell him she's a slut, tell him she's seeing someone else, I don't know, I can get witnesses, I can threaten her, I can say she stole from me, put a wad of notes in her handbag, threaten her with prison ..."

Four months later, as he was walking with her down the Calle Marqués de Urquijo and realised that he was going to marry her, Julio Carrión González remembered all this, and he remembered what had happened on the morning after that dark night of fear, that long sleepless night that left him with his nerves on edge. When he ordered her into his office, he completely forget what he had intended to say, the harsh tone he had planned to adopt.

"So?" Angélica put her weight on one hip, and held her chin a little too high, and looked down at him behind the desk. "You wanted to talk to me?"

"Yes." That was all he managed to say before he got to his feet and strode over to her, gripped both of her hands in his left hand, and held her chin with his right, his fingers digging into her cheeks, forcing her mouth into the caricature of a kiss.

"You're a piece of shit, Angélica, do you hear me? That's all you are, a piece of shit." She stared at him, but made no attempt to struggle free of his grasp, "You're an insect, I can crush you anytime I feel like it, do you understand me? You think you're so clever, Angélica, but you don't know who I am, you don't know what kind of friends I have, you haven't the slightest fucking idea of what could happen to you if I decided to pick up that phone, is that clear?" He waited for her to nod, for her to weakly mumble "yes," to see a flash of fear in her eyes, but she didn't move. "Is that clear?"

And, at that moment, Angélica Otero Fernández brought her mouth close to the mouth that was raining abuse on her, and without knowing how, without knowing why, Julio Carrión González kissed her, and went on kissing her, he let go of her arms because he needed his to embrace her, needed his hands to touch her. He ran his hands over her body and felt a strange tingling in his fingertips as though he already knew this skin, this flesh he was tasting for the first time with growing passion which she frustrated at just the right moment.

"Enough," Angélica guided the uninvited hand from her bra and took a step back. She looked Julio Carrión in the eye, grasped the hands that had recently imprisoned her own and placed them on her waist. "I have to go... I've got a lot work to do."

"Angélica..." he whispered.

"Yes?" Her voice was serene, charming.

He could think of nothing to say and she opened the door to leave, but before she did so she looked at him and her eyes bore that same look of triumph they used to have when he agreed to do the Russian trick.

"I've split up with Emilio," she announced a week later, "That what you wanted, isn't it?"

Julio simply smiled, but some time later he found her and invited her to dinner. She told him she couldn't come "I'm busy," she said, without elaborating, but she suggested another date. Over dinner, Julio Carrión confirmed what he already suspected: Angélica was not going to create any problems for him as long as he was prepared to resolve the main issue.

"Let's see if I've got this right, Julio…" Angélica interrupted his long-winded explanations, "You're suggesting I take the place of Rosi, and order two dozen roses – red roses, I think - for myself once in a while?"

"No, that's not it at all, Angélica," He found it difficult to stay calm, and had to resort to cliché to mask his true intentions. "You know perfectly well what kind of woman you are, and what kind of man I am."

"That's exactly why I said it…" as she spoke she shook her head from time to time. "It's unbelievable, really! You're a very intelligent man, Julio, but you never seem to understand anything."

"OK." The offended party fixed his eyes on the tablecloth. "Forget I said anything."

But he knew what he had said, and Angélica - who flung her arms around his neck as they left the restaurant and kissed him with the wild abandon she had, until now, reserved for his office - also knew. All summer, things ebbed and flowed – from passion to indifference, bravado and more bravado, then indifference, then passion - until their relationship entered its most delicate stage in September, by which time they could swing from boiling point to tepid in a heartbeat. Angélica knew precisely the right moment to invite him for a drink on the terrace of the café Rosales, where she launched into the carefully rehearsed speech that began "Listen, Julio, you may be rich, but you're not respectable."

"Shall we get the bill?" she said, when she tired of looking at herself in the mirror of his silence.

"You get the bill. You invited me, remember?"

"You're right."

He had said it only to make her blush and having obtained this meagre satisfaction, he got up, found the waiter, paid the bill, then went back and took her in his arms.

"Are you walking home?" for the first time in months he was in complete control and he decided to use the situation to his advantage. "It's such a beautiful night…"

"Why are you asking me that?"

"I was going to suggest I walk with you. If you don't mind, that is."

"No, of course I don't mind."

As they walked along the Calle Marqués de Urquijo, Julio already knew that he would marry her. It had nothing to do with Angélica's impeccably marshalled arguments. He had already known he would marry her sooner or later, and why not sooner. These were the rules of the game, and he had already rebuffed too many pushy mothers, too many daddy's girls. Romualdo, who was a lecher and had already fathered three children, had warned him that people were starting to talk. There were gossips who insinuated that he was homosexual, or had some incurable social disease, that his tastes ran to the perverse. Weddings bring peace, his father had always said. Angélica still wanted to marry him, she had always wanted to marry him, and her boldness in saying it to his face was not only admirable, it also cleared up of a number of obstacles. If he chose Angélica, he would be spared the trouble of a courtship. If he chose Angélica, he would be marrying into the aristocracy, the family might be destitute and full of undesirable elements, but it was unarguably aristocratic. No one would raise the slightest objection to the marriage, and he found Angélica attractive, had always found her attractive, he had always understood her and she was a lot like him. He knew that now.

By the time they arrived at the Calle Princesa, he had already decided to marry her, but he did not tell her until they reached the Glorieta de San Bernardo. As they stood, waiting for the traffic lights to change, he gently put his hand on her shoulder and asked:

"What will your mother say?"

Angélica gave him a wary, uncertain look.

"What will my mother say about what?"

"What will she say when she finds out you're marrying me?"

She smiled, a smile that blossomed slowly into something so exquisite that it was overpowering.

"Oh," she said, "Are we getting married?"

"Of course," Julio smiled, "I thought you knew that."

"No. You haven't even asked me."

Pedestrians had begun to cross the street, but neither of them moved. "Angélica, will you marry me?"

"Yes." The traffic light had changed to amber, to red,then to green again by the time they had stopped kissing. "I expect my mother will pretend to be happy. You're a good catch."

On 5 May, 1956, Don Julio Carrión González married Señorita Angélica Otero Fernández at the church of Santa Barbara in Madrid; Doña Mariana Fernández Viu was maid of honour. Neither then, nor at any time later, did she dare say a word about this wedding, every detail of which was planned, arranged and controlled by the bride, who not only chose a wild silk dress designed by Cristóbal Balenciaga, but also chose the date, the flowers, the music, the guests, the menu for the reception, the bridegroom's suit, her own engagement ring and, of course, the conditions of the marriage contract.

"Maybe we should go back to my place for a *siesta*," Julio would suggest from time to time, after they had lunched with Eugenio, or in Torrelodones with his father. He had already introduced her to the wives of a number of government ministers, and, having seen the diamond on the fourth finger of Angélica's right hand, everyone at Carrión Construction knew they were engaged.

"Absolutely not, Julio!" she shook her head, "We couldn't possibly! You go and have a nap at your place and I'll go to mine. You know it's for your own good. Can't you wait four little months?"

"No, I can't wait..." In the taxi, he would fondle her, squeeze her, paw her, and she would let him, right up until the moment when she would stop, always perfectly calculating the time, the risks and the benefits.

He could not wait, but he waited all the same. What he needed was to marry a pretty little virgin from a good family and that was precisely what awaited him at the altar. It would also be good for him to give her two or three children, but Angélica knew what was good for her, and waited almost a year before she got pregnant. By the time she told him the news, she had become something of an expert in the contraceptive properties of certain sins that are never confessed and her husband, who had by now spent almost twelve months far from his subterranean pleasures, smiled when she asked him if it had been worth the wait. At the time, the only thing beyond Angélica's control was the reason for that smile, because she could never have imagined that what Julio loved most about her in bed was precisely what he loved most about her anywhere else in the house. Through his long, steep, dangerous ascent to glory, Julio Carrión González had considered everything except whether he had someone to love him. It was when he realised how much his wife loved him that he appreciated that fact. And he grew accustomed to Angélica's love, her passionate, unconditional devotion. Her love became vital to him, later it would be indispensable, until he missed it in every woman with whom he cheated on her, while he, in turn, learned to love her after his fashion.

In 1958, Rafael, their first child, was born, he was blond and pale with blue eyes like his mother. A year later, Angélica arrived, with green eyes and a complexion of translucent pink, utterly unlike her father. Finally, in 1961, he had a son who seemed to look like him, and they christened him Julio, after his father. But although Julio had dark eyes and resembled his father in his gestures, as time went by his hair grew lighter and his skin paler. Then, in 1965, Angélica became pregnant for the fourth time.

In November, she gave birth to another son. He had black hair, olive skin, and beyond the usual ambiguity of all babies, he had something about him that made all those who came to see him at the hospital exclaim" He's the spitting image of you, Julio, honestly, I've never seen a baby who looks so like his father..."

Julio would simply smile, but he felt a particular satisfaction when he held his fourth child, Álvaro Carrión Otero, who would, in time, become his favourite son.

"I never slept with your father, Álvaro."

Suddenly I felt a terrible urge to laugh and a terrible urge to cry, but I did neither. I sat motionless, unable to think, to speak, to feel anything at all. I was here, and I had heard. Raquel was here and she had spoken. This was all that I knew, all I could grasp. Then, seeing her curled into a ball on the far edge of the bed with her back to me, like a lost, abandoned girl, I knew I had to do something.

I moved towards her, put a hand on her shoulder and turned her towards me, and she let me, not helping, not resisting, as though her body was uncoupled from her spirit. Raquel Fernández Perea, the love of my life, belonged to me and me alone, she belonged to me not to my father, she was mine more than she had even been. I hugged her hard, pressed her to me, I held her for a long time but I could not save her from this stillness as absolute as the that of sleep or death. I watched her breathe, felt her breath against my neck, savoured the peace of this embrace but I could still see the eyes of the man who had shadowed her through the streets, in doorways, by telephone as though searching for his own life. The man who at this very moment should be kissing this woman, wanted to kiss her, yet couldn't.

I had to do something, but my mind was teeming with memories, some static, some moving, whole scenes and fragments of scenes, whole sentences and isolated words. *I'm sorry, I was expecting your mother...Álvaro, for a physicist, you have a vivid imagination... Aren't you scared?... When he smiled, your father looked like a child's drawing of the sun ... What must you think of me?... She is right for you, Álvaro, you're right for each other. But you're nothing like your father. The person she's wrong for – I mean absolutely wrong for – is him. Don't tell me it hadn't occurred to you...*

Somewhere beyond my consciousness, beyond the shock, the urge to lash out, the blind fury of a bull that, having realised the cape is just a decoy now longs for revenge, I could feel the faint throb of my pride, this useless but persistent relic of the honest, ordinary guy I used to be. I didn't want to think, but I could remember the sequence of my intuitions, and I remembered the moment when I realised that the worst thing that could happen would be for me to know the true nature of Raquel's true relationship with my father. Now, on the brink of that abyss, I was overjoyed to know that I had never shared this woman with Julio Carrión

González, and that joy terrified me, it threatened the future I had been prepared to live out in the unbearable shadow of a repugnant passion.

Without wanting to, I thought about all these things as I held Raquel in my arms. I could tell she was more terrified than I was, because she knew everything, she had known from the start, known everything except maybe that she would fall in love with me, and that I would fall in love with her. It was then that I realised the true extent of my misfortune, the pitiless cruelty of a defeat I had not even begun to suffer because love, my love, would never be enough to slay the dragon, because all my love, all my ordinary words would never be enough to fill the silence it was born in, the silence in which it had grown strong. And I was guilty of not wanting to know, of not asking, of evading those questions which had only one answer. It would have been easy: when did you first meet my father, Raquel? Where? How did you end up having an affair with him? How long did it last? It would have been easy, but I had chosen an easier path.

For a moment, I thought that maybe I could choose to do nothing. I pictured the scenario: "It doesn't matter, nothing matters, I don't need to know, all that matters is that I love you Raquel, so let's get up, get dressed, and let's go home, let's go and sleep in your apartment on the Plaza de los Guardias de Corps, and we'll never mention this again…"

It's not easy to bury the dead, to watch the gravediggers, the predictable, hypocritical, expression of condolence they put on when their eyes accidentally meet those of the bereaved, the sound of the shovels, the grating of the coffin against the sides of the grave, the quiet whisper of the ropes being paid out. It's not easy to bury the dead, but it is easy to put them in a tomb deeper than the earth, deeper than any cemetery. *Your grandmother was a schoolteacher, she was good woman, she loved her husband, she loved to play the piano.* I could do the same thing, I could take my head from Raquel's shoulder, kiss her with all the care that such a kiss requires then, asking no questions, I could lay my head on her shoulder again, in the warm security my love had built for her.

I could choose to do nothing, I could pretend to do nothing, behave as though I had forgotten her dishonesty, convince myself that I had not colluded in her lies, and go on living in the convivial silence of those who prefer not to act, not to know, not to ask. But I loved this woman. Loved her so much that, sometimes, the love I felt for her confused and overwhelmed me. I loved her so much that I could not disregard the reason she had run away, her secret, nor could I condemn her to some half–line life, a fantasy content in what it did not know.

543

"Talk to me, Raquel." I lifted my head from her. "Say something, please…"

"I don't know where to start…"

I leaned back against the pillows, lit a cigarette and waited.

Raquel is hurting more than you are, Berta had told me, and I hadn't believed her, I couldn't imagine anything could hurt more than the uncertainty I felt, but now as I watched her suffer, watched her grow paler, and more distraught, as frightened as a lab rat in a cage, I did not like it.

"It doesn't matter where you start. I'm on your side."

"You don't know that yet, Álvaro."

"I do know," she was right, I didn't know, but I could compensate for this lie with a greater truth, "Because I don't want you to leave me again."

She closed her eyes and nodded several times like a little girl accepting her punishment.

"The first thing my grandfather Ignacio did after he slept with my grandmother Anita was to teach her to read and write." She spoke calmly, with no hesitation, with no trace of shame, or tears. "She was eighteen years old, but she was illiterate because she'd grown up in the mountains, miles from the nearest village. Her father was a forester, and he couldn't afford to send her to school. Ignacio was six years older than she was, he was a law student, but he gave up his degree in his third year in order to enlist. They met in Toulouse, during the Second World War, my grandmother had no papers and my great-grandmother had taken her in, and he was hiding there, because he had just escaped from a labour camp. He escaped a lot of times from a lot of different places. Since they didn't have any Spanish reading books, my grandfather sent Anita out to buy two exercise books and then he made one for her. He'd taught a lot of soldiers to read and write, so he knew the books by heart. The first sentence my grandmother ever read by herself was: Anita is a little apple. He wrote it to make her laugh."

She stopped with her grandmother's laugh and looked at me to gauge my reaction. I was in no hurry, and when she saw this, she nodded again.

"This was the first thing I should have told you. And I nearly did tell you that afternoon when you took me to the museum, when that ugly little girl who'd found something she didn't understand came over to talk to us…"

"Was she ugly?" I interrupted her, and saw her smile for the first time in a long while.

"Very ugly. Don't you remember?"

"I remember her, but I don't remember thinking she was ugly."

"Well she was. She had a face like a fish ..."

"And was very intelligent."

"Yes," Raquel said, "That's what you said at the time, an intelligent girl, it makes all my work worthwhile. Remember? And you were so happy that I nearly told you about my grandmother, about the exercise books because... suddenly you reminded me of them, of the people I was always hearing stories about ... It was like I'd seen it before, no, it was like I'd been told the story before. When I was little, I heard a lot of stories like that. Maybe you don't understand, but that was all they had left, their culture. Education, education, education they always said, it was like their motto, it was like a magic spell that could change the world, make everybody happy. They'd lost everything and they'd come through it by working in schools, in bakeries, as telephone operators, things they were grossly overqualified for, but at least they had their education. At least they'd always have that, and they never forgot, not even afterwards when my grandfather finished his law studies, when he got a job with a legal practice, or when he set up on his own with a French friend and finally started to make some money. My grandmother was even more amazing, because she qualified as a nursery school teacher. She did it for years and years, she was the one who taught me the alphabet, well not just me, my brother, my sister, all our cousins..."

"She taught Annette?"

"Yes. Actually, now that I think of it, Annette really liked you. When she came to say goodbye and gave me your note, she was completely on your side. She said you were very charming, and practically suicidal. She asked me how I could treat you like that, what you'd done that I was being so hard on you. And I told her you hadn't done anything..." Her voice trailed off and she looked away. "I told her I was the one who had done something... I should have told you about my grandparents that first afternoon, Álvaro, but I didn't dare. I was afraid you'd ask questions ... That's why I always said I didn't want to talk about your father. I really liked you, it had been a long time since I'd really been attracted to someone and I didn't want to spoil it, I didn't want to ruin everything before it had even started, and since you'd said you didn't want to talk about him either, I just thought, fine. I was an idiot. I should have known. Everything that happened after that point was my fault. I should have told you the truth from the very beginning. But I was afraid and now... It's all my fault."

Until that moment, the smiles in Raquel's voice had soothed my bruised soul, had sutured my wounds with the promise that they would heal completely. We were in the apartment on the Calle Jorge Juan, the apartment my father had given Raquel, though I didn't yet know when or why. I hadn't forgotten, but I didn't want to lose Raquel, I didn't want to give up on this story which seemed too long, too long ago to end up in a place as small as the distance between us. So I sat up and hugged her, pulled her to me, and I threw her a lifeline she had not asked for.

"You were at your grandmother's place in Madrid?"

"Yes."

"I knew it, I swear I knew you were there..."

"Why?"

"I don't know, I just knew. And I drove through Canillejas often, believe me. Not for any particular reason, obviously, I don't know the area well, I was just driving around hoping I might see you. Did you see me?"

"No."

"But you wouldn't have spoken to me anyway."

"I don't know."

"If you were at your grandmother's place, I'm sure you would have, I'm sure she would have sided with me..."

"Don't you believe it. She... oh..."

Then she did exactly what she had done when I had begged her to say something, as though she couldn't talk and hold me at the same time; she pulled away, covered her face with her hands then let them slip down her until they were resting on her thighs.

"Tell me one thing, Álvaro." Her voice was suddenly grown-up, serious. "Do you know who I am?

"Well..." I was so flustered that I couldn't bring myself to give the obvious answer, but she understood my silence.

"No, I don't mean that, obviously, you know who I am, I'm Raquel Fernández Perea, I live on the Plaza de los Guardias de Corps. I mean... before you knew me. Didn't you ever hear the name Fernández Muñoz? Did your parents ever mention it?"

"I don't know..." I thought for a moment because I sensed that this question was vitally important, and I wanted to be certain before I answered. "No, I don't think so. I mean, they're common enough names, but... No, I don't remember my parents ever mentioning it."

"You didn't talk about us at all," she said with a sad, bitter smile. "Well, that's better for me, but not so good for you."

"Why?"

She didn't answer straight away, as though she needed time to think.

"Because what I'm going to say will catch you off guard, and you won't like it," she spoke very slowly, "But otherwise it would have been worse for me. I've been thinking about it for a long time now, and I knew it wasn't possible, I knew you couldn't have known and had an affair with me without saying something... I knew it wasn't possible, but I was afraid to ask you. Though, of course it was possible, because..." I didn't dare interrupt because she was somewhere far off, in a place where all I could do was see her, hear her voice without understanding what she was saying, and then she suddenly looked up, looked into my eyes. "Do you remember me, Álvaro?"

"You know very well I've been doing nothing else for the last month..."

"No, a long time before that," she paused and glanced around her like a hunted animal, "It was in May 1977."

"May 1977?" I laughed at the absurdity of this date so far in the past that it didn't even seem real. "But Raquel, in 1977 I was only..."

"You were twelve," she interrupted me, "I was eight. You were living on the Calle Argensola, in a huge, beautiful apartment with a long corridor and right at the end of the corridor was the kitchen, it had folding wooden doors painted white with round windows like the portholes on a boat."

Now it was my turn to look away. I did not know how to respond.

"It was a Saturday," Raquel went on, her voice clear, each word carefully chosen, "I came to your house with Ignacio, my grandfather. I didn't know who you were, I'd never heard of you before. Every Saturday afternoon, my grandfather would take me for a walk, and that day he told me he had to go and see a friend. That's not going to be much fun, I said, and he told me it would be fine, he said his friend had children the same age as me. When we got there, your mother asked if I wanted to go into the kitchen to have a snack with you and your sister Clara. I didn't really want to, but my grandfather said I should and I didn't dare argue because it was all so weird. Your mother was scared stiff when she saw us, she was really nervous." Raquel paused and I heard a tremor of fear in her voice. "You don't remember?"

"No."

"There was a wooden table in the middle of the kitchen and you and your sister were already sitting there. The first thing I remember thinking was that you didn't look anything like each other, then I thought how pretty she was, blonde with deep blue eyes and pale skin and long eyelashes. Then the maid, her name was Fuensanta, gave us hot chocolate and she put two bowls on the table, one with *ensaïmadas* and one full of *picatostes* and she told us not to eat them all because your brothers would be back from football soon. We ate quite a lot, because the chocolate was really good, and you asked me if I was your niece."

"Me? But why would I have asked you that?"

This nonsense made me react, but she didn't seem to notice, she just nodded her head as I struggled with the obscure urge to reject this ridiculous story which couldn't possibly be true however much she insisted that it was, as she went on nodding slowly.

"What are we playing at, Raquel? Don't talk such rubbish, honestly... I don't see what you're getting at, I don't know where all this is coming from, who told you all this stuff, how you know Fuensanta's name and what the house was like, but I don't believe a word of it, OK? That's enough now ..."

"You don't remember anything?" her persistence had made me furious, and she realised this but the fact that I could not remember affected her much more and, as she began to rattle off details like machinegun fire. "I can't believe you don't remember, Álvaro, you have to remember, I was there for ages. After we had our snack we went into a room where there was an electric train set on a big platform between two balconies. Your bedroom was on the left, Clara's was on the right. She wanted me to come and play with her dolls, they were twins, she got them for Christmas, a blonde doll in a blue dress and a red-haired doll in a green dress, but you wouldn't let her play with me, you wanted to show me the train set, you were really proud of it, you had two engines and you showed me the tunnels and the signals and then your father showed up and he made two lollipops appear from my ears, an orange one and a strawberry one and then your mother came to get him. You have to remember, Álvaro. When I was leaving I was still holding one of the dolls and Clara wanted it back, but your mother made her give it to me as a present, I didn't want it, but your mother wouldn't let her take it back and you sister was crying. "'But Mamá, they're twins! If there's two of them how can I give her one? And then..." Raquel saw my face change, "You remember now?"

"That was you?" I said, hardly able to believe my own voice, "The little girl with the doll, that was you?"

"Yes," she closed her eyes and her body suddenly went limp. "That was me."

"But I don't remember you, Raquel," I shook my head, too stunned to think, "I didn't know it was you... Talk about fate... All I remember is the doll, actually, my sister throwing a tantrum when she saw the caretaker's daughter, Mariloli with it. I remember she went and asked for it back and Mariloli wouldn't give it to her, she said she'd found it in the street."

"I didn't throw it away, I left it on a bench with a lollipop on either side."

"It doesn't matter. All I remember is that Clara was really upset. Clara was the youngest and she was completely spoiled so she went and told my father, but Mamá was there, and she didn't even let her finish, she gave her a slap across the face. I'd never seen my mother slap any of us before and I never saw it happen again. I remember that, and my sister remembers it. She still talks about it sometimes. We all laugh about it now, but at the time she cried for weeks."

"I'm sorry." Suddenly, for no reason, Raquel's eyes welled with tears, "I'm really sorry. Clara was right. I said so to your mother, but she wouldn't listen."

"But that means..." It was only now I knew that the story was true that I realised the consequences, "That means you and I..."

"We're cousins..." she said with a simplicity that to me seemed almost insulting. "Second or third cousins, I don't know... My grandfather Ignacio's father, Mateo was the brother of Lucas, your grandmother Mariana's father. Our great-great-grandmother was clearly very religious and named her sons after the apostles..." She faltered again and I could hear real a mounting anxiety in her voice, "But you didn't know any of this, Álvaro, did you? You couldn't have known. When you asked me if we were related, that first time we had lunch together, you didn't know..."

"No, I had no idea..." I was still shaken by the words 'our great-great-grandmother'.

"But, that afternoon, when I first met you and Clara, you both liked the idea. I remember Clara saying 'We haven't got any cousins.' And I told you I had lots of cousins, that some of them lived in Paris, I told you about Annette, and I told you I was born there and you decided that meant I couldn't be Spanish. You said 'People who are born in France are French.' You don't remember?"

"No, but it hardly matters, you seem to remember enough for both of us."

"I remember everything. I'm sure for you it was just an ordinary Saturday, some little girl comes and has a snack with you and goes away again... I've often thought about it. I wouldn't remember either, if I were you. I don't remember the children who used to come to my house when I was little, I don't even really remember my parent's French friends who used to stay with us for weekends. But I remember everything about that day because it was important to me. That afternoon, when we left your house, I saw my grandfather cry... And my grandfather never cried, never... He didn't cry the day Franco died or the day the came back to Spain after thirty-seven years of exile, or even when he ordered *vermú de grifo* on the terrace of a café in Vistillas, because that meant he really was back in Madrid after all those years, even then he didn't shed a single tear. But, when we left your apartment that Saturday in May 1977, he sat down on a bench on the Plaza des las Salesas and he cried..."

Now she was crying too, but she did not let it stop her.

"I asked him what had happened, I asked... He'd bought us ice creams, he was calmer now, we were walking down Recoletos towards Cibeles eating our ice creams and I said 'What happened, grandpa?' I thought he wasn't going to answer..."

I watched her cry and I did nothing, I didn't comfort her, I didn't dare touch her because her tears were utterly unfathomable to me.

"I was only eight, but he liked talking to me... We talked about everything, all the time. I was sure he wasn't going to answer but he did. He said, 'Oh, it's a long story. A very long, very old story. You wouldn't understand, and anyway, I think it's for the best if you don't know.' I asked him why and again I thought he wouldn't tell me but he did, he said... he said..."

Suddenly, she broke down, sobbing uncontrollably with the catastrophic inevitability of a dam bursting. Tears flooded down her face, but still she went on speaking, trampling down her grief with words, and I listened, I went on listening.

" 'OK...We've come back, haven't we?' this is what he said to me. He said if things had been different, if things had been normal I would lived here all my life. But to live here... To live here there are some things it's better not to know ... That's what my grandfather told me, and he knew why he was telling me this, he knew and it's... It's the most important thing... Nobody's ever told me anything as important as that in my life... But time passed and he died ... I didn't listen, he was right, but I didn't listen ..."

Then she paused, but this time it was deliberate, very different from those moments when her tears had forced her to stop.

"And if I had listened, if I hadn't forgotten his words, what they meant, I'd never have met you, Álvaro, I'd never have met you..."

By the time Raquel fell asleep, it was almost daylight. I found it harder to get to sleep than she did, and I woke up before her.

It was late, the room was hot, the sun insinuating itself through the closed venetian blinds, and I could hear the faint sounds of rush hour from the street below, the horns, the brakes, the trucks. These sounds surprised me and I didn't know whether to welcome them as proof of the outside world, or regret the fact that they had interrupted my perfect solitude. I was alone, Raquel was sleeping next to me and I liked to watch her sleep. Raquel was still sleeping and I was alone. Absolutely, terrifyingly alone. Alone in the middle of a desert, a battlefield laid waste, at the centre of the void. Alone.

"Why did you bring me here?" I had asked Raquel towards the end, as the truth began to take shape like a giant mass of grey dust, a shapeless ball of filth spattered with dried blood, old blood, but blood just the same. "I don't like this place."

I had begun to gauge the sickening nature of this ugly mass of frozen truth that blackened my tongue and slipped down my throat, infecting my gullet, my stomach, my lungs. I was inhaling dust, could feel it weighing on my eyelashes, sticking between my teeth, see it under my fingernails, feel it filling every cavity, and still I asked her why she had brought me here, I thought this, I said it, it was my voice, my eyes looking at her. I felt the sting of tears, I who almost never cry. "Take this," I remembered my sister Angélica saying on the morning of my father's funeral, "You haven't cried, Álvaro, take this, it'll help." I never cry, I hardly ever cry. That night I didn't cry, but I could feel the sting of Raquel's tears in my own eyes.

"I don't like it either," she said, "But I thought that if one day, we manage to come through this thing... If some day you can forget what sort of woman I am, what I'm capable of, if you can look at me without thinking that I'm cheating on you, that I've been cheating since the start well... I thought it would be good for us to have talked here, because neither of us likes this place, and we'll never come back here."

We'll never come back. When I woke, it was late but Raquel was still sleeping and I was alone. I couldn't stand myself, couldn't stand my memory, its intolerable, relentless activity now that I no longer knew who I was, now that everything had expanded until it burst the bounds of chaos, a small, domestic quantity faced with the incomparable vastness of order. I'm a physicist and I need to be able to predict. This definition had imploded like all the calculations, all the principles, all the axioms I'd ever learned, loved and wielded in the first part of my life. The only thing I could be certain of now, at this moment, as Raquel slept and the sun warmed the room through the closed blinds, was that the second part of my life was beginning, a blank, empty horizon with immense boundaries I could make out only hazily, like a newborn, my eyes not yet conscious of their purpose.

My life had changed so much, so quickly. And yet my memory bombarded me with images, gestures, words, some old, some recent, but all ancient, all obsolete now, and I could feel the joy of ignorance, the excitement and the exhaustion of the man who had arrived here only a few hours earlier. I no longer knew who I was, what I should expect, what I should do, when the woman sleeping next to me woke up. "Forgive me, Álvaro, please, forgive me…" I hadn't said anything, but I had taken her in my arms and had held her for a long time. I loved this woman. The only thing I knew was that I loved this woman and still I did not know what to do, what to decide when she woke up. It had been almost daylight when Raquel fell asleep, but it was harder for me.

"Make no mistake, Álvaro, it wasn't revenge," she said, "I wasn't looking for revenge. Too much time had passed, I was too far from Paris, from 1946, 1947… I'm not saying that to defend what I did, on the contrary. Revenge is noble, it's a passion. A stupid, feeble, useless passion because you never get back what you invest, but it's an emotion nonetheless, and I… What I did was without passion, Álvaro, it was all calculated. I'm an economist, you know that."

And she went on, taking no short cuts, stripping me of every consolation, pointing out one by one every pothole, every tree stump, every quagmire along the only path out of this maze.

"When I saw your father's name on the contract, I had no idea what had happened with Paloma. I knew about her husband, I knew that one of her cousins had turned him in and that he had sent her a love letter from prison. My grandfather always said that he had never seen a man love a woman more than his brother-in-law loved his sister. And I met her, she was a strange woman, she seemed a lot older than her brothers and sisters and she hardly ever spoke. I only ever remember seeing her sitting in an armchair at María, her sister's, place. María was amazing, she was charming and funny and a she was great cook, she had a big house and a garden teeming with children and grandchildren, and her husband, uncle Francisco, he was great too, he was from a village somewhere in Toledo…"

Then she looked at me, shook her head as though she wished she had bitten her tongue.

"What?" I asked.

"Nothing, I was about to say something stupid."

"What?"

"Just…I was just going to tell you that uncle Francisco used to make marzipan sweets for everyone at Christmas. And I hate marzipan, but I always ate one of them so as not to offend him. That was all I knew at the time. When my grandmother finally told me what had happened, I understood why Paloma was the way she was... a sort of living corpse... but it wasn't real to me, because I was too far away. Too far from those tragic widows, that strange, theatrical world of a life lived in mourning ... I understood her in theory, in practice all it taught me was that revenge is not worth it. 'I'm sick to death of the civil war' my father used to sing every Sunday when we came back from lunch. Grandma Anita used to make paella every Sunday and invite us over.

"My mother makes paella on Sundays too."

"Well, there's nothing better than a good paella. But as soon as we were outside, my father would start singing 'I'm sick to death of the civil war,' and my mother and my aunt Olga would join in, and all the kids laughed, because to us it was like blasphemy to a Catholic, it was something you weren't suppose to think, let alone say out loud. We'd be in fits and uncle Hervé, Olga's husband, who was French and didn't understand anything would look at us like we were mad. And maybe we were, but that madness was the reason why I couldn't really understand Paloma, couldn't really understand what my grandfather meant when he said 'To live here there are some things it's better not to know. Things it's better not to understand..." I didn't want revenge, Álvaro, but I'm worse than my grandparents, worse than Paloma, or at least I was when all this started. We're all worse now, the Spanish I mean, worse than the generations that came before us. 'This country has gone to the dogs', remember? That's what you and Berta said that night when I said I didn't feel well, because I couldn't listen to it any more, Álvaro, I was sick with shame. There you were, talking about your grandmother, and I felt so awful I couldn't bear it any more. I wasn't looking for revenge, I'm a typical modern Spanish woman, I was just thinking about business, I wanted to make a pile of cash, wanted to pull off the best deal of my life, oh I wanted to cover my back, all those old grievances, but it was all so long ago I barely understood them. But your father died before I could pull it off and that ruined everything. That's what happened, Álvaro, believe me."

She had stopped and looked up at me, dropped the corner of the sheet she had been twisting between her fingers. I studied the creases one by one, I couldn't think of anything to say. Of everything I had learned that night, what had hurt me least was Raquel's attitude: it was cold, more than cold, it was cunning, ruthless, not like my father but more like my mother, like my grandmother Mariana, but I couldn't reject them or push them away. My parents would always be my parents, I couldn't cut them out of my life, but she didn't realise this, she didn't know what I was

553

thinking, what I was feeling at that moment.

"None of this has anything to do with you, Álvaro. I didn't know you'd be the one to come and see me, I didn't even know who you were when I went to the cemetery the day of the funeral and saw you standing away from the others. You do look a lot like your father, you're the spitting image of the Julio Carrión in the photos of birthdays and Christmases I saw, but I thought maybe you were a nephew or something, because otherwise you'd be standing beside your mother. I had to count your brothers and brothers-in-law before I realised there was one missing, and until I saw you go over and kiss the others at the end, I wasn't sure. I was looking for the dark-haired boy I'd seen when I visited that huge apartment when I was eight years old, and that was you. But I didn't intend you to see me. I wanted to see you, all of you, that's all. That's the only reason I went to your father's funeral, to see your faces, to know what your mother looked like so I could be prepared. But things didn't go the way I'd planned."

She stopped again and when I looked up at her I saw that she was looking at me, cautiously stretched out the fingers of her right hand to stroke mine. I took her hand and squeezed it.

"It had nothing to do with you, it was your mother, I...I wanted to hurt your mother. That sounds awful, doesn't it...?" She tried to smile but it didn't quite work. "I had nothing against you, I just wanted to ruin your mother... And then... then you changed everything, Álvaro. That's the most ridiculous part, because I had a plan to make a pile of money and your mother wouldn't have known anything about it, but then your father died and she sort of inherited it... When your father died, I turned against her, but she'll never know, because you were the one who came to the meeting and nothing turned out the way I planned, which is good for everyone, except you, you're the only good guy in this sorry mess... You saved your mother – because she doesn't deserve to live in peace – and you saved me, because if you hadn't ruined everything without even realising it, I would have been ruined too..."

She paused again, tried to smile, and this time she succeeded. But I couldn't smile. The cold, calculated way she had laid everything out had begun to pain me, though I hurt more for her than for myself.

"At the start, I didn't realise what was happening. I was so sure I knew who the good guys were, who the bad guys were, where I fitted into this story... I wasn't looking for revenge, it wasn't my style, and it wasn't my revenge to take... I'd make the deal of a lifetime and in the process, I'd ruin what was left of your father's life, and I was glad about that, I was completely sure about what I was doing, I knew he deserved it… I wasn't looking for revenge, but still the idea of revenge was reassuring, it was there in the background … Until that afternoon when we went to the museum, Álvaro, when I saw you talking to that ugly little girl, but she was so clever you didn't even notice she was ugly. It was like a switch being turned on - I saw you through my grandfather's eyes, Álvaro, I stood there seeing you as my grandfather would have seen you and I realised he would have approved of you, he would have really liked you. After that, I couldn't stop, because there I was with you, and my grandfather was there with me, and I saw myself through his eyes and I realised he wouldn't have liked what I was doing, he wouldn't have liked it at all. I know it's hard to believe, I know it sounds like a lame excuse, but until that moment I didn't realise what I was doing, what my plans really meant, what I would have to lose to make all this money. Oh, I know my grandfather was long dead, but that didn't matter, I was still his granddaughter, and what I was doing to him was worse than anything anyone had ever done to him when he was alive. I loved him and here I was destroying everything he held dear by becoming like your father…"

"No…"

I had not said anything for a long time, trying to take in what I was hearing, but the word came out of its own accord.

"Yes…"

"No, Raquel." I took her in my arms and I remembered the half-burned candles around the jacuzzi, the purple rubber dildo, the blue pills in the scuffed silver box. "No."

"Forgive me, Álvaro, please forgive me …"

It was almost daylight and she fell asleep. I stayed awake, envying her her guilt, her sleep. "It's good for everyone except you," she'd said, and she was right. She had fallen asleep knowing I was there beside her, knowing I was on her side, but I was alone. Now that I finally knew all the variables in the equation, solving it was more difficult than ever. So much so that the first thing I was able to establish with any certainty, though it pained me to do so, was that it would have been better if Raquel had been my father's mistress. The traditional, not to say biblical hypothesis which during the good times I had managed to forget, and during the bad times had only appalled and disgusted me, had placed me in a more comfortable, more civilised place than the wasteland in which the truth had left me.

Utter solitude is not a good place to think. I could picture Raquel talking to my father, laying out her conditions in the same neutral tone she had used that first afternoon when I first went to her office, the confident, self-assured, sterile tone she had mastered during so many meetings with clients just like him, so many heirs just like me. I could easily imagine the tense squalid stand-off between them; what I found more difficult was picturing her here, in this apartment, planting her land-mines for my mother to find, mines which had exploded in my face. Her clever little *mise en scène* - the hash, the half-burned candles, the unwashed dressing gowns – this troubled me more than her grand plan for blackmailing my father. Because this was not about the past, it was about the future.

This conclusion meant that I had already come to a decision, but I didn't realise that before I fell asleep. I realised it in the morning, although my decision was not complete, it was only a husk. Because, if forced to choose between being left with something or with nothing, everyone would choose something. It was not a choice, it was a non-choice.

"How do you feel?"

Raquel woke long before she opened her eyes. I could sense the change in her breathing, saw her turn over, felt her foot brush against mine.

"Fine," I said, although it wasn't true.

"You're not fine. You can't be fine. I knew it, that's why I left. And I wouldn't have come back, you know, if you hadn't kept looking for me."

I ran my fingers through her hair, marvelled at how beautiful she was in the morning. "I came because you said goodbye, If you hadn't wanted me to find you, you wouldn't have said goodbye."

"I know, but it doesn't matter now, does it? I've had a lot of time to think. You'll never be able to trust me again, no one will trust me, and it's not your fault, it's mine. I've thought about it every which way, but it's true. I've made too many mistakes.... You deserve better than this..."

"Let's leave," I said suddenly. "Let's get up, get dressed and leave."

The last time I had asked her to leave with me, she had been struck dumb. This time, she did exactly as she was told.

We didn't meet anyone in the hallway or in the lift. The caretaker didn't seem to be around. It was 2.30pm. When we stepped out into the street, a surge of warm air enveloped us.

"God, it's hot." She looked at me and I nodded, not just because I agreed with her, but because the triviality of the remark made me feel better.

It was true, it was hot. The sun beat down, and it wasn't just the sun, there was the blare of horns, the smoke, exhaust fumes from the cars, children struggling with schoolbags, a fifty-something couple kissing on the corner of the street, the shrill jangle of a slot-machine as we passed a bar, three men standing in a doorway laughing, a mother scolding her son, two drivers arguing over a parking space, fragments of conversation, the street, life itself, the blissfully anaesthetising effects of chaos.

I put my arm round Raquel's shoulder and she shrugged momentarily when she felt the weight of it. "It's really hot."

Raquel had been right to meet me at that unfamiliar apartment which, now that we were away from it, seemed artificial like a stage set. We both knew that everything would be easier away from the floor to ceiling windows, the air conditioning, the stultifying atmosphere of a place no one lives in. Raquel had made a lot of mistakes, but on this point she had been right. We walked down the Calle Jorge Juan in silence, enveloped by the heat, the noise, the smells, walking in a straight line towards the other side of Madrid, our side. When at last we saw it on the far side of Recoletos, silence gave way to reality.

"I'm hungry."

"You're always hungry, Raquel."

"That's true..." she sounded apologetic "Aren't you hungry? I didn't eat yesterday and we didn't have breakfast this morning. It's nearly three o'clock."

"I could murder a coffee."

"Just a coffee?"

We sat on the terrace of a café and when the waiter brought the menus she held him back. "Don't go, we'll order straight away. Two white coffees, and a bottle of mineral water and I'll have some tapas. I'll have a large portion of Iberian ham on wholegrain toast, and a *tortilla*.

"Would you like bread with the *tortilla*?"

"Please..." she turned to me, "What are you having?"

"Um, I don't know... I'll have the *tortilla* as well."

When the waiter disappeared, I looked at Raquel. I knew how to tell when she was hungry, recognised the supremely confident way she addressed waiters only to profusely thank them later for their attentiveness, as though she had some reason to apologise, but today everything was different. 24 hours ago, 36 hours ago, or 72, or 120, I would have given anything to be here with her. Her disappearance had reduced my life to a single sentence, 'anything to be with Raquel', anything to be find Raquel, anything to hear her say she was hungry, anything to be sitting opposite her at a table on the terrace of a café, to watch her eat. But now the happiness was gone, and I didn't know what to do.

"I told you," her expression faded, her eyes became troubled, shifting from the sky to the tablecloth, the trees, before settling on me again. "I told you it would be hard ..."

"It's not you, Raquel. At least you're alive, I can talk to you, ask questions, listen to your answers, I can stay with you or I can leave. You're alive and you're slightly problematic." The half-burned candles around the jacuzzi, the rubber dildo, the blue pills in the scuffed silver box, "But you're a problem that's easy to solve. There's so much more than that, a lot more, and I can't get my head round it. That's what's hard."

Hearing myself say this aloud made it easier, but I didn't continue; I sat, trying to work out how much of what I had said was true, the part I wanted to believe, the part that would save me. My father was a more extraordinary man than we, his children, would ever be, I remembered, and I knew this better than anyone, since of his children I was the only one who had never tried to be like him. The waiter came back with the coffees and the omelettes. "I'll be right back with the ham," he said. Raquel didn't look at him, she went on staring into my eyes with an expression of abandon, of fear and love that I knew well. Very well. Now, I knew everything there was to know about those eyes which burned me, hurt me, and which should have been able to heal me.

"Aren't you going to eat?" The waiter had just set down a slice of toast half the size of the table, but she hadn't even picked up her knife and fork.

"I'm not hungry."

"I don't believe you," I smiled.

"Really," she looked as though she was about to cry again, "I'm not hungry any more..."

I observed Raquel, the line of her jaw, her neat chin, the gentle perfect curve of her long neck, the curious, shadowy colour of her big, dark eyes. A clever girl, so beautiful you had to look twice to take it in, because the perfect harmony of her beauty was invisible to the casual glance, to eyes that did not deserve to see it. I looked at Raquel, and everything was so sad, so arid, so grey, and so fearful and we were so used to laughing, that there would never be a moment worse than, crueller than this terror, louder than this silence.

"Eat, Raquel," I heard the sound of my voice and I was astonished to find that my tongue still obeyed me.

"Really, I'm not hungry..."

"Eat!" I never cry, I hardly ever cry, but I could feel my tears about to well and I was not going to let them fall, not here, not in front of Raquel, even if I had to carry her too, even if my shoulders ached from the weight of all these bodies. "Go on!"

"You're very bossy all of a sudden, Álvaro." She cut a piece of the toast, piled some ham onto it, brought it to her mouth. "That was a stupid thing to say."

"Yes," I wasn't hungry either, but I forced myself to eat, and felt better for doing so. "I like it when you say stupid things. Say something else."

"Like what?"

"I don't know, it doesn't matter." She was disconcerted, she seemed afraid and I didn't like to see her afraid. "Just talk, Raquel, tell me something, anything you like.

"But I don't know what..."

"Talk." She sat racking her brain, her toast suspended in mid-air, but I couldn't wait, I couldn't bear the clamour of this silence any more. "Tell me what the Wise Men brought you at Christmas when you were little, what your favourite toys were, the teachers you didn't like, anything, it doesn't matter..."

"The Three Wise Men did bring me presents at Christmas – well, not just me, all of us – because even though we were living in France, my parents celebrated on 6 January and we didn't do Santa Claus... I'm really scared, Álvaro."

"It's OK, just keep going."

"It was really important to us, you know, keeping up the traditions while we lived in France, like the twelve grapes, we always had grapes on New Year's eve. Grandma Anita always complained 'It's so difficult to get them here and they're terribly expensive'. Then I'd see a single tear in her eye, but she'd brush it away quickly and go back to eating her grapes. My grandparents had a clock that chimed the hour, it was in the living room, and after dinner, we'd all pile in their with our twelve grapes to wait for midnight. One year, my grandfather Ignacio phoned Aurelio my other grandfather, who was living in Spain then, in Torre del Mar, and listened to the chimes from the steeple at Puerta del Sol over the phone, but he hung up after the fourth or fifth bong, and we all kicked up a fuss so he never did it again..." Raquel brought her hand to her mouth and bit her lower lip. "I'm so stupid, maybe it's hard for you, talking about this kind of thing, maybe it would be better if I talked about school..."

"No," Her irrational fear, her need to feel guilty brought a genuine smile to my face. "I'm enjoying it."

"Really? Well, anyway, all my friends in Paris thought the thing with the twelve grapes was weird, and the thing about the Wise Men ..."

By the time I asked for the bill, we'd got to a little plastic stall on wheels with a striped awning and a cash register with fake money and coins, her favourite toy when she was seven, which might have gone on being her favourite had it not been broken when they moved house.

"It's amazing, it was the only thing that got broken. It wouldn't have mattered if it had been that horrible lamp with the crocheted lampshade grandma Rafaela sent my mother. One of her friends had crocheted the lampshade, but Mamá always hated it... Anyway, I was upset, I couldn't understand how it happened, because it was solid plastic, you know? How does a solid piece of plastic just crack down the middle? Shall we go...?

"Yes." I'd paid the bill and was already on my feet, "Let's take a taxi."

"OK."

I gave the taxi driver the address and she didn't say anything. The radio in the car was turned to a station playing hits from the 1980s so we didn't feel the need to talk. Raquel slumped against me, took my hand and started singly along softly. Then a new song came on about *terror in the supermarket/panic in the grocery store/my girlfriend has disappeared/and no one can tell me where she's gone*. At the end of the chorus my girlfriend looked at me and we both burst out laughing. It was the first time we'd laughed since finding each other again, and yet, for me, the laughter left a sad taste in my mouth. The taxi turned into the Calle Conde-Duque, Raquel took her purse out of her bag and insisted on paying. "I've got all this change," she said.

"OK, well..." we stood there on the pavement, not saying anything, and I saw her lips tremble, but she was not going to cry again, she was simply so nervous she was shifting from one foot to another. "Well... I'm going upstairs, obviously and you're... I don't know."

"I'm staying with you," I added quickly, "I mean, if you don't mind..."

"No, of course not." she pulled me into the doorway, "Of course I don't mind, I want you to stay. I just thought... you might want to be alone."

"I'm already alone, Raquel."

"You're with me," but she didn't dare look at me.

"I'm with you and I'm alone."

"OK then..." she said as she opened the door, "Let's say I'm with you too."

It was a silly play on words, but it felt good to hear it, it felt good to step into the cool, dark foyer I had watched so often from across the street. And yet, as we waited for the lift to arrive, I was keenly aware of the booming silence as the motor groaned into life, the ordered grinding of the gears, the hiss of the doors as it reached the ground floor. The lift was long and narrow. Side by side, we would have been pressed against each other, so we went in Indian file, me behind, Raquel in front, and watching her guarded movements, the care she took not to brush against me, the sudden gracelessness of her arms, I felt a terrible, wrenching pain.

We arrived at the fourth floor stiff, silent, as detached from each other as men and women often are before their first time together. But this was not our first time. When she opened the door to her apartment, she went in and stepped aside to let me pass .I knew that I should kiss her. You should kiss her, Álvaro, I thought, but I did nothing. I stepped into the hall, walked past her, and Raquel looked at me as though I held her life in my hands, and I knew that this was true, and so, awkwardly, clumsily, I moved towards her just as she came towards me and our shoulders collided.

She lifted her face to mine just as I bent my face to hers and we collided again. But then her mouth found mine and, standing there, arms wrapped around each other, we kissed for a very long time, as long as it took for my body to make a decision for me. Before, I could lose myself in her, entrust myself to her with no limits, no conditions, merge my will with her, negate my being until it was reduced to its strict organic dimensions, to flesh and bone. But that was then; 'now' seemed to begin again in this apartment, and as I looked at her as we were distinct, as though we were not one thing, my body liberated itself from me and my hands began to undress this woman, my feet to move through apartment, leading her down the corridor, instinctively remembering the steps, never bumping into the furniture. I was me but it was not me, because I could see with my eyes closed, all my attention was focussed on Raquel's mouth, her skin, the lithe, golden splendour of her naked body sprawled across the mattress.

Nothing was the same now, nothing was innocent, we were a little older, perhaps a little wiser, but the Earth still remembered its orbit and still surrendered to the gravity of Raquel's hips, and I surrendered too, like a river overflowing its bed. My body recognised Raquel's body, and I recognised myself in Raquel's body, it still worked, the miracle of cancelling time, but sex had become a trap, a dangerous weapon, an exhausting exercise that could somehow still soothe me, could even transport me to a place beyond pleasure, a place vaguely akin to happiness. Then, for two or three hours I slept soundly, deeply, and when

I woke I found Raquel's eyes staring into mine.

"I made coffee" she said, running her fingers through my hair, "You want some?"

I nodded. She got up and I watched as she walked out of the room naked, and I tried to remember how many times I'd seen her do this. The television had never been turned on before but now it projected a gray glow against the wall. While I'd been sleeping, Raquel had watched an old black and white film with the sound turned down so low you could barely hear the dialogue. I thought of Mai, then remembered that she had been watching a film when I had gone into the bedroom to get a clean shirt less than twenty-four hours ago. And then there was Miguelito.

I propped myself up on my elbow and looked at the alarm clock. It was 6.50pm. Miguelito would be in front of the television now, watching cartoons. I had prepared myself for this. I had imagined these scenes a hundred times, the offices and lawyers, rough drafts, the finished documents, strangers coming and going in a corridor like shadows detached from their own bodies, words of encouragement, cold stares, silence. Joy had made me strong, because Raquel had taught me that there is no task, no problem, no lawsuit, no mistake that cannot be overcome when the ultimate goal is happiness. I had steeled myself for this, for these moments when I would think about my son, lying in this bed with the television on, and having made it this far, it all seemed so hard, so unfair, so cruel for me, for everyone that I suddenly wanted to give up, to disappear, to go away and never come back, alone, as though I could somehow stop being my father's son, my mother's son, Raquel's lover, Mai's husband, Miguel's father. As though I was not Teresa's grandson – as though I was a coward.

Raquel reappeared with a tray and I realised I hadn't thought about my grandmother Teresa for a long time. Her gentle presence hovering over me like a good fairy had played no part in the complicated negotiations I had been having with myself since the night before.

"I brought some biscuits," Raquel said balancing the packet on my knees, "Chocolate chip, you like them, don't you?"

I nodded.

"Can I ask you something, Álvaro?" Raquel curled into a ball and her voice trailed off into a whisper.

"Don't talk in that little voice, Raquel, anyone would think you were scared of me."

"I am scared of you, well, not you, but…" she sat up again and looked at me.

"When are you going home."

"I'm not going home."

Very slowly, I ate one of the biscuits. Her body was tense, her fists clenched but still she said nothing.

"I can't go home," I said, biting into another biscuit, "Last night, Mai said that if I left I needn't bother coming back. She stood at the front door and asked me if I'd heard what she said, asked if I was leaving anyway, and I said yes. Then I left."

"Oh..." Raquel tried to collect herself, but she couldn't get over what I'd said. "You know people say these things, but they don't mean them. Mai only said that to try to stop you from leaving. I'm sure she'd take you back."

"I'm not going back, Raquel, I can't," I looked at her and she suddenly seemed so sad that I was confused. "Especially not now. There's nowhere I can go, I don't have anywhere, I don't have anything, I'm alone, I told you that. My whole life has been blown apart, and the pieces are so small that there's no way of putting them back together... I can't go home and tell Mai that I'm coming back because my father was a bastard, a thief who destroyed the life of a widow who was no better than he was – maybe worse, since she turned in her cousin's husband and had him shot, just so she could rob the family of everything they possessed, and that that same woman went on to be my grandmother, and her daughter betrayed her, married her worst enemy and became my mother. Don't you understand? If I can't even bring myself to believe it, how can I tell anyone else? But mostly... mostly, I don't want to go back, Raquel. Last night, I walked out on my family with the intention of never going back, and I didn't know anything, the only thing I knew was why I was leaving ..." I looked at her again, but she had buried her face in her hands, "But, if it bothers you, I can go to a hotel."

"It's not that, Álvaro, I don't want you to leave ... It's just... it's all so fucked up, everything is so completely fucked up..."

She hugged me and I couldn't see her face any more, but in her voice I could hear my own defeat.

"I knew it would turn out like this, and it's all my fault... but I love you, Álvaro, I've never loved anyone as much as I love you... I nearly went out of my mind, I was thinking, I don't know, I imagined what it would be like if everyone else was dead, your mother, your wife, and it was just the two of us, that you'd had an accident and lost your memory... It sounds stupid, doesn't it? I thought about us meeting in a different country, imagined we weren't related, I pictured us meeting at some dinner or at a party, because sooner or later things were bound to turn out like this ... But I couldn't, I couldn't bring myself to imagine

563

this… all this pain. That's why I imagined everyone was dead, that it was just you and me, living in this apartment, with the sun streaming in through the windows on Saturday morning, me bringing back flowers from the market, the two of us laughing because we were happy, because I'd never gone insane, because I'd never filled a box full of things, gone round to the Calle Jorge Juan, bought two dozen candles in the little Chinese shop next door, never arranged them around the jacuzzi, never lit them and blown them out one by one, as if it were my birthday…"

This sadness, as much mine as hers, coursed through me like some deadly, merciful drug I was powerless to resist.

"And I imagined us being happy because you trusted me, Álvaro, because I'd never lied to you. That's how I pictured it, not this… not this fucked up mess, even though I knew it would turn out like this, that it would never be just the two of us, Álvaro, that it would never be just you and me. There would always be too many people with us, the living and the dead, ruining everything… I knew it would turn out this way, but it's just so unfair, so horrible…"

I never cry, I hardly ever cry, but I was crying now.

She wiped away my tears, pulled me to her and buried her face in my neck.

"Can you get through this, Álvaro?"

"I don't know, Raquel," My brief, meek, silent tears had stopped. "I honestly don't know."

# III

# THE FROZEN HEART

The old folks *(sic)* say that in this country
There once was a war *(sic)*,
That there are two Spains now that nurture
Old grudges and old doubts
[…] But all I have seen are people
who suffer in silence, pain and fear
people with just one desire
their bread *(sic)*, their wife *(sic)*, their peace. *(sic)*
[…]The old folks *(sic)* say
that we do what we please *(sic)*
and that this means its impossible
for a government to govern anything *(sic)*
[…]But all I have seen are people
who are obedient even in their beds
people who ask only
to live their lives, with no more lies *(sic)*, in peace.
Freedom, freedom without anger
Keep your fear, your anger to yourself
Because there's freedom without anger, freedom
And if there's not, there will be *(sic)*.

Rafael Balads, José Luis Armentero and
Pablo Herrero
*Libertad sin ira*, (1977)

In the last days of summer indolence, I was twice reminded of a poem by Antonio Machado which I had not though about for some time: the sonnet *To Líster, Chief of the armies of the Ebro* [...] Any poetry written for specific circumstances can be terrible, but this reservation aside, all poetry is specific. Jorge Manrique's *Lines on the Death of his Father* is specific, and is García Lorca's *Lament for Ignacio Sánchez Mejías* and Antonio Machado's poem about the assassination of Lorca. [...] Why then was this particular sonnet so badly received? Why, nowadays, does anyone who wants to praise its beauty have to find some excuse...? [...] Later, during the second world war[iv], Líster[v], true to his vocation, found on the battlefields of Europe, now, so many years later, his loyalty may seems anachronistic; these days, the sonnet Machado dedicated to him inspires a feeling of vague disquiet. We are so discreet these days! We're so much above such things!

Francisco Ayala (1988)

Mai had tidied the house before she left, but as I stepped into the bedroom, I tripped on a little yellow cement mixer with plastic wheels hidden in the doorway. I picked it up and put it back where it belonged, between the fire engine and the red Ferrari on the shelf where my son kept his fleet of cars. Everything about the room pained me, its smell, the duvet cover that matched the curtains, even the web that Spiderman was climbing. I left the room quickly, soundlessly, as if it were night-time, a different time, but Miguelito wasn't in his bed sleeping, and I didn't feel any better. As I moved down the corridor towards what was now my ex-wife's bedroom, I could almost see him, see his mother, hear her voice, the laughter, the footsteps, the echoes of my former life. I could remember ever word of the conversation we had had the night before.

"Hello?"

"Hi, Mai, it's Álvaro..."

"Yes, I do still recognise your voice."

A conversation that brought to an end one of the cruellest, most brutal, most unpleasant days of my life, although I'd lost count of the contenders for that title. "I thought you weren't coming back," Raquel said when she opened the door at 8pm on that fateful day, 30 September. It was a Friday, a day that had begun when the alarm rang at 7am.

"I have to go to work," she announced. "I took the day off yesterday because I imagined I'd need it, but today... I don't have a choice."

"It's OK." She waited for a minute to see if I had anything else to say, but I could think of nothing.

Watching her get up and leave without turning back, I remembered her words, the brilliant, terrifying prognosis of what awaited me. *I knew things would turn out this way, they were bound to turn out this way, but I didn't want it to be like this, I imagined that it was always Saturday morning, always sunny.* I didn't get up to have breakfast with her. I should have, but I was too tired. I hadn't slept any better at the Plaza de los Guardias de Corps than I had at the Calle Jorge Juan.

At five past eight she came back into the bedroom in her business clothes – trouser suit, high heels, brown leather briefcase – but this time I didn't pull her down onto the bed, creasing her clothes. Not that she had been expecting me to. She appeared with a piece of toast in her hand, popped it into her mouth and then sat down on the bed.

"What are you going to do?"

"Today? I'm not sure... I should go home, take a shower, get some clothes, though I don't feel like it. Afterwards, I honestly don't know."

"Well," she kissed me, "When I get out of work, I'll be here…"

I simply nodded. She left and I found myself alone, surrounded by the stillness of things, the silence of the empty house.

I realised the second part of my life had not begun in that strange, uninhabited room with Raquel's confession. The second part of my life would begin when I got out of this bed where I had so often slept to face the routine which Raquel was lucky enough to have recovered already.

We had slept next to each other, and made love silently, feverishly at about four or five o'clock when our mutual insomnia coincided, but this was of no help when the alarm clock went off. I looked at it again and realised it was already 9.40am. I couldn't spend the whole day in bed, so I told myself the best thing to do would be to begin at the beginning.

I should have phoned Mai. This was the first thing I should have done that day, but it was the last thing I did. I didn't regret it. "You're the only good guy in this sorry mess, Álvaro," Raquel had said to me. This was not exactly true. To my wife, to my son, I was the bad guy. This was why I should have phoned Mai, but I had a shower instead, rummaged in the wardrobe and the drawers until I found a blue t-shirt of Raquel's that fitted me. Then I sat down to breakfast at the kitchen table and surrendered to the fantasy time-travel, reliving the tender scene a few hours short hours after I had left her that first afternoon, when nothing was at stake, almost nothing, on;ymy freedom and her perfect skin velvety as a rare peach.

I should have phoned Mai, but I didn't feel like it. I needed to phone Fernando but I couldn't. If I can't bring myself to believe it, how can I tell anyone else? The bitter echo of my own words floated over the flowers Raquel hadn't bought; it wasn't Saturday morning, even if the sun was streaming through the windows with an infuriating, almost cruel joy. I finished what, under normal circumstances, would be my one cup of coffee and poured a second one. There would be a third cup later.

I was an ordinary, reasonable guy whose only quirk was a morbid aversion to funerals. My life was a little patch of garden, where there was nothing to trouble my eyes or my conscience. It's a long story. A very long, very old story and to live here, there are some things it's better not to know. Things it's better not to understand. If I wanted I could choose to do nothing. It's always possible to do nothing, to learn to live with no questions, no answers, no anger, no pity. It's always possible not to live but to pretend to live, at least it's possible here in Spain, a country where the laws of gravity, the laws of cause and effect, did not apply, a country where no one had ever seen an apple fall from a tree, because the apples had always been on the ground, it was more practical that way, it was better for everyone, for as long as the hand was quicker than the eye, as long as the simplest illusions worked in favour of those who held the lense, as long as the good name of the little people who did what they had to in order to survive was held in contrast to the outmoded reputation of 'honourable' men and women, who were so ineffective in reality, so boring in the sterility of their sacrifice, because if they had done nothing, if they had simply surrendered, if they had not vainly risked their lives again and again, nothing would have happened anyway. They might not have been honourable, perhaps, but we would have understood them just the same.

Little Spanish boy being born into this world, may God protect you. Because to live here, there are some things it's better not to know. But I love you, I have faith in you, I know you will grow up to be a good man, an honourable man, brave enough to forgive your mother who will always love you and who will never completely be able to forgive herself.

Little Spanish girl coming into this world, may God protect you. You don't even have the right to know who you are, because to live here, there are some things it's better not to know. Best to leave everything as it is: the bare branches of the apple tree, the fruit carefully arranged, a clever trick by a set designer who likes to work when there are no witnesse, for those who remain are already dead from fright. Not even the right to know who I am because, in those days it was difficult being the child of certain people, it could even be dangerous... Through love or sheer calculation, so many years come down to this, one, two, three whole generations, almost a century of pain and pride. This is the point where the memories of the victors and of the vanquished meet, different viewpoints, but with only one result for the children, the grandchildren of everyone.

Little Spanish boy born into this word, don't count on God to protect you. Protect yourself from the questions, from the answers, from their reasons, or one of the two Spains will freeze your heart.[2]

There was a third cup of coffee, then a fourth. I called my brother Julio. When I left the house, I felt like a stranger in my own body, as though I wasn't sure that this was me, this man standing on a corner, raising his hand to hail a taxi. But this man was me, the same yet

---

[2] A reference to *Proverbios Y Cantares* No. 53, the poem by Antonio Machado that is reinforced in the book's title.

different, and I would never be anyone else. This was the one thing I knew for certain.

Julio told me to meet him in a café near his office on the Paseo de la Habana. I arrived thinking there wasn't much more that could go wrong, but a few hours later, as I crossed la Castellana, I was so angry that I decided to walk home. The walk did me good, but by the time I was half-way there, my knuckles and the side of my face started to hurt and, the pain was so bad I had to stop. I went into a bar, had a drink, but afterwards I couldn't find a taxi. I was too tired to go one walking, so I took the *metro*. I was so late back that Raquel didn't have time to compose herself when she buzzed me through the front door and I found her standing waiting for me, tearful and with an indescribable expression on her face.

"I thought you weren't coming back," she said, and I remember thinking it sounded as if she were talking to a soldier coming home from war.

"But I did come back," I said, I was home from the war.

She hugged me and I hugged her, I could feel her warmth, her pleasure, the pale echo of an ancient happiness.

"What happened to you, Álvaro?" Raquel looked at me and frowned, "Did you fall or something?" she brought her fingers to my face and gently touched my eyelid. "Your eye is all red and swollen."

"It's nothing, I just… I talked to my brothers," I was laughing, though I didn't know why, "I got into a punch up with Rafa. It's funny, you know, I haven't been in a fight for twenty years and I thought he'd come off best, but in the end, he was the one who came off worst, I'm sure he'll need stitches. I've had a lot to drink, but I could do with another. Do you fancy one?"

Shetook my hands and looked at my grazed, swollen knuckles. "My God… What did you do, Álvaro, tell me…" She was scared and my smile did little to reassure her. "Are you drunk?"

"A bit, it's nothing serious."

"I'm just going to get myself a drink because I have to phone Mai. I'll be right back."

I went into the kitchen with my mobile phone and slowly, deliberately, clumsily, I put a tray on the counter with a glass, some ice and a bottle of whiskey. 'This isn't going to help', I thought; it wasn't going to help and I hadn't had any lunch. But the first sip warmed me from inside and settled me.

"Hello?"

"Hi, Mai, it's Álvaro…"

"I do still recognise your voice."

"How's Miguel?"

"He's fine, He's been asking for you."

"I'd like to see him."

"OK, we'll talk about it…"

"Of course, but I was thinking…"

Until then, everything was fine. Until then, I had managed to accomplish what I'd set out to do: to accept the harshness in her voice calmly, speak in short sentences, avoid any aggression or intimacy that might be misunderstood. Until then, everything had gone well, but I was a lot drunker than I thought I was, I got bogged down, and Mai took advantage of my hesitation.

"Well don't think, Álvaro. You didn't think when you walked out on us, so don't start now. You'll get to see Miguelito when the judge decides you can."

"I don't think it needs to come to that, Mai…" I heard my voice, it was slurred and thick, so I made an effort to speak more clearly. "We should be able to deal with this like…"

"…like civilised people? Fuck you, Álvaro!"

I thought she had hung up, but I could hear her breathing on the other end of the line, agitated at first, like an echo of her anger, her bitterness, and I nearly said I was sorry, and it would have been true. I was sorry I had hurt her, she was one more body I had to carry on my shoulders. I almost said I was sorry, but she exploded just in time, sparing me the insults my compassion would have deserved.

"I don't want to be civilised, do you hear me? You've destroyed me. You're a bastard and a liar and I don't deserve this, Álvaro, I don't deserve this. I loved you, Álvaro. Now all I want is for you to die, I want you to rot in hell with that fucking b…" I heard her sobs begin, then end, silence. "I'm sorry. I shouldn't have said that. I've spent my whole life criticising women who… I'm sorry, honestly. I'm in a bad way."

"It's OK." I preferred the slight moral superiority conferred on me by her insults, but I made no attempt to take advantage of this ceasefire, I couldn't do it, I was too drunk, and in too much pain. "I need to come over, Mai. I need to get some things."

"OK. But I'd rather not see you, so… Tomorrow morning first thing, when Miguelito wakes up, we're going to the mountains for the weekend. You can come by anytime after 11. The sooner you take away all your things the better."

"I'll call you on Monday, to see how Miguelito is…"

"OK."

The conversation hadn't lasted more than two or three minutes, but by the time I finished I was exhausted. I finished my drink, not thinking of the consequences, then went to the bathroom to splash water on my face. When I emerged I bumped into the wall, but that didn't hurt nearly as much as the look I got from Raquel, who was sitting on an armchair, leaning forward, her elbows on her knees.

The love of my life was looking at me like a convict hoping for parole. It pained me, Her anguish pained me, and I was struck by the discrepancy between this scene and the scene as Mai must have imagined it: violins and plump blonde cherubs with fake wings, flowers falling from the ceiling and a faint, coloured spotlight picking out a couple dancing and whirling and smiling and kissing. This was probably what Mai was imagining and it was the dream I should have been living, the most saccharine, pathetic love story, the best moment of my life. I still remembered when I was happy, when the sun split the stones from pure pleasure when Raquel laughed, the smiles that were an intimation of some small private joy, the way she told me she was happy to be with me, of celebrating my presence in her life. She was still the same woman, but her presence was not enough any more for me to be that man

"Does it hurt?" Raquel indicated her own eye and I made a vague face, as though I didn't care. "Do you want to take something? I think I've got some ibuprofen somewhere."

"No," I almost told her I was grateful for the pain, because it kept me conscious.

I collapsed on the sofa and tried to work out how long my hangover would last, the depth of the quagmire of silence we were trapped in. Raquel tiptoed around me with every word, every look, every caress. She had known things would turn out like this, she'd known from the very beginning.

"Come over here, beside me…" I said.

There were no violins, no flowers raining down from the ceiling, no chubby blonde cherubs fluttering around out heads. The only light came from three 60 watt bulbs, but still Raquel came and sat beside me, took me in her arms, pressed her face into my neck and I kissed her the way I usually kissed my son.

"Are you going to tell me what happened?"

"No," I said, "I don't feel up to it, Raquel, I don't want to talk about it… I'd rather wait and tell you everything together when it's all over."

"What do you mean, Álvaro?" There was a tremor in her voice.

"It's not you…" I said. "What I mean is… I'm here, I'm with you, Raquel, I've had too much to drink and I just want a bit of peace. I've had it up to here with meaningful conversations, do you understand what I'm saying? I'm tired of secrets and guilt and tears. I can't stand it any more, I can't keep doing this…"

"All right," she said in a whisper.

"Do you want to go out?" she suggested after a long silence, all our silences seemed to be long now. "We could go to the cinema. It might take your mind off things."

"I've already been."

"Really?" she looked at me, surprised. "When?"

"Three o'clock, something like that, I'm not sure… When I left Julio, I wasn't hungry. It was hot out, I had two hours to kill before meeting Rafa and I didn't know where to go, so I went to the cinema."

"What did you see?"

"I don't know…" This was true. "I don't remember. I left before the end.

"You didn't have any lunch?" I shook my head, "Well, let me make you some dinner."

I could almost hear the bells ringing out, celebrating her relief, my relief that one of us had finally found something to do. Raquel was a good cook, though she always made too much, but tonight I was glad of the excess. I needed to eat, more than that I needed the domestic warmth of this scene, needed to hear her talk about spinach, fish, potatoes.

"It doesn't look as if it was frozen, does it? The sea-bass, I mean…" I nodded and went on eating, "It's because of the mayonnaise, the mayonnaise you buy in supermarkets ruins everything, it gives everything this artificial flavour, like it somehow manages to transfer all the artificial flavourings and preservatives to the fish or the vegetables. It only takes a few minutes to make fresh mayonnaise and there's no comparison. I can kind of understand instant mashed potato, because…" She feel silent, looked at me, and bit her lower lip. "I'm burbling…"

"No. Go on… what were you going to say about instant mashed potato?"

"Are you really interested?"

"No, but I like listening to you."

"Like rain…"

"Yes, I love listening to the rain too…"

And it went on raining, it rained for a long time, it rained all night about mashed potato and artichokes, about *tortillas* with potatoes that were too hard and potatoes that were too soft, with or without onion, about the advantages and disadvantages of cookbooks ancient and modern, the miraculous status of chocolate, the disaster that was Raquel

Fernández Perea's first dessert, when she was 17, and her *Sachertorte* which was better than any you could buy in Vienna.

Raquel's voice trickled like warm, gentle rain, over truths and uncertainties. It rained all night, this strange night when all our secrets were used up, our guilt, and our tears, and all that remained was silence, the subtle but implacable force of its blade. I was drunk but Raquel went on talking, her voice raining over me, over the aspirin she brought me before collapsing into bed next to me, raining over my eyelids, my body, her body, it on into our long, deep sleep. It rained, and then a sunny Saturday dawned, a morning that seemed made for sex and indolence. The sheets were warm, the blinds half-open, and Raquel was naked, her skin golden, soft, there were no flaws on the soft skin of her belly, her magnificent breasts, her hips that were capable of driving the planet from its orbit.

"I have to go," I said eventually.

"Where?"

"To see my mother."

"Don't go, Álvaro."

She clutched my hand, squeezed it as though determined not to let go.

"Don't go," she said again, still gripping my hand. "What good will it do? You already know all there is to know, and it's true, I swear, everything I told you is true. Leave it, Álvaro, please, I've already made enough mistakes for both of us ..."

I shifted closer to her, kissed her on the lips, then freed my hand from hers, and started to get dressed.

That morning I went to see my mother for me, but for her too, so I could buy her the sun of other Saturdays, so I could see her come through the door with shopping bags and flowers, so I could buy her crystal vases to put them in. So that she could live with me, I could live with her, and not just pretend to live.

I walked to the Calle Hortaleza and got there at about 10.40 am, but I buzzed first to make sure no one was home. Mai had tidied the house before she left, but as I stepped into the bedroom, I tripped on a little yellow cement mixer with plastic wheels hidden in the doorway. I put it back where it belonged and went inside, and saw the large suitcase on the bed.

A closed suitcase can be as heartbreaking as a dream that has died, stripped of the hope it contains when it lies open on the bed. I opened the suitcase and looked at the impeccable geometry of my neatly folded shirts, incongruous in their perfection, Mai hands folding them, always the same way, a hundred times, Mai's hands folding them last night or

574

maybe even this morning, a single image with diametrically different meanings. I had prepared myself for this, I had steeled myself to face it because happiness is priceless. As is grief. And as I looked through them, carefully lifting each one so as not to disturb their perfect order, I realised that what I needed was not in here.

My one grey suit, the one I wore to my viva examination, to conferences, was still hanging in the empty wardrobe, together with a white shirt, the tie I usually wore tucked into the breast pocket. I hadn't worn it for more than a year. "Álvaro, *hijo*, you could have worn a tie…" The day we buried my father, the day we met with the lawyer, and before that banquets, commemorations, birthdays: "Álvaro, *hijo*, you could have worn a tie…" "I know, but I forgot… didn't think of it, you're right, sorry Mamá…"

I'll wear a tie today, Mamá. As I stepped out of the shower, I wondered whether it was worth it, but it didn't matter any more. Methodically, reluctantly, I put on my suit, the way I used to when I was nine, ten, eleven and had to go up on stage at school to collect my prize for mental arithmetic. That Saturday morning, looking at myself in the mirror, my right eye already purple, I thought about Julio, Rafa, Angélica, just as I had the night before. We'd never resembled each other less.

"For fuck's sake, Álvaro, you could have warned me! All hell is breaking loose, and of course everyone assumes I knew all along…"

My brother Julio came up to me, smiling, but before he finished the sentence, he frowned and took me by the shoulders.

"You look like shit," he whispered, "What's going on?"

When Raquel told me that she had never slept with my father, I hadn't thought about the rest of them. It was not just that this truth was brutal, squalid, bitter; it was my truth. It was my love at stake, my life. It had been an implosion, a subdued, silent blast detonated by men and women who were long dead, leaving everything in ruins, like a building suddenly disappearing in a cloud of dust. This was how I saw things, and it concerned only me, it had only ever concerned me, from the moment my mother sent her good son to that meeting where it had all begun. It was pure coincidence, a chain of trivial, insignificant events, a series of accidents utterly unrelated to each other except for the unfortunate fact that I was always present. Raquel had nothing to do with anyone but me, she was mine and mine alone.

When she told me she'd never slept with my father, I didn't think about the rest of them. The truth had scorched the earth around me, razed it like a spring frost leaving me alone, with no one behind me, only the faint form of Raquel, curled into a ball, somewhere on the distant horizon, And yet, beyond this shadow, they had still been there, my mother, my brothers and sisters, those cut-out faces on the family tree that hung in the living room at La Moraleja. My mother had been obsessed with arts and crafts, something that, at one point, had taken up all her free time. There was restoring old furniture, then needlepoint, paintings, napkins, towels and baby blankets carefully embroidered with her grandchildren's. My son's bedroom was filled with the fruits of his grandmother's hobbies. At one point, she had become interested in genealogy and drawn up dozens of family trees, for her children, her sons- and daughters-in-laws, her friends. The largest of them, she had kept, painting the branches and the leaves with the skill of a miniaturist in special metallic paint. There we all were, our little heads carefully cut out, forming an intricate design. The tree was moderately leafy at the crown, choked in the middle, with a profusion of lower branches, a gap here, a gap there, then suddenly the Carrión Otero family, my parents, my brothers and sisters, each detail mapping out the highs and lows of marriage, births, more births, then at last a death which would never remove the embarrassing smile from the board it was stuck to.

That morning, Raquel had gone to work leaving me alone on the threshold of what would be the rest of my life. I sat at the kitchen table and had a coffee, and another, and another, smoking like a trooper. I thought about my father, about weighty subjects and trivial things, until I remembered the family tree, the green leaves, the smiling faces, the empty spaces my mother had left for and the future marriages her children might have, the little comments that sounded like warnings addressed to no one in particular, though when she made them she was always looking at Julio. *You can leave me in peace, because I have no intention of re-doing it ... Anyone who doesn't fit in there now will just have to be left off it...*

My father was out of our life now, but my mother would never take his photograph from the tree. Raquel was part of my life now, but no one would ever cut out her face and stick it in its rightful place. As far as my father was concerned, Teresa González Puerto died on 2 June, 1937, when she was most alive. To my brothers and sisters, maybe even to my mother, I would begin to die the moment I managed to get up from this table where I was sitting drinking coffee and smoking compulsively in an attempt to bring myself back to life.

Time had passed, a lot of time. When Raquel told me, the main events were so devastating that I hadn't noticed the loose ends. "My grandfather met your father again in a café in Paris, invited him home, he spent a lot of time with the family, he was so charming that they all became very fond of him and before long he was part of the family..." Between the third and fourth cups of coffee, I reminded myself that I should phone Mai, that it was the first thing I should have done that morning, but I dialled Raquel's number instead.

"Álvaro, hi... Is something wrong?" she said, her voice choked with panic.

"Everything's fine. I just wanted to ask you... When your grandfather and my father met up in Paris, how did they know each other?"

"From Torrelodones," she sounded calmer now, "My family used to go there on holiday before the war. They had a house there."

"I know that, but there must have been a lot of children in Torrelodones, even if it was only a village... And before the war, my father would have been... well, he was born in 1922. I'm just surprised your grandfather would have remembered him after all those years..."

"Yes, but his mother, your grandmother Teresa, was friends with everyone; not so much with my grandfather Ignacio, because he was the youngest, but with Mateo and Carlos, his brother-in-law. They were all socialists, they were in the same chapter of the party as her, they went to the same meetings at the Casa del Pueblo ... All I can tell you is that my grandfather knew your grandmother, and so he was able to recognise your father as Teresa's son. I don't know if that makes sense..."

"It does, yes."

The last coffee did nothing to shake me out of my inertia – barely two fingers of thick, lukewarm glop, the grounds stcking to my palate. My grandmother Teresa, her little smiling cut-out face, maybe I was the only one who knew the truth about her, or maybe Rafa and Angélica knew, maybe they'd always known, my mother never knew what happened to her mother-in-law, but she knew the rest of it, she had to.

*Why? What good will it do?* Raquel had asked these same questions twenty-four hours earlier in an attempt to dissuade me from making the visit that would close the circle. Now I was asking myself Why? What good will it do? The questions were hardly original. They had been asked by so many, answered by the silence of millions of voices who had said nothing for over thirty years.

Why? Because of me, a treacherous son who listens to stories put about by the enemy, Álvaro, the ingrate, the traitor. Perhaps I didn't have the right to think only of myself, but this wasn't about my father, my memories of my father, any more. It was about my own identity, my own memories. Perhaps I didn't have the right to think only of myself, but

577

thinking about myself was thinking about all of us, freshly washed, our hair combed, dressed in our Sunday best, posing in front of the camera for the family album my mother kept in the attic with our school reports. Portraits, group shots, a family – my family. There was still time for me to save it, to preserve the smiling face of this model family, to spare them the aggravation of finding out who they really were. Or maybe not. In all probability they already knew and didn't care.

There was no coffee left, but I kept on smoking. I thought about the word 'generosity', the word 'responsibility', the word 'selfishness'. I thought about order and chaos, about the past and the future, I thought about Teresa, and I thought about Raquel. How could we begin to live like this, how could we rise above it. It would never be just the two of us, Álvaro, it would never be just you and me. There would always be too many other people, the living and the dead, going to bed with us, getting up with us, eating and drinking with us. Why? What good would it do? Just because. Because thinking is the antithesis of action and I couldn't think any more. Julio picked up as soon as I called, his voice sounding both cheerful and worried. Then, as I left the apartment, crossed the square and hailed a taxi, I realised that Mai would have talked to him. It was then I also became aware that I had forgotten something vital – the need to protect Raquel, to find an alibi for her, to minimize her role in this ugly, squalid, sordid mess.

"Let's get a table. I need to talk to you." I suggested.

I'd already warned him over the phone, but he followed me without saying anything.

"First off, I've left Mai, but you already know that, don't you?"

"Of course I know," he said, smiling as if he hadn't heard the first part of the sentence. "Mai called Angélica yesterday and as you can well imagine half an hour later Mamá knew. She gave me a real bollocking, too. 'You must have known, Julio, I'm sure you knew, he always covered up for you and now you're covering for him, you men are all the same, you're pigs, the lot of you.' That's why I said you could have told me beforehand."

"I know. I'm sorry. What exactly did Mai say?"

"To Angélica? I don't know. All I know is that I got a earful because you left your wife for a younger woman."

"She's not younger. Mai's not even a year older than she is."

"Well, to hear your sister talk, you'd think she was straight out of school, that's all I know…"

"Raquel is thirty-six but… she's very special …"

"I'm sure she is," he laughed.

"No, I don't mean like that. I don't know how to explain it... You remember Papá's funeral?"

"Papá's funeral?" Julio raised an eyebrow, "Of course I remember, but what's that got to do with anything?"

"You remember we went for lunch afterwards and I asked you if any of you had seen the girl who turned up at the end, and you said you hadn't?

He looked at me, confused, thought for a moment then shook his head.

"I vaguely remember something... I don't know, does it matter?"

"Yes."

"You mean that's her?"

"Yes."

"What was she doing at Papá's funeral?"

"She's our cousin."

"A cousin?" he looked impressed.

"A third cousin or something. Her great-grandfather was the brother of our great-grandfather."

He put his elbows on the table and rubbed his face a couple of times. "Jesus Christ! So how come we don't know her?"

"That's precisely the point... why don't we know her."

I paused, then let him have the whole story.

"Remember after the funeral when I found the little silver pillbox with the Viagra? And I was wondering what sort of man Papá was... You had a lot on at the time and Mamá asked me to go to La Moraleja instead. I'd already been there once, but I hadn't taken any photos or anything. Anyway, when I arrived no one else was there, Lisette was off doing some course or other, so I was looking around in Papá's study and I found a cardboard file with his papers from the Blue Division. Some notes had been scribbled on them quite recently, names and dates and things I didn't understand, and there was a phone number. That's how I met Raquel. I phoned her and I asked her who she was and she said she'd prefer to tell me in person." I wondered if I was lying convincingly; from my brother's expression, it seemed I was. "It was all a bit cloak and dagger, but in the end I agreed to meet her and she told me that she'd met Papá by accident, because she owned an apartment in Tetuán that Papá's company was trying to buy because they already had the one next door and wanted to knock through the wall to make a bigger flat, I'm sure you remember..."

"Wait a minute, that rings a bell... But we bought a lot of property in Tetuán, so I don't remember exactly."

579

"It doesn't matter. You probably wouldn't remember anyway because she refused to sell for ages. She works in a bank, so she's quite clever about these things and she thought the longer she waited, the more you were likely to offer, and that's what happened. In the end, Papá swapped her apartment for one of the ones Rafa tried to sell to Mai and me, the one on the Calle Jorge Juan. She was worried because the deal was done only a couple of days before Papá went into hospital and she wasn't sure if the sale had gone through. That's why she came to the funeral. She had to talk to one of us sooner or later, and she wanted to get a good look at us... Anyway, that's what she told me. It all sounded weird, and it was pretty weird, but I didn't care, it seemed harmless enough, and anyway, I fancied her. About ten minutes later we were flirting and, well, what happened next doesn't really matter. When we went to the reading of the will, I noticed that the apartment she was talking about wasn't listed as part of Papá's estate, I even had an argument about it with Angélica, remember?"

"Oh yes, I remember that all right."

"Anyway, that night, I phoned Raquel and we arranged to meet up again, and I was still attracted to her. So much so that we started seeing each other, and before I knew what was happening I became obsessed, I'd fallen completely in love with her and I told her I was going to leave Mai. Then suddenly, she disappears and I went crazy, I mean really crazy, I was in a very bad way. It was all a coincidence. It could have happened to Rafa, or to you, or a different company might have bought her apartment and we'd never have met. But that's how it was, and I fell for her. And now I've found out there was something else she wasn't telling me."

My story was full of holes, but I'd already gone too far when I realised that sooner or later Rafa was bound to meet her, and although he'd only spent ten minutes in her company, there was a chance he would recognise her as the investments advisor he'd met at the bank, in which case my whole story would collapse like a house of cards. At that moment, it was the least of my worries, and if my relationship with my family survived the weekend, it would be the least of their worries too. Anyway, Rafa never really noticed women, and Julio had swallowed the story hook, line and sinker.

"I think I know the girl you mean," he said, "I never actually met her, because I wasn't dealing with the contract, but I remember there was one of the buildings in Tetuán where this girl was driving us mad. What I don't understand is.... Why would Papá trade an expensive apartment for her place? I mean he was old, but he wasn't stupid. And why are you looking so depressed, Álvaro? The girl came back again didn't she, you should be happy."

I rubbed my eyes and ordered another beer.

"Julio, do you remember Mariloli?"

"Mariloli?" he nodded, looking at me as thought I was insane, "The caretaker's daughter from Calle Argensola?"

"That's her. The one who found Clara's doll in the street and wouldn't give it back."

The story of the red-haired doll in the green dress was one that had survived the ages, and the expression on my brother's face changed. At that moment, I realised he knew, that he had probably always known, maybe since that day in 1977, but I told him anyway, who our father was, just how honourable he was, what he had done to become a self-made man, everything from the two separate ID cards right up to the moment when Raquel forced him to face up to what he'd done just before he died.

"It was a dirty trick," he said, yet he was still smiling. "What I don't understand is why this girl feels bad, why she feels guilty for sleeping with you without telling you. I mean, if meeting each other was just a coincidence... She has to be as weird as you, Álvaro ... So she knew Papá was a bastard? So what? I've known that for years, I told you so myself. I can deal with it. She suddenly had the chance to fuck him over and she took it? Good for her... Maybe Papá died because some girl showed up at his office one day with a pile of papers he was hoping he'd never see again? It doesn't change anything, Álvaro. She didn't kill him. He was 83, he was bound to die sooner or later. What difference does it make now?"

"Dead men have no friends."

"Never a truer word," Julio raised his glass.

"But... I don't understand" I looked at my brother and saw his smile fade. "I mean, don't you care?"

"I already knew, Álvaro. I've known for years. I've known since that afternoon when your girlfriend – Raquel isn't it? –showed up at Calle Argensola with her grandfather." He finished his beer, then signalled to the waiter. "I think I'll have something stronger... fancy a Gin and Tonic?"

"No." This didn't mean I didn't want a drink, and my brother knew it.

"A whisky then? I'd scored three goals that afternoon, I remember it like it was yesterday. I'd played really well and Papá was proud of me, and back then, that was all I cared about. I was supposed to have a try out for the Madrid junior squad the week after that, remember?"

"Of course, I spent three months bragging about you at school. I bet all my friends they'd sign you."

"Mamá was terrified, but Papá liked the idea of having a footballer for a son. We talked about it after the match, just Papá and me, Rafa was sulking, he didn't say a word the whole way home. He was very jealous of me at the time, because he'd spent the whole season on the subs bench. Anyway, we got home and there was this girl playing with Clara and... And nothing. I had no idea what was going on. Then, before dinner, Mamá came and got Rafa, Papá wanted to talk to him about something, and I was sure it was about me, I was sure he was going to tell him not to be so jealous, to accept the fact that he wasn't as good a footballer as I was. But it wasn't that. At dinner, everyone was solemn, Papá, Mamá, Rafa and Angélica."

"Where was I?" This section where Julio's and Raquel's stories overlapped was part of a time that to me had been insignificant.

"In the kitchen, I suppose. You and Clara still ate in the kitchen back then. You certainly weren't with us. I remember everything because... Well, that night, Angélica came into our bedroom."

"I suppose I was already asleep?" Fate was a poor ally, I thought again, astonished that I had been systematically missing during this episode which would later prove much more important to me than to either of my brothers.

"Yes, you were asleep, I was nearly asleep myself, but they woke me. Rafa and Angélica said they had something to tell me, something really important. We went into the playroom and they wouldn't let me turn on the light. We sat on the floor, we could hardly see a thing. The bedroom door was open, and there was a glow from your nightlight. Then Rafa started talking, telling me this strange story, and at first I didn't understand..."

Julio had been toying with the ice in his glass for some time, but now he put it down. I looked at him, astonished that my brother, who was never really interested in anything, could remember the details so precisely, could recreate – without the slightest hesitation or doubt – everything that had happened that night so long ago.

" 'We're in an extremely serious situation,' Rafa told me, like a complete jerk, 'You need to be informed because the whole family is in danger, especially Papá, but he did it for us...' This is how he talked, and I nearly laughed because he was talking like a character in a B movie. 'Papá did what he did for us, because he was very poor and he didn't want us to be poor...'" Julio started to act out the scene, talking in a whisper, waving his hands around as he played the part of Rafa that night. " 'He wanted us to have the best in life, and anyway the other people were the bad guys. They burned churches, and then they ran away because they were all criminals, so whatever they had didn't really belong to anyone…'" Julio rverted to his normal voice. "'I don't understand, Rafa,' I said, 'What did Papá do? Who were these other people? Angélica said 'Let me tell him.' She was much calmer than Rafa, less nervous. She got up, opened the door quietly and went out into the hall, and a minute later she came back on tiptoes carrying this big book, 'Here, look,' she said. The book was called *Spain in Flames*. Have you seen it?"

"Never even heard of it. We had it at home?"

"Of course… Anyway, it's all very well complaining that you were too young to know anything about it, but you were lucky because it was a catalogue of atrocities. Corpses and more corpses and children with their throats cut, men being shot, women crying… And fires, there were lots of fires, burning crosses, statues of the Virgin knocked down… You get the picture. Rafa wanted to go on telling his story but Angélica wouldn't let him. She wanted me to look at every photo. 'What is all this?' I asked and she explained it to me better, more clearly than Rafa. 'This is what the Reds did during the war. Today, this man came, he's Mamá's uncle, and he was a Red. He came to tell Papá that he had come back to live in Spain, and that he knew that it was Papá who ended up with everything…' 'What do you mean ended up with everything?' I asked. 'It's like Rafa said, the Reds ran away and they left everything behind,' she said calmly. 'And Papá took all their stuff?' 'Not exactly,' she explained, 'it was all auctioned and it went to lots of different people and then Papá… it was Mamá's family too.' 'Oh,' I said, I felt a lot better about it now, 'as long as it was Mamá's too…'"

"I think I need another drink," I announced.

"You're going to get drunk, Álvaro."

"I don't care… Anyway, that's not the worst of it because…"

"Yes." He reached across the table, put a hand on my arm and squeezed it. "I'm sure it's not. The bottom line is they told me it all belonged to Mamá anyway, but I didn't believe them. I knew that couldn't be true, because if it was, why would that man have come? And why was everyone so on edge? I asked them but they didn't tell me. They couldn't, of course, and I only found out later."

" 'The most important thing is not to talk to anyone about this, especially not the little ones, but you need to tell me if anyone asks you questions, because Papá could be in serious trouble. Now that Franco is dead the Reds think they can do what they like…'"

The waiter set down the first glass over the limit I would drink that day. Julio, who had ordered a tonic water, waited until he'd left before continuing.

"I was shitting myself, Álvaro, I'm telling you," and then, as though he felt he needed to justify his reaction, "I wasn't even sixteen. When I went back to bed, I still had all those photos going round in my head. Back then... everything was political. There were posters all over the streets for this side and that side, people were always talking about politics, even the priests used to talk to us about it in school. And our side... I don't know, but Mamá and Papá and their friends were really worried, they were scared to death half the time. They didn't like what was going on, the Communist Party had just been legalised, it was as if it was the end of the world. I couldn't get back to sleep that night, and you know why?" I shook my head. "On account of that little girl."

"What little girl?"

"Your girlfriend. Raquel, isn't it? The little girl who'd come round..."

"I don't get it, Julio..."

"It's simple... Of course, I'd seen the photos, the blood, the dead bodies, but before all that I'd seen her. It's funny you don't remember, because I remember it as if it was yesterday. She was wearing a white dress with small dark red flowers, a jacket the same colour as the flowers and her hair was in braids tied with ribbons. She looked just like Clara, she dressed like her, even talked like her... I only saw her for a second, and she never even spoke to me, but that night, lying in bed, all I could think about was her and Clara playing with the dolls, and ... I don't know how to explain it, but I couldn't connect her with all the stuff Rafa and Angélica had told me. I never saw her grandfather, but she... She was so normal, so little, so innocent, she was just like us... Do you understand?"

"Yes." I did understand, but I could find no other words to thank him for siding with that little girl, a girl I still couldn't remember even now he'd described what she was wearing that day.

"Well ... I thought, that all the stuff we had really belonged to her. She didn't look like she was poor but... I couldn't help thinking that her grandparents had been left with nothing, that her parents had grown up with nothing, in a strange country, while all of us - Mamá and Papá and all the people we knew – had been living like kings in Spain. Seeing that little girl mad me sad, made me feel ashamed, even though it wasn't my fault. I thought it was unfair. So I said to Rafa – he wasn't asleep either – 'Is Papá a thief?' And he was really angry.'Of course Papá's not a thief. You're an idiot, a stupid little idiot.' That's what he said, and I didn't argue, because you know what he's like. Nobody was going to change his mind, not me, not anyone."

"So what did you do?"

"When?"

"I don't know, the next day, afterwards..."

"Nothing. What could I do? There was nothing anyone could do. The next day was Sunday and Papá drove us all to Torrelodones for lunch. While we were walking around the village, everyone stopped to say hello to Papá, and I looked at him and he was smiling and I thought: they know. They had to know, Mamá knew and the woman in the tobacconist, the guy who owned the restaurant on the square, all those people who said hello to us, everyone knew but nobody had ever said anything. I remember feeling like that for days afterwards. If I met someone in the street, or in the metro or in a shop, I'd wondered if they knew too, if everyone knew that my father was a thief..."

"What about Rafa? And Angélica and Mamá? They never talked to you about it?"

"No, no one ever said. Until you mentioned it just now, no one has ever talked to me about it..." He smiled. "It's not as if I forgot, because I never forgot but... I learned to live with it, just like everyone else, to act as if it didn't matter to me. But I failed my tryout for the Madrid junior squad."

"That's right..." This unexpected conclusion made me smile. "I lost all my bets."

"I mean I was nervous and everything, but, to be honest, I didn't want them to sign me. I didn't know exactly what Papá had done, but that didn't matter, because I knew it was something bad. Don't get me wrong, I'm no saint, I'm not even sure that I'm a good person... But after that, I didn't look up to him any more, I didn't care if he was proud of me."

"But..." I didn't dare say any more, but he knew what I meant.

"But I'm here?" I nodded and he smiled. "I got where I am with without having to sweat, without having to say anything, and I'm happy. I'm not like you Álvaro, you know that. Although I'm not the one sleeping with the girl in the flowery dress – actually, you should introduce me, I'd be interested to see what she's like – but, essentially, I don't really care. It's not my life, Álvaro, and it's not yours. Papá was not a good man, I've told you that before, but that has nothing to do with you or me. There's nothing we can do. Anyway, what difference does it make now...?"

My brother Julio was the first person to tell me it was useless. Then I thought of Teresa González Puerto, her life, her death, her smiling face pasted into the family tree, the legacy I shared with this smiling fair-haired man who looked at his watch and asked for the bill.

Julio was her grandson too, even if her letter would have meant little to him. Maybe it's best if it's just you and me, grandma, I thought, maybe it's better if I spare you the indifference and the resentment of my brothers and sisters. But he was her grandson too. Perhaps the best of those who were left.

He'd already closed his mobile phone and slipped it into his pocket and was patting his jacket to make sure he hadn't forgotten anything. "There's something else, Julio. The day I found the blue folder, there was a letter in it from grandma Teresa, Papá's mother. It was the letter she wrote the day she left, because she didn't die in 1937, she died four years later, in 1941, in a prison in Ocaña."

"Jesus!"

"And that's not all..." I was about to go on, but he held up his hand.

He glanced around him again, as though he was afraid. "Some other time, Álvaro. Please don't be angry, but I really can't stay . I'm having dinner with someone, it's important..." He paused, saw me smile," OK yes, it's a woman... I'm not going to sleep with her or anything like that, honestly, but I like her company, and I don't want to be rude... I'll call you later, because I'm interested, honestly, but I have to go."

"Whatever you want."

"You're not angry?"

"I'm not angry with you."

"OK, but before I go, let me give you a bit of advice... two bits, actually...The first is the most important. Listen to me, Álvaro, you need to get away from here. Just leave - tonight, tomorrow and take your girlfriend with you. Go somewhere nice, somewhere beautiful, lock yourself in a hotel room and fuck her. Screw her until you can't get it up, then screw her some more, fuck her until you don't feel anything. Forget about who her grandfather was, how she knew Papá, forget that she's your cousin. And when you feel like your cock is about to fall off, then decide. Stay with her, or go home, go back on bended knee, put you head in Mai's lap and beg her to forgive you. I've tried both, and they both work. Listen to me, Álvaro, I know what I'm talking about. Deal with your own life, think about yourself. Don't think about Papá. Now I really have to go ..."

He got to his feet, put his arms around me and kissed me on the cheek.

"What about the second thing?" I said, "You said you had two pieces of advice."

"The second thing is don't talk to Rafa about this." He was suddenly deadly serious, "Don't even think about it, Álvaro."

But I'm not like you Julio, I thought as I watched him dash out of the bar, I'm not like you, you said it yourself.

The letters began to arrive in the last week of April 2004, but Raquel Fernández Perea, who had spent the May bank holiday in Istanbul with Berta, already knew what they said before she opened hers.

She was still fumbling in her pocket for her key when Nati came out to talk to her, as though she had spent all afternoon waiting for Raquel to get back. "Have you heard?" What a nightmare, I don't know what we're going to do..."

Raquel paid little attention to Nati since theatrical, almost hysterical outbursts were part and parcel of her neighbour's character; she was, an elderly woman, who was in good health despite suffering from some chronic condition.

Nati lived on her own. She had been married and widowed by the age of forty and had had two children, but her son had died in a motorcycle accident. By that time, her daughter was living in Tenerife, where she had found a job as a chamber maid, then she had met a boy, married him and now lived there permanently. She visited her mother whenever she could and had often suggested that Nati come and live with her, but Nati did not want to leave her apartment. "As long as I can still cook and clean for myself, I've no intention of going anywhere," she would say. But her loneliness meant that she lived in exile, in a fantasy world borrowed from so-called reality TV.

Raquel opened her door, set down her suitcase and turned to hug Nati. "What's the matter, Nati? It can't be that bad."

"You don't think so?" Her neighbour clapped her hands to her face and closed her eyes. She looked as if she were about to cry, but Raquel knew she was only mimicking something she had seen on television. "They're throwing us out on the street, that's what they're doing."

"What are you talking about?"

"You'll see ..."

When they had moved in eight years before, Raquel had only been married for three years and still got on well with her husband. The apartment was to be the subject of their first real argument. He had not wanted to buy the place at first, because he did not think it was a good deal. In the end, he realised that it was too good an opportunity to miss, but he was never happy living there. She, on the other hand, loved the apartment and immediately added it to the long list of favours she owed Paco Molinero, her best friend at work. He managed a different department, and in dealing with a couple who were about to default on their mortgage, had suggested that, before foreclosing, he would try to find a buyer. The building - neither new nor old - was unremarkable and there was no lift. The second floor apartment, 70 square metres with ceilings that were very low and two small bedrooms that overlooked a gloomy courtyard, was not much better. But the price more than made up for its flaws. Raquel did not plan to live there for long, she intended to sell it in three or four years' time and use the profit to buy an apartment she really liked, but when the time came, she found she felt at home here. Since the summer of 1999, she had had the place to herself. That was the year she and Josechu had decided they needed time to think, and took separate holidays. Both got what they wanted: Josechu never came back, and Raquel was delighted.

That summer, Raquel thought long and hard about her life. She would never really understand why her marriage had fizzled out. She had married for love, at least that was what she believed, and she had never regretted doing so. But at some point, Raquel realised she liked living on her own better than living with Josechu, and from that moment, her frustration at her husband's little quirks, the trivial arguments they had about what to watch on TV or where to go on Friday night blew up out of all proportion. There was no particular reason, they did not need one. Eventually they split up with no heartbreak, no bitterness, almost without noticing, in much the same way they had lived together for six years.

Nati, who lived opposite, was the one person who genuinely benefitted from this amicable divorce. She became one of the few stable things in Raquel's life, as all her attempts to find someone else failed. After the divorce, Paco Molinero made a play for her. He had done it before – before and after her wedding, so often, in fact, that Raquel had stopped counting. Raquel knew he could not help falling for a woman the moment he saw a sign of weakness. She knew this, but she loved him anyway because he fulfilled every definition of the word 'loveable'. He was gentle, generous, funny, good company, loyal, caring, charming without being clingy, and very attractive. From a distance Raquel almost found him handsome. And he was handsome, other women recognised it, and so did Paco. He was tall and well built, almost precisely the sort of man she might fancy. This was why, every time he came back into the fray, Raquel thought that the problem must lie with her and she racked her brain to discover what flaw, what deficiency, made the relationship impossible.

She would marshal her arguments and resolve that this time it would be different, but it was always the same. She found Paco Molinero attractive with his clothes on. She found him attractive with his clothes off. But that was as far as it went, because the moment he touched her,

Raquel felt uncomfortable, so alienated from her own body that it was as though he were touching someone else, taking some other woman to his bed. It was even worse afterwards because, as she lay there, feeling guilty that her mind had been elsewhere, she would look up at him and realise that he hadn't even noticed. Every time the frustration was worse, the guilt and the depression were worse, but above and beyond that she felt a growing sense that for her sex was impossible, horrible, ridiculous. The next day, Raquel would feel awkward with Paco and before long she would suggest they they go back to planning the multimillion dollar scam they had been working on for years. What had started out as a joke, a game neither of them took seriously, had become a codeword for their failure. Every time she dropped by his office and, instead of whispering, 'last night was wonderful', suggested that she thought she had found a solution to the traceability of wiring money to a bank in the Cayman Islands, Paco knew that he should let things drop for a while.

"Where's that boy?" Nati would drive the nail in every time.

"What boy?" Raquel would say innocently.

"The boy who was here last weekend. He's been here before, too... Paco, isn't it?"

"That's right."

"Where is he?"

"He's at his place, Nati, where do you think he is?"

"Such a shame ..."

"What's a shame?"

"He seems like such a nice boy, I think you could do a lot worse..." Raquel sighed. "Oh, *hija,* don't look at me like that! I won't say another word!"

At moments like this, Raquel would remember Josechu and almost found herself agreeing with his complaints about their daily visits from this lonely, meddlesome old woman who was capable of turning almost anything into a crisis so she would have an excuse to ring a neighbour's doorbell. But Raquel did not really mind Nati's campaign in favour of Paco Molinero, and her exasperation rarely outlived Nati's apology. In practice, when she was not plotting her great banking swindle, Raquel's life alternated between periods of annihilation and moderate firs of promiscuity, never reaching a happy medium. The theatre had bored her because of its excess, banking bored her by its very nature. Berta knew lots of men, many of whom were very good in bed because they were so desperate to please, but they only ever talked about themselves, their successes, their reviews, and how much they would like it if she came to see them rehearse. Her clients at the bank were deathly dull, usually married and rarely good in bed because they were in too much of a hurry and too rich to care whether they pleased anyone or not. In the end, Raquel would always find herself looking at Paco Molinero and realising that he was the only suitable man she knew.

But this was not the only reason for her perpetual indulgence towards Nati. She was used to spending time with her grandmothers and had grown up in a family in exile, obsessed with creating support networks. Nati needed her, and Raquel felt sorry for her, but she also genuinely liked Nati. She was funny, friendly, lively, willing to do anything for a bit of company, and Raquel enjoyed the fifteen minutes they spent chatting when she got home from work - or rather the fifteen minutes Raquel spent offering monosyllabic countrpoints to Nati's theatrical account of the most recent goings on.

"Have you heard the news?"

If a politician had been taken to hospital, that must mean he was dead, if a gas tank had exploded at Leganès, the whole neighbourhood would burn to the ground, if an actress walked out on her husband, it had to be because he'd been cheating on her with her best friend, it there was a tailback on the M-30, it was because a school bus. Nati always talked this way, not because she lied but because she was bored and it was her way of adding a little spice to her life – admittedly by sowing imaginary death and destruction. Nati had worked out for herself that happiness did not make for gripping fiction, so she enthusiastically cultivated misfortune, oblivious to the small, constant humiliation she heaped on herself by doing so. But that afternoon in April 2004 Nati had a piece of terrible news which, for once, she had not heard on the television.

"Here, take a look at this..." Nati hurried into her apartment and emerged with a piece of paper and an aluminium cake tin. "Oh, and I baked you a cake."

Raquel smiled and held the door open to let her pass. "Thanks. Come in for a minute. I'll make some coffee."

"I can do it if you like."

"That would be nice."

She was exhausted after her flight back from Istanbul. It was almost 8pm and she still had to unpack, do a load of washing, take a shower, wash her hair and get herself ready for an early start in the morning, so she didn't really feel like talking to Nati, but when she sat down in the kitchen and read the letter, she was glad she had.

"Don't worry, Nati," she said, "This is just the first..."

"That's all very well for you to say." Raquel looked at Nati and realised it would take more than a couple of platitudes to reassure her.

"I'm worried sick."

She had good reason to worry. Raquel had already heard rumours and read an article somewhere about this, but it had all been so vague she had dismissed it. Yet it had been bound to happen sooner or later, because her apartment and Nati's, their building, the whole area was ripe for speculators.

When Paco Molinero, who was always keen to score points with her, had first told Raquel about the apartment on the Calle Ávila, she had told Josechu that they would be living on the Avenida del General Péron. While not exactly true, this was not quite a lie. The celebrated Avenida del General Péron which ran through the poshest part of the city did begin near the abandoned warehouses, the nineteenth-century factories, the derelict villas and the cheap houses of the Calle Ávila. From the Tetuán, you could see the lights of Paseo de la Castellana, the skyscrapers of Azca and the Santiago Bernabéu stadium, but still, Tetuán was Tetuán, an old hodgepodge of an area that appealed to Raquel, but not to her husband. Recently, she had been thinking that it was only a matter of time. If urban renewal continued at this rate, the street would soon be more to Josechu's taste than her own, but it had never occurred to her that it would happen so quickly.

"Have you talked to the president of the housing co-op, Nati?"

"Yes... There's going to be a meeting, I think, I'm not sure." She nodded to the letter Raquel was holding. "They're going to evict us, aren't they?"

"That's not what it says," Raquel shifted her chair closer to Nati, took the woman's hand and spoke to her slowly and carefully. "It says that our building has been zoned for urban renewal. That means the city council," or some other bastards, she thought, "have decided to modernise the area, you understand? To knock down some of the old buildings and build new ones."

"But this isn't an old building," protested Nati, her voice choked as she realised that her neighbour, who was young and knew how to work a computer, had come to the same conclusion she had.

"It's hardly new, though, is it?"

"Well I don't know," Nati was not indignant, she was close to tears, "then why don't they knock down the buildings in Puerta del Sol? They're a lot older than anything here."

"I know, Nati, but they're listed buildings, they can't tear down the city centre because..." Raquel decided that it was pointless trying to explain. "Listen, there's no point in talking about it right now. The city council have laid down certain norms – rules if you like – but they still

592

have to be discussed, they can't just be applied to everything. We can appeal, and we will appeal, but if we lose, well… They still have to *buy* our apartments, because that's your apartment Nati, and no one is going to take it away from you,OK? If we have to sell, then we'll sell, but they'll have to give us a small fortune, or one of the apartments in the new building."

"OK, but then… where will I live while they're building all these new apartments?"

"Well, you could go to Tenerife," Raquel smiled but Nati did not smile back, "Your daughter would love to have you…"

"If I go to Tenerife, I might not come back." This was Nati's worst fear.

"Don't worry… these things take time. There's the appeal, the verdict, another appeal… I'm sure by then you'll want to go and see your daughter."

"Are you sure?"

"I'm sure."

That evening, Raquel managed to calm Nati's fears, but they did not survive contact with the outside world. Forty-eight hours later, she accompanied Nati to the meeting of the residents association, at which Raquel's predications were systematically toppled like dominos. The chairman argued in favour of unconditional surrender with as much passion as if he had already received a bribe from the construction company, but his arguments sounded unassailable. They were. The building suffered from a while series of structural problems which were more than enough to have it condemned, and even if the resident's association had wanted to repair these faults, no bank would ever lend money on a condemned building. However, there was one possibility. A construction company had offered to buy the apartments in order to secure the rights to the land. The chairman recommended that they accept this offer and sell as soon as possible, since there was no other solution. "We'll see about that," said Raquel before leaving. She had argued strongly against the recommendation. "And what else can we do?" the chairman asked, and she knew from his smile that everything had already been decided. "Everything…" she said. But by the following morning, she realised that 'everything' amounted to two phone calls.

"You can't appeal against the decision, Raquel," Her brother Mateo, a lawyer, called her back fifteen minutes after she first spoke to him. "I'm sorry."

"Why not?" She was not prepared to give up so easily. "All laws can go to appeal…"

"No, not all of them. There are some laws – rulings, in this case - that can't be appealed. Rulings deemed to be in the general interest cannot be brought to a standstill by individual interests."

"The general interest?" the words repulsed her. "Let me tell you what..."

"No, Raquel," Her brother interrupted her. "You're not going to tell me anything... I didn't draft the law, and there's nothing I can do about it. I'm just telling you how it works."

Hardly had she hung up when the phone rang again. It was her contact in the Mortgage Department.

"There's nothing we can do, is there?" Raquel said before her colleague even had the chance to speak, "We're screwed."

"'Fraid so. I'm sorry. And I'll tell you something else, even if you could get the money, you'd be a fool to do any work on the building, you might as well flush the money down the drain..."

"Because there's no way to appeal the decision?"

"Exactly."

"I just heard. Thanks for getting back to me so quickly."

"No problem. Good luck."

We'll need more than luck, Raquel thought.

She mulled over the problem all day. She wasn't worried about herself – she had bought her apartment so cheaply that she was bound to make a profit – she was thinking about Nati and the old man on the first floor, about Maruja two floors up, a single mother with three teenage kids. None of them had spoken up at the meeting, but she had watched them, seen their faces fall, their shoulders sag, their eyes fixed on the floor. Their home was the only thing they had, they had spent years and years paying for it, buying themselves some measure of security. We're fine now, they had thought, there's nothing else that can go wrong. And now they were going to lose it all because of some greedy fucking speculator wreathed in the laurels of the 'general interest'. It's always the same old story. Well not this time.

Raquel Fernández Perea repeated these words to herself over and over until they finally rang true, then she picked up the phone again.

"Don't get so worked up, Raquel." Paco Molinero, the best negotiator she knew, tried to calm her down. "Tell me the whole story, slowly, from the beginning..."

"What do you think?" she asked him when she had finished

"Well, it doesn't sound good," he attempted to temper his verdict, "At least on the face of it."

"I know, but I have a plan."

594

If they were incompatible in bed, over a desk, with a problem to be solved, they were all but invincible. Raquel was the more imaginative, the more daring, Paco more shrewd, more realistic. They enjoyed working together precisely because when they pooled these talents, they could come up with innovative solutions. The one they came up with that day – *resistance is victory*, was hardly brilliant, but at least it seemed like a solution.

"So?" Nati appeared that evening just as Raquel stepped out of the lift. "It's bad, isn't it? They going to throw us out on the street."

"Of course not!" But looking at her, Raquel suddenly felt such a surge of pity that she put her arms around her, and hugged her harder than usual. "No way! I've taken steps... I've spoken to my brother, who's a lawyer, and to Paco and I'm about to go up and talk to the surveyor on the top floor, because I thought he was good at the meeting last night, didn't you?"

Until the chairman had asked him several times to calm down, Raquel had not even known the man's name. Sergio was short, skinny, almost insignificant and younger than Raquel, but she had the impression that she could count on him. Something he immediately confirmed.

"We can't appeal the ruling," he said as he opened the door."

"I know. But we have to do something," she said, dispensing with formalities.

"Of course," he emphasised his words with a vigorous nod, "By any means necessary."

It took them two hours and a six-pack of beer to come up with a detailed three-point plan: storm the bastions of power, bureaucratic wrangling, dogged resistance.

Sergio had also found the chairman's willingness to capitulate, his rush to negotiate an overall price for all the apartments, suspicious. "I'm sure someone's greased his palm." Raquel nodded, taking her notebook out of her bag. They decided that he would be their first target. She jotted down some notes: *inform neighbours, mount secret campaign to unseat chair, form administrative council, contest chairmanship, trigger election, stand as a team - Sergio chair, me, vice chair. Other way round. Sergio prefers me as chair, him vice-chair. Once elected: never file documents on time, ignore formal demands, never talk to developers, keep paying community charges etc, get independent valuation on every apartment, add 10%, eventually settle for 20% less, keep our heads down, contact media, go on TV, stand our ground even if they cut off the electricity. They can't demolish the place with us inside, they can't do anything while we're still inside.* When they had finished, Raquel underlined this last sentence, then got up and said goodnight to her disciple.

"Let's take twenty-four hours, think about it," he said walking her to the door, "We can meet back here tomorrow at the same time."

"See you tomorrow, then," Raquel smiled and kissed him on both cheeks, "And remember: resistance is victory."

Resistance is victory, she repeated to herself, resistance is victory. Jesus, it has to work sometime…

And for a long time, she was convinced it would work, because, their plan got off to a good start. They had the support of all their neighbours which the exception of the former chair and a woman who rented out her apartment and was never there, and the week after they were elected, someone called from Promociones del Noreste S.A. to say invite them to lunch.

"No way!" Raquel said, "If you want to see us, then you can come and meet us at my apartment. But it can't be this week, or next, because the vice-chair is on holiday at the moment…"

They made them wait a month and showed up to the meeting with two lawyers, Mateo Fernández Perea, whose righteous anger his sister found terribly amusing, and Sergio's girlfriend who had just finished her studies and was scared to death. The developer's spokesperson was a thirty year old lawyer in an Armani suit with John Lennon glasses, hair cropped short to hide the fact that he was prematurely balding. His name was Sebastián López Parra, and he handed each of them a business card before they sat down. He began by reeling off the mutual benefits of collaboration for all parties concerned, his tone polite, almost smarmy, but it became hard-edged as he attempted to persuade them that they had no legal recourse. He did not dare explicitly offer them money, but his every word obliquely hinted at the lustre of corruption. When he had finished, he surveyed them and stopped when he came to Raquel, as though he realised that she the principal stumbling block.

"Well, if you've finished, I'd like to say a word or two…" she gave him her most charming smile before putting forward a figure to which he responded with an even broader smile.

"Señora, please… I thought this was a serious negotiation!"

"Oh, I'm deadly serious, believe me," she paused and her smiled faded, "I'm an investments advisor working in asset management, I've been in this business for years and I know a lot of people. I've consulted a number of them and – as I'm sure you already know – their estimate is a lot closer to our figure than it is to yours. If you're not prepared to take this offer seriously, we can stop now and start looking for another buyer.

I'm sure yours is not the only company interested. The fact that you already own the building on either side is your problem rather than ours. We may be forced to sell our apartments, but we're not compelled to sell them to Promociones del Noreste."

Sebastián López Parra smiled again, took off his glasses, cleaned them with his tie, then put them back on and looked at Raquel.

"You do realise," he said serenely, "that if you fail to negotiate a deal with us or with some other company before the ruling is passed, your property will be expropriated at which point you will lose considerably more..."

"Of course," Raquel was as calm as he was, "but, as I'm sure you're aware, this is not prohibition Chicago, so I am not aware of any legal recourse, you have to prevent us from selling to another buyer. And if we should lose, as you say, then in all probability your company will lose considerably more."

"Very well," Sebastián López Parra's glasses were shining, but he cleaned them again with the same care and attention before getting to his feet. "We will, of course, have to give the matter some thought."

"Of course," Raquel stood up.

"I'm still inclined to think that the price you are asking is excessive, and does not reflect the current state of the market, but I would ask that you do not talk to other potential buyers while we consider a new offer. I believe it is in all our interests to reach an agreement." He shook hands with Mateo, Sergio and Sergio's girlfriend, and walked with Raquel to the door.

"Goodbye," he said simply, giving her an ambiguous smile tinged with surprise and something which, in other circumstances, Raquel might have interpreted as complicity.

"See you soon." Madame chair replied, thinking that at least they had sent someone intelligent.

"Girl, you were amazing!" Sergio's girlfriend rushed over and hugged Raquel.

"But why did you hike up the price? That's not what we agreed," Sergio said.

"I know but suddenly... I don't know... I got the impression that they weren't going to cut off the water and the electricity. I'll bet you anything they'll want to settle long before it comes to that. That's why I jacked up the price, because if I'm right, we've got a decent margin to play with."

"Let's hope so."

This was what she thought, but she did not think it would be easy. It wasn't easy, but resistance still seemed to be the surest path to victory. There were other meetings, with lawyers and without, with experts and without, both sides bluffed when they needed to, and sometimes the game seemed to go one way and sometimes the other. Spring ended, summer passed, autumn came and it began to grow cold.

Until this point, Sebastián López Parra who had begun negotiating with the owners individually the day after he met the new chair of the residents' committee, had only managed to persuade the pensioners on the first floor, who were terrified and who immediately moved to their house in Guadalajara to avoid any trouble. The others preferred to trust Raquel when she assured them that, if they stood their ground, victory was theirs. It was a simple calculation and she was convinced that they would win out. They had to: 2004 was about to end and the ruling was due to come into force early in the new year. Resist, resist, resist. On 10 January, 2005, Sebastián López Parra made his final proposal. It was 4% below the figure which Sergio and Raquel had decided was their bottom line a year earlier, but they treated it as if it were a victory. Which it was. Resistance is victory, and they had been victorious.

"Don't even think about baking a cake today, Nati," Three days later, a courier delivered purchase and sale agreements to each apartment and when Nati called to tell Raquel she had received hers, Raquel decided they should celebrate. "I'm going to buy cakes and some of that Majorcan chorizo you really like. And a bottle of Baileys."

"*Olé!*", Nati somehow managed to applaud into the telephone.

"You go and invite Maruja, I'll talk to Sergio."

In fact, it was no big deal. Raquel smiled as she hung up. But at least they weren't going to be thrown out on the street. What they stood to make for each apartment would not be enough to buy a similar apartment in the new building, but it would be enough for a large deposit, leaving them with a small mortgage. When Raquel looked at it like that, it seemed a pyrrhic victory, but they had negotiated a much better deal than any of their neighbours in Tetuán, all those who had given up without a fight.

The strangest thing was that none of them intended to live in this place they had so staunchly defended. Nati had decided she would just take the money, and if she didn't like living in the Tenerife, it would give her the freedom to come back. She now talked excitedly about the move because it no longer seemed like a surrender but a change of scenery. Sergio was moving to Aluche to live with his fiancée. They had already put her apartment up for sale and planned to use their combined resources to buy somewhere else in Madrid. Raquel was almost certain that her grandmother would sell her the apartment on the Plaza de los Guardias de Corps, which had been standing empty for a year, since Anita had decided she couldn't bear to live there now that her husband was dead.

Anita had moved to Canillejas to live with her daughter Olga, who had come back from Paris, unable to go on living there after the traffic accident that had left her a widow. Everyone, including Raquel, had tried to persuade Anita to rent out the apartment. 'Maybe later,' she would say, 'maybe later,' but the truth was she could not bear the thought of a stranger living there. This was why Raquel was convinced that she would sell to her, even though at first her grandmother refused.

Anita was nervous whenever Raquel mentioned the subject. "You're family, how can I do business with you? I can't sell you the apartment, *hija*. I'd happily give it to you if I could…"

"But you've only got one apartment and you have two children, four grandchildren and five great-grandchildren and it wouldn't be fair on them. Am I right?"

"Yes," she nodded without much conviction.

"Then sell it to me grandma! I'll buy it, you can keep the money, and give it to whoever you like."

"But you're family, how can I do business with you?" Anita would say and it would start all over again, until the day when Ignacio Fernández Salgado decided he was tired of listening to the same thing.

"It's easy, Mamá, you just sign a contract." He faced down his mother's shocked glare. "Don't you see, it's better for everyone. Nobody wants the apartment except her, and she's about to be chucked out of her place… Do you really want Raquel to live somewhere she won't be happy and have a stranger buy your apartment? After her father intervened on her behalf, Raquel knew it was just a matter of time before her grandmother agreed to sell. That afternoon, as she arrived home laden with trays, she was more excited at the prospect that she would be soon be moving to the apartment where as a girl she had spent every Saturday with her grandfather Ignacio, than she was at having negotiated an agreement with the developers. For her, this was the happy end to her relationship with Sebastián López Parra, his tie and his John Lennon glasses. She kissed Nati, Sergio, his girlfriend, and Maruja, the single mother from the third floor, set the trays down on the kitchen table, poured drinks for everyone, and began to read aloud:

"Madrid, 17 January, 2005, We the undersigned Doña… "

"But today is on the 13th," Nati protested.

"We'll go see and the lawyer on Monday," Sergio said, " Let her finish reading, we can ask questions afterwards."

"We the undersigned Doña Natividad Melero Domínguez, vendor, and Don Julio Carrión González, purchaser..." It's impossible, Raquel paused, it can't be him, it's too much of a coincidence.

"What is it?" Nati asked

"Nothing, it's just..." Raquel quickly recovered her composure telling herself that it couldn't be him, the word was full of people named Julio, named Carrión, there was even a vineyard called Bodegas Marqués de Carrión, it had to be a coincidence. "I just thought I recognised the name... Anyways, Don Julio Carrión González, purchaser, hereby agree..." She read the contract to its conclusion and smiled and clapped with the others, but although Nati, Sergio and Maruja signed their contracts, having checked that each copy mentioned the same amount, Raquel did not sign in the space reserved above her printed name. For two hours, she looked after her guests, she laughed, she talked, she listened, she topped up their glasses but never for one single moment did she stop thinking about the name Julio Carrión González.

She was almost certain that she had never known the complete name of the man you had made lollipops magically appear from her ears that distant afternoon in May 1977, because she rarely heard the name after that day. At her parents house, no one talked about the war, about their years in exile. It was as though none of it had really happened, as though the Fernández family had never left Madrid, as though the Pereas had always lived in Torre del Mar, as though her father had not been born in Toulouse and her mother in Nîmes.

Her parents did not like to talk about such things and when they had no choice but to talk about that period of their lives, they couched the experience in words so vague that it sounded as though they had gone to France to study, or on holiday. Julio Carrión was a particularly good example of this tendency to obscure the facts. 'During that whole thing with Carrión', her father would say or, 'before that whole Carrión episode,' and if one of his children asked who he meant, he would say, no one, just one of his father's colleagues who had done the dirty on him. Raquel, however, knew more about the story than her brother and sister. She had heard her grandfather call the man a bastard and she had seen him cry, she also knew what Ignacio Fernández Muñoz had told her years ago, as they walked hand in hand down the Paseo de Recoletos.

"Would you like an ice cream?" She had been nineteen at the time, though she still spent every Saturday afternoon with her grandparents. "I'm buying."

"No, I'll buy."

600

"OK, but…" she realised that this was as good a time as any to ask him. "Tell me something *abuelo*, do you remember that day we went to visit the apartment with all the children, the place where they gave me the doll?" He smiled bitterly, which she took for assent. "You're never going to tell me, are you…?"

"Tell you what?"

"What happened that afternoon."

"You're so stubborn, Raquel." Ignacio Fernández Muñoz stopped in the middle of the boulevard and looked at his granddaughter. "You must have asked me…"

"…a thousand times, I know," she nodded, "But you've never given me an answer."

"That's not true." He handed her an ice cream, tasted his own, and walked on. "I always answer. I went to see that man because I needed to talk to him. And I talked to him. That's all there is to it."

"So, you talked to him just like we're talking now."

"And you think that doesn't mean anything?"

"You see?" Raquel smiled in spite of herself, "There you go again, trying to sidetrack me. I don't know why I even bother to ask."

He laughed and they walked on for a bit, eating their ice creams. Raquel thought that, as usual, she would not get another word from him. But this time, it was different.

"I'll make you a deal." Ignacio suggested as they reached the Plaza de Cibeles. "I'll tell you the important parts if you don't ask any questions, OK?"

"Why?"

"That question is not part of the deal."

"Oh, granddad, you can be so stubborn."

"So can you…"

They both laughed, but Raquel was the first to speak.

"Agreed. No questions."

"Let's walk down the boulevard, it'll be nicer." Raquel nodded. "That afternoon I went to see a man named Julio Carrión. We'd been friends years before in Paris, at least I thought of him as a friend. So when he said he was going back to Spain, we asked him to sell the family properties and send us the proceeds. You see, when they lived in Spain my parents were rich, but in Paris we were poor. Julio promised to take care of it, but he kept everything for himself."

"He stole from you?" Raquel asked, and her grandfather nodded. "Everything? But how did he…?"

"We had a deal, señorita."

"I know, but…"

"No buts." Ignacio Fernández put his arm around his granddaughter's shoulder. "A deal's a deal."

This was all Raquel Fernández Perea knew about Julio Carrión when she saw his name next to hers on the contract. It had been sixteen years since that afternoon when she had persuaded her grandfather to confide in her, and in the meantime, she had barely thought about it, because when they got to the Neptune fountain, her grandfather had made her promise that she would never mention it to anyone. Raquel realised that the reason he did not want to talk about it had nothing to do with her grandmother, but with her father, and she was happy to agree. Her father did not like his daughter knowing things he would prefer not to talk about, and since he could not criticise his father, it was Raquel who bore the brunt of his anger if she let slip some name, or some date she was supposed to keep to herself. In 1988, by the time Raquel finally discovered what the phrase 'the Carrión business' actually meant, talking about the past was considered to be in poor taste, and Raquel had lots of other things she was happier to think about.

At nineteen, Raquel Fernández Perea had been happy about most things, even about Spain. At thirty-five, however, Julio Carrión's name bothered her so much that, after her neighbours left, she sat down at her computer, crossed her fingers, and typed in the name of the company that was buying her apartment.

Promociones del Noreste, S.A. had a stylish, modern website with some sophisticated animation. It had clearly been designed to persuade people to buy: there were comprehensive floorplans and virtual tours of the apartments. In the navigation bar on the left was a button that read *Who We Are* which directed her to a link to the Grupo Carrión, which owned the company along with five others. In the section marked *Human Resources*, Raquel found a link to the management team: Don Julio Carrión González, President, Señor Rafael Carrión Otero, CEO, and Señor Julio Carrión Otero, Managing Director. Next to each name was a link *Find out more…* She clicked and found out more. There they were, the magician who made lollipops appear and his elder sons, still almost as blond as they had been as teenagers, though they had considerably less hair. She read:

> "Don Julio Carrión González was born in Torrelodones, Madrid, in 1922. A self-made man, he founded his first company, Carrión Construction, in 1947…"

She stared at the photos for a long time, read the biographies over and over, wondered what had become of the dark-haired boy, the youngest son, then sat, staring at the screen. She thought about her grandfather who had died of a brain haemorrhage in the spring of 2003 as he was about to celebrate eighty-five years of a life that had been both beautiful and terrible; beautiful, because he had made it so, terrible because of what others had done to him. The death of Ignacio Fernández Muñoz had been the hardest blow his granddaughter had ever suffered, because she loved her grandfather more than anyone in the world and still needed him. Now, sitting in front of her computer, she missed him more than ever, and she didn't know how to react to this joke that fate had played on her.

"What should I do, granddad?" She said it aloud, but there was no answer, so she gathered up the dirty glasses, emptied the ashtrays, washed them all and went to bed, but she could not get to sleep.

She could choose to do nothing, sign the contract, sell the apartment, move to the Plaza de los Guardias de Corps and get on with her life as though she had never seen the name Julio Carrión González on the agreement. She imagined could hear her grandfather: *Don't do anything, Raquel. Why? What good would it do?* This had been more or less the advice he had given her when she was eight. "We've come back here, haven't we? If things were different, if things had been normal, you would have lived here all your life. But to live here, there are some things it's better not to know. Things it's better not to understand," She could choose to do nothing, it's always possible to do nothing, to know nothing, to want nothing, but she was not eight years old any more, and it was her grandfather who had made her the strong, determined woman she had become. *Don't do anything, Raquel, there's nothing to be done.* Raquel felt exhausted, ill at ease in her own body. *But I have to know, granddad, even if I don't do anything about it, I have to know, can't you see?* She fell asleep still talking to her grandfather and dreamed that her alarm was ringing. Then she woke up, and her alarm went off.

"What should I do, granddad?"

As she made breakfast, she heard his voice again, but in the cold light of day, what she had found out last night seemed so cruel and unfair. The same name, the same man, the same story all these years later, and nothing had changed, he still had the law on his side. She needed to know. If she was to judge calmly, even if she did nothing, she had to know.

"What are you doing tonight, Grandma?" By now, it was 11am and she'd had a lot of time to think but had come up with nothing that would change her mind.

603

"Raquel! I'm so happy you called... I was just about to call you."
Anita Salgado laughed and her granddaughter felt the warmth of her
voice. "I think you know why..."

"Really? Oh, that's wonderful," but at that moment she wasn't
particularly interested in the apartment on the Plaza de los Guardias de
Corps. "I need to talk to you, grandma. Can we meet up this afternoon?"

"I can't, Olga and your mother and I are going to the theatre this
afternoon."

"Well, let's have lunch tomorrow then. I'll take you to that Chinese
restaurant."

Anita thought it was a wonderful idea. Raquel had discovered that
both her grandmothers had a weakness for Chinese food, and she still got
a kick out of taking them. "It's all so pretty," Grandma Anita had said.
"The little bowls, the porcelain spoons and the colours, the deep red of
that sauce just makes you want to run up a dress in the same colour, and
it's so delicious." Her granddaughter smiled and nodded. At the end of
the meal, she would always say: "Let's not mention this to your
brother..."

Ignacio, the doctor of the family, was constantly worried about his
grandmother's weight, because she suffered from high blood pressure.
Raquel knew her brother was right, but she more worried that Anita, who
was almost eighty now, might give up on life altogether, something she
had almost done after her husband died, refusing to dye her hair, paint
her nails or leave the house. That period, when she had taken to her bed
for days, had scared everyone. Since then, her daughter, or her daughter-
in-law or both, would take her to the theatre once a week, her son took
her to bullfights when they were on, and her grandchildren would visit on
Saturday or Sunday. Mateo would take his children along, Ignacio would
show up with his daughter and a blood pressure monitor. But it was
Raquel, who had no children and didn't work afternoons, who spent the
most time with her. They saw each other twice a week and went to the
cinema or to the hairdresser and sometimes, they had lunch at a Chinese
restaurant.

That Saturday, Raquel booked a table at one of the best Chinese
restaurants in the city before going to collect her grandmother. Anita was
waiting downstairs, and gave Raquel a smile so radiant that her
granddaughter felt guilty that she was about to ruin it. She kissed her
granddaughter on both cheeks, loud, quick kisses like machinegun fire,
then took Raquel's arm and they walked out to the car. The weight
problem which so concerned the third Ignacio Fernández in the family
had not limited her mobility until recently.

"*Hija mía*, I'm so happy!" she said contriving to slide into the passenger seat unaided while Raquel held the door open.

"Are you all right."

"Of course, why wouldn't I be?" Her grandmother looked at her as though surprised. "What are you waiting for?" Not until Raquel was sitting next to her, and the engine was running, did she decide to explain the reason for her happiness. "So, I talked to everyone about the apartment. I talked to Jacques, but he's got his head in the clouds as usual, he didn't even know what I was talking about. 'But I'm going to Milan, grandma,' he says to me, 'Why would I want an apartment in Madrid?' So he's fine... And Annette seems happy with the idea, 'That's cool, grandma,' she said, "That way when I come to Madrid I can stay with Raquel, she'll have tons of space, I'm sure she won't mind...'"

"Of course not, grandma, I love Annette, you know that, we're great friends."

"Anyway, then I had a word with your brothers, they were the ones I was really worried about, because Mateo is always saying that your parents spoil you and I spoil you and that's why I gave you your grandmother María's bracelet."

"Grandma, he's only teasing you," Raquel parked the car, got out and opened the passenger door as Anita extricated herself.

"Anyway, I had a word with him, just in case... I said: Mateo, now tell me honestly, if you want the apartment, if you'd rather I didn't sell it to your sister, please tell me. But Ignacio's reaction was priceless, he said 'Listen, grandma, what I think you should do is sell the apartment and split the money with me on the sly, then the two of us can go off to Las Vegas for the weekend and blow the lot!' He's such a funny boy. He wears me out talking about diets all the time, but I'll have to admit he does make me laugh. He doesn't really like the idea of living in the city, nobody really wants to live in the city apart from you. You're like your grandfather... That's why I think it's best if you keep the apartment because... It's what he would have wanted... He really loved you, you know, you were always his little girl."

Raquel saw her grandmother waver.

"We're not going to cry, are we?" Raquel said, blinking back tears herself.

"No, no..." but it was too late for Anita, who was already wiping a tear from her eye. "I'm so glad we came here. Isn't this the place where they do that sticky rice I like?"

"That's right..."

Anita smiled broadly, then squeezed her granddaughter's arm as the waiter showed them to their table. Raquel looked at the menu and picked an excellent red wine, which her grandmother refused to taste until they had made a toast.

"To your apartment."

"To *your* apartment," Raquel countered and they both laughed.

"So, what did you want to talk to me about?" Anita asked.

"Well, the thing is..." I'm about to ruin your lunch, Grandma, Raquel thought, "Oh, let's talk about that later. Why don't you tell me about the play you saw yesterday?"

In doing so, they rescued the main course: the prawns, the noodles, the rice, the Peking duck with pancakes, but as they were about to order dessert, Anita Salgado looked at her granddaughter the way she used to when she was a little girl.

"Thank you, that was lovely. Now, are you going to tell me why you're so jumpy?"

"I'm not jumpy, grandma."

"Oh yes you are," Anita smiled, "Maybe I'm an old woman, maybe I have trouble chewing, I'm half deaf and there are times when my memory's not so good, but I'm no fool."

"No, you're right."

"So?"

"The company that's trying to buy my apartment is called Promociones del Noreste, does that name mean anything to you?" Her grandmother shook her head. "The man who owns it is called Julio Carrión González."

"It can't be..." Anita shook her head vehemently, as though she could somehow erase this name from every conversation present and future. "It must be someone else, I mean there's even a wine called..."

"I know," her granddaughter interrupted, "I thought about that too. But I looked it up on the internet and..."

"Oh, the internet..." Anita pulled a face. "You can't trust anything your read on the internet ..."

"Grandma," Raquel's expression was serious and Anita fell silent. "It's him. I visited the company's website. Julio Carrión González, born in Torrelodones in 1922, founded his first construction company in 1947. Take my word for it. It's him."

"1922..." Anita was no longer looking at her, she was murmuring to herself as she brushed imaginary breadcrumbs from the tablecloth. "That would be right, he came between Ignacio and me. I was born in 1924."

"It's him, Grandma," Raquel took her grandmother's hand, "There was a photo on the website. I recognised him."

Anita's dark eyes widened in astonishment. "How could you know what he looked like, *hija*, you've never even met him? I suppose you might have seen a photo of him back in Paris, but you couldn't know for sure..."

"I could, grandma, because I have seen him, I met him. It was much later, in 1977, granddad took me to their house one Saturday. He told me he was visiting a friend."

"Granddad?" Anita Salgado who was two months from her eightieth birthday was astounded. "My husband Ignacio went to visit Carrión...? In 1977? The year we came back?"

Raquel nodded. The ensuing silence was so long, so impenetrable, that it was as though the shouts of children, the conversation and laughter of the other diners existed only to underscore the anguish of this old woman, who had pressed her hands to her face as if she was trying to shut out the world. And yet all around her the world went on existing.

"He promised me... over and over he promised me. I told him I wouldn't go back unless he swore he wouldn't go and see him, that he wouldn't look for him ... On your children's lives, I said, and he said 'I swear on my children's lives', and then he goes... And he took you with him ... he was so pigheaded. He was the most pigheaded, most reckless man I ever met, he always had to be the strongest."

Rage turned into grief and Anita began to sob. It pained Raquel so see her there, so small, so alone, in so much pain, so she got up and sat next to her grandmother, and hugged her.

"I'm sorry, grandma, please forgive me... I'm so sorry;"

"You've got nothing to be sorry for, *hija*. "You haven't done anything wrong." She took Raquel's hand and breathed deeply as though to steel herself. "And what happened? He didn't take a gun, did he?"

"A gun?" Raquel, still upset at having made her grandmother cry did not know what scared her more, the word itself or the casual way Anita said it. "No, of course he didn't... what are you talking about?"

"No, I suppose not, not in 1977," Anita's almost gentle tone shocked Raquel even more. "But then, why go to see him?"

"Well..." Raquel had to think. Unbelievably, she had never asked herself this question before now. "I don't know, I really don't know grandma. He had an old leather briefcase with him full of papers. Carrión's wife took me into the kitchen to have a snack with her children and afterwards we played for a bit. I only saw Carrión himself for a minute or two, but I really liked him. He did a magic trick for me, he..."

"...he made sweets magically appear out of your ears?"

"Something like that..." Raquel said and Anita nodded bitterly.

"Lollies. Then his wife came to get him and he went off, he talked to granddad for quite a while, but I didn't see him afterwards. When we left, granddad..." Raquel looked at Anita and thought she had suffered enough. "He asked me not to say anything to you about it, he said it was an old story that I wouldn't understand, and that I didn't need to understand it because I was going to be living here now and to live here there are some things it's better not to know."

"Just as well," Ignacio Fernández Muñoz's widow finally smiled.

"I suppose... But I need to know, grandma, I need you to tell me what happened, even if it is all in the past., I'm not eight years old anymore."

"But why?" Anita looked at her in genuine amazement. "What good would it do?"

Raquel had prepared some questions of her own.

"What good does it do me to know my own name, grandma, or your name, or my parents names, or why you don't eat apricots any more? What good does it do me that I've never once heard you mention the name of the village you come from? What good does any of it do? None, I suppose, but it helps me to understand who I am. Isn't that enough?"

Anita Salgado Pérez looked at her granddaughter and could think of no answer. She brought a trembling hand to Raquel's face and stroked it gently.

"Let's go," she said, "This is not the place to talk about such things..."

Raquel asked for the bill and settled up.

"Where do you want to go?"

"Take me home." Before Raquel could protest, Anita explained. "Olga's not there at the moment, she and your mother have gone out to the sales"

The two of them walked back to the car in silence, then they drove through the deserted early afternoon streets of Madrid until they were almost half way home.

"I'll tell you the whole story. I'm not sure it's the right thing to do, but I'll only tell you if you promise me two things..."

"Not to talk about it to anyone?: Raquel smiled.

"Yes. That's the first thing. Why are you laughing?"

"I'm laughing because it's always the same story, every time Julio Carrión's name comes up, someone asks me to promise never to talk about it. First granddad, now you..."

"But you promise?"

"I promise. And the second thing?"

"The second thing is I don't want you to do anything stupid after I've

608

told you. So Carrión wants to buy your apartment? Fine, it's a small world, what can you do? Sell him your apartment and move into our old one and then we'll never have to mention his name again, agreed?" Raquel simply nodded, but it was enough. "It's unbelievable… But I'll tell you something, it's a good thing your grandfather is dead. I never thought I'd hear myself say those words, but if he was still alive I don't know what he would have done…"

"Would you like me to make some coffee?" Raquel asked when they arrived back at Carillejas.

"We've just had coffee. Why don't you get out the bottle of cherry brandy instead? You know where it is."

Anita sat in one of the armchairs by the window and didn't speak again until her granddaughter had poured the brandy. Raquel sat on the little stool she'd always sat on as a little girl, when the two of them watched old films while Ignacio had his *siesta*.

"You know what happened, don't you? Carrión robbed us. Well, he didn't rob me, I didn't have anything to steal but he stole from Ignacio's family."

"I know that much," Raquel admitted, "But that's all. I don't know how he did it or who he was or how you knew him."

Anita Salgado raised a hand as though to say 'not so fast'.

"Your grandfather never really got over it… He blamed himself, he thought that it was his fault, though we told him it wasn't. We all told him, his parents, his sisters, I must have told him a thousand times that it wasn't his fault, that the only person to blame was the crook who had swindled us…but Ignacio… He didn't care about the money, well maybe a little, but that wasn't what really hurt him. What he couldn't bear was the fact that Julio had fooled us, that he had lied to us so that he could rob us, that's what really hurt. It if had been… I don't know… If it had been a stranger, some lawyer we'd hired in Paris or some friend of a friend, he would have thought it was a dirty trick… 'but that Julio could do something like this, after we'd been so good to him, we were like a family to him, he was always round our house…"

"Of course," Raquel suddenly realised who Carrión was. "That's why you said I might have seen photos of him in Paris, Carrión is the one in the white shirt in those photos of you posing with a big birthday cake - it was Papá's birthday I think, or Olga's…"

It was Aída's birthday, María's daughter, but yes, that's him."

"Of course, but you never said anything…"

"Why would we? We certainly wouldn't have talked about him… As I said, your grandfather never really got over it, so, at some point we just stopped mentioning him, we pretended that we'd forgotten all about it and in the end, mercifully, we did forget, although I don't think it changed anything... I'm sure Ignacio went to his grave still feeling he was to blame. I remember the first days after it happened, the first nights. He didn't let it show in front of his family, he felt he had to be strong. His parents – and they were the ones who had lost everything, who owned the properties – they took if calmly. 'Franco could have taken it all in '39,' his father said, 'it would have been just the same.'"

"Yes," Raquel interrupted gravely, "But it's not the same."

"Of course not, but what can you do?" her grandmother smiled sadly, "Their son had been killed, their son-in-law had been murdered, they had a grandson in Madrid they had never even seen, so what difference did money make? Ignacio understood, he agreed with them, but at night, when we were in bed... 'Another betrayal," he'd say, 'another traitor, I can't bear it any more, Anita. Why am I even alive? I'm alive so that I can be betrayed again and again and again and I can't go on like this, I'd rather be dead...' That's what he said to me, the poor man, and I'd say 'I don't want you to die, Ignacio, please don't die...'. because I didn't know what else to say, how to comfort him. 'Why does this always happen to us, why is it always the same story? We're the wretched of the earth, Anita, the wretched of the earth...' He said it over and over again, and he was right, because everyone had abandoned us, nothing was going right, we were more and more isolated, there were fewer of us and Franco was becoming increasingly powerful, and now Julio, one of our own had betrayed us..."

Anita fell silent as she saw her own grief reflected in her granddaughter's eyes. She knew it would take time for Rquel to digest what she had heard, and this was only the beginning.

Quietly, almost fearfully, Raquel asked: "Was Carrión a member of the Party, Grandma?" Anita looked at her as though she didn't understand, "Was he a socialist, an anarchist, was he ...?"

"What do I know?" her grandmother interrupted her, then she shrugged her shoulders. "Of course he was. That's what he said, anyway, and I believed him, we all believed him. He definitely had a JSU card, I saw it with my own eyes, it had been issued in Madrid during the war. But I don't know who Julio Carrión really was... What I do know is that he was an opportunist, a user, a cynic. He was an evil man."

"Raquel could not find the words to express her confusion. "I don't understand. How could he have...? Nobody ever suspected anything?"

"Nobody," Anita smiled "We never thought there was anything strange about him. Julio's mother was a socialist, one of those

610

Republican teachers everyone admired. Your grandfather met her and he always said that she was a wonderful woman, a brave, dedicated communist. She was from Torrelodones and my parents-in-law had a house there, they used to go there every summer, so when Ignacio met her son in a café in Paris, and realised he was lost alone, living in exile, he brought him home. His mother had been friends with Mateo and Carlos, she'd been sent to prison for thirty years, and had died there. Back then, that was enough. Why would we have been suspicious?"

Some months later, Raquel Fernández Perea would discover that this woman was Teresa González Puerto and she would hear her speak through her grandson, a dark-haired man who was the spitting image of the traitor she remembered. She would also discover that Julio Carrión's capacity for betrayal was boundless, and the love that had performed the miracle of bringing this dead woman back to life moved her all the more. Teresa González Puerto was alive again the man Raquel loved, in the lips that spoke her name, and this new life would be good. When it happened, Raquel would realise why she had fallen in love with this woman's grandson, why she had never loved another man as she loved him, why her need to fuse her body with his was as elemental as the need to drink when she was thirsty, and sleep when she was tired. When it happened, she would also realise that her sleep was damned, that there would be no sunny Saturday mornings, no coming back from the market with a huge bunch of fresh flowers.

Anita Salgado had promised to tell her granddaughter what had happened, and she kept her promise. She talked for three hours, sometimes relating incidents chronologically, sometimes as they came to her. She confessed that she had forgotten certain names, and certain dates, but she gave a coherent, detailed and comprehensive account. Through her eyes, Raquel could see Julio Carrión as he had been at twenty-five, the most charming man in the world, brilliant, intelligent, a man so irresistible he managed to overcome Paloma Fernández Muñoz's resistance. Her grandmother insisted that everyone had liked Julio Carrión, but although he had an easy rapport with men and children adored him, it was women who found him the most attractive. It was his this, she believed, that had led her sister-in-law to give in to him, something she would not have done with any other man. Using Carrión to revenge her husband had not been a motive, merely a pretext for the attraction Paloma might not even have recognised and would certainly never have admitted to. But Anita was sure that Paloma had been attracted to him, and in the end, she told Raquel, it was Paloma that she felt sorriest for.

"She suffered more than anyone, because of course we later found out that Julio had married Angélica, the daughter of the woman who had informed on Paloma's husband. It didn't matter to us, but for her, it was the last straw. Paloma felt so humiliated, so ashamed at what she'd done that she refused to speak, she refused to eat, she could go for days without saying a single word. I tried to talk to her, because I'd always been fond of her, I still am..."

"You used to work together, didn't you?" Raquel remembered a photo of the two of them in white aprons, standing behind the counter of a bakery.

"That's right, when we first met in Toulouse... She was the only person who helped me with my mother, and she was the one who supported me when Ignacio had to leave for fear of being turned in. I used to visit her whenever I could, and if we were alone, I'd say: 'You were a widow when it happened, Paloma, a free woman, what difference does it make that you slept with him? You couldn't know what that bastard was going to do, none of us knew,' and she'd say, 'Don't, Anita, I don't want to talk about it.' But I'd insist for her sake, 'The man you slept with isn't the Julio Carrión living in Madrid, you fell for a man we all liked. You know she tried to commit suicide?"

Raquel shook her head sadly, "No, I didn't know. Nobody ever told me anything."

"She slashed her wrists with the razor that night we found out that Julio... Poor Paloma...," every word seemed to pain Anita, "Your grandfather had me, he had his children, but Paloma... She was completely alone... And she was so pretty, she was a real beauty, a lot of Spanish men in Paris were in love with her, and French men too. That's how we met your uncle Francisco, you know, back in Toulouse. Every night, he'd stand outside the bakery, waiting for her to come out, and then he'd follow her home. Never said a word. We used to make fun of him, especially María, she always was a minx, but that's how they got together. One day, poor Francisco realised that he preferred María's teasing to her older sister's airs and graces, and she said yes and they're still together to this day. But I don't think Paloma was ever interested in another man, and that's why... When she realised that of all the men she could have had, she chose the worst..."

"Well, well," Raquel, hanging on her grandmother's every word, had not heard the door open, but she recognised the voice immediately. "What's this little gathering in aid of?"

Her mother, carrying various bags and with a broad grin that indicated the shopping trip had been a success, entered the room before her sister-in-law Olga.

"Grandma's selling me the apartment," Raquel got up to greet them both. "We had lunch at a Chinese restaurant to celebrate."

Olga kissed her niece and then her mother. "Good for you, Mamá, it was about time you made up your mind."

"Now maybe we can talk about something else at mealtimes..." Raquel's mother chimed in. She asked if they'd made coffee. Raquel said they hadn't, Olga said she would make some, then the phone rang, and as Raquel Perea Milan began emptying her shopping bags to show them what she had bought at the sales, the afternoon suddenly slipped into being an ordinary day.

"I nearly bought a dress for you, *hija*, it was a little denim dress with sequins, but I can never be never sure with you, I thought you'd probably think it was kitsch, so..." She began to pack everything back into the bags, then looked at the clock. "Oh my God, it's twenty to eight! Did you bring the car?" her daughter nodded. "Could you give me a lift home, then you could come up and say hello to your father."

"I'll give you a lift, but I can't come in. I'll see Papá tomorrow, I was thinking of coming over to yours for lunch... Grandma, could you give me the keys to Plaza de los Guardias de Corps?" Anita raised an eyebrow. "Now that I know it's really going to be mine, I'd like to look at it again... Actually, now that I think of it, what's going to happen to the furniture? Can I keep it?"

"I wouldn't get your hopes up," Her mother said, "There's not much furniture left."

"No, but what's left is the things nobody wanted, isn't that right, Mamá?" Olga said, "Those little beds, that big sofa in the living room that wouldn't fit here, a couple of lamps and Papá's old desk. You said you wanted that, didn't you Raquel?"

"I did, but there was no space for it in Tetuán." She didn't look at her grandmother, "That's why I'd like to go over now and have a look round."

"Now?" Anita sounded surprised, "But it's getting late."

"There is electricity, isn't there?" Raquel said, ignoring the note of suspicion in her grandmother's voice "Or did you have it cut off?"

"No, we didn't ... Jacques said his family would be coming for Christmas and there wouldn't be room for them all here," her grandmother stared evenly at Raquel who held her gaze. "Your grandfather's keys are in the drawer of the bedside table." When Raquel got to her feet, her grandmother added: "Just a minute. Remember what you promised me."

"Yes."

"Yes what?"

"Yes, I remember."

"Eight months later, when Raquel came and told her the last story she'd ever have wanted to hear in what little remained of her life, then asked if she could stay for a while, Anita had simply nodded. Then she took her granddaughter in her arms and told her she could stay as long as she wanted and that when she had seen her walk out with the keys that afternoon in January, she had known that Raquel would not keep her promise. Raquel had known it too; perhaps it was the fact that her grandmother's tale weighed too heavily on her, the terrible despair of a man who was now dead.

Raquel Fernández Perea would never be able forget these words, but perhaps they might have remained just that, words she could not forget, had her grandmother not given her the keys to her apartment, had she not immediately recognised the key that opened the drawer in her grandfather's desk, something she had seen him do only once in her life, had she not found an old pistol and a box of ammunition in that drawer, and with it, a battered brown leather briefcase that contained more than papers.

"You would have found it anyway," Anita told her eight months later, "It's my fault, I should have thrown all that stuff out. I didn't want to give it to your father, or to Olga, it would only have upset them, you know how much they hate that sort of thing, I should have thrown it away... I thought about it, but it was too painful, because all those things had belonged to Ignacio, they were Ignacio, so I just decided to leave things as they were... and now look what's happened."

Raquel did not disagree, but she could not help thinking that if she had kept the promise she had made to her grandmother she would never have met Álvaro Carrión Otero.

Álvaro did not yet exist for her when Raquel took the leather briefcase from the drawer, careful not to touch the gun. Her hands were shaking so much that she decided to take the contents into the living room to read. There were title deeds in the name of Mateo Fernández Gómez de la Riva and deeds in the name of María Muñoz Palacios. There were certified copies of their wills, a copy of the power of attorney signed in Paris on 27 March, 1947 by Mateo Fernández Gómez de la Riva in favour of Julio Carrión González, and a copy of a second power of attorney issued in Paris on the same date by María Muñoz Palacios in favour of Julio Carrión González. Raquel read half a dozen letters, date stamped and posted in Madrid, in which Julio – no surname - sent his love to the whole family, telling them he had begun the process and explaining the various bureaucratic difficulties he was encountering. She also found a receipt for a bank transfer of 5,000 pesetas issued in February 1948 at a branch of the Banco Español de Crédito, to a current account in the name of Mateo Fernández Gómez de la Riva, along with half a dozen other letters written in the autumn of 1948 bearing the letterhead of a legal practice in Madrid in which a certain Manuel Rubio Martínez informed his clients that as of that date, their name did not appear on the deeds or titles of any of the properties about which they had enquired. The lands and properties in question had been the subject of a series of extraordinary seizures in accordance with the expropriation laws, and thereafter had been sold on to third parties by their owner Don Julio Carrión González.

"Sebastián?" it was eight o'clock in the morning but she decided there was no point in waiting. "It's Raquel Fernández Perea, the president of the…"

"Yeah, yeah…" he was awake, she could hear a smile in his voice, "I know who you are. How are things?"

"Fine. I was just calling to tell you I won't be at the meeting with the notary this afternoon." She said this in as neutral a tone as possible.

"OK… If there's a problem we can meet later in the week, morning or afternoon, whatever suits. The others will still be there, won't they?"

"Yes, everyone else will be there, but my case is a little different. I didn't realise that Promociones del Noreste was owned by Julio Carrión. My family has a complicated history with Señor Carrión, and I need to speak to him before I decide whether or not to sell."

Sebastián López Parra began to lose his patience: "Raquel, for Christ's sake, we've been working on this deal for over a year, I thought we were past the stage of petty tricks."

"It's not a trick, Sebastián, I assure you." From her voice, he realised this was true. "And it has nothing to do with you. I need to meet with Julio Carrión, I need to talk to him, and until I do, I'm not signing anything."

"OK, if you're determined, I can try to set something up. I've just seen him – he's a lawyer too, so I don't think there'll be any problem."

"I'm not sure we're talking about the same person, Sebastián. I don't mean Julio Carrión Otero, it's his father I want to talk to, Julio Carrión González.

"That's impossible!" Sebastian was beginning to sound nervous. "Don Julio is an old man, he's over eighty, he can't be disturbed… Listen, Raquel, I think I've been very fair to you throughout this whole process, so don't go making trouble for me. Don Julio is the president of the company, but he only comes in for a couple of hours a day, and that's only because he's bored, he doesn't have anything to do with the running of the place any more. His sons are my bosses, and they'd never forgive me. I could lose my job over this, I'm telling you..."

"I suspect Don Julio won't want his sons to know," Raquel Fernández Perea was astonished by the composure in her own voice. "In fact, I'm sure of it, so let me make a suggestion. Have a quiet word with him, or leave a note with his secretary. Just tell him Ignacio Fernández's granddaughter would like to see him. Nothing else. And tell him if he doesn't want to see me, I'll have to talk to his sons."

When she hung up, the panic and the fear she had suppressed during the conversation overwhelmed her, and she felt an excruciating cramping in her stomach. She had banked on the fact that the Carrión family were not so different from the Fernández family, and if the victims had kept their ruin a secret for all these years, their executioner would have had all the more reason to keep quiet himself. A second ago she had been sure of this, but now she realised that not only did she have no basis for her assumptions, she also found herself hoping that Julio Carrión would not take her threat seriously, and that he wouldn't agree to see her so that she would never have to look the man in the eye.

"What have I got myself into?" The question plagued her all morning. "How the hell did I come up with such an insane idea?" What had seemed clear to her on Saturday night, what on Sunday had dazzled her as she studied the framed photographs in her parents house now seemed like foolishness, an act of madness. Carlos and Paloma's wedding photograph, Mateo wrapping his coat around Casilda as they looked into the lens, Ignacio in his French army uniform with Anita holding their son, the two of them in a park in Toulouse, five smiling men showing off the German tank they had captured, Ignacio Fernández Salgado and his sister Olga in costume, Ignacio dressed as an Aragonese peasant and Olga as a flamenco dancer, her mother in Córdoba in a mini-skirt posing in front of the Cristo de los Faroles, and the photographs of her great-grandparents, of her grandparents, her aunts and uncles, her cousins, her parents, photos that spoke to her, photos that made her smile, photos that made her eyes well with tears. As she was looking at them, talking with the people in the photographs, everything had seemed so clear. Now she also began to pity Sebastián, who had been so good to her, and who had not missed an opportunity to hint that he could be better still if only she would let him.

Raquel Fernández Perea, who had talked about so many things with her grandfather Ignacio, did not know that, in the heat of battle, brave men and women fear nothing and no one. The fear comes later, when they begin to wonder how they could have been so foolish, so insane. That evening, when she stepped out of the shower and noticed there was a messaage on her mobile phone, she immediately recognised the number and dialled her voicemail. "Hi, Raquel, it's Sebastián. I talked to Don Julio's secretary and she got back to me. Don Julio can meet you at his office the day after tomorrow at half-eleven. Let me know as soon as possible if that's OK with you." She was grateful for the unruffled tone of his voice, and replied by text message: *'Good. I'll be there.'* When she tried to put the phone down, her hands were shaking so much that she dropped it on the floor.

The rest was easier. There was no way of backing out now and necessity is the mother of courage. On Wednesday morning, Raquel Fernández Perea showered, ate breakfast, put on her business suit and left for work with ice in her veins. At 11am, with the same icy determination, she hailed a taxi, gave the driver the address of an office on the Paseo de la Castellana and tried to clear her mind. She couldn't stop her knees from trembling as she stepped up to the reception desk, but managed not to sound flustered as she gave her name. Julio Carrión González's secretary was waiting for her as she stepped out of the lift on the third floor. Having greeted her tersely, she led her in silence down the long carpeted hallway.

"If you would like to wait here," the secretary said, gesturing to an armchair, "Don Julio will see you right away."

Raquel realised that these offices were utterly unlike the rest of the building, with its modern glass-and-steel façade, but she did not have much time to ponder the difference.

"If you'd like to go in…" A moment later Raquel found herself in a room so vast that she had to walk sa certain istance to make sure that the man behind the desk was really him. She felt no different than she did when faced with a new client and her host did nothing tochange that impression. Julio Carrión González did not get up from his seat to greet her, and she responded to this discourtesy by remaining standing, looking down at him. She remembered her grandmother's description, something that had been borne out by the photo on the website; Julio Carrión was old, but he was an attractive man. He still had the same shock of hair he had had as a young man, though it was white now, the same fierce intensity in his expression, the same sparkling eyes.

"You look at lot like your aunt Paloma." He was the first one to speak and his remark caught her off guard. "I'm sure people are always telling you that. Her hair was a little darker than yours and her eyes were a brilliant blue, but the shape of your face, the chin, the neck, that elegant jaw-line... You're very like her..."

Raquel said nothing, she went on staring down at him, a sharp metallic taste in her mouth.

"Please take a seat, Raquel." Julio Carrión yielded to politeness, "Tell me, what can I do for you?"

"You can start by not calling me Raquel, I have no desire to be on first-name terms with you," She listened to this voice as though it were not her own, and drew strength from her words.

The old man laughed and his face looked like a child's drawing of the sun, a big yellow ball with sunbeams streaming out from it. Raquel did not know that Julio Carrión had always been attracted to brave women, she didn't yet know that she would be the last, and that she would be the exception.

"I didn't mean to offend you," he said, "But you are considerably younger than I am. So, Señora Perea would you like to tell me why you're here?" Though he had just turned eighty-three, he was still a charming man and seemed to revel in that fact, "I'm guessing you wish to tell me that the price of your apartment has just gone up considerably, am I right?"

"No." His face was suddenly serious. "Not exactly. I don't know if you remember me, I'm the little girl who came to your house with Ignacio Fernández Muñoz one Saturday afternoon in May 1977." She paused to study the effect of her words and saw him nod. "He had this briefcase with him." She picked up the briefcase and showed it to him. "I'm sure you recognise it. It's the same briefcase and it contains the same documents. I want you to tell me what you and my grandfather talked about that afternoon. That's why I'm here."

"And why should I tell you?" Raquel noticed the tone of this question was markedly different from his previous remarks. She saw him stiffen, he was bolt-upright in his chair now, and there was a hardness in his expression, but far from inhibiting her, his manner spurred her on.

"For a start, because if you don't tell me, I won't sell you my apartment."

"Now listen to me, Señorita." His lips curled into a sarcastic smile underscoring the contempt in his voice, "Don't you threaten me. I don't give a shit about your apartment. I can buy a hundred buildings like yours..."

"Fine." Raquel Fernández Perea felt much better now, and the blood in her veins began to thaw. "In that case I'll contact Señor López Parra

618

and let him know that my apartment is no longer for sale. He'll be terribly upset, because he's put a lot of work into negotiating this deal but you're the boss. Don't worry, I won't tell him why, I'll leave that to you. I think that would be best, don't you?"

She let the question hang in the air and saw that although the contempt on his face had not entirely faded, it had dissolved into something more complex.

"I don't know what you're trying to do, but if you think you can frighten me, I can assure you, you're sadly mistaken... But I'm loathe to ruin the hard work of one of my best employees or run the risk of bringing something as ambitious as the Tetuán project to a standstill. I have no intention, however, of wasting all day with you, so just name your price and I'll pay it."

"I want to know what you and my grandfather talked about that afteroon. That's my price."

Julio Carrión González clenched his fists, making no attempt to disguise his irritation.

"Your grandfather is dead," he said, after a moment, "How will you know whether I'm telling you the truth? That I'm not conning you?"

"Go ahead, try," she said, "I don't think you can fool me, Señor Carrión. I knew my grandfather extremely well, so well in fact that having spoken to you only for a minute, I'm fairly sure I know what happened that afternoon."

"Really?" he paused and looked at her with disdain, "Why don't you tell me?"

"You offered him money, didn't you? And he wouldn't take it."

She knew she had hit the mark when Julio Carrión looked away, his eyes moving slowly around the room as though seeing it for the first time.

"I'm going to tell you something that may surprise you," he said at length, "Señorita..."

"Raquel."

"Fine, I'm going to tell you something that may surprise you, Raquel. I had a lot of respect for your grandfather. Ignacio was a good man, honest and generous." He looked at her and saw that her expression had not changed. "I've met few men like him in my life, and I genuinely admired him. The fact that we weren't alike, that we didn't think or feel or believe in the same things never stopped me from respecting him."

"I didn't ask you what you thought of my grandfather," – and I'm not going to get angry until I'm good and ready – "And I have no interest in your opinion."

"Yes, but…" Julio Carrión tried to smile but it faded under the forbidding glare of the woman sitting opposite him. "I just wanted you to know… that afternoon…" He paused, and rubbed his forehead before continuing. "Ignacio came to tell me he'd come back to live in Spain, in Madrid, and he still had all the documents relating to his parents properties. That's all he wanted to do, as far as I know. And you're right, I did offer him money, a lot of money, but he wouldn't sell me the briefcase. 'I'd rather rob you of your sleep,' he said to me, 'I'd rather you spent every day worrying about what I might be doing, what I might be planning to do. I'm going to ruin you, Julio, but you'll never know how or when or where I'll strike. I just wanted you to know that.' And that was it. He got up and walked out without saying goodbye. Oh, he called me all the names under the sun, and I'm probably paraphrasing a little, but I swear that was all he said."

Now it was Raquel's turn to be silent. She had been caught off guard by what he said, even more so by her conviction that Julio was not lying to her. It had to be the truth. It was the only thing that fitted with what her grandfather had told her, but she needed time to take it in.

Julio Carrión watched her. A moment later, he made a mistake.

"Aren't you going to ask me what I did?" his tone was sarcastic again, mocking.

Had he not asked that question, Raquel Fernández Perea would have had time to remember the advice her grandfather had given her, his example in forgoing his revenge, reducing it to a threat he had no intention of ever carrying out. When she had opened his desk drawer, his granddaughter had found a gun and a case of bullets, one of which had had Julio Carrión González's name on it for thirty years, but her grandfather had elected never to use it. Raquel understood Ignacio, she understood his reasons, and suddenly she felt a terrible surge of grief, pride, and love. *'To live here there are some things it is better not to know Things it is better not to understand.'* Maybe he was right, and she was about to accept this fact when she heard his question and looked up and her resolve was shattered by Julio Carrión González's condescending smile.

"I never took Ignacio seriously," he said, I never felt the slightest fear, believe me. Oh, I offered him money, because at the time, things in Spain were complicated, and I didn't know who was advising him. Back then, we didn't know whether the courts might intervene in these matters. That was what worried me, not him. Because I knew Ignacio, maybe not as well as you did, but I knew that he was too good, too sensible to ruin his life simply in order to ruin mine. Back in 1947, he would have killed me, there's not doubt about it, but in 1977... Even courageous men grow soft in old age, even the communists were prattling on about national reconciliation. Your grandfather is dead, and here I am chatting to you. That's the way life goes. So why don't we call a halt to these fantasies and talk business, because the only place the good guys win is in films, Señorita."

Bastard. You vile bastard. You vile fucking bastard.

Raquel got up, took her handbag and the briefcase and headed towards the door.

"I don't... Where are you going?"

She stopped halfway and turned. Julio Carrión González was finally on his feet, leaning over the desk and staring at her.

"I need to think things through," she said in the clipped, professional tone she used with her clients, "As you can imagine, I'm not about to make a decision right now, but don't worry, I'll get back to you." Then she walked quickly out of the office, closing the door behind her. The secretary looked up from her computer.

"Excuse me," Raquel asked with a smile. "Could you tell me where the toilets are?"

After throwing up her breakfast, she felt slightly better. When she stepped out onto the street, the icy stab of the wind from the mountains felt like a caress, and she took a deep breath. She wasn't afraid any more, her legs felt strong, but what she had just experienced had left her in a curious state of detachment, a sort of spontaneous anaesthesia which made it possible for her to go back to work, sit at her desk, and deal with the business of the day as efficiently as a well-programmed machine. She felt as though she were outside her own body, but her mind was working perfectly and could deal with anything, anything other than the office she had visited that morning. Perhaps this was why, when she left the bank, she did not go home but to her grandparents' apartment. There, sitting on the sofa, she slowly regained control of her nerve endings and wondered whether she truly was Ignacio Fernández Muñoz's granddaughter.

Even the most straightforward negotiations could be stressful but she dealt with them every day at work. She had never learned to play poker, but she knew how to bluff, knew how to bet on nothing more than a hunch. Sometimes she managed to make a great deal of money for her clients, and she was rarely wrong. So she decided to wait. She analysed the situation carefully, and concluded that the ball was not in her court. Carrion would do something. Quickly.

"Hey, Sebastián," Raquel greeted him as though his call – less than forty-eight hours after her meeting with his boss – was a complete surprise. "Good to hear from you."

"Fine…" he said, sounding uncertain, "Listen, are you at work?" His voice sounded uncertain.

"Of course … aren't you? It was still Friday the last time I checked…"

"Yes, no… That's not what I meant. Are you in the office right now? I'd like to come up and talk to you for a few minutes?"

"You're here?" Raquel was surprised "Plaza de las Descalzas?"

"Yes, that's why I'm asking… I mean if you have a minute…"

Raquel checked her diary, then her watch, then repeated the operation a second time.

"I have a meeting at one o'clock, but I can spare you a few minutes…"

Six minutes passed before Sebastián López Parra knocked on her office door. Raquel could not guess why he had come, but she was certain that this new development worked to her advantage.

"Come in, come in," She got up to greet him and saw that he was nervous. "Please, take a seat… So, then… it's strange you being on my patch."

"Yes, it is, I suppose. But actually, I'm just a delivery boy…"

He was carrying a white envelope, which he now put on the table together with a key. Then he looked at her and frowned, as though unsure of what the words he was about to say actually meant.

"Don Julio Carrión asked me to bring you this. He insisted I deliver it to you in person, and  said it couldn't wait. He's obviously decided to deal with your apartment himself. He didn't explain what he was doing and I wasn't about to ask, but I have to say…" He took off his glasses, looked at them, and decided against cleaning them. "Listen, Raquel, I don't know who you are, or what's going on, or why everything is suddenly so urgent, but…"

His words trailed off again, as though he couldn't bring himself to say them aloud.

"That envelope contains a contract proposing an exchange. Don Julio gets your 70 square metre apartment overlooking the Calle Ávila and in exchange you get a 180 square metre penthouse with a 60 square metre terrace, in a luxury development on Calle Jorge Juan within walking distance of the Retiro. And as if that wasn't enough, he'll also pay the taxes and conveyancing charges, yours and his. These are the papers and I've brought you a key because Don Julio thought you might like to look at it first, though personally I don't think you even need to see it…"

"Really?" Raquel smiled, "You've seen the place…?"

"The apartment? Of course..." He relaxed now, like a student who has just finished his oral exam ..."

"Look, Raquel, this is the weirdest, most unbelievable thing that's ever happened at Promociones del Noreste, take my word for it. I've been working there for ten years and I've never seen anything like it. You know yourself that Don Julio Carrión is no saint, and his son Rafa is worse, he's a shark. Of course he and his brother know nothing about this, that was the first thing Don Julio said 'the most important thing is that no one else finds out.' Just so you know, it's not a simple swap, it's much more complicated. He's giving you the apartment and you're giving him yours, then he's selling yours back to the company for the same price everyone else in the building is getting. Why? So there's no paper trail, obviously, so no one can ever find out he gave you this fabulous apartment in exchange for a shitty little apartment and start asking questions. Look, I'm going to tell you something, because I really like you..." He looked at her and laughed, "You're about to make a killing on this, Raquel, You're going to make an absolute fucking killing on it."

Raquel laughed along with him, playing for time, but she could already feel a tingling euphoria beneath her skin.

"Good," she said, picking up the envelope and the key and slipping them into a drawer, "Well... I'll go and have a look at the place, but it won't be for a couple of days because I'm moving in to my grandmother's apartment over the weekend, it's been standing empty for ages ... I'll call you Monday, OK? Tuesday at the latest."

Sebastián López Parra nodded, but he made no move to leave.

"That's it? You're not going to tell me anything?" he ventured at last, "Please ..."

"It's a long story, Sebastián," she cut him off,, "a very long very old story. You wouldn't understand. Anyway, I think it's better if you don't know."

She got up to signal that the meeting was at an end and walked him to the door. It was only 12.45, but her one o'clock appointment was already waiting. As she chatted with him, going over the figures of his current investments, she found it difficult to ignore the fact that the envelope she had not even opened and the key that came with it were sitting in her desk drawer. She had lied to Sebastián, she would not be able to move into the apartment on the Plaza de los Guardias de Corps for at least another fortnight because her grandmother had decided to have it repainted, but she now knew that Julio Carrión did not like to wait, and when she had checked that the contract was exactly as Sebastián had

623

outlined, she decided to persevere in her strategy. This, however, did not prevent her from wolfing down a *tortilla* in the nearest bar as soon as she got out of work, then rushing off to see her brand new apartment.

The building was indeed within walking distance of the Retiro, the most expensive part of the Salamanca district. But the building was nothing compared to the apartment itself. The hall was so huge that at first she mistook it for the living room. When she had recovered from the shock and went to explore the rest of the apartment, she found herself in a room so vast she didn't know what it was. Divided into separate living spaces by three small steps, the room contained a dining table and eight chairs and in the other section, three huge white sofas laid out in a U. There was only one bedroom, the back wall curved like the apse of a cathedral. The most surprising thing was the size of the bathroom, also in two sections, the first enormous in itself and the second completely taken up by a jacuzzi the size of a small swimming pool with spectacular floor-to-ceiling windows and a view almost as spectacular as that from the terrace. This was the room she liked best. The kitchen, on the other hand, was so ridiculous that she had trouble finding it, in fact at first she thought it was just a corridor with a built-in wardrobe on either side. This she didn't quite understand. The rest, she understood perfectly.

So, you're not scared of me, you little bastard?"

She wandered through the new apartment, more slowly this time, focusing on the details. An antique pink and grey marble fireplace which must have been salvaged from some mansion, two huge plasma screen televisions, one in the living room, the other in the bedroom, a parquet floor, probably original, like the ceiling roses and the cornices. More marble, more expensive hard wood, high-tech fittings even in the bathroom. At first, Raquel felt like a little girl in an amusement park; she spent the whole afternoon here, looking, touching, turning everything on and off until she grew used to the space. Then she sat on one of the sofas, staring straight ahead, as if Julio Carrión González was watching her and she laughed.

"You're going to shit yourself, you bastard," she said it again slowly, articulating every word, "You're going to shit yourself ..."

By now, she had managed to stop listening. It had not been easy, because from the beginning, from the moment she realised what was happening, she knew that she was going to betray both her grandfather and her grandmother. She had promised her grandmother that she wouldn't doing anything stupid, the same promise Ignacio would have extracted from her had he been alive. Ignacio Fernández Muñoz had forgone revenge, reducing it to a threat he had no intention of carrying out, preferring to think of his children's future, his grandchildren's future, his serene old age and, all these years later, his wife had made the same choice with a smile. But this was different, this was business, their granddaughter thought, just business. It did not occur to her that the current owner of this apartment had thought the same thing in the spring of 1947, because he too had stopped listening.

It was not easy, but she managed to convince herself that this had nothing to do with her family and everything to do with her talent. After all, for the past ten years she had been perfecting a get-rich-quick scheme that would never come to fruition, she would never board a plane with Paco Molinero, split the proceeds down the middle and deposit her three or four million euros in a bank account in the Cayman Islands. That had only ever been a game, but it was her favourite game. Raquel Fernández Perea mentally calculated the value of this apartment, which would be hers the moment she signed the contract. This way, I cend up with almost as much money, she thought, and I don't have to break any laws, I barely have to lift a finger. Then she thought of Julio Carrión, the last words he had said to her:

"That's the way it life goes, *macho*."

After that, everything was brilliant, easy, simple.

"What's happened, Raquel?" Nati asked when she saw her on Monday, "You've been acting very strange."

"Me? Nothing... it's nothing."

"Don't give me that, ever since you didn't show up at the notary's office with us, you've been acting like a lunatic."

"Don't be ridiculous, Nati," Raquel forced herself to smile, "Nothing's happened."

And it was true, nothing had happened yet. Nothing happened until Sebastián López Parra, tired of waiting for her to phone, called her on Tuesday afternoon. She was perfectly charming. She told him she'd seen the apartment and she loved it, that the view was magnificent, and that she would drop by on Friday morning to sign the contract.

"You needn't trouble yourself," he protested, "Surely you noticed that I've already signed both copies on behalf of Don Julio, so all you need to do is sign one of them and send it back by courier. We can sort out the rest at the solicitor's office."

"I know, but I'm free all Friday morning," she went on, sounding like an excitable teenager.

"Whatever you like... You know it's always a pleasure to see you."

Poor Sebastián, thought Raquel as she hung up, and she thought it again as she left his office on Friday morning.

"So, I'll see you at the solicitor's office, then..." he looked at her, blushing. "Now that this whole thing is over, I was hoping maybe we could have dinner some night?" He kissed her on both cheeks and walked her to the lift.

"OK, so you'll call me?" Raquel turned, and realised he was about to come with her, "You don't need to see me out, Sebastián, I know the way, I'm hardly likely to get lost..." She went to push the button for the ground floor, but when the doors closed, she pushed the button for the third floor instead.

This time, there was no one waiting for her, but she remembered the way and walked quickly towards the waiting room. The door was open, but there was no sign of the secretary who had been there the previous week. She thought perhaps she had made a mistake, perhaps Julio Carrión had decided not to come to work that morning, but she did not stop to think about it. She turned the handle, pushed the door and found him sitting at his desk, telephone in hand.

"She's right here in front of me." Raquel heard him say, "Yes, she's here. I'm telling you, I'm looking at her right now..."

"Sebastián has nothing to do with this," she said, in the same tone she had used a week earlier when she asked him not to use her first name.

"He thought I was leaving."

"OK, OK," Carrión attempted to reassure Sebastián, "It doesn't matter. I'll call you later."

He hung up, and stared at her, and Raquel stared back, calmly with a slightly impudent smile.

"I thought we had nothing more to discuss."

"We don't. Not about the Tetuán apartment, anyway," she said, "as I'm sure Señor López Parra has told you, I've accepted your offer – a very generous offer, I might add – so I have no problem with you on that score."

"I'm delighted to hear it, because I have no intention of wasting any more time answering your questions.

"Oh, don't worry about that, I'll be doing the talking today. All you have to do is listen. And it won't be a waste of your time, I assure you. In fact I think I can say it will be time well spent."

"I'm sorry, señorita," he looked down his nose with the condescending smile she recognised, but this time it had no effect "But I don't believe you have anything to say that will interest me."

"Well you are wrong, Señor Carrión. and not for the first time. Even courageous men grow soft in their old age, to quote what you said the other day. I'm sure you're right, but let me give you another little saying:

Even the cleverest, most cunning men can become fools as they grow older." She smiled. "I always thought it was true, but you've given me ample proof. For example, the apartment you have just given me in exchange for my little place in Tetuán. As I said, it was a very generous offer, but so disproportionate, that it made me think. I've done a lot of thinking and I've come to a number of conclusions. The first is that you are clearly a bigger liar than I am. Last week, you told me I couldn't frighten you and, at first, I admit, you had me fooled. But now, thinking about the manner in which you have dealt personally with this matter, I don't believe you. You are frightened of me, Señor Carrión, very frightened. And you were mistaken enough to let it show."

She paused, the first of a series of strategic silences.

"Oh, don't get me wrong, I understand your motives, your reasoning... For a rich man like you, a few hundred thousand euros hardly matters, does it? You calculated that, given the value of the apartment, I would go away happy, but you were wrong." She feigned an expression of affable surprise. "Did you really think that Ignacio's grandchildren didn't go to university?" She smiled. "Didn't Sebastián tell you what I do for a living? No, Señor Carrión, a genuinely intelligent man would have put himself in my shoes, anticipated my reaction, but you... you didn't even try. I, on the other hand, tried to put myself in your shoes, tried to see the situation through your eyes. It was not terribly difficult and it allowed me to draw some conclusions. That is why I was fairly sure that, after talking to me, you would think that peace and quiet were priceless."

She paused again, but he said nothing, simply looked at her with the same attentive curiosity he might have lavished on some exotic artefact in a glass case. You're hard as nails, she thought, but she was not discouraged.

"And there, too, you were mistaken. But I can understand, honestly I can. In fact I understand so well, I'm going to propose a deal. I've come to offer you the peace and tranquillity my grandfather refused to sell to you. I admit it, I'm not a good person like Ignacio. I'm not as brave, as deserving of your respect, but I don't suppose you care, in fact, you probably find that comforting – after all respect has no place in business." She looked at him again but could not fathom his expression. "As you can imagine, it's not going to be easy for a poor soul like me, moving from the Calle Tetuán to life on the Calle Jorge Juan, there'll be a lot of expenses: furniture, clothes, accessories... It's going to cost me a fortune to live up to my address."

Now he chose to speak, though he kept it as brief as possible.

"Are you attempting to blackmail me, Señorita Fernández?"

"Blackmail you?" Raquel's eyes flew open and she gazed at him, all innocence. She shook her head and smiled. "Good God, no, I wouldn't think of trying to blackmail you. I'm simply proposing a business transaction. I have something you want and I'm prepared to sell it to you, that's all. I've scanned the documents we talked about the other day so that you can check them and see that I'm not lying to you…" she took a thick white envelope from her bag and pushed it across the desk. "I've put them in chronological order." As Junio reached towards the envelope, she picked it up and took out the contents. "It's all there. All my great-grandparents title deeds, the powers of attorney made out in your name, the letters you sent, 'with love to the children', a receipt for the bank transfer of 5,000 pesetas you sent to stall them, the letters from the lawyer they engaged and all the attendant documentation…" He flicked through the documents one by one as though they barely interested him. "Everything. Your peace and tranquillity. A million euros and they're yours."

"A million euros?" Julio Carrión burst out laughing, "Are you mad? It's not 1977 any more."

Raquel remained calm, "I realise I promised you earlier that I wouldn't ask you any questions but… Tell me, Señor Carrión, do you read much?" She looked at him curiously, but he did not bother to answer. "I didn't think so, so I'm guessing that you don't spend much time in bookshops. It's a pity, really. I think you might find it interesting. You wouldn't believe the number of books being published in Spain these days about people like you, lives just like yours… It's amazing. You only have to look at the covers: *brigadistas*, militiamen, women too, of course. It's an interesting phenomenon and one that can't really be explained, not even by me, and I'm the daughter of Reds. Anyway, I don't have to tell you, that you know my family's story by heart…So, no, it's not 1977. You see, in 1977, people were still scared to death to talk about these things. Not today."

"Indeed," he said, "That's what I've been trying to get you to understand."

"Yes, but I think it's you're the one who doesn't quite understand. I think we're talking about a different kind of fear. You really should let me finish… Do you mind if I smoke?"

She wanted a cigarette, but that was not why she asked. Taking the packet out of her bag, lightinga cigarette, picking up the ashtray on the desk and setting it next to her, was all a carefully calculated ploy to cover another strategic pause.

"It's not just books, there are films too, they're making documentaries about the war, about the post-war period, about the Spanish camps, the French camps, the children that were taken away from Republican prisoners, the disappearances..." She feigned surprise. "Back in 1977, nobody ever mentioned these things, did they?" She allowed a hard edge to creep into her voice. "Judges these days are happy to issue an exhumation order for anyone the fascists summarily executed during the war, or after the war. They've been digging them up from ditches on the roadside, finding them in wells and canyons... Have you seen it in the papers? They even mention it on TV sometimes. Imagine what the killers must feel like, because most of them are still alive, the Falangists, the members of the Civil Guard... They'd be about your age now, though some of them would be younger. Imagine them, retired, happily, watching TV and suddenly a judge makes an order and *bam!* it all comes out..."

Raquel Fernández Perea was betting everything on a single card. It was her one shot and she was making it up as she went along, but she put her trust in fear, this ancient fear that had been slowly curdling since a warm May afternoon in 1977. Her rival's impassivity made it impossible to judge the success of her performance, but at least he wasn't laughing.

"Oh, I know nobody's going to do any more than that, nobody's going to put them on trial or lock them up, but their children, their friends, their neighbours, the grandchildren's classmates..." She closed her eyes, and shook her head. "Not a pretty picture, is it? Not that I think they don't deserve it, but it can't be pleasant, especially in this country. But, you know, everything changes, nothing stays the same, especially here in Spain." She smiled, her courage returning. "I won't lie to you, I'm delighted. I think of it as justice, but I realise that justice is something that is rarely done here in Spain. That's why I said that I understand you, I understand why you feel you should be allowed to get away with it. But I think you're mistaken Señor Carrión, I have to tell you, in all honesty. You're mistaken, like all those other men, and for them it's too late to stop their grandchildren finding out who they really were, the crimes they committed, the people they tortured or kidnapped."

Raquel Fernández Perea stubbed her cigarette out into the ashtray and realised her heart was pounding. She had shown her card. It was there on the desk, and it was all she had. "On the other hand, I've given this a great deal of thought, as I told you, and I think one million euros is a fair price. I know no one is going to put you on trial, Señor Carrión, at least not at the moment. I hope by now you've realised I'm no fool. I know that nobody is going to take away what never belonged to you, because it's one thing, the political parties and unions taking back what was stolen from them, but "private individuals are a different matter. Don't think for a moment I don't know that. But if we can't come to some arrangement, you are leaving yourself open to severe repercussions – not prison, I'll grant you, but deeply unpleasant nonetheless."

Julio Carrión loosened his tie and opened the top two buttons of his shirt. He was deeply uncomfortable now, and he could not have chosen a worse moment to show it. Raquel Fernández Perea felt her body relax, her smile broaden, her foot shifting easily to the accelerator.

"If we don't come to some arrangement, I might be forced to publish these documents. I'm sure they would make a fascinating addendum to a book, a book that told the story of your life, Señor Carrion, and that of your mother-in-law, the woman who gave Paloma's husband up to the Falangists…"

She forced herself to take an unscheduled pause to calm herself a little.

"My family still has photos of your mother-in-law, and of your wife Angélica when she was a child. We might even publish the beautiful love letter Carlos sent to Paloma when he was in prison a few days before they shot him. Maybe it wouldn't be a bestseller, but I'm sure it would sell, it's a popular subject these days. I wouldn't make much out of it because I'd have to split the money with the author, but that doesn't matter. I've made enough money out of the Calle Tetuán apartment so… Just think about it, Señor Carrion. I wouldn't be famous, but you would be." She gave a little laugh as though this last thought amused her. "I know that a scandal in a large city is different to a scandal in a little village, because in a place like Madrid everything gets watered down, and your children probably already know that you're a crook, I mean you all work together, but I'm betting it would make your company famous…"

When she had stepped into the office, she wasn't sure that she would have to go this far. She had rehearsed this part of the speech as carefully as the rest, but she was aware that it was more precarious, more risky than personal threats. She had been prepared to wait for a more propitious moment, to wait for him to explode, but Julio Carrión was not looking well, he was very pale, and his breath was coming in gasps.

"I don't think it would be to your advantage, because like all big construction companies you're very dependent on public investment, commissions, subsidies… If people were to find out who you really are, where your money comes from, there would be no more motorways, Don Julio, no more building permits allowing you to build luxury developments as long as you agree to a percentage of social or affordable housing should be built on site." He didn't even smile. "That's how it works, isn't it? No political party would risk the backlash of continuing to line your pockets, and to be perfectly honest, I don't think many private companies would risk it either. I've thought long and hard about this and I think a million euros is very reasonable. I'm not trying to ruin you or even to leave you in poverty. I could have multiplied that amount by any figure I liked, but then you would have had to explain things, sell off assets, leave a big hole it would be difficult to account for. Of course, that would be the perfect revenge, but I don't want revenge. All I want is a fair deal.. I'm sure it won't be too hard for you to lay your hands on a million euros without anybody noticing. I can give you a hand myself, if you like. As I'm sure Sebastián told you, I'm an investments advisor, and you're one of our clients; I checked our files. You'd simply need to sell off a few shares."

Now Julio Carrión began to move. His hands were shaking as he reached into his shirt pocket and took out a scuffed silver pillbox and poured the contents onto the desk looking for a small white pill which he picked up with trembling fingers. He put it in his mouth and swallowed it without water, although there was a bottle and some glasses next to him. Suddenly, Raquel was scared. She saw him close his eyes, saw his head fall back against his chair and realised that this little drama was over.

She gathered up the photocopies, slipped them back into the briefcase and got to her feet. She was sure that nothing else would happen, but just then Julio Carrión opened his eyes, leaned forward, gripping the arms of the chair, and finally spoke:

"You're nothing but lowlife scum..."

"I know," Raquel smiled, "But I think its about time that the lowlife scum was a Fernández, don't you?"

Then she headed for the door. She was so excited, she wanted to scream, but when she reached the door, she turned and said: "Sebastián has my details. I'd be grateful if you could get back to me as soon as possible.."

But Julio Carrión González would never get back to Raquel Fernández Perea. This was the one detail she had not reckoned on, the one eventuality she had not foreseen as she began to plan her future.

At work, nobody saw any problem in giving her a mortgage against the Calle Jorge Juan apartment so she could pay for her grandmother's apartment in cash. When it was all over, Raquel decided, she would sell the apartment, pay off the mortgage and keep the profit. The rest – the million euros she expected to get any day now – she would give to Anita so that, when the time came, she would inherit no more than her rightful share. The mechanics of how this would work was the only weak point in her plan. She had not worked out how to restore some part of the Fernández Muñoz fortune without her grandmother realising she had broken her promise, but there was plenty of time to think about that. When Carrion did not get back to her immediately she was not worried. It's difficult to raise a lot of money without raising suspicion, she knew this better than anyone, and she assumed that the president of Promociones del Noreste would once again ask Sebastián López Parra to handle the matter. So, when she showed up at the solicitor's office for their meeting, she was quite certain the documents to be signed would not be the only thing they had to discuss.

"I suppose you heard?"

"What?" she tried to sound jokey, but she realised something serious had happened.

"Don Julio had a heart attack about a week ago, not this Friday but the Friday before, the day you came by the office."

"You're not serious!" Her alarm was palpable. "That's terrible... I thought he looked a bit pale ..."

"Yes." Sebastián nodded. "Me too. When I went up to see him he said he was going home, that he didn't feel well. He said I shouldn't be angry with you, that you'd just stopped by to ask some silly question..."

"Yes, it was just a family thing, it's a long story..." Raquel paused and looked at Sebastián. She realised that he had no way of knowing the truth. "Anyway, it's not important. The poor man, how is he?"

"Not good, not good at all. He'd already had a serious heart attack six months ago and a couple of close calls before that – his heart is weak and ... I don't know, but I don't think the doctors expect him to come through this time."

He did not come through. Two weeks later, the Carrión family published his death notice in three Madrid newspapers. The notice was simple and tasteful and gave no date or time for the funeral, but Raquel Fernández Perea had an idea. While in Madrid, no cemetery would have given her the information she asked for, in Torrelodones, they did not even ask for her name.

The first day of March 2005 dawned, the sun was shining, the sky a deep cobalt blue, so pure, so intense it looked like an illustration in a children's book - a perfect sky, clear, deep, translucent. Raquel arrived in the village before the funeral cortege and stopped to let it pass. When the hearse turned in to the cemetery, she locked her car and went into a bar for a coffee, but it was so cold that she couldn't get warm.

A quarter of an hour later, she went back to her car and drove to the cemetery. There, standing apart from the others, halfway between the cemetery gate and the grave a dark-haired man turned towards her and looked into her eyes.

I was eleven years old, and my parents had a summer house in a little village in Navacerrada. It was a two-storey house with a garage and a garden in a development divided into half-acre plots, all exactly the same although some of them had swimming pools. It was set on a hillside surrounded by pine forests , the classic summer resort for the aspiring middle-classes. There were no gates, no security of any kind, the streets were little more thantracks, but there was an open space the size of a football pitch and about a dozen kids of my age.

"Rafa?"

"Yes?"

"Hi, it's Álvaro."

Four years later my father built a house in La Moraleja where we could live all year round, with a garden so big we never really used all of it and a swimming pool three or four times the size of the one we had had in Navacerrada. His family was no longer part of the middle-classes so he sold the summer house. Nobody seemed to miss it apart from me. My older brothers were too old now to enjoy the monotony of summers in the mountains and Clara hadn't yet discovered the bicycle, but I had always been happy there, and I still have a scar on my left leg to remind me.

"I've been expecting you to call."

"Are you at the office? I need to talk to you."

"Not now, Álvaro, it's nearly half past two…"

That afternoon, a few of us had taken our bikes down to the dam. We had been expressly forbidden to go there, which is why we went. To get there, you had to cycle along a busy road and then cross it to get to the finish line - the bridge over the reservoir. The fishermen didn't even look round at us when we arrived, but we felt proud, a feeling that quickly dissipated when we realised there was nothing to do there but look at the water. We left our bikes by the path and lay down on the grass on the far bank of the reservoir, reminding each other that we were now in Becerril rather than Navacerrada, and thinking about the ride home which was much steeper than the toure we had taken to get here.

"OK, then. Why don't we have lunch?"

"No, I can't, I've got a meeting with someone from the Castilla-La Mancha Department of Public Works."

"What time will you be back in the office?"

Until one of us realised that there were a lot of different ways to race. The idea probably came from the stages of the Tour de France or the Vuelta a España which we would watch on television in the afternoons, each day in a different house, scrupulously following a specific order so that nobody's mother got angry, and avoiding houses that had a swimming pool as much as possible so that we could continue to go swimming in the mornings. We'd didn't have stopwatches, but we always synchronised the second hand of our watches and raced against the clock along the last street of the development, although to celebrate the finals, we always went to the bridge over the resevoir.

"About 5 o'clock... I don't know Álvaro, I don't think there's much point us meeting today, do you? I already know you've left Mai, I know that you've left her for another woman, and I'm not having a go, I have to assume you know what you're doing. Isabel and I have no intention of getting involved, so..."

"But there are other things I need to talk to you about."

"Really? OK then..."

That week, I hadn't come in the top three, but I sprinted onto the bridge, standing on the pedals, the bike wobbling all over the place. Maybe I just wanted to prove to myself and anyone watching, that just because I'd had a bad day, it didn't mean I wasn't still up there with the best of them, the quickest. I was probably never faster than I was that afternoon, because my tyre only had to brush the edge of the bridge and suddenly the bike tipped up and I was thrown over the handlebars. I landed on one of the pedals of a bike being wheeled along by a boy, knocking it and him over. It was one of those old bikes with open spokes and one of them went into the calf of my left leg like a piece of shrapnel.

"I'll see you at five o'clock, OK? Oh, one more thing, do you mind if I ask Angélica along?"

"I don't mind, but I'm surprised. She's livid with you. You know she's the first person Mai called when you left?"

"I know, Julio told me. I've just had a drink with him. But I have to speak to Angélica one way or the other, I have to talk to all of you."

When I first tried to move my leg, the whole bicycle came with it. The metal spike was too deeply embedded and my friends had to help me. When they pulled it away, I howled in pain, but the pain didn't impress me as much as the river of blood spurting from the wound. I had cut myself badly and here I was, all on my own, eleven years old with a group of other eleven year olds, miles from my house, miles from the village, on the bridge over the reservoir. My arch-rival – the only other boy in the gang who cycled as fast as me – had already set off to tell my parents, but the blood was still pouring out, and I thought of the pictures in*Exploits of War*, and the films about the war in the Pacific that Papá, Julio and I used to watch on Saturday nights. I'd seen this kind of thing lots of times and I knew exactly what to do; I took off my t-shirt and ripped it along the seam, wrapped it like a tourniquet just above the wound and tightened it using a stick. When I got up, the pain was so bad I thought I was going to pass out, but I didn't cry because I was more worried about the telling off I was going to get. Even back then, I never cried, almost never, but I knew my parents would be at the house, and I knew Papá would be the one to come and get me because Mamá didn't drive.

"Fine. I'll see you at five o'clock.... Actually, can we make it half five?"

"Half five it is."

"I've got to go, I'm running late…"

It was Papá who showed up, and he showed up quickly. When his car pulled onto the bridge, I could hardly breathe, but I saw his face before he got out, and realised he wasn't angry. He closed the door but didn't lock it and almost ran over to me frantic with worry but also compassionate, like Mamá. It was an expression I had never seen on him, nor had I ever heard this quaver in his voice. "What happened, *hijo*?" He slipped his arm around my shoulder, and kissed me on the forehead. "I fell and hurt my leg," I said and in a second he was on his knees examining the wound. "What's this?" he gestured to my t-shirt. "It was bleeding a lot, so I made a tourniquet." He stood up and looked at me, smiling. "You're a brave boy, Álvaro," he said, and took me in his arms, and suddenly I felt so happy, so proud to be a Carrión, to be his son.

"Hello?"

"Hi, Angélica, it's Álvaro."

"Oh, I've been wanting to talk to you. I hope you're happy!"

He supported me with his right arm and told me not to put ant weight on my leg as we walked back to the car. My friends moved aside to let us pass, all of them looking symapthetically, almost admiringly at this grown-up who still knew how to behave as if he were one of us, as if we were equals. Having turned fifty-four that winter, my father wasn't much younger than some of my friends' grandparents, but he didn't look his age, and when I told them how old he was it inspired a respect almost akin to fear. They all found it easier to deal with my mother, who was the same age as their mothers and who was very blonde and seemed very gentle. That afternoon, they discovered that Julio Carrión was an extraordinary man, more extraordinary than they might ever have guessed, as he eased me onto the back seat of the car, then climbed into the front and thanked them all for helping his son. After that, they would have walked over hot coals for him.

"Listen, Angélica, I don't want to argue with you."

"Well, I'm afraid you don't have much choice, because I can't think of a word for what you've done. Have you any idea the state Mai is in? You've destroyed her... And your son? Did you even stop to think about Miguelito? Honestly, I don't know how you could..."

"Remind me, Angélica, weren't you already sleeping with Adolfo before you left Nacho?"

As we left the bridge, I asked him where we were going. "We'll go home first," he said calmly, "Let Mamá know you're alright and get you some clean clothes ... Then we'll take you to Madrid so we can get that leg stitched up." "But why don't we go to the doctor in the village? I suggested, eager to minimise my culpability, but he shook his head. "No, I don't trust him. I'd rather take you to a hospital, you've only got two legs the last time I checked, and it's no bother..." When we arrived back at the house, my mother rushed out to the car, pulled open the door and showered me with kisses. Then she looked at the wound and started screaming. "Jesus Christ, Angélica!" my mother was the only person my father scolded that afternoon, "Are you trying to scare the lad to death? Go and get him a clean t-shirt and put pyjamas and toothbrushes for both of us in a bag in case we need to spend the night in Madrid."

"Yes, but Nacho had already left me before, if you remember, he had an affair with that nurse. He walked out and didn't come back for three months and when he came back... Oh, it doesn't matter. It's not the same, Álvaro."

"It's a little bit the same."

"It's not remotely the same. My marriage was a fuck-up, it had been over for years and you know it ..."

He was like that, able to reassure, to inspire confidence. It was almost impossible to get him to change his mind and that day, Mamá didn't even try. So I stopped feeling guilty and started to consider what was happening as a kind of adventure, which it was. On the drive to Madrid he only asked me if my leg hurt twice and I lied. "Not really", I said, and he told me an exciting story, one I'd never heard before and would never hear again, a story that sounded like something out of a film, about Romualdo Sánchez Delgado who'd played football with us only a couple of weeks ago, in a coma with terrible frostbite and Papá and his friend Eugenio, both of them waving guns, screaming in Spanish at this German doctor, saying they'd put a bullet in him if he so much as thought about amputating Romualdo's leg. "So you see," he said as the tower of the Hospital La Paz came into view, "I'm something of an expert in saving people's legs, and this time, I don't think I'll even need to pull a gun." I laughed and told him again that it didn't hurt much, and I was happy, I was proud of him, proud to be his son.

"OK, Angélica. But that doesn't change the fact that you fell in love with another man and I've fallen in love with another woman. Back then it was your life, this time, it's mine. We all make our own decisions."

"It's not the same, Álvaro."

"Maybe not, but I have to say it looks the same to me."

"He made the tourniquet himself, doctor, with his t-shirt and a stick he found lying on the ground. What do you think?" The young doctor smiled at my father then examined the wound. "You're very brave, Álvaro," I heard this for the second time that afternoon, "It must have hurt a lot." I didn't answer and the doctor turned back to my father. "We'll just give him a little local anaesthetic before I stitch it. He'll have a scar, but as long as it heals well, he shouldn't have any problems..." My father nodded, still smiling. He wasn't afraid and that was enough for me not to be afraid. When he'd finished putting on the spectacular bandage, the doctor looked at me gravely and told me that the most important thing was not to put any weight on my leg. "I know it's boring having to lie around during the summer holidays, but it's the only way." After that, Papá taught me how to walk with crutches and I quickly got the hang of it so by the time we went out to the car, I was sure he was going to take me back to Navacerrada. Instead he drove in the opposite direction. We went to a seafood restaurant on the Calle Fuencarral near the Glorieta de Bilbao. I'd only been there once, for my parents' wedding anniversary, but clearly he went there regularly because the few waiters who weren't on holiday came over to speak to him. "It's a pleasure to have you back, Don Julio."

"I don't think so,"

"Well I know so. Anyway, I'm nothing like Julio, it's not like I used to cheat on Mai, I didn't go running around after every woman I met. I'm sure you know that because I know she does."

"Yes. That's why she's prepared to forgive you, she wants you to come home. Think about it, Álvaro. Don't throw your whole life away on a whim."

"I'm sure you can come up with something for this cycling hero here." Papá said when the maître d'hôtel appeared. "Certainly," said the man, and the dinner we had was magnificent, but although I loved the

638

langoustines, the barnacles, the spider crab, what I loved most about it was being there with my father, eating together as if we were friends. I had never spent so much time alone with him, and I had never thought it would be so easy, that we would find so much to talk about, that we would laugh so much. It was one of the most beautiful nights of my life, certainly the best up to that point, or at least the best I can remember now. It was very late by the time we left the restaurant, and the only light came from the streetlamps, but I could see a warm golden flow envelop my father, an impossible halo picking him out against the trees and the buildings, the cars and the passersby, and this glow enveloped me too isolating the two of us in a world of our own. I can't remember it any other way, my father and me, shining together in the deserted city the summer I turned eleven.

"It's not a whim, and I'm not going back."

"Well you're making a terrible mistake. Because you have a wonderful wife, a wonderful life, Álvaro. You and Mai have always been happy, it was great just seeing the two of you together, and now…"

"Listen, Angélica, I don't want to talk about this any more. You don't know anything about my life and I'm not about to tell you. But I do need to talk to you. It's about Papá. That's why I phoned."

I've never forgotten that glow that followed us home to the Calle Argensola and sustained me as I waited in the doorway while Papá parked the car. My father helped me put on my pyjamas, tucked me in as though I were still a baby, kissed me goodnight, and slept in the bed next to me just in case the sleeping pills didn't work and I woke up in the night. The glow did not even disappear as we lay there in the darkness and suddenly I realised that I wouldn't be able to fall asleep until I said something: "I really love you, Papá." "Me too, *hijo*." That's what he said, and happiness stung my eyes, brave boy that I was, but I didn't cry that night, even then I never cried, I hardly ever cried.

"About Papá? What exactly?"

"I don't want to talk about it over the phone. I'm meeting Rafa at his office at half five, could you come along?"

"OK. But only if you promise to think about what I said."

The next morning we were in a good mood. We went out for breakfast, not saying much. We listened to the radio all the way back in the car, and I remember the sun, the wind whipping in through the window, the summer songs we hummed as he drove. When we got back, Mamá took me in her arms and kissed me a million times. Then she put a wicker chair out on the porch with a stool for me to rest my leg on and asked if I wanted to read or listen to music, was I hungry, was I thirsty, suggested she could play board games with me. I let her spoil me, but returned a smile for every smile her husband gave me, commenting on all this fussing. Two weeks later, Mamá insisted on coming with us to Madrid. She screamed when she saw the scar, a 'Z' in the middle of my left calf. Papá laughed. "Angélica, please, he's not a little girl. Anyway, when he gets hair on his legs, you won't even see it." On this point, too, he was right. I was the only one of his sons who looked like him and shortly afterwards my legs were covered with dark downy hair which could hide anything, anything except who I am: the son of Julio Carrión González.

"Angélica, please... I'm forty years old."

"Exactly. The age at which everyone makes this kind of mistake."

"OK, that's it. I can't promise anything, but if you want to come, I'll see you there at half past five."

As I hung up, I could feel my leg throbbing. I could feel the scar, its form, the pattern it traced on my skin, the fear, the courage and the old pain, the shrapnel deep inside. I hadn't thought about it for years. I hadn't wanted to think about it today, but still my leg throbbed, I could see the glow lighting my way as though it had never dimmed, as though nothing would ever be over. Sitting alone in a bar on the Paseo de la Habana at a table made of some dark wood that Mai could have named without batting an eyelid, I could still see my father sitting opposite me, the huge seafood platter between us, his big smile, his handsome face. I saw my father as he had been that summer evening, his face framed by a golden halo, and I could see myself as I had been, short and brave, happy to be there with him, to be the son of this extraordinary man. I had not chosen this memory, I hadn't wanted to dig it out, but I couldn't take my eyes from his. My memory had chosen to give me back this pain, this love, so real, so powerful that nothing and no one could ever defeat it.

"Can I get another whiskey, please? And something to nibble?"

"I'll bring you the menu."

"No, I don't want to eat, just some nachos or something."

I loved my father. I loved him, I admired him, I needed him. I hadn't forgotten him, but I had managed not to think of him when I read my grandmother's letter, and later, when Raquel talked to me about Julio Carrión González, young and effortlessly charming in victory and defeat, even in the final, calamitous disaster. A liar, a swindler, a traitor, a thief, a conman, an opportunist, a man devoid of morals, emotions or scruples, an evil man. That had been easy, it had been easy to listen, take in each new piece of information, fleshing out the profile of a fictional character, a stranger with a familiar name who was my father, true, and the father of my brothers, my sisters, my mother's husband, but nothing more. For as long as my love for him was absent, those words, 'my father', were simply a label, a meaningless title. Julio Carrión González had been my father, I was his son, his heir, but not his accomplice. Until my memory betrayed me, and words took on their meanings once more.

"Can I get the bill please?"

I had learned to love Raquel Fernández Perea in spite of my father's love. Now I would have to learn to love her in the knowledge of this love and all these lies. Meanwhile, I had begun to break up inside, slowly at first, a small crack in my conscience, the blunders of my imagination, the rage with which I decided to obliterate them. It hadn't been easy, but it had not been too complicated, until the truth latched on to my arms, and my legs and began to gallop away in every direction. Determined to put myself back together as best I could, I had to accept that my limbs would never be the same again, that my bones would never knit at the same angles and my body would forever drag behind it the consequences of this process, amputated limbs of unequal length, a slight limp, an unending ache, on overcast mornings. Love is capable of anything, and when forced to chose between being left with something or with nothing, everyone would choose something.

"Could I get a ticket for the 15.30 screening?"

"Which screen?"

"It doesn't matter, I don't know, Screen 2..."

Love cannot abolish itself for as long as it exists. No matter how inconvenient, how unwelcome, however terrible it is. It had been hot out in the street, in the cinema it was cold, but my father's smile lit up the screen and I could hear his comforting voice: *You're very brave, Álvaro*, my own voice hoarse with emotion, *I really love you, Papá* and his voice again, *Me too, hijo*. Nothing that had happened, nothing that would ever happen in the future could blot out that face, or silence that voice. My leg was hurting so much that I had curled into a ball, my eyes were stinging with all the tears I had choked back since that summer, since that night when I had felt happy, proud to be the son of Julio Carrión González. Almost thirty years had passed and I had never stopped being proud, it was one of the few things that would never change, though recently, as the whole world collapsed around me, I had managed to forget that I loved him. And here in an air conditioned cinema showing some film I would never remember, I realised the meaning of this love that had conquered everything, withstood everything, which would not give in to head or heart, because it was part of me, like Raquel, like my body, like my name.

"Excuse me, I was supposed to meet my brother Rafa, but he's not in his office..."

"That's not his office, he's taken over Don Julio's office, I mean your father's office."

"I see... and Julio?"

I had had to learn to love Raquel in spite of my father's love and now I would have to go on loving my father alongside my love for Raquel. And nothing would be as difficult and strange as adapting to this love I did not want but could not stop myself from feeling, no matter how much I despised this man, no matter how ashamed I was of him, no matter how much his life, his greed humiliated me. He did not deserve the love of a son like me, but he was my father and that explained everything, ruined everything. He was my father. I realised it at that moment, just as I was about to squeeze the trigger, light the fuse, push the detonator that would explode Julio Carrión González once and for all. The most charming man in the world, the inveterate seducer, the snake charmer, the wizard, the brilliant autodidact, the undefeated champion was about to vanish from his family's life, at least for a few hours, and even the wilful blindness of his children would not bring him back safe and sound, unsullied, the man on the piece of gilded card his wife had pasted alongside our smiling faces.

"Julio is still in his old office. Well, you know yourself, he's not bothered about things like that... would you like me to show you through?

"No, that's all right, thanks."

Julio had warned me not to call Rafa, and he knew why. I knew too. That was why I'd called him. If I hadn't arranged to meet Rafa and Angélica nothing would have happened. Julio would never have mentioned we'd had the conversation and after a while he'd probably forget since it was the sort of thing that didn't really interest him. In that respect, he was a lot like Clara, but not like me, not like Rafa. But I knew what I intended to do and why. Rafa and Angélica would later question my reasons. They would think I was trying to get back at Papá through them, that I had suddenly gone mad, that I was lashing out, that I had been motivated by hatred or some fanatical ideology, or driven to it by this sexual obsession that was going to ruin my life. They would think all these things, but I was completely calm, I knew what I was doing and I knew why I was doing it. I wanted to talk, I wanted to listen. Just that, nothing more. I wanted to tell aloud this story that no one had ever told me and heard them say aloud what I had never hear. I wanted them to know what I thought, how I felt and wanted to know what they thought, how they felt when they had discovered these things about the man who had been their father. It didn't seem like much, but it was a lot, because a lot of time had passed and the silence intended to cover up the truth had, over time, displaced it. I was about to break that silence.

"Hi, I have a meeting with my brother Rafa…"

"Of course. Go on in, he's expecting you."

"What about Angélica? Is she here?"

Rafa's secretary nodded and as I pushed open the door I remembered my birthday, it must have been my seventh or eight birthday. I had asked my parents for a table football game, but none of the toyshops had one in stock so when I got home from school that afternoon I got a consolation prize, a magic set, a predictable present all of my siblings had received at least once. I was so disappointed that I started whining even before I'd finished taking the paper and my mother became angry with me. My father said nothing, but the next morning he showed up with a huge box. "One magician in the family is more than enough," I heard him say as he opened it. Then, years later, he gave me the table-football game again, though I hadn't even realised he'd kept it. It was just after Miguelito was born, he showed up at the hospital with it. "I thought… seeing as it's a boy," he muttered as we kissed him.

"Hi."

Rafa, sitting in Papá's chair, made no attempt to get up, nor did Angélica, who was sitting in one of the two chairs reserved for guests, but I insisted on greeting them, Rafa first, then Angélica, and they both kissed me but with a stiffness, a coldness that made me think they already knew why I had asked to meet them.

Rafa immediately confirmed the fact, toying with a slim, elegant mechanical pencil identical to the one Papá used.

"Listen, Álvaro… I know you've had a lot of serious stuff going on in your life, so it's hardly surprising you're worked up… But when you said you'd already spoken to Julio that surprised me, so I had a chat with him… The first thing he told me was that he'd warned you not to call me, and, to be honest, you should have listened to him …"

He paused and looked at Angélica, but she said nothing. He went on in the same slow, considerate tone though it already held more than a trace of disdain.

"There's nothing you can tell us that we don't already know. What happened is ancient history, and after all this time it has no importance whatsoever. We shouldn't judge, because we can't. Not you, or me, or anyone who didn't live through those times, anyone who didn't have to make decisions in circumstances that were so appalling we can't even begin to imagine them. So before you start, let me tell you two things. The first is: nothing you can say will change the way I feel about Papá. And the second…" he gave me a sardonic smile "Julio told me the whole thing about finding the phone number on some note in a folder, but I don't believe a word of it, Álvaro. Let me tell you right now, there's something not right about this girl. I'm sure she was the one who came looking for you and I'm even more sure that all she's out for is your money."

He spoke with such assurance, such gravitas, that I laughed.

"Would you like to tell me what you're laughing at?" Rafa asked, irritated by my reaction.

I didn't want to rush him so I asked him a question. "Tell me, since you know everything, did you know that Papá's mother Teresa died of pneumonia on 14 June, 1941 while imprisoned in the detention centre in Ocaña?"

"That's not true!" Angélica finally spoke.

"Grandma Teresa died during the war," Rafa said, "the summer of '37 I think, and she didn't die of pneumonia, she died of tuberculosis. You know that perfectly well, Álvaro, we all do."

"No Rafa. All we know is what Papá told us, what he wanted us to believe, but it's not the truth. In June 1937, grandma Teresa walked out on her husband, but she was very much alive. She wrote a goodbye letter to her son, because he refused to go with her. I have the letter. It was in his office at La Moraleja, in the blue folder you seem to think I've made up. I applied for a copy of her death certificate, I can show it to you whenever you like, Grandma Teresa died in Ocaña, a prisoner. She was tried in 1939 and sentenced to death for aiding and abetting the revolution, but the sentence was later commuted to thirty years.

My brother did not flinch but his face was white. Angélica had no political nous and simply got angry.

"I don't understand… What do you mean prison?" she asked shifting nervously in her chair "What did she do?"

"Do? She didn't do anything. They put her in prison for what she was. A socialist. And a Republican, obviously."

"What the hell are you talking about, Álvaro?" she gave a nervous laugh, "That's impossible… grandma, a socialist?"

"Yes, socialist," I smiled to see that the working-class left-wing values my sister had acquired through marriage were so weak you did not even have to scratch the surface to watch them disappear. "She was a militant activist in the Socialist Workers' Party, the Torrelodones chapel. Like your husband's grandfather, the one they shot and dumped in a well in the Canaries, because he was a socialist too, wasn't he?"

She refused to admit to this, but I didn't care, because I knew. I turned to my brother and noted that his colour had returned, and his cheeks were flushed.

"What right do you have to go snooping around, taking things out of Papá's study?" he leaned over the desk, fists clenched.

But he didn't scare me, and he knew it.

"The same right as you have, Rafa. When I got there, there were a lot of gaps on the walls. Lisette told me you'd taken some of the pictures, and Julio had taking the photo of Mamá and Papá in the silver frame. I thought it was a free for all."

"That's not the same."

"You're right, it's not the same. You didn't have the simple curiosity to look for anything, and I did. That's why I was the one who found the folder, though as you can see, I never planned on keeping the contents to myself. I'll tell you everything that was in it, I'll even make photocopies of the documents if you like. There's a lot of interesting stuff in there."

"Don't go to any trouble on my account," Rafa sat back in his chair, trying once more to seek refuge in arrogance. "So, Grandma Teresa was a socialist? Big deal. It happens in the best of families, everyone knows that. So they put her in prison after the war? Hardly surprising, I mean that was why they won the war. If it had been the other way round the Reds would have done the same. What else?"

"Oh, there's lots more, but I'd rather take things slowly. You have to admit that I've already told you at least one thing you didn't know. Two, actually. First: who our grandmother was. Second: who Papá was. A man capable of denying his own mother, burying her alive, lying about her to his own children..."

"No!" Angélica interrupted me with sudden vehemence: "That's not true, Álvaro, it can't be true. Papá must have had his reasons. Why are you siding with her against him? We knew Papá, we didn't know her. We don't know the first thing about her, we have no idea what sort of person she was..." she turned away from me, seeking consolation in Rafa. "Back then, everyone did horrible things, even women... Maybe she was... I don't know. If they sentenced her to death, she must have murdered someone, or turned someone in."

I looked at my sister, at my brother and, I took a deep breathe.

"Grandma Teresa was a teacher. She taught infants in Torrelodones. She was very militant, and was a senior figure in the local branch of the Communist Party. She was also a liberated woman, and very brave. She spoke at meetings, chaired committees, helped refugees... Franco and his cronies sentenced lots of people like her to death, leaders of left-wing parties who had done nothing, and they always used the same excuse: incitement to rebellion, although obviously they were the ones who had rebelled. They presided over a systematic, ordered reign of terror which had nothing to do with actual crimes committed in the Republican areas. I'm sorry, Angélica," I smiled at my sister, "but your grandmother never murdered, never tortured, never informed on anybody. Everyone in the village loved her."

Rafa was not prepared to put up with my smile.

"You don't know the first thing. This is all just fantasy…"

"No," I cut him off, "I'm telling the truth. There are still people in Torrelodones who remember her, Encarnita, who runs the chemist shop for example. You remember her, she came to Papá's funeral. I went to see her and she told me about grandma Teresa – 'she was a dyed-in-the-wool Red, but she was a good woman," that's what she said. She knew her quite well, she went to the school Teresa taught in and she was great friends with Teresita. They were the same age."

"Teresita?" my brother's composure deserted him again.

"Oh, shit! Of course, that's something else you don't know… I paused to savour the moment. "You see, Papá wasn't an only child. He had a younger sister, Teresa Carrión González, born in 1925. I've got a copy of her birth certificate, if you're interested, I got it from the registry office in Torrelodones. And I have a photo of the two of them together, her and grandma and the other kids from the school in Torrelodones. Encarnita has kept it all these years, her daughter made three copies for me Teresita, would have been… I don't know, about twelve at the time. There's no mention of her in Papá's papers, no photographs, no letters, nothing. I don't know whether she died during the war or afterwards, she might even still be alive. But Papá certainly never tried to track her down, nor did his father. He doesn't even mention her name in the letters he wrote home from Russia…"

"But…" Angélica was now completely lost. "That can't be right, because that little girl… well, she must have lived with him, mustn't she? I mean she was…"

"…part of his family?" My sister looked at me and nodded. "Of course. They lived under the same roof until grandma Teresa left her husband in June 1937. Teresita went with her, but Papá didn't. Encarnita said she never really understood why, because Papá was very fond Manuel, that was the name of grandma Teresa's lover, the man she went off with. He was a teacher too, a socialist and an amateur magician. He was the one who taught Papá to do magic tricks."

"So…" Rafa smiled, "as well as being a teacher, a socialist and a Republican, grandma Teresa was a slut?"

"No more than your sister," I smiled too, "who's sitting right here."

"Can you stop talking about that, Álvaro?" my sister did not see the funny side. "Anyway, it's not the same," Rafa came to her rescue, "Things were different back then. There must have been a terrible scandal, I mean imagine it, a married woman committing adultery, abandoning her son … It must have been humiliating! I'm not surprised Papá didn't want to have anything more to do with her."

"I am. Because she didn't abandon him, he was the one who chose not to go with her…"

I forced myself to stop, because my brother's little smiles were beginning to infuriate me and I didn't want to get angry until I was ready. "Back then, what grandma Teresa did was no more or less serious than it is nowadays. Even then, divorce existed in Spain, Rafa, and so did civil marriage. Divorced women were entitled to live on their own or even remarry without losing custody of their children…" I turned to my sister. "That's why I compared it to your situation, Angélica, I wasn't trying to criticise you, honestly, I mean how could I given the position I'm in right now …" I paused again, turned back to Rafa and stared at him. "It's not like things changed with the Republic. And I'm sure grandpa Benigno was thrilled that Franco won, because he was a complete fascist and a sanctimonious prig. You only have to read the letters he wrote when Papá was in Russia. He couldn't get enough of the executions or religious processions, and maybe as far as he was concerned, his wife was nothing but a slut and a communist, maybe he thought he was well rid of her… But it couldn't have been just that, I mean he wasn't like that with his son…" Fuck you, Rafa, I thought before saying, "Because Papá enrolled in the Socialist Youth Movement a month and a half after his mother walked out."

"That's a lie!" Rafa got to his feet and came towards me, his hands quivering with rage like a bad actor playing a Spanish nobleman of the Golden Age whose honour has been besmirched. "You're a liar, Álvaro! I don't believe you."

"Come on, Rafa, sit down. It's not a lie, it's the truth. I know because I found his membership card. I'll make a colour photocopy for you, one side is red with a five-pointed star and JSU in capital letters, and on the other side there's a photo of Papá when he was fifteen, his full name, date of birth, all the usual stuff…"

My brother did not move. He had never been a nice person but now, ridiculous as it seemed, I pitied him.

What exactly was the JSU" Angélica saved the situation, her voice like a frightened puppy.

"It was an amalgamation of the Socialist Party and Communist Party youth groups. They merged shortly before the war."

"And Papá was a member?" she sounded as though she was no longer sure of anything.

"Yes. He was also a member of the Falange Española de las JONS. There was another identity card, issued in 1941. Late June, to be precise, he obviously liked joining things in the summer..." I smiled, but my brother and sister were stonefaced. "Papá became a Falangist when he joined the Blue Division. They obviously knew nothing about his past, I suppose the JSU must have burned their archives to protect their members before the Fascists marched into Madrid. There's something else you didn't know."

"I didn't," Angélica said

"Neither did I," Rafa walked back to his chair, but the confidence was gone from his voice. "I suppose it's not really that strange. Papá just changed his mind, that's all."

"Of course he did, that was something else he was really good at. He was so attached to having more than one opinion that he never gave up on any of them, he just shifted from one to the other, careful never to get rid of his membership cards in case they would prove useful in the future. He kept them both all his life. I found them in a little velvet pouch. They were with his mother's letter and a photo of Papá taken in Paris in 1947 with a beautiful woman, Paloma Fernández Muñoz, another relative, she was grandma Mariana's second cousin and the great-aunt of the woman I'm seeing, because I'm sure Julio has told you that the woman I'm having a relationship with is our cousin.."

"But..." Rafa was still worried about what I'd said first, "Papá never spent any time in ..."

...in Paris?" Of course he spent time in Paris. He lived there for over two years, from late 1944 until April 1947. When he realised the Germans were going to lose the war, he deserted and instead of coming back to Spain, he stayed in France. He thought the Allies would invade Spain, topple Franco and restore democracy, everyone thought so at the time. It seemed logical, it was what should have happened. So Papá dusted off his old JSU card, that way he could fit in with the Spanish exiles and go back with them in triumph."

I stopped and looked from Rafa to Angélica, both were pale and struck dumb.

"That's how he met the Fernández family. They were from Madrid, and before the war they spent their summers in Torrelodones. The only surviving son in the family was a communist, but his brother and his brother-in-law – who were both shot near here, at the cementerio del Este – had both been socialists and had been friends with grandma Teresa. Ignacio Fernández had known her too, and one night in Paris, he recognised Papá in a café. He brought him home, and the family protected him, fed him, helped him get a job. When Papá decided to go back to Spain in 1947, they asked him if he would oversee the sale of their lands and properties, because back in Spain they had been rich, but they had had to leave everything behind, when they crossed the border into France. So he agreed to help them, the way they had helped him, and he came back to Spain with powers of attorney signed by them. Then he robbed them of everything they had. Everything." I stared at my brother and he held my gaze. "They were difficult times, I grant you, but I think we are allowed to judge, Rafa, I think we do have the right to an opinion even if we didn't life through those times."

"Shut up," the first time he said it, it was barely a.whisper.

"I don't feel like shutting up," I said, "And I don't think it would be good for you if I did, because there are a lot of things you need to know, and there are things I need to know too. For example, what did Papá tell you about the day Ignacio Fernández came round to our in May 1977, with his granddaughter Raquel. And how do you think Papá met grandma Mariana, and Mamá?"

"Well…"

"Shut up, Angélica!"

"I won't shut up Rafa." My sister staunchly met his gaze, then turned back to me. "Why do you ask?" He didn't really say much about it. He told us he met grandma Mariana in Torrelodones because she used to spend the summer there, he said he helped her to sell off her some property that belonged to her family and they split the profits. Then, later on, when she was older, Mamá went to him for help. Grandma Mariana wanted her to stay at home but she wanted a job, and he hired her as his secretary, they started going out together and… But you know all this, don't you?" She was right, I did know this. "That's what he told us. He said that when her family went to France, they left everything to grandma Mariana, and now they wanted it all back, but they had no right…"

"Of course, I murmured, "Of course."

I paused again and for a moment I wondered whether all this was worth it, whether it would do any good. I was tired and I felt disgusted with myself, sickened by my father, his life, my family, everything. A lot of time had passed, and I had not even known these people. I was about to stop, to get up and say that none of it mattered. I needed to get out of this office, to breathe something other than this stifling air, to go back to Raquel and be with her. And I might have done it if I hadn't seen my brother's face, seen the way he was looking at me.

I went on, now, dispassionately.

"That's not how it was. Grandma Mariana kept everything for herself because she was the only one of the Fernández family who didn't leave. When the war started, she was living in an apartment in Arguelles, but the building was destroyed in an explosion. Her uncle suggested she come and live with them near the Glorieta de Bilbao, and she stayed there even after they left. She kept a low profile, made sure that no one tried to take the place from her. A few months before Franco's troops marched into Madrid, Carlos, her cousin Paloma's husband showed up around midnight. He was twenty-eight and a lieutenant in the Republican Army. He walked with a limp, and his right arm was paralysed, he'd been badly injured at the front in late 1936. All he wanted was somewhere to stay, somewhere he could get some sleep, have something to eat. He wasn't armed, and there was no one else he could turn to, so he asked Mariana if he could stay the night. The next morning, she turned him in. The Falangists showed up and found him in bed, they dragged him out in his pyjamas, and put him in prison. He was charged with military insurrection, sentenced to death and executed - that way grandma Mariana managed to ingratiate herself with the fascists, so that no one would bother her and she could keep all these things that had never belonged to her," I turned to my sister, "So you see, it wasn't grandma Teresa who informed on people, it was grandma Mariana. She thought she was so clever. But she hadn't reckoned on Papá, Julio Carrión González who was on his way to becoming a self-made man."

"Don't say things like that, Álvaro..." Angélica clicked her tongue irritably, "The way you tell the story, you make it sound... OK, the Republicans had property confiscated, but it wasn't theft, there were laws, judges, courts...it was... Well it was one of the consequences of the war, the circumstances were exceptional, I mean, they weren't there, they'd left everything behind, they'd given up their property ..."

"No, Angélica, they hadn't abandoned their property, they ran for their lives – and they were right to go. The only two men in the family who stayed were put up against a wall and shot."

"OK, but... You can't just talk as if it happened yesterday..." Her expression changed, as though she had finally found the line of reasoning she had been seeking. "If what you've said is true, what grandma Mariana did was horrible, that poor man... But what Papá did was different. He wasn't a thief, Álvaro, everything he did was legal."

"Legal?"

I should have left as soon as I said this, because all the blood in my body had rushed to my face, I felt my ears burning, my throat was dry, my tongue was parched, and everything seemed tinged with orange, this office, the furniture, my brother, my sister, the whole world was on fire.

"This whole fucking country was illegal, Angélica! Every single thing about it was unlawful, don't you get that? The laws, the judges, the courts, the whole fucking thing."

I felt a sudden blow to my back. I turned and saw Rafa, saw in his eyes the flames that were devouring me. "Shut up!" He grabbed the collar of my shirt and I could feel his spittle on my face, his face pressed so close to me that it was as if he was going to kiss me. "Shut up, shut up you fucking bastard, shut up right now."

"Get your hands off me," I struggled free of him and, perhaps unconsciously, I realized that although he was bigger than me, I was stronger than him.

He stepped back, but he was still too close, and I could still feel this nameless heat, the flames dazzling now, they seemed to envelop everything, flaring higher, reaching an intensity I could not have imagined.

"I'm sick of you," Rafa went on screaming insults flecked with spittle, "I've had it up to the back teeth with the spoiled little boy, the brains of the family, Mamá's little fucking scientist. What the fuck do you know about the real world, Álvarito? What would you know about the price of anything? Fuck all, that's what. You're like a parasite, forever sponging off Papá, you were happy to spend his money, and now you come here with all this shit..." He paused for a moment and gave a bitter laugh, his face a rictus of contempt, "And the worst of it is he did more for you than he did for any of us, you were always his favourite, Papá's little boy. 'Álvaro is the brains of the family,' he used to say, 'Álvaro is the best of you, he's the only one like me.' You ungrateful bastard! Don't you get it? Papá didn't want you to suffer the things he suffered... He didn't want you to have to grow up penniless, and Jesus Christ he knew what it was to be poor. You have no idea, Álvaro... Did you ever wonder how much rent Papá shelled out for your apartment in Boston? I was the one who had to go to the bank to set up the standing order you got every month. Because poor little Álvaro couldn't get a job like everyone else after university, oh no, he had to do a doctoral thesis, and then another one, because he got a grant so it was *really* important. Only proper scientists get to go there. But he couldn't live in halls like everyone else.

Oh no, poor Álvarito had to have his own apartment, and Papá had to pay for it …"

My blood was pumping so fast it felt as if my veins were about to collapse.

"That's not true, Rafa. I did my first thesis with a scholarship from the university, and by the time I went to Boston, I was a professor and I'd been earning a salary for four years."

"Oh yes, your salary! I'm sorry, I forgot," he laughed again, "You get a state subsidy, Álvaro, as if you were a motorway… You'd prefer to think it was that instead of thinking it was Papá's money. That way you can be pure and good and enlightened, that way Álvaro can concentrate on important things and all the little immigrant kids from San Sebastián de los Reyes get to enjoy the fruits of capitalism once a month pissing about in your fucking museum: 'Why does the ramp thing go down? Why does that light go out? Why is it moving more slowly now?'"

"Shut up, Rafa!" I launched myself at him, grabbed the lapel of his jacket in both hands. "You should be ashamed, talking like that, I'm ashamed to listen to you. You don't know what you're talking about."

"Oh, look," still mimicking a high-pitched voice, his eyes wide in feigned astonishment, "The Earth is going round and round."

"Shut the fuck up." Then suddenly I found myself saying what I had long thought. "You're the lowest of the low, do you know that? You're contemptible, Rafa. You disgust me. You're proud of being what you are, an animal. You're ignorant and you're happy knowing nothing, you wish everyone was like you, you want people to live without ever wondering why things happen… You're worse than Papá."

"Get your hands off me, Álvaro."

"Much worse, you're harder, more cynical… And it's different for you, because you had the choice," I relaxed my grip, "You represent everything I despise in this world, you and people like you…"

"Let go of me!"

I let go, and he punched me. He swung hard and hit my right eye, but I didn't feel anything, because by now my body was filled with violence, power, anger. I took the blow and ran at him like an enraged bull. He fell and I hurled myself on top of him, lashing out with both fists, so focussed that there was nothing he could do to defend himself. He covered his face with his hands but I went on hitting him, one two, one two, his head juddering from side to side as the blows rained down and I felt the sinister thrill of my strength, his weakness, the insatiable desire to keep hitting him and never stop.

"Álvaro, please… for God's sake"

My sister's voice brought me back from that distant place. I heard Angélica screaming, saw her fall to her knees beside me. She was crying now, tugging at my sleeve, I could hear her, feel the pressure of her fingers, but I didn't look at her. I couldn't, because I could not take my eyes from Rafa, lying there under me, his face covered in blood, his arms lying lifeless by his sides. There was blood on my hands, I could feel an ache in my knuckles, but there was nothing more. Suddenly all the confusion, the anger, the emotion vanished and I found myself alone with my own version of horror. It had been more than twenty years since I'd been in a fight, and I had never hit anyone the way I hit Rafa.

"I knew it."

Then I heard someone come up behind me, grip me under the arms, and haul me off Rafa.

"I told you, Álvaro, I knew this would happen, I know him a lot better than you do…"

It was Julio. As soon as we had started yelling, the secretary had opened the door and was so terrified by what she saw that she had rushed off to find him. Now, here he was, his arm still holding me in a bear hug. Rafa struggled to sit up, brought his hands to his face and howled in pain. "You've broken my fucking nose, you bastard!" His voice was thick and slurred.

"Let me have a look…" Angélica touched his face gingerly, ignoring his protests, "No… I don't think it's broken, but it's very swollen. We'll have to put something on it. Come on, get up, here let me help you." She tried but she could not move him. "Julio, give me a hand."

They each took one arm and pulled Rafa to his feet. I watched, like an innocent bystander looking at the pain someone else had caused.

"I'm taking you to the hospital, Rafa, you need to be checked over. That cut on your lip is going to need stitches, and your eyebrow too, but it's nothing serious, there are no broken bones, so there's no need to worry…" For the first time in my life, I was grateful for my sister's punctilious, overbearing character, "But first I need to clean up your face, let's go to the bathroom, Julio, you come with us…" Then she turned to me. "Don't go anywhere, Álvaro, please… I want to talk to you."

Julio turned to me as though he'd forgotten I was still there and before I could follow them, he came over, put his hand on my head and kissed me on the cheek. He didn't say anything, he just walked away, leaving me alone in this vast office where it had all started, Papá and Raquel, truth and lies. My sister quickly reappeared.

"Álvaro…"

I was expecting her to read me the riot act and I was prepared to accept it, because I deserved it. Rafa had hit me first, but I didn't just hit him back, I had lost control. As she said my name, however, wiping her hands on a paper towel, I sensed in her voice a nervous tremor of confession.

"Álvaro, I just wanted to say..." she twisted the paper towel in her hands, staring at it as though it demanded all her attention, but then she had a better idea. "Here, let me take a look at that eye first."

She came over to me and wiped my face with a clean corner of a tissue, then touched it gently.

"It's fine," she said, "You'll have a black eye, but there's no bleeding... Álvaro, I want to ask you a favour, all those things you told us about Papá, about grandma... well, I realise how important it is to you, honestly, I do, but... Maybe you don't understand, I know he wouldn't understand but I'd really rather Adolfo didn't find out, I'd be grateful if you didn't say anything, because..." By now the paper tissue was a sodden mass and she balled it into her fist. "A lot of time has passed and Adolfo, well, he still thinks about his grandfather a lot, he's obsessed with him, and it wouldn't do him any good to know..."

She finally looked at me, and what she saw in my eyes spurred her on. A moment earlier, I felt no more solid than the paper towel she had just ripped to shreds, but now I could feel a warmth coursing through my body and a sudden, mysterious serenity.

"Go to hell, Angélica."

I said it calmly, without raising my voice, then I turned and walked out.

When Mariví buzzed through to say someone had arrived to discuss the letter she had sent to Julio Carrión's widow, Raquel Fernández Perea was so nervous she felt sick, but she composed herself quickly as though her visitor was already sitting on the other side of the desk. She picked up the phone and quickly dialled an extension number.

"Aunt Angélica is here. She's here."

"But," Paco Molinero hesitated only for a second, "Surely she should have phoned to make an appointment?"

"She should have, but she's clearly decided just to show up. It can't be a good sign."

"Why do you think that? Don't worry, Raquel, I'm sure everything will be fine."

But it was Álvaro Carrión Otero and not his mother who was knocking on the door of her office.

"She's here. I've got to go…"

"Good luck."

When she had left the solicitor's office, the proud owner of a luxury apartment she had no intention of ever living in, Raquel had already sensed that Julio Carrión would not survive his heart attack. She knew that there was a good chance her second visit had been the death of this man, but although she found it hard to believe, she didn't care. If he had spent fifty years without feeling so much as a shred of guilt, she was not about to start feeling guilty now. On the contrary, it would have been a fitting, even a happy ending to her grandfather's story were it not for the fact that Carrión's death would put paid to her plans.

Dead dogs don't bite. As the man who should have been her victim lay dying, Raquel often thought of this expression which she had heard so often in Paris in every Spanish accent possible after Franco died, as her family dragged her to visit hundreds of friends, and each time there would a glass of champagne, a slice of tortilla, and always the same toast: "*Muerto el perro, se acabó la rabia*". But it was not true, and she felt a rage well within her at the thought that Julio Carrión was going to win again, though it would cost him his life. Just the thought of it made her angry but her anger provided the solution. When she realised that the anger she felt was not her, but a passion she had inherited from her

655

grandfather, it reminded her that while neither sin nor blame cant be inherited, debts can be. Working as she did for a bank, it was something she knew better than anyone.

It would have been easy for her to attack Julio Carrión's children since she knew what they looked like, where they worked. Sebastián would kick up a fuss, but in the end, he would take her to their offices. It seemed a workable hypothesis, but she shelved the idea, not because it was unfair, but because she thought she might be wrong about them, because she had never forgotten the incident with the red-haired doll in the green dress. Clara Carrión was the same age as she was, and though her brothers were older, they were all of the same generation, the first generation of Spaniards not to live in fear. And fear was key, it was a necessary condition if her plan was to succeed. Were it not for the fact that Julio Carrión González had been afraid - that same fear that had paralysed Anita Salgado Pérez at the mere thought of her husband visiting Carrión thirty years previously - then the speech Raquel had learned by heart, rehearsed in front of a mirror, would barely have raised a worried smile. Everything she had said was true. The bookshops were full of books about the war and the post-war period, every month there was some new documentary about it, judges were constantly issuing exhumation orders for victims of Franco's reign of terror, the State was paying reparations to Republican organisations and unions whose assets had been seized after the civil war, but to take advantage of this upheaval would require more than a battered leather folder full of documents in the hands of an economist with no publishing contacts.

What Raquel had, though important to her, would have seemed trivial to a journalist because there were so many stories like it – stories more shocking, more incredible, more spectacular - that the tragedy the Fernández Muñoz family had suffered would seem unremarkable in the face of the great national tragedy. It was brutal, it was hard, but that was how it was. She knew this, and she knew that even if she went out herself and staked out the offices of every publisher and newspaper in the country and finally found someone prepared to publish her story, the consequences, far from destroying the Carrión family, would be little more than a temporary hitch. The future of the Grupo Carrión would not be tainted by revelations about its founder's past, Raquel Fernández Perea was certain of that, but she had played and she had won, or she would have had death not snatched victory from her.

Raquel had bet everything on Julio Carrión González's fear and he was afraid, he had always been afraid. That morning, in his office, Raquel realised that his reaction had nothing to do with her threats, it was the result of a deep-rooted fear. For years and years, Julio Carrión had been waiting for Ignacio Fernández Muñoz to carry out his threat, steeling himself to withstand the final blow. Her grandfather had been right after all. He had robbed Julio of his sleep and in doing so he had fostered the ideal circumstances in which his granddaughter could finish the task.

But what had worked on the father would not work on his children. Raquel could picture herself giving her little speech and imagined their response: 'Really? Fine, you go ahead, do what you like.' They would not be afraid, and their equanimity would leave her defenceless. All that remained was the mother, the widow, the chief beneficiary of Julio Carrión González's fortune, the daughter of 'the Toad', the blonde, blue-eyed girl whom everyone in the house had been worried about because she was never scared when she heard the air-raid sirens, she would stay wherever she was and go on playing. For Angélica, born in 1935, the wail of the sirens was so routine there had seemed little point in being scared. This was all that Raquel knew about this woman, that and the fact that she had found fine food difficult to digest. Her constitution was so accustomed to eating black bread and lentils that the first time they gave her anything more nourishing, she went to bed with severe stomach cramps.

Anita, her grandmother, had never told Raquel how Angélica had come to marry Carrión. She did not know that Mariana Fernández Viu did not contact her uncle and aunt either before or after Julio Carrión came home, but in 1949, the night before she took the train back to her parents house in Galicia, Mariana had gone to see Casilda García Guerrero, her cousin Mateo's widow. Casilda had kept in constant contact with the Fernández Muñoz family since the war ended, even after she remarried. During the hard times, when she lived alone with her son in a dingy attic flat on the Calle Ventura de la Vega, she had sometimes been forced to go cap in hand to Mariana when she had no work, or her son was ill. Whenever she did, 'the Toad' gave her barely enough to survive on and she had never dared ask for more.

It was through Casilda that the Fernández found out what was happening in Madrid. It was Casilda who wrote to relay what Mariana – having tracked her down through one of her brothers who worked in a café - had told her. By then, Mateo Fernández Gómez de la Riva and his wife and children already knew, from the lawyer they had hired, that Julio Carrión González had robbed them of everything they owned except the house in Torrelodones. It was Casilda who informed them that Julio Carrión had just thrown their niece out on the street, that Mariana had suggested she might represent their legal interests in Spain to try to claw back what she could, and that Casilda had told her to go to hell. "Maybe I was wrong," she wrote, "But I'm sure that bastard Carrión has arranged things so that there's no way of getting anything back. If you want me to write to the Toad, I have her address..." They all knew there was nothing to be done, and that even if there had been, it would have been to Mariana's advantage, not theirs. They did not trust her any more than they trusted Carrión, and they somehow felt happier to think that things had ended like this, rather than the two of them dividing the spoils. And so when the news came, they were caught unawares.

By the time they opened a letter from Casilda to find a press cutting from the society pages of a Madrid newspaper, it was 1956 and the Fernandez family had attained a standard of living that was comfortable enough for them not to think about Julio Carrión every moment of the day. This did not make it any easier for them to read the news: *"On Saturday 5 May, 1956, Don Julio Carrión González, thirty-four, was joined in holy matrimony to Señorita Angélica Otero Fernández, twenty-one, in the church of Santa Bárbara..."* On the cutting, Casilda had scribbled in pencil *'what do you think of this? I was speechless...'* The Fernández family was speechless, too, though they quickly forgot about it, all except Paloma, who sank even deeper into depression.

These few stories that her grandmother Anita had told her had taught Raquel more about fear than she would otherwise have learned. A fear that was impossible for her, for any of her generation to truly understand.

"But I don't get it, grandma..." she said the same thing over and over. "If Casilda was still in Spain, if you and she were writing to each other all the time... How is it that Mariana ended up with everything? Why didn't she hire a lawyer, file a claim against her..."

"Who, Casilda? Oh, *hija mia!* Casilda couldn't have stood up in court …"

"Maybe not, but surely she could have found someone to represent her. Surely the courts would have had to do something..."

"Oh yes, they would have put her in prison."

"But why? She had already been in prison and they let her out at the end of the war. I don't mean she should have gone to the police but... I don't know... she had nothing, she was penniless, she was working every hour of the day and night, and there was Mariana with everything ... The war had been over for eight years by the time Carrión came back!" The more she talked about it, the less she understood, "I mean surely you must have thought about it before then? I mean your husband was a lawyer, and his father was an engineer who had worked for the ministry... They must have known lots of people in Madrid, they weren't helpless, surely there were people they could have turned to ... That's why I don't understand, how could this have happened, grandma."

"Because we were afraid, Raquel." Anita looked at her granddaughter and smiled, "Everyone was afraid, whether they were rich or poor, educated or illiterate, we were all afraid. You don't know what you're talking about, Raquel, you can't begin to imagine."

Maybe this was why Raquel said nothing.

"Look," her grandmother came to her aid, "when the fascists marched into Madrid, Paloma's husband Carlos went to see a close friend to his, a professor at the university who had become a communist during the war, and, from what he said, ended up being more radical than any of them. I don't remember his name, but I do remember he was from a family of fascist army officers. That was the only reason he was still alive, and the reason Carlos thought he might be able to help him. He had to walk all the way to Aranjuez to see him, and his friend heard him out, promised to help him and asked him to wait. Then went inside and informed on him. It was his little sister who came and told Carlos, to get out of there as fast as he could, she even gave him money for the train back to Madrid. She saved his life, even if it was only so that Mariana could turn him in the next day. Do you understand?"

"But the girl, she was a Nationalist?" said Raquel.

"Of course. She may have been right-wing, but she was a good person, a better person than her brother. This was why we were afraid, because we couldn't trust anyone. The only person we trusted was Julio, because he was like family to us, and look what happened..."

Raquel had known Casilda all her life. Every year, on the way back from their holidays in Torre del Mar, they would stop off for lunch or dinner with her. Casilda was an elderly, affectionate woman who would always hug her then hold her at arms length and marvel over how much she had grown. After her parents went back, they saw her more often. Casilda invariably came with them if they were lunching out of town, and sometimes Raquel would stay over with Casilda and Mateo so that her parents could go out. This was why Raquel did not understand what happened the day her grandparents came back to live in Madrid, that day that had begun with vermouth on tap on a terrace in Vistillas. At six that afternoon, the doorbell rang. Raquel answered it and found Casilda in tears. "What's the matter, auntie? Are you hurt?" Casilda shook her head and asked if her grandfather had arrived yet. "He's in the living room.", Raquel said. He wasn't in the living room any more, but standing behind her, and when she realized, she had to step aside quickly so as not to be crushed, because her grandfather and Casilda threw their arms around each other and stood there for a long, long time, Casilda crying and whispering, "Ignacio, Ignacio…"

When her grandmother told her everything she knew about Julio Carrión, Raquel remembered that scene and the many others that had made her childhood the most intense, the most exciting, the most emotionally charged period of her life. After the war, Casilda could not have left Spain, even years later, it would not have occurred to her to try, just as it would never have occurred to her in-laws, to Ignacio and his family, to take the simple but dangerous initiative of sending her a plane ticket. It was too late for Raquel to ask Mateo's widow whether she had had a passport before 1976 since Casilda had died a few short weeks after her brother-in-law Ignacio, but Raquel was certain that she would not have run the risk of going to the consulate to apply for one, since she would have had to present her police record. It was absurd, but that was how it was.

Time had passed for everyone, but the fear remained, as powerful, as formidable, as insuperable as a range of snow-capped mountains. To these people, fear had been a landscape, a country, unvarying condition not to be questioned. And that, thought Raquel Fernández Perea, was what fear must also be to Angélica Otero Fernández.

"But does the widow know?" Paco asked her on the day they settled down to plan her coup in earnest.

"She must know," Raquel answered, "I know what you're thinking, The minute I tell her my name she'll know who I am and what I want, she'll be as scared as he was, agree to meet me straight away without telling anyone. I know her sons don't know who I am, Sebastián told me. He said the one thing Carrión insisted on was that they weren't to be told anything, and even if my surname is Fernández, my mother's name is Perea, so…"

Seeing Paco shake his head she let the sentence trail off.

"No," he said, "That's not what I meant. How can you be sure that she knew what was going on?"

Raquel couldn't answer that question. All she had were, her suspicions, the memory of that distant Saturday afternoon, her intuition as a girl of eight, the blonde woman wringing her hands and glancing around, feverishly looking for her cigarettes. Ignacio Fernández Muñoz's visit had made her nervous, sick with fear, that was the only thing Raquel knew for certain.

"When my grandfather took me to the Carrión's house in 1977," she continued in a more circumspect tone, as though trying to convince herself, "she was the one who came to the door. She smiled and asked what she could do for us and when my grandfather told her his name she fell apart, I thought she was going to faint."

"OK…" Paco smiled, "That means she knew *something*, Raquel, I mean she must have known something, mustn't she? When Carrión came back to Spain she was a little girl, living with her mother, she must have known him, at least by sight. But we still don't know how they met seven years later. Maybe she only knows part of it, and you can't know which part."

"Does it really matter?"

"Of course it matters," he said seriously, "It's the one weak point in your plan."

Julio Carrión González had been buried for eight days when Raquel sent Paco Molinero an email inviting him round to her new flat for dinner. "So, what is it?" he appeared in her office a few minutes later " what's happened? You couldn't walk twenty yards to my office to tell me?" Raquel smiled, " I could have, but I think the occasion calls for something more formal."

When Raquel finally explained the story to Paco, it was easy because, not being Julio Carrión González's son, he did not interrupt her with questions. Even so, he was so amazed by what she told him.

"Wow, that's serious… I'll need to think about it."

She nodded, but masked her disappointment with a smile.

"Hey," He came over and shook her gently by the shoulder, "I just mean I need time to work out how to get the widow to hand over a million, not whether you should sell her the documents."

"So you still think it's a good idea?"

"Me?" he pointed to himself and burst out laughing, "I think it's brilliant."

For the next week, Paco called her or sent emails every day, sometimes several times a day, looking for details, names, dates, amounts that Raquel did not yet know. She had told him that neither of them would get a penny of the money, they had to treat it like a game, like a mini version of the great swindle they had been planning all these years, and he had agreed without a second thought. He already had a notebook full of charts and figures, names and dates and only when he was ready did he suggest they have lunch together after work.

"That's your one weak point, Raquel, you need to think about it. With the information we've got, you can't just show up to meet the widow and say you're her long lost niece and that her husband had agreed to pay you a million euros for some documents that prove he's a crook. What if she

661

knows nothing about it?"

"It's impossible," Raquel said, though she was not completely convinced.

"Of course it's possible. Suppose her mother kept everything about her relationship with Carrión from her? Suppose they met up later by which time he was already rich... There's no reason for her to know where he got his money from. Even if she suspected, she might never have had the guts to ask him straight out..."

"That's impossible..."

"You think so? Back then? In this country?" Raquel looked at him and she hesitated. "Listen, Raquel, all most people want is a quiet life, you know that. So your grandfather shows up at her house one day... of course she was scared, he was like a ghost from the past, because it was all over now, Franco was dead, the exiles were coming home, political prisoners were being released... Your grandfather would have been the last person she expected to see when she opened the door. But the fact that she was scared just means she was unnerved, it doesn't mean she knew her husband's role in the whole thing. I'm not saying she didn't know, all I'm saying is we can't be sure."

"What about him? He must have been hysterical, he must have been beside himself, and his wife would have noticed something, wouldn't she?"

"Maybe, but that night when they were in bed, all Carrión had to do was take her in his arms, and tell her he wasn't not going to let anyone harm his family. That's what the men of his generation thought masculinity was. And the women thought femininity meant saying nothing and blindly trusting your husband. Think about it, Raquel... Maybe the widow thought the real villain was her mother, that Carrión's only mistake was helping her. It's possible. Or, if she knew everything when she married Carrión, that means your aunt Angélica betrayed her own mother. That's possible too, and if it's true, it works in your favour. But what if Carrión had a heart attack at the mere thought of his wife finding out what he had done to her mother after all these years? Or maybe Angélica knew everything that happened between 1940 and 1970, but doesn't know about you going to visit her husband a month ago. You said yourself he didn't want anyone to know. That's why I'm saying we can't be sure. If you go and see her, it's quite possible she'll throw you out, or send for her sons, or call the police ... None of which would be good."

Raquel Fernández Perea listened carefully to his reasoning, cursing herself for her own carelessness, for the weakness which had suddenly, treacherously taken over her mind.

The day she had gone to Julio Carrión González's funeral, she had no specific plan. She intended that Carrión's debt would be repaid by his heirs, but she did not know when or how. Nor was she in any hurry. The estates of the rich are notoriously long and complicated to sort out, requiring detailed inventories, a complex division of assets and considerable fiscal acumen, it was something that would take months, perhaps as much as a year. But there would not be another occasion when she could observe the Carrión family together. It was this, rather than any urgency on her part that prompted her to go to the cemetery in Torrelodones that freezing March morning. She was not sure that any information she might glean would prove useful, but she had only ever seen these distant relatives once before, almost thirty years ago. She was expecting nothing more than an ordinary funeral, black coats, dark glasses, handkerchiefs clutched in trembling hands, love, pain, a family caught overwhelmed by grief, but she had not discounted the possibility that there might be sibling rivalry, family squabbles, something that might prove useful.

When she saw a man standing away from the rest of the mourners, halfway between the gates and the grave, she assumed he was an acquaintance, possibly a colleague of Carrión's, someone unrelated to the family. But he had turned to look at her and as he did so, Raquel Fernández Perea felt the ground open up beneath her feet, because this was a stranger she already knew, a stranger she had seen in a handful of old photographs. Though the man she was now looking at was older than the young man who had smiled so charmingly for those group portraits, he was considerably younger than the old man who was the author of that smile. Had she known both of them when they were the same age, she might have noticed subtle differences between them, but the thick, dark, slightly wavy hair looked identical as did the face, the chiselled jawline, the olive skin, the long thin nose, the well defined mouth. His eyebrows were dark and thick and in time would turn white without detracting from his glittering eyes. Because this man, who could not possibly be Julio Carrión, was Julio Carrión, a carbon copy of the face that was about to dissolve into the earth.

She was so worked up that she could not hold his gaze for long. She looked away and lit a cigarette. It can't be his son, she thought, otherwise he'd be at the graveside with the others. She easily spotted Angélica, her hair still dyed the same colour, though she was a slim, frail old woman now. Next to her stood her two elder sons whom she recognised from the photos on the website, both tall, blond, pale-skinned, though balding

663

now. They looked exactly as Raquel had imagined them and markedly different to the other two men in the group. One of them, a tall man with dark hair and a beard had his arm around a good-looking blond woman who looked very much like her mother. The other, shorter, with cropped hair and a black tie, was Clara's husband. Raquel recognised Clara immediately, because she still had the gentle, ingenuous beauty that had first captivated her when they were girls. Next to her were two other women, but there was no dark-haired man, the grown-up version of the twelve-year-old who, even in 1977, was the only one of Julio Carrión's sons who looked like him.

She stubbed out her cigarette and turned to look at the man who stood apart from the gruop. He was smoking now, still looking at her, his expression a mixture of curiosity and surprise. Raquel realised it was Álvaro, that it had to be Álvaro even though he was standing on his own, away from everyone else, although he looked as though he did not want to be with the others. Had she been able to think about things coldly, she would have exulted in his isolation, it was more than she had been hoping for when she arrived at the cemetery, but she could not think coldly.

This man was not Julio Carrión, though he looked like him; she was not Paloma and yet she could not take her eyes off him. It wasn't rational, it wasn't logical, and it wasn't good, but Raquel Fernández Perea, together with her intelligence and all her plans, folded before this sudden attraction to a man who was not even himself but the shadow of someone else. Before Raquel had time to digest this, the ceremony ended, the sobbing grew louder as the coffin was lowered into the grave, the widow crumpled and the lone man rushed forward, hugged her and kissed her, reclaiming his place among the mourners. Raquel left quickly, suddenly intensely aware of the risk she was running in being here uninvited.

Since then she had made little headway. She had spent a lot of time thinking about what she knew and what she did not know, about Angélica and her children, she prepared a dozen different variations on the speech that had made it possible for her to triumph over an old man caught unawares, but she liked none of them. The memory of those eyes which were but were not Julio Carrión's disrupted her plans, emphasising her weakness, her vulnerability.

Raquel Fernández Perea, who had been born with ghosts, grown up with ghosts was now too old to believe in them, she knew now that what she had seen had been the result of her transporting herself into a time and passions that were not her own. Yet this did not prevent her from sensing that those dark eyes held a warning. This was why she had called on Paco Molinero, who was loyal, intelligent, and unbiased.

"You're right," she said after his speech, it seemed so obvious to her now that she said it again "Acually, you're right. But there is another possibility…"

"The investments."

"Of course," she nodded enthusiastically, "I don't know how I can have been so stupid."

This had been the only irrefutable truth in the speech Raquel Fernández Perea had made to Julio Carrión González on her second visit. Before going to see him, she had gone to the records department of the bank and had found accounts in his name and in those of several of his companies. She was not particularly surprised, the president of Grupo Carrión fitted the usual profile of the clients who approached the bank to manage some small part of their personal wealth so as to forge relationships with an investment manager in case they should need them when times were hard. For Carrión, as for most of the others, these personal investments represented only a small percentage of their businesses investments, not because the funds invested were negligible but because the amount of traffic – and therefore of commission and fees – was almost nonexistent. Raquel had quickly realised that taking over the management of the portfolio would not be difficult, but the death of Carrión had made her abandon a possible route before she should have.

The following morning she went to see Miguel Aguado, a shy, amiable, ugly man some years younger her with whom she had barely spoken in the course of ten years. She knew nothing about his work, but it did not take her long to figure out that he was hardly a brilliant investment manager.

"Given what you've said I don't see any problem passing on the portfolio, but I warn you, you won't make a penny out of it. As I said, I don't really know the sons, I always dealt directly with Don Julio, but I'm fairly sure they will want to liquidate the stock. I don't know how many of them there are, but I know it's a big family and they're rich. It's always the same, you never make any money out of big families."

"I know," Raquel smiled, "I'm sure that's why Clara phoned me. She'd forgotten I even worked here. We've met up a couple of times, mostly at class reunions, and we were best friends when we were little. But I'm sure she wouldn't have called me just to sell off the shares … Anyway, I'll just have a look, I won't do anything, and if I manage to persuade them to reinvest, I'll send them your way, after all they're your clients."

This was not the first time she had done a deal like this with a colleague, nor would it be the last. Writing to Angélica was even less difficult. She could have asked her secretary to do it, but she had a form letter on her computer and it only took five minutes to fill in the blanks. She was careful to sign it R. Fernandez Perea, then she sent it off, crossed her fingers and waited. If Angélica realised who she was from the letter, she would call immediately. If not – and at this point it hardly mattered – she would have to wait. She knew from experience that it usually took heirs about a month to reply, very rarely less and quite often more, so she decided to leave it until mid-April before she began to worry. Julio Carrión González had died on 1 March, 2005, and it was on the last day of the month that Mariví buzzed through to say the widow had arrived.

I'm not ready. This was the first thing she thought. She was not ready, although she had rehearsed exactly what she was going to say, every inflection, every gesture. This was just a preliminary encounter, an excuse to set up a proper meeting, at which Raquel would, at a judicious moment, place the documents in their battered leather folder on the table.

Raquel was accustomed to dealing with beneficiaries, and she invariably rattled off the same speech Angélica Otero Fernández would hear that morning, but Raquel had envisaged a very different kind of meeting: first a brief phone call, just long enough to get a sense of the woman she was dealing with, then a long series of offers and counter-offers all couched in exquisitely polite terms. She had wanted to meet with Julio Carrión's widow in her office since it played to her advantage but she had anticipated the fact that Angélica might decline, pleading illness or exhaustion, in which case Raquel had planned to say that, she would be only too happy to come and see her at her home.

This was what she had planned to say. She had carefully chosen every word, every phrase: of course there's no pressure, take all the time you need, I know how difficult these things can be, though it is a considerable sum of money and I would not advise leaving it too long, shall we say a month, shall we pencil in a date? This was how she had planned it, and had it gone according to plan, everything would have been fine. But she had sent the letter of March 20, and now, nine days later, here she was knocking on the office door without even phoning first to arrange a meeting. Raquel did not understand, but she could not keep Angélica waiting any longer.

"Come in" she said finally, her voice as bright, as confident as she could make it. And Julio Carrión's doppelganger stepped into her office.

When she saw him, she got to her feet, though she had not

consciously told her body to do so. It's impossible, this can't be happening, but she closed her eyes, opened them again and Álvaro Carrión was still standing there, looking as surprised, as shocked, as she was.

"I'm sorry, it's just... I was expecting your mother," she said eventually

"Yes, I came instead." His voice calmed her as it was nothing like his father's. " And since your charming receptionist didn't even both to ask my name..."

"Yes," she managed to smile as though amused, "Mariví is a real character." She tried to think what she should do next, then remembered. "Please, take a seat."

After he left, she walked back to her desk, and slumped into her chair. She felt awful but could not think why. The phone rang before she had time to compose herself.

"Is she gone?" Paco said.

"Yes."

"So, how did it go?"

"It didn't..." she took a deep breath, "she didn't come, her son came, the youngest, the one I met that day I went to their place with my grandfather."

"That's hardly surprising. So, what happened?"

"Nothing happened, Paco. I gave my little speech, gave him the documents, told him to look over them and then he left." She took another breath and felt a little better. "It's over."

"What do you mean over?"

"It's over, there's no way I can get to the sons... besides... I was nervous, I didn't know what to say. Maybe if he'd called to arrange an appointment I could have come up with something, but when he just showed up. And now... I don't know..."

"What's the hell's the matter with you, Raquel?" Paco's tone changed, "Honestly! You're starting to sound like a complete beginner..."

In her profession the term 'beginner' was the worst possible insult.

"You're right," she admitted, then repeated it to convince herself. "You're absolutely right. Nothing went wrong, I was just a bit nervous... I don't even think he noticed."

"Good. Don't worry, we'll find a way of getting to the widow. We can talk about it later. Are you free for lunch?"

She was free, and suggested she book a table at the restaurant they usually went to.

After she hung up, she went to the toilet and splashed water on her face. She had been born with ghosts, had grown up with ghosts, she knew they had form and heft and more character than many living people. She also knew that she should not tell anyone about what had happened that morning. That she had sat down next to Álvaro Carrión and had not been able to look him in the eye. That the whole time she was talking, she had been more conscious of how close his arm was to hers than of what she was actually saying. That when her assistant brought in the coffee and Álvaro Carrión said "Just as well Mariví didn't bring it. I'm scared to death of her," she had looked up at him, saw that he was looking at her, and had felt something like a fizzing inside her. She could not allow her body to fizz again.

This was something she could not tell anyone, especially not Paco Molinero. She couldn't tell him that fifteen minutes of conversation with Álvaro Carrión had done more to turn her life upside down than a whole night in bed with him. It was at precisely that moment that her Department Director chose to call her about one of their more problematic clients. She had to put the director on hold when Álvaro reappeared in her office to ask why she had been at his father's funeral but fortunately, her boss did not take kindly to being made to wait and rang back immediately, the call as welcome to Raquel Fernández Perea as the sound of the bell to a boxer about to collapse.

"But why did you go to the funeral?" Paco seemed worried at this new information. "You didn't mention anything to me about it."

"Well … it didn't seem important until now. I went to the funeral to see what they looked like, how Angélica looked … I mean playing hardball with a merry widow is one thing, but with a broken-hearted wife who was in a wheelchair or something would be…. I was just curious, I wanted to check a few things."

"I can understand that, but you didn't have to go to the cemetery, you could have gone to the service, it would have been a lot less risky.

"But a lot less useful, Paco. There would have been too many people, Aguado was probably there…," she paused to collect her thoughts, "At the time, I didn't know Aguado handled Carrión's portfolio, but there was bound to be someone from the bank. I didn't want to draw attention to myself, and I could hardly go up and offer my condolences… The Carrións are a big family and their father was a rich, successful businessman. with the church would have been full with all those people, I wouldn't have been able to get a good look at the family without being noticed."

"You're right."

"I was fairly sure there would be a public church service and a private burial, and I thought why go to a public service when I could go to the private burial in a tiny village cemetery where I was bound to see everything?" As she spoke, her reasoning sounded logical, sensible. "It was obvious, at least I thought it was obvious. The death notice mentioned the service but not the burial, which meant that they weren't expecting anyone but family at the cemetery, that's why I showed up late, so that they would be too busy listening to the priest to notice me. How was I to know that one of the sons would be standing on his own away from everyone else, that he'd notice me and that he would be the one to show up at the meeting instead of his mother? It's just a coincidence... It's unbelievable. I mean, it's the sort of thing you wouldn't bet on if your life depended on it."

"True," Paco smiled at her.

They ate their starter in silence, and ordered another bottle of wine.

"So," Paco spoke first, "What are you going to do now?"

"Well, obviously I can't tell him the truth, so I'll have to make something up."

"You have to work out some plausible excuse for being at the funeral, Raquel."

"I know, I know..." She looked at Paco and felt trapped, "Don't think I haven't thought about it. I need a reason that doesn't involve Aguado, doesn't drag up the entire family history, and still allows me to go ahead with my plan to get a million from the widow... That's about right, isn't it?"

"That's about right. It's not going to be easy."

"Not to mention the fact that this could cost me my job."

"Of course."

Have I gone completely mad? Raquel Fernández Perea thought, not for the first time. How the fuck did I get myself into this mess? People don't go to cemeteries to see strangers being buried. It had been stupid, completely stupid, and now it was now a noose round her neck, a sword hanging above her head. The easiest thing would be to tell the truth, or at least to say that Julio Carrión had been an old friend of the family. But she certainly couldn't present herself as the avenger of her grandparents and her great-grandparents, explain that she had been motivated by pure hatred, that she had come to glory in her enemy's defeat.

She had introduced herself to Alvaro Carrión as his father's investment advisor, something she was not. She had told Aguado that she and Clara had been to university together, that too had been a lie. Either of these details, which at the time had seemed as trivial as her visit to the cemetery, would be enough to get her fired, it could even get her blacklisted, making it impossible for her to find work. If she was found out, the company she worked for would be curious to know why she had lied, and she could hardly tell them that Julio Carrión, one of their most valued clients, was a thief, a swindler and a bastard, precisely the sort of person whose funeral no one would want to got to. Nor could she tell them part of the truth without revealing everything, which would amount to confessing to something that might not be a crime, but sounded very like one.

"This is a nightmare," she said aloud, "I've no idea how to get out of this mess."

She was not expecting a response, but Paco offered one which was so categorical it seemed obvious.

"By going forward. Always move forward, you can't retreat now, Raquel. Don't think about defending yourself, think about your attack."

"Really?" she managed to find her smile again, "But how?"

"I don't know," Paco admitted, "but we'll think of something. We've got three days, four actually, since we still have half of today and half of Monday."

Paco tried to pay the bill but Raquel insisted on paying, though she allowed him to drop her home in a taxi. When she was alone, she wondered where to begin. Though it had never been her method of working, she decided to adopt Paco's technique and sat down at a desk with a stack of paper and a pen. But having quickly filled half a dozen sheets, she realised she did not know where to go next, she also found she could hardly keep her eyes open. She had had too much wine with lunch. As soon as she lay down, she fell asleep and woke up almost an hour later, her brain befuddled and her throat dry. She splashed cold water on her face, picked up the sheets of paper she had scribbled on and brought them back to the bed.

She had always done her best thinking lying down, something she was reminded of when she read through the notes, which were nothing more than a list of obvious points she knew by heart. It was obvious that a burial was an intimate ceremony, obvious that she needed to divert Carrión's son as far as possible from her work, it was blindingly obvious that there was nothing to be gained by admitting the true nature of her interest until the right time, consequently she needed to concoct some personal relationship with the deceased or better still, with one of his relations. She had already considered inventing some link to Carrión's grandparents, his parents or his children, she had also considered some work connection, some complicated favour he had done, platonic friendship, intolerable jealousy, but everything she thought of was embarrassing: I was in love with your brother-in-law and I just came to see hello, he doesn't even know me... my grandfather knew your father when he was young... we're from Madrid but we used to spend the summer in Torrelodones and your father lent my grandfather some money, I just wanted to pay you back... I was very fond your father, though I only met him once or twice, he used to magic sweets out of my ears...I ended up at the wrong funeral, I was supposed to be at a funeral in Guadarrama but I got the names mixed up...

She could have gone on inventing pathetic excuses all night, but now that she was sober she remembered something else. She could not make up some vague, trivial excuse, Carrión's son already knew where she worked, he had been to her office, had asked her already and her only answer had been a nervous silence and a blush that was deeply unprofessional, and he would remember this. She had to think of a different means of attack , had to concentrate on Álvaro, think of something he would never expect. It was only now that she looked at the situation through his eyes that she felt composed again, that she imagined a very different scenario, something bold, something risky, something worthy of her.

It was the best idea she had had all afternoon, and it was something that played to her strengths. After all, I used to be an actress, she thought as she pictured the scene; Álvaro waiting for her outside the bank, her taking him to a bar, sitting at a little table, looking into his eyes and saying: 'I really can't talk about it, and it's best if you don't know the details, but all I can say is that your father got himself into some deep trouble. Only two people know the details, I'm one of them, and I was afraid that the other person would show up at the cemetery and cause a scene. That's the only reason I went to Torrelodones. When they didn't show, I left without saying anything because I didn't want to worry you needlessly. You probably shouldn't mention this to anyone else, but if over the next few months a tax inspector tries to contact you about your father's dealings with us, call me. If not, then just forget we ever had this conversation. I can't tell you any more, I have to be discreet for the sake of the other clients involved. Goodbye Señor Carrión, it's been a pleasure...'

"Sounds good," she said aloud.

Just then, the phone rang.

"Hello?"

"I've thought of something." It was Paco Molinero.

"Me too." She felt a relief akin to euphoria. "Well, it might need a bit of work…"

"Come on then, tell me."

She rattled off the speech she had just made up and as she did so, she was keenly aware of all the flaws she had not noticed earlier. But when she had finished, Paco whistled in appreciation.

"Not bad, not bad at all…"

"You think?" Raquel was no longer sure.

"Absolutely," Paco agreed, "The plan I thought of is similar…"

"Really?" Raquel's euphoria deflated like a burst balloon. "The thing is, as I was saying it just now, I didn't believe it. I mean it would get me out of a bind, but it's a story without an ending… What I mean is, he might be satisfied, but if he's not…"

"He'll go on asking questions."

"Exactly."

"Look, right now it's better than nothing, OK?" Paco was still trying to sound upbeat. "Let's go over it again tomorrow, OK?"

After she hung up, Raquel lay stretched out on her back, arms folded across her chest like a corpse. This was her thinking position. Playing the mysterious woman was all very well, but this man was careful, circumspect… Raquel pictured Álvaro Carrión, his eyes, the profile he had inherited from his hard-as-nails father, his own hardness towards her, his tone at first vague, even complacent, then bitter and uncompromising when he came back to her office This was all she knew about him, and it was not enough to gauge how he would react to the scenario she had imagined. She had assumed that Carrión would simply accept what she told him without asking questions, but that was a big assumption to make. "Don't talk to anyone, I'm saying this for your own good…" If her little speech didn't frighten him and he did ask questions, she would have to come up with some sort of financial malfeasance. She could easily come up with something convincing, but as for providing proof… She had no idea how she was going to bring up the idea of money and she had to accept the fact that there was still Aguado to consider. If she had learned anything in her years at the bank, it was that in any financial scandal there were always too many people involved.

And at that moment, a spotlight flickered on in her head and suddenly she could see the whole chessboard.

"No…" she said aloud, trying to get her head around the idea. No …"

It had been a natural association of ideas. Financial scandals, almost by definition, involve several people; she had been looking for something more private, more intimate. Nothing was more intimate than sex. Sex would take Aguado out of the equation and now she remembered something else: the girl who had been there before Aguado, a mousy little thing called Regla didn't work for the bank any more because she had been sleeping with a major shareholder from Unión Fenosa who was old enough to be her grandfather. She was now married to him.

She sat on the edge of the bed, prepared to give up on the idea, but now that her brain was running, she couldn't make it stop. The ideas fell into place, the pieces moving forward in harmony. Sleeping with a client might be crass, but it was not a crime. Everyone did it, especially the women, since they had more opportunity. The relationship between a multimillionaire and the person who manages his finances is an intimate one and can very easily end up in a bed. Nobody was ever fired for sleeping with a client, mostly because by the time anyone found out, it was too late. Secrecy was as much a part of the game as the sex itself. Having to deal with so many zeroes every day made financial professionals careful about such details. If nobody knew about a financial advisor sleeping with a living client, they were hardly likely to know if she had slept with a dead one. Álvaro Carrión would have no way of finding out that she was lying to him, all she had to do was get the key to the apartment on the Calle Jorge Juan.

"No, I can't do it."

She got up, went into the bathroom and as she looked at herself in the mirror.

"Well, if my grandmother ever finds out," she thought eventually, "The shock alone would kill her..."

The idea seemed too risky, too complicated, but it would solve her problems once and for all. Álvaro Carrión would not be happy to find out that his father had had a mistress, he might even disapprove, but he could not discount the possibility. At the end of the day human beings were boring and predictable, and sex wasn't the only thing they had in common. From the Bible to the latest romance novels, human beings were obsessed with conquering old age, with cheating death. Julio Carrión had been eighty-three years old, but he certainly did not look his age. He had been a strapping, virile, attractive man, an older version of the charmer he had been when he was young. Surely Álvaro knew that. He would probably not be thrilled to discover that his father had had a mistress young enough to be his daughter or indeed his granddaughter, but Álvaro was a man - she thought with an investment advisor's unerring instinct – with an eye for the ladies himself. It was therefore reasonable to assume that while he might be annoyed, he might also feel complicit in his father's last fling.

"This is madness," Raquel thought, "it's completely absurd." She went into the kitchen, made egg mayonnaise, then went into the living room And found old black and white film on television.

It was risky, it was complicated, but most of all it was perfect. She had been to Julio Carrión's burial to see the family, to draw whatever conclusions she could, and she had done well. On that freezing, bright March morning she had noticed one of Carrión's sons standing off to one side, away from the rest of the mourners, not wearing a formal grey suit or even a tie. When he had come to her office, she had noticed the jeans, the suede jacket, so out of keeping with the usual attire of a millionaire's son. Even if there were some reactionary Catholic sects who dressed like trendy liberals, and even if Álvaro Carrión were a member, no amount of anger or indignation would allow him to hurt his father's last lover. Whether he liked it or not, he would simply have to accept it, because along with the key to the Calle Jorge Juan apartment, he would find the documents detailing this overly generous, but perfectly legal, gift. Whatever had induced an old man to make such a gift shortly before his death did not change the fact that he had done so. Dead men don't talk. It was unlikely that the Carrión family would create a scandal since the apartment represented a drop in the ocean compared to the money they would inherit, and even if they did, Raquel Fernández Perea's superiors would never be able to challenge her version of events. She was certain that Julio Carrión had been very careful, and that Sebastián, following Carrión's orders, had made sure there was no link between the Tetuán apartment and the one on the Calle Jorge Juan.

When she finally went to bed, she thought she would have trouble getting to sleep, but she nodded off quickly. She had decided that the great advantage of this plan was that it resolved her current problems, whilst leaving the future entirely open. Now, everything depended on Álvaro's reaction. If he was angry or offended, it might be more difficult to get to his mother, but if his clothes were any indication of his outlook on life, he would probably keep his father's secret, and Angélica would once again take the position her son had usurped when he walked into Raquel's office.

And that was that. Later, when the lie began to snowball, when it began to grow and grow, to shift and change, to infect everything, Raquel was shocked to think that all this deception had been born between her bed and her bathroom. Later, when she felt she as if she were a prisoner of this lie, she wondered where her reservations had been, her fears, when she had begun to enjoy this madness, or rather when she had stopped disliking it. Later, she would never be able to understand what had happened, but she would temper her judgement, reminding herself

674

that she had not been motivated purely by ambition and greed. In fact, she had been motivated by fear, an intimately familiar, intensely Spanish emotion. And perhaps time, too, which had gone too quickly, leaving her no time to stop, to reconsider her actions.

Her plan was not only risky, complicated; over breakfast, she realised it was also going to be hard work The apartment on the Calle Jorge Juan was the key to her plan, the piece that would guarantee checkmate in the imaginary game of chess she had been playing against the Carrión family since the previous afternoon. The scene she set had to be convincing. She had to dress it up with things, plant landmines, leave a few red herrings and some genuine clues. Everything that would happen later stemmed from the fact that she did not have time to have second thoughts, but simply threw herself into this task – in fact it had been fun.

"How are things?" Paco was late into work that morning, but the first thing he did was call her.

"Much, much better… thanks to me everything is perfect."

"Really?" he sounded surprised.

"Everything. The Great Financial Swindle is set to go."

"Well, tell me…"

"Oh, it's a long story. Are you doing anything this afternoon? If you like we could have a quick lunch and I'll explain everything, then I need you to come with me somewhere…"

"Somewhere?" He sounded even more surprised, "I don't understand, you're starting to scare me Raquel."

"There's nothing to be scared of. And it won't be dangerous. I just need you to come with me to a sex shop. I mean I could go on my own…"

"A sex shop?"

"Look, I know it doesn't make any sense to you, but you haven't heard the best bit. You are talking to Julio Carrión's mistress." She waited for a response but Paco was speechless, "Aren't you the one who said attack is the best form of defence?"

When they met up that afternoon, she stared at Paco for a long time before launching into her story. She knew him well, she knew they made a good team because their talents complemented each other. Raquel was more imaginative, more daring, Paco more shrewd, more realistic. Consequently Raquel was expecting questions, possibly even criticism, his usual reaction to her dangerous flights of fancy. But when she finished, Paco did not simply laugh, he clapped.

"Fucking genius!" he chuckled, "It's absolutely brilliant…"

Raquel was so excited by his enthusiasm than when she entered the huge sex shop on the Calle Atocha, she felt a giddy excitement, the same reckless, giggly thrill she had always felt playing pranks as a girl. The shop assistant must have noticed because he came straight over and asked if he could help.

"Um, well… I need…" she stopped to think. "I'm not sure, eight or ten DVDs, pornos obviously but tame. You know boy girl fucking. No transvestites, no animals, no S&M… Above board, so to speak."

"Well, they're all there," he said gesturing, "Right behind you in these two aisles."

"I know, but I don't know much about this stuff so I'll probably get it wrong. So I thought, I mean if you don't mind, you could pick them for me?"

"OK…" he looked puzzled, "It's usually down to personal taste, but if you want…"

She followed him with a plastic basket as though she was shopping for a new cheese at a supermarket. She was on her own, as Paco had gone to have a look around.

"Lesbians yes or no? Threesomes? Group sex?"

"OK, that's all classic stuff. Just not too hard, because the guy they're for is getting on a bit and… well, I wouldn't want him to give me a scare."

"We have got some special offers. They're older films, but the quality is much the same."

"No, I'd rather spend a bit more. Ordinary stuff, but classy. You know, nothing tacky, young, beautiful people…"

Her basket was half full when Paco showed up with another basket.

"Pick one." He showed her what was in the basket and she laughed. "I think Don Julio would like the metallic ones, but the coloured ones are prettier, they'd suit you…"

"Paco, honestly!" she looked at the dildos. "Do you really think we need one?"

"When your lover is eighty three?" he laughed, "Let's just say, I don't think it's too much."

"Let's take the purple then, it's more Republican."

"I was thinking …" but the assistant, whose eyes had opened wide when he heard the age of his customer's lover, did not say what he was thinking just yet.

"What?" Raquel asked, seeing his expression as he watched her put the dildo in her basket.

"No, it's nothing" The assistant shook his head, "I forgot what you said earlier – everything legal and above board, right?"

"Well, actually..." she leaned over and whispered in his ear, "It was just a figure of speech."

"I've got a friend next door who sells Viagra," he said looking at Raquel, "You can normally only get it on prescription. I mean I have herbal stuff here, but it's not really up to much. And I just thought maybe..."

"Yes, I'd be interested."

"How many do you want?" he asked taking out his mobile phone.

Raquel thought for a minute "Two would be fine for the moment..."

At this point, Raquel Fernández Perea realised that everything would be fine, that luck was on her side. Paco went with her to the bar where the dealer was waiting, but he left immediately afterwards.

"I'm meeting a girl and I'm running late," he said, looking at the ground as though ashamed he had not mentioned it earlier. "I probably won't be in Madrid this weekend, but if you need me you can get me on the mobile, OK?"

"OK," Raquel kissed him "I'm very grateful, honestly, I can't tell you..."

Just then the light turned green, and he dashed off to hail a taxi.

"He disappeared just as Raquel was about to give in, invite him for a drink, then dinner, and end up in bed.

She had been so sure that this was what would happen that she had actually wanted it to. As she paid for the pills she worked out that she hadn't slept with anyone since 31 December  when Berta had taken her to a party where's she'd met an actor who she'd fancied at the time, though not afterwards. Since then, her campaign of resistance, the negotiations with Sebastián López Parra, meeting Julio Carrión González again, her grandmother's secrets, her visits to the Grupo Carrión and everything had kept her too busy for sex. Even so, Paco's lack of interest was a nudge from fate, because if she had spent the night with him, she would not have been able to get rid of him until Monday morning, and she preferred to work alone. Now that the fear and the worry were over, she trusted her own abilities more than she trusted anyone else. She did what she needed to do and she did it well. She did not need to call on anyone's, except for her brother Ignacio, who explained to her the following day that the small white pills you put under your tongue were called Sustac, and were to prevent heart attacks, and that the big white ones were probably statins for lowering cholesterol.

"Do you want to see them," her grandmother asked taking a pillbox out of her bag, "You can keep them if you want, I've got a whole pharmacy back at the house, but I don't know what you'd want them

677

for…"

"Nothing, I was just curious," she said slipping the box back into her grandmother's bag having pocketed three pills.

The following morning, she bought a small silver pillbox with a scuffed lid similar to the one she had seen Julio Carrión tip out on the desk at their last meeting and a silver retracting pencil like the one she had seen in the pocket of his jacket. She also went on the most extravagant spending spree of her life, buying expensive cheese, *foie gras*, olives and crackers, chocolates, a bottle of whiskey and a bottle of gin, coke, tonic water, napkins… She had toiletries at the apartment on the Calle Jorge Juan but she took them home with her, since it would be more convincing to keep the new stuff and put her old half-used ones in the apartment. Her only concession to thrift was to stop by the Chinese supermarket on the corner where she bought some glasses, some plates and cutlery more cheaply that she could in Salamanca. She bought a DVD player there too, since operation bachelor pad was already costing her a fortune, although she knew that sooner or later she would sell the apartment and make her money back. She also happened on votive candles in plastic containers that seemed ready made to place around the jacuzzi.

On y Sunday afternoon, with all the white goods working, ice in the fridge, the bed made and the ashtrays dirtied, she poured herself a drink, undressed, ran a bath, placed the candles around it then slipped into the water with the dildo. "If you're not planning on using it, you'll need to wash it a couple of times to get rid of the new smell,," Paco had advised her. She didn't use it, but she let it soak for half an house, until the candles had burned down halfway, then she blew them out one by one as if it were her birthday and congratulated herself. She was certain she had made no mistakes, but she checked everything one last time before she left.

The following morning, Paco Molinero dropped by.

"How are you?"

"Good," she assured him, but seeing his face she corrected herself, "Not as good as you, but quite good. I'm a bit nervous."

"Do you want to have lunch?" He did not give her an update on his weekend.

"I can't, I'm having lunch with Álvaro Carrión."

He looked surprised, "I didn't know you'd be having lunch together."

"Nor does he," she laughed, "But I thought it would be a nice touch. I can hardly tell him I was his father's mistress just like that, and besides, if we have lunch I might be able to get some for information out of him."

"OK, well call me and let me know how it goes."

That morning, she had tried on half her wardrobe before settling on a dress. She did her make up just before leaving, and did not bother to wonder why she had not got back to Sebastián who had phoned on Saturday. When she saw Álvaro, still wearing jeans, on the far side of the glass door, she smiled without having to think about it, and everything else flowed just as easily. She hadn't planned on calling him by his first name, but as she walked up to him, she decided she could hardly call him Señor Carrión. This was the last conscious decision she made before taking the key to the Calle Jorge Juan apartment from her bag and placing it on the table.

Leaving the restaurant, she should have realised that it had been years since she had been so attracted to a man, but she was no longer thinking straight. She was worried that her legs would not carry her home, when she got home, she shut herself in the bedroom, closed the blinds, threw herself on the bed and laughed. She wanted to laugh, she didn't want to think about what had happened. She did nothing else until the phone rang.

"What happened?" Paco sounded panicked, it was 6.15pm. "You didn't call me."

"No ... I just forgot."

"So?"

"Very bad. And very good."

"What do you mean?"

Raquel sat down, took a deep breath and attempted to adopt a serious tone.

"Álvaro Carrión is a physicist."

"A physicist?" Paco sounded confused, "You mean his father's a multimillionaire, and he's a scientist?"

"Yep."

"That's the weirdest thing I've ever heard in my life."

"I know," Raquel understood her colleague's reaction, "His older brothers both work for their father's company, all very dynastic, but not him. He's a professor at the university. He has nothing to do with the family business, so I couldn't get any information out of him. And he didn't take it badly when I told him his father and I were lovers, actually he didn't react at all. And he seems to be a bit of a liberal. I was pretty lucky on that score."

"And on the other?"

"What other?" She was confused now.

"What do you think? The money?"

"Oh, that... I've no idea. I'll have to play it cool, see what side he's on. For the moment, he doesn't seem upset or offended, he didn't call me a slut or accuse me of lying. He kept the key, so I'm fairly sure he'll go round to the flat."

"I hope so, that's what we're counting on. But I don't understand... Why didn't you just tell me it went well?"

"Um... because it was fun, a lot of fun."

"Jesus, Raquel," Paco's surprise quickly turned to impatience, "You didn't go to lunch with the guy to have fun."

"No, you're right, but what can you do? I had fun."

She could not think of any other way of explaining it and she spent the rest of the evening imagining Álvaro Carrión falling into the traps she had set for him, a pastime that both amused and excited her. She had thought she was completely in control, but forty-eight hours later, she was already lost.

Rafael Carrión Otero called her on Wednesday 6 April to inform her that Álvaro was not president of the Grupo Carrión. Before she had time to digest this news, he told her that he was taking over responsibility for the investments, that he was very busy and that he would like to meet with her the following morning, because in the afternoon all of the heirs were meeting, he would therefore be grateful if she would put together all the necessary documents because he intended to liquidate all the stocks and investments at his mother's request.

"Nothing you can say is going to change my mind," he said in conclusion, so Raquel did not even try. Goodbye investments, she thought, good riddance. Paco Molinero agreed with her.

She did not much care for Álvaro's older brother. He was so unlike Álvaro that she made no attempt to keep him any longer than was absolutely necessary. He was tall and thin, but had a beer belly, his shoulders were stooped, and his blonde hair was so thin and sparse that he would have been better getting rid of it altogether. Otherwise, he was arrogant, condescending and so abrasive it was as though he intended to be rude.

"I thought that some young man was dealing with my father's investments, Aguado," he said as he was about to sign.

"He was. But he's been working on a rather delicate project these past few months, so he asked me to take care of..."

"Doesn't matter," he signed before Raquel had even finished speaking.

As he said goodbye, Raquel realised that he was looking at her as though she were a piece of furniture. At the time, she did not think about it, but she was reminded of his expression a week later when she compared it to the focussed, smiling, slightly worried face of his brother as he sat across the table from her in the Japanese restaurant.

She had been expecting Álvaro to call her to return the key, but aside from buying a short dress with a plunging neckline and a pink jacket which admirably highlighted what it appeared to conceal, she had prepared no strategy, no new offensive for their next meeting.

If someone had shown her the scene two weeks earlier, if she had been able to see herself, hear what she was saying, she would have laughed and said. "It's ridiculous, he's the last man in the world I'd consider sleeping with." But Álvaro Carrión Otero knew how to look at her, he was funny, he was charming as he struggled to find the right words so as not to hurt her, he was touching when he told her he had packed up all the stuff in the apartment so his brothers and his mother wouldn't find out, and he was disarming when he lowered his voice to a whisper and stared into her eyes and asked her if she had loved his father. It had been years since she had felt such electricity in her body, and he could set it off so easily that, by dessert, she was already thinking about the worst possible plan the world had to offer.

He was thinking the same thing, she could tell, and that evening, this gave her pause. But even as she glanced at her watch, pretending to be worried about how late it was, muttering about some early morning meeting, already she was no longer sure of anything. That evening, Álvaro Carrión Otero had been himself, not a ghost, not the shadow of his father, and Raquel Fernández Perea could no longer use her aunt Paloma's fragility to mask her own vulnerability. She had managed to brush him off, gently, wordlessly, burning no bridges, and she was certain she had done the right thing. She didn't want to think about the fact that never in her life had she wanted to sleep with someone as much as she did with him. When she got home, she was so depressed that she did not even have the energy to lay into herself for being such a fool.

As she fell sleep, she tried to absolve herself of her sins. It doesn't matter, I'll get over it. When she got up the next day, she consoled herself with the same words. But it did matter, and she did not get over it. The days passed, and her conviction that she would get over it began to dissolve in the acid of her unsatisfied desire, to which she offered an antidote.

'So what? So I sleep with him? I'm not about to tell him anything and it's not like anyone in my family will ever find out…" this first small dose was so exhilarating that she began to take the antidote by the spoonful, "It would only be a one-off, anyway he's married, it would just be an affair…" until she realised it was easiest to drink straight from the bottle. "It's not as if I'm going to get addicted, is it? I'm past that stage … I mean it should just be a quick fuck, and that's it done, it's not like it would happen again… Actually, it's much better to sleep with him and get it out of my system instead of mooning round for the rest of my life thinking he might have been the one, I mean, obviously he's not, how could he be, I mean what are the chances that one of Carrión's sons would turn out to the The One? It's ridiculous… I don't know anything about him, about his life, I can't just… The easiest thing would be if he knocked me back, that way it would be over and done with… I'll call him, tell him I have a couple of thing belonging to his father, though he might ask me to send them by courier, I mean that's what they're there for…'

Raquel Fernández Perea would never know that on 4 April, 1947, as he stepped off the train at the Gare du Nord in Paris, Julio Carrión González had had a similar conversation with himself although the outcome had been very different. And yet she realised that, whatever else might happen, Álvaro had saved her, because it was only after that dinner when he had begun to be himself that Raquel had realised she was dealing with a man, a delicate, defenceless creature of flesh and blood as innocent of the guilt of the ghost he resembled as Paloma had been the moment Julio betrayed her. Álvaro's words, his smiles, his looks convinced her that she was not dealing with his father, but with him. And the more she thought, the more she shuddered and things began to fall apart, her plans, her ambitions, her desire for revenge

"I didn't say anything about the money." The morning after her dinner with Álvaro, Paco Molinero reacted to her news with a stunned silence. "It just wasn't the right moment. Anyway… It doesn't matter, I don't care anymore, I honestly don't care. I'm starting to think the whole thing was a mistake. I think a lot about my grandfather, you know? I think he would have wanted it this way, and I'm starting to understand him, to understand his reasons…"

Paco was unconvinced.

"What do you mean you don't care about a million euros, Raquel? It's impossible, nobody just loses interest in a million euros."

At that moment, Raquel realised they were no longer a team, more like two radio stations on different frequencies. It was her fault, because she had not told him the truth. This was why Paco didn't understand, he couldn't.

"You're hiding something." He said a couple of days later. "There's something going on. What did I just say to you?"

"Um?" He can tell, Raquel thought, he can see it, this is terrible because it means we won't be able to work together. "I don't know, I didn't catch it. Something about the cement works?"

"You see?"

"There's nothing going on... I'm just a bit preoccupied..."

A chaos pendulum had appeared in her life.

A week after they had sushi together, Raquel Fernández Perea called Álvaro Carrión Otero and suggested they meet the following day. He did not say no, but Raquel had forgotten that she was supposed to be spending the afternoon with Berta.

"I thought you said Jaime was an insufferable egotist who never talked about anything except himself," Berta rattled this off before she even said hello.

"What are you talking about?" Raquel was surprised to see her friend show up at her place at 5.50pm.

"You're wearing your lucky skirt"

Raquel looked down and saw that she was wearing the skirt with the small yellow flowers, her favourite, the one she called her lucky skirt because it suited her. But that did not explain why Berta was here or why she was talking about some actor Raquel had slept with on New Year's Eve.

"So, I'm wearing my favourite skirt... That doesn't mean..." Then she remembered, "Oh God, we're supposed to be going to the theatre to see Jaime tonight." She clapped both hands to her face. "Jesus, Berta!"

"You forgot?"

"Yes... I don't know, lately I've been all over the place."

"You're meeting someone."

"Yes." Raquel looked at Berta and laughed, "Listen, I'm meeting him at a quarter past six, why don't you come down with me and I'll introduce you. We're going to an exhibition about black holes."

"What?"

"Black holes," Raquel laughed again, "Outer space, you know... He's a physicist —science, levers, pulleys, forces, all that... He's the one organising the exhibition."

Now it was Berta's turn to laugh.

"And you fancy him?"

"Something rotten..."

Later, fate, in the form of an ugly little girl who couldn't work out some contraption with water jets and levers, provided Raquel with a moment to think. As Álvaro was explaining the machine to the girl, Raquel felt two intense but contradictory urges. 'Either I kiss him right now,' she thought, 'or I get the hell out of here.' There was a third possibility – she could tell him the whole story – but she immediately discarded this one. Nor did she want to run away, so she decided to trust the intuition that had so dazzled her the last time she had seen him. Álvaro was not upset to be told that he was nothing like his father, and he agreed with her that it was probably best if they didn't talk about him. This would have been the moment to show her cards, to tell him some part of the truth. 'The first thing my grandfather Ignacio did after he slept with my grandmother Anita was to teach her how to read and write.' She composed this sentence in her head, but she knew that Álvaro was Spanish too, he was well used to mysteries and silences, and she wasn't lying to him any more. It was true that at school there had been a science test in which they were shown two almost identical drawings of housewives hoovering and that one of them was holding the handle much higher than the other, that she had made a mistake which had cost her a good mark in science. Álvaro knew the right answer, of course, he was a good teacher and she genuinely liked him, liked him so much she wanted to sleep with him, after all, it was just a fuck, an affair, nothing important. But inside the gift-wrapped box he placed on the table before dinner were two pendulums, a classic, ordinary pendulum that swung predictably over and back over and back, and a second pendulum that was chaotic, unpredictable, yet they moved in harmony, and in all eternity, even with an infinite number of decimal places, it would have been impossible to predict what happened to Raquel Fernández Perea that night.

"Are you mad?" Berta looked at her, astonished.

By the time Raquel told Berta, but only Berta, the whole truth she was already in so deep she did not even know what madness might mean.

She had told nobody until now, she did not even want to think about it, did not want to gauge the dimensions of this trap in which she felt so comfortable, so happy. When she was alone, she preferred to imagine a different scenario, a Saturday morning, light spilling in through the balcony widows, Álvaro in the kitchen in his pyjamas as she came back from the market carrying bunches of flowers that she arranged in crystal vases. This was what she preferred to imagine, but the night before, the three of them had had dinner and Raquel had pretended to feel ill in order to stop Álvaro and Berta to stop talking. But she knew that Berta had not been fooled. She could have phoned her, made something up, she could have said she and Álvaro had had a row before they came out or that the story he was telling was so touching it had made her cry. She could have told Berta anything, but time had passed, barely three months in ordinary time but to her they felt like a lifetime. The night before, when he was talking about himself, Álvaro had been talking about her too, because it was bound to happen some day, and some day she would have to tell somebody the truth. She had decided to start with Berta.

"Jesus Christ, Raquel, what are you saying?" Berta who could never pick a man who was right for her, stared at Raquel, her face as pale as wax. "I don't believe this. How did you get yourself into such a mess?"

"I didn't get myself into a mess," At first Raquel tried to defend herself. "It just happened... How was I supposed to know I was going to fall in love with him? I don't understand any of it... it all seemed so simple, everything was going so well and I didn't realise..."

She was not a good person, she knew she was not a good person, that she would never convince anyone that she was blameless in all this, but Berta did not challenge her, she simply came over, put her arms around Raquel, and tried to sound upbeat.

"It's OK, it doesn't matter," Raquel could tell Berta did not believe this, "It's not so bad, because... well, you can still make it right."

"I hope so."

"Of course you can," Berta hugged her again. "So what are you going to do? Just see how it goes, I suppose?"

"What else can I do?" Raquel felt better. "He's married, he has a kid, he's not going to give all that up for me, is he? Married men never leave their wives. Besides, we've been seeing a lot of each other recently because he doesn't have lectures, but when term starts, things will go back to the way they were before. I'm not going to say anything... I can't tell him, Berta, I can't tell him the sort of man his father was, the things he did, he'd end up hating me... And if he ever found out, he'd never be able to trust me again. I'd never be able to face him, I'd die of shame. I love him, Berta, I love him so much that I couldn't bear him to think any less of me.

Raquel realised that if she carried on, she would end up crying, and she could not let herself cry because to do so would be to admit that it was all over, that her relationship with Álvaro was doomed to fail sooner or later, so she shook her head and tried to look on the bright side.

"But if things go on the way they're going, if we're still together and he gets to know me properly, forgets about his father, then maybe... Maybe I can just never tell him... Or maybe a time will come when it doesn't seem so important. And if it's going to end, then it's going to end, I just want it to last as long as possible. I don't know Berta, I don't know what to think..."

"I'm guessing you've got to be the only woman in history to sleep with a married man and hope that he doesn't leave his wife," Berta said philosophically and they both laughed

But that night, when she was alone Raquel thought about things again and she felt drained, empty, as though there was a gaping void eating her up inside, because she loved this man, loved him more than anyone in the world, but all her love was useless. She no longer dreamed of sunny Saturday mornings, of bouquets of flowers in crystal vases, but until that night she had not realised that this dream with which she had lulled herself to sleep, was much more than a simple fantasy, some vestige of her romantic teenage dreams. The imaginary flowers she arranged in imaginary vases were her life-line, a guarantee that she would survive.

That night, when Berta left, Raquel Fernández Perea died a little. And when the life that she had dreamed of lay before her, when Álvaro Carrión Otero laid like a carpet it at her feet, when he offered her everything he had, and she refused him, Raquel felt herself die a little more, and she did not want to die, not tonight, not in front of him.

Berta had told her that there had to be some way of making things right, and Raquel wanted to believe it. "I've got to find some way to make things right," she told Álvaro the next morning as they were having breakfast together and she went on saying it to herself, a hundred, a thousand, a million times. She sprawled on her bed, lying on her back, arms folded over her chest like a corpse, her thinking position, but even this was useless. The word 'disappear' seemed to lurk round every corner, behind every door she opened, trying to escape from this brutal, cruel fate that meant giving up on the only thing that mattered to her.

This can't be happening, it can't be happening, she thought. She got up, went into the bathroom and splashed water on her face. But this time, she could not come up with a plan.

Clara, my sister, was waiting for me on the porch steps. I hadn't said I was coming, but I wasn't surprised to see her sitting on the same step she had sat on as little girl when there was trouble at home.

I said hello and sat down next to her, the way I used to when I was the only brother who knew she was upset because she'd ruined a library book or lent her watch to some friend from school who had lost it.

"Hi," she smiled, ignoring my black eye. She took my face in her hands and kissed me on both cheeks. "What are you dressed like that for?"

I was wearing the grey suit I wore at my viva examination, a dress shirt and a tie. On the rare occasions I wore a suit, I never managed to feel comfortable enough to forget I was wearing it, but that morning I had forgotten

"I came to talk to Mamá." I said, as though this was sufficient.

"Really? What about?" She looked at me and I saw that her eyes were shining, "Weren't you even going to call me?"

I had an appalling hangover, though I only realised this when I climbed into the car, the big suitcase packed into the boot, my breath steaming up the windscreen with a foul-smelling mist. I felt intimidated by the pure blue of the horizon, the blue of my mother's eyes which was always deepest, loveliest when she was angry or upset. "Don't go, Álvaro." Raquel had said. Her dark eyes flecked with green were suddenly so dark they seemed black. "Don't go." But I did go, I had to go. When I closed the door of the apartment on the Calle Hortaleza, a place I had always loved and would now never come back to, I thought that maybe it was better this way, better to get it all over at once, like when we were children and one of us had chickenpox and Mamá piled all five of us into the big bed so we would all get it over with at once.

When I closed the door of the apartment on the Calle Hortaleza, I thought about the time Miguelito had chickenpox. I remembered the fever, his little body limp and sweaty and then, almost before I realised it, he was bouncing around with the wonderful, inexhaustible energy of a healthy three-year-old. It was better this way, better to get it all over with at once, I thought, the tears, the guilt, the questions, the secrets. "I'm tired of deep meaningful conversations," I had said to Raquel the night before, and it was true. I couldn't take any more, yet there I was driving down the road to Burgos while my memory bombarded me with images of the life I was leaving behind, my wife's naked body, my son's irrepressible laughter, my mother's soft fingers as she held my hand in the street.

"Of course I was going to phone you." This was why it did not bother me, running into Clara, even though I hadn't called her, "It's just that you are the youngest, so if I didn't know anything about it, you were hardly likely to know anything either."

"I'm never going to know, Álvaro," she said, not looking at me, "Never."

"Don't you want to know?"

"Of course, you know me…" she looked at me now and smiled, "But I'm a coward, aren't I? That's what you always used to say when we

687

were little. Come on Clara, talk to Papá, talk to Mamá, just tell them what happened, you can't keep hiding forever, you can't sleep out here on the porch... Remember when I broke the porcelain dancer? The day I failed my exams? The night everyone was out and it was just you, me and Fuensanta and I got ink all over Angélica's dress and it wouldn't come out? That was the worst, I'd never been so scared in my whole life, do you remember?

"Yes." I remembered everything, and I smiled back. "'It wasn't me, it wasn't me,' Whenever anyone couldn't find something, it was because you had wrapped it up carefully in a plastic bag and put it in the bin, and you'd always say the same thing: 'It wasn't me, it wasn't me.' But it didn't matter, you always gave yourself away in the end. This time it's different, Clara."

"No," she shook her head, "It's not... Last night, talking to Angélica, I could hear Papá's voice, you remember 'Little mouse, little mouse...' Then I called Rafa and I could still hear him 'Little mouse, little mouse, will you marry me?' I didn't even call Julio, there was no point, he always takes your side even when you're wrong, and you're wrong, because you can't be right, and Rafa can't be right..."

'Little mouse, little mouse, will you marry me?' When Clara was about three or four, it had been her favourite story, and Papá was the only one who was allowed to tell it. Every night she would appear in the living room of the apartment on the Calle Argensola carrying the same book and she would go over to Papá and say 'Little mouse, little mouse,' and Papá would say 'Little mouse, little mouse' and sweep her up in his arms and read the short poem. He did it so often that eventually they both knew it by heart, and they would recite it all the time, wherever they were. Clara always played the Vain Little Mouse, and Papá would put on the different voices for the other characters including the shrill voice of the little boy mouse that always had Clara rolling around laughing. Clara became 'Little mouse, little mouse,', my father always called her that, even on the most solemn occasions. The day she stepped out of the house in her wedding dress, he took her by the shoulder before she left and said 'Little mouse, little mouse, why are you marrying someone else?' and they both burst out laughing.

"How is Rafa?"

"Well..." She pulled the face she always did whenever she had to talk about something unpleasant. "He's furious with you, obviously. And his face is a mess. He had to have stitches, and they've put something in his nose to keep the septum in place. You knocked it out of place when you punched him. He said it was very painful."

"I'm sorry." She did not react yet, so I went on, "I swear, I'm sorry… but he was the one who started it."

"I know, Angélica told me, anyway, you only have to look at your eye. But what I don't understand is how you could fight with Rafa, Álvaro. I mean, I'm not surprised at him, that's what he's like, but you… And all over some stupid remark, just because he made fun of your museum."

"No, Clara, that's not what it was about. It's true, he did laugh at the museum, at me, and my work, but the worst thing was…" I wondered whether I had it in me to explain, and even if I had, she probably would not understand. "It's not because he attacked me, he attacked what I stand for, everything I believe in… I wasn't bothered by what he said about me, but to attack science and scientists and what we do… I just lost it."

My sister looked at me, the disbelief on her face almost comical and I realised how ridiculous what I had said seemed to her. "I know it sounds stupid, Clara, but it's not. There's nothing I hate more than people who brag about their ignorance, people who are proud to be nothing more than animals, I can't stand it. That's what Rafa did, and he did it deliberately, he knew exactly what he was saying. I may not be religious, but I don't go round blaspheming and insulting people who are."

"You can't compare the two!"

"I'm not…" I smiled, trying to comfort her, "But that's what happened. Rafa attacked me, he was looking for a fight and I gave him one."

"When I heard, I couldn't believe it, honestly, not you… He's more violent, well maybe not violent - he's more antagonistic, more controlling, you can't have a simple conversation without him getting all worked up but you just have to let him, we all know that, and then he calms down."

"I've been taking this shit all my life, Clara," I interrupted her, "I've been putting up with it for years, Rafa screaming and me saying nothing so as not to spoil things for everyone, but that doesn't mean I'm passive and it doesn't mean he has the right to have the last word even when he's wrong. Its just habit, it's the way we do things in our house, it's the way we do things in this country."

I had been careful to control my anger, careful not to raise my voice even as I felt the flames licking at me, the stifling heat of this rage I had hoped never to feel again. But for all my efforts, Clara must have seen some small spark, because she looked terrified.

"I don't understand, Álvaro."

"It doesn't matter... I'm not proud of what happened yesterday, in fact, I'm not even sure I understand myself." This was true and she realised it. "Nothing like that has ever happened to me before."

Clara said nothing and I began to feel guilty again, sick with shame as I pictured the scene, Angélica rushing into casualty, finding some colleague she could trust, whispering that her brothers had been fighting; Rafa slumped on a plastic chair, his face swollen, hating me and Julio next to him, not knowing what to say. It must have been horrible, humiliating for everyone. I felt so ashamed just thinking about it that I made the mistake of trying to justify what I had done.

"And it's not that bad, is it? I mean, people fight all the time because they've had too much to drink, or someone's rear-ended their car, or because of some woman..." Seeing misery well thick and watery in my sister's eyes, I stopped.

"This whole this is driving you crazy, Álvaro."

I tried to see myself through those eyes that still looked like drops of honey, Clara's eyes, the baby of the family, the little mouse who had understood me better than anyone when we were children and who then began to look at me as though I were an alien with a bizarre job and bizarre opinions but who had never stopped being her brother Álvaro, one half of the team doomed to lose every game we ever played against our arch-rivals, the big kids. She was grown up now, she was thirty-five, she had just told me I was going crazy and perhaps she was right because she was staring at me from the serenity of a perpetual childhood, in which nothing was difficult, nothing was nasty, a universe of pastel coloursin which, if emotions were not intense, at least they were never confusing or unpleasant. To Clara, this was what life was like, she would not allow it to be any other way.

"This story would drive anyone crazy," I said.

"No, Álvaro, not me." She shook her head. "Not me, you know that. That's what I told Angélica last night when she tried to explain that this woman you've left Mai for is our cousin and that she's told you... horrible things about Papá and Mamá and grandma Mariana. I told her I didn't want to know, and now I'm telling you, I don't want to know, not now, not ever. I'm not going to fall out with any of you, because you're my family, but Papá was my father and to me he was the best, no matter what anyone says."

Tears made it impossible for her to say more, and I could have asked her why she was crying, what reason there could possibly be for these tears that belied her faith, the gentle certainty of her words, but I didn't. I knew the answer, and I knew that she would give me a different one.

"I'm crying because this whole thing upsets me, I can't stand to see you fighting, I love you all so much." It was true, she loved us, we all loved each other, what else could we do, we were a family.

"Let it go, Álvaro, please." She took my hand and squeezed it just as Raquel had done that morning when she had asked me not to go. "Forget this nasty, ugly story... We can't understand it. I know you think you do, but I think Rafa is right, we can't know what we would have done if ..." she did not want to continue, so she changed tactic. "The thing I really don't understand is, what difference does it make? What does it matter what Papá did before we knew him? When we knew him he was a good man, a good father, he was clever and ambitious, but he was honest, everyone loved him, you most of all, Álvaro, you loved him more than any of us... That's the saddest part, Julio and me, we were always on Mamá's side, but you were the one he loved best, then Angélica, then Rafa... Poor Rafa!" her eyes filled with tears again, "And you did love him, Álvaro, I know you did, you can't hide that kind of thing."

"I loved Papá, Clara, and I still love him, " I said, "I could never stop loving him, even if I wanted to, forget him... Julio told me it's possible to forget, but I don't think I can. I think about Papá all the time, more than I ever did, and I always remember the good times, the times he helped me, took care of me... It's about the same with Mai. She has never seemed as beautiful or as wonderful as she does now in my memories." I looked at my sister and smiled, "It's all my fault, I know that, and I know I'll get over it. I know that if my relationship with Raquel wasn't so complicated, that if she hadn't blown our world apart, my memories of Mai would not be as powerful. But with Papá, it's different. With Papá, there's nothing I can do."

"Then let it go, Álvaro. Don't do it for Papá's sake, or even Mamá's, do it for yourself... And for me. Just leave things the way they are, because it's pointless, Papá is dead, and we have to go on living. We have to try to be happy. Look at what you've done... Rafa hates you and he'll end up hating Julio because he stuck up for you, Angélica is in pieces and as for me..."

Clara began to cry again and I put my arm round her shoulders. I thought about her, about what she had said, about the words that mattered to us: generosity, responsibility, selfishness, and I thought of other words, words that Clara would never know *be a good man, an honourable man... Maybe I am wrong, but I am doing what I feel I have to do, and I am doing it out of love...* Clara did not understand, but I did. Clara did not want to know, she was determined to live, or at least to pretend to live inside her little glass house. It was not terribly original, but it was a path she had the right to choose, to add her deafening silence to the silence of the millions before her who had chosen to say nothing, to close their ears to a silence more piercing than any scream. It was a choice I had had. From the very start, I knew that I could choose to do nothing, pick up the pieces of the porcelain dancer, put them in a plastic bag, and throw it in the bin, pile some rubbish on top of it and stamp it all down. This had always been her approach when she was little. She could run away now, but sooner or later the future would catch up with her and she would end up knowing what she did not want to know, hearing what she did not want to hear. Some small shard of truth, this enemy she was trying so hard to outwit, would slip beneath her skin like a splinter of wood that draws no blood. This was what would happen, I knew that. I was her big brother and I had been through every stage already.

"Don't worry, Clara," I whispered, hugging her still, "If you don't want to know, I won't say anything. I love you too, I'll always love you... little mouse, little mouse..."

At this, she looked up at me and smiled, we hugged again and I got to my feet.

"Please, Álvaro, don't go in to see Mamá..." I closed my eyes so as not to have to look at her piteous, pleading face. "Not today, wait for a while. She's seventy years old and she's not well, Papá's death has been very hard on her and now all this..." I opened my eyes and saw that her expression hadn't changed. "That's why I came, to make sure you were all right, and to ask you, to beg you not to upset Mamá. Please, Álvaro..."

I took my sister's hands in mine, and answered her in a firm voice. I was completely calm because I had known from the beginning, long before I arrived at La Moraleja, that I would hear these words, that someone would come and say these words, would hand me on a plate this perfect excuse, this ideal alibi.

"I haven't come to upset Mamá, Clara, I just want to talk to her, that's all. I just want to hear her side of the story."

"But there's no rush, is there?" Clara looked at me again and with a great deal of effort managed to smile. "Nothing's going to change if you wait for a week or two, just so you have time to calm down, to think about what you're doing ... This is all ancient history, Álvaro, it happened long before we were born. I'm not asking you not to talk to Mamá. I'm just asking you to wait for a while till things calm down, the whole situation with Mai and this woman, and Rafa..."

"I can't wait, Clara." I was still calm. "I have to get it over with once and for all, so I can get on with my life, so I can go back to being a normal person... It's not about Mamá, or you. It's about what I am, what I'll be when I come through this." What I was about to say was so obvious that I did not even stop tom think of the consequences. "You have the right not to know, but I have the right to know."

"No, Álvaro," Her voice and her expression hardened, "You have no right to hurt her, to tell her all these horrible things about Papá, to hurt us. And you have hurt us, you know, all of us and for what? That woman has saddled you with all this guilt and now you want to play the hero, that's all this is, and you have no right ..."

"What I have, Clara, is no guilt, none at all." She didn't understand, but I continued. "I haven't hurt anyone, or robbed anyone, I haven't informed on anyone or betrayed...

"La-la-la-la!" She took a quick breath and began to scream "La-la-la-la-!"

Eyes tight shut, her fingers in her ears, my sister stood there screaming. It was another of her strategies, like sitting on the porch steps, neither inside nor outside, or making something she had broken disappear. She didn't want to listen, and I didn't want to talk any more although I still had one or two things to say. I knew that my mother would not fall apart, her heart was not going to stop just because I talked to her, and that was all that mattered. But Clara did not want to hear, so I left her standing there, though her voice piped up just as I was about to step through the door.

"Wait for me, Álvaro." She ran her fingers through her hair, tugged at her skirt and rubbed her eyes.

Together we went into the neat, deserted house. The sun streamed in, across the polished floor of the hall. At the far end of the room, sitting on a sofa with her back to the light Mamá watched us come in. Her legs were crossed, her hands lay casually in her lap, and as we approached her, she sighed.

"Leave us alone, Clara."

My mother's heart was not about to stop simply because I talked to her, this much I knew, but I had not expected her to smile at me, or to repeat her order in a calm, almost pleasant voice.

"I want to talk to Álvaro alone, Clara."

"But, Mamá..."

"Why don't you go and wait in the garden? Lisette took the children out a few minutes ago. The weather is beautiful, why don't you make the most of it?"

My sister looked from Mamá to me then turned away without saying a word.

"Close the door on your way out, darling…"

She waited until we were truly alone, then she smiled and said, "Well, aren't you going to kiss me?"

"Of course, Mamá…"

As I walked over, I noticed her jewellery, the sheen of her silk blouse, the almost geometric perfection with which her skirt lay across the sofa like a well-trained pet. Her hair was salon perfect and there was a touch of blusher on her cheeks. My mother had dressed up and put on make up in preparation for my visit, but her actions meant something different from the grey suit, the shirt and tie I was wearing. Seeing her, I felt bewildered, lost in the confusion of my expectations and I surrendered to her authority with the same meek docility I had had when I was a child.

"You've gone to a lot of trouble just to visit," she was not smiling now, but her face still seemed relaxed, pleasant, "You know how much I love it when you wear a suit." She gestured to the nearest armchair. "Sit down. I've been expecting you."

We looked at each other as though we were strangers, as thought we needed to weigh each other up, and I wondered who this woman was, this woman who had always been my mother. I realised that if my mother's attitude was not like mine, it was also not like that of my brothers or sisters. When I had met Clara on the steps, I had not paid much attention to what she was wearing, but I could remember now, her hair was caught up up with an elastic hairband, her boots were dirty and spattered with mud. "You've hurt us, all of us." Clara had said and I knew this was true, that it had been painful for Julio to speak to me, more painful still for Rafa, that Angélica had not slept all night and that Clara too had suffered, sitting alone here in the garden. According to the basic measurement by which we, her children, calculated suffering, being alone, a widow, old, and defenceless put my mother at the pinnacle of the scale. But it was beginning to look as if the five Carrión Otero children had made the same mistake.

I had not taken on my mother's pain, I hadn't wanted to think about it. I had decided to leave it until last, the vague, fabulous moment when I could tell myself it was finally over, that it was time to draw a line on the ground, jump over it, and start again on the other side. I hadn't wanted to calculate my mother's suffering, her despair, to measure it against my guilt because if I had, I would have been unable to move. I was going to be a good man, a brave man, an honourable man and maybe I was wrong, but I was doing what I felt I had to do, and I was doing it out of love.

I knew that my mother was a strong woman, a hard woman, that she would not fall apart or break down in tears, but the scene as I had imagined it was very different and the absence of anxiety, pain or bitterness made it impossible for me to interpret what I was seeing. Her calm seemed almost offensive, it unsettled me, so much so that for a moment I thought perhaps it was not just her, not just me, that it was not just us, because I could not know how many times and in how many rooms this scene had been played out. As I realised this, I suspected that it had been my biggest mistake, my greatest miscalculation because things were not simply different to how they appeared, they were often the complete opposite and this had to be the result of some phenomenon, some variable that I had not allowed for in my calculations. This was why, until this moment, it had not occurred to me that what to the rest of us was a tragedy might to her be nothing more than an irritating nuisance.

Optics is a paradoxical science. Often, distance makes it easier to focus, heightens our ability to distinguish the shape or volume of an object just as sometimes proximity can be a hindrance to unaccustomed eyes, but these rules apply to things, we cannot apply them where people.

I did not have time to develop this thought since my mother got in before me, answering a question I had not yet asked her.

"Your aunt Teresa, your father's sister, lives in Germany..." She paused, to leave me the opportunity to say something, but I could say nothing so she carried on in the same simple tone. "Well, I suppose she might be dead now, we haven't heard from her since about 1978... At the end of the war she was in Algeria. Your grandmother managed to get her onto a boat leaving for Oran with one of the sisters of the man she was living with, and she stayed there. Then, after the Second World War, she married a Spanish man who had been a prisoner in one of the Nazi camps in French Africa. They had children, I don't know how many, and they stayed in Oran until Algeria became independent. Then they lived in France for a while and sometime in the mid-60s they moved to Germany. They settled in one of the big cities, I don't remember which, Stuttgart, maybe, or Düsseldorf, her husband worked for Volkswagen. Your father hadn't heard from her since he came back from Russia, but after Franco died, when the exiles started to come home, he found out through some Spanish Republican organisation, some men who had been building railways in the Sahara or something like that, I don't really remember..."

She talked and I listened, forcing myself to take it all in, to remember every word, all this information I had not asked for.

"Anyway, Teresa's husband had been one of them, some of the men

695

who came back remembered his wife, and they gave your father her address. Papá wrote her a long letter, telling her about his life, saying he would like to see her again. She wrote back straight away. Half a page. She told him what I've just told you, that she was fine, that she didn't need anything, that her children had grown up and married and living in Germany, that if her brother hadn't thought about her for forty years, she didn't know why he was bothering now. That was it."

She looked at me again, her lips curling into a strange, indeterminate expression that looked as though it might be a laugh, an expression of surprise or one of disdain.

"I thought maybe she had some strange idea." Papá thought it would be useful to have sister who was communist, I don't know, something stupid like that... Her letter was so short, so curt, that he didn't write back. I could tell you he was upset, but that would be a lie. The truth is I didn't understand why he had written to her in the first place, and I still don't. They hadn't seen each other since your father was fifteen and she was twelve... But one night, he was watching an interview with a writer living in exile, and they showed all these photos, and footage of people crossing the border. Suddenly your father got up and said, 'I'm going to look for my sister.' 'Your sister?' I said, 'Why?' but he didn't answer. He just went ahead and did what he wanted, as he always did, you know what he was like."

"But you never said anything to us about it." My voice sounded as if I had not spoken for years.

"Of course not," my mother looked surprised, "Why would I have said anything to you? If your father's sister had shown up, it would have been different. He wanted her to come and meet you all, he suddenly felt sentimental, you wouldn't believe it, afterwards he could hardly believe it himself ... Papá never talked about it, but I think he often thought about his mother... It had been so long and we'd had no word from them, then suddenly," there was a note of irritation in her voice, "suddenly it was Republicans this and Republicans that, dead Republicans and exiles in México, France, Argentina, the children of Russia, the children of Belgium, it was Republicans all day long, in the papers, in magazines, on television... It was boring beyond belief, it was like there'd never been another war and we were somehow guilty of something... Anyway, your father got it into his head to look for his sister, but when he got that letter, it was obvious she wanted nothing to do with him. We never heard from her again. Nor did we want to."

"Why are you telling me this now?"

"Because it's the only thing you don't know, isn't it?" She folded her

696

arms and we looked at each other. "And because it's the only thing I'm going to tell you."

In the silence that followed, I realised that nothing had changed, nothing had trembled or hardened inside her. She remained motionless for a moment, as though posing for a portrait, but then Clara's oldest son, who had been playing football with his brother came up to the window, tapped on the glass and mouthed "Cuckoo! Grandma!" My mother shifted, turned towards the window and waved, pursing her lips again and again to blow kisses to him. She went on waving and blowing kisses to Fran until Iñigo noticed and ran up to the window too, and I thought about Clara, Rafa, Angélica and Julio, I thought about my son, my nephews, about all the children yet to be born, about my father, his money, this house, and I thought about my mother. Suddenly I felt there was no air, I couldn't breathe, I couldn't spend another minute in this room. But the children ran away again as quickly as they had appeared and their grandmother regained her composure.

I needed to talk, I knew I owed it to her but I could not bring myself to do so, I didn't dare ask her to suffer, and yet this was the only thing that my mother could do for me, the only thing that would have comforted me, would have reconciled me to my name, my past and their past, to the love that I could not pluck from my memory.

I should have spoken, but I couldn't bring myself to say the words, only to think them, 'suffer, Mamá, please,' I repeated it to myself once, twice, three times, 'suffer just a little, for Clara, the little girl out there all alone as – little mouse, little mouse will you marry me –the whole world comes crashing down around her. Suffer for Rafa, suffer for him, Mamá, because his face is a bloody mess and he has a prosthesis in his nose because of me, because of you, because he stood up for you, suffer just a little, Mamá, even if it's only for Julio, the one who says he doesn't suffer, who doesn't take life seriously, he was always your favourite, and mine, suffer once and for all, Mamá, please, for Angélica who's torn apart by this, torn between what she thinks she should think and what she can't help feeling, suffer for her, Mamá, and suffer for me too, even if I am the most ungrateful, the most cruel of your children, suffer for the terrible loneliness you've condemned me to.

"What are you looking at me like that for, Álvaro?" She smiled at me. "I knew this would happen. Your father and I were sure it would happen some day. Nothing stays secret forever and our secret has always been so complicated. There were too many people involved, too many grudges. What we couldn't possibly have imagined was how you'd find out but… Well, I suppose life's full of surprises."

"Explain it to me, Mamá" I hadn't planned to speak but the words burst out of my lips. "You don't need to tell me the details, because there's no point, I already know everything, but tell me how this could have happened, because I don't understand, I've tried and I don't understand … All this cruelty, this greed, this cynicism…"

She leaned forward, rearranged her skirt, closed her eyes for a moment then opened them again.

"You were the one who taught me right from wrong, Mamá, the one who taught me not to be selfish or greedy, not to be jealous of my brothers and sisters, to share what we had and to forgive each other. You taught me the Our Father, do you remember? 'Forgive us our trespasses as we forgive those who trespass against us.' I know that's not how they say it now, but I can still recite the old version by heart… But I can't do it any more, I can't, Mamá, I can't believe that you could lower yourselves like that, that you could sink so low. I have to find some way to make sense of it, because you are my mother and Papá was my father, and I can never stop loving you, I'll never be another man's son, another woman's son, I'll never have any other family, but I just don't understand …"

Her eyes were so cold, so clear.

"I feel so alone, Mamá," I needed to look at her, but I didn't dare, "I need you to explain so that I can believe it, do you understand? I need you to tell me why Papá swindled everyone, why he betrayed the people who trusted him, why he never believed in anything, why he never loved any, why he stole and lied and cheated and why afterwards he was able to love you, to love us, explain it to me, tell me something that is better than what I know … Explain to me why Papá buried his mother, why he disowned her. Tell me how it's possible to inform on a starving, unarmed man who's exhausted and just wants a place to sleep for the night, tell me how your mother could have sent her cousin's husband to his death, because she knew they would shoot him… Tell me, or at least tell me that she never slept after she'd done it. You taught me the Our Father, Mamá, tell me that her conscience tormented her to her dying day, that she would have done anything to turn back the clock and spare his life…"

I heard footsteps, laughter, then Lisette's voice calling out "Iñigo!", proof positive that reality still existed beyond that doo.r

"I know it can't have been like that, Mamá, but I need you to tell me, even if you have to lie to me… I don't understand my father, I don't understand my grandmother, I don't understand you, my own mother, I don't know how you could marry the man who threw you and your mother out onto the street, who stole everything you had, a man your mother hated more than anyone in the world. Papá was her worst enemy, you were her only daughter, and didn't it occur to you to look for someone else? You raised five happy children, and we were all well behaved and good at school and responsible and reasonable and we grew up to be good people, good workers, good citizens, and good parents to your grandchildren... It's unbelievable, Mamá... Don't you think it's unbelievable?"

I heard footsteps again, more laughter, and the sound of the front door slamming.

"That's why I need you to explain. Please, Mamá, explain it to me. Tell me what everyone else tells me, that I can't possibly understand, that I didn't live through those time and I have no right to have an opinion, to judge ..."

My breathing was painful now, my tongue sore.

"Tell me this wasn't a country, Mamá, tell me it was the Wild West, tell me everyone was prepared to sell his soul for a plate of lentils, that a man's life wasn't worth the price of the clothes he stood up in, that nobody remembered what dignity was, tell me I don't know what I'm talking about because I was born into a world of privilege and I should be grateful. Tell me anything, tell me you didn't know what was going on, what your mother did, what Papá did..."

Finally I looked at her and saw that her eyes were closed, barricaded behind her hands.

"It must have been hard to live with your head held high, with your eyes open, ears alert, I can imagine that, because fear debases everyone, depravity can only breed depravity... It must have been like that... I can imagine that, but it doesn't comfort me, because you were alive, Mamá, you had eyes and ears, and there are families who survived with no secrets, no one to cry over, no one to worry about, people with no sins and no deaths on their consciences, but you... for you to tell me, that you never asked questions, that Papá died with a clear conscience... I'd rather you told me something else, I'd rather you told me that it was a long time ago, that you don't remember, that you don't understand what I saying, that you don't know why I want to rake up the past after all this time. That I'm naïve, a fool..."

She took her hands from her face then, and opened her eyes.

"At least tell me that, Mamá"

She was so quiet it was as though she had stopped breathing, and her eyes, bluer now, not just cold but frozen in their fury, held the gaze of a young woman,. My mother was beautiful she had always been beautiful, but now, as callousness stole over, up through her skin, I did not find her beautiful. For a moment I was afraid of her.

"Could you give me a cigarette?"

"What?" At first, I thought I had misheard, but she nodded to my pack of cigarettes.

"Can I have a cigarette?" she said again in a neutral voice.

"Of course," I said, "Here. But I really don't think you should smoke…"

"I shouldn't," she lit a cigarette, her hands trembling, "But I enjoy it."

We smoked in silence and I had time to regret what I had said to her, and to realise there was nothing else I could have said.

"You know something, Álvaro?" She stubbed the cigarette out in the ashtray, and now she was a different woman, she was the mother I had always known. "You really should get your hair cut. It's such a shame you wear it long because it eats into your face, and you're a handsome man, you've always been the most handsome one in the family…

And the most intelligent, Mamá, I was about to say, don't you remember? But I get the message, don't worry, I'm going… I got to my feet and didn't open my lips until I pressed them to her forehead. I had never experienced a moment as difficult as this.

"Goodbye, Mamá…"

I headed towards the door and realised I felt better than I had expected, maybe because I was no longer capable of feeling anything, the astonishment whitewashed everything inside me, within and without.

"Listen, Álvaro…" But there would be no mercy, not yet. "I forgot to mention. Not next Sunday but the Sunday afterwards, the 16th…" she frowned, "That is the 16th, isn't it? Anyway, we're having a barbecue for María's twentieth birthday, I can hardly believe it, twenty…"

Suddenly I found myself smiling. I was smiling from sheer astonishment, because I could not believe what I was seeing, what I was hearing, it couldn't be happening, but I had eyes and ears too and I trusted them, and this woman was my mother, I thought, and I was her son. She was saying these simple, affectionate words and looked at me with those eyes.

"It's amazing isn't it," and this man was now me, and she smiled too, "I remember when Angélica was pregnant, my first grandchild, I couldn't believe it, sometimes I think it was just yesterday… but it's not… Anyway, your niece wanted a barbecue, but I'm not sure, this late in the autumn it might rain, but, we'll do what we can… And I was thinking that… Well, obviously I hope you'll come, and maybe you could bring Miguelito, Álvaro…"

And at that moment, precisely at that moment, not a second earlier or later, her eyes filled with tears.

"I'd love to see him. That's the hardest thing about divorce, it's terrible, really, not being able to see your grandchildren... So I'm counting on you, and on Miguelito. Don't worry about Rafa, I'll have a word with him."

She looked away, smoothed her skirt.

"I just wanted you to know that if you want, you can bring this girl, Raquel, isn't it?"

The whiteness dazzled me, blinded me, shot through my temples like a razor-sharp needle.

"I remember her name because I was really surprised at someone in their family having a biblical name. I'm sure she's very pretty, because she was a very pretty child, and I'm sure she's very educated and refined and that she'll know how to be..."

Everything past and present was white, within me and without. My fingers were white, my hands were white, the tie I took off and the pocket I stuffed it into were white, my eyes and everything they saw, my ears and everything they heard, and my brain in its bleached-white uselessness.

"Don't look at me like that, Álvaro" My mother too was white, she smiled at me with white lips, "You'll always be my son, whatever happens. I know you think all of this is serious, but it's not, I know it's not. Time will put things into perspective and after I'd dead you'll regret the things you said to me a moment ago, but until then I have no intention of losing you. As for this girl... Well she can hardly be any worse than your sister-in-law Verónica. Now she's the mother of two of my grandchildren. Just like anyone else."

Don't suffer, Mamá. Don't suffer for me or for anyone, don't even suffer a little, never seek consolation in suffering, that's the only thing I wouldn't understand, now that things have begun to take shape and form again, get back their colour, now that I have regained control of my body, not that my eyes, my ears, my brain can see something other than whiteness, don't suffer, Mamá, don't even think about suffering, because I won't suffer for you.

I left without saying a word. I started the car without putting on my seat belt and drove away as quickly as I could. I drove without knowing where I was going until I came to myself and parked at a bus stop. My legs, my hands, my whole body was trembling, and it would have done me good to cry, but I didn't even try. I rarely cry, very rarely, almost never.

I don't know how long I sat there, but I know I eventually drove back to Madrid, that I parked as if by some miracle in front of the Cuartel del Conde-Duque, that Raquel buzzed open the door without saying a word, that I stepped into the lift with the big suitcase and my story over my shoulder.

I know that at that moment I was thinking that maybe it wasn't so serious. My mother's heavily made up cynicism, her pitiless smiles, the stony husk of her soul, the hard, dry scar where her heart should have been stung my eyes. And yet mine was just one more story, one of many, so many, so similar, great and small, sad, ugly, squalid stories which always seem like lies at first and always turn out to be true.

Just a Spanish story, the kind that ruin everything.